TERMINAL VELOCITY

Vassily Petrov swore as the stealth suddenly lost altitude and precipitously nosed down. He tried to emergency restart, but both his engines were now dead. His altimeter line, white numbers flashing on the right upper portion of his main screen, showed he was dropping like a stone with the fierce storm swirling around him, pelting the cockpit canopy windows with hailstones.

Petrov tried to restart one final time. His engines briefly caught, but then died of infectious flameout. Now, he knew, there was but one option left: He had to land the plane dead-stick, on the desert, with all the risks to which such an emergency landing would expose him. The choice was as clear as it was Draconian—crash-land or simply crash. There was no longer any in-between for Shadow One.

SHADOW
DOWN

David Alexander

BERKLEY BOOKS, NEW YORK

This is a work of fiction. Names, characters, places, and incidents are either the product of the author's imagination or are used fictitiously, and any resemblance to actual persons, living or dead, business establishments, events or locales is entirely coincidental.

SHADOW DOWN

A Berkley Book / published by arrangement with
the author

PRINTING HISTORY
Berkley edition / February 2000

The Penguin Putnam Inc. World Wide Web site address is
http://www.penguinputnam.com

ISBN: 0-425-17305-4

BERKLEY®
Berkley Books are published by The Berkley Publishing Group,
a division of Penguin Putnam Inc.,
375 Hudson Street, New York, New York 10014.
BERKLEY and the ''B'' logo
are trademarks belonging to Penguin Putnam Inc.

PRINTED IN THE UNITED STATES OF AMERICA

10 9 8 7 6 5 4 3 2 1

Acknowledgments

A number of good people helped with research on this purely imaginary work, though none of them would like to be identified by name. They would prefer to inhabit the realms of the imagination, where gremlins and gnomes, but also spooks and moles, live, work, and play. To these imaginary friends, my genuine thanks.

For the unsung war heroes in my family: my great-grandfather, infantryman; my uncle, bomber crewman; and most of all my father, secret saboteur of Hitler's deadliest "victory" weapon.

*For heaven is parted from thee, and the earth
Knows thee not . . .*

—John Keats

Nothing is true. Everything is permissible.

—Hassan i Sabah

*For we wrestle not against flesh and blood,
but against principalities, against powers,
against the rulers of the darkness of this
world, against spiritual wickedness in high
places.*

—Ephesians

Author's Introduction

The scenarios described in this novel take place in the very near future, where the paths of current events and future technological, political, and military challenges converge. Yet the concept on which the novel is based has interested me for a long time.

When I was a kid, the nuclear submarine *Thresher* disappeared on her maiden voyage. For months, nobody had a clue about her fate. The idea that this complex piece of big-ticket military hardware could simply vanish into the depths of the ocean with all her crew aboard captured my youthful imagination. To me it was a real-life *Flying Dutchman*. As the years passed, the revelations concerning our country's covert actions in the *Thresher* incident, and in connection with Soviet submarines, began to leak out of secret files. These, too, went into the mental hopper.

In the late eighties the concept that the then just-rolled-out stealth fighter might also be lost one day and become the subject of a rescue operation, in this case a clandestine mission on the ground, took form. But publishers scoffed at the notion that this could ever happen to the then newly minted superplane, invisible to radar and thus invulnerable to attack.

I remember sitting across the desk from one editor at a paperback house in New York's Chelsea district, an editor then known for his acumen regarding military and action thrillers, who spontaneously began shaking his head and clenching his fists as I pitched my concept. His body language declared loudly that my ridiculous idea was turning him off. Funny that he now seems to have vanished from the publishing scene like a human *Thresher*.

As it turned out, about six months after I began working on *Shadow Down* for Berkley, and ten years after I first began pitching the book to editors, my dumb idea turned into the six o'clock news when an F-117A stealth was downed over Bujanovici by what—at this writing—was presumably a low-altitude SAM strike. The rescue mission, proclaimed by the media as a humanitarian effort to save a downed airman, but likely as much intended to retrieve or destroy classified components of the F-117A, also became reality. Judging by the experiences of many downed fighter pilots in the Persian Gulf, the rescued pilot was fortunate indeed to have been in the cockpit of a stealth, instead of an F-16, F-4, or virtually any other aircraft in the USAF inventory when "whatever-it-was" brought him down over Yugoslavia.

Since even real events have their gray areas, especially those concerning military actions, it should come as no surprise to readers if in the course of this book they find I have taken occasional liberties in treating doctrine, technologies, politics, weapons systems, and other elements of the plot.

I've striven at all times to base characters and events as closely on real-world situations as possible. But I've also made various exceptions to this rule because I've found that whenever life imitates fiction, the closer it comes the more interesting it gets. Yet when fiction imitates life, the opposite is generally the case. This is also why, as Zarathustra was once said to have spake, any resemblance to persons living, dead, or otherwise, is purely and completely coincidental, and everything in this novel is totally a work of the imagination. That, and absolutely nothing more.

DA
March 1999

Book One
Low Observable

One
The Votrin Algorithm

Like daggers in flight, two black-hulled aircraft cleaved the predawn darkness. They showed no lights as they crossed into the mountainous northeastern tier of Iran from the low-lying steppes of Azerbaijan and began to climb and turn their way through the high, rocky passes.

Each plane carried a single missile in its conformal weapons bay. It was all the mission would require. One missile, one kill. After being a dream since the days of Douhet's World War I theories on airpower, after showing itself possible at Ninh Binh Bridge in North Vietnam, and then becoming accomplished fact in the Desert Wind air campaign, it had established itself as air combat doctrine.

But the missiles that would be launched when the stealth aircraft reached their pinch-off coordinates were unlike rounds fired from any planes that had been part of the Gulf air tasking order. They were far more sophisticated than the LGBs that, their targets painted by invisible laser radiation from emitters on the undersides of

F-117As, were seen on bomb camera footage wreaking surgically precise destruction on targets in Baghdad, Kosovo, and other enemy bastions.

In fact, the rounds nestled in the belly of each aircraft were not even bombs at all—smart, dumb, laser-guided, or otherwise. They were true fire-and-forget weapons. Deployed from extreme standoff range, they would autonomously find their way to their targets and trigger their high-explosive conventional warheads once in place.

The missiles, called JASSMs, were closer in lineage to the Tomahawk cruise missiles that were launched from ships, submarines, and bomber aircraft in the Gulf. The joint air-to-surface standoff missiles were air-breathing predators, steel-skinned sharks with silicon intelligence, uplinked to global positioning satellites, capable of flying a low-trajectory path to their targets inside Iran.

They had been programmed with three-dimensional data from a KH-14 photoreconnaissance satellite orbiting one hundred miles above the Middle East some thirty-six hours before. When released, and after a brief booster stage burn, the JASSMs' ramjet turbofan engines would ignite and their navigational systems would place them on increasingly serpentine flight vectors toward their targets across the arid desert of Iran.

The stealth planes that flew the mission were also unlike any flown before in combat, but for somewhat different reasons. In design, they were similar to the F-117A stealth fighter and, like the F-117, deliberately misnamed because neither plane would ever intentionally engage in a dogfight, and was therefore no true fighter.

The subsonic stealth aircraft, depending on a sophisticated inertial navigation system linked to an onboard computer processor array to keep the plane stable, and incapable of anything like the rolls, turns, wingovers, and other high g-loading maneuvers of true fighter jets like the F-22 or MiG-29, would not last a minute against an airborne interceptor aircraft that had it in his sights. It was a ghost plane, flying under cover of darkness only, destined never to see combat by the light of day.

The two planes that crossed into Iran this night at four hundred twelve hours, Greenwich mean (or "zulu") time, precisely according to the timetable prepared by the mission commander, were not F-117s, however. They were not even part of the United States Air Force inventory.

Though similar in appearance to the F-117, the planes had rolled off the assembly line at the Mikoyan-Gurevich plant at Krasnovodsk, C.I.S., on February 19, 2002, where they were emblazoned with the red star of the Russian air force on their rear stabilizer fins.

The stealth aircraft were MiG multirole fighters, designated MFI-19 by the former Soviets, dubbed "Eclipse" by NATO, and each single-seat plane was flown by a Russian pilot. Their mission, however, was a joint undertaking by the air arms of both the United States and the former Soviets against a common threat. Its objective was to destroy the nuclear warfighting capability of the Islamic Republic of Iran.

Four hundred feet beneath the sand desert of western Kuwait, Brigadier General John "Stick" Yarwood of the U.S. Air Force sipped coffee from a porcelain mug that bore the image of a cartoon character from a prime-time television comedy show. The coffee tasted like a sock boiled in sweat. The incongruous thought that this is what Yarwood's own nerves would taste like right now if they were brewed in a twenty-dollar electric coffeemaker flashed through the general's mind.

Yarwood glanced at his wristwatch. Four hundred twenty hours, zulu. He'd been up without sleep for the preceding nineteen straight hours. He needed some sack time, but that would have to wait awhile yet. Not until the targets had been destroyed and both planes were back in their hangar would Yarwood permit himself some downtime.

Yarwood stopped his pacing and cast a look toward the operation's joint commander, General Mikhael Korniyenko of the Voiska Protivovozdushnoi Oborony, or C.I.S. Air Defense Force. Korniyenko was scanning the

center display panel of a three-screen array on the wall
that faced the two-tiered command and control pit—the
battle cab. The mission's ground support personnel went
about their duties below. The commanders and their staffs
oversaw everything from the upper level.

The command, control, communications, computing,
and intelligence—C-4I in military jargon—center was
still under construction. It was one of the concessions the
U.S. had made in order to mount the operation. Kuwait
was the ideal place from which to launch a strike on targets across the Persian Gulf. But it had cost. The base, as
well as a sizable arms package including tanks, planes,
and mechanized artillery, was part of the price paid the
tiny but avaricious oil sheikhdom.

If the operation succeeded, the expense would be cheap.
Yarwood well knew the risk it was designed to eliminate.
Iran had emerged as the biggest winner in the late twentieth century's Mideast power sweepstakes. Quietly, with
exquisite patience, the revolutionary government in Tehran had played both Eastern and Western power blocks
against the EEC and reaped a harvest of military hardware
and weapons technology for their pains.

The U.S., wishing to continue the thaw in relations that
had come about following the election of the moderate
Rasulali to the Iranian presidency, had rewarded Iran with
fighter aircraft and computer technology. The Iranians had
paid court to the Russians as well—more accurately paid
them large sums of money—and in return gained important nuclear reactor and ballistic missile expertise. As long
as Iran continued to overtly snub Iraq and make friendly
overtures to its distant suitors in Washington and Moscow, it continued to harvest a bumper crop of war machinery. East and West both believed for a time that the
Iranians would be content to savor their toys and leave it
at that. Both were wrong. By the late nineties, Iran had
made rumblings about taking over swathes of Azerbaijani
territory toward creating a Persian superstate.

In 1998, Iran had mobilized its forces along its shared
northeastern border with Afghanistan, and sent secret

shock waves through the intelligence communities of both the Americans and Russians. Iran had not only mobilized its land army, it had placed its nuclear forces on standby alert as well. Overhead surveillance satellites tasked by the CIA's National Photographic Interpretation Office, under the Directorate of Science and Technology, had shown beyond doubt that Iranian MRBMs—medium range ballistic missiles—were aimed northward. HUMINT or human intelligence resources revealed that Iran's Strategic Rocketry Forces had its collective finger on the figurative launch button.

These revelations were nothing new to the Israelis, who, by way of their national intelligence agency, the Mossad, had warned Central Intelligence for years about the burgeoning threat of Iran's nuclear weapons capability and her growing will to use those weapons of mass destruction. But Mossad's warnings about Iran were ignored, much as Israel's own nuclear weapons program had been ignored some thirty years before.

It was only now, when the Israelis, claiming that Iran was on the verge of launching a major regional power bid and would not hesitate to strike at Israel in the process, threatened to mount an attack of their own, that the U.S. had finally been moved to act.

On June 7, 1981, the Israelis had launched a daring mission to destroy SAAD-17, an Iraqi nuclear reactor then under construction outside Baghdad, with a sortie of F-16 fighters. The planes demolished the plant in under two minutes before sweeping back across the Jordanian border. The international complications caused by the raid threatened to undo U.S. policy in the Mideast because, for one thing, the Israelis had been secretly provided sophisticated KH-11 satellite imagery by Washington which was used to target the strike. A strike by Israel today against Iran, even if successful, would have far more ominous consequences. Nor could the U.S., given its new détente with Iran, risk even indirect involvement.

The solution came with the downing of an Aeroflot commercial jet by terrorists financed by Iran. That was the straw that broke the camel's back, or more accurately, angered the bear. At the U.S.-C.I.S. summit in 2001 held directly after the accession to the presidency of former General Dimitri Pavlovich Grigorenko, the strike plan was broached. Grigorenko, an ex–military officer and Afghan war veteran, approved the plan. It would give his forces a chance to outshine the Americans for once, even if only a select few would ever know of it—and none beyond a handful ever would.

Furthermore, there was a legalistic pretext that appealed to the Russians—the obscure 1926 Tehran Agreement, signed by Reza Shah Pahlavi, father of the shah of the same name deposed in Iran's 1979 Islamic Revolution, which permitted the U.S.S.R. to enter Iran should, according to the wording of the document, "circumstances develop which constitute a danger to Russia." Until now, the Russian-Iranian treaty had never been invoked since its signing, with one near exception.

In 1981, the Soviet Union, looking on as Iraqi forces penetrated into Iran during the Iran-Iraq War, had concentrated fifty mobile divisions in the Caucasus and Afghanistan near the Iranian border, poised to cross into Iran had the Iraqi penetration continued and Iran found itself in serious danger of defeat. Then the Soviets were prepared to move with or without Iran's consent, invoking the terms of the 1926 treaty.

Events never required this move, but neither had the Russians lost their keen interest in a region which Leonid Brezhnev had described in a 1977 speech given in Mogadishu, Somalia, as "one of the great treasure houses on which the West depends." Strategically, Iran's importance remained as great to the C.I.S. as it had been to the Soviet Union that preceded it. The buildup of Iranian nuclear forces was a development that the Russians would never tolerate for long.

The surgical interdiction operation would have to be conducted in total secrecy, and be completely deniable. Russian stealth aircraft carrying American cruise missile technology would serve the purpose. The planes would launch from a point hundreds of kilometers distant from their targets, and the missiles would never be seen until they exploded. Iran would know the truth, of course, but it could never prove it had been hit by a peacetime air strike. Tehran would have been sent a message it could understand in no uncertain terms.

Flying time–on–station on a broad circular track high over the southeastern quadrant of Saudi Arabia, a USAF E3-A Airborne Warning and Control System or AWACS aircraft scanned the airspace out to a distance of 320 klicks with its suite of computer-linked air defense radars. The thirty-foot-diameter parabolic rotodome situated on double struts atop the forward fuselage revolved continually, providing coverage deep into Iran via the newly upgraded RSIP radar suite to which the antenna was linked.

Over a thousand miles to the northeast, across the low mountain chains that formed a natural barrier between Iran and Khazakhstan in the Urals, a plane with a silhouette remarkably like AWACS's and an identical purpose, an A-50 Mainstay, was flying an almost identical circular track across the still-dark skies.

Both surveillance aircraft were linked by secure military satellite relay to the C4I center in Kuwait, where the coded telemetry from their computer-enhanced radars was viewable separately on the two flat-panel side screens, or as a composite on the larger central screen of the command post.

The tactical picture showed that the airspace surrounding the projected track of the Shadows was free of fighter aircraft. Eavesdropping on Iranian communications also indicated that enemy ground tracking radars had picked up no hint of the impending strike. The large screen also displayed the projected track of the stealth aircraft, which, though invisible to radar, were not quite as invisible as most would believe.

On the other side of the vast ar-Rub' al-Khali or "empty quarter" of the Saudi Arabian desert, others were monitoring events. They, too, knew the truth about stealth, and had known from the first. In the C4I center, part of a DUF or deep underground facility buried in a remote corner of the Negev desert, communications specialists attached to the Directorate of Signals Intelligence of the Zahal or Israel Defense Forces, also studied the imagery on their own screens.

Officially kept out of the loop, the Israelis knew about the coordinated strikes anyway, just as they knew about the Votrin Algorithm, the so-called antistealth algorithm that formed the nucleus of a sophisticated computer program that made antistealth radar possible.

The Americans had their own version of the algorithm. They had possessed it from day-one, because stealth had never been intended to blind friendly eyes, only becloud the vision of the enemy. The myth of stealth's near invisibility to foe and friend alike has been, and still is, one of the most effective disinformation operations of the United States government, and one that has had willing accomplices in global defense establishments, which see it in their interests to perpetuate the long-standing myth.

Because of the disinformation surrounding the capabilities of stealth, few outside of a select group of warplanners have ever asked this question: What military force commanded by sane individuals would ever build a sophisticated weapons system that they did not have the power to detect and destroy should it ever fall into unfriendly hands?

The Americans had designed stealth, and had simultaneously designed the capability to defeat stealth. This capability was one of the most closely held secrets of the United States government—so closely held that there was a termination order applicable to anyone attempting to reveal it, one that had been used on at least two occasions, as far as the Mossad knew, and maybe more.

The counterstealth secret was U.S. property—until Votrin came along in 1989. The Russian mathematician had led a group working for the Soviets during the Gorbachev era tasked with finding a way to defeat stealth. Acting on the fact that stealth does not make planes invisible, but only reduces their radar cross section, or RCS, to a fraction of its actual size, Votrin devised his algorithm. It could be used to computer-enhance radar images and show where stealth was located in the skies.

The Votrin Algorithm wasn't as good as its American counterpart, but it was good enough to make at least the initial "angular stealth" aircraft designs visible to the right radars—and they had to be powerful enough radars to begin with, linked to powerful enough mainframe computers. If you had these, then you could see stealth. It was that simple.

The system wasn't as effective against later upgrades of stealth, and useless against the more advanced "curved stealth" of the American B-2 bomber, nor did it work against the new active electronic measures that the Americans had begun incorporating into their upgraded stealth after the Gulf War. But against the original angular stealth of the F-117A, it worked well enough to paint a usable picture.

The Israelis had been working on the Votrin Algorithm for over a decade, enhancing it and the computer-linked radar systems necessary to make it work. Votrin himself had been found dead in a Brussels apartment block in 1999 where he had lived since after escaping the Soviet Union following the fall of the Berlin Wall and the end of the Cold War. The official explanation had been death by natural causes, a heart attack suffered in an open-cage elevator rising between the fourth and fifth floors of the building. The Israelis put a different spin on it. They called it a KGB *mokri dela* operation, a "wet job" by Department K of Line S, the Komitet Gosudarstvennoy Besopastnosti's efficient assassinations directorate.

But whatever had killed Votrin, his work lived on. The Israelis retained a full set of his technical papers giving the essential parameters of the antistealthing process. The problem was, at least for them, that the Iranians had it, too. The Russians themselves had sold them the basics of the system, and their own petrodollars had financed the rest from the best of the brains of the expatriate Russian scientists who fled their homeland in the wake of the Cold War.

Against the American Block-III upgrade of the F-117A that was still under wraps at Nellis Air Force Base in Nevada, far from prying eyes, Iran's Votrin-enhanced radar would be nearly useless. But against the more primitive stealth of the Russian clone of the U.S. jet, the Eclipse, it was an enhancement that would increase the stealth's RCS by as much as 35 percent. That could make all the difference in the world, the Israelis knew, as they continued to cast probing beams of electrons at the equivocal night skies above the Middle East.

Two
Of Sales Reps, Radars, and Stealth

In the cockpit of the stealth plane code-named Shadow One that was now flying its programmed "black line" toward the nuclear reactor at Kasjhan, there was little for Vassily Petrov to do except detachedly observe. On autopilot, the plane practically flew itself, its inertial navigation system taking bearings from the array of GPS satellites overhead and matching these against onboard sensor data.

Protracted inactivity changed Petrov's focus, and his attention began to wander. His mind cast back to the two-month training period that had preceded the mission. Preparations had taken place in strictest secrecy. The joint U.S.-Russian team had been based at Vnukovo, a military rocket base at Kapustin Yar, in a remote section of the Urals. It had been agreed that Russian pilots would fly the mission in Russian planes, but the Americans had brought along their own personnel, including technicians and pilots who had flown actual missions in stealth aircraft during the Gulf War and in Yugoslavia.

Captain Chuck Covington had been one of those pilots. Covington had taken part in the opening sorties of the Desert Wind air campaign. The destruction of an Iraqi chemical weapons plant with laser-guided bombs had been his baptism by fire. Petrov had found a friend in Covington, and the American stealth driver had added personal details concerning his combat flights to those in his regular briefings.

Covington described the terror of his flight over the night skies of Baghdad, a city that glowed in the distance with an orange radiance like live coals on a barbecue grill, due to the density of antiaircraft fire flung at the skies. The streams of triple-A were so thick, the pilot said, that they blended into glowing sheets. As he approached the Iraqi capital, the acrid stench of cordite that had slowly seeped into the Nighthawk's cabin had become a choking cloud. Covington was convinced that he would die.

"They fired more bullets than I thought were ever made in the history of the world," Covington had told the Russian. "The only way I can describe it is if you turn a room into the world's biggest popcorn popper—with popcorn going off all over the place—and try to walk from one end to the other without getting hit by a piece of popcorn. That's what it was like."

"But then how did you succeed in not getting hit?" Petrov had asked the American pilot.

"By thinking, 'they're not going to hit me,' over and over again, like some kind of mantra," Covington had replied, "and just keeping on moving."

Then Covington told about the elation of hitting the target, seeing it blow sky-high in a mushrooming pillar of flame and heat, and realizing that he could not be seen by the enemy, that he was invisible and therefore untouchable.

Tonight, Petrov's flight presented none of the tension and terrors that Covington had described. The view through the cockpit windows of Shadow One was of a sky jet black and crystal clear, flecked with the countless ice chips of blue, white, and yellow stars.

There was darkness below, too, occasionally broken by the flash of headlights from vehicular traffic on one of the tributary roads crisscrossing the desert floor. Produce and consumer goods from Haifa, Amman, Cairo, Tehran, Damascus, and places far removed from the Mideast were trucked to commercial centers in Iran at all hours, just as they were in the C.I.S., Europe, or the U.S.A.

Although the stealth flashed through the sky at a velocity approaching the speed of sound, there was virtually no sense of physical motion for its pilot. Unless he chose to look out the cockpit windows, Petrov's only impression of movement was a purely psychological one, produced by the muffled roar of the plane's twin turbofan engines, and the color visuals on the multimode display screen at the center of the console, which showed a pictorial representation of the plane's flight path on a moving map display.

The plane's avionics suite was in large part a product of French technology. It had been designed and built by the French aerospace firm, Aerospatiale, in a deal that had mated French expertise in electronics miniaturization with Russian breakthroughs in high-power radars. The Phazotron Zhuk-PH system in Shadow One incorporated a stealthy synthetic-aperture laser-radar, or ladar, moving-target identification, and terrain-avoidance modes.

The result of the collaboration was a rate of cockpit miniaturization that was unprecedented in Russian aircraft design. The breakthroughs meant that for the first time Russian aircraft could begin to approach some of the sophistication that had put American military aircraft light-years ahead of them for so long, and even exceed it in certain realms.

Unlike true fighter aircraft, or the F-117A Nighthawk, for that matter, the Eclipse did not have a heads-up display or HUD, which overlaid the pilot's line of sight through the cockpit window with navigational references, target acquisition data, and other pictorials. The Eclipse didn't need a HUD. Though called "multimode," it was neither an air-superiority nor an air-dominance fighter. It flew one mission and one mission only—that of a silent, unseen platform for air-to-ground ordnance of various kinds. That was it.

Instead of a HUD, the plane's console was divided into a complex of three 9.7-inch active matrix color screens, with smaller dedicated displays for target information and navigation data at either side. The left and right screens gave configurable air-combat imaging and radar readouts. The center display was a multimode monitor linked to a RISC processor-based CPU that integrated all the data the pilot would need into a comprehensive whole. Right now the multimode screen showed Petrov a green-and-pink trough that undulated and curved toward a distant horizon line.

The trough represented the plane's trajectory, with distance and altitude, in klicks and degrees, marked off by black intersecting lines. To either side of the winding, snaking flight path was a representation of terrain out to a distance of one hundred klicks, and on this terrain field were pictorials that showed waypoints, terrain features, and threats, each color-coded according to their threat priority.

Petrov's most immediate concern as the plane flew past the first of its three waypoints were the two threat balloons—balloonlike wire grid representations in glowing orange—about fifty klicks ahead, representing SAM sites. The orange color indicated threat-rich environments with overlapping radar coverage, to be avoided at all costs.

Each of those SAM installations was equipped with a battery of surface-to-air missiles. The latest intel had shown a mix of SA-6 "Gainful" low-to-medium altitude missiles and the much newer 90Zh6 upgrade of the Soviet SA-10 "Grumble," which could reach high into a fighter's altitude envelope. A typical Iranian battery, he knew, would be made up of two or three launchers sitting atop tracked armored vehicles. Each mobile launcher was a self-contained unit including tracking and guidance radars and up to four missiles ready for deployment on pneumatic-actuated launch pylons.

The SA-10 upgrade in particular had a number of improvements that worried Petrov. Among them was its new 64N6 long-range, 3-D phased-array surveillance radar that bore the NATO code designator "Tombstone."

Unlike other SA variants, the 90Zh6 utilized two separate system components. The transporter-erector-launchers, or TELs, which fired the new 48N6 missiles, were carried on the trailers of the 54K6 command modules, which contained the radar and were mounted on a heavy MAZ-543 truck. About the same length as the earlier 5V55 series, the 48N6 was a much fatter missile, carrying more fuel and giving it greater range than previous versions.

The 64N6 radar upgrade, which was good enough to allow the SA-10 to engage tactical ballistic missiles at medium altitudes, was linked to a new-generation fire control computer with multiple scan modes enabling the simultaneous engagement of six targets with up to two missiles per target. All things being equal, the 64N6 radar stood a minuscule—but genuine—chance of detecting Shadow One in flight.

In an electronically cluttered environment such as a multiple sortie attack would create, the small, pigeon-sized radar cross section that the stealth returned to probing radar lobes might never be detected. But in an empty skyfield, in an electronically sterile environment, there was a chance of radar engagement, however small. The SAMs would have a hard time acquiring the target, but they had formidable range, and even a lucky near miss might prove fatal because of the blast radius of the missiles' high explosive fragmentation warheads.

As the threat balloons grew larger on the Eclipse's multimode screen, Petrov's thoughts turned in other directions. It was pointless to worry, and besides, the envelopes of the balloons were far from the perimeter of his projected flight path. Many kilometers separated those deadly missile launchers from his plane, and as he approached them, he knew INS would decrease the aircraft's ceiling to further maximize his low observability. Terrain-following radar would take over then, the stealth would dip low and hug the contours of the desert. Amid the ground clutter of reflected radar side lobes, it would be hidden from detection.

He would never be seen. Under cover of the night, he would ghost right past those SAMs.

Still many kilometers from the black arrow streaking toward it, Petrov's intended target lay exposed on the flat tableland midway between the Dasht-e-Kavir desert and Iran's capital, Tehran. The venting stacks of the nuclear power plant at Kasjhan now were cold and silent. Ordinarily the stacks vented nonradioactive waste steam produced by the plant's three-hundred-megawatt reactor into the night air. But tonight the French-built plant operated on only a skeleton staff, as it had been doing for the past two weeks.

The plant was undergoing a periodic downtime during which its spent uranium fuel rods were replaced and routine maintenance and inspection were conducted. The air strike had been calculated to coincide with the final week of these maintenance procedures, when the facility would remain functionally idle and understaffed. Apart from reducing the loss of human life and other collateral damage, this also significantly lessened the hazards of the explosive release of radioactive contaminants into the atmosphere as a result of the missile strike.

None of the estimated annual ten kilograms of plutonium produced by the plant would be found on-site. HUMINT, or human intelligence assets, had confirmed that all the plutonium had been transported to the Iranian Nuclear Technology Center some five hundred kilometers to the southwest, not far from the Isfahan processing complex, which included a uranium hexafluoride plant using high-speed centrifuges to enrich uranium into weapons-grade material.

Isfahan, too, was on the night's air tasking order. As

Petrov flew his heading toward Kasjhan, his fellow pilot Lavrenti Samsonov flew the other stealth aircraft in the direction of Isfahan, where another JASSM would be launched to destroy the facility. Both the CIA and KGB's estimates placed the amount of bomb-grade plutonium at the facility in the vicinity of thirty pounds. While the amount of enriched uranium already processed was not precisely known at the time of the raid, the available plutonium was estimated to be enough fissionable material to make ten Hiroshima-size bombs, or single warheads of about one megaton each. In the scale of the Mideast target set, that was easily enough for Armageddon.

The Isfahan site was a windowless four-story concrete building on the surface, and a five-story underground complex directly below where the plutonium was processed, stored, milled, and machined into warheads. Estimates placed the number of operational warheads in Iran's nuclear arsenal at somewhere between ten and fifteen. Were the reactor at Kasjhan not destroyed, the number could rise to twenty or more within a matter of months. Coupled with Iran's growing arsenal of medium-range Shihab-3 ballistic missiles, each with an approximate two-thousand-kilometer range—enough to threaten the flanks of Central Europe—the nukes presented a major regional power shift in the making, one that threatened both East and West.

The strike on Isfahan posed no danger of triggering a nuclear detonation. On the contrary, the explosives stored at the complex would help cook off the plutonium and prevent it from forming fissionable critical masses. The danger of the explosions releasing a toxic, radioactive cloud was there, but the risk was deemed acceptable. The plutonium was stored on the lowest level of the plant and would be buried beneath tons of concrete rubble.

The blast would, in effect, entomb the plutonium underground.

Or so it was hoped.

● ● ●

At the al-Rash'd ground radar station, all was quiet. The lonely outpost in the arid desert landscape was a node of the Iranian air defense system garrisoned by a small contingent attached to the Iranian 21st Signal Corps, headquartered at Mehrebad Air Force Base near Tabriz.

The personnel assigned to al-Rash'd included radar operators and technicians, missile crew for the single SA-10 launch system, and a mechanized detachment of Warsaw Pact BRDM-2 and BTR-70 APCs, heavy trucks and Jeeps from the 2nd Regional Command of the Iranian People's Army that provided security. Apart from the two monthly deliveries of food and the contraband, including forbidden liquor, purchased from Bedouin traders that regularly sold to the base, the duty was tedious, and personnel usually rotated out as soon as possible.

Tonight, at four hundred twelve hours, life at the remote desert station was no exception to the general rule of monotonous drudgery. Apart from the scopeman monitoring the radar display in the station's control room and the sentries walking their posts around the fence surrounding the installation, no one was awake.

Izmir Albrouny, whose surname was Turkish, reflecting his family's southward immigration after World War I, was twenty-six and had trained as a radar operator at the Iranian military academy in Tehran. Because Albrouny had showed himself to be skillful at his job, he had been selected to train on the new, Valkyr-II digital pulse Doppler radars that had been built by the German firm of Oberlikon under a contract with the Iranian military.

The Valkyr-II radar was linked to a Siemens mainframe computer system running SNA-Unix that could process the radar returns at ultrahigh speed, comb and filter the returns, and display the data on the high-definition color screen. The system also incorporated Votrin algorithms under a feature Oberlikon called its "advanced antistealthing" feature set.

Oberlikon had demonstrated its new radar at the Defense Services Asia Exhibition in Kuala Lumpur, Malaysia, in the spring of 2001, at the IDEX arms trade show in Abu Dhabi, UAE, the following summer, and then at the Paris Air Show at Le Bourget Airport. Its sales representatives at these and other global arms bazaars had aggressively marketed the enhanced radars, and their efforts had not been in vain. Oberlikon sales reps in the firm's Bonn headquarters had set up appointments with a number of interested buyers representing the military branches of their respective governments.

Later that season, the Iranian government had clinched a multimillion-dollar deal with Oberlikon to retrofit their French-made radar system with the VK-II upgrade package. The enhancements in the retrofit would make the Iranian air-defense system the best in the region, barring that of the Israelis, which was built by a consortium including Oberlikon, the Israeli firm IAE, and the U.S.-based McDonnell Douglas Military Electronics Division. The retrofit of the Iranian system was only partially complete, which was another reason for the timing of the strike mission flown by the Shadows.

Nevertheless, the retrofit was more complete than intelligence available to the U.S.-Russian coalition had indicated. The radar defense node at al-Rash'd was not listed as among those scheduled to receive the Valkyr-II upgrade until the fall. The Israeli military intelligence agency, AMAN, had confirmed this through intelligence from a highly placed informant in the Iranian military, but though true at the time the intel was received, it had been rendered false by a step-up in the pace of the retrofit program.

The net result was that tonight, as Vassily Petrov cleared the first SAM site along his flight path and approached the second to his right, the presence of his aircraft was picked up by the air defense radar node at al-Rash'd and seen by Albrouny at precisely four hundred fifteen hours, while Shadow One was passing thirteen kilometers to the east at an altitude of ten thousand feet and a sub-Mach speed of seven hundred miles per hour.

The radar contact did not register as a blip, nor was the radar scope that Albrouny watched a round, green screen dominated by a moving sweep hand of white electronic snow. Albrouny's screen was a large, modern computer monitor equipped with a keyboard and mouse that showed a full-color digital relief map of the roughly two hundred klicks of territory covered by the radar node.

The view from the screen was the airspace looking down from an imaginary point above the earth. Instead of the blips of yesterday's technology, symbols and lines indicating the type of threats and vectors of approach flashed into being on the screen, and slid across the map as radar tracked them.

At four hundred fifteen hours, zulu, Albrouny was surprised to see an icon he knew only from training exercises appear on the extreme left of the screen. The symbol was a yellow triangle with the approximate speed and heading of the aircraft it represented listed beneath it as it crossed the map.

"*Madergenduh!*—motherfucker!" Albrouny muttered in Farsi as it appeared. He knew the yellow delta icon stood for a radar contact with a stealth aircraft.

A split second later the contact disappeared from the screen, but then reappeared in under a minute, already many kilometers from the point of the first sighting. Then it disappeared and was not seen again.

Since the new radar system was equipped with several advanced, computer-aided options, Albrouny used them to the fullest. While he waited for the contact to reappear, the scopeman clicked on the histogram button on the toolbar atop his screen. This feature enabled operators to replay, then analyze, recent contact data that was stored in computer memory.

Albrouny found the first and then the second stealth contacts, playing each back in slow motion in a window superimposed over the main digital map, which continued to show real-time radar returns. He next ordered the system to display the lobes and ellipses of the recorded contacts and to analyze their signatures against a library of aircraft radar signatures stored in the system's extensive database.

The results of the analysis gave Albrouny a textual and pictorial match on several points of convergence between the actual contact and the statistics the database contained about low-observable aircraft.

The pictorials were good, but not conclusive. The bottom line for Albrouny was that he'd maybe had an actual stealth contact, but it might just as well have been atmospherics, a glitch in the software, an electronic hiccup, or a radar lobe bouncing off a natural object with a radar cross section small enough to fool the system into thinking it had seen a stealth. A cluster of hailstones in the midst of a *shamal,* or severe storm, could account for this. Other things could, too.

Still, there it had been. Albrouny pondered awhile as he continued to process and analyze the contact data, displaying lines of bearing, estimated speed, and other information.

Did he want to wake "the Beast" from his slumbers and risk his commanding officer's legendary wrath? This was the question. Albrouny knew very well that he had replaced a radar officer who had dared to disturb Major Kuraytem while he was enjoying the company of one of the women smuggled into the base from the regional capital, Semnan, and had paid for his indiscretion with a hasty transfer to the hard-duty garrisons in contentious Kurdish strongholds in the mountainous region north near Tabriz.

Staring at the screen, Albrouny rhythmically drummed his fingers on the edges of the computer keyboard. Finally, he picked up the phone beside his console, taking a chance on rousing the base commander from his nightly drunken sleep, and hoping that tonight the major slept by himself.

Three
Ghosts in the Machine

Vassily Petrov heard a warbling, two-note chime announcing that the stealth had reached its final waypoint, in this case its initial point for ordnance release, or IP. The IP is generally keyed to a prominent terrain feature. Here the landmark was part of a system of deep culverts with steep, poured concrete sides, lying athwart the north-south axis of the Tehran to Isfahan highway approximately ninety-six klicks from the target site.

The glowing blue triangle indicating the boundaries of the zone that overlaid the plane's position on the flight path display echoed this new situational development. Though Petrov's left scope showed a thermal imaging view of the landscape, enhanced with pseudocolor to bring out contrast, he straightened in his seat and glanced directly out Shadow One's cockpit window at the terrain below.

Now Petrov could just discern the unlighted four-lane strip of blacktop highway some two thousand meters below the plane, with the steeply inclined concrete walls of the culvert a few hundred meters directly ahead. The twin headlight beams of a big lorry barreling down the highway toward the culvert lit the way for him.

Petrov armed the stealth's missile launch system as he checked the kilometers-to-go readout at the top of his main scope that counted down the distance to the ordnance release point. The estimated time of arrival at the heart of his launch envelope was also projected on the multimode display: six minutes.

Shattered by the sound of the IP warning tones, forgotten as he went through his checklist of procedures, Petrov's broken reverie was now replaced by an all-over alertness fed by the rush of adrenaline that coursed through his veins. Suddenly all the implications of the mission, of where he was and what he was about to do, stood out in stark definition. This was combat, not an exercise. He was soon to launch a live round on an actual target.

An unexplainable fear swept over him, the ancient fear expressed in tales of letting the genie out of the bottle, and of taboos about crossing thresholds, that have always been attended by a sense of deep foreboding. The human who first picked up a burning stick must have known this fear, and the human after him who saw the sharp point the fire had formed and then fashioned an arrow, surely also experienced it. On and on through the ages that fear had become familiar to those who had crossed thresholds in peace and in war.

Vassily Petrov was just another in a long line, stretching backward and forward to vanishing points in a dark infinity, who was destined to know it. Covington, his American briefer, had certainly known it, too. Petrov wondered if his own fear was greater than Covington's. Did the absence of the sound and fury of war that the American Nighthawk driver had experienced over Iraqi airspace during Desert Wind make a difference? Or was it simply the primordial psychological fear of threshold crossing that brought it on?

Petrov would have to think about this later. For the moment he was a pilot, not a philosopher, and he had a job to do.

As Shadow One's icon neared the center of the glowing green box depicted on the screen, Petrov continued the missile arming and prelaunch procedures, first initializing the computer link to the JASSM's onboard processor that interrogated its multiple systems, including the missile's ring laser gyroscope, which took positional readings and backed up data from GPS.

Only when all systems read in the affirmative did Petrov open the conformal carriage bay doors and lower the JASSM down from the belly of the stealth. Then, in the heart of his launch envelope, he hit the pickle button on his joystick and held it down, a signal to Shadow One's battle management computer system to take over the remaining launch procedures that were to vector the missile in on its target.

The plane lurched as the JASSM's chemical booster stage ignited, thrusting the stub-winged, snub-nosed robot bomb from beneath the black abdomen of the aircraft. The rocket's exhaust whooshed out in a steaming, smoke-gushing contrail as the departing JASSM quickly outstripped the plane. Seconds later the booster stage burned out and the missile's air-breathing ramjet propulsion system took over, hurling the JASSM into the night at supersonic speeds.

Petrov felt the plane lighten as the fifteen-hundred-pound tube of metal, computer hardware, and high-explosive warhead separated, and sideslipped left. Coming off the vector, Petrov saw the missile's jet exhaust flare on his right as the bird disappeared into the darkness. It was soon visible only as an arrow-shaped red pictorial gliding down the wire-grid flight track on the central multimode cockpit screen.

Petrov kept his eye on the right visual display unit showing nose-camera TI video from the missile as it flew its course. Headers on the video feed displayed GMT, elapsed time, and the presence of an active lock on GPS satellites, which augmented the JASSM's terrain contour matching or TERCOM and digital scene matching correlator or DSMAC programming to enhance the accuracy of delivery on the target.

The nose-camera video showed a colorized image of moving terrain features slashed in half by the ruler-straight vertical line of a highway below. An eerily glowing rectangular object, like some luminescent deep-sea shrimp caught in the glare of diving lights, slid past on the highway before being lost to view. The object, Petrov knew, was a truck whose path JASSM had just overflown less than fifty feet below it.

Until the missile struck its target, or until a failure of the plan warranted its premature detonation or retargeting, Petrov would scan his TI nose-camera screen to track the JASSM's progress. During the approximate six minutes until the missile reached its delivery point, Petrov would loiter near his IP, ready to take any of several actions. When the TI image registered a kill, he would turn, burn, and head back to his RV or rendezvous point across the Iran-C.I.S. border with an Ilyushin-78 Midas fuelbird.

The next few minutes were the most unnerving of Petrov's career as a military pilot. Though he'd practiced the launch procedure many times in flight simulations, doing it for real was an entirely different experience. The eerily soundless moving imagery on the TI screen continued to depict the ghost landscape passing beneath the JASSM, terrain features looming larger, then smaller, as the missile executed dips and turns on its preprogrammed flight trajectory that would make it nearly invisible to radar by losing its signature in the ground clutter.

Trucks and other vehicles continued to appear in the final minutes before delivery, eerie spectral forms that passed soundlessly beneath the hurtling cruise that had looped back to confuse ground detection radars and followed the rift of a wadi for several kilometers, then popped up again and flew a course along a lateral road. This was not surprising—as in the Gulf War, roads were used as reference points for the missile's homing system because they were easy to follow and led unerringly to the assigned targets.

And then, in the final sixty seconds of flight, Petrov began picking up the target itself on his feed.

The venting stack and dome of the main reactor building were clearly visible, as were the four outbuildings placed on a circular access road that serviced it and the vehicles in the parking area outside.

Suddenly the view shifted as the JASSM, which had been paralleling the road on a low trajectory at nearly twice the speed of sound, shot upward to commence its terminal engagement phase.

Now Petrov was looking downward at the gaping mouth of the venting stack, lit with a ring of small, flashing red aircraft warning lights, and the broad, stressed concrete cupola of the main reactor dome beside it.

Two more seconds passed. Suddenly the image of the dome filled the entire screen. Now there came a bright flash of obliterating whiteness and the missile's nose-camera feed snowed to a maelstrom of electronic noise.

Petrov stared at the now empty display for a second more, aware that he was soaked with sweat, then switched it over to standby mode. Banking sharply, he turned Shadow One around and reset the plane's inertial navigation system for the return track of the covert flight. The first boom of the multiple explosions at Kasjhan reached him a full minute after the actual destruction took place.

The explosion that reduced the Kasjhan nuclear reactor to a charred and melted mass of heat-fused wreckage and killed five staff members who were on duty on the night watch at the plant, was thorough and all-consuming.

The incendiary system the JASSM used was an FAE or fuel-air explosive, recently developed to utilize a payload of jellied explosive that filled most of the one-ton missile. The FAEs deployed in the Gulf were monsters, but the technology had matured to the point where a lot more bang could be had for a lot less buck and took up

considerably less volume using heavy-density, jelled incendiary sources.

The JASSM's terminal velocity had propelled it downward into the center of the reactor dome, where its hard-
ened-steel penetrator head punched a hole in the
twelve-foot-thick steel-and-concrete vault. Milliseconds
later, now inside the reactor building, the FAE warhead
detonated in two coordinated phases.

First, a cluster of very fast electronic switches akin to
the kryton switches that trigger nuclear explosions, fired
a ring of small plastique charges that air-dispersed the
jelled explosive in a spherical cloud. Milliseconds after
that, the main charge aft of the primary charge detonated,
igniting the fuel cloud, which exploded in a fierce chain
reaction equivalent in power to a one-kiloton nuclear
blast.

Many kilometers to the south, at almost the same time,
the nuclear weapons processing plant at Isfahan was sub-
jected to a similar cataclysm from the second coordinated
JASSM strike. In this case, the presence of a full night
shift on duty resulted in many more human casualties,
most of them buried under thousands of tons of the same
concrete-and-steel wreckage that sealed off the plant's
plutonium reserves forever. Apparently in Isfahan's case,
the intelligence estimates had been somewhat faulty.

Vassily Petrov heard the second, and louder boom of the
final explosion as he swung Shadow One in a broad circle
and headed back toward the mountainous borderland. This
time the noise was accompanied by a shock wave, riding
a bubble of supercompressed air, that buffeted the plane
and resulted in a momentary warning of imminent engine
flameout on his console gauges. The brief loss of power
gave Petrov a queasy feeling in the pit of his stomach.

But then, seconds later, the crisis was past and he was
vectoring along his return flight path, all systems now
back to normal. Except for one development, the flight
back was identical in all respects to the flight in. Now the
night sky was less black, less clear outside his cockpit

windows; a film of dust seemed to hang in the atmosphere.

In a moment Petrov understood the reason for this. He was flying into a desert storm, but one of nature's own this time. What the inhabitants of the region called a *shamal* was blowing up, a tempest of sand, wind, rain, and sometimes even pelting bullets of ice, that could become very bad at times.

There it was again. Another group of radar returns classified as a stealth contact by the Valkyr-II system. This time it held for a moment longer. And now, to top it all, the track was approaching the station.

Albrouny had roused the Beast from his lair, and now Kuraytem was standing over his shoulder, watching the screen, too. The major, looking unkempt in his hastily donned olive-drab fatigues, was rocking a bit and he reeked of hashish smoke and the chewed stimulant called *naswar,* but his attention was focused on the screen and he was not shouting.

Then, just as before, the contact disappeared from the scope. Yet this time Albrouny was told to keep his eye on the display. The base's SA-10 missile battery was activated, too, just in case the contact turned out to have been real.

Suddenly it was back again. Major Kuraytem grabbed the phone beside him and punched a three-key internal number. He was immediately connected to the SAM battery outside.

"Sergeant, I want your crew to put radar on coordinates delta-nine-zero-seven. You are to synchronize fire control with my instructions."

Kuraytem continued issuing orders to the Grumble crew. To Albrouny, he now seemed as sober as a mullah at morning muezzin, and shouting just as loud.

"Sir, I have another contact on my scope," Albrouny told the major. "It's the stealth again." The scopeman read off the new coordinates, which Kuraytem relayed to the SAM crew. Seconds later they had launched a missile.

• • •

The situation had changed again, changed for the worse. Petrov realized he was now in serious trouble. The *shamal* was buffeting Shadow One with incredible force, freezing rain and blinding sand pelting the aircraft's thin metal skin. He pulled back on the throttle, gaining altitude, pushing the plane above the worst of the weather, but using up precious fuel reserves in the process.

Petrov's tactical situation had also deteriorated by this point. The plane's Zhuk-PH threat-fingerprinting ladar popped a SAM symbol onto his field of view, simultaneously shrieking out tones of warning. The missile was vectoring in his direction, the round's active radar seeker head emitting a telltale electronic signature. Intellectually, Petrov knew there was no chance that the missile could achieve a terminal guidance lock on Shadow One, but his gut instincts flew in the face of reason. Again, he throttled back, clawing higher to move out of the path projected on his main screen.

To his surprise the missile changed course and began to close. Petrov took further evasive action, now flying down into the center of the storm. The missile continued to close but suddenly became erratic. Petrov didn't know it, but on the radar screen back at al-Rash'd, the stealth pictorial had also disappeared from the map display.

The SA-10 warhead was moving at Mach 2.5, almost three times Shadow One's velocity. Its trajectory brought it close enough to the plane so that when it exploded, a mixture of circumstances ensured that the concussion wave caught the aircraft on its leading edge.

The combination of the *shamal* and the warhead's adaptive detonation feature was enough to cause a flame-out of the stealth's left engine. The warhead's onboard processor used a best-guess approach to direct the fragments of detonation in the direction of the contact as opposed to the conventional spraying of blast fragments in all directions. In this case, the warhead guessed right.

Petrov swore as the stealth suddenly lost altitude and precipitously nosed down. He tried to emergency restart, but both his engines were now dead. His altimeter line, white numbers flashing on the right upper portion of his main screen, showed he was dropping like a stone with the fierce storm swirling around him, pelting the cockpit canopy windows with hailstones, some the size of mothballs.

Petrov cursed and tried to restart one final time. His engines briefly caught, but then died of infectious flameout. Now, he knew, there was but one option left: He had to land the plane dead-stick, on the desert, with all the risks to which such an emergency landing would expose him. However, the choice was as clear as it was Draconian—crash-land or simply crash. There was no longer any in-between for Shadow One.

Four
A Sea of Brown Sugar

"Missile detonation, sir," Albrouny informed Major Kuraytem. "Near the last radar contact with the bogie."

"I can see that for myself," the major replied dourly.

Kuraytem picked up the phone and was answered by a crisp: "Armored brigade headquarters, Lieutenant Gosaj speaking."

"It is possible that an enemy fighter aircraft has been damaged or destroyed by a SAM strike," Kuraytem told the lieutenant, measuring his words. "I want you to put everything you have into a search for wreckage."

Kuraytem read off the grid coordinates of the likely wreckage scatter zone from the digital radar's map display.

"Yes, Major," Gosaj replied. "Is there anything else I should know about the aircraft?"

Kuraytem considered for a few moments, then said, "Nothing else. Except I want to be informed the moment you find anything, no matter what. Understood?"

"Yes, sir," Gosaj replied, and rang off. He, too, paused a few seconds to reflect on what he had just been told. To order up a mechanized search detachment in the middle of one of the worst winter storms to hit the region in years meant that something big indeed was up. He'd have to keep his eyes open and his wits about him.

Picking up the handset, Lieutenant Gosaj punched in four numbers, soon dictating a series of instructions of his own.

Few alternatives remained. With all thrust gone, Petrov had only his inertial navigation system to stabilize the aircraft via movements of wing flaps and tail rudder. The Eclipse, like the American F-117 Nighthawk stealth fighter, was a hard plane to control even with all systems functioning normally. Under the present circumstances, it was like flying an iceberg over Yellowstone Park. But for three very sound reasons there was no possibility of Petrov ejecting.

The first was that the plane was cruising too low to the ground for his ejector seat's chute to reliably open, the second was the howling hell of ice and sand that surrounded the plane, and the third was that Petrov could not be certain that pulling the hazard-striped ejection lever beneath his seat would not simply result in detonating a large explosive charge that would blow him and the plane into a cloud of fragments.

The last consideration was the same one that Francis Gary Powers had faced almost forty years before in a U-2 spy plane some twenty-five thousand meters above the Soviet Union, and had resulted in the same decision Petrov now made—not to pull the ejection lever but instead land the plane if he were able.

Petrov could only succeed in this by attempting an instrument landing. The view from the cockpit was a dark, swirling chaos, punctuated by the steady rat-a-tat of hailstones drumming against wings, fuselage, and canopy windows. The only reliable picture Petrov had of the environment outside the plane came from its thermal imaging screen. He kept his eyes fixed on that. *Thank God I still have electrons,* he thought.

The TI sensors linked to the screen looked downward through the storm, revealing the flat desert floor below in shades of black, white, and polychrome. Petrov could see a mountain range off in the distance and surmised that he had enough taxiing room to land the plane. But the resolution was by no means sharp enough to tell him if any small boulders, shallow wadis, thorn trees, or other hazards that could snap his nose gear lay in the plane's line of approach.

Buffeted by the storm's intensifying fury, the aircraft violently lurched and pitched, and the stick bucked in his hand, so he could hardly hold it. Petrov continued to scan the TI screen. He was searching for a highway. It would be a far safer place to touch down than open desert. Time was running out, though, and he was pushing the envelope. Shadow One was losing altitude fast. He had to start his approach now. He'd be hitting the desert crust one way or another damned soon. Whether he did it landing or colliding was up to him.

Petrov lowered the landing gear, and angled Shadow One's nose down into the weather. It was not easy. Apart from the wind that was trying to flip the plane over the way a cat savages a mouse in its claws, the plane was still doing better than four hundred miles per hour. With its angular fuselage design, the Eclipse was an inherently unstable aircraft. This was why it needed a fly-by-wire flight control system. Without it, the plane was the aerodynamic equivalent of a fallen leaf caught in a strong wind, albeit a leaf equipped with ailerons and tail rudder. *And I have no engines,* he thought.

Within seconds, after the nose and aft landing gears extended and locked into position, Petrov had dropped another two hundred meters through a dangerous, swirling soup of sand, rain, and ice. He could see the ground jumping up at him in the TI scope, and though the altimeter showed he had cut his descent rate in half, he was still moving forward at tremendous speed.

In a heartbeat his nose gear dug into the desert crust. The stealth rolled along the flat surface of the Dasht like a bullet on wheels. Petrov ejected his braking chute and felt it deploy out the plane's rear with a bone-crunching lurch. The chute caught the wind with a savage jolt and the plane skewed to the right. It was still moving at better than a hundred miles per hour, and going sideways in the bargain.

Suddenly Petrov felt an even greater jolt, and the plane's nose pitched over. The horizon tilted crazily as the plane seesawed, its tail section flung in the air. The forward landing gear had struck a boulder, he at first surmised. But as his world was stood on end, Petrov realized the truth: he'd rolled right into a wadi.

Petrov's next sight was of sand being dumped over his canopy windows, as though a malevolent giant were shoveling great heaps of it onto a tiny black insect that had fallen by his feet and howling with laughter while burying his victim. Petrov had the perverse sense that he was sinking in a dry, granular sea, a sea, it seemed to him, that was made of dark brown sugar.

By seven hundred hours the *shamal* had largely petered out, leaving the desert floor encrusted with a thin film of ice and piled with heaps of sand where no dunes had existed scant hours before. In the lead APC of the armored detachment that was already many klicks from its base, Lieutenant Gosaj scrutinized the desert through high-power binoculars.

The *shamal*, he realized, had also obliterated all traces of anything that might have rolled, walked, fallen into, or sunk beneath the area overnight.

Just the same, Gosaj had another twenty kilometers' worth of vacant desert to cover before he could report back that he had found nothing. After that, helicopters would take advantage of the more suitable flying conditions now prevailing in which to conduct a thorough search by air.

Expecting to find nothing, Gosaj continued to peer through his binoculars as the tracked vehicle lumbered forward, followed by a GAZ heavy transport truck carrying a detachment of Iranian regulars in case there was trouble.

It was going to be a real son of a bitch. Both men could sense it in their guts. The American air-force general and his Russian PVO counterpart had seen enough missions to know when things had gone sour, and this one had just curdled like day-old cream. The initial jubilation following the successful strikes on the two targets was followed by a tense wait for the planes to return.

Only one of them had come back so far. Samsonov had made his run, turned around, and flown a course back across the Iran-Azeril border to rendezvous Shadow Two with a waiting fuelbird.

After tanking up, Samsonov had been escorted to the staging base by two MiG-29s. Directly on landing he had been debriefed.

But Petrov had never made it home across the border. Shadow One had not been sighted by any of the MiG fighter patrols sent out to scan the border for the MFI's return. There had been overhead surveillance by a KH-14 photoreconnaissance satellite, but this had showed only the possibility that the plane had been shot down.

Maybe it would return after all. For now, though, the plane was missing. Lost was a better way of putting it.

Petrov couldn't bring himself to do what he had been ordered to do. He had received clear instructions: if he made a forced landing and the stealth was still intact, he was to trigger a special demolition charge that would blow up the plane and then attempt to escape on foot.

Supposedly Petrov would have five minutes between activating the demo charge and the explosion to get clear of the blast zone. But Petrov entertained lingering doubts about this. He reasoned that on a mission as secret as his had been, it might have been deemed prudent to obliterate all traces of the aircraft, including the pilot. Twice Petrov had steeled himself to activate the destruct sequence, but both times he'd faltered and held back.

Petrov came to the conclusion that he was neither brave nor patriotic nor suicidal enough to execute his orders.

He then decided on a different approach.

Daylight found him crouched against the lip of the wadi in which the plane had crashed, shivering in the bitter morning cold as he set up the portable satcom unit he had been provided in case he'd had to eject and needed to be rescued. Petrov understood that the command center would be listening on all emergency frequencies. The satcom rig used an advanced signal hopping, spread spectrum transmission mode that would make the call harder to detect and impossible to eavesdrop on even if detected, although any form of transmission posed a risk.

Petrov had climbed up the side of the shallow wadi and peered over its edge. Beyond lay an empty expanse of desert, the sky above vacant of any man-made object. Either the Iranians hadn't seen him go down, or if they had, they were not yet within visual range of his aircraft.

With no reason to hide, he ascended the sloping embankment to the level of the desert floor and took stock of his situation.

The plane appeared intact from this vantage point, but that could be deceiving. All he could see of Shadow One was the top half of the peaked fuselage and the projecting two thirds of its canted wings. The flat underside of the plane was buried under a few hundred kilos of windblown desert sand that had been funneled down around it by the *shamal*. Thankfully, the wadi had been shallow, or he'd never have gotten out.

Petrov was willing to bet that Shadow One's nose gear had been damaged during the last few seconds of landing; in which case, even if he could restart the engines, it would make getting airborne again highly problematic to say the least.

Still, with a little help it might be possible. If a rescue team could be gotten in somehow . . .

Petrov let the thought trail off without troubling to complete it in his mind. It was all academic, and no doubt wishful thinking. He had his orders, and he should have followed them to the letter. And yet . . . let any of the bastards sitting on their padded rears across the border find themselves in his position, Petrov had no doubt that they would think twice about blowing up the plane. Fuck them, he thought. Let them cut him a second set of orders. He wanted to live.

Breaking open the gray metal container, he extracted the satcom unit. The unit was far smaller than previous units he'd seen, roughly the same size as the original cellular phones designed for cars, which it closely resembled, with a large rectangular base and separate handset. In fact, the unit's main difference from old-style bag phones was in the shape and size of its antenna, which was a mini–satellite antenna like those found in commercial satellite television systems.

Once Petrov had unpacked and set up the antenna, which unfurled like an umbrella, it went through a scanning procedure that aligned its beam with a Russian communications satellite in low earth orbit or LEO and executed an electronic handshake protocol that established the secure uplink. The Cyrillic letters on the unit's small monochrome LCD display told Petrov he was ready to transmit.

General Korniyenko's phone buzzed.

"Sir, we have just received a satcom transmission from Major Petrov," the voice of one of the communications technicians working in the pit below the installation's upper, tactical level announced. "Would you like to be patched through?"

"Yes, at once," he replied.

Korniyenko motioned to Yarwood, whose translator listened in on the conversation despite Yarwood's textbook-fluent knowledge of conversational Russian.

Seconds later Petrov was in touch with the general.

"Greetings, Vassily Ivanevich. What is your situation?" asked Korniyenko, addressing Petrov by his patronymic in informal fashion, a sign the pilot took to indicate that the general did not suspect the true and serious nature of events.

"Not good, sir," Petrov replied guardedly, aware that he was sure to provoke the general's wrath before long. "The plane lost power. It might have been due to a near miss by a homing missile, the effects of last night's severe weather, or both, but the upshot is that I was forced to land the aircraft."

"You have not destroyed it, then?" the general asked, and Petrov could not fail to note the new edge of suspicion that had crept into his voice.

Petrov took a deep breath. "No, sir, I have not," he replied. "The plane does not appear badly damaged. It may even be flyable. But it is partially covered with wind-blown sand as a result of the emergency landing during the storm. I believed it was my duty to try to contact you before carrying out the destruct order."

Korniyenko thought over what Petrov had just told him. His first impulse was to threaten the pilot with court-martial for insubordination, for his orders had been unmistakable and not subject to interpretation. In the old days this is what he would have done, at the top of his voice. But these were new times, and Korniyenko tempered his reply accordingly.

"Say your position and then destroy the plane," he spoke into the handset. "A search-and-rescue mission will be flown out tonight. A team is waiting on standby. At hourly intervals from nightfall on, listen for instructions on emergency channel number three. We will get you out. But you must destroy the plane at once. Is this understood?"

"Understood, sir," Petrov replied. "I will do so immediately."

"Very good," the general replied. "We will see each other later. Now do as ordered, Major." There was no mistaking the general's intention in these last words, nor, Petrov noted, was the patronymic being used anymore. He had been addressed in the businesslike form of "Major." So be it then. An order was an order.

The satcom unit's LCD display showed that the uplink had been terminated. Petrov saw no other choice. Whether or not he died as a result of triggering the destruct sequence, he was duty-bound to do it. In any case, he would rather die carrying out orders than return home in disgrace and branded permanently as a coward. There would be no point in living such a life. He would forfeit his career and military benefits. His life, in effect, would be as much over that way as if he'd been blown up with the stealth.

Petrov stowed away the satcom rig and got his survival kit and gear out of the downed plane's cockpit. He reached in again and pressed the arm button for the detonation charge.

All at once hell broke loose.

A sudden staccato burst of automatic fire made Petrov start reflexively. He thought at first he'd been hit. But he felt himself and discovered with relief that he was unharmed.

When the pilot looked up he saw a heavily armed Mil-24 Hind-F attack helicopter hovering overhead, its fuselage painted in a desert camouflage pattern of grays and browns. A wisp of smoke curled from the four-barrel rotary cannon beneath its cockpit that had fired the 12.7-mm warning salvo.

For a brief instant Petrov incongruously thought that a Russian rescue party had somehow reached him. But that moment flashed past him as quickly as it had arrived.

Right chopper, wrong army, he thought. The helicopter bore the green-white-red insignia of the Pasdaran Air Corps, and Petrov could now see a pillarlike cloud of dust trailing behind tiny black specks on the horizon that he knew was surely a mechanized armor column following on with additional troops. Although he didn't understand the commands, in Farsi, being barked at him by the amplified voice of the helo's pilot, he was well enough aware of their connotations.

Petrov raised his hands high over his head.

Many kilometers away, his superior officer was mouthing the Russian word for traitor, sotto voce, out of earshot of his American colleague.

Major Kuraytem heard Lieutenant Gosaj's distant voice over the radio set's speaker. Static and interference played their usual tricks with reception, but even so there was no mistaking the excitement that had seized hold of Gosaj.

"Sir! Excellent news," he declared. "We have discovered a plane intact. It appears to be a highly advanced aircraft, possibly experimental—a stealth aircraft even, perhaps."

"The Americans have attacked us?" Kuraytem asked, perplexed at his subordinate's talk of stealth aircraft. Who else but the Americans flew them?

"No, sir, I don't believe it is the Americans."

"Then who?"

"*Shuravi,*" Gosaj replied.

Kuraytem was stunned. Gosaj had just used the Farsi word for "Russians."

"Explain," Kuraytem ordered.

"Sir," Gosaj answered, "the plane bears no markings or other insignia of nationality we can see. And it is partially buried in sand. However, the instrumentation markings are in Cyrillic characters and the pilot appears to speak only Russian." He paused. "What are my instructions?"

Kuraytem thought a moment. "The pilot has been captured and he is alive, you say?"

"Yes, sir," Gosaj answered. "The pilot is alive and apparently uninjured."

"Very well," Kuraytem answered. "You are to guard the crash site pending the arrival of reinforcements. Until then you are to let nothing come between your men and the plane, is this understood?"

"Completely understood, Major," Gosaj answered crisply.

"As to the pilot of the plane, he is to be placed onboard one of the two Hinds under armed guard and immediately flown back to base. The other helo is to remain with your detachment. I will issue the appropriate orders."

"Very good, sir," Gosaj said, and replaced the radio handset as the conversation ended.

Within a matter of minutes Petrov had been searched for weapons. Then, with his wrists cable-tied behind his back, he was pushed into the open side hatch of the low-hovering Mi-24.

As Gosaj watched the helicopter rise to its cruising altitude of nine meters and chug off to the west, trailing faint brown contrails from its port and starboard engine exhaust vents, Major Kuraytem was already thinking about his next posting—to the military academy in Tehran if things worked out right. After this coup he would be promoted, he would make certain of that. Then it would be good-bye to this lonely desert hellhole.

"I shall be in my quarters," the major told the radar operator. "Keep me posted, Albrouny. And good work."

"Thank you, sir," Albrouny replied, and smartly saluted.

Major Kuraytem returned the salute and left the command center. It was time for a shower and shave, and maybe even a pinch of *naswar* to celebrate his good fortune, and the still better things yet to come, thanks to the ill-starred adventurism of his country's foes.

Five
Stratagems of Power

The president's ten A.M. briefing in the Oval Office was not what he'd anticipated. Travis Claymore had received the reports of the downing of Shadow One via the morning's National Intelligence Estimate sheet from the CIA, which he normally skimmed at his six A.M. breakfast.

This morning the intel briefing was accompanied by Critic-coded cables from Defense and the Pentagon. All concerned the joint U.S.-C.I.S. mission inside Iran and the loss, and presumed capture, by Sepah-e-Pasdaran or Iranian Revolutionary Guard forces, of the Russian stealth plane.

By nine o'clock Claymore was at his desk in the Oval Office, with his planned weekend getaway to Camp David canceled and fresh intelligence reports littering his desktop. By nine forty-five the president had placed and received a half-dozen phone calls, concluding with a twenty-minute-long conversation between himself and Russian President Grigorenko.

Claymore had sounded the Russian leader on his country's plans, aware that in the seven-hour time lag between Washington and Moscow there would have been time for Grigorenko and his staff to explore several options. Specifically, he wanted to know if the Soviets were considering an operation to retake the plane.

"Yes, candidly we are considering such an alternative," Grigorenko had told Claymore. "I'm sure you will agree that the possession of the aircraft by Iran poses grave risks to regional and world security."

"I do agree," Claymore had replied. "No question. But I have to tell you, Dimitri, that from the information I have available, I have my doubts about the wisdom of a military option. First of all, we don't really know yet what the Iranians will do with the plane. For example, there's a question in my mind about whether they'll just take the plane apart and reverse-engineer or go for a deal. In my opinion we should try a little old-fashioned horse trading first."

"We don't think this is likely," Grigorenko returned, trying to remember that the U.S. president, like most Americans, could be at times extremely naive concerning global political realities. "We have committed an act of aggression against them, indeed an act of war. We have set their cherished nuclear weapons program back a decade. It seems unlikely that they will have any inclination to bargain."

Claymore paused a moment to gesture to his secretary in acknowledgment that the chairman of the Joint Chiefs had just arrived for their scheduled ten A.M. meeting.

"Sorry, Dimitri. You still there?"

"Right here, Mr. President."

"Glad to hear it, partner," the president replied. "Now, I hear what you're saying, and it makes sense. But the way I look at this problem is, 'Well, hot damn. They got the plane.' We've got to accept that. But we have other things they might want to trade for it."

"Such as what?" Grigorenko asked. "Oil? Iran is awash in crude. Wheat? They have more than sufficient staples.

Technology? They have stolen plenty of it and have bought the rest. Weapons? This, they might want. But do we wish to offer them weapons after we have gone to such extreme lengths to take their weapons away?"

"Well, now let's back up, here, Dimitri," suggested Claymore. "In fact, there may be an option in there you've missed. It's an open secret that the Iranians have been negotiating major arms upgrade packages with the U.S. and C.I.S. both. Now, we have warned them repeatedly about repercussions concerning nuclear proliferation. On the other hand, we have always been willing to provide arms for legitimate defense needs."

"And you are suggesting that things can go back to normal if they return the plane? Just like that?"

"That's an oversimplification, but essentially that's exactly what I'm saying. Look, Iran knew damn well that their possession of nuclear missiles capable of hitting Tel Aviv, let alone Belgrade, Bonn, or Kiev, would not be tolerated. So they took a gamble. Well, they lost. My position is that we've gone and hit them with the stick, so why not dangle the carrot before giving them another whack in the teeth?"

Grigorenko considered the American leader's words a moment. "Your point is well taken, Mr. President," he replied. "I will bring it up at a meeting of my cabinet later today. But I must tell you in all frankness that I do not think a political solution will find acceptance in Russian legislative circles. Unlike your country, Russia is not blessed with a secure southern border. Iran is behind guerrilla factions in Afghanistan and insurrection in the Caucasus. Imagine Mexico, armed and belligerent, and you will appreciate the threat as we do. However, I will look into this."

"Thanks, Dimitri," replied Claymore. "I know we can work this out advantageously."

"Good-bye, Mr. President."

When Claymore hung up the phone it was already ten minutes past the briefing hour. He punched a button on his intercom and told his secretary to send in the chairman of the JCS as well as the secretary of defense and national security advisor, who also waited outside in the Oval Office's anteroom.

In his Moscow office, President Dimitri Grigorenko, looking and feeling considerably more tired than Claymore at the end of a long day, also had a visitor cooling his heels outside. He did not plan to discuss any horse trades, though, no matter what he had told his opposite number in the White House. Politically, the Americans drank Pepsi—his drink was Stoli Kristall.

The sprawling farm occupied hundreds of cultivated acres in the north of the scrub desert Israelis call the Negev. Craggy mountains, looking for all the world like immense mud pies left by the Creator to bake in the searing desert sun, loomed in the near distance. Yet where the tractor rolled along at its snail's pace, near the terminus of an irrigation pipeline that sprayed jets of cool water across a field of vine-ripening tomatoes, the air was pleasant, and the farmer sitting in the shade of the tractor's sunroof could gaze over his well-tended crops with justly earned satisfaction.

The farmer had only returned to the land in the past few decades, working it as he had once done as a much younger man on the *moshav,* or community farm, where his family had settled a year or two after the Russian Revolution of 1917. Former IDF general and minister of defense during the Begin government's second term, Assaf Gilad had been out of politics for the last two years, and out of the military for at least a decade. To all intents and purposes, he was a farmer now, and the farm was his home, his *bayit shehu bayit,* as the Israeli saying went.

But Gilad had more than tomatoes on his mind as he sat on his tractor and ruminated. Farming was in his blood, it was true, but so were the soldier's calling and Israeli politics. Gilad had lost his taste for neither of the three. In recent months he had become as determined to regain his lost place at the helm of Israel's ship of state as he was to bring in the winter's bumper harvest of, in the Old Testament phrases, the fruit of the vine and the bread of the earth.

As to the military, the old-boy network in the Israeli Defense Forces is stronger than many of its foreign counterparts. Gilad had current contacts with Israeli military intelligence, known by its acronym, AMAN—strong ones—and he made sure to keep them strong. His contacts did him favors and he returned those favors. It was the unofficial way of accomplishing certain things in Israel, as everywhere else, though here more especially so.

What Gilad had recently learned through one of these contacts could be his ticket back into the center of regional and global events, he believed. A Russian stealth aircraft had gone missing. The plane had been tracked covertly as it entered Iranian airspace, but it had never returned. Human intelligence—HUMINT—sources in Iran confirmed that the plane and its pilot had both been captured intact. The Zahal could not officially conduct a mission to retrieve the stealth, were that even an option, but Gilad might be able to do so—unofficially.

If so, he would be able to pile up many favors owed him, including placing the current Israeli prime minister deeply in his debt. Israel would never overtly acknowledge the technological windfall that possession of the Soviet stealth plane would afford it, just as it had never overtly acknowledged its massive nuclear weapons development program over the decades. But Israel would covet such stealth technology and make good use of it both in its regional fight for survival and in its global fight to gain economic markets with high-end military technology.

If anyone knew this, and was in a position to exploit this knowledge, it was he, for Gilad had been one of the prime movers behind the now defunct Lavi project of the 1980s. The Lavi was to have been Israel's home-built advanced technology fighter plane, a jet optimized for the high-endurance and long-range bombing missions that Israeli military needs dictated. Apart from its combat role, however, the Lavi could have also be used as a potent political weapon.

The U.S. had been using its fighters for just that purpose for decades, postponing, reassessing, and even embargoing fighter sales to Israel every time Israel did something that ran contrary to the United States' Mideast policy. This was a potent form of pressure on Israel to conform to U.S. wishes, but it could work the same for Israel against other countries should Israel sell them the Lavi, tying them to future upgrades and supplies of spares.

The Lavi had proven too costly to build in the end, but there had been a raft of high-technology subsystems developed for it that Israel had successfully and profitably marketed to other countries' defense establishments. Now, with a Soviet stealth fighter in Israel's possession, the potential gains could prove enormous. The windfall in stealth technology, advanced radars, avionics, and other subsystems would alone guarantee tremendous strides in Israel's defense sector. But even more than that, Gilad thought he saw the key to a revival of the Lavi project, or even something far beyond it, in the capture of the stealth.

Gilad brought the tractor's slow creep to a stop and switched the ignition off. Glancing across the tomato field at the flat mud cake of Mount Haran in the middle distance, he unclipped the satcom phone from his belt. The phone was the best in the world, as secure as state-of-the-art electronics could make it. It needed to be, considering the number at the headquarters of Israel's elite Nahal Brigade which he dialed and would erase from the phone's memory as soon as the call had been completed. Most of Israel's commando forces were drawn from the Nahal. Like the Lavi project, it, too, was a unit Gilad had helped found.

A few seconds later Gilad heard a clipped voice answer.

"In Tel Aviv," Gilad said, "the beach umbrellas are opening on Dizengoff Street."

He paused and waited for the expected reply.

•　•　•

The television news special was headed by veteran news-anchor Scott Dunnelsford, whose deadpan delivery style was familiar to millions of American TV viewers. The report, which ran a week after the strike on the Kasjhan and Isfahan nuclear facilities, delved into the theories concerning what actually took place.

"Now from foreign correspondent Bradley Pearsall, who reports live from Tehran," Dunnelsford said. "Brad, you've been in Tehran for two days, what have you found out?"

"Well, Scott, for one thing the Iranians are not saying much. Though theories abound concerning a secret mission involving the United States in bombing the reactor complex at Kasjhan and the nuclear facility at Isfahan, this is no replay of the 1979 storming of the embassy. The Iranians are keeping mum and their new détente with the U.S. is holding steady."

"Now, you say U.S. involvement in the bombings, just what do you mean by that?"

"By involvement, Scott, I mean that the United States might at least have some complicity in the bombings, meaning again, that if not actually sending U.S. planes to strike the facilities, it might have contributed targeting data to some other country."

"What other country? Do you know?"

"No one's saying, but the implication is that Russia might have been the nation that actually sent the planes."

"Thank you, Bradley, please keep us posted," the news-anchor concluded. "And now from our Israeli correspondent, Chaim Bar-Lev. Chaim, what's the word in Tel Aviv?"

"Well, Scott—"

"Just a moment, we'll have to interrupt, Chaim. Ambassador Marlene Dockweiler will soon be meeting with Iran's President Rasulali, and she's on live remote feed. We'll get back to you. Madame Ambassador, good evening . . ."

•　•　•

In Tehran's bustling Zarnegar Street, in a multistory glass-and-steel building fronted by a driveway protected by a heavy iron gate and speed bumps that is well known to the Tehranis, is located the southern military district headquarters of the Iranian Vezarat-e-Ettela'at va Amniat-e-Keshvar, or military intelligence directorate, which is more commonly known by its acronym VEVAK. From this building it is a short and, in good weather, often pleasant walk to the Presidential Palace situated only a few city blocks away, and similarly, though far more noticeably given the presence of armed soldiers, protected from unwanted intrusion.

Today, punctually at 9:15 A.M., local time, the chief of VEVAK, General Katayoon Shadrokh Choubak, met with Iran's president, Othmar Beheshti Rasulali, in the president's spacious and well-appointed fourth-floor office at the Presidential Palace.

Nominally accountable only to the Ministry of Defense, VEVAK was in fact solely under the control of the Iranian president and *faqi,* or chief religious leader, and answerable only to Rasulali and his coterie of loyal and discreet bureaucrats. So, for that matter, was the Iranian General Intelligence Directorate, otherwise known as the P-ID or Political-Ideological Directorate, or secret police. It was responsible for detecting and punishing dissent among Iranian citizens, and boasted a detachment in every police station in the country.

President Rasulali had welcomed Choubak and bidden his Uzbeki servant to pour the general a cup of *chai siah,* or Iranian-style black tea from the ornately chased silver samovar that stood on a serving table near the president's desk. The *faqi* often took *chai* at this hour, as he sat on the Louis XIV chair with red velvet back and arms carved in the shape of lions' heads that had once belonged to Iran's deposed ruler, the shah-in-shah, Reza Pahlavi. The *faqi* liked to sip his tea as he scanned his desk calendar to prepare for the day's appointments, and the tea was generously sweetened with sugar in the traditional manner he favored.

Choubak, who preferred *chai sabz,* a green Afghan-style tea more popular in the north of Iran, took a courteous sip from the china cup and then set it down on its saucer. Apart from the clinking of Delftware and the turning of the pages of the president's desk calendar, the only other sound was the hum of the ceiling fan turned high against the stuffiness of the room. Though luxuriously appointed, the windows of the *faqi's* office were made of bulletproof glass and were never opened when the *faqi* was present, as a security precaution.

At last, Rasulali looked up and regarded Choubak. Despite his gray unkempt beard, worn in the style of the mullahs, Rasulali was as distant from the Ayatollah Khomeini in the spectrum of Iran's internal politics as Jimmy Carter had been from Richard Nixon in the U.S.'. Rasulali had run as a moderate with an agenda of political and cultural reform. The people had given him an overwhelming mandate to implement liberal change in Iranian society. This included a new détente with Iran's regional neighbors and global adversaries, including the former "Great Satan," the United States.

Iran was on the road away from isolation and pariahhood. Paradoxically, this also made her far more dangerous to the world at large. A revitalized Iran more and more saw herself as a regional military and economic power. She was as big geographically as she was rich economically, with oil revenues only surpassed regionally by Saudi Arabia's. Iran wanted to grow economically and territorially, and every step away from the religious parochialism of the past decades was a step closer to potential regional conflict.

"How is the business with the plane proceeding?" Rasulali asked his intelligence chief.

"Well, Excellency," Choubak replied. "The aircraft which, as you know, is in a secure location, is being studied by our Directorate of Technical Affairs. Its officers report important discoveries in the areas of military electronics, miniaturization, semiconductor design, and computing, to name a few."

"I understand the pilot was taken alive," Rasulali went on. "I would assume that this *Shurav* is being interrogated with respect to any additional information he can provide."

"That's correct, Excellency," Choubak answered. "For the time being it has been decided to keep the pilot at the location of the aircraft. We considered bringing him to headquarters here in Tehran, but rejected this option."

"Why is that?"

"Too risky, for one thing, and also he would probably know very little. After all, he was merely a pawn in a far larger strategic game. The pilot's greatest knowledge asset would be in operating the aircraft. We could best exploit this knowledge at our base in the Dasht-e-Kavir at which the stealth is being kept."

"Very well," Rasulali replied, and asked what steps were being taken to attend to security concerns brought about by the plane's capture.

"As you are aware, *faqi,* the military brigade controlled by VEVAK includes a rapid intervention battalion that is trained to deal with any threat that may arise. It is commanded by Colonel Farzaneh Hossein Ghazbanpour, who is an able leader. I suggest he be given any additional men and equipment he requires to carry out his task."

The president raised his teacup to his lips and sipped, his heavy-lidded eyes half closing as he reflected on what he had just heard. After a few seconds he nodded his assent, and turned his full gaze on the general.

"The American ambassador is scheduled to meet with me shortly after your departure," he said. "I want to be completely prepared."

"Understood, your excellency," Choubak said to the Iranian leader. "And you will be, *faqi.*"

Choubak decided to take another sip of his *chai.* The president was known to ask many questions, and he might be occupied with answering them for some time yet.

Dimitri Pavlovich Grigorenko sat brooding in his oak-paneled Kremlin study. He looked up, studying the mantel above the fireplace, which gave the room a comforting cheer. He had not yet decided whether he would keep the fire burning during the summer, as Nixon did and as Brezhnev also had done during his tenure as general secretary of the party. Something about the fire in the summer bespoke the character shared by those two world leaders. He was not of their stripe. He was of a new breed.

Grigorenko presided over a new Russia. He was an ex–military man, the Eisenhower of his generation. Russia would have its stealth and its new brigades of tanks. It would be militarily on parity with the West, and would compete in the lucrative global defense market.

But it would not be building up its nuclear arsenal and it would be scaling back its conventional forces. Grigorenko had vowed that he would no longer be cowed by the ancient fear of invasion. If Russia was to continue into the twenty-first century, it would have to forge stronger links with the West. From this point on there was no turning back.

Nevertheless, the stealth mission would have to be salvaged somehow. And it could be done, certainly it could be done. Grigorenko was a soldier first, foremost, and always. Eisenhower had also been a soldier and had nearly been brought down by the exposure of the U-2 spy plane flights over the Soviet Union. Grigorenko could face political difficulties over this, during a far more critical time in his country's history.

But there was a way out. Grigorenko pressed the intercom button and summoned into his office a man in paratroop uniform who had been waiting in the anteroom for some time. He regarded this man. He had known him for many years, in Afghanistan.

"Sit down, Viktor Sergeivich."

Captain Arbatov of the GRU's Spetsnaz forces removed his red beret emblazoned with the paratroops insignia and took a seat opposite the president's desk.

"You are looking well, Mr. President," he said.

"There's no need to be formal, Viktor," Grigorenko replied, "so you needn't subject me to your usual sarcasm."

"I have never uttered a sarcastic word in my life, General," he replied.

"You are a lying son of a bitch, Captain," Grigorenko said, handing one of the glasses of Stolichnaya vodka he had just poured to his visitor. *"Prosit,"* he said, and knocked it down, watching the Spetsnaz officer do the same. "Now to business," Grigorenko resumed. "Viktor, you and I have known each other for a long time, since Afghanistan."

"Before that, General," Arbatov cut in.

"Da, before that, I forget," Grigorenko said. "So what I am about to tell you will go no further than this room until the appropriate time, understood?"

"Perfectly, General."

"Good. Now listen carefully. We are in deep shit, my friend. You have no doubt heard rumors concerning the loss of a stealth aircraft somewhere in Iran."

"I might have heard a thing or two about this, yes," Arbatov replied.

"Since I know that your 'thing or two' probably amounts to more than I myself know, I'll skip that part of it," Grigorenko told his guest. "But I doubt if even you have heard that our political gray eminence, Yeltsin, has succeeded in circumventing my executive powers. On his own, he has managed to sell the general staff of the GRU on his independent choice to lead a raid into Iran to retake or destroy the plane."

"Who is it?"

"I cannot tell you yet," Grigorenko equivocated. "All I am willing to reveal at this point is that it's one of Potapenko's fair-haired boys. You know the kind the old *'pidar gnoinizh'* favors."

"It must be Nemekov, then," Arbatov said, nodding to himself as if in confirmation of a good guess. "In that case, God save us all. He hasn't seen a day of real combat. He's a fucking *shavski* who got lucky one fine summer day and made his reputation." Arbatov used the slang word for a major incompetent and fuckup; *shavski* literally meant a "shit-eating dog."

"But a politically connected *z'opolit,* for all of that," he added. "This ass-kisser will probably get the job no matter what you try to do. And I *am* right about Nemekov, eh, General."

"Yes, you are indeed," admitted the Russian president. "Still, there's no arguing about the operational soundness of a raid as opposed to other alternatives, wouldn't you agree?"

Arbatov smiled. "You are sounding me out, General, I, a lowly captain, on matters of such strategic importance?"

"Viktor, I am too tired to fence right now and too depressed to joke," returned Grigorenko. "I am well aware of your undeserved demotion in rank and the persecution you've suffered. I promise you I will see to righting all wrongs, once I am able. Now please answer my question."

"A colonelcy, Dimitri. That is the least I deserve. I am now the oldest captain in the Russian army, dammit!"

"You'll have it, Viktor. And a full pardon."

Arbatov nodded, sipped at his vodka, and began, "There's no question about it, Dimitri. A raid is the only possible recourse at this stage. A few men on the ground, a few light infantry vehicles—quick in, quick out. That's the way to do it."

"But surely attack helicopters—"

"Are a needless complication, and a risky one," Arbatov cut in. "Remember the dangers and complexities of the American hostage rescue mission of 1980? It was unbelievably elaborate. Each level of complexity was one more reason why it could not possibly work, one more nail in the plan's coffin."

"Quite true," said Grigorenko.

"Also," Arbatov went on, "force-on-force symmetries tend to escalate matters rather quickly. You send in helos, the opposition answers with missiles and other aircraft. The thing can snowball into a major incident if even the slightest problems arise. But with a small Spetsnaz force, there's little risk of this happening. Also, if the men are captured or killed, it's far easier to deny."

Grigorenko poured them both another glass and said,

"We are of the same mind, Viktor. That is why I want you to prepare to lead precisely the sort of commando mission you have described."

"As a colonel?" Arbatov asked.

"After the mission I'll be able to make you a damned marshal, Viktor. For now, you'll have to remain a captain. Pick your men and start training. And mind not to pass Nemekov on the way out. He's scheduled to arrive next."

"You are meeting with him, too?" the visitor from Spetsnaz asked incredulously after drinking the last of his vodka.

"*Da,* I must," Grigorenko replied. "I have not yet consolidated my position to act autonomously. Don't forget his connections. Now go—it's best your paths don't cross."

The portly, gray-haired farmer from the Negev had changed from his comfortable jeans and T-shirt to his best Savile Row suit for the meeting. His wife had assured him that he looked better than she had seen him in a long time and suggested he wear suits more often. Gilad had produced nothing concrete as yet, but this meeting was still a triumph. They, the mandarins, had come to him. Finally, after these lonely, painful years of political exile in a desert both figurative and real, the big shots from Tel Aviv had come to Assaf Gilad for help, just as they had in '68 and in '73.

Gilad was now the only one they could come to with such a problem, the *mamza'rim,* the double-crossing bastards. Gilad would be there to pull the rabbit out of the hat when nobody else could do anything but wring their hands and cry out to the heavens above.

The prime minister himself had groveled before him. Gilad had been respectful to that pompous windbag, although he had no reason to be. Who was the prime minister anyway? A nobody. A Johnny-come-lately. A rich, well-educated, Ivy League nobody from a well-to-do American family.

He should still be sitting in his posh apartment on New

York's Upper East Side, spouting his bilge before the network news cameras during every crisis involving Israel, as he did in his old days as UN ambassador. That's all he had ever been. A face and a voice. What war for Israel did he ever fight in? What blood had he ever shed for the Jewish State? None, that was the answer. Gilad had shed more than his share of his blood for Eretz Yisroel.

It had been Gilad who had been a true warrior, with the vision to see over the horizon what those putzes in the Knesset could not discern. *Wait, just wait,* Gilad said to himself. In a few weeks' time they would all learn a lesson from an old warhorse who still had a thing or two to teach them. They had chosen to brand the mark of Cain upon his forehead. What Gilad planned would remove that stain of infamy forever.

Six
Horses and Tree Heads

Anatoly, acting as spotter for the sniper squad tasked with taking down the sentries guarding the hangar, spoke into his throat mike. "Twenty degrees to your right, Leonid. Guard in the tower."

"I see him."

Anatoly was positioned on a rise that gave him a good vantage point on the hangar through the bipod-mounted image intensification scope in front of him. Cammied up and wearing black BDUs like the rest of the three squads that made up Captain Arbatov's handpicked Spetsnaz company, he was low observable in the predawn darkness.

The mission's objective was to breach the base's perimeter defenses, storm the hangar, and destroy the Eclipse stealth fighter guarded by the Iranians inside it, killing anyone and anything that stood in the way.

At three hundred forty hours, zulu, the squads had moved into position with squad one, the sniper detail and machine gunners, taking the point. Squad one's two snipers would eliminate guards on the perimeter while the two machine gunners, each equipped with a bipod-mounted RPK-74 light machine gun, set themselves up for intersecting fire lanes a hundred meters down the road leading to the base.

As Anatoly gave targeting instructions to the squad's second sniper, nicknamed "Tanker," he saw Leonid's man slump across the barrel of the machine gun high in the crow's nest of the guard tower off to his left, struck in the head by a well-placed 7.62-mm bullet from Leonid's bolt-action Dragunov SVD sniper rifle. A few moments later the lookout in the second, right-hand tower went rag-doll limp.

The two kills were followed in quick succession by volleys of sound-suppressed fire taking down more sentries walking their posts. A last pair of Iranian regulars manning a sentry booth at the main entrance were killed as one stood outside smoking a cigarette; as he fell dead, his partner in the booth rushed out and was stopped by a round from Tanker's Dragunov SVD. The attack dog he'd held on a leash was also silenced.

Once the guard and lookout detail had been dealt with, the motorized second squad moved in through breaches in the perimeter fence. Some Spetsnaz dismounted to aim RPG-18 Strela shoulder-fire missiles. The mounted troops opened up with rockets and heavy-caliber automatic fire from their assault vehicles.

The successive salvos discharged high-explosive warheads into the barracks building, the radio tower, and the motor-pool area. Helos were destroyed on the ground and stray vehicles were shot up. Before the echos of the explosions had a chance to die down, squad three, beefed up to platoon strength, punched in through the breach, taking advantage of the pandemonium to storm the hangar at the center of the enemy compound.

Led by Zil Larovich, Arbatov's second in command, the third squad mowed down the scattered opposition and soon reached the hangar. Fast armored vehicles rolled in behind them, machine guns throwing fire, cleaning up whatever was left over.

"There she is, *moj' drugoi*," he shouted to his men. "Boris and Lev, double quick."

While the squad's gunners formed a cordon of fire around them, the team's two sappers rushed toward the aircraft. Placing the demo charges at key points between nose assembly and tail rudders of the stealth plane, they armed the charges and set a four-minute delay.

On Larovich's signal they hustled from the hangar toward the waiting main team element outside, where they took cover behind a screen of APCs.

The hangar exploded behind them with a thunderous report. A pillar of fire reared up into the black skies. In seconds it had risen fifty meters and was still climbing.

In just under twelve minutes following the snipers' opening salvos, the dismounted squads were piling into the two infantry fighting vehicles and driving hard to their preplanned LZ, where the Antonov AN-72 Coaler transport plane would be warming up.

They met no opposition on the road and were soon inside the belly of the plane, where Arbatov was waiting for them.

"Not bad," he said, checking his stopwatch. "Under twenty minutes this time." Arbatov lit a cigar and tucked the stopwatch into a pocket of his black BDU trousers. The technical staff was getting better at combat simulation, he noted. "At nine hundred hours tomorrow I'll have reviewed the video of the exercise and have my criticisms ready. I think there'll be plenty. You have about four hours to get some sleep. Pleasant dreams."

Brussels was never warm, or at least Raful Barak had never been in Brussels on a job at any time other than winter, and he had never been to Brussels for any other reason than to do a job. At one time Barak's jobs had been on company time, so to speak. These days he free-lanced.

Sometimes he did jobs for Israel's Mossad, other times

for what originally had been called Sayaret Matkal, before it became AMAN, the Israeli military intelligence bureau. Still other times Barak did jobs for select individuals, those who'd stood for him as what were called *susim* or "horses" in Israeli intelligence circles—people who had helped Raful move up through the ranks and covered his ass when he got into trouble or protected him from the predations, machinations, and arcane schemes that were part of business and survival in Israel's secret intelligence establishment.

One of Barak's most influential horses had been Assaf Gilad, whom he had known since his days in the elite Egoz or special forces units. The old soldier of Israel's hard-line right political wing had used Barak's services or a number of occasions during his term as the Begin government's minister of defense, and before that while head of Unit 101's Egoz. But Barak was not on a job for Gilad at the moment.

Today, Barak's employer was Mossad's secret assassination directorate, called Komemiute, for which he'd jumped as a contract *kidon*, which translates into English as "bayonet" and which is slang for an expert skilled in what is otherwise known as wet operations or wet jobs. This jump—and to "jump" in Mossad parlance means to insert into a foreign country under false cover to do a job and then quickly extract—was one of many he routinely freelanced.

Though not especially tall, Barak stood out in a crowd due to his cadaverous face, shaven skull, and lips set in a kind of perpetual grin that resembled nothing so much as the death rictus of a corpse. The long, gaunt face he'd been born with, and the ravages of time and war, had molded deeper furrows into the hollows of his cheeks.

But the death grin was the result of a sniper's bullet that had struck Barak in the face during the war in Lebanon and resulted in permanent damage to the trigeminal, the large nerve that runs along either side of the head and controls the facial muscles. In the war's final stage, after the car-bomb assassination of Bashir Gemayel, when the

Egoz were involved in uprooting nests of PLO guerrillas from the bomb wreckage that had once been the city of Beirut, Barak had gone out to hunt down the man who had disfigured him for life.

He had found the rifleman partying in a discotheque, for even amid the rubble of war-torn Beirut the nightlife for which that city was famed had never stopped for a moment, even during the worst of the fighting between warring PLO factions and between the PLO and the Christian Phalangists. It was surreal, like something out of Poe's "Masque of the Red Death"; but there it was, a continuous party in the midst of death, bomb rubble, and daily chaos. That was Beirut in 1982.

Barak had patiently waited until his quarry had filled himself to the brim with imported French champagne and then gone off to relieve himself. Later that evening they found the rifleman with his lips and mustache cut away from his mouth, encircling his severed penis, which had been jammed between his teeth.

The woman PLO member who had been the shooter's companion for the evening, a young recruit from Weisbaden, Germany, full of revolutionary ardor, had vomited at the sight of the corpse as she caught a glimpse through the disco's open toilet door. The sight had made it impossible for her to have normal sex again; her future contacts were limited to women. Barak had left the Ka-Bar knife he'd used to do the sniper buried in the former PLO shooter's heart as a reminder of his visit. He had never felt sorry about his damaged face again.

A sharp, quick knife had been Barak's weapon of first choice from that day on, but circumstances occasionally called for other means to be used, sometimes a silenced pistol, other times poison or a bomb. Still other times it was the spike, Barak's next favorite method of dispatching his targets. On the crowded Brussels street, the target had never seen Barak approach, had never suspected that he was marked for death, or that the execution would be carried out with the swiftness and anticlimax of a twinge of heartburn.

The *kidon*'s target, a Swedish national named Uwi Sondergaad, had often contemplated his own death, the nature
of his work as an international arms broker specializing
in big-ticket transactions—tanks, APCs, SAM transporter/
launchers, and the like—and the forged end-user certifi-
cates that rendered such transactions possible, made him
naturally prone to such musings. Sondergaad had never
suspected that he would go out with scarcely a whimper,
though. Yet that's just what happened.

Sondergaad's offense was in providing television reporter Bradley Pearsall with secret documents he'd stolen
from an office in the Israeli Bureau of Defense. Sondergaad had often used the office in which to work and the
safe was not locked. He had microfilmed the copies of
Israel's stealth development efforts for a series Pearsall
was planning on the arms race in the Mideast in the decade following Desert Storm.

Pearsall had promised Sondergaad total anonymity, but
had burned him without a second thought by revealing
enough about him in his series to make the identity of his
informant read like an open book to those with the right
needs to know. Sondergaad's duplicity was being punished by his death not so much to protect Israeli defense
secrets as to send word that another member of Israel's
old-boy network, a former Mossad head whom Sondergaad's revelations had embarrassed, would not be trifled
with.

The spike Barak would use was already in the hand
that was hidden inside the pocket of his zipped nylon ski
parka. At close range, the spike was deadlier than any
bullet or explosive. Plus it had the benefit of leaving no
visible marks. Even a sharpened pencil could be pressed
into service as a spike weapon, providing it was properly
braced against the heel of the hand when put to use—this
was the now infamous "Liddy pencil trick."

The gangland killers of Murder Incorporated had favored ice picks sharpened to a razor edge, but modern
synthetics had devised far better weapons. Today, spike-
men could choose from an array of slim Kevlar spikes

whose tips could be honed to perfection and had tensile strengths high enough to puncture the bone of the skull with effortless ease that would have made Lepke Buchalter salivate with envy.

As he followed his quarry and watched Sondergaad hail a cab, Barak savored the moment. He had dropped a letter bomb in a mailbox a short distance away. The charge was only a quarter ounce of C-4, but when it exploded it would create a sizable commotion. Barak tensed himself for the moment of the coup de grâce, the moment of supreme pleasure for him. The letter bomb exploded twenty seconds later, causing all heads to turn in the direction of the smoking mailbox across the road. Sondergaad's head was one of them.

The mailbox with its plume of smoke was the last sight Sondergaad saw on earth. The five-inch Kevlar spike in Barak's palm had already punched through the thin membrane of bone at Sondergaad's left temple and pierced the temporal lobes of his brain, cutting off his centers of balance, breathing, and blood circulation. As Sondergaad's knees began to buckle, Barak's spike was already hidden inside his head, and the small puncture wound in his temple was masked by his shock of graying hair.

Barak was already passing Sondergaad as he collapsed, a smile on his thin lips. Anonymous in muffler and woolen watch cap, he paid no attention to the sudden commotion that the corpse lying in the middle of a busy street in central Brussels produced. He was already hailing a cab on the other side of the street, on his way to the airport, bound for Tel Aviv.

Halfway around the world, within the space of the same hour, it was start of business at Fort Bragg, the commencement of another day at the United States' main training center for special forces troops, including the still officially secret Delta Force.

Bragg was still home to Delta, but the unit's facilities, like Delta itself, had changed dramatically since the early days of its formation by Colonel Charles "Chargin' Charlie" Beckwith.

One of the ways that Delta had changed was in its culture. It had begun to recruit a more laid-back type of operative, one that would have given the spit-and-polish-minded Colonel Beckwith cause for one of his well-known cussing fits. Those in the classic snake-eater-and-tree-head mold were not as popular on campus as they once had been.

However, Delta's outgoing commander, Colonel Armand Pellegrino, looked down on this trend. For one reason, Pellegrino could point to Major Peace Mitchell, who, in Pellegrino's opinion, was a disgrace to his flag, his country, his uniform, his president, and even his first name.

Mitchell once had listed his military occupational specialty as "guitarist." He had a nasty way of pronouncing the word "sir." His troop seemed to have been handpicked on the basis of how badly they had flunked their psych evals. He smiled at the wrong things. He was also too short, in Pellegrino's estimation, and he had a foul mouth. But since he was about to be transferred overseas, Pellegrino didn't give much of a damn anymore. Mitchell would soon be somebody else's headache.

"Major, I have some good news and bad news," Pellegrino told Peace as he stood in his office. "The good news is that you and your unit will not face court-martial charges for kidnapping General Swann and holding him hostage for seven days."

"Boss, that's wrong. We held him for eight days."

"You interrupt me again, Major," Pellegrino said, "and I'll put you in the stockade, is that clear?"

"Yes, boss," Mitchell replied.

"And don't call me 'boss.' It's 'sir,' got it?"

"Yes, *sir*."

"Now," the colonel continued, "I am sick and tired of you and that bunch of prima donnas you call a troop exceeding all rules of professional military conduct. The general could have pinpointed his acknowledged security leaks without such dangerous theatrics."

The colonel shifted in his seat.

"Now for the bad news," he went on, and this time he was almost grinning. "You and your troop are about to begin training for what I would characterize best as a suicide mission. Unfortunately I'll be gone by then. Maybe it'll be on *60 Minutes*."

Pellegrino pushed a set of orders and the mission plan across the desk at Peace, thinking that he would not want to be in the major's shoes at this point, because Mitchell was caught between a rock and the hard place.

Mitchell picked up the report and simply asked, "When do we start, boss?" He was smiling now, too.

The farm was remote enough to be safe from prying eyes, the ones that could cause problems, that is. Other prying eyes, in the form of recon satellites in orbit, he didn't worry too much about. They might see what was happening but they belonged either to the Americans, his own people, or maybe to the French.

The Russians didn't have a bird tasked with this region, as far as his knowledge went, and the old man's knowledge in these matters was as up-to-date as the knowledge of how his prize hybrid sheep were being bred, maybe better. As to the sheep, he had begun with a herd of Persian Blackhead, and developed a breeding program that crossbred them with the native Awasi variety, producing an entirely new strain.

Old Man Gilad's sheep, which he had named Colchis, after the fabled land in the story of the Golden Fleece, had reaped him a fortune, but this was only part of his sizable holdings. His farm had been as blessed with good fortune, with *barak,* as his political career had been cursed by ill luck, bad timing, and treacherous bedfellows, like the contemptible Begin, who had turned him out as a political scapegoat after the Sabra and Shatilla massacres of the Lebanon War days. His lemon and olive groves, his fields of wheat, corn, and barley, had made Gilad an extremely wealthy man.

He would never again want for material comforts, and he was not without friends in high places, nor did he fail to note that he had earned his place in the history books as the hero of two wars, ranking in achievement with his old mentor and sometime rival Moshe Dayan.

Still, Gilad was not content to be a name on the page of a book, a subject of schoolchildren's history classes. As long as he breathed, he thirsted to be in the spotlight, to be part of the forces shaping not only Israel and the Middle East, but the world as well. It was as much in his blood as the farm was, and although he had grown up on a *moshav,* or communal farm, with the smell of earth in his nostrils, he had known from the first that politics and fame were the two greatest loves of his life.

He would no longer be denied these. Yet there was more.

Gilad believed he had never been more needed by his country than he was today.

Now, when Israel faltered on the brink of sanctioning a full-fledged Palestinian state on its West Bank, history itself cried out for him to step forward and stretch forth his strong hand, like the patriarchs of old. His so-often-misguided people had profaned the Eternal and risked kindling His wrath. He would save them from the consequences of their wickedness.

And like the patriarchs of old, like Abraham, like Isaac, like Jacob, and like Joseph and Moses who came after them, Assaf Gilad had the means at his disposal to make his plans manifest. His sophisticated video surveillance system showed one of them arriving right now. It was Raful Barak, just back from Brussels, and now driving through the gates of the farm and up the long road that led to the main house.

As Barak walked toward Gilad's door, another elder statesman who had played a role in global political events, in a dacha many kilometers to the north and east on the birch-forested outskirts of Moscow, also prepared to receive a visitor.

Like Gilad, the ill and aging political mandarin was still well connected, though he had been out of office for the better part of the past year. And also like his Israeli contemporary, Boris Yeltsin still thirsted for power and a direct hand in the way Russia, and to a lesser extent the world beyond the *Rodina*'s borders, was run.

Indeed, Yeltsin had arranged it so that when the ex–Colonel General Grigorenko became Russia's second democratically elected president, he would be making decisions contingent on Yeltsin's advice and approval. But the wily general had outfoxed his patron and to Yeltsin's chagrin had gone off on his own, moving ahead with reforms at a pace far faster than the former Russian leader believed practical, let alone possible.

Still, Yeltsin held cards he could play. One of those concerned this recent blunder in the Iranian desert, which he knew all about through his many sources. The secret report on the crash of the stealth plane had reached him at the same instant as it reached Grigorenko, and Yeltsin had immediately made his plans based on the opportunities he deemed it presented.

"Come in, sit down, Valery Fedorovich," Yeltsin said, nodding to his servant who poured both him and his visitor a glass of aged Napoleon brandy, which Yeltsin still drank despite strict doctor's orders. "How is everything at home? Your pretty wife Elena has received the small household gift I sent?"

"It was overly kind of you, sir," the younger man said to the former president. "Far more than we deserve."

"Nonsense, it's the least I could do," Yeltsin said. "Now drink up. We must talk business before my doctors arrive for their afternoon torture session. Tell me all that you have learned since your last visit."

Yeltsin watched Valery Nemekov take a strong belt of the brandy, the way a man should drink his liquor, and set the glass on the coffee table. Yeltsin immediately filled it again, and would continue doing so throughout the conversation, as much to enable himself to enjoy the sight of good whiskey being drunk as to loosen the other man's tongue.

Nemekov still had the boyish good looks and fair hair that Yeltsin had recalled from the turbulent days of the 1991 democratic revolution. Then it had been Nemekov who had headed the *boyevaya,* the hit men of the KGB Alfa team that, under orders from the reactionary cabal headed by the accursed Kryuchkov, was to break into the Russian parliament building where Yeltsin had barricaded himself. Alfa was to assassinate him and his close associates in a hail of automatic fire and grenade shrapnel.

Kryuchkov, who had been appointed chief of the KGB under Gorbachev, and who later aligned himself with hard-liners and recidivist Communists when the reforms under glasnost and perestroika had seemed to falter, was to have assumed control of a resurgent Soviet Union in a coup d'état that would have swept Yeltsin, the new president-elect, from power. But as a moving wall of tracked armor flowed into Moscow one workday morning, and pressed toward the Kremlin to the shock of Center-bound highway commuters, the Russian *nomenklatura* had gotten the word out and the people took to the streets, erecting barricades against the tanks of August, stopping them in their tracks with often no more than their bodies as living barriers.

Yet the confrontation might still have ended with the Kryuchkov faction victorious had it not been for Nemekov's refusal to carry out the assassination directive the KGB head had given him. In the end, it had been Kryuchkov who had—at least to the outside world—committed suicide in the wake of his defeat.

Yeltsin, and many others, knew that Kryuchkov's "suicide" had been what Russians called *vyshera mera,* "up-against-the-wall time." Not without irony, this had been the same form of punishment that had been meted out to so many "enemies of the state" during the tenure of Kryuchkov's KGB leadership.

Like his own victims, Kryuchkov had been led into a

room in the basement of KGB headquarters in Moscow's sprawling old Lubyanka prison building, made to kneel in a corner with his face to the wall, and executed with a single nine-mm hollow-nose round fired from a Makarov pistol to the back of his head. Akhromeyev, Pugo, and Kruchina, the other three members of the Kryuchkov cabal, had met the same fate as their leader, first watching his brains explode in a wet red nova, then taking Kryuchkov's place against the blood-streaked wall.

Due to his courage in defying the KGB *chekisti,* the opposite fate was in store for Valery Nemekov. Yeltsin had rewarded him for his courage and promoted him to head the C.I.S.'s elite special operations unit, Vasaltnik Force G. Nevertheless, there was one problem with the young man, perhaps a grave one in light of the reason Yeltsin had summoned him to his dacha today.

Nemekov's entire fame rested on what he had not done as opposed to what he did do. With the Vasaltniki, he had proven himself inept, and had survived only because he was Yeltsin's chosen favorite and protégé, and could meet with the old man directly, virtually any time he wished. Now, however, it was a different story. Yeltsin was being eased out of his advisory position by Grigorenko. Soon enough he would be a forgotten and sick old man in full retirement, with no voice in Russian affairs, breaking wind in his dacha as he waited for the end.

The host continued to wait for Nemekov's story. The younger man began by stating what Yeltsin already surmised.

"Grigorenko has chosen Arbatov to head the mission into Iran. I have been passed over once again."

"Arbatov?" Yeltsin said, his brows crinkling in thought. "Is he not the vodka-swilling miscreant who was courtmartialed for unsoldierly conduct in Afghanistan?" He thought back to his days as party chairman under Gorbachev, and the prosecution of the Afghan War, in which he had played a minor political role.

"Yes," said Nemekov. "The same one. But you should

know, since it was you who agitated for court-martial, was it not?"

"So I did," Yeltsin replied, and the memory returned from across the gulf of years. "He had killed his superior officer, a Colonel Panshin, I think it was."

"Yes, Panshin was his name."

Yeltsin's brows furrowed deeper.

"This Arbatov had been ordered to carry out a revenge attack for terrorist atrocities against our forces in the Khunduz region. He was to lead Spetsnaz into a village harboring CIA-trained Mujahideen killers and destroy their stronghold. Instead, he ended up murdering his superior officer."

"Correct, sir," Nemekov replied, drinking another glass of brandy. "Arbatov refused to obey his orders, and when the colonel drew his gun, Arbatov took it from his hands and struck him down with a single blow. The colonel never got up again."

Nemekov was somewhat drunk by now, but not drunk enough to add to his story that Arbatov, though demoted in rank from major to lowly captain, was found to have acted in self-defense at his trial and had enjoyed the support of many other officers, who by then were fed up with the cycle of atrocities that marked the later stages of the war. Arbatov's troop had been ordered to kill every man, woman, and child in the village and then raze it to the ground.

He had killed all of the Mujahideen he could locate, but refused to permit his men to execute innocents and noncombatants. Arbatov's defense became known as the Mai-Lai defense; he pleaded he would not become the Lieutenant William Calley of Afghanistan. His plea was accepted by his peers, and though Arbatov was punished, he was not executed as a traitor as Yeltsin and supreme commanding officer of Afghan forces, Army General Vladimir Potapenko, had wished. In the end Arbatov became a hero, though none who valued his career was foolish enough to admit this in public.

Yeltsin poured his guest another glass of brandy, almost

draining the bottle. "Don't worry, Valery Fedorovich, my good friend," the old man told his young protégé, "it will all be taken care of. Wait a week or two. You will see that I am still not without my helpers and supporters in many high places. Arbatov will never lead this mission, you can be sure of this. I give you my pledge that you and only you shall be the one. *Prosit!*"

Boris Yeltsin lifted his glass and drained it dry.

Seven
Bumps in the Night

The guard sullenly shoved the bowl of thin soup and the hunk of stale bread through the narrow slot in the door of Petrov's cell, stared at his charge a moment through the Judas hole above it, rammed shut the latch, and went down the hall. When the cadence of footsteps and the jingle of keys died away, Petrov left his cot and examined his supper.

The bread was a sex club for maggots and the soup looked, smelled, and tasted like it had been freshly ladled from the prison latrine. Nevertheless, Petrov wolfed down his meal with a gusto that nobody unacquainted with his predicament could be expected to fully comprehend. By now he'd learned the amazing fact that starvation held the miraculous power to transform even filth into caviar, and in his weeks of captivity the stealth driver had become no stranger to starvation.

Petrov had already spent time as the guest of several Iranian military encampments, being shuffled around like a walnut shell on a monte player's table. They had blind-folded him with each move, but they had not plugged his ears and nostrils. Petrov had heard and smelled and tasted the desert around him. He retained his pilot's sense of time, speed, and distance. He doubted if he had traveled more than a hundred klicks in any direction.

At each new stop he had been questioned about the operation of the plane. Usually the interrogation was pre-ceded by a beating or a mock execution. The Iranians seemed either to take a perverse enjoyment in holding an unloaded pistol to his head and dry-firing the gun or to believe that after several exposures to this pretense Petrov would still think they were serious. This time there was a new wrinkle. After the *de rigueur* snap of the hammer against firing pin, Petrov was actually brought from the stockade to demonstrate some of the aircraft's instrumen-tation to his captors.

He had been taken under guard from his cell, frog-marched blindfolded through a compound alive with motor-pool noises, sour cooking odors, and, at one point, the sound of a television or radio playing the theme song of the universally recognized American TV show *Bo-nanza,* into a large and busy aircraft hangar, where his blindfold was removed. It was night, but the floodlit han-gar swarmed with technicians, soldiers, and officers, their collective attention focused on the black aircraft that oc-cupied center stage. Like the holy Ka'ba stone of some high-tech priesthood, it seemed to hold them all spellbound.

Petrov could see at a glance that some internal gear from Shadow One had been removed for examination. Modules from the rack-mounted secure communications system lay on a steel trundle table near the fuselage, where technicians with a sweep oscilloscope touched diagnostic probes to the ICs of the exposed printed circuit boards. But virtually everything else about the exterior of the plane appeared intact.

The Iranians sat Petrov down and told him they were interested in the MFI's inertial navigation system. They wanted Petrov to demonstrate how the pilot interacted with its menu-driven command interface. Would he be willing to do so?

Petrov gave them what they wanted, but volunteered nothing whatever. This was not just out of patriotic duty or a flier's *esprit de corps,* but derived from an instinct for self-preservation. Petrov reasoned that the more information he provided the Iranians and the more quickly he downloaded useful data into their brains, the less he was worth to them, and the sooner his meager rations of thin soup and maggoty bread would become a fast bullet between the eyes and an unmarked hole in the ground beyond the floodlit perimeter of some isolated desert camp.

Nevertheless, Petrov also noticed that they had fully refueled the plane, which they would want to do in order to taxi it from hangar to hangar, and in order to perform other tests on its onboard systems. When they threw him back in his cell again, Petrov decided that if it were at all possible, he would try to get back into the cockpit and fly the plane to freedom. He could sense that his days as a captive were numbered, in any case.

If death awaited him, he thought, then it was better to meet it as a soldier than as a whipped cur. He would make a run for it. This he swore.

Viktor Arbatov found himself summoned to the base commander's office from the training area in the midst of a training exercise. However, instead of his normal commanding officer, Colonel Golovsky, another officer sat behind the oaken desk.

Arbatov already sensed what was going to happen, but he saw no other choice than to play the farce out to its inevitable climax. In some regards, Russia would always be Russia, and nothing would ever change the innate love of intrigue and backstabbing that characterized everything from politics to art in the intensely and hopelessly Slavic country.

"Captain, I won't mince words with you," the newcomer began. "I am Colonel Putilin, your new commanding officer."

"What became of Colonel Golovsky?" asked Arbatov.

"He was transferred suddenly on medical leave," Putilin answered gruffly. "Anyway, this does not concern you."

"No? Then what does—sir?"

"Your record of insolence has not gone unnoticed, Captain," Putilin replied. "You would do well to adopt a more soldierly tone. It might be of help to your career—what is left of it, anyway."

When Arbatov said nothing, Putilin went on. "In any case, you have been ordered to stand down from mission training at once. You and your men are to return to your headquarters until further notice."

"Then the mission has been scrubbed?"

"No, not scrubbed, nor did I say that it had been," Putilin answered testily. "Your unit is to be replaced with one led by Major Valery Nemekov."

"Nemekov? How can this be? He is a Vasaltnik, not even Spetsnaz. He is a paratrooper trained to do grunt work. That is good soldiering, in its place, make no mistake. But we Spetsnaz are surgeons, specialists at what we do. It is ludicrous to send mere crunchies to do our kind of work."

"Guard your insolent tongue or I will personally see to it that you are court-martialed. This time you will spend the rest of your life in prison, I guarantee it. Now get out of here. You have received your orders. Obey them."

"Yes, sir," Arbatov told his glaring superior, saluting smartly, then turned on his heels and strode into the hall. But he thought to himself that if Putilin believed that this was the end of it, then that posturing little martinet was very much mistaken.

The red light atop the camera glowed, a signal for him to look up, speak in rich, cultivated tones, and show some of the expensive caps that covered his front teeth. That, and reading from the TelePrompTer, was what they paid him for.

"Thank you, Linda. I'm sure those Korean orphans will never forget the first lady's surprise visit."

Newsanchor Scott Dunnelsford faced the number-two camera, which pulled in for a close-up head shot, beaming his familiar smile to millions of dinnertime TV viewers—the same ones who had long since forgotten his failed stint as a daytime soap opera actor many years before.

"Next, the crisis in Iran heats up," he said next, his voice crisp and modulated. "Today the United Nations Security Council voted unanimously for sanctions against the United States and Commonwealth of Independent States in the wake of the destruction of two Iranian nuclear facilities.

"At a press conference earlier today, White House Press Secretary Helene Goldthwaite denied U.S. involvement in what Iran has called 'naked aggression' against its territory, instead claiming that the explosions that destroyed the two nuclear facilities were the result of accident or sabotage.

"So far there has been no comment from Russian officials on the Iranian claims. But Iranian President Othmar Beheshti Rasulali, in a speech before the Iranian parliament, has threatened military action in retaliation for the alleged attacks. Just what form this would take has not been made clear."

Camera two pulled back for a long shot while camera one dollied into position for a close-up of the female anchor. As soon as she saw the red light come on, she began reading from the TelePrompTer screen below the camera lens.

"And we'll be following that story as it continues to unfold," Linda Bailey said, the thirty thousand dollars the TV station had spent on speech instruction to remove all traces of the accent she'd grown up with in the slums of Brooklyn's Brownsville section replaced with the bland but perfect diction of a media clone.

"In Belfast, the death toll continues to rise after the explosion of a bomb at a packed rugby stadium. The Irish Republican Army has claimed credit for the bombing.

British Prime Minister Harley Peters, fresh from his court-room defense in the number 10 Downing Street sex scandal, pledged that Britain would not take this matter lying down. In Colombia, a resurgence of narcoterrorist activity has government forces on alert . . ."

The ancient trade route known as the Silk Highway meandered through the Caucasus Mountains and down its granite flanks into the flat grasslands of Azerbaijan. From there it wended its way steadily southward, into Afghanistan and Iran. Ancient though it was, the Silk Highway followed the far more ancient tracks laid down by the Crusaders, who had trudged on foot toward Constantinople and down into the Holy Land by way of Libya and the Sudan.

In the twentieth century the route had been trodden by Gypsies and heroin smugglers, arms traders and clandestine travelers shuttling between Europe, Asia, and the countries of the Middle East.

Along the tortuous, zigzagging route, diverse peoples who were basically stateless had sprung up over the centuries—Tatars, Khazars, Uzbeks, Kurds, Sabians, Yazedis, Druze, and many others. Citizens of their respective countries mainly by decree, they were often willing to turn a blind eye, shelter fugitives, or smuggle them across their porous borders, if the price was right or other considerations were met.

Even during times of war, which came often to the region beset by the shifting winds of nationalism, dictatorship, and ever-changing political affiliations, the borders remained porous, and though the price of the bribes could drastically increase, the border guards could always be counted on to do business as usual.

To the Russian military forces, embroiled in the civil war in Afghanistan throughout most of the 1980s, this ancient road had become the latter-day equivalent of the Ho Chi Minh Trail that had bedeviled the Americans in Vietnam during the 1960s and early 1970s.

Like the Ho Chi Minh Trail, the overland mountain

route was an open channel for thousands of tons of weapons, spare parts, and ammunition for Mujahideen forces throughout the war years. Unlike it, however, there was no hope of even token bombing of the route, which stretched across a dozen countries and even more ethnic regions, and which could never be stopped at its source. With the right couriers, contraband of every kind was virtually guaranteed to reach its destination intact.

As the sun rose on a barren stretch of mountain road in a high mountain pass one fog-swept morning in late March, its rays burned through the tatters of fine, drifting mist and reflected off the dull, dust-caked chassis of a Land Rover that rolled toward a nearby Azeri town, a village of stone houses and narrow, unpaved streets called Kushtam. Inside the vehicle were Raful Barak and a squad-strength detachment of handpicked mercenaries, all of them Israeli and all of them drawn from Nahal Brigade Egoz forces loyal to Gilad.

The group's destination had been planned and mapped out during their preparations by elements of AMAN's Unit 504, which specialized in cross-border intelligence, and they bore forged papers that identified them as Turkish merchants, modern-day counterparts of ancient traders who plied the region in centuries past.

They, said their papers, had been on a buying mission for a prestigious Parisian antique dealer. The papers and cover story had been prepared by Unit 8520's Development Directorate, which specializes in false identification, counterfeit currencies, special covert weapons, and other nonstandard items and services for agents abroad. Both were flawless.

Any check on the dealer, which was what the Mossad called a *sayan,* or an unaffiliated helper, would confirm the cover. The Mossad maintained contacts with *sayanim* throughout the world who, though themselves not members of the intelligence organization, were willing to provide support for its operators. Their ranks included business people and professionals from all walks of life.

Usually these were fellow Jews, but not always.

The Egoz team did not carry arms other than a single Pakistani-made variant of the AK-47 and a few handguns, but these weapons would not attract undue concern in this rough and remote mountain country, no more than scimitars would have done in the days of the ancient caravans that had once trod this same route.

There was a full consignment of military weapons, ammunition, and special electronics, including commo and GPS awaiting delivery for Barak's team, but that would come near the end of the journey, just before they crossed over into Iran in search of the downed plane. Carried with them now were only a few rugs, seemingly purchased during their travels, but really bought in the large collectibles market of Istanbul.

As Barak rode in the front seat of the first Land Rover, he thought back on his final days at Gilad's farm, just before the team's departure. Gilad had been jubilant, more full of his old energy and confidence than Barak could remember in years. They had drunk a glass of aged French cognac, the Old Man's favorite drink, and smoked imported Cuban cigars, talking about the mission and its importance.

Apart from Gilad's messianic belief that by retrieving the secret of Russian stealth, he could somehow bring peace to the Mideast and save the world, which Barak regarded as megalomaniacal nonsense, the Old Man's plan had a far more materialistic side to it. If they could succeed in flying the plane out, or even in dismantling enough of its electronics and fuselage to bring it back to Israel, they would have struck a gold mine.

Once reverse-engineered, the Russian stealth technologies could be improved upon and sold individually to any buyer with the money to afford them. It was the old equation known to junkyard dealers—in pieces, a car was worth many times more than it was worth whole. The Mossad had become expert at this practice, and Gilad had been one of its inventors.

It was settled that Barak would be Gilad's agent in selling the technology, and they discussed ways of contracting out stealth to various countries. The Chinese, the Koreans (both North and South), and the Swedes, who wanted to enter the fighter plane market with an upgraded, first-line version of their Gripen second-line fighters, were all on the short list.

And why not? In a year or two, maybe five, the secret of stealth would be out anyway. By 2010 the Americans and the Russians would be selling stealth openly at global arms shows, the way the Americans now sold laptops, electric guitars, refrigerators, and their inane pop culture, and like the Soviets sold Kalashnikovs and vodka.

And furthermore, who really owned stealth, after all? Probably the Nazis of Hitler's Third Reich, who had invented the concept back in the early forties, Barak thought. The original stealth plane was the so-called Horton Wing, prototypes of which the Americans had found along with so much other technology amid the ruins of Nazi Germany and transported to their country for development. It was ironic how much—including helmets identical to those of the Nazi Wehrmacht, save that they were made of Kevlar instead of steel—the Americans had taken from their former enemies and made as Yankee as apple pie.

Barak's thoughts snapped back to the present. The Land Rover was now approaching the stone hill town on the dusty mountain road. Yigael, at the wheel, honked at an old man leading a flock of shaggy-pelted, long-horned goats that blocked the road. The villager stopped and smiled, revealing a set of *naswar*-stained teeth in a gaunt, unshaven, and craggily windburned face. He held out his hand in an okay sign and moved it back and forth indicating, in sign language, that he wanted a cigarette if the car was ever to pass his loudly baa-ing flock.

Colonel Farzaneh Hossein Ghazbanpour was a rarity in the Iranian army or Pasdaran. His tenure in its ranks dated from the final days of Shah Reza Pahlavi's doomed kingship.

Somehow, he had survived the worst excesses of the Khomeini years, distinguishing himself as an able field commander during the bloody eight-year-long war with Iraq, to emerge during the more moderate period that followed as a highly decorated military hero and a well-known figure to most Iranians.

Ghazbanpour was even more unusual in having received military training in the United States at the U.S. Army's Academy of the Nations, which had trained military officers of the shah's regime during the 1970s, just prior to the fall of the house of Pahlavi.

Because Ghazbanpour was an expert on air warfare, and considered a prime example of the new style of Iranian military operations and tactics, he was given command of the remote base in the Dasht-e-Kavir, the high desert in central Iran, where the captured Eclipse aircraft was being kept.

Ghazbanpour was uncertain of many things, but he was sure of one: that the Russians, or even the Americans, would mount a mission to retake the lost stealth fighter. Too much was at stake for both nations simply to leave the plane in Iranian hands and shrug their collective shoulders at the consequences. He himself, Ghazbanpour thought, would lobby for such a mission were he in the places of those who made military decisions in the U.S. and C.I.S. And since such a mission was inevitable, in Ghazbanpour's opinion, he would plan for it in advance.

The stealth plane, he decided, would make excellent bait with which to reel in his adversaries. Ghazbanpour was a student of the ancient Chinese tactician Sun Tzu. He recalled that the old General Sun had advised that in order to prevail on the battlefield, a good commander needed to first attack his enemy's strategy. Ghazbanpour would follow the sage's wise counsel. All he needed to do was to set the mousetrap and listen for the sound of a snap in the night.

Precisely at seven hundred hours on a Sunday morning, the *chekisti* invaded the barracks of Spetsnaz Group G and marched down the double row of wooden bunks. Men looked up and said nothing, for they knew better. The contingent of KGB, with a colonel at their head, proceeded to Captain Arbatov's private quarters and stopped. The major did not bother to knock. He signaled to the two men behind him who carried fire axes. They rushed forward and viciously swung them, shattering the wooden door to flinders.

The two men with axes rushed into the room but quickly regretted their haste. Arbatov sent the first man sprawling with a butt smash of the Avtomat Kalashnikova AKS to the side of his head, and impaled the second man through the arm with the compact autoweapon's fixed bayonet.

"Stop!"

It was the head *chekist* who barked the order. The Makarov pistol in his hand gave it teeth. Arbatov pulled the bayonet from the bleeding wound into which its tip had bitten deep and kicked the man against the wall in the groin to hasten his slide to the cold wooden floor.

"Drop your weapon and step forward or I shall not hesitate to shoot!"

Arbatov tossed the AKS onto his cot and stepped out into the barracks as the KGB colonel backpedaled. Arbatov saw a potentially disastrous situation in the making. The *chekisti* had chosen to beard the lion in his den. They had brought along a troop that surrounded the barracks and was inside it, but his own men would be willing to fight if he gave the order.

"What is the meaning of this?" asked Arbatov, though he already suspected what would happen and knew he could not prevent it.

"We have received reports that you are dealing heroin from your quarters, Captain," the colonel answered. "Step aside. Your quarters are to be thoroughly searched."

Arbatov said nothing. There was no point, especially now that the martinet Putilin had put in an appearance and was glaring at him with open hostility. He was to be set up and there was nothing to be done about it—at least not at the moment.

Expectedly, the major's underlings returned clutching a kilo bag of a white powdery substance.

"What is your explanation for this?" asked the *chekist*.

"My explanation is that your lackeys just planted it. Why didn't you simply shoot me and get it over with?"

The colonel pulled his lips taut in a kind of grin.

"You deny dealing dope, then?" he asked.

"Get fucked, you *chekist* scum-eater!" Arbatov cursed. "You can shove that bag of shit up your faggot's ass." A roar of laughter rose up from the barracks at this remark.

At this point Putilin stepped in. He made Arbatov's choice a simple one. Either face court-martial, and risk execution for what was a capital offense in the army of the C.I.S., or accept transfer to a punishment battalion in the Caucasus for a year of hard labor. Boris Yeltsin had made good on his pledge to Valery Nemekov, and Arbatov had been left with no cards to play. He left the barracks under armed guard.

Eight
To Each Their Own

The command center was located at the former Strategic Rocket Forces base at Kapustin Yar in the Caucasus. The large military map was secured to the broad tabletop, lit by overhead fluorescent panels. Major Valery Fedorovich Nemekov and his aging mentor, Army General Vladimir Illich Potapenko, who had pushed hard for his commanding the mission, supporting Boris Yeltsin's wishes, stood beside the map table discussing the operational planning of the impending strike.

Both were attired in stiff, new camouflage fatigues, the bottoms of their BDU trousers bloused into the tops of their high black paratroop boots. Nemekov's uniform was completed by the maroon beret of the Vasaltniki, worn at a rakish angle to complement his angular features. If clothes made the soldier, both men would have ranked as Napoleons. But soldiering took more than a good custom tailor and a pair of shiny boots.

Potapenko was a doddering throwback to the Neanderthal age of the Brezhnev political era, too well connected to be forced out of his sinecure just yet, and determined to hang on as long as possible. Privately, though, Potapenko had been planning his imminent retirement for the last several months and had already announced it to his inner circle of close confidants.

This mission, in which his young protégé would use the storehouse of warcraft the old general had passed on to him like a Zen swordsman to an ardent young samurai, would be a fitting end to his long and illustrious career.

At least in uniform, Potapenko was still an imposing presence. His six-foot-two frame gave him an august stature, and his broad chest, still looking muscular thanks to adept tailoring, was draped with at least a kilogram of shining medals and colorful campaign ribbons. They were decorations won in a host of engagements stretching back to the heyday of Soviet domination of Eastern Europe and the U.S.S.R.'s strategic involvement in the Middle East and Central America.

Potapenko had been the liaison man in Cairo for Gamal Abdul Nassar in the mid-sixties, and had helped train the Egyptian army that was to launch what soon became known as the Six Day War. A year later he had helped defeat the 1968 Prague Spring uprising in Czechoslovakia, pouring Soviet T-72 tanks, BTR assault vehicles, and other mechanized armor into the rebellious East Bloc satellite state to create a juggernaut of steel that crushed all opposition.

Today Potapenko was dressed in the camouflage fatigues of a Russian field commander, and wore only shoulder flashes as insignia of rank. He also wore a general-issue Makarov PM nine-mm automatic pistol holstered at his waist, though the only thing worth defending oneself against here were the hordes of fat blueblack bottle flies that infested the southern region of the Eurasian landmass.

An aide suddenly entered the command post staff room and handed the old campaigner a sheaf of printouts that had just been downloaded from the tactical computer system installed at the base. The lieutenant saluted smartly, the way Potapenko required his staff to salute, and promptly withdrew. Potapenko scanned the printouts, then handed them to the younger man similarly attired in fatigues who stood at his side.

"The latest reports from our forward observation team of ground agents," he told Nemekov, who skimmed through the pages while the general summarized. "Conditions on the ground are currently highly favorable. There is little chance of adverse weather, and optimum flying conditions will likely continue through the next three days." Potapenko smiled at his protégé, flashing a set of perfectly capped front teeth. "A great time for daring," the general concluded.

"The plan is sound," Nemekov told him. "That's the most important thing."

The older man turned back to the large military map on the table. Clusters of multicolored pushpins had been inserted to represent targets and waypoints, and lines of march had been drawn between the fixed coordinates. Move by move—it was there, all laid out in front of them—an inexorable progression from the landing of troops and equipment to the storming of the base and the destruction of the stolen stealth fighter-bomber. Simple, by the book, and as certain to be effective as anything could be in combat. All in all, one could not hope for a better chance at success.

Potapenko had no use for military revisionists who wanted to adopt so-called modern Western procedures and doctrine. As a young disciple of the extraordinary Marshal Zhukov, he had helped draft the warfighting manuals after the Great Patriotic War. They were as sound today as they were back then, he knew.

Potapenko pointed to the landing zone marked on the map where two all-weather Antonov transport planes would touch down, carrying sufficient Vasaltniki and equipment for a high-mobility assault force of company strength.

Such a formation would be the perfect size for an operation that called for high mobility and rapid insertion and extraction from the combat area. Also—and though he had said nothing of this to Nemekov—should things go wrong, there was an excellent chance that a force so small would be wiped out entirely, reducing political problems in its wake.

But this would not happen, he reminded himself. The plan was sound and the mission was destined to succeed.

The old general continued to smile as he fixed his clear blue eyes on the face of the younger man. "From here you must follow the timetable to the minute," he advised the major. "If you do, it will all fall into place."

The pointer moved to the first cluster of red pins, indicating the initial waypoint, a deep wadi, actually a rift, situated midway between the base and the LZ. "From landing to Wadi Kumar is twenty-six minutes. From there a scout detachment is sent. Who is its leader, I've forgotten."

"Lieutenant Trapezhnikov," Nemekov told the general, "an able leader. He served with honor in the Afghan campaign."

"Yes, I know the man, yes," Potapenko said, thinking of a young recruit in one of the Vasaltniki detachments. "Next, the main strike follows. There are no reports of new defenses being installed since our last photographic reconnaissance satellite pass."

Nemekov checked his watch. "The latest data should have been ready by now. I'll look into it."

He picked up a phone and called an aide for the satellite imagery. The aide said that he would check back. He soon came in and placed the large sheaf of acetate printouts that had just come off a color plotter on clips above a light box stationed near the main tactical map.

Nemekov and Potapenko studied the orbital photoimagery. Blown up by a factor of three, the overhead surveillance data showed a great deal of detail, comparable in quality to the U.S. Keyhole series output at low resolution. The two soldiers could clearly see that defenses at the base had not significantly changed in the last twelve hours.

Most important, there was still no armor guarding the ground approaches to the base. Either the Iranians had not yet brought in their mechanized equipment, or they were deliberately not trying to attract attention to the installation by signs of beefed-up activity.

Nevertheless, a series of photos taken the previous morning, when the angle of the sun was just right, clearly showed the sharply angled nose assembly of the stealth plane projecting from between two open hangar bay doors. The plane was apparently there, and they would soon make sure the Iranians no longer possessed what they had stolen from the former Soviets.

Potapenko was pleased at the high-grade satellite photointelligence. "Good. Nothing material has changed," he told the younger man. "I am more certain than ever that this mission will go smoothly."

Nemekov smiled. As usual, he was in complete agreement with his mentor.

Already inside Iran, and far closer to the target of the impending operation, Raful Barak was not as blandly certain of success as the two men who finalized their war plans far away across the chain of mountains to the east.

The Egoz team's photointelligence or PHOTINT was not as good as that available to the Russians. It might have been better had they had access to American overhead surveillance data from a Keyhole, Lacrosse, or one of the other half-dozen types of birds the Pentagon, NSA, and CIA had in orbit. These spy satellites could use multiple cameras, lasers, and radars, or combinations thereof, along with specially polished and movable mirrors, to produce amazingly accurate and detailed imagery of sites on the ground that no other force on earth came remotely close to having.

What the Americans could do with their satellites was incredible, which is why Gilad had lobbied the Reagan Administration years before for Keyhole satellite imagery back in the early eighties. The U.S. spysat imagery was not only good in its raw, unprocessed real-time form, but could be further enhanced by computers to produce three-dimensional graphics of target sites, accurate down to the last millimeter.

Gilad's Ministry of Defense had desperately wanted Keyhole access so it could aim Israel's then fledgling offensive nuclear missile force at targets inside the Soviet Union. The strategy had been to threaten the Soviets with nuclear first strikes if they did not keep their Arab client states on a short leash. Though Ronald Reagan amiably complied with the request, the Weinberger-controlled U.S. Defense Department had withheld access, and had made the decision stick. The president's mind, stricken by Alzheimer's, had by then deteriorated to the point where virtually all policy decisions were made by his subordinates and rubber-stamped by him.

Gilad got his Keyhole data anyway, through convicted espionage agent Jonathan Pollard's spying, and also by other, yet more secret means. The farmer in the Negev still had a back channel into the American National Security Agency today when he needed more of the satellite intelligence in which the NSA specialized.

But nobody was supposed to know about this mission, least of all the Knesset or the prime minister. Both, Barak suspected, would have heart attacks if they had the slightest inkling of what the former general was up to. Israel officially wanted no part of Russian stealth technology, nor did the long-beleaguered Jewish state want to anger the Russians, the Americans, or the Arab states, with all of whom they now had increasingly cordial diplomatic relations. This is why most of Barak's intelligence came from HUMINT rather than orbital PHOTINT sources.

Gilad's private network of *katsas,* or undercover agents on the ground, stretched from one end of the Mideast to the other. It included the east and west coasts of America and everything in between, as well as the capital cities of Europe. Gilad had worked for decades to build up this formidable private intelligence service, and he considered it his personal fiefdom, which he ruled as the laird of the manor.

The Old Man had assets on the ground that nobody could match, not Mossad or the KGB, and certainly not the CIA, which had always run the most laughably inept agents in the business, such as the clownish Aldrich Ames, and then usually sold them out in the end. It was from these assets, including the *marats* or "listeners," who picked up stray bits and pieces of useful intelligence and sold them for a price, that Barak had been able to build up a strategic picture of where Shadow One might be found and the steps necessary to retake the plane. Tonight, in the desert darkness at twenty-one hundred hours, Barak entertained nothing resembling the certainties that the two Russian soldiers held at their Azeri staging base while poring over their mission maps.

The Egoz's vehicles had already begun to fill with the rugs that the caravan of "merchants" had bought at the towns and hamlets along their route. Now Barak's men were halted at a small cooking fire lit in the desert. They might have spent the night at a Kurdish village only about fifty klicks behind them, where they had freshened their fuel reserves, but it was important that they be away from prying eyes and ears. Tonight, weapons and gear from a hidden stash site had joined their inventory.

At each stop, more than fresh gas and rugs were purchased. Fresh information from confidential sources, concerning the whereabouts of the plane, troop dispositions, the names of bribable border guards, the schedules and habits of desert patrols, was all bought and paid for by the merchants from Istanbul. At the last of the towns, Barak had also taken on two guides well versed in the roads, weather, and general conditions of the Dasht-e-Kavir, ones who knew every wadi, rock, *sabkah,* and tree in the desert by heart.

Barak had decided that he needed these guides because of his uncertainty about the target—for the moment, anyway. There seemed to be reason to believe that the plane was at a small base at al-Kabriz, where workers had seen an aircraft resembling it.

But Bedouin contacts told another story. Some had traded at a more remote, and more heavily secured, base equipped with bomb-resistant hangars. Their informant had seen nothing. But one of the soldiers had griped about the "damned black plane" he had to guard, then quickly fell silent. The Bedouin had been well paid for their information.

Barak had decided to form two reconnaissance groups, one going to the smaller base at al-Kabriz, and the other, which he would command, to the secure base at Wadi Quom. The two teams would leave as soon as preparations were finalized, and the guides would lead them. They would keep in touch by secure satcom transmissions at regularly scheduled intervals. When the time came, the guides would be killed and buried, having seen and known too much for their own good.

Barak saw one of his men gesture. The teams were ready to roll. He spilled the dregs of his coffee into the sand, and placed the porcelain cup in the pocket of his fleece-lined sheepskin coat, where for some reason he had carried it throughout most of the journey.

Then he climbed into the Land Rover and gave the signal to move out into the cold desert night.

One after the other, their immense turbofan engines crying out their barbaric songs of naked power, the two Antonov transport planes had roared to safe landings on the hard-packed desert crust. They had been guided to the landing zone by a prepositioned operative, a Kurdish national in the pay of the Russians, who had been paradropped in with a portable radar homing beacon a few days before.

The beacon transmitted course information to the flight decks of the transports, guiding them to within a few meters of the LZ. The man on the ground then used chemical light sticks tossed onto the sands to mark the landing zone, and the planes touched down, between the glowing red, green, and blue dashes that softly lit the night.

No sooner had the planes' landing gear touched earth than the rear ramp of the first Antonov slammed down amid a cloud of swirling dust, and men and machinery spilled onto the desert floor, a process repeated moments later, following the second Antonov's landing.

Before the planes had taxied to a stop, with well-trained precision, the BTR-70 armored personnel carriers and two BRDM armored command vehicles were rolled onto the turf and the Vasaltniki assembled into ranks. As soon as the planes had off-loaded, and with engines still hot, the Antonovs took off again, disappearing into the black night skies.

The transports would return just before dawn the following day to pick up the men and equipment for the return trip, but until then they couldn't afford to sit on the ground, where they would be as vulnerable as beached whales. The Antonovs would fly back across the border, tank up from Ilyushin fuelbirds, and orbit their stations until they were ordered back in for the return leg.

But all of this was still several hours away. Now Nemekov issued final instructions to the reconnaissance unit he was sending toward al-Kabriz as a forward observer team. If what it saw on the ground indicated conditions that were favorable for an attack, then Nemekov's main force would engage the enemy. If not, he would weigh whatever alternative options presented themselves.

Nemekov saluted the commander of the recon team and watched the BRDMs roll off into the night. Once the vehicles were out of sight, he turned toward his aide who was setting up the satcom rig.

"General Potapenko is on the circuit, sir," he told Nemekov, who snatched at the handset.

According to an old Bedouin expression, when Allah created the desert, he laughed. The nomadic tribesmen understand this to mean that the desert is always unpredictable. It can be capricious and cruel. It can be beautiful, bountiful, and life sustaining. But it is always changing, and it never assigns its fidelity to a creature as humble in its eternal eyes as man. With mercurial suddenness, it can change from friend to foe, exposing those it had concealed from enemies and rendering them vulnerable to ambush and destruction.

This it did tonight, before the recon patrol sent out by Nemekov had gotten halfway to its first rally point.

Lieutenant Aksel Trapezhnikov, who had led the scout team, returned with his men to the safety of a ravine on the flank of one of the low, arid hills that began about two klicks from the desert base at al-Kabriz. He at once radioed his superior. He had good news to report.

"Scabbard, this is Saber," he said into the handset. Moments later he heard Nemekov's voice in his ear.

"Say your situation, Scabbard."

"The situation is better than expected. The merchandise is still on the shelves."

"Are there any new buyers?" asked Nemekov, meaning, in their prearranged transmission code, had there been any new negative developments that might abort the mission.

"Negative. No new buyers. Goods are on the shelves and the doors are open, but no interest from any new buyers."

"Excellent news," Nemekov responded, understanding that there was some new development that made attack even likelier to succeed. "Will arrive in time for business. Out." Trapezhnikov would fill Nemekov in when the main force arrived at the hide site.

Nemekov smiled and rubbed his hands, as much in anticipation as for the warmth it would generate in the chilly night air. He turned to his XO.

"It's a go, Baylin," he said to the young lieutenant, attired as he was, in the standard Warsaw Pact variant of the NATO "chocolate chips" desert camouflage pattern fatigues, as popular today on Manhattan streets as they were during the Gulf War months. "Instruct the men that we move out in ten minutes."

"Yes, sir, at once," Baylin replied, saluting smartly. He loped off to transmit his superior officer's order.

• • •

The main contingent of the Iranian ambush force lay in wait amid the rocky landscape of the desert. Colonel Ghazbanpour himself commanded them from the field.

He had sent out patrols, all of them on foot, and all of them naturally adapted to use the desert for concealment and attack. Most had grown up in this environment and called it home. Ghazbanpour's patrols were under orders to report in at half-hour intervals.

The patrols had not seen the landing zone, which was beyond their area of operation, but one of them had spotted the Vasaltniki scout team on its way to the base. Though their running lights were off and though the team navigated by night-vision equipment, the noise of the vehicles carried across the desert, and to well-tuned ears, it was as loud as thunder.

It was not long before Nemekov's advance unit was being watched as it was conducting its own recon of the base.

Now, back at the patrol's hide site, the force was under constant observation by Iranian troops.

Ghazbanpour's orders were to wait and permit the enemy to concentrate its forces, then allow it to launch its attack unhindered. Afterward, it would be counterattacked, encircled, and, if luck held and strategy was sound, completely annihilated.

Nine
Hell Was a Diamond

Dawn was still at least several hours away. Plenty of time to launch a strike that in training exercises had never lasted longer than thirty minutes from start to finish, with an additional forty-odd minutes to make it back to the LZ, and maybe another ten sacrificed to Murphy, which is what even the Russians called the personification of the ancient military law stating that if anything can go wrong, it probably will.

In the case of Nemekov's mission, Murphy would play one of his cruelest jokes ever. But as he issued orders for the team to move into its preattack positions, Nemekov had no inkling of this yet.

As far as the major was concerned, the base was wide open for an unchallenged assault. The approaches had been checked for land mines, perimeter booby traps, and intruder warning devices, and these had been cleared or neutralized where found. Lieutenant Trapezhnikov had been correct in his promising assessment of the odds favoring success. Nemekov had seen this right away. The base was lightly defended, and there was no indication of heavy armor either on the road leading up to it or within the confines of the eight-foot-high chain-link fence surrounding it.

It was not prudent to take matters at face value, of course, and Nemekov was well aware that this could be a deception maneuver on the part of the Iranians. They might have hidden several tanks and APCs in a nearby wadi, ready to provide fire support. But it would have to be close to be effective, and surveillance had detected no sign of any armor on the road or surrounding terrain.

There was a ZSU-123 quad-barreled cannon mounted on an AMX light armored vehicle, but it did not seem operational at the moment. Either it was unmanned or its crew was not paying attention. A lightly armed Hip-H helo sat nearby, also apparently unmanned. Both could be quickly and easily destroyed in place. Ordinarily this would be too good a development to be true, and give grounds for suspicion. But in this case, Nemekov believed that appearances were not at all deceiving.

Nemekov reasoned that in a fight in Europe or in Chechnya, suspicions might be in order, or in the middle of a war practically anywhere else. But this was Iran, and it had been a long time since the American attempt at an airborne rescue that was launched in 1980. His assessment was that the Iranians were simply not expecting a commando raid and did not believe anyone knew that the aircraft was being sequestered at this isolated base. They were simply running true to form—belligerent but careless in critical aspects of warfare.

Nemekov was wrong, however. Appearances here were most deceiving. For this error in judgment his force would pay dearly, and the first installment would be made in a very short while.

Unaware of what was to be, Nemekov issued immediate orders for the assault to proceed.

• • •

The attack commenced swiftly at three hundred eighteen hours, and it continued with clockwork precision after that. Everything came together at once. All the weeks of planning and exercise jelled into a single paroxysm of combat synergies as the assault was put in motion.

There were two attack teams, each striking from the opposite direction. Snipers attached to the teams sighted on ground and tower sentries and took them down with precisely aimed head shots. Guard dogs were fired on if they did not run. Even as the Iranian soldiers dropped, squads of RPG shooters fired shoulder-launched missiles into the base compound.

The HEAT or high-explosive antitank rounds struck one after another, pulsebeat after pulsebeat, producing thunderous reports and blinding strobe flashes of blazing light. Concussion waves shattered glass and pulverized concrete, tore limbs and heads from Iranian soldiers caught in the lethal rain of spinning shrapnel, and reduced military vehicles to burning heaps of twisted wreckage. Cobra heads of flame and tarantula clouds of acrid cordite smoke loomed skyward in the aftermath of the missile hits, and everywhere things had begun to burn.

In the strobing, flashing, splintering light of many high-explosive strikes, hell was a diamond, and each new instant revealed another crystal facet of carnage in monochrome. In jittery, Chaplinesque frames, men died, or were maimed, or burst into flame, or were ripped apart by shrapnel. Only the sounds of battle had continuity.

The screams, the crumps of the initial explosions and the hot whoosh of the fireball, the blunt thudding of the Avtomat Kalashnikov AK rifles ported by both sides, the calls to action and the yells of terror and pain ran out of sync with the flickering images of battle as behind the rocket team the BTR fighting vehicles rushed in, hurling forty-mm cannon fire and hosing down the base with sustained 7.62-mm machine gun bursts.

Minutes after the lightning attack commenced, Lieutenant Trapezhnikov and his team rammed their armored BTR-70 carriers through the wall of the hangar where missiles had blown an opening. Quickly dismounting the BTRs, they charged inside, cradling their weapons. They immediately came under fire.

As they broke for cover or crouched behind the armor, unit members could now clearly see the black stealth plane within the center of the hangar, surrounded by a cocoon of computer and electronic monitoring equipment, worktables and coils of thick power and data conduits.

There were more Iranians within the hangar's recesses manning rifles and machine guns, already set up behind sandbags in prepared defensive fire positions. These troops were better trained, motivated, and equipped than those previously encountered. As soon as they had seen the Russians enter, they opened up with rifle grenades and automatic fire.

Trapezhnikov saw three of his troops take immediate hits as they fired back, and he instinctively knew that these enemy forces were the best troops the Iranians had, ones committed to a final showdown. They could slow the strike up long enough for reinforcements to arrive. Surely that was their purpose, and perhaps there was mechanized armor hidden in the desert after all. But they would not succeed.

"Back! Fall back!" Trapezhnikov hollered, and waved at his men to follow him from the hangar entrance into the flame-drenched night. There they would regroup for a counterattack.

As soon as his men were clustered in a defensive ring behind the armored personnel carriers, Trapezhnikov outlined his plan. The carriers were to storm the hangar again and lay down cover fire while another team set up a typically Russian weapon, the AGS-17 Plamya automatic grenade launcher.

The Plamya cycled belts of fifty thirty-mm high-explosive canister grenades at high speed. It had a range of almost three thousand meters. The Plamya could saturate the hangar with blast and concussion sufficient to kill every living thing inside. The squad carried two Plamyas.

The rest happened extremely rapidly with foreordained consequences.

While the two Plamya teams set up their rigs, small-arms suppressing fire killed those defenders it caught and forced the rest to keep their heads tucked down. Then, when they were ready, the Plamya teams fired off one thirty-round grenade belt after another into the sand-bagged positions in front of the plane, shredding anything living or already dead.

At the same time machine gunners manning the heavy MGs mounted on the APCs raked the steel catwalk running along the top of the hangar on four sides where snipers had been sited. A whirlwind of steel chewed up metal and living flesh without discrimination. The catwalk sections soon broke free at the corners with groans and snaps of shearing metal, and dangled vertically above the hangar floor like Damoclean swords over the heads of the doomed defenders.

"Break fire!" Trapezhnikov shouted at his men. A little more than five minutes had passed from the time the guns had opened up, and thousands of rounds of ammunition had been expended. No answering fire was heard from the emplaced positions. Only corpses now manned the sandbags. The hangar was secure. The first phase of the assault was now complete.

Trapezhnikov risked standing up and quickly surveyed the smoke-choked interior of the hangar. Lights from his vehicles outside shone through the perforated plate-metal skin of the place, while bodies were slumped over the bullet-riddled sandbags, damasking them with blood.

Above, one of the catwalks had broken from its fastenings and hung at a ninety-degree angle to the hangar floor. On a section of steel platform directly across it that was still intact, a corpse in the olive-drab uniform of an Iraqi regular was slumped over the railing, its arms dangling pendulously.

Lieutenant Trapezhnikov permitted himself a grim smile. They had won the day. The victory had been expected, but what is expected does not always materialize. Trapezhnikov felt that pride was justified by the achievement.

He issued rapid orders for his sappers to place bricks of halvah-textured Semtex high explosive around the plane's fuselage and set the digital detonation timers. While he waited for this action to be completed, he radioed the news back to mission commander Nemekov who was with the team outside the hangar.

"Do nothing until I arrive," Nemekov told the lieutenant. He wanted to make sure the demolition work was carried out to his specifications.

Minutes later Nemekov entered the hangar and noticed the hollow look on his subordinate's face.

"What's wrong?" he asked.

"Sir, the plane, it's, well—"

"Spit it out, what is the problem?"

"It's not the stealth, sir. It is a *maskirovka*. The Iranians have tricked us."

Nemekov pushed the younger man aside and ran toward the plane, to where the sappers had already stood down, their faces grim. At a distance it still looked real enough, and Nemekov willed himself to believe that his subordinate was mistaken, in which case the imbecile would have hell to pay. But up close Nemekov saw that it was he who had been mistaken. Much now seemed amiss with the aircraft.

First, there was the paint job. It was not the characteristic Styrofoam-like coating bonded to a composite metal hull, it was merely flat black paint, sprayed on by an air-powered applicator. The angled surfaces of the wings and fuselage were wrong, too. Through the cockpit window, there was no instrumentation on a crudely fashioned replica of a console. Other than this and the vacant pilot's seat, the cockpit was empty. *Yes,* thought Nemekov, *a replica, and a crude one at that.* Trapezhnikov was right. This was indeed a mock-up, a *maskirovka*.

The Iranians had played them. Played them for suckers. The white-hot ball of anger that exploded inside Nemekov's stomach and flooded him with a sense of almost maniacal rage forced saner thoughts from his mind. All he knew for the next few seconds was an intense anger at having been conned. His men winced as he raised the AK-47 in his hands and fired off a full clip into the dummy plane, then beat the glass of the phony cockpit to splinters with the rifle's heavy wooden buttstock, and kicked at its flimsy fuselage with his steel-toed boots.

When his rage had been vented, Nemekov stood on the mounting platform set up beside the mock-up, breathing heavily and looking down at his assembled troops. As the rage passed, it allowed the saner realization of what would happen next to come through, and although this realization also caused Nemekov anger, it brought with it as well a sobering sense of caution. If the plane had been a *maskirovka*, then . . .

"Let's get out of here, fast!" Nemekov shouted as he ran down the steps and palmed a fresh clip into his Kalashnikov.

Jumping into the lead command vehicle, Nemekov opened up a satcom link while the column retreated toward the road.

The sky was lightening into the false dawn that comes to the desert before sunrise. A chill wind swept across the land. Nemekov transmitted the bad news to the staging base many kilometers distant.

The Antonovs were on their way to pick them up at the LZ, he was informed. Nemekov only hoped they would live to reach it.

There was no point in striking the misled enemy when he was caught in the trap. At the sham base, the *Shuravi* would have a defensive perimeter to dig in, and it would make his destruction all the more difficult. Ghazbanpour might then have had to call in reinforcements and this would have robbed him of the shining glory of being responsible for his own victory, from start to finish.

Fortunately, the Iranian saw that the Vasaltniki had fallen straight into his trap. He had wanted to decimate

their forces and deal them a psychological blow before
striking; otherwise he would have chosen to hit them on
the way toward the base, well before they'd even reached
it.

The purpose of letting them find out that it was a Trojan
horse—a kind of inside-out Trojan horse—was to wear
them down, whittle away their numbers, cause them to
panic, and ultimately to flee.

This, Ghazbanpour seemed to have accomplished. The
forces defending the sham base had died shedding the
blood of martyrs.

His one great fear, and the single flaw in his plan that
he had been able to detect, was that the Russian commander might show the presence of mind and dig his men
in at the base, rather than withdraw in panic. From entrenched positions, they might have called in reserve
forces.

The transports might have also been able to land closer
to the base or even bomb or strafe the Iranian forces. But
none of this had happened. The Vasaltniki had panicked
as Ghazbanpour had guessed they would, and had fled
back into the open desert.

They would have no defenses here, only many kilometers of thirsty sand to soak up their spilled blood. Ghazbanpour owned the desert, and before the sun had risen,
he predicted that victory would be his.

Army General Vladimir Illich Potapenko slumped back in
his seat. He could not believe what he had just heard. The
attack had been carried out against a diversionary mock-
up, a phony base and plane, a shrewd *maskirovka*. He
listened through his radio link for real-time coverage of
the battle.

The shouts of his men, coming to him through the invisible ether of space, filled him with a gnawing dread
that seemed to attack his bones with acid. What would
happen now? His great victory was tarnished. Soon his
political enemies would begin to circle, and bring him
down.

He gave no thought whatever to the beleaguered men in the Iranian desert. There was only one ray of hope. If the Antonovs did not reach them in time, the Vasaltniki would be obliterated. The planes would be delayed if the MiG fighters being held in reserve were not sent as escorts. Later, Potapenko could find a way to repair his reputation.

Potapenko picked up a secure phone and began to issue a series of rapid orders in the crisp military tones for which he was famed throughout all of Russia. The Vasaltniki would be sacrificed to his own survival.

Ten
An Ode to Deception

Nemekov realized his double mistake as the Iranian ambush commenced firing on his force. As soon as the opening volley of mortar rounds began to hit with characteristic *crump-crump* sounds, blowing shell craters in the desert and gouging chunks from the wrinkled gray hills of extruded bedrock, Nemekov knew that he should not have given in to his emotions.

Instead he should have dug in and fought, using the wreckage of the destroyed desert base for shooting cover. He could then have called in a cross-border air strike of MiG-29 Fulcrums and decimated the attacking forces, per one of his backup options. The fighter sortie could have bombed and strafed the living hell out of the Iranian bastards who had set them up using the *maskirovka*.

This still could happen, but it would come at a heavy price for his force, and also for his career, once he finally returned home.

But to hell with that. Survival was what counted. Nemekov would return home, and he would take as many of his men along with him as possible.

The Iranian mortar crews out on the desert were sighting in on them, getting their range taped, placing their high-explosive canisters closer and closer to the column with each salvo. Nemekov knew they had to be spotting by light amplification or thermal imaging because it was still predawn twilight, and this would give him precious minutes to deploy to safer ground. There was no substitute for the human eye when it came to calling in mortar strikes. It would be a while yet before they got his range down.

Up ahead, the desert track passed before several immense piles of prehistoric rock that the earth had thrust skyward during its volcanic past. Nemekov told the driver to run hell-bent for leather toward one of the defiles between these rock formations where they would have some cover; pitifully little, but at least some.

The Iranians, he could see, were trying to prevent this with all their might. They were walking their mortar fire toward his force, and getting dangerously close with each successive round they lobbed.

Crump!

Nemekov could now feel the ground shudder as gouts of gravel, dirt, and sand were flung against the sides of the APC, and the clouds of dense cordite smoke grew thicker outside the front slit windows. The armored personnel carriers were not immune to high-explosive strikes, simply more resistant than other vehicles. Their hulls were made of thick plate steel, but not thick enough to withstand a direct HEAT hit.

Nemekov had chosen the BTRs and BRDMs more for their mobility than their armor, forfeiting weight for speed. He hoped the trade-off would not accrue to the destruction of himself and his force as he raced toward the gap in the rocks.

Crump!

Suddenly the light armored vehicle to his right was hit by a near miss. It proved to be close enough.

The BRDM disappeared in a detonation flash and clouds of choking black smoke, reappearing a moment later strangely transformed. It was now a blazing, blackened mass of charred metal wreckage.

The bodies of the five Vasaltniki who had been riding in it were flung here and there, sprawled in death like rag dolls. Nemekov's vehicle was rocked by another brace of mortar shells hitting close by the BTR. He doubted he would live long enough to reach the safety of the defile ahead, or that it was anything but a stopping point before death overtook him.

The pilot and copilot of the lead Antonov transport plane had been in the process of tanking up as the orders to recross the Iranian-Azeri border came over the secure radio circuit. The crew of the Ilyushin fuelbird pumped in the last remaining kilograms of aviation gasoline and pulled up the hose-and-drogue assembly that had been linked to a receptacle at the top rear of the twin-engine transport aircraft, midway between the wings and the tail rudder assembly.

As the Antonov's pilot applied forward thrust, the two huge turbojet engines uniquely mounted at the tops of the swept-back wings, near the fuselage, cycled out thousands of foot-pounds of jet thrust.

From a stationary point below the flight deck of the fuelbird, the Antonov began to move quickly, speeding on a southwesterly course. The second transport plane flew behind it, spaced at approximately one half kilometer.

The planes soon became black specks against the slowly lightening morning sky as the refueling planes returned to base to take on more avgas and then return to fly circles in the air, awaiting a rendezvous with the returning Antonovs on their cross-border flight with their Vasaltniki passengers.

As the fuelbird turned and lumbered back to the base, its pilot noted the white vapor trails of three MiG-29 air superiority fighters at an altitude several thousand feet above them. The Fulcrums were turning in the sky, just as they were, and heading back in the same direction, only at a much greater speed.

The Ilyushin driver supposed that they were no longer deemed necessary. The mission was obviously proceeding according to plan.

Such thoughts would never have crossed his mind had he eavesdropped, only a few minutes before, on the secure channel through which the fighter pilots were linked to the command center on the ground below.

"Talon Leader, this is Scabbard command center," the voice of the ground controller had told the lead pilot.

The fighter pilot acknowledged the transmission and was ordered to return to base. He asked for a repeat and was again told to immediately break formation and head back to the airstrip. The flight leader acknowledged his orders and heeled his plane around.

"What do you make of this?" asked his wingman, whom he could see in the cockpit of the MiG off to his left. "Didn't even ask us to escort the Antonovs."

"Who knows?" the leader returned. "Probably nothing."

"I say let's go have a look," the wingman declared. "Fuck the orders."

"You do anything like that and I'll have you up for court-martial," he said back. "This is a spook operation and I don't want to stick my neck out any further than it is already. Clear, Yevgeny?"

The wingman said that it was clear, but not until after a moment's pause. The fighter pilots picked up no further chatter as the planes made the short run back to base.

So, they were to be made sacrificial lambs, Nemekov thought. He should have seen this coming, too. He and most of his men had safely reached the defile, realizing that they were in fact in a twisting warren of gullies, small wadis, and box canyons cut into the bleak gray folds of the barren desert hills.

He had deployed his vehicles and men along one of the rock galleries, protected by outcroppings and overhangs of weirdly sculpted sandstone. As the sun rose in the sky and it became full daylight, the enemy shelling stopped for a short while. But the lull was all too brief.

Very soon, Nemekov had heard the telltale *thuk-a-thuk* of whirling rotor blades and the banshee whine of powerful diesel-turbine engines.

The soldier was familiar with that particular sound.

Before seeing the choppers appear over the top of the rock galleries, he knew what they were—Mil-24 Hind-F gunships of Russian manufacture, sold to the Iranians in a package deal shortly after the ascent to power of the Khomeini regime in the early eighties.

The Mil-24s were heavily armed with rockets and a thirty-caliber machine gun. The choppers could also carry troops that could be dropped from a low hover to scale the side of the bluffs below which his force was sheltered.

Soon the sound of the rotors and engines swelled to a deafening crescendo in the heat of the desert air.

Nemekov looked up and saw the Hinds just skirting the edge of the defile system, not daring to come overhead in range of his guns.

"Hold your fire," he ordered his men.

Had the helos intended to hit them, they would have swooped in fast, and in formation, firing their rockets and automatic cannons as they converged. Since they weren't doing this, it was something else, probably a surrender ultimatum, that was their objective. Nemekov had no intention of surrendering, but it cost nothing to listen, especially since he needed to buy time until the Antonovs came within rescue range.

The transports couldn't land right on their position, of course, but their pilots might be able to arrange an alternate LZ close enough for at least a contingent to break away and make it back across the border. At this point Nemekov would consider this a token victory.

In the seconds of silence as the Hinds hovered ominously overhead, Nemekov thought back to the events of a few minutes ago, events that now seemed to have taken place at some distant point in another life.

He recalled how, once his men had reached the dubious safety of the defile, he had contacted the mission staging area on satcom, ordering in the MiG fighters that he hoped would neutralize the Iranian ambush. And he recalled how he had been stunned both by what he had heard and by the voice to whom he'd been speaking.

"Negative, the planes have been recalled to base," the ground control officer had told him. It should be Potapenko on this circuit, Nemekov thought. Yet it wasn't. He suspected then that the old bastard had sold him out to save his own neck. That was just now becoming crystal clear. Potapenko didn't want his men to return, dead or alive. Not if they dared fail him.

"What the hell do you mean the planes have been recalled?" Nemekov shouted into the handset's mouthpiece. "And where is Potapenko?"

"The general has instructed me to deal with any further requests for assistance," the voice resumed calmly. "The transport planes are on their way. They should reach their landing zones by seven hundred hours."

"The Antonovs will do us no good if we are all dead, you imbecile," Nemekov shouted again. "I want fighter cover. I want those MiGs sent in!"

"I'm sorry, sir, but as I have said, the fighters have been recalled to base."

"Why?"

"Problems with their communications systems necessitated their abrupt return. We are now working on getting them back into the air. Please have patience."

Nemekov forced himself to keep his voice level, despite his hatred for the nonentity on the other end of the line and the sound of high explosive impacting on the rock faces of the cliffs surrounding them.

"What's your name?"

"First Lieutenant Zotov, sir," the voice said.

"Lieutenant, I want you to find Potapenko and put him on right away," Nemekov said.

"As I said, sir—"

Nemekov cut the other man's voice off.

"Listen here, you maggot," he shouted. "You tell the general that unless he immediately gets on this line, I will order my men to lay down their arms and hoist the white flag of surrender. I will then personally reveal every aspect of this operation to my Iranian interrogators. Have you got that, Zotov?"

"Yes, sir, I—"

"Do it, maggot!"

Nemekov's wait seemed like an eternity, although less than a minute had passed before his mentor was on the line. He had, of course, been right beside Zotov all along, Nemekov knew with sudden certainty.

"Valery Fedorovich, how sorry I am for your predicament," came the old man's mock-soothing voice on the commlink. "Please do not let me down. The Antonovs are on their way."

"I want the MiGs sent over here," Nemekov shouted. "I am told they were recalled? Is this true?"

"I am afraid so," the general replied. "There were some unsolvable problems."

"Liar!" Nemekov shot back. "You've sold us down the river."

"Take care. You are losing control, my young friend."

"I want those planes in here, you stinking old *bizh-denok*!" yelled Nemekov. "Send them in or I will surrender my men."

"If you do that, then I will see to it that your wives and loved ones are severely punished. It's not like the old days, but there are still ways to do such things, if one has the means."

"Fuck you, you bloody murderous bastard," Nemekov shouted, aware that his men were watching him with amazed stares. "If I survive this, I will wring your withered neck. That is a promise."

The general paused a beat. Such a sickening lack of courage in one he had personally raised up by his own strong hand. Besides, the odds strongly disfavored Nemekov ever keeping that particular promise.

Potapenko thought he had been wrong in selecting Nemekov for a protégé. The young man should have been willing to give his life for his superior officer, for the general considered himself the living embodiment of his nation in all its greatness.

"*Do svidahnya, moj' drug.* I hope we shall meet again," was all the old man said before severing radio contact.

In the lead chopper, Colonel Ghazbanpour sat in the co-pilot's seat and received the nod from the pilot that indicated his lip microphone was patched into the helo's public address system.

Ghazbanpour had not yet decided whether or not he preferred to take the Russian commando forces alive or dead. He could conceive of making excellent capital for his career if it turned out either way. So he could afford to show some measure of mercy. He would let the gods of war decide the outcome.

"Attention, attention." He spoke into the rice-grain mike, hearing his amplified voice thunder even above the sound of the rotors. "This is Colonel Farzaneh Hossein Ghazbanpour of the Iranian People's Army. You are surrounded by superior forces on every side. Escape is impossible. Surrender is your only option—that or death."

He paused for effect, pleased at his command of spoken Russian. "Surrender terms are unconditional. Lay down your arms and leave the enclave with hands raised above your heads. When you reach the road you will be issued further instructions. That is all. You have five minutes to decide."

Nemekov kicked the satcom unit to the ground and faced his men. He had not meant the threat to surrender he had made to Potapenko. It had been a bluff. Still, he thought it only fair that the men should unanimously decide their fate.

"What will it be?" he asked them now. "If we choose to make a stand, our only hope is that some of us can break free and reach the Antonovs by some other route. The defile network we are now within may prove to have other exitways. But many will surely not make it. I therefore leave the choice up to you—surrender or fight."

One by one, the verdict came in. Somebody called out, *"Odin 'ebetsya, druoi draznitsya—kakaya raznitsa?"* and raised a chorus of laughter. The old proverb went, "One fucks, the other teases; what's the difference?" But the point had been made.

The choice was to fight and die rather than surrender.

When the five minutes were up, the Hind pilots saw the Vasaltniki forces begin to disperse along the galleries in the defile complex below them. It would be like shooting fish in a barrel, thought Ghazbanpour, almost too simple. But that was the decision of the trapped commando unit and the Russians would pay a heavy blood price for it.

In the end all would be killed, of this there was no question in Ghazbanpour's mind.

It was impossible to say which side fired the first volley that shattered the brief cease-fire.

As soon as the Vasaltniki's mechanized armor down in the defile started up, shooting broke out. Machine gunners atop the BTRs and on the back of the BRDMs fired up at the Hinds, which dodged and jinked to and fro, loosing high-explosive rockets and automatic cannon bursts in answer.

Men screamed as they were hit and died, and the reek of cordite soon filled the smoke-choked stone galleries as the Vasaltniki scattered for cover.

Nemekov eventually found himself and three other commandos emerging from one of the rock galleries and suddenly out into open sand desert. He could hear bursts of small arms fire and rocket explosions in the distance, but somehow his vehicle had evaded the choppers. This surprise reprieve would not last very long, he knew, but at least for the moment they were out of the maze of death.

Nemekov consulted the portable global positioning unit tethered to the BTR, and saw that they might reach the landing zone in time if they moved quickly and had some luck on their side.

The BTR was dangerously low on fuel, but they had no other choice. Their luck continued to hold, however. The clear blue sky remained free of Iranian gunships.

Now in the distance they heard the sound of the powerful jet engines of the incoming Antonovs.

"We're almost directly below you," Nemekov radioed the crew of the assault transport planes on the preassigned emergency frequency they had kept open for rescue transmissions. "Do you see us?"

The pilot in the lead plane scanned the terrain below.

"Affirm. I see you. Hold steady. Commencing landing approach."

Nemekov breathed a deep sigh of relief. He could see the lead plane begin a landing pattern, and although the BTR's fuel gauge read a little below the empty point, he knew they could probably make it on the fumes. The planes were on their way. Their amazing luck had held.

Then another sound made Nemekov realize that the promise of rescue and safety had been a false one all along.

The Iranian Mil-24 Hind appeared from behind the towers of stone. Either it had been "masking" itself, as pilots used the term—playing a brutal hide-and-seek game of lying in wait for the transports to arrive—or it had just breasted the low desert bluffs on a search path for any stragglers that had not been captured or killed in the fighting. Either case spelled death for Nemekov's small force element.

The lead Antonov saw the Hind gunship and immediately pulled up its nose, trying to claw its way back to the skies and freedom. But that would not happen. The Hind immediately opened up with a rocket salvo and struck the transport aircraft dead center in its unprotected flank.

As the lead plane exploded, whirling pieces of burning wing debris and fuselage fragments, skirling and wheeling outward and downward in a mad tangle of mangled steel, struck the second aircraft that could not turn in time to avoid being hit. It, too, exploded in a second fireball, whose concussive blast front was powerful enough to shake the desert as a pancake of shocked air slammed into the flat ground.

Pieces of burning wreckage and flaming gouts of ignited aviation gasoline poured down onto the rock and sand, turning the desert into a crackling cauldron of flame. Within the amphitheater of fire, the BTR struggled on, a pathetic gray-brown beetle crawling through a flaming brazier of live coals.

Nemekov wasted no time in climbing behind the BTR's 7.62-mm heavy machine gun and pointing it up at the giant steel dragonfly that he saw wavering in the shimmers of heat distortion caused by the superheated air that surrounded him. The metal insect danced and dodged as he cooked off everything in the belt-fed magazine, watching the red tracer bullets that were loaded one to every fourth armor-piercing slug bolt skyward in a stream of crimson dashes.

Suddenly Nemekov saw the Mil-24 dip its nose. A puffball of oily black smoke belched from one of its two side-mounted turbofan engine exhausts. Another followed, and another. The center of each black puff was a blazing yellow.

"I hit the bastard!" he shouted in jubilation as the smoke clouds thickened and the enemy helicopter heeled over sideways, firing a salvo of its remaining rockets at the BTR. It tried righting itself, but failed and began a slow, arcing plunge to the jagged rocks below. Moments before it crashed, the pilot had emptied its rocket racks down on the fighting vehicle.

Nemekov and the two other Vasaltniki who rode with him in the BTR did not live to see the Hind strike an outcropping of stone pillars that towered from the flat desert floor and erupt into a soaring, fifty-foot fireball, as falling wreckage hammered the ground with a shower of blazing steel. The multiple rocket strikes on the BTR reduced Nemekov and his Vasaltnik companions to spinning chunks of charred meat and bone. Seconds later their Iranian enemies were also blown to bits as their helo went up in flames.

Eleven
A Court They Could Play Ball In

The U.S. president wore a light blue *Air Force One* windbreaker emblazoned with the Great Seal of the Republic over a monogrammed golf shirt and blue jeans, his favored attire on longer flights on the executive jet. Dubbed the "Flying Taj Mahal" by some, the mammoth plane contained a plush presidential suite in the nose, two galleys equipped for gourmet cooking, eighty-five telephones, a press room, hospital, two conference rooms, six bathrooms, and enough electronic gear for computing, communications, and defensive electronic warfare to require 238 miles of wiring hidden in its airframe.

Cruising over the midwest at thirty-five thousand feet, en route to the G-5 economic summit in Tokyo, the chief executive's sneakered feet were propped on the edge of the teak conference table as he drank black coffee and faced the large, flat panel display screen. Arrayed around the table of the wide-body 747's conference room were Chief of Staff Lew Baldridge, National Security Advisor

General Oscar E. S. Throckmorton, and Secretary of State Marston Everett Carlysle.

Though there were two other members of his cabinet onboard, the three were the only ones with a need-to-know; nor would Throckmorton have been onboard had the president not decided to hedge his bets against being caught without a knowledgeable staffer close at hand as the C.I.S. commando mission into Iran unfolded. The rest of the traveling presidential entourage, like the group of pool reporters in the aft media cabin accompanying the officials overseas, was occupied elsewhere and thoroughly out of the loop.

As it turned out, and as President Claymore was now learning in detail as the teleconference progressed, the action had turned into even more of a tar baby than had America's 1980 Iran hostage rescue mission. The two-way electronic conference net linked those onboard *Air Force One* with a hastily convened meeting of the National Security Council in the White House Situation Room buried some thirty feet beneath the foundation of the executive mansion. Here the directors of the CIA and NSA, the chairman of the Joint Chiefs, and various other representatives of the U.S. government and military gathered for an emergency crisis management session.

Ordinarily the president would have chosen to remain in Washington until the Russian mission had run its course, but there was no question about missing the Tokyo summit. Fortunately, the president was used to working in the recently refurbished presidential jet. Originally opposed to the jet, which was delivered during the last year of the Bush Administration at a cost of almost $300 million, he now considered it an extension of the Oval Office, where he worked, and the East Wing, where he slept.

Travis Claymore had listened to the briefings from the Pentagon's and intelligence community's representatives that told about the C.I.S. mission's failure. The Russian commando force had been annihilated and the stealth aircraft was still in Iranian hands. This had, to some extent, been expected and Claymore could at least keep a clear conscience, having warned C.I.S. President Grigorenko against the mission. But that was not all. There was a new and unexpected development that overshadowed everything else.

"How can you be telling me those missiles are armed, General?" he asked the JCS chairman, General Parris "Jack" Thibodeaux. "That was the entire point of the mission, wasn't it? To prevent them putting nukes on those things. Am I right or wrong?"

"Mr. President, you're right. Absolutely right." The chairman looked into the camera, aware that all eyes in the Situation Room were on him. "And that should have been what happened, and it didn't. But there is always the possibility of their having outstripped our intelligence, and in this case they did."

"You're sure those are nuclear warheads on those missiles?" the president asked. "How many were there again?"

"Two, with a third possible," the chairman replied. "And we are very sure. The director of the CIA can explain."

"Mr. President."

"Hello, Cliff."

"Mr. President," CIA director Clifford Merrick began, "we know there are nuclear warheads on those Iranian birds because we have watched them being prepared in a manner consistent with procedures for nuclear warfighting. As you know, we have been keeping our eyes on Iran during the last few weeks, with special attention devoted to the missile batteries. In three cases, we noticed conventional warheads being removed and replaced with new warheads bearing markings which indicate they are nuclear devices."

"Could this be some kind of trick?"

"It might be," the DCI replied, "but we don't think it is. We have human intelligence sources, that is, people in there, highly trusted people, who have verified that the Iranians had at least two, and maybe three, nuclear warheads in transit to a test facility at the time of the air strikes, and that they have now placed these on the missiles."

Travis Claymore paused a moment, then asked, "What kind of damage are we talking about here? How big are these nukes?"

The DCI deferred to General Jack for the reply.

"Mr. President," he said, "the best way to answer your question is to put the matter in perspective. We estimate the size of each warhead to be in the three-kiloton range. The burnout zone for such a warhead would be about twenty square miles. Depending on population density and other factors, the casualty rate would be about sixty thousand per warhead. To put it another way, each warhead would have the stopping power of approximately ten Hiroshima bombs."

"Jesus Christ on a fucking raft," the president said.

The DCI added that the missiles appeared to be in a state of readiness for launch. The president then asked for options.

"We have a plan available, Mr. President," said the chairman of the Joint Chiefs, who again held the floor.

The president listened, and then nodded.

"Put it into operation," he told the chairman. "We'll talk again just before I land in Tokyo."

As the big screen blanked, the president picked up the phone and announced to his aides seated at the table that it was time he placed a call to Moscow. This thing had really snowballed.

Army General Potapenko had returned to the Kremlin to brief his political masters on the mission's grave consequences. He knew their displeasure, but he also well knew that they could admit nothing publicly about the matter. He informed them of his decision to retire, further putting himself out of harm's way.

He would escape this fiasco unscathed and withdraw to his dacha on the Moskva River in the unsullied forest country near the Moscow suburb of Archangelskoye.

There he would live out his remaining years in comfort and write the memoirs of his Afghan War exploits. Potapenko had already made arrangements with a Moscow-based literary agent for the rights to his life story. So far, he had heard that publishers in London, Paris, and New York were preparing offers.

Of some of the general's exploits, however, his intended memoirs would never speak, although these were well known to his contemporaries. As the general lay back comfortably in his bed, completely naked, he awaited the evening's enjoyments with growing anticipation.

After this ordeal, in particular, he needed to relax. He was still in perfect health, and though his doctors had advised him to moderate his drinking, he could still comfortably put away more than many a younger man's share of *pertsovka,* the spiced vodka that he, like Stalin, especially favored.

Sipping from his glass, Potapenko now trained his eyes on the doorway to the bathroom, where his guest for the evening was freshening up. He was not too old to enjoy the vigorous pleasures of sex either, and here, too, he had no doubt that he could outlast many a younger man, especially in today's Russia with its so-called new breed.

Disgusting, this current generation! They were weak, like Grigorenko and his bunch of misnamed "modernists," and destined to be overrun by the barbarians of the West in time. This invasion might not be a military one. It could be economic. But it would come. Potapenko was glad he would not be around to see its full development.

But enough of such thoughts. Now was not the time for dark sentiments. As his pretty guest for the evening came out of the bathroom, he smelled the scent of the expensive French cologne he had bought as a gift wafting in his direction.

How sweet it smelled. And how sweet was the appearance of his long-limbed bedroom companion, how beautiful were the sculpted breasts and rounded buttocks. The general cast his eyes across the fetching young body and patted the bed beside him.

"You are a vision, Misha," he said to the muscular young blond man. "Come, sit here beside me."

The old general ran his hands along the youth's body as Potapenko's companion returned his intimate caresses. Potapenko closed his eyes as he lost all track of time.

Long after the rapturous climax that made the air catch in his lungs, however, the general continued to gasp for breath.

This time it resulted from the smothering darkness of the pillow that powerful, unseen hands held down over his face. As he wheezed and panted like a landed fish, Potapenko heard voices above his head, gruff voices that were somehow familiar to him, voices that mocked him bitterly as his lungs strained to inhale the life-giving air that was being denied them.

"This is for the men you sacrificed, traitor," the voices swore.

There was a network, a kind of *nomenklatura* among Afghan veterans, and though Nemekov had not been the keenest of military men, he had belonged to that network nevertheless. It took care of its own, and avenged wrongs done to its own. The betrayal of Nemekov and his Vasaltniki force would be repaid tonight—in full.

On the bed, Potapenko continued to writhe and struggle pathetically. Despite his years he was strong, and he fought hard for his life. But the men holding him down were stronger still. Even Misha had pitched in, for he, too, was one of the *nomenklatura*. The old warrior's last experience as the blackness around him became permanent and he left the scene far sooner than he had ever anticipated, was hearing the sound of his assassins curse his name.

Brigade commander of Iranian Islamic Ground Forces, Western Operational Area Command (field headquarters Karbala), Colonel Farzaneh Hossein Ghazbanpour stood on the catwalk of the underground hangar facility and observed the activity some thirty feet below him. There, in the center of the five-hundred-meter square enclosure,

surrounded by technicians and linked by umbilicals of
electrical cabling to banks of diagnostic equipment, stood
the black plane that had been captured by an incredible
stroke of luck.

Ghazbanpour dragged hard on the Marlboro cigarette,
one of the twenty he daily smoked, and considered the
immense good fortune that had dropped this windfall into
Iranian hands. Others, of course, would say that it had
been Allah who had been responsible, especially the both-
ersome Major Meshkati from the Political-Ideological Directorate who was attached to the brigade.

Fortunately, the power of Meshkati and those like him,
once so great that the zealots had overridden the commands of competent military leaders during the Iran-Iraq
War and sent scores of thousands to needless battlefield
deaths, had now waned considerably. Soon such parasites
would be gone entirely. For the moment the P-ID's representative still hung on, his duties actually little more
than those of a chaplain, although in theory he could go
over Ghazbanpour's head directly to the Islamic Revolutionary Court of the Armed Forces should he deem it necessary.

The malignant little parasite watched, but could do
nothing. Even in the days of the P-ID's greatest power,
chances were he would have had to keep his nose out of
the colonel's business. Ghazbanpour's authority came direct from the *faqi* himself, via General Choubak in Tehran. Apart from head of the Majlis, or supreme legislature
of Iran, the president was also the country's holiest cleric,
who, as master of the Koran and interpreter of the *hadith,*
or traditions of the Prophet and the Twelve Imams, determined how the codices of Shia Islamic law were to be
realized in the world of living men. By the *faqi*'s decree,
Ghazbanpour was to have absolute control of the operation to guard the plane, and he enjoyed a direct channel
to the office of the president in Tehran. None could stand
in his way.

This, reflected Ghazbanpour, was ironic in the extreme,
considering how deeply the colonel loathed the revolution

and all it had represented, and how he had lived most of the last two decades with the fear of imminent arrest, trial, and execution. Though a Muslim who believed in Allah and the three pillars of the faith, Ghazbanpour had also loathed fanaticism in any of its manifestations.

At the time the revolution had swept across Iran, he had been a major in one of the northern garrisons, commanding troops riding herd on the Kurdish separatists in the rebellious hill towns. One day he learned that his entire family in Isfahan had been wiped out in one of the political purges that were common during that time.

Fearing for his own safety, and in any case powerless, Ghazbanpour had said and done nothing about it. Somehow, he'd remained untouched by what had happened. It was much later, when his place in the military pecking order was assured, that he had approached the Israelis and offered to spy on his country. A thirst for revenge had tempted him, but he had ultimately changed his mind and recanted.

In the end, the colonel had stayed loyal to Iran, in part because of wise counseling from his friend and mentor General Choubak. He had been able to live with himself these long years, to keep sane and whole, by viewing it all as a global game. Now, after much reflection, Ghazbanpour was certain that he was not far from wrong.

It was indeed a game. One in which lives hung in the balance, but a game for all of that. Ghazbanpour would play his part. As a loyal Iranian, he would see to it that the stealth aircraft was used to benefit his country. But the colonel would continue to provide information, as he had been routinely doing, to his immediate superior, General Katayoon Shadrokh Choubak. And, though close to the ear of the *faqi,* Choubak had for many years been the double agent whom the Israelis knew by the code-name Ahriman.

Book Two
Last-Extremity Solutions

Twelve
A Sierra Oscar in Mind

It had turned out to be a day full of surprises. Major Peace Mitchell still could not believe the VIP treatment he'd pulled. Since leaving Delta's headquarters at Bragg at six hundred hours that morning, it had been one surprise after another, almost like a birthday party.

First off, there was the VC-35A Learjet awaiting him at nearby Pope Air Force Base, tanked up and ready to fly him north and east across the Alleghenies into West Virginia, where a DOD staff car would be waiting to shuttle him to the Pentagon. It's a rare day that the U.S. Army springs for a Lear instead of a rustbucket DC-9 for the sorry likes of a special-forces major. Generals pull rides on those aircraft, other ranks usually take what's left over, which usually means the ghost of *Memphis Belle.*

Were this not surprise enough for Mitchell, there was the spanking-new Lincoln with blue-and-white military tags waiting for him when his plane landed at Washington National Airport less than an hour later. The black government-issue chariot was driven by a helpful young second lieutenant from JCS staff who welcomed Mitchell and even held the door for him. Mitchell considered asking him where the wet bar was, but thought better of it.

Mitchell's driver then chauffeured him the short distance of his journey's remaining leg along the Jefferson Davis Highway through the rolling green countryside of Alexandria, Virginia, confining his respectfully banal remarks to the weather and the colorful autumn foliage.

The lieutenant hadn't even cussed once, hadn't uttered so much as a "damn" throughout the entire half-hour drive. This was another wondrous sign to Mitchell. On previous visits to the Puzzle Palace, Mitchell had either driven himself or pulled a loudmouthed NCO with inevitable obsessions about one or more parts of the female anatomy, who thought the driver's seat of a military staff car was little more than a psychiatrist's couch on wheels.

Not that Mitchell didn't know what underlay today's VIP treatment. He did as surely as the Lord made green apples. It was the downing and capture of the Russian stealth fighter that had taken place weeks before.

The incident had been keeping Mitchell busy around the clock lately since his new boss, Colonel Mike Armbrister, had called him into his office at Delta's home base at Bragg in what had been previously known as Range 19.

This was a secluded, pine-forested area six miles in circumference within the sprawling Bragg military reservation, encircled by a sensor-studded, double-row, razorring-topped fence, and patrolled night and day by armed sentries who carried their weapons locked and loaded even in the latrine. Delta had moved out of its original headquarters in the old Bragg Stockade, where "Chargin' Charlie" Beckwith had founded it, and into its new, $75 million Range 19 complex in 1987.

Armbrister had told Peace that the president wanted a mission plan ready to roll in case the White House found a way to co-opt the Russians from going in themselves and trying to retake their lost stealth plane. Unlike the departed Pellegrino, Armbrister was supportive and unafraid to take chances.

The president had tried selling Moscow on the deal, but the former Soviets wouldn't even consider it. It was their aircraft, they'd stonily protested, and they were going to take it back themselves—period. The U.S. was told to butt out, which is precisely what it did.

Nevertheless, the White House still wanted an armed intervention force held in readiness against a possible last-minute change of heart, or some other unforeseen contingency, and the Joint Chiefs had concurred. Delta had been given the job of crafting a credible game plan for a mission into Iran to destroy the Russian aircraft on the ground, and Armbrister had put Mitchell in charge of making the plan take shape. The plan would be for an armed reconnaissance mission, a special recon, as it was called.

Then the Russians had sent a Spetsnaz detachment in with disastrous but—from what the twice-daily intel dumps that came into "Jaysock," the Joint Special Operations Command headquarters at Bragg's neighboring Pope AFB showed—unsurprising results.

Mitchell recalled the morning the Russian operation had commenced, and the amazement he'd experienced when he'd read the intelligence briefings that had come in from the CIA, NSA, and other national and foreign intelligence sources, including British MI6 and Israel's AMAN.

Incredibly, it had not been one of the Spetsnaz companies that had been sent in, but a detachment from one of the GRU's second-string Vasaltniki or assault brigades, which were good at what they did, but simply did not have the training that the mission called for. It was obvious that arcane Kremlin politics, which had changed only superficially since the days of the Communist Politburo's hegemony, had determined the choice. When the mission failed, and failed miserably, Mitchell had felt no surprise, only a numbing shock.

Nor was there much surprise about his being summoned to the Pentagon today in order to be briefed on the role he'd been ordered to play. Mitchell had expected to be called to Joint-Chiefs-of-Staff headquarters the moment he'd learned of the failed Russian operation.

He'd also been certain he would be expected to tell his superiors that his men were good to go for a U.S. mission into the Iranian desert to pull the Russians' chestnuts out of the fire for them.

In the aftermath of the first attempt, the follow-on mission would be twice as impossible to bring off, but that was not Mitchell's lookout. He just went where they sent him.

The headquarters of the Joint Chiefs of Staff, which includes the Pentagon offices of the Joint Special Operations Command, is reached at the Pentagon via the River Entrance, which is also the JCS entrance.

Mitchell's courteous young driver pulled the Lincoln into a numbered bay in the five-sided building's vast north parking lot and saluted smartly as his passenger left, reminding the major to phone the motor pool to arrange for transportation back to the airfield when he was ready.

Once inside the building, Mitchell flashed his military ID, turned right on the E-Ring, and walked a short distance down the bustling corridor, past portraits of several presidents. He recognized Jackson, Grant, and Teddy Roosevelt, but gave up on the others, who glowered at him for neglecting his American history lessons as he crossed beneath their merciless gazes.

Mitchell continued along the hall, passed Corridor Eight, and continued past more portraits and depictions of great nineteenth-century land and sea battles, until he passed the offices of the chairman of the JCS, where he immediately turned left onto Corridor Seven. A few minutes later, after another walk past more noble portraiture, Mitchell reached the closed, unmarked oaken door that opens into the Special Operations Division of the Joint Chiefs of Staff.

Unlike most depictions of the command center of

America's special-forces arm, which includes Army Rangers and Green Berets, Navy SEALs and Delta Force itself, the Pentagon headquarters of the Joint Special Operations Command does not boast a darkened, sunken pit filled with banks of electronic screens and overlooked by enormous television screens. These can be found at NORAD headquarters inside Cheyenne Mountain, Colorado, at Stratcom's underground command post beneath Offut Air Force Base in Nebraska, and some other places, too, but not here.

JSOC's Pentagon headquarters is in reality a warren of meeting rooms and open-plan staff areas sectioned off into modular work zones. The complex also has a few specialized rooms, such as the cipher room, the computer room, which contains a specially made Cray X-2000 hypercube mainframe, and the room with downlinks to real-time and near-real-time satellite imagery, which are all restricted. Otherwise—and with the exception of its many uniformed staffers—the nerve center of America's ultra-secret special-operations capability could pass for the main office of a large insurance company.

It was into one of the large meeting rooms of the JSOC complex that an orderly ushered Mitchell on arrival. As Mitchell entered the bustling enclosure, he saw that he was probably the last person to get there. The massive oval table of dark, polished mahogany was occupied by a half-dozen military brass and as many civilian representatives of the Defense Department, the National Security Council, and the various spook agencies with their cryptic, three-letter names that made up the U.S. "intelligence community."

Mitchell was directed to his place, one duly outfitted with a yellow legal pad, pencil, and nameplate, where he took his seat. He recognized few of the others in the room with him, with the notable exception of Major General Orville B. Childers, who Mitchell knew had been appointed head of the joint task force responsible for the mission and who reported directly to the chairman of the JCS, General Parris "Jack" Thibodeaux. Thibodeaux was

Colonel Mike Armbrister's direct superior, which made him the boss of bosses, as least as far as Mitchell went.

Thibodeaux soon rose and brought the meeting to order. As the general spoke, Mitchell listened with rapt attention. So far, his only source of surprise had been the Pentagon's uncharacteristic travel arrangements. But less than five minutes into Thibodeaux's speech, Mitchell knew that he had gone far beyond mere surprise, into the realm of pure amazement.

The most amazing part of all was that Thibodeaux, who had both airborne and Ranger experience dating back to Vietnam, obviously meant every word he was saying about the sierra oscar, or secret operation, he had in mind.

"Get up!"

The words, barked in Arabic, roused the sleeping men on the cold, hard ground. The two Bedouin guides awoke to find themselves in the middle of a circle of standing men who glared down at them with open menace.

Before they could rise, they were grabbed by the arms and jerked to their feet. The hilts of combat knives were pressed into their hands and the circle around them broadened to give them more room. The Bedouin looked uncomprehendingly at the serrated blades gleaming dully in their hands, then at each other with dawning awareness.

As they traded their wordless glances, a hunk of rope approximately four feet long and knotted at both ends was flung between them, into the center of the circle. Each Bedu knew what was expected of him, and knew why, and both men cursed the need for the few Iranian ehatys that had led them into this trap when they had known better from the first. But there was no turning back, not now.

One man, then the other, stooped and picked up an end of the rope in his free hand. Warily scrutinizing each other, the men placed the knotted ends between their teeth and clamped down hard. Moments later the knives swung and slashed as each man sought an opening through which he could slice up the belly or stab into the heart of his opponent.

Sitting atop the roof of one of the parked Land Rovers, Raful Barak watched the gaunt figures dance their deadly pavane. It was unlikely that either antagonist would survive. But should this happen, the winner would earn the privilege of taking him on next.

Barak unsheathed his Ka-Bar and ran the edge of his thumb along the honed cutting surface of the heavy steel blade, feeling the sharpness of the metal bite the fragile skin. One Bedu had already cut the other in the eye and blood was now pouring from the man's injured face onto his shirt. Barak knew the remainder of the blinded one's life was numbered in seconds.

Then both men went down and Barak could no longer see what was happening above the heads of the men forming the circle that penned them in. More minutes passed, and then one of the Egoz looked his way, holding out two downward-pointing thumbs. Barak nodded and put his knife back in its sheath, then climbed down from the roof of the vehicle. The team would proceed from here on its own, with no outsiders to bear witness.

Sergeant Maggard's beeper went off just as the topless dancer was doing something interesting with the twenty-dollar bill he'd just given her. Various other warbles, trills, and beeps were sounding from the pockets of the four other men sitting on either side. The chorus of electronic noises was already drawing the hostile stares of other dance enthusiasts in the audience.

Although the five men would have had little trouble in cleaning out the bar with their bare hands, they did nothing except switch off their beepers and get up to leave. The paging meant that Delta G-Troop's Blue Team was being assembled for a mission without delay. As Maggard stole a backward glance at the girl on the stage, his one consolation was that, wherever they were and whatever they were doing, the rest of Blue Team had also gotten the same message and, like him, were already on their way back to Bragg.

Thirteen
Boar Hunting in Novosibirsk

Three time zones, two thousand miles, and approximately two hours prior to Mitchell's appointment at the Pentagon, Captain Viktor Arbatov was leaving the center of Russia's military-intelligence-and-special-forces command on the outskirts of Moscow. The Glavnoe Razvedyvatelnoe Upravlenie, or Military Intelligence Agency of the former Soviet Union, is commonly known in the West by its acronym, GRU.

The organization can still be found in the location it occupied during the heyday of the Communist superstate. This is the central building at the old Khodenka Aerodrome, surrounded on three sides by buildings housing the apparatus of several other government service branches of Moscow Center.

While its title might give the impression that the GRU serves the same function as U.S. military intelligence, such as the Army's DIA, the Navy's ONI, or Air-Force Intelligence, this is not the case at all. On hearing the acronym GRU, most Westerners automatically assumed it to be a military counterpart of the KGB. In fact, the GRU has no direct equivalent in the American military force structure, nor is it merely a clone of the better-known Russian KGB.

For one thing, the GRU's functions exceed the mere collection of intelligence, the practice of espionage, and the collection of what the Russians call "cosmic intelligence," that is, intelligence derived from orbital surveillance platforms, including satellites. The GRU is also responsible for active measures, "special" or "tactical" reconnaissance, and other so-called "special assignments."

In order to carry out these varied functions, the GRU also serves as the command center of the former Soviet Union's special forces, including Spetsnaz and Vasaltniki, which are under the control of the Third Department of the GRU's Sixth Directorate.

Viktor Arbatov had just emerged from a briefing given by General Gennady Kirpichenko, and his mind was still spinning out the implications of what he had learned and the orders he'd been handed. All in all, the general's brief had been the culminating moment of an incredible thirty days for Arbatov.

First, there had been the unexpected pardon from the so-called punishment battalion in which he'd languished for the better part of the last month. This was a strange euphemism for a prison, but so it went in Mother Russia. Then there had been the sudden and unexpected death of Army General Potapenko, and now, to cap everything, these new orders he'd received, orders that called for Arbatov to begin training with a troop of American Delta Force commandos for a second mission into Iran.

Arbatov could still hear Kirpichenko's grating voice as it emerged from the round Slavic face of his superior officer, head of the Spetsnaz companies, the elite of all the Russian special-forces units.

Kirpichenko had promised Arbatov everything he required to get the job done—only the job *must* be done, the stealth fighter must be destroyed before the Iranians could make any major strides in copying its advanced systems.

This time, no slipups. The general had made this crystal clear. This time, *khui pinat',* he stressed, slamming his hamhock fist against the top of his desk—asses must be kicked.

Since the abortive first mission, the damned Iranians, the *chernozhopyi,* or "black bottoms," had been increasing their efforts to reverse-engineer the MFI-19 Eclipse's main systems components, and before long it would be too late to deny them the fruits of their research. This time the Americans would have to be directly involved, Kirpichenko added.

First, they had a legitimate stake in the outcome of the mission, both because U.S. planning, targeting, and weaponry had been involved, and also for geostrategic considerations. Second, the C.I.S. needed U.S. bases in the Gulf region from which to stage, because another mission could not be launched from the east—the Iranians were watching their eastern borders like hawks.

Finally, the Americans had sold the Russian president on their plan, and Grigorenko, like any shrewd politician anywhere, had also seen a way to deflect further blame should the second attempt also fail in a joint operation with the U.S.

The damned fools, Arbatov thought as he listened to Kirpichenko's briefing, though he kept his mouth shut. It was nothing short of a suicide mission that the *papakhas,* the big hats, were asking him to now undertake. The Americans were idiots to have become involved in this madness; and so was he, for that matter.

However, Arbatov had little choice but to follow his orders and somehow make it all come together. He had no intention of going back to the cramped, foul-smelling prison cell, with the bad food, the fat rodents, and the sadistic *bugori,* or prison bosses, who had been his companions for many long weeks. Even suicide was preferable to that.

Besides this thought, Arbatov also had the no-doubt-insane notion that there was indeed a way to make the impossible thing work out.

At least Arbatov was guaranteed to have company in this coming fool's crusade.

Kirpichenko had also revealed that Arbatov would doubtless be glad to learn that his old comrade, an American major named Mitchell, would be part of the fusion cell, for the GRU had adopted the American phrase for the mixed special-forces group originally coined during the War in the Gulf when mixed cadres made up of American, British, and French commandos conducted deep-strike missions inside Iraq.

Arbatov would not have used the term "comrade" to describe Mitchell, either in the standard sense of the word or its old, Communist-era sense, but he did think of Mitchell as a kindred spirit. There had been secret liaisons between U.S. special-forces cadres and Spetsnaz since the start of the Yeltsin political era in Russia in December of 1991. Although not openly publicized by either East or West, the special-forces liaison had been ongoing since then.

In the same way that Delta engaged in joint training with European SOF cadres, such as the French GIGN or German GSG-9, it also trained with Spetsnaz, once perhaps the greatest of the adversaries it had been geared up to fight. Arbatov remembered Peace as a real *muzhick,* what Americans would call a "regular guy," and there were not many whom he honored with such a tag. More important, the Russian also respected the American's soldiering skills.

The mission, thought Arbatov, might be doomed to failure, but it was also sure to be an interesting one. Besides, the American Marines weren't the only group of fighting men who held the question "who wants to live forever?" as an article of faith.

With this thought in mind, Arbatov's musings turned to the recent funeral of the coward and traitor Potapenko, who had been buried two days before in Moscow's grand

Ivovkensky Cemetery in the section reserved for military heroes of the Rodina or Motherland. Arbatov knew the truth behind the old *bizhdenok*'s supposed "heart attack" while "boar hunting" in the hills of Novosibirsk.

Boar hunting, indeed! The general had betrayed the Spetsnaz one time too many, and because he no longer wielded the kind of power he once had done, accounts could be settled. Like many another Spetsnaz who had served in the Afghan War and had known Potapenko back then, Arbatov would not have missed the funeral for the world. He had attended not to pay his last respects to the legendary military leader, but to jeer, if silently and with an outward show of respect, one of the most hated scumbags in recent Russian history.

As the Zhiguli MT-40 sedan from the GRU motor pool carrying Arbatov back to the Spetsnaz training site rolled through the wooded suburbs of Moscow, covered with a frosting of one of the last large snowfalls of the receding but still deep Russian winter, Arbatov's mind cast back to the final days in Afghanistan, the days of the desperate Russian retreat back across the border.

It was one of the great retreats of military history, surely the equal of Napoleon's retreat from Moscow or the German withdrawal over the Rhine in World War II. But the history books would never teach it and only a handful would ever know the full story concerning it.

During the war Potapenko had been the supreme commander of all Spetsnaz detachments in the Afghan combat theater. As a chief, he had been capricious, cruel, and arrogant. If not for his commanding officers taking matters into their own hands on more than one occasion, disaster would have befallen many an operation.

But during the pullout Potapenko had sunk to the lowest depth he'd reached in that sorry affair. He had cut a deal with the commander of the Hesb Nasr, the hated Omar Tousek. The Hesb Nasr were not true Mujahideen. They were bandits who infested the rugged mountains of the Panjshir, loyal to no creed but the lust for plunder and following no leader save Tousek. The Hesb Nasr preyed on Afghans and *Shuravi* alike and were hated by both.

The Spetsnaz had occupied the Soviet garrison at Pul-e-Khumri, a fortified hill town that had been built up into a regional command center. The withdrawal was to begin in the morning. But in the dead of night, a Hip transport chopper dusted off, escorted by two heavily armed Hind-F gunships. The Hip carried Potapenko and his retinue to safety.

When they were gone, GAZ trucks appeared at the gate, their drivers bearing military passes. The trucks carried hundreds of Hesb Nasr armed with rifles and rocket launchers. Hundreds more waited in the surrounding hills, ready to storm the base once the shooting started.

The Hesb Nasr had the advantage of surprise and they used it without mercy. Virtually all the occupants of the garrison were slaughtered that night. Thousands of tons of military equipment fell into the hands of the Hesb Nasr as a result. The weapons and hardware formed the nucleus of the arsenal that the fanatic Taliban would use a few years later to enslave the Afghan people, once the Russians had left.

Potapenko had sold the Spetsnaz forces for a handful of gold. They had died for nothing, or as the saying went, *ni za khy sobachy*—for less than a dog's dick. The few Spetsnaz that escaped that night of slaughter found they could not touch the general, legally, politically, or otherwise, until just now. He had been too well connected, first to the Politburo, and then to the corrupt *nomenklatura* that ran the "new" Russia.

Not that Potapenko was alone in his treachery. If he was merely one of the worst, there were still others almost as bad. Still, the old soldier had stood as a glaring symbol, not only of the corruption of the *vlasti* or kingpins of the old regime, but of the apathy and decadence of the new. Arbatov bid him good riddance.

There had been no snow in Jerusalem that winter, although snow was not unknown to that storied city on the Mediterranean coast. But the nights were still cold out in the Judean hills where the *kibbutzim* stood like bastions around the ancient land and where Assaf Gilad had his sprawling farm.

The aging warrior was busy with the winter harvest of Jaffa oranges, winter wheat, and the fruit of his large olive groves, and he carefully took note of the weather, whose capriciousness at this time of year was well known to the *moshavniks,* those perennial soil tillers of the reclaimed desert lands that included Gilad's own family.

This season's early frost could wipe out his entire crop of oranges, the best in all of Israel, and Gilad's personal attention to the harvest was critical to its success. But he had been summoned to the whitewashed building complex on the suburban outskirts of Tel Aviv, and it was a summons that even the lion of the Six Day War was not in a position to ignore, because that summons had been delivered in a phone call from the prime minister himself.

And so, early one morning, farmer Assaf left his harvest in the hands of his sons and hired farm-hands and traveled the narrow blacktop roads that twist and wind their way through the wrinkled, arid hillsides of northeastern Israel, heading toward the warmer, greener, lusher Mediterranean coastal plain.

By late afternoon he had reached his destination—the headquarters of Ha Mossad le Modiyn ve le Tafkidim Mayuhadim or the Institute for Intelligence and Special Operations, most often shorted simply to "the Institute" or Mossad, by which name it is commonly known around the world. The white buildings that house the Mossad stand in plain view of anyone passing them on the A-9 Highway that runs from Tel Aviv to Bethsheba along the Mediterranean coast. In fact, the complex looks like a resort, complete with a large and well-maintained Olympic swimming pool, occupying the palm-topped crest of a hill around which the highway slowly curves.

Unlike the CIA's Langley, Virginia, headquarters, however, there are no road signs conspicuously indicating Mossad's presence to travelers on the highway. In fact, one Israeli intelligence operative was known to have mar-

veled about the sign on the Washington-to-Baltimore ring
road that read TO CENTRAL INTELLIGENCE AGENCY, and
gave the number of the next turnoff on the highway during a trip to the States. There are no signs that point to
the fact that the Mossad headquarters is actually Mossad
headquarters and not a country club or hotel set on a hill-
side amid plantings of date palms. It even boasts a swimming pool.

Unlike a hotel, however, nobody gets through the main
gate of the complex without either an invitation or a job
at the Mossad complex, and there are even watchers in
cars and on foot positioned amid the surrounding neighborhoods whose task is to keep track of suspicious vehicles or pedestrians, especially those with cameras. Such
parties find themselves photographed and license-plate
numbers are noted. All data is fed into the Mossad's central computer system, nicknamed the "Beast" by those
who use it.

But Assaf Gilad was one of the invited few, and on
presenting his Israel Defense Forces or IDF ID to the gate-
keepers, he was permitted into the Mossad compound,
where he parked his car and entered the main building
lobby. He was soon on his way up to the fifth and top
floor, in the company of an escort and with a name tag
pinned to the breast pocket of his sport coat, for a meeting
with the head of the Mossad and members of the Israeli
cabinet.

Had it been the CIA and Gilad were an American, it
would be unlikely that the meeting would be attended by
as senior a group as this particular assemblage. But Israel's intelligence, political, and defense establishments
are far smaller and much more closely knit than those of
its much larger Western counterparts, and the relationships between members of the Israeli elite are far more
informal than elsewhere in the world.

Since familiarity can also breed contempt, the meetings
between these various branches, when they happen, can
also become heated and turn into verbal, and sometimes
even physical, brawls. This was close to what took place

a few minutes after Gilad entered the secure fifth-floor conference room, whose walls were impervious to electronic listening devices and in which no notes were permitted to be taken.

Gilad soon found himself in a shouting match with the current head of the Mossad, Yitzhak Bar-Illon, an argument that was all the more acrimonious to Gilad since Bar-Illon had served under him during the Yom Kippur War as a lieutenant, and although he had long ago attained the rank of general in the Israeli Defense Forces, Gilad still considered him his underling.

Bar-Illon was also to blame. He had no intention of stroking the Old Man, who he had learned was off on another one of his now infamous cowboying escapades. Who was he to single-handedly write Israeli foreign policy?

The personnel whom Gilad had pulled out of the AMAN and other places had been noticed and little by little the true story of Gilad's operation had leaked out. It wasn't just that the prime minister was livid over Israel's interference in a Russian-American operation, and wanted no part of the stealth plane or confrontation with the Iranians, it was also that Gilad's operation could compromise one of the Mossad's most important espionage assets inside the Iranian military, an agent code-named "Ahriman."

Ahriman, Gilad was told, was a deep-cover mole highly placed in the Iranian defense establishment. Ahriman was already in contact with Israeli intelligence and had reported back on having heard rumors of an Israeli move to retrieve the plane. If so, his life and the precious intelligence he fed the Mossad could be jeopardized. Unfortunately, it was now too late to stop Gilad's mercenaries inside Iran; indeed the moment Gilad had revealed the plane's existence to such men as they, it was already too late to stop them.

But Gilad was informed that he was no longer running the show on his own. He was now working for the Mossad, as a middleman. From now on Bar-Illon would be giving the orders and Gilad would be obeying them. If not, there would be repercussions.

"I built this party with Begin," Gilad had answered. "Ben Gurion, Golda Meir, Moshe Dayan—I knew them all. And now you Johnny-come-latelypishers are shoving me around, threatening me, giving me orders—"

Gilad broke off and stormed out of the meeting, livid with rage. To hell with Bar-Illon and his *minyan* of pishers, he thought. No mere lieutenant was about to tell him what to do, and never would.

Fourteen
Backdoor Recon

Their hulls painted matte black, with the dull white stars and bars of the USAF visible only at close range and invisible in the almost total blackness of the cold, moonless night, the three boxy, rotary-wing aircraft churned northeastward less than one hundred feet above the desert floor.

They were MH53-J Pave Lows, enhanced Block III versions that had been optimized for special-operations missions, with a beefed-up avionics suite and more powerful radars than previous helos of the class. The ships had also been upgunned, with fifty-caliber Browning MG-3 heavy machine guns that could be fired through side windows or the helo's rear ramp in addition to the pintle-mounted door guns, one of which was a 7.62-mm Minigun.

The helos were flying in what their pilots referred to as "turf mode." Others called it NOE, for nap-of-the-earth, or mud-moving. These terms, and others like them, referred to the technique of traversing at extremely low altitude where an aircraft's radar signature is more likely to become lost in the so-called ground clutter, the jumbled reflection of radar echoes bouncing off the terrain.

Helicopters were especially good at exploiting this weakness of radar's ability to see incoming threats, especially those equipped with terrain-following/terrain-avoidance radars. The Pave Low III was especially good at this stunt, because its TF/TA radars, and the computers that controlled them, were the best of the breed.

The same went for the Pave Low's enhanced navigation system, ENAV. As long as its uplink to the suite of global positioning satellites or GPS remained intact, ENAV could bring the bird to within a few feet of its programmed destination point, and do this trick in total darkness with no navigational aids.

This is why the Pave Low is the chopper of choice for special-forces and special-operations missions and why the bird is high on Delta's wish list. But Delta's aviation squadron, added to the force in 1998, doesn't include any Pave Lows yet and probably won't in the future. When Delta needs a Pave Low, it knocks on the door of the USAF's 1st Special Operations Wing, as it did during the Gulf and Kosovo wars, and as it will probably continue to do in future wars and future covert missions.

The Air Force, like the United States' other armed services, likes to keep at least one finger in any given pie, and if its own special operations branch isn't in as great demand as the Navy's SEALs or the Army's Delta, then at least USAF pilots will be in on the action.

The three Pave Lows participating in tonight's mission were owned and operated by the 1st Special Operations Wing's 20th Special Operations Squadron, which was based at al-Jouf, Saudi Arabia, a few dozen miles from the Iraqi border, though the mission would stage out of Kuwait. For the chopper crews, what had at first appeared to be a routine training mission turned out to be the most incredible thing to happen since the hot-shit glory days of the Gulf.

• • •

In the pilot's seat of the lead chopper, Captain Richie Johnson unwrapped a Snickers bar and popped it into his mouth. Chewing the bite-sized junk food snack helped calm his nerves when he flew.

The minute he'd been briefed by his commanding officer, Colonel Marty Applebaum, that the training exercises his squadron element had been flying for the last month were about to go hot and live, Johnson knew it was time to break out the bag of candy he'd been saving for a special occasion.

Now, having just passed his second waypoint ten minutes out of Kuwait and thirty-five miles inside the Iranian border (the first waypoint had been at Kuwait, where the ship's ENAV system had fixed its exact position on the surface of the earth), Johnson still couldn't quite believe that this run wasn't simply another training exercise like all the others.

But the scene in the aft cabin behind the cockpit argued differently. No longer was it empty, except for his flight engineer, Sergeant Sam Williams, who also doubled as tailgunner/backender and his right and left doorgunners, Doug Tallish and Ron Smith. All three also doubled as scanners. As such, they were the chopper's lookouts, regularly calling out the altitude and eyeballing the ground below for obstacles the terrain-avoidance radar didn't pick up.

They also kept their eyes peeled for any Bedouin bands below that might fire a rifle or even a shoulder-launched SAM at the low-flying bird. At the ground-hugging altitude the Pave Low flew, even a single bullet could bring the chopper down by hitting a weak spot in the airframe or penetrating the cockpit window and killing or seriously wounding the pilot.

Bedouin tribesmen roamed all over the deserts of the Middle East, as they had been doing for thousands of years. The sand wastes were their home; moreover, it was their turf. As a general rule, the desert nomads usually minded their own business and kept their noses out of the shifting winds of regional politics. But some bands did not, and many such tribal groups went about their wanderings armed to the teeth.

When driving a flying bungalow only a few-score feet over the heads of potential snipers, it paid to be careful.

As Johnson heard the scanners call out their regular sightings, he also heard the occasional sounds of others in the cabin with them, and the odd creaks of heavy objects shifting as the giant chopper pitched and lunged up and down and left and right above the uneven desert floor. The unfamiliar voices belonged to the team of Delta Force commandos that was webbed down against the sides of the chopper, below the metal "pizza racks" that held the modular component units for the Pave Low's navigational, communications, radar, and other critical onboard systems.

The creaking that from time to time penetrated the steady drone of the chopper's diesel engines belonged to the two fast attack vehicles, or FAVs, that were strapped down to the deck in the center of the bird's vibrating steel belly. Johnson could feel the distinct inertial effects of the additional load, too. The extra few tons of cargo altered the way the chopper handled, making the aircraft feel more sluggish in Johnson's hands.

Although Johnson never let it show in his voice as he called out instructions to his copilot and crew, he was nervous. Johnson was flying a steel house over hostile territory, and it was loaded to the gills with more extra payload than he'd ever carried in his entire career. The only things holding all that matter up were the rotor blades spinning overhead. Suddenly those thirty-foot-long reinforced polycarbon blades seemed as thin and as frail as plastic toothpicks.

Although Johnson had worked out the fuel requirements for the flight to the last pound of avgas, his eyes kept flicking to the chopper's fuel gauge, glowing a dull green in the view field of his night-vision goggles. The flight into Iran would tax every ounce of fuel the chopper carried, even with the extra tanks that the Block III carried and the increased lightness of the helo as the fuel load continually burned off. Mathematics were one thing, but reality could often be another, and usually was a bitch.

Johnson knew that even with the chopper's fuel supply good to the last drop and no unexpected hitches to spoil the party, his bird and the two other Pave Lows trailing behind it would not have enough fuel to make it back over the border to Kuwait. Their returning home depended, in large part, on nonpilot spooks getting all their ducks in line, and this was not a fun thought.

The Army's Intelligence Support Activity or ISA was supposed to have a crew of stay-in-place agents prepare the landing zone. The ISA's assets were native Iranians who had been working undercover since after the abortive Carter-era hostage rescue mission and were considered reliable. ISA's people were supposed to truck two huge bladders of avgas out into the desert for refueling the Pave Lows once they landed.

Supposed, supposed, supposed. That was the scary part. Too many damned supposeds for Johnson's liking.

Johnson had no faith in anyone but himself and his own people. He knew his capabilities and he knew theirs. He did not know the people on the ground from the hole in his rear echelon, and what Johnson didn't know he didn't trust, especially when his life and the lives of his crew depended on somebody else getting it right.

But there it was, and he'd just have to live—or die— with it. Johnson popped another Snickers into his mouth and chewed, scanning the softly glowing readouts on the panel in front of him through the light-amplifying lenses of his NVGs.

The choppers hung and danced, strung like sing-along notes at the bottom of an old-time movie screen, as they rose and fell to the cadence of an inaudible music score. With Johnson's Pave Low in the lead, the sortie flitted through the Zagros mountain range that jutted up along the Iranian border like broken teeth in a bleached donkey's jaw, weaving their way through the tortuous line of serpentine twists and turns between the dark basaltic hills on either side.

The USAF and the Russian Air Force had prepped the invasion on both sides of the Iranian border with a series of near incursions on a daily basis for the last two weeks. Antonovs to the east and F-111s to the west would edge up near Iranian early-warning radar sites to put the Iranians on the defensive, and then abruptly pull back.

After fourteen days of this game of hedge and dodge, the Iranians' edge had been dulled and they would not be as likely to interpret a chance radar contact with the Pave Low fleet with the requisite alarm.

Beyond that, the course flown by the chopper sortie had been planned to exploit a weak spot in Iranian radar coverage shown up by Rhyolite radar satellites and RC-135 electronic intelligence aircraft, both of which had been busily watching the border testing to see where coverage was thin.

The analysts at the National Security Agency's vast computer farm at Fort Belvoir, Virginia, had found a sizable gap in the southwestern sector of the radar shield, an approximate thin spot of five miles where the coverage of two sites didn't quite overlap. That's where the Pave Lows had snuck inside.

From that point on, they had flown through the mountains, lightening somewhat as their extra loads of fuel burned off and handling better in their pilots' hands.

Some forty minutes out of Kuwait, the helo squadron came out of the mountains and skimmed across the open desert of the Dasht-e-Kavir, the great salt pan occupying most of the northern quarter of the country. In the lead chopper Johnson heard the series of warbling tones from ENAV signaling the approach of the third and penultimate waypoint, where a fresh navigational update was taken and minor corrections made to the course.

As the birds passed the waypoint and skirted the last of the brooding, strangely folded hills, they dropped down to fifty feet above the desert floor, their cruising altitude for the remainder of the trip.

As the altimeter showed the drop, and the green-tinted view through Johnson's light-amplifying visor changed from mountains and valleys to the floor of the Dasht rising up all around the cockpit window, he called out to his scanners to keep their eyes peeled and their calls crisp and intelligible.

This was probably the most hazardous leg of the in-bound flight, Johnson knew, and he didn't want any mistakes. He could see the desert floor below in detail now, and every boulder, every thornbush and Joshua tree, and every rise and dip in the arid landscape could pose serious hazards for the mission.

He was also picking up some weather, too. Nothing heavy, especially for the deserts of the Middle East in winter, where storms of freezing ice, rain, and sand might appear from out of nowhere, but he could see and hear the pellets of ice and specks of windblown sand strike against the windshield, and he felt the Pave Low rock slightly as it passed through eddies and air pockets.

Johnson turned on his windshield wipers and held back a curse. He didn't need a shitstorm on top of everything else. Fortunately the weather never got much worse than the little bit of hail and soon it stopped altogether. Johnson relaxed a little and ate another Snickers, telling himself that it would work out all right.

It could have been the weather that prevented anyone from seeing a thirty-four-year-old Bedouin tribesman named Hamdi Feroz bin-Tukali who had been sheltering amid the boulders of a sandstone formation about thirty yards abreast of the oncoming path of the choppers. The young Bedu had been awakened from a dream in which his older brother, Achmed, had appeared to him, riding on a donkey and beckoning Hamdi to follow.

Hamdi had pursued his brother across the desert, and stopped to point at a strange rock formation that rose in the distance, shaped something like a woman's naked body yet also something like the body of a poisonous scorpion. Though Achmed had said nothing, only pointed,

Hamdi knew without being told that this rock formation held the key to enormous wealth, somehow even of life itself.

Hamdi was about to ask Achmed why he had shown him this vision when suddenly the rock formation exploded with a thunderous boom, and an immense geyser of black oil gushed forth, spewing high up into the sky. At this point Hamdi awoke with a start, but still heard the thunder in his ears.

Suddenly he realized that the noise was coming from overhead, swelling to a crescendo from out of the west, and that it was made by the huge black forms that swept across the desert.

Helicopters, he thought as the four other members of the band awakened at the sound and stared toward the western horizon. Hamdi was the first to recognize the helicopters as American flying machines.

He had seen many aircraft pass overhead in the desert, including Russian ones, but nothing like this. That meant Americans, or English or French, which to Hamdi were all the same. At the same time he realized that his brother Achmed had warned him of their approach in the dream. Achmed, who had been killed by fire from an American helicopter such as this during the Gulf War, had called him to take vengeance.

Before the others could raise their guns, Hamdi had lifted his AK-7 autorifle and fired off a burst as the dull, bulky black shapes came streaking overhead. In another heartbeat they were gone. Hamdi and the others stared after them as they lowered their weapons, hoping against hope that at least one of the American warplanes would come crashing to the desert floor and explode in a fireball, but nothing happened.

The black shapes disappeared, and soon the thunder of their passage had faded to the nocturnal silence of the desert once again. Only when the birds had returned to Kuwait and the ground crews inspected them and found the places where two of Hamdi's bullets had creased the hull of the second chopper in the sortie, would there be evidence of the helos having been fired upon.

But although Hamdi believed that he had done the American gunships no damage, he had at least not hesitated to shoot. Of this he was proud. And besides this, there was the second part of his dream yet to fulfill. Calling to his comrades, Hamdi mounted his camel and set off in the direction of an Iranian military encampment not far from this place where he had dreamed his dream of wealth and vengeance.

The mission reached its final waypoint and proceeded toward its landing zone unaware that the choppers had been sighted and that the mission was compromised, hitting more weather as the LZ and H-hour both drew closer.

As the lead Pave Low skimmed the desert, Johnson swept his eyes from his instrument panel to the view through the cockpit window.

The moving map display, a circular panel located below and to the right of his altimeter and FLIR or forward-looking infrared displays, and just above his ENAV display screens, showed him that the Pave Low was on course and approaching the LZ.

At the same time the fuel gauges, located on the topmost portion of the control panel, showed him that the fuel supply of his bird was getting dangerously low. The chopper had consumed almost 90 percent of its available avgas load and would be left with less than 10 percent capacity as it approached the landing zone. There was no way short of a miracle rivaling Christ's resurrection for the sortie to make it back to Kuwait if there was no fuel awaiting them at the end of the run.

Yet the creeping, sickening fear that had begun to gnaw at Johnson's entrails and that no amount of Snickers therapy could hope to wipe away (besides, the bag was almost gone by now) was that there never would be any fuel. As the circle representing the helo moved across the dully glowing map display and approached within a mile of the LZ, there was no indication that anybody was down there waiting for them.

By now he should have seen an infrared strobe flashing somewhere below and just ahead, to indicate where the choppers were supposed to land, but there was nothing except the artificially glowing darkness through his light-amplification goggles. Johnson's crew was getting jittery, too. The doorgunners had been craning their heads out into the night, looking for a strobe, and nothing was there except for the wind and the hail and the fine white dust particles that blew into their faces.

"What's up? Where's the fucking strobe?" asked Williams from behind the cockpit.

"Relax. It'll be there," Johnson said, using his calmest tone of voice and hoping nobody sensed the nervousness he, too, felt.

He was also well aware that the flight crews in the two choppers behind him were also just as edgy, but would not break radio silence to express their fears. When another series of warbling tones sounded in the cockpit, announcing that they had reached the LZ, there was still no sign of the ground support team. But by now there was no choice. The chopper's fuel supply was almost totally eaten up.

Johnson was about to announce that they were about to land and fend off any questions about the absence of ground support from his crew, when he saw the flashes dead ahead.

Twice, once, twice—in the prearranged pattern. Johnson took a long, relieved breath and keyed his mike, announcing that the ground crew was waiting and the choppers were about to touch down.

A few minutes later the force was on the ground, the helos' rear access ramps fully lowered, and men and transport rolling out into the darkness.

Fifteen
On a Fast Train

The grounded birds took on avgas from two enormous rubber blivets that slowly deflated on the desert floor as they were emptied of their contents. A perimeter security detail was already walking post, cradling bullpup Kalashnikov AKS-74 autorifles that were standard issue to the cell. Mitchell stood watching the chopper crews refuel and recalibrate their instruments. As soon as the Pave Lows had drunk their fill, they would dust off again. It was still winter in the Dasht and his breath left vapor plumes in the cold night air, whose temperature was a chilly thirty degrees Fahrenheit.

Hundreds of cubic feet per minute of aviation gasoline gushed through the flexible rubber hoses connecting the fuel bladders to the helos' intake receptacles. The chopper crews in their brown nylon jumpsuits had asked for nobody's help in getting their hardware airborne again. They had done their part of the mission and were in a hurry to get out. On the ground they felt vulnerable and exposed, and with good reason; they *were* vulnerable and exposed.

The intelligence support activity or ISA crew that had set up the fuel dump had already melted into the desert. These were local agents in place who for weeks had been storing fuel and equipment smuggled down from U.S. supply depots in Turkey. Having done its part, the advance team was no longer needed. Its continued presence in the operations zone would jeopardize the safety of these nationals, who were all CIA contractors.

As the birds were gassed up, the U.S.-Russian fusion cell checked its weapons and equipment and loaded gear and supplies into the FAVs that had been ramped off the back ends of the choppers. The FAVs were the key to the mission's success, one reason being that there was no reasonable way to march on foot across the hostile desert environment and expect to wind up in any kind of shape to take down a target.

During Desert Storm, the British SAS had been the first ground troops to go into Iraq and clandestinely hunt Scuds, and they did so contrary to CENTCOM's express orders that no ground troops leave Saudi Arabia until the air campaign's conclusion. Britain's special-forces commander, General de la Billiere, had convinced his American opposite number to make a special exception for his SAS, and the Brits had gone in, but they'd paid a heavy price for their boldness.

When the first Anglo-American fusion cells were set up later on in the battle, the SAS warned that between the severe cold, almost lunar terrain, lack of landmarks, and armed Bedouin bands, it was suicide to go into the desert on foot. Ride or fly in, but never walk, they had advised. Walking will get you killed.

The Brits had come up with a solution—LSVs or light strike vehicles. These were essentially Land Rovers stripped down to resemble oversized, heavy-frame dune buggies with a sturdy tubular steel cage welded to the chassis in place of the normal passenger compartment. There was space for two men riding up front, while the frame could be either crammed with gear, carry another team member, or be equipped with a pintle-mounted heavy machine gun, such as a fifty-caliber Browning LM-3 or a forty-mm multiple grenade launcher.

Heavy MGs, thirty-mm cannon, or a variety of surface-to-air and surface-to-surface missiles such as Milan, Dragon, or TOW, could also be mounted up front, over the passenger-side seat, with spare missile tubes, shells, and ammo carried in back within easy reach.

The LSVs quickly became a staple of desert commando warfare and of any special-operations mission requiring high mobility under rugged terrain conditions. Delta later produced LSVs of its own, moving the steering wheel from right to left and rechristening them FAVs, which, with some modifications, were what the fusion cell brought with it into Iran aboard the Pave Lows.

The cell had trained on the FAVs in Kuwait for weeks prior to the mission launch date. By now its members were familiar with every quirk and tick of the machinery. In fact, Mitchell had selected Delta's Blue Team for the mission partly because it was a mobile warfare team that specialized in desert operations on dune buggies.

Delta's policy was to divide its fifteen-to-twenty-one-man troops into four-to-six-man teams, each with a unique MOS or military occupational specialty. Some specialized in sniping, others in counterterrorist ops, but Blue Team's specialty was the one needed for the Iran mission. The team had taught the Spetsnaz everything it knew on the subject, and the Russians were fast learners, devising some new wrinkles of their own that might in the future become part of standard Delta operating procedure.

As the last few kilograms of avgas were pumped from the blivets into the choppers' thirsty storage tanks, Mitchell's glance fell on Arbatov, who was also looking on. Together the two mission commanders watched the refueling of the aircraft and the deployment of the troops. The growls of revving engines, the curses and shouts of busy soldiers, the shrill tones of battlefield communications and computing devices being energized, and the clatter of weapons being loaded and gear being stowed away and lashed down broke the spectral stillness of the desert night.

"They're looking good," Mitchell said to Arbatov, who, like himself, was attired in standard NATO desert camouflage BDUs and U.S. "Fritz" helmet with their black, gray, and white "chocolate chips" patterns. The battle dress had been adopted as standard issue for the cell.

"I would be disappointed if they were not," the Spetsnaz replied. "My men were handpicked, as were yours. They are the best, and the training they received at your Disneyland facility at Bragg is light-years beyond anything we have back home."

The troops' movements communicated a sense of high morale and confidence. There is a difference in the way poorly trained and badly motivated soldiers behave, even when constantly drilled, and commanders can tell at a glance if they have "the right stuff" or not. These guys had it.

It had been agreed that the Delta operators and Spetsnaz company troopers would train in pairs and ride together in the FAVs; otherwise there would wind up being two teams instead of one. Force integration was as important and basic as ammo in small unit operations, and the force would not be a true fusion cell unless it learned to fight, think, and react as a single, cohesive unit.

This was easier said than accomplished, especially at first. Delta and Spetsnaz not only had fundamental differences in doctrine, training, and weaponry, but there were major cultural differences as well. Where the American troopers had been trained to take their own initiative in all situations, the Russians never acted without clear-cut orders, and relied more on brute force than stealth and mobility in their combat style.

The Russians didn't like the American M-16 rifle either, preferring the heavier Kalashnikov AK-47, which had more stopping power than the somewhat underpowered Armalites. A compromise was struck in issuing the lighter, short-barreled AKS-74 Kalashnikov to the fusion cell as its standard assault weapon, which the Americans had already trained on as part of the Delta course. The light machine gun version of the AKS-74, the RPK-74, was also adopted as a squad automatic weapon or SAW, as was the American standard machine gun, the M60A1.

There were many other problems, too, hundreds of them, in fact. But solutions had been found to most of these and compromises worked out for the rest. The men soon formed strong bonds. When H-hour came they had been welded into a fourteen-man squadron under the joint command of Mitchell and Arbatov. By now—Delta's boss, Colonel Armbrister, had acerbically noted during a training review—they even farted in the same key.

They wore the same uniforms, packed the same gear, and shouldered the same rifles. They even cussed alike; most, by now, in two languages. The only noticeable difference in kit between GIs Ivan and Joe were the small shoulder patches high on the right fatigue sleeves—stars and bars for the Americans and the C.I.S. flag for the Russians.

Since Mitchell outranked Arbatov, it had been decided by their respective bosses that while each would cocommand, Mitchell would serve as recognized troop CO and Arbatov as his unofficial "horse handler" or XO. Mitchell would have final say, but both he and Arbatov could issue independent orders applicable to all members of the cell. Neither Spetsnaz nor Delta troopers seemed to have any problems with the arrangement.

Some twenty minutes after the troop had touched down on the sandy floor of the Dasht, the Pave Lows had been refueled for their return journey and all the fusion cell's gear had been broken out and squared away. Mitchell and Arbatov shook hands with Johnson and soon watched the black helos ascend into the even blacker night sky above them.

Within minutes the Pave Lows were swallowed up by mother night, and the final cadenced echoes of their rotor blades had died away completely. An eerie silence descended over the men on the ground, and the clandestine landing zone in the Dasht suddenly felt like a very lonely place to be, and one very far from home. Mitchell gave orders for the cell to mount up, and the six FAVs rolled away from the LZ, heading outbound toward the team's assault positions. The night soon covered over their tracks with a windblown blanket of sand.

The CIA's Langley, Virginia, headquarters are located on 219 wooded acres approximately eight miles from downtown Washington in a campuslike setting envisioned by its first civilian director, Allen W. Dulles, a bas-relief bust of whom can be seen on the marble North Wall of the foyer of the Headquarters Building. This same wall of the central lobby also displays a chevron of silver stars commemorating CIA agents who died in the line of duty. A glass-encased Book of Honor beneath the engraved stars gives the dates of death for all, and the names of a few, of those whom the stars on the memorial wall represent.

It was half-past three in the afternoon when the Director of Central Intelligence, Clifford Merrick, received an urgent call on a secure, scrambled phone line in his seventh-floor office in the one-million-square-foot annex to the Headquarters Building's West Facade that went up in the Orwellian year of 1984. The call originated from Tel Aviv, and Merrick found himself mentally calculating the time difference even as he lifted the handset to his ear.

With seven hours separating the two time zones, it would be about ten-thirty at night in Israel. Merrick braced himself for an unpleasant surprise. His secretary had told him the call was from the head of Israel's Mossad, Yitzhak Bar-Illon, and Merrick knew his opposite number in Israeli intelligence wouldn't be phoning at that hour, local time, if there wasn't some kind of bitch abrew. Merrick didn't turn out to be wrong, either.

As he listened to the voice of what was obviously a very tired man on the other end of the line, Merrick clenched and unclenched his right fist, a nervous habit he had when he was hearing bad news. The worse the news, the more he worked his fist, and he was working it into a white-knuckled ball as the words came out the ear end of the secure phone connection to Tel Aviv.

Some ten minutes later, when Merrick had fired a few questions back at Bar-Illon, and had listened to the Mossad chief's answers, and the conversation was over, Merrick sat at his desk, deep in thought.

We know about the mission to take the plane, the Mossad chief had warned. *Cancel it. There is a leak.*

After a while Merrick picked up the phone and dialed the special direct number to the Joint Chiefs at the Pentagon. It was the chairman himself that he got on the line, after General Thibodeaux was rounded up by his staff members, who could not get the DCI to leave a message. But when he'd finally secured the chairman of the JCS on the wire, Merrick's last shred of hope evaporated.

General Jack informed Merrick that it was too late to recall the Pave Lows. In fact, they had already refueled and dusted off from their desert landing zone. The team was on the ground. The helos were being tracked by satellite at the moment, and were about fifteen minutes away from their point of arrival in Kuwait.

Other measures would have to be taken, the chairman said, and told Merrick to hang in there. The situation on the ground was still salvageable. He'd get back to him. Merrick signed off and telephoned the White House. The chairman's words had not assured him, and the DCI seriously doubted if any part of the mission could be salvaged. Not anymore.

The deserts of the Middle East are not all alike; in fact few deserts are clones of one another, just as few forests are identical. The one thing Middle Eastern deserts do share in common is that they're all arid places without large trees, except for petrified ones. The Dasht-e-Kavir is a case in point.

Unlike its close neighbor, the ar-Rub' al-Khali, or Empty Quarter, of Saudi Arabia a few hundred miles to the west, the north-central desert of Iran is a vast expanse composed of many *sabkahs* or salt flats of alluvially deposited gravel beds, towering rock formations of hard black stone, wadis of varying shapes, sizes, and depths, and some sandy and rocky territory, changing eventually to jagged ranges of low, stickleback mountains that rise up on the distant horizon.

The Dasht is not strictly a sand desert, like the Empty Quarter, the Sahara, or the Sinai farther to the southwest, with sand dunes, barchands, and the other features of the "sea of sand" familiar to anyone who's ever seen a Hollywood epic set in the desert. In winter and early spring, the Dasht can also get extremely cold, with sudden *shamals,* or desert storms, that can rival the oft-capitalized one in severity on a small scale.

As Delta found out on its original mission into Iran in 1980, the topography most characteristic of the Dasht is the Martian crust of sand and gravel that covers most of its flat places. Unlike a true sand desert, which is murder on the tires, suspension, and transmission systems of any wheeled vehicles that have to cross it, the surface crust of the Dasht affords vehicles good traction where the rubber meets the road.

Mitchell had strung out four of the fusion cell's six vehicles in a star formation, with his command vehicle on one starpoint and Arbatov's dune buggy bringing up the rear. The other two FAVs that made the lateral points of the star were spaced out at half klicks from an imaginary centerline running through the lead and rear buggies.

The remaining two vehicles had been sent ahead as scout patrols, leading the main body at a distance of between one and two kilometers and in touch by global-mobile or GloMo communications links. These links incorporated SINCGARS secure radio channels with real-time video transmission and downlinked satellite telemetry, including GPS, all of which could be accessed from portable TRAVLER field units that resembled highly ruggedized laptops, and also from fixed companion units mounted on the FAVs.

The formation was a good way to scope out the area and see oncoming threats before they were right on top of your troops, and it also kept your people from bunching up. Mission data, including a route to the target with multiple waypoints, had been programmed into GPS. The waypoints were spaced approximately ten klicks apart, and when the final one was crossed, the cell would be at the perimeter of the strike zone, which was an imaginary thirty-meter circle drawn around the desert outpost at al-Kabir. It was at this base that Delta's final intel briefing had conclusively pinpointed the missing stealth fighter.

The plan called for the fusion cell to rendezvous at the final waypoint by four hundred forty-five hours, local time, then form up and attack the base in two highly mobile attack formations of three FAVs each, firing Milan antiarmor missiles, fifty-caliber machineguns, and LAW rockets at anything that moved. Once inside, they were to hit the downed Eclipse with more Milan strikes, confirm that the plane was destroyed, and hare out of the burning base before Pasdaran reinforcements had time to arrive.

Before dawn, at around five hundred twenty hours, the returning troopers were to be onboard a Russian Antonov AN-72 all-weather transport aircraft that was tasked with ferrying them out of Iran through the back door—that is, across its eastern border. If the FAVs could not be stowed aboard the Antonovs in time, they were to be left behind at the LZ with five-minute satchel charges tossed in the driver seats.

Mitchell had programmed the dash-mounted GPS on his lead FAV to sound a low-pitched alert tone each time the cell reached its waypoints, at which time he was to make any course corrections necessary and listen in on the secure satcom uplink for any changes in plan. Otherwise the cell was to observe radio silence.

The cell had passed the first GPS waypoint, at Wadi Omar, after under ten minutes of travel, and was midway to the second waypoint at Nay Tabas when the satcom line came to life. Using the keyboard on the dash-mounted comms unit, Mitchell piped the voice transmission through the compact headset he wore while visuals appeared on the TRAVLER unit's color LCD screen. Since the transmissions were accessible over the entire global-mobile communications net, Mitchell knew Arbatov was in on it, too, in the rear FAV. What they both heard was extremely bad news.

It was Colonel Mike back in Kuwait, calling from the Gallant Echo command center. Armbrister was telling them that the mission had been scrubbed. General Yuri Rostovich, the Russian CO for the mission, repeated the orders for Arbatov's benefit. All the general would say was that the intel on the plane's location had turned out wrong, and that the cell was to abort and make for the planned extraction site, where the Russian transport planes would pick them up with an ETA of one hour.

As he spoke to the men out in the Dasht, Armbrister wished he could say more about why the mission had been canked. He also wished he could have gotten word to the team sooner. When CIA Director Merrick had told President Claymore that the Israelis had an agent high up in the Iranian military chain of command who had warned them that the desert base was a trap, he had canceled the mission.

Then Claymore was reminded that he had to act in tandem with the Russian president. It was almost another hour before both leaders reached a mutual decision to pull out the cell, and by that time the Pave Lows had returned to base. The Antonovs, however, were fueled and ready on their Caucasus landing strip, and though not as stealthy as the MH53-Js, they were faster, longer-ranged, and more resistant to bad weather than any helicopter. The planes were also manned by fresh air crews.

Mitchell and Arbatov called a halt and turned the team around. The mission had been scrubbed, they told the troop. All knew they would have to move fast in order to reach the extraction zone by the time the Antonovs came busting in through the back entrance. If the assault had been burned, there could be troops out scouring the desert for them at that moment. Nobody mentioned it, but many in the cell felt like someone had just walked across their graves. Though the feeling was quickly pushed out of mind, it turned out to be prophetic.

•   •   •

Colonel Ghazbanpour had sent out tripwire patrols as soon as he had received the report from the army outpost located at Khaneh Kvodi garrison, some two hundred kilometers distant. Major Salubesht, the commander of the outpost, was personally known to him, as was the Bedouin band that had warned the major of the presence of American helicopters in the area.

The Bedouin had been on their way to the base, which was one of their regular stops, where they had steady customers for hashish, cigarettes, whiskey, Western porno magazines and videos, and the occasional item of flashy electronics to sell to the bored troops who were stationed on duty there.

Major Salubesht had not told Ghazbanpour about anything except the cigarettes, as he himself was a customer of the other wares sold by the Bedouin. But he did mention to the colonel that he had paid the *mohajer* a reward out of his own pocket amounting to fifty Iranian ehatys. Ghazbanpour assured him that he had done well, and that he would personally reimburse him.

If the report turned out to be accurate, the commander's information would be worth much more than a few ehatys to Ghazbanpour. From the Bedouin's description of the helicopters, he had made a sketch in pencil on the pad in front of him on his desk. After hanging up with the major, Ghazbanpour looked at his drawing.

The sketch looked more like the Pave Low than anything else, and if that were true, it meant that the Americans were inserting their special-forces commandos into his backyard. Which also meant that they had fallen neatly into his waiting hands. It would be too much to expect for the legendary U.S. Delta Force to have been sent in, but the more Ghazbanpour pondered it, the greater the likelihood of this very development became.

Colonel Ghazbanpour lit one of the English Player filter cigarettes he favored, rubbing his hands with glee—what a coup it would be! It would be a second hostage rescue disaster, another embarrassment for a sitting U.S. president. This time there would be no demonstrations outside a captured embassy compound, no mob scenes, no histrionics; the new spirit of détente between the U.S. and Iran would mean that the matter would be handled with far more discretion, indeed, he guessed, in strictest secrecy.

But there would be leaks to the media, and in global political circles, too, and there would be prices that would have to be paid to keep the leaks from widening into common knowledge. Iran would come away the great winner, more powerful than before, while Ghazbanpour would have become the man of the hour, the man who had rubbed the noses of both the Americans and the Russians into the desert stones until they bled.

Ghazbanpour wasted little time in his reverie; he was a doer, not a dreamer. Before his cigarette had half burned to gray ash, he was on the secure line to his troop commanders, ordering out the many patrols. Ghazbanpour didn't have long to wait for results.

The first of the tripwire patrols he had sent into the desert had already reported contact with a formation of fast, military-style commando vehicles moving rapidly in the direction of the Dasht's eastern border.

The patrol had clashed with the formation but was all but wiped out in the flash firefight that ensued. Still, a second, larger contingent of Revolutionary Guard Corps, or Pasdaran, forces had closed with the invaders a few kilometers down their line of advance. They had killed some of these interlopers, forcing the remainder of the foreign commando force to take refuge in the Semnan. This was a region of arid desert broken by low hills and defiles and known for its mineral hot springs and craterlike wadis that marked the flow of underground rivers and streams.

The commando force was presently dug in at one of these naturally fortified areas and under heavy attack by Pasdaran troops. Ghazbanpour knew the region fairly well. He informed his field officers that he would personally oversee the assault, and ordered a helicopter to be ready to shuttle him to the scene of the fighting. Minutes later he was on his way.

Sixteen
Ne Znayu

Petrov's dream was of Vladivostok. Of this he was sure.
Yet he couldn't remember another thing about the dream.
For a few seconds after jolting awake in the dark, bitterly
cold cell, he lay in a semiconscious state, trying to recapture something of the dream vision before he floated back
to his bleak reality. It was somehow important that he take
something of the dream state back to the waking world
with him, though he couldn't say exactly why this should
have been.

But after minutes of fishing in the dark lake of his
mind, willing himself to recall what he had dreamt, almost
nothing would emerge. The only scrap of dreamstuff he
could retrieve was incongruous: the sound of a thunder-
clap or an explosion that had cut short his dream and
brought him back to his living hell.

Petrov sat up on the metal slab, set on four poles and
bolted to the wall, that served as his bunk. The slab resembled nothing so much as a mortician's gurney, which

Petrov suspected it had once been before being pressed into service in the installation's brig. His first act was to reach for the stinking, louse-infested army blanket that was his sole article of bedding and wrap it around his now gaunt shoulders. The blanket had fallen off when he'd awakened, and he desperately needed the pathetic warmth and meager comfort it would provide.

Not that it could provide much—even the few weeks of starvation rations had weakened him considerably and turned him into an emaciated wretch smelling of sweat, dirt, and urine. In the first hours of his captivity Petrov had demanded better treatment and had been quickly disabused of this approach.

The Iranians had beaten him half-senseless, then spat on the bleeding form they had tossed onto the hard concrete cell floor. One, who could speak a few words of Russian, made it plain to Petrov that he was lucky not to have been lined up against a convenient wall and shot as a spy—in fact, the guard had pointed to a nearby wall outside the cell that was pockmarked with bullet holes and streaked with caked, dried blood, to help make his point.

After a few days of starvation and nights of shivering cold, a new man appeared at his cell door. This one was fluent in Russian. In fact, he spoke with a distinct Moscow accent—and with good reason, Petrov later learned, since the man was a Russian national like himself. The newcomer, whose name was Dikushkin, told Petrov that if he cooperated he would live and receive better rations; ultimately he would be repatriated. If he did not collaborate with the Iranians, then he would be immediately shot without trial as punishment for espionage.

In the beginning Dikushkin stuck to his original cover story of being an Iranian air-force engineer, despite the fact that he was an obvious ringer. What he wanted from Petrov was his assistance in explaining some of the finer points of the MFI-19's advanced stealth and avionics systems. After some show protestation, designed to gain him better treatment, the pilot finally agreed to help. In fact, it was apparent from the first that he really had no other choice. Yet Petrov decided that he would continue giving the Iranians as little aid as possible, and keep an eye out for any opportunity to escape that came his way.

Petrov rubbed his eyes and tried to get his bearings as he drew the filthy, itchy blanket closer against his by now scrawny shoulders, shivering in the cold of the desert night.

Svoboda—freedom. That, he now knew, was the meaning of his dream of home, of Vladivostok; and with that realization something of the dream began filtering back to him. He had been riding on one of the brightly painted tram cars that climb to the Funicular Terminal, and was approaching the hilltop from which one gets one's first view of the bevy of merchant ships riding at anchor in the harbor.

Then there had been—then he had done—what was it? Something wonderful, something . . . he could no longer remember, only that then the dream had ended with a loud and startling noise.

Petrov turned back to his musings. He had been taken from the cell and marched at gunpoint to the large hangar where the multirole fighter was kept under armed guard. It was night, or early morning, just like now, and floodlights lit the interior of the hangar while a contingent of heavily armed Pasdaran soldiers stood their watches. Dikushkin had accompanied Petrov to the cockpit of the plane and immediately began bombarding him with questions.

What was the purpose of this bank of switches? That scope? That readout panel? When putting the plane into a high-g turn, how stable was its angle of attack? Were there any fail-safe devices built into the aircraft to thwart unauthorized tampering, and if so, where were they found and what did they do?

Petrov realized that the Iranians were as much in awe of the aircraft as if a flying saucer had unexpectedly dropped into their laps. They were desperate to learn the secrets of the stealth fighter so they could reverse-engineer the aircraft for their own air force, but they were also totally perplexed by its many technological innovations.

Petrov laughed inwardly. After spending untold millions of dollars since the breakup of the Soviet Union in trying to recruit the best Russian scientists possible, the Iranians still had not gotten themselves a viable brain trust. Or did they know more than they were telling Petrov, trying to confirm what they already guessed?

Whatever the case, the Russian pilot gave them as little assistance and information as possible. *Ne znayu,* I don't know, was his stock reply. The Russian traitor they had used to interrogate him sensed this, though, and there were more beatings. After these, Petrov became somewhat more cooperative, but only as much as traffic would bear. Resisting the bastards was bound up with retaining his last shred of humanity. As long as he could tell himself that he continued to put up a fight, he could stay human. If he capitulated, he might as well slash his wrists, he reckoned.

Then, after nearly two weeks, the pilot sensed a certain urgency about the questions coming from the turncoat, Dikushkin. He was bold enough to ask him why, but Dikushkin's answer was now *ne znayu.* Yet Petrov suspected that something major was in the offing, because among other things the guard detachment protecting the hangar had been doubled, and there were more signs of the base having been put on full alert.

Sirens wailed and searchlights came on at unpredictable hours of the night. Guard dogs barked outside his cell and the engines of mechanized armor coughed and cranked in the shattered desert silence. Although Petrov had been consistently denied any news of home or of current global events, he suspected that a rescue mission had been launched.

Petrov got confirmation of this when he chanced to glimpse a new prisoner being brought into the stockade. A single look told him everything he needed to know.

The prisoner was wearing desert camouflage fatigues of the elite commando forces, Vasaltniki or Spetsnaz from the looks of him. That, and the fact that he himself was still a prisoner, told Petrov that while a rescue mission had been mounted, it had either failed or had been aborted.

The following day his guards boasted of this very thing to him. They laughed and told Petrov that the Russians had been slaughtered like flies as they tried to escape the wrath of Allah's ordained fighters. Only one of his countrymen had survived, and they had him now, too. The Iranians celebrated this event by giving Petrov extra food and cigarettes.

Then had come a small glimmer of hope. When the stench of his cell had become a problem for his guards, Petrov was removed from it long enough for the narrow cubicle to be hosed down. Standing a few feet away, near the door of the adjoining cell of the stockade, was the commando whom Petrov had seen brought in a few days before. A glance told him the man had been injured but not properly treated.

His face bore the signs of a badly healed scar, covered by a dirty bandage. The lone guard in attendance cautioned them not to speak, but for a few moments his attention was diverted by the appearance of an officer who began dressing him down in Farsi. The soldier took the chewing-out like a docile cur, and paid Petrov no attention.

Petrov knew it was to risk a beating, which, in his severely weakened state, might very well kill him, but he was determined to speak to the other man. Though he had no way of knowing it, the captured soldier was Lieutenant Trapezhnikov, second in command of the Vasaltniki team led by Nemekov, and lone survivor of the engagements that had destroyed it.

Petrov sensed the wounded soldier had the same idea as he. When the soldier collapsed in a heap, and suddenly began thrashing as if suffering a seizure, Petrov got ready to act. The officer looked their way, shouted something at the guard, and the guard ran down the corridor to the phone, leaving them momentarily unattended. The officer then followed the soldier and did not return. As Petrov suspected, the Vasaltnik had only put on an act.

"Who are you?" he asked. Petrov told him. "Trapezh-nikov," the injured man said back. "I was part of a rescue attempt. All the others were killed. The plane is here?"

"Yes, I have seen it," Petrov said.

"Then it is imperative that we at least attempt to destroy it."

"I agree," replied Petrov.

"Listen," Trapezhnikov went on. "I'll keep my eyes open. If there's a chance to stage an escape, I'll get word to you somehow."

"I shall do the same," Petrov agreed.

"Could you fly the plane out of here if the opportunity presented itself?" Trapezhnikov next asked.

Petrov had long ago thought this over.

"Not unless the plane were fueled and onboard electrical systems powered up, and even then I would need appropriate gear, at least a flight helmet, for comms if nothing else. Still, it would be a closely done thing."

"But you might try given those conditions?"

"Yes," Petrov answered without hesitation. "It's better than rotting in this hell, even though the chances are slim, to say the least. As for the first two points, the electrical systems and the fuel, I believe they may be workable. But I've seen the plane when they brought me for questioning, and the flight gear is nowhere in evidence."

"How much did you tell them?" Trapezhnikov's eyes became gimlets.

"That's my affair," Petrov replied.

The brief conversation ended with the shout of the original Iranian guard, now accompanied by another two new latchkeys and the base medic, who were rushing down the corridor toward the stricken man. Petrov feared that he'd be dragged off and beaten to death for his brazenness, but all he got was a rude shove out of the way as the other men rushed toward the Vasaltnik.

Later Petrov was asked about what he'd been doing near the other prisoner, but his reply that he'd only been attending to an unwell fellow soldier was accepted. Either the Iranians believed him or they didn't care; Petrov assumed the latter.

Now, in the dark confines of his cell just before dawn, Petrov suddenly noticed something new. He had lived in this hell-stricken place so long that every contour of its broken concrete floor and filthy cinderblock walls, even in pitch darkness, was etched in his memory.

Yet something was wrong, he now saw, something was different than usual. But what? What was out of place? In time he perceived that it was a tiny anomaly in the darkness. A section of deeper darkness, like a scab on a body, that should not be there. Slowly, his malnourished body's joints creaking, Petrov heaved himself off the mortician's gurney and warily crossed the cell to the point near the heavy iron door.

There, on the concrete, he saw it, and at first didn't believe it was actually there. But moments of staring down at it convinced him that it was no hallucination. And then, when Petrov had stooped and picked up the key, he knew at least that it was solid, and that it was in fact solid and real.

His heart began to race—there was something else he hadn't noticed about the cell until just now—up close he could detect the absence of a few centimeters of darkness between the iron jamb and the heavy door that meant the bolt was not latched.

What had he to lose, anyway? Only his life, and that was slowly being stolen from him anyway.

Petrov reached forward and gingerly tried the handle of the door. He was only half surprised to see it swing open and the light from the deserted corridor spill into his cell like milk from a ladle. Then, as Petrov stepped hesitantly out into the corridor, he suddenly remembered.

He had dreamed of flying.

Yes, he thought. *That's it.*

Flying!

It was a spot of desolation amid a world of desolation. The desert barrens stretched away on every side, boundless and disorienting. But for the fusion cell, hunkered down like jib rats in the sand, it was a city of refuge. The hide wasn't marked on any of the military maps the team had brought with it, maps supposedly produced from the latest satellite photosurveillance updates. But it was there just the same.

From the looks of the place, it was literally as old as the hills off in the distance—the ruins of a desert fort dating back to the late nineteenth century, the days of what the British called their "Great Game" with the czarist Russian empire for control of the Transcaucasian landmass, a contest of weapons and will that eventually extended from the Khyber Pass in Afghanistan down into the Arabian Peninsula.

One of the scout patrols Mitchell had sent out the previous night had picked the place up on a thermal imaging scan of the terrain through a binocular scope that could be quick-mounted on any of the tubular bars of the FAV's superstructure. The TI scope contained some processor circuitry that also gave estimated range and enhanced the image. The desert floor radiated the solar heat it had accumulated throughout the day back up into the air at its own unique rate. Other objects with their own unique thermal coefficients did the same.

Stone, mud brick, metal, wood, what-have-you, all radiated at different rates. The structure in the distance showed up white against the dull gray of the cooler, less radiant sands. It looked like some kind of run-down adobe building, made of stone, mud brick, and wood beams, part of which had fallen down, with various other smaller and equally dilapidated outbuildings surrounding it. It turned out, under closer inspection, to be a small caravansary—the tactical maps showed two in the region, but none in the general vicinity of the fusion cell. Yet there it was.

Caravansaries dot the deserts of the Middle East, and while they evoke images of camel trains laden with spices and silks, they are the desert equivalent of the lodges found in the world's mountainous regions, from the Alps to the Rockies—places of refuge for wanderers in desolate regions, whoever they may be.

The Mideast's larger and better known caravansaries straddle ancient trading corridors that are well traveled to the present day, and over time many have become small towns and trading posts rather than isolated rest areas. This unknown place wasn't one of these; it lay in the remote desert off the beaten path and was little more than a pile of weather-beaten ruins.

Using secure commo, the patrol had radioed back to the wadi where the main element of the team had set up a hide site. Mitchell and Arbatov checked their maps and decided the caravansary was a better place to hole up than where they were at present. After the firefight, this part of the Dasht was crawling with Iranian patrols, and it was only a matter of time before the game of high-tech hide-go-seek the cell was playing with their hunters ended in capture or annihilation of the force.

The fusion cell was moving cautiously by night, using thermal and low-light imaging, as well as a number of other special technical aids, with which to navigate and avoid detection. These would keep them out of harm's way for an estimated twenty-four to thirty-six hours, but after this, their odds of evading their pursuers diminished steadily down to a flat, bleak zero. The cell either had to extract by then or face the inevitable consequences.

Now, as dawn began to paint the sand, stones, and rock with a wash of yellows, golds, and crimsons, it was satcom time again, the magic moment when Mitchell and Arbatov prepared to give another of their scheduled situation reports to the Gallant Echo command post in Kuwait, which would be satlinked to JSOC operational headquarters at Pope AFB, adjacent to Bragg.

The satcom uplink was a secure, encrypted circuit relayed over military communications satellites using global-mobile protocols. The GloMo links were high bandwidth; the links carried any kind of data, fax, multimedia, not just voice alone. GloMo hardware was a far cry from the walkie-talkies and PRCs used in Korea and 'Nam. The hardware took the form of TRAVLER's shock-resistant laptop unit, equipped with a variety of peripherals including color camera and wireless mikes, and other gear, including SINCGARS frequency-hopping radio units, hard-copy printers, and additional monitors and portable transceivers resembling ruggedized cell phones. Everything was modular and interoperable.

One of the advantages of the TRAVLER portables was their multimedia capability. Mitchell's troop could upload and download more types of data than ever before, including real-time video and still photo imagery from overhead surveillance assets, like the LaCrosse and Keyhole satellites the Pentagon had jockeyed out of their normal orbits to keep an eye on the proceedings below in the Dasht. It was the real-time imagery that Mitchell's crew had been able to view on their TRAVLER screens that had been key to keeping them out of the hands of the Pasdaran search teams combing the desert for them.

Using TRAVLER, they could look down and see their situation from one hundred miles up in geosynchronous orbit, a God's-eye view that showed them precisely where the opposition was searching and—in some ways more important—where it was not. To the Iranians, it was as if the fusion cell had uncorked a djinn from a bottle and cloaked itself in a shield of invisibility. But it was simply that the troopers had eyes that could see in ways the opposition could not. By comparison, the Pasdaran were blindfolded and groping about in the dark.

When the satcom link was operational, Mitchell and Arbatov faced their commanding officers back at the distant command post via two-way teleconferencing. An extraction plan was being put into effect, they were told. But they were ordered to remain in place until given further orders. The political winds had shifted somewhat and new orders were being cut. If there was any possible way to destroy Shadow One, the cell would be ordered to make the attempt, regardless of the risk factor involved.

But the stranded troops might get some extra help in performing this feat, and this was now being worked on.

At the moment new surveillance and tactical assets were the subject of high-level discussions in Washington and elsewhere. The cell was to stand by for further instructions regarding this development. Colonel Mike signed off, and Mitchell shut down the link and put TRAVLER into sleep mode. Next scheduled transmission was in two hours, and he wanted to grab some sack time if he could.

Seventeen
Last-Extremity Solutions

In Washington it was somewhat past three in the afternoon. In the eighteen-by-twelve foot White House Situation Room, which is buried deep beneath the executive mansion, a tense and often acrimonious debate concerning what the cell had just been told was now taking place.

President Travis Claymore was flanked at the large oval table by National Security Advisor Throckmorton, and his secretary of defense, Robert Gooch. The contingent from the Pentagon included the chairman of the JCS, General Jack Thibodeaux, with aides occupying chairs at the rear of the cramped room, ready to wade in with documents and charts when and if their bosses deemed it necessary.

The conclave of mandarins also included two representatives from Israel—the ambassador to the U.S., Shimon Halevi, and Yigael Bar-Zion, of AMAN. Neither wanted to be where he was at the moment, since their inclusion was the result of a last-minute phone call from their Prime Minister Simchoni to President Claymore.

The call had provoked Claymore into one of what the White House staff called his "LBJ blue-streak cussing" attacks after signing off. The president did not like surprises, especially the unpleasant kind, and he found the warnings of moles, cowboy operations, and burned cover distinctly unpleasant.

After some preliminary paper shuffling, the president got the meeting under way and heard situation reports from various staffers. It was now the JCS chairman's turn at bat.

"General Jack," the president began, having dubbed Thibodeaux this to avoid tripping over his last name, which Claymore could not pronounce without a stammer, "we were talking about contingency plans to get this supreme stew of bullshit over with. What have you got for us today?"

"Well, sir, we at JCS have been working to develop a number of options and have prepared three packages for review." The chairman half turned in his seat and gestured to one of his aides, who jumped up and brought over the charts and a stand.

"Package one is what we call the 'Breakfast Special' option. Basically, it calls for tactical strikes using sea-launched cruise missiles from our carrier battlegroup in the Strait of Oman. Once we know the location of the plane, we could pursue this course of action."

"I don't like it," the president avowed. "Too many risks in there. What's package two?"

The chairman motioned at his aide again and a page of the chart was flipped as he explained another option. The president heard out the chairman, but shook his head as he listened. After the chairman had finished his presentation, the president said, "You left something out. How the hell are we gonna know where that plane's at? We don't have any confirmation yet, now do we?"

"No, sir," the chairman admitted. "But we're pursuing various options."

"My information is that you're about as close as a blind

man in a coal hopper to finding his asshole and that the satellites aren't worth a shit, is that right?"

"Well, essentially that's the case," the chairman was forced to concur. "Satellite imaging has its inherent limitations. Normally we would want to rely on surveillance assets that could fly in for a closer look, such as TR-1—"

"That's the spy plane, Mr. President," said Claymore's national security advisor, breaking in.

"Right, that's the spy plane," continued the chairman, "and we'd want to use that type of high-altitude aerial reconnaissance asset in a tactical situation like this, which is what I suggest that we do."

"No can, General Jack," the president told the chairman. "No more pilots getting shot down in Iran this go-round. Had enough of that horse manure over Kosovo. And hell, it's practically raining bodies on the goddamn Iranians by now. What else you got up your sleeve?"

"Well, there is another option, an asset called Tier III—"

"That's a robot surveillance aircraft, Mr. President," said the national security advisor to Claymore, who had glanced his way again for clarification. "But it's supposed to still be under development."

"General, I hear the Tier III's still supposed to be under development," the president said to the chairman without missing a beat.

"Yes, well, technically that's right, sir," Thibodeaux said right back. "Actually, we are at the stage where Global Hawk's roll out is imminent and we at the Pentagon think we can reliably use this UAV, or unmanned aerial vehicle as a solution in the present scenario."

"Global Hawk is what they call Tier III, Mr. President," the national security advisor told his boss, who squinted with annoyance.

The chairman of Joint Chiefs went on to describe the various selling points of using Tier III, such as the fact that it was an unmanned vehicle with a ten-thousand-mile end-to-end range which could fly from the U.S. to Iran transmitting real-time data at any point.

He also pointed out that with its classified cruising altitude—he refrained from stating it was better than ninety-two thousand feet because of the mixed company—it flew too high to be hit by SAMs or even high-performance fighter planes, but that in the unlikely event it ever crashed, there were numerous self-destruct options that would make its falling intact into enemy hands highly unlikely.

The president said he'd consider that while the next speakers had the floor.

"Gentlemen, I believe most of you know Ambassador Shimon Halevi," said the president. "Shimon, please tell us what you've come here at your prime minister's urging to say. And by the way, Shimon, please thank his lovely wife personally for that delicious homemade layer cake she sent over. The first lady and I served it when President Mubarak was at the White House recently and he raved about it."

"Thank you, Mr. President," Halevi began. "I will personally convey your thanks to the prime minister. Now"—he glanced at the briefing papers in front of him on the table, having permanently forgotten about the cake—"as you but nobody else in this room is aware, there are some aspects to the situation that bear on what has just been discussed."

He proceeded to tell the NSC about the cell of highly trained Israeli commandos that was now operational in the Iranian Dasht-e-Kavir, but that they were working for Assaf Gilad, who was staging what was basically a one-man operation. At the cussing that followed this revelation, Halevi tried to blunt some of the rancor by making comparisons with Oliver North's White House basement operation during the Reagan presidency, which in foreign policy terms was practically a shadow White House, but these didn't go over well.

Still, he'd made his point. Nobody's skirts were clean. America had had its Nixon-era Plumbers and its Colonel North and Israel had its Assaf Gilad. As different as they were in other outward aspects, both men were cut from the same cloth.

This point having been made, Halevi dropped his next and even more devastating bombshell. The Israelis had an agent in place, a HUMINT or human intelligence asset who was close to the action on the ground in Iran and in a position to contribute high-level intelligence on the location of the aircraft and perhaps even assist with an extraction plan for the fusion cell on the ground.

There was more cussing and commotion after this news, and the chairman of Joint Chiefs asked why the Israelis hadn't told anybody about this until just now. Halevi brought up the Eilts Affair, which took place during the Carter era. This involved the last-minute exposure of an American intelligence agent in Libya in order to protect then U.S. Ambassador Herman Eilts from a Qaddafi-sanctioned assassination plot, burning the covert U.S. agent in the process.

Halevi, who also hinted that there were other, more secret examples he could also cite, had again made his point, and he'd done his homework.

Now it was the president's turn.

"General Jack," he told the JCS chairman, "you go ahead and use that bird of yours—"

"Global Hawk, Mr. President," said the national security advisor.

"Global Hawk, right," said Travis Claymore. "You get that Hawk in gear, General, until we know more about the location of that sumbitchin' Russian plane. This meeting's adjourned, gentlemen. Same time, same place tomorrow, unless some more shit hits the fan, and we'll see what happens."

President Travis Claymore rose and straightened his jacket, and left the Situation Room. Attended by his entourage, he strode in his trademark cowboy boots toward the private elevator that would whisk him several stories to the White House above where he had a taped address to make to the nation, defending himself against a fresh round of charges by the opposition party.

By now, President Claymore had already forgotten the events in the Mideast and his mind was focusing on concerns of a more personal nature, involving a financial killing he'd made in pork-belly futures trades, some of which had wound up in the coffers of his recent campaign's slush fund, though he suspected that all that was going to change in a very short time. San Antonio's favorite son knew the lumber was about ready to hit the spinning buzz-saw blade, and when it did, Katy, bar the door ... — Iranian nukes would blow pork bellies clean off the media's anti-Claymore playlist. Maybe for good.

Petrov felt alive for the first time in weeks. Every nerve tingled with heightened awareness—awareness of risk, of danger, but also of the tantalizing promise of *svoboda*. The pilot's hope was far more than a state of mind. It was something tangible, as real as the sharp scent of moisture on the wind that heralded the approach of a cleansing rain.

The fatigue, hunger, and despair of his imprisonment faded away as Petrov stole down the deserted cellblock corridor as quietly as possible, praying one of the Iranian turnkeys from the checkpoint around the corridor's L-shaped bend would not choose this moment to begin his late-night rounds. These were seldom predictable, he had found, from many nights of listening and watching.

But no one came to challenge his escape. Not so far, anyway. His pulse racing, he passed one, then two, then three steel cell doors. Outside the fourth door in the queue, he drew up and gave two short raps with his knuckles.

It opened in a flash and a strong hand pulled him quickly inside, into pitch darkness.

"Shhh," he heard a gruff voice in his ear.

Petrov nodded. The warning hadn't been necessary. He had no intention of crying out. Why should he?

The hand released his arm and the commando gestured toward the bunk at the far end of the cell. Petrov sat beside him in the dark.

"You, too, have been freed, I see," he said.

"Yes, it seems we have a friend on the inside."

"Or an enemy who is manipulating us for purposes of his own," the Vasaltnik added.

"You want to stay and rot here, then be my guest," Petrov angrily replied in a loud whisper. "For myself, I have other plans."

He held up the key he'd found on the floor of his prison cell and showed it to the soldier in the semidarkness. "I've seen the storeroom where my flight gear is stored. I'm betting my life that this key fits its lock."

"It's not digital?"

"You're joking, aren't you?" Petrov shot back, having grown tired of the man's posturing. "Here camel dung is used for cologne and you think they have cipher locks?"

"What are the chances?" the commando asked, still unperturbed.

"Maybe thirty percent," Petrov answered. "You want better?"

"Yes, I do," he answered, nodding. "Though I suspect we will have to live with thirty percent odds."

"Or die."

"Yes," the Vasaltnik said.

"By the way, Trapezhnikov, what is your first name?"

"Call me Aksel," the Vasaltnik told Petrov.

"I am called—"

"I already know," said Aksel. "Let's get started."

The two men soon were moving stealthily toward the door of the darkened cell.

Minutes later they had acquired the olive-drab uniforms of two Iranian regulars who had been subdued by Aksel. The first soldier had been the unluckier of the two. Aksel had been forced to take him down without benefit of a weapon, which meant he had to hit him, and hard—sleeper holds and arcane kung fu pressure points are as much the stuff of fiction as related techniques from the planet Vulcan, unless, of course, you prefer running the risk of having to hit your opponent a second time as he comes back at you, mad as a hornet.

A roundhouse right with plenty of steam behind it to the solar plexus, or a swift kick in the groin with a steel-toed combat boot, followed up quickly with a forearm or elbow smash across the bridge of the nose is the best prescription for sending an opponent to dreamland in a hurry—providing, of course, that the element of surprise lies in your favor.

In the case of the hapless Iranian soldier, who'd been grabbed as he passed Aksel's cell a few moments after he and the pilot concluded their escape plan, this was certainly the case. Before the guard could pass the cell door, it was flung open, two powerful hands caught him by the tunic, and he was hauled inside into darkness, where he was soon put to sleep by the generous application of pummeling fists to the appropriate soft spots.

After Aksel had changed into the guard's uniform, which was fortunately loose enough to fit his somewhat larger frame, he left the cell in search of a surrogate for the pilot. He found the second soldier having a smoke against the side of the tunnel wall that was part of the base's underground bunker system. This soldier, too, paid the price for relaxing his vigilance while on watch.

Aksel used two of the phrases he recalled from his premission refresher courses in conversational Farsi. He, like many an Afghanistan veteran, had become fluent in Farsi, which was a lingua franca during the days of Soviet involvement there, and also in Dari, Farsi's Afghan dialect.

The first phrase was *ta kan na khor,* meaning "don't move," which was used in tandem with the application of the muzzle of his commandeered AKS-74 autorifle against his captive's chest as he stripped him of sidearm and rifle. The other was *man koja hastam,* which meant "walk this way," and preceded the guard's being frog-marched down the brig's tunnel toward the cell where the other guard was now bound tightly with strips of the lice-infested blanket that Petrov had cut into thongs with the bayonet of the captured rifle.

With a change of clothes and the other guard now joining his comrade on the filthy floor of the murky cell, Petrov and Aksel made their way toward the storage room on the installation's ground level. The key fit the lock as Petrov had predicted, and the pilot's flight gear was soon retrieved with Aksel's help.

They also found some spare ammo clips and a case of antipersonnel grenades, which they stuffed into a musette bag along with the spare AKS taken from the second downed guard. Perhaps more important, they found food, in the form of canned rations. They scarfed down what they could and carried as much of the rest as they could cram into their pockets. Almost instantly they felt new energy flowing through their bloodstreams and into their starved cells.

Minutes later Aksel was marching Petrov at rifle point toward the hangar where the stealth plane was being fueled.

"This one is wanted by the eggheads again," Aksel said in Farsi to the Iranian guards stationed outside the cellblock.

"What happened to Hossein?" asked the head latchkey, a lieutenant seated at a desk.

"His syphilis is acting up again. He's off vomiting somewhere."

"His what? You say he has syphilis?" The guard stopped chewing his kebab and rice balls in midsentence.

"Yes, didn't you know? Hossein has had it for years. It acts up every now and then. Don't worry, he'll be back as good as new as soon as he's finished puking out his guts. It's the mercury they give him for it. Fucks up the whole system. Gives him fierce spasms sometimes."

The guard eyed Aksel, openly skeptical. The look on his face said, Is this man joking? But there was not even a hint of a smile. The Vasaltnik's face was completely deadpan. Here was a man who was as serious as an imam at the muezzin's evening chant. But this story he was telling . . .

"What is your name, Sergeant?"

"Nateghi, sir."

"Papers, please, Nateghi."

His hand was already reaching across the desk.

"I have no papers. You see, I don't need papers with my brother on the People's Islamic Revolutionary Council, close to the ear of the *faqi* himself." Aksel leaned in close and glared at the seated man. "Maybe you want to speak to him concerning my papers, eh, Lieutenant?" Trapezhnikov picked up the phone and offered the handset to the seated man. "Go ahead. Call my brother and ask him about my papers. He'll tell you all you want to know."

The guard stared at Aksel's deadpan face and then at the receiver in his outstretched hand. Tense moments passed. Finally, the guard took the handset from Aksel and gently placed it back in its cradle.

"That won't be necessary, Sergeant. You may proceed. Of what concern is this prisoner to me, anyway? Take him away, Nateghi."

The head guard waved them through the checkpoint dismissively. They walked toward the door set in the cinderblock wall at the corridor's end. Aksel reached to pull it open, when the lieutenant at the desk shouted for them to stop.

"Just a moment, Nateghi," he called out.

Aksel turned, his finger tightening on the trigger of the rifle in his hands. His heart pounded, but neither his eyes nor his expression betrayed his wariness.

"Yes," he said evenly. "What is it?"

The head guard stood up and slowly walked toward them. He stood abreast of Trapezhnikov and stared hard into his eyes.

"Your brother, Nateghi," he said. "He is a big shot in Tehran, you say?"

Though tensed for action, the Vasaltnik remained outwardly calm. He dared not look at the pilot, but prayed that Petrov would not betray them with a show of panic. Trapezhnikov kept his eyes on the Iranian's as he answered.

"One of the biggest shots," he told the guard.

The sergeant nodded and gestured at one of the armed soldiers stationed nearby. The Pasdaran walked over. Trapezhnikov could almost hear Petrov's heart thud in his chest. He tensed his muscles for action and got ready to take both men down with a burst of autofire.

"Private Razouk here has a wife in Tehran," the sergeant said. "She's with child, but our commander won't give him maternity leave. Think you might have a word with your brother about this for a brother in the ranks? Maybe he can pull some strings?"

Trapezhnikov instantly relaxed, though the lieutenant didn't know it.

"You can be sure that I will," he answered with feigned outrage. "You have my promise, Razouk, that matters will be fixed. I'll let you know by tomorrow."

"Good man, Nateghi," the lieutenant said, and gestured for Private Razouk to return to his post. "I'll not forget this."

"My pleasure," Traphezhnikov said. "Anything for a *baradar*—a brother in arms."

They mounted a flight of concrete stairs behind the door without incident as the head latchkey returned to his desk and his dinner. So Hossein had this disease? the lieutenant thought as he began to knead the moist rice in the bowl before him into a tight ball. Well, that was certainly news. He put the rice ball into his mouth, followed it with a piece of kebab, and resumed reading the newspaper on which the bowl sat while he chewed his meal.

"You damned fool! What was the meaning of that stunt? You could have gotten us killed!" Petrov took the opportunity to whisper to the commando, whose expression remained as flat and unperturbed as ever. "Had that guard seen even the smallest trace of a smile, and had luck not been on our side this once, it would have been all over!"

"I *was* smiling," Aksel said, his expression grim. "But

on the inside. And our luck held, didn't it? Now shut up and don't play Jesus with me—your halo's covered with shit. Do what I say if you want to fly your precious black plane out of here."

Eighteen
The Hammer and the Anvil

They emerged from the passageway and found themselves standing in a corner of the hangar. Suddenly the two escapees caught a good look at Shadow One. It was only a few hundred meters away, though as Petrov had found before, it was the center of attention for numerous military and technical personnel.

Petrov noted mentally that the Eclipse looked ready for takeoff. It was connected to an auxiliary power supply unit and its cockpit canopy was canted up and back from the fuselage, as if the plane awaited a pilot. Were the Iranians planning a test flight in the dead of night? Possible, very possible, he decided. Now he also realized the hangar door was open. It had never been so before when he had been summoned to the plane.

Then, without a chance to turn his face aside, Petrov spotted the turncoat Dikushkin across the hangar, seated at a worktable. The engineer had been crouched over a sheaf of printouts, talking to two other men in Pasdaran khakis and red berets. The table was piled with waveform generators, oscilloscopes, high-speed raster printers, and other electronic gear. Dikushkin did a double-take and stared at the newcomers for a shocked, lingering moment.

"Quickly—the traitorous bastard's seen us!" Petrov stage-whispered to Aksel out of the corner of his mouth, while Aksel slipped him the second AKS he'd kept hidden in a large musette bag. The bullpup autorifle was cocked and locked, and a 5.45-mm blunt-nosed round was already cranked into the firing chamber, its safety catch set to automatic burstfire.

A second or two passed, and then Dikushkin unfroze. Jumping to his feet and dropping his papers, he hailed the nearest soldiers in his vicinity. Petrov and Aksel couldn't hear what he was blustering at them, but Dikushkin was gesticulating wildly, pointing their way, and shouting toward the khaki-clad Iranians who'd run up to him. The soldiers immediately rushed the duo. Other troops dropped down and aimed their rifles.

"Go!" shouted Aksel. "Don't stop for anything!"

He whipped the bullpup Kalashnikov to navel height and squeezed off a multiround burst. Flame erupted from the lateral vents in the weapon's muzzle brake as he wrenched the barrel to and fro. Bullets sprayed the running Pasdaran before the soldiers could return fire. The wounded Iranians staggered and hit the concrete bleeding, but the troops who had already taken cover had begun to shoot. The hangar had come alive with crisscrossing steel.

Petrov reached the stealth unharmed. But as he grabbed for the railing of the access platform whose steps ascended to the cockpit, he heard the whine and spang of ricocheting bullets. Pivoting reflexively, he fired back from a half crouch, his index finger tightening on the trigger before he even thought to sight the weapon.

Answering with a panic burst had saved his life. His bullets tore into the midsection of an Iranian army major who'd been leveling a mean-looking, long-barreled Magnum at the back of Petrov's head. Petrov had beaten death by a trigger squeeze and a split second. Now it was the major who struggled to push his digestive organs back into his abdomen. As Petrov looked on, his knees buckled and he collapsed in a heap, his intestines uncoiling in a bath of blood.

Petrov whirled and remounted the steps of the platform. Now level with the stealth fighter's cockpit, he turned to see Aksel hurl two canister-type antipersonnel grenades. The grenades exploded as airbursts, raining shrapnel down on everything within a thirty-foot splinter radius. Aksel reloaded his AKS with a second banana clip, then cut loose with a sustained burst of autofire as a trio of soldiers tried to rush him, forcing them to hit the deck. In the momentary lull that followed, Aksel turned toward the plane.

"Cover me!" he shouted to the pilot.

Petrov propped the muzzle of the AKS on the iron bars that surrounded the platform. He dropped to a crouch, the most natural firing position, and got off a long, steady burst.

Too many bullets, Petrov thought as Aksel ran for the aircraft. They had taught him in the survival course always to fire many short bursts instead of a few long ones, but his fear had made him forget his training.

He wondered how many bullets were left in the magazine. Petrov had forgotten the number this weapon's clip could hold. *Is it thirty? Forty? Fifty, perhaps?* But what did it matter now?

Petrov continued to fire, but went to shorter bursts to conserve ammo as Aksel closed the distance to the plane, bullets sniping close at his heels as he sprinted a broken-field run.

"Inside!" the Vasaltnik shouted, taking the platform's metal steps double time. "I'll cover you." He reached out his free left hand. "The weapon," he demanded. Petrov's AKS was soon in Aksel's practiced grip.

Aksel turned and fired sweeping, side-to-side bursts of autofire from the twin Kalishnikovs while Petrov hustled into the stealth's cockpit. Quickly plugging into Shadow One's oxygen supply and comms, he fired up the engines

and energized the avionics, relieved that both were functional. He then turned to Aksel and gestured for him to
get into the plane. There was enough room between the
pilot's seat and the bulkhead, if Aksel was prepared for a
very bumpy ride. If necessary, he could breathe from the
backup oxygen supply. The Vasaltnik shook his head.

"Get going!" he shouted. "That's an order!"

Petrov was about to shout back in protest when a three-
round burst struck Aksel in the side. Part of his rib cage
dissolved in an aerosol of blood and bone that spattered
the black flank of the aircraft's hull, christening it with
martyr's blood. Though he was dying, Aksel found the
strength to throw two more grenades and continue crank-
ing out steel, thereby slowing the determined advance of
the Iranian force that was pressing in on the plane.

"Go, Vassily," he shouted. "Dammit—go now!"

Petrov couldn't bear the sight of the stricken man who
was expiring before his eyes. Filled with emotions he
could not name, the stealth driver turned his head and
tugged back on the throttle, feeling the black plane's engines roar to brute wakefulness. A moment later he saw
Aksel shudder as more bullets riddled his body, the two
weapons he'd clutched clattering to the concrete a moment before his corpse hit the bloodstained concrete.

Now! Petrov screamed inwardly. *Go now!* A paralyzing
fear had overcome him. Yet he had to summon the nerve.
Now! the inner voice continued to demand. *It will work!*

Yet Petrov knew it would be futile in the end. There
was surely no time to get the plane airborne before they
cut him down. Even so, at least Shadow One would be
destroyed in the process. The Iranians would still lose.
Then Petrov realized that they weren't shooting any
longer and risked a look out the cockpit canopy window.

He saw an Iranian officer with arms in the air, ordering
the troops to break fire. They clearly weren't prepared to
risk hitting the valuable plane. At the same time red hazard lights flashed and sirens klaxoned. The hangar's steel
plate door had begun to slide closed again. It was now or

never, the pilot realized. In minutes he might as well open the canopy and give himself up.

Petrov advanced the throttle to its middle power stop and the twin turbojet engines roared more loudly than before. The jet leapt forward with a savage lurch, pulling away from its access platform and sending tables supporting diagnostic equipment crashing to the hangar's concrete floor. Like a once captive bird of prey, Shadow One shrugged off its fetters and bolted for the freedom of the night, which was its natural element, screaming out its yearning for the sky.

Petrov's total attention was focused on the moving hangar door that loomed up ahead of the plane, slowly shearing off the night beyond. It wasn't that far from the nose of the aircraft—less than thirty meters if he estimated correctly—but the gap was quickly shrinking. He knew he had only a matter of seconds to reach it before it had rolled shut to a point where he would be caught like a moth in a sparrow's beak. Even the most minor damage to the fuselage could abort his flight, and if the hangar door closed too far before he reached the entrance, it would be the same as striking a steel wall at high speed.

Yet he was committed now.

Live or die, there was no turning back.

Petrov advanced the throttle forward again. Centrifugal forces slammed him back in his molded seat. Twin plumes of burning exhaust gases seethed from the plane's thundering turbofans, setting men and equipment afire. As the black arrowhead streaked toward the hangar door, two-legged torches did a flailing, screaming dance in its wake, like human sacrifices set afire to appease some ancient god of death.

Petrov saw the edge of the armored guillotine rushing toward the fragile glass bubble of the cockpit, coming so close it almost scraped the thin transparent skin. And then he had crossed the threshold between light and darkness, then he was hurtling across the flat pancake of the desert sands, gaining velocity and greater lift with each elapsed second and already feeling the landing gear begin to elevate off the ground as the black spearpoint he rode shot through the air at fantastic speed.

But now, above the roar of the turbofans, Petrov could also hear the staccato chattering of automatic weapons fire. The sound was like a choir from purgatory, mixed with high voices and low, the alto voices belonging to scores of carbine rifles and light machine guns hurling glowing red-and-green tracers at the hurtling plane, the basso-profundo voices belonging to the heavy, vehicle-mounted machine guns loaded with armor-piercing slugs that sought his range.

Personnel carriers, Jeeps, trucks—anything and every-thing that rolled and could carry troops and weapons—sped toward the plane from the four corners of the airstrip. Shadowy man-figures behind the big guns triggered off a vortex of steel at the escaping prisoner and the coveted prize he was about to snatch from their grasp. Petrov saw they meant to stop him on the ground if they could, and were throwing everything at him but the kitchen sink in order to do it.

Pulling out all the stops, Petrov shoved the throttle for-ward to the hilt, applying full military power, and yanked back on the stick, feeling the plane gain immediate lift and its belly turn at a sharp angle toward the sky.

Built for stealth and not speed, the MFI did not have the thrust-to-weight ratio of a MiG-29 or an F-16—its engines weren't powerful enough for Petrov to stand the plane on its tail and shoot into an almost vertical ascent trajectory, and its wafered airframe was far too fragile for any kind of hotdog stunt like that.

But Petrov pushed the stealth's airframe to its design limits, feeling its bulkheads, control panels, and the stick in his hands shudder and buck like the whole plane was about to come apart around him. His mind was intent on gaining as much altitude in the shortest possible time, on putting the earth and the death and madness that infested it like crawling lice as far below him as possible, on es-caping the hellhole in which he'd rotted and stunk and suffered for end-to-end weeks.

The moments passed as the numbers ascended on his digital altimeter gauge and his rate of climb increased. Soon all indications of firing had stopped, and even the yellow puffballs of Triple-A the Iranians were sending up were many meters below his ceiling. He was alone with the sound of the stealth's engines now, and he knew he was out of range of anything they could throw at him from the ground except their longest-range SAMs.

Petrov leveled off at sixty thousand feet, near the top of his envelope. The aircraft was stable now, and the stick no longer bucked in his gloved fist. Below, night mantled the earth and he was all but invisible to radars, including those of the Russian-built SA-10s with which the Iranians would even now be trying to pinpoint the runaway plane.

The Iranians would be scrambling their fighters, too, and these would also pose a significant threat, because although they couldn't see him, the planes could concentrate in the approximate area of his flight path and have a better chance of making visual contact, from which point they could effectively attack.

Petrov plotted an evasive course vector that would bring him within range of the northeastern border while he scrolled through the satcom frequencies. The Iranians, who had forced him to give them the encryption keys to the frequencies during his captivity, would be listening on all channels, but that couldn't be helped. He'd have to get off a message, or even if he made it across the border, there would be no refueling aircraft waiting for him and his tanks would run dry.

Someone would be listening. Someone *had* to be listening. If they were not . . . he pushed the thought from his mind and continued to transmit. But as his pleas for acknowledgment went unanswered, even this hope began to fade. He had less than a half hour of fuel reserves, according to his readouts, and after that, he would drop to earth like a stone.

And then—

"Shadow One, this is Whiskey Bravo Delta control. Say your situation."

The signal had been faint at first, but electronic warfare officers aboard a Mainstay airborne warning-and-control aircraft flying a figure-eight track above the Caucasus had picked it up at the very edge of airspace identification range. Now the crew dogs had a lock on the signal and could pull it in clearly.

"Am airborne and proceeding on flight vector delta eight-point-zero-zero-seven." The course coordinates were coded and the Iranians had no reason to have asked Petrov for them. Even if his transmissions were intercepted, it would do the opposition no good. "Fuel reserves are critical. Will require immediate AAR. Can you provide?"

"Affirmative, Shadow One," the Russian voice answered. "We have a bird with plenty of fuel waiting to RV with you at coordinates six-zero-niner-point-gamma-six. Can you make it?"

Petrov consulted his fuel gauge and did a fast and dirty course plot on the keypad linked to the plane's flight computer.

"Roger, Whiskey Bravo Delta," he said. "I can just make it. With a little luck."

"We will cross our fingers, Shadow One. May lady luck crouch between your legs the rest of the way. Out."

Petrov smiled, and corrected his course as he made for the refuel RV point. But as he flew his plot, he began to have fresh doubts that he would reach it. As his heartbeat slowed and his adrenaline rush subsided, he realized that an intermittent sluggishness of the flight controls that he'd noticed earlier was now noticeably worsening.

The inertial navigation system that controlled the ungainly, angular aircraft was malfunctioning, he knew that now with certainty, and it had begun to destabilize. Petrov flipped switches and punched buttons on the console, shunting to redundant systems, but the backups didn't fix his problems.

He surmised that either the plane had been hit by gunfire in a vulnerable spot on takeoff, or that the Iranians had tampered with the electronics—a loose connection header, an IC zapped by static, any number of small glitches of that order could damage the delicate, interconnected systems that controlled the aircraft in flight.

Seconds later the plane had become almost too unstable to handle, a black Icarus burned by the heat of the night, its waxen wings beginning to melt. Dropping from his cruising altitude of sixty thousand feet—a ceiling proof against SAM launches—Petrov descended down to lower altitudes, risking the chance of visual contact, or even contact with enemy tracking radars, against the hope of gaining greater control in the heavier air closer to the ground. The maneuver helped somewhat, but not enough. The plane's controls had begun bucking again in Petrov's hands, and this inability worsened by the minute.

The plane shuddered and began drifting off course, and then suddenly, the pilot felt the sickening lurch he had been half expecting as the stealth's left engine flamed out. Then came a second, more severe jolt as the condition pilots called "infectious flameout" made the second engine sputter and die as well.

Pushing the lighted restart button did nothing—the stealth's avionics were now behaving the way the electrical system of an automobile with a dying alternator behaves on the road—the illuminated dials and buttons on his console blinked off and on, flashing to an epileptic rhythm. His tactical displays froze, and then kaleidoscoped into sheets of electronic noise. His systems were shutting down all around him, sliding into shock, crashing like plates from a cupboard.

No doubt about it.

His plane was going down.

On the four-lane highway below the emergency landing approach of the stricken stealth fighter, its amber running lights aglow, a diesel truck hitched to a long, low trailer called a HET, or heavy equipment transporter, was making the dreary northbound return run from Masshad in the east to Tehran.

Behind the wheel of the slow-moving lorry was a tired man named Omid Farzaneh, who had spent the last five hours on the desolate desert road and was anxious to complete the final leg of his trip back to his home in the outlying suburb of Kaf Amal. Not long before, Omid had trucked his cargo—a medium-sized crane—to a construction company in Masshad, and was now highballing it back home with a signed manifest.

It was just shy of four o'clock in the morning and the long, straight blacktop highway was devoid of traffic, as it had been for many uneventful kilometers. Farzaneh hadn't seen a headlight for what seemed like ages. He was feeling mentally drained and physically fatigued, but that went with the territory, and besides, the radio was keeping him from dozing off behind the wheel. He'd make it all right—he'd made this run often enough to almost do it in his sleep. There was no point in pulling over, not for a while yet. He could go at least another fifteen klicks before he was too dazed to drive without a nap, he reckoned.

But tonight's run would be considerably different from any Farzaneh had ever made before in his lengthy career as a long-haul trucker. It was as he lit the end of his bogarted cigarette with a plastic butane lighter that Farzaneh saw something in the sky that seemed to blot out the stars. As the lighter flame snapped off, leaving the cab in total darkness, Farzaneh saw that he was not hallucinating.

A large, black, saucer-shaped object—some sort of plane, maybe even a UFO, it seemed to the startled driver—was hurtling down, directly in the path of his truck. In a heartbeat he would collide head-on with the thing.

The trucker panicked and acted without thinking. Had he been more alert and less frightened, he might have averted the disaster to come, but that wasn't to be. Acting from blind hysteria, Farzaneh violently jerked the steering wheel to the left, hoping by this maneuver to evade the path of the oncoming airborne object.

It proved to be a fatal mistake.

Had he turned the wheel to the right instead, the truck

and its long trailer might have fishtailed onto the flat gravel surface that was graded level with the road and probably stopped without further incident.

But to the left of the highway was an incline—not a steep one, even for the desert, but steep enough to send the mammoth rig careening nose-first onto the sands below the level of the highway. In the process, Farzaneh was catapulted from his seat, over the steering wheel, across the top of the dashboard, and squarely into the windshield with enough force to shatter the small vertebrae of the upper neck, killing him almost instantly. The truck was not equipped with an airbag.

As the black, discoid shape passed only a few scant feet overhead, the truck continued rolling for several minutes longer, until it plowed headlong into a rock outcropping, crushing part of its front end. Then it came to a full, juddering stop, with the body of its deceased driver flung half out the shattered window to wind up sprawled across the hood.

Petrov's landing was not much smoother, but fortunately for him it did not prove fatal. The stealth plane set down on the flat desert pan with its landing gear extended, and for a minute its nose dipped sharply downward and almost plowed into the soft, dark sands. But then, still rolling, it straightened up, and with wing flaps distended, Petrov managed to slide to a shaky stop only a few hundred meters from the disabled HET.

The stealth driver undid his harness webbing, unbuttoned the cockpit canopy, and pulled himself out from under it onto the boxy left air scoop. He checked his watch, or rather the Japanese watch he had taken from one of the Iranians they had bushwhacked for fatigues in place of the flight suit his captors had stolen from him, reading the time from its backlit LCD dial.

The black numerals on the glowing green display showed the time was precisely four A.M.

Only half of Vassily Petrov's dream had come true. He had lived to fly. But he had flown to nowhere.

Nineteen
The Falcon and the Falconer

At Nellis Air Force Base, which sits just southeast of the hotel and casino towers of downtown Las Vegas, a HET roughly twice as long and considerably wider than the hapless Farzaneh's had arrived in the dead of night. It carried a cargo in a special formfitted container.

Civilian employees of the U.S. Defense Department with high security clearances had been expecting the delivery and quickly got to work unpacking it from its crate, once the HET had driven into a security-screened hangar facility, a facility in the heart of Nellis that is the headquarters of the USAF's 11th Reconnaissance Squadron, the first operational unit formed to fly long-endurance unmanned aerial vehicles to distant regions of the globe.

The personnel who surrounded the HET were employees of DARO, the Defense Airborne Reconnaissance Office, a department of the larger organization known as DARPA, which stood for Defense Advanced Research Projects Agency. DARO had been involved in the initial development of the UAV or unmanned aerial vehicle programs for the Air Force, and it had recently finished conducting its final ACTD or advanced concept testing and development trials of the Tier program's advanced UAVs some months before.

Hours later, when they had uncrated the delivery, Global Hawk was rolled into a section of the enormous hangar where the process of programming the UAV and fitting it out for its clandestine mission commenced. The long-range remote airborne surveillance system was a thirteen-ton aircraft the size of a single-engine plane with a 116-foot wingspan. Its fuselage blended seamlessly into a huge ramjet intake at the rear and flared into a rounded sensor bulge at the front, with long, slightly backswept glider wings sprouting from the hull's midsection.

The combination of design elements gave the robot plane the look of a winged monster blindworm imbued with cold, sinister intelligence—which is not very far from what it was. In addition to downloading digital maps into its memory, the preflight maintenance process, which would take several hours, would upgrade Global Hawk's hardware and ROM software and comprehensively test all its systems, including its classified imaging payload.

Global Hawk was built to fly long endurance missions that required it to stay airborne—or, as it's said in military parlance, "loiter"—for as much as twenty-five hours before returning to base. During that time it could aerially survey approximately forty thousand square nautical miles, a target area equivalent to the state of Illinois, with a resolution of objects as small as three feet in diameter. Utilizing spot-mode scanning, it could surveil a much smaller area with a resolution of objects down to one foot in size, if necessary.

The UAV was also equipped to carry EO, or electro-optical, and SAR, synthetic aperture radar, imaging payloads as well as a third infrared (IR) system simultaneously while operating at altitudes of greater than sixty thousand feet. The UAV could be crammed with up to a ton of cameras, radars, and other sensors. Global

Hawk could also transmit real/near-real-time data via line-of-sight datalink and satcom relay. As already stated, it could also be armed, which this bird most definitely was, with both air-to-air and air-to-ground capabilities.

As the crew of technicians worked on the plane, another crew labored to set up a command-and-control area for the remote operation team that would be responsible for the flight of the Hawk. A series of tall Plexiglas screens had been set up to cordon off an area about thirty feet square. Behind this soundproof, and indeed bulletproof, glass barrier, banks of rack-mounted communications equipment and miles of thick power and data cables were being installed to enable long-range control of Tier III Minus.

A portable stereo sound system was also being set up, including a CD changer stocked with two hundred of the loudest rock albums ever recorded.

But that was for the Hawkman.

Petrov gave up on the plane's satcom unit. He'd wasted precious time in trying every conceivable combination of settings, but nothing but static repaid his struggles. He surmised that the antenna element had been damaged during the forced landing, but couldn't be sure.

Whatever the case, his communications link was down for the present. Nor were there now any means available to him to destroy the aircraft. This time Petrov had not hesitated to trigger the MFI-19's autodestruct sequence, but nothing happened. The Iranians had either removed the explosive charge or pulled out the circuit modules that controlled the detonation sequence. It was now either destroy the plane with his bare hands or leave it alone. Petrov decided to leave it alone.

He stood looking around him, at the desert on all sides, at the pale white skull face of the leering moon that seemed to mock him from its perch in the black, star-filled sky above, at the asphalt highway that ran ruler straight across the sand desert to the distant line of the faraway horizon, at the two black skidmarks of peeled tire rubber, illuminated by pale moonlight, that skewed off the roadbed and into the dark, and the metal behemoth that had made those tracks now motionless in the distance against a jumbled heap of strangely twisted and deformed rocks.

Petrov was suddenly overwhelmed by the alien weirdness of it all; he felt he was living a moment in hell caught in amber. He thought that if ever there were a perfect time for a man to lose his sanity, this was it. He seemed to have been catapulted through Alice's looking glass into a surreal world where nothing made sense anymore and where all his bearings on reality had been stolen from him.

The profound disorientation he experienced, Petrov knew, was the combined effects of stress, sleep deprivation, hunger, and probably illness, too, and he also knew that in order to survive he would have to turn off all parts of his mind that weren't directly connected to his military training and instincts for survival. He knew also that he had to move, to get away from where he was, and to do so before sunrise. He'd already wasted too much time in his futile efforts to phone home.

But what to do? And where to go? Petrov needed to admit to himself that he'd been defeated. He was as good as dead. In a few more hours it would be fully light, and with each continuing hour of daylight, his hours of freedom steadily dwindled down to the zero mark. Before the next day was out, he was certain of recapture. This time the Iranians would have no more use for him and would give him no quarter.

He would be executed on the spot and the plane retaken, and when the final reckoning came, his death would be reported as an "accident" to his wife and children back home in the port city of Vladivostok. It now dawned on Vassily Petrov that his own personal survival was bound up with the survival of the plane he'd piloted.

If he could only find some way to hide the aircraft from discovery, he would have gained a bargaining chip, might even be able to work a deal in exchange for his freedom.

But how would he do such a thing? Lift the damned machine on his back? Plow up the desert crust and bury it in a huge hole? Maybe even summon some sleeping djinn from a magic lamp to pry apart the crust of the earth and swallow the plane in its hidden depths.

In anger, Petrov picked up a handful of small stones from the desert scree and hurled them at the side of the plane, hearing them go *plonk, tink, plonk, tink* as they struck the composite-material fuselage with hollow thuds. What was the use? He was through, and that was a no-shit judgment call. Petrov might as well admit it to himself. There was no way to hide a plane in this flat, almost featureless desert country. He might as well try to draw water from one of those rocks in the distance, the way Moses had done in the Bible.

He reared back to hurl the last of his handful of stones at the half-buried monster cockroach when he got hit with what they call a BFO at the Pentagon—a blazing flash of the obvious. Petrov simply called it *nomskaya,* intuition. By whatever name, its effect was to stop him cold and spin him around, as he suddenly recalled an image of the area from his descent and forced landing that matched something else he had seen on his flight into Iran.

The stone that he'd been about to hurl in impotent rage thumped instead to the sandy desert floor as Petrov ran toward the higher ground of the roadbed and surveyed the encompassing terrain by the electric blue wash of ghost-pale light from the shining lunar skull.

It was amazing, he thought. But yes, there it was. Right in front of him all the time. Time and the odds both ran against him, because the darkness would soon give way to the rising sun. But with a little luck, he might just be able to pull it off. Dear God, how he prayed that he might!

The black Camaro, with blue federal tags and a huge bird of prey with outspread wings painted on its hood, that pulled up to the guard post at 11th Recon's gate at Nellis wasn't new, but it had seen a lot of the detailer's shop. The air scoop protruding from the front of the hood bespoke a heavier, more powerful engine than the car had come off the assembly line with. The tinted windows weren't standard either. Sergeant Everett Loomis, who'd been watching the car pull up, was instantly on the alert.

This wasn't the usual type of vehicle that came and went through the portals he guarded. That was good by him. Loomis was in a shit mood. His wife had found out about his affair with a waitress in Reno. She'd already taken the kids and left for her mother's in Tempe, Arizona. Then the waitress had dumped him for a Mexican dishwasher. Doing a number on some smart-ass punk would make his day. He hoped the driver gave him an attitude. He really hoped the driver was high. That might give him an excuse to point his rifle at the car and maybe shoot it up some, after which he'd see the motherfucker handcuffed and arrested by the base MPs.

Please, let me beat the shit out of this guy, he prayed silently as he stepped from his booth.

Loomis glowered down at the Camaro's driver's side as the electric window slid down into its recess in the door. One look at the driver told Loomis that his ship had come in. Long, lanky black hair, those kind of Ray•Bans with round lenses, and fingerless driving gloves. Loomis inhaled, hoping for a whiff of pot to go with the rest, but was disappointed. The car interior smelled like new leather. He bet the guy used one of those bullshit fake leather sprays to make it smell like that. Never the fuck mind. At least he could tell the punk to turn down that loud rock music that was blasting out of the car stereo. What the fuck was that shit? Definitely not music, that's for sure.

Before the MP could say a word, though, the driver hit a button on the dash and the music dropped several decibels in a heartbeat. Undaunted, Loomis fixed the driver with his most daunting scowl and asked him to state his business at the base.

"My business? Guess you'd have to call it saving the world from its own bad karma," is what he answered.

"What was that?" Loomis asked, with tightening jaw,

omitting the "sir," with which he normally concluded questions to visitors. This dude did not rate a "sir," not from Loomis.

"Check this out, my man," replied the driver, and shoved a base pass into his hand.

Sergeant Loomis's frown deepened as he read the name on the pass—Bartholomew Simpson. What was this, some kind of joke? Man, he was going to kick old Bart Simpson's smart ass if that name didn't match his manifest, which Loomis was sure it wouldn't.

Except, there it was. Bartholomew Simpson. In black-and-white. Still, this had to be some kind of bullshit. It had to be. Somebody was pulling Everett Loomis's chain. Just to make sure, Loomis told the visitor to wait. He was going to check it out. Take his sweet fucking time doing it, too. But a phone call convinced Loomis that he was to pass the car through immediately, and Loomis was smart enough to know that he'd been wrong about the profile—this guy was some kind of spook.

"Sorry to keep you waiting, Mr. Simpson," Loomis said to the driver, who simply grinned at him in response and stuck out his hand for his pass.

Loomis handed back the base pass and saw the window roll up, failing to keep the sound of thudding bass from infecting the hot desert air with its mad vibrations as the muscle car rolled into the parking lot of Nellis's high-security Section Three.

"Oh, one thing," the driver said, rolling his window down again.

Loomis turned to listen.

"Go fuck yourself, asshole."

Everett Loomis was soon enveloped by clouds of exhaust fumes as the sound of peeling tires screeched in his ears.

Loomis didn't know it, but the Hawkman had just arrived.

It was better than Petrov had dared to expect as he neared the place he had reconnoitered from the air and spotted from the road. It was far enough from his landing site not to be overly obvious to pursuers, yet close enough to have allowed him to reach it on foot in a relatively short time.

As it was, he had made it with bare minutes to spare. The false dawn had already arrived, and with each passing minute the deep black sky lightened by half tones to shades of gray and blue and the air temperature imperceptibly climbed. Petrov crept closer, past the ubiquitous camel thornbushes and rock outcrops dotting the landscape, examining this place of refuge in every detail, while part of his mind replayed the events of the past few hours.

After his flash of inspiration, the pilot had climbed down the embankment and ran toward the crashed truck that had come to rest nearby. It became obvious that the big rig's engine was still kicking over as the winking amber running lights along the sides of the cab and flatbed grew nearer.

The faint sound that Petrov had heard in the distance was fast becoming the deep, throbbing idle sound of a powerful diesel engine. The plume of exhaust seeping from the tailpipe confirmed this to Petrov as he finally reached the truck, out of breath from the desert jog in his weakened state, and saw Omid Farzaneh's mangled corpse sprawled across the hood through the shattered windshield.

He would need to turn off the engine, probably, which would entail pulling the cadaver's legs free of the cab and rolling it onto the desert floor, but this ghoulish task would have to wait until Petrov had satisfied himself that the truck met his needs. Convinced that the rig was in no danger of rolling away from him after chocking its rear wheels with large rocks, Petrov walked around to the back of the HET and lifted himself onto its steel-plated deck. As he paced it with arms outstretched to measure its length and girth, he estimated that it was wide enough for his purposes, though barely.

At the front of the trailer, just behind the cab, was a heavy-duty electric winch that was operated by a pushbutton remote-control unit. Petrov switched on the remote, and tested out the winch, which moved up, down, left, and right, paying out and reeling in the heavy woven steel cable with flawless efficiency. The duty ratings of the winch were printed on the remote unit in English and Arabic. Petrov knew enough of the former to understand that the maximum load the winch could safely handle roughly matched his specifications. From this end, at least, the job seemed doable.

Petrov next went around to the front of the cab to see about the feasibility of the rest of his plan, but this would involve removing the driver's already rigor-mortis-stiffened cadaver so that Petrov could check the fuel gauge and move the truck.

With the door swung open and one foot perched on the running board, he paused to consider the best way of accomplishing this task. A few test pokes at the body told Petrov that it had become too stiff to easily force back down into the seat and be dumped out the door, so the best approach would be to drag it from the cab. This proved to be much harder than he had anticipated.

Rigor mortis was advanced, and the jackknifed posture of the corpse around the dashboard meant that Farzaneh's bloating legs kept catching on the steering column, brake pedals, shift, and bottom of the dash. Extracting Farzaneh's mortal coil was really a two-man job. Petrov had alternately to pull from the front of the truck and push from inside the cab, working back and forth like a dog worrying a large bone, until the legs of the dead driver finally came free of the cab's interior.

At least another hour was to pass before Petrov succeeded in freeing the corpse from the cab. By this time he was badly winded, but he knew he couldn't stop to rest more than a moment. He also knew that apart from concealing the body as best as he was able, he needed to take its papers. He didn't want anything to lead back to him.

Now, seated behind the wheel, Petrov restarted the truck's diesel engine, backed away from the boulders, and

drove the juddering semi across the uneven desert landscape toward the squat black shape that loomed in the
ebbing darkness.

It took him almost another hour to winch the stealth
plane up onto the bed of the carrier and lash it down in
a way that was secure and as unobtrusive as he could
make it. There was plenty of tarp in a storage locker on
the back of the carrier, and tie-downs of various kinds.
Petrov was able to cover enough of the plane with tarp
before lashing it deckside to make it reasonably hard to
spot. It would take more than a single glance in the dark
of night from a passing vehicle to identify the new cargo.

Now, back behind the wheel of truck, he shifted into
first gear and juddered his way again across the desert
floor until he found a low part of the embankment where
he thought it reasonably safe to pull up onto the flat surface of the highway. Praying that the plane would not
snap loose from its cables or that the truck wouldn't over-
turn under the uneven load it carried, he applied power,
felt the triple rows of wheels find purchase, and moments
later was crawling onto the highway in growling low gear.

From there, on the level roadbed, the remaining ride
was smoother and considerably faster. Petrov pushed the
rig for as much speed as he dared squeeze from it, because
it was getting close to dawn. He could see the horizon
faintly lighten to a blue hairline toward the east, in the
direction he was heading, and the once bright stars begin
to grow dim. With no traffic on the remote stretch of
desert road, he made good time, and found a shallow-
graded turnoff onto the spot he'd seen from a few kilometers' distance.

He took another shallow-graded turnoff and heard the
tires splash in the brackish water of the mud through
which he rolled, watched the steep concrete walls towering up on either side of him. He could kiss those high
walls, because they would hide him from the light of day,
and from the sun, and he knew the place would provide
even better hiding places as he pushed deeper into it.

This place to which Petrov had driven the truck was a

huge concrete culvert built to funnel the precious seasonal outflow from the distant mountains to the parched cities to the north of the Iranian plateau. The culvert was part of a system that fed the taps of Tehran, Yazd, and smaller towns in between. In some places, the watercourse dove underground, but here the form it took was a deep, square-bottom channel, in the form of an exaggerated *U*, reinforced with poured concrete, and dug into the desert floor by foreign engineers in the 1970s.

The walls of the main channel were honeycombed with side tunnels for the inflow from other water sources, including seasonal rains, and the huge ditch was entirely covered over in places to prevent evaporation by steel plates that had become buried underneath sand through the years.

Culverts like this one had been used successfully by Iraqi Scud crews during Desert Storm to hide Saddam's missiles from satellite and aircraft surveillance. The culverts had made ideal hiding places for the Scuds for a number of reasons. For one, they were wide enough to easily accommodate the Scuds' transporter-erector-launchers or TELs, and their shape, construction, and proximity to water meant that they combined a mix of temperature gradients that radiated a kind of thermal stealth, making the TELs hard to spot on IR or TI scans.

Petrov hoped this culvert on the edge of the Dasht would offer him a similar sanctuary. He had no other choice, in any case. The winter sun had already risen, a leprous orange blotch on the far horizon, wavering in the thermals that had begun to rise from the desert floor—another day in the Dasht-e-Kavir had begun.

In the distance, the pilot thought he could hear the wavering thud and drone of attack-and-surveillance helicopters, but that might be his imagination, he knew. Fatigue and hunger played tricks with the mind, and he was suffering from both. As the sun parted from the horizon line and swam toward the center of the brightening blue sky to become a yellow Cyclops eye, Petrov fell asleep in the cab of the truck, and dreamed of nothing.

• • •

Several hours after Petrov had found the culvert in which to hide the truck, and many kilometers distant from his hiding place, Barak and his squad of Israeli Egoz renegades were changing into the uniforms of the Iranian regulars they had ambushed and killed. As a result, some of the uniforms were bloodstained and bullet-riddled, but that couldn't be helped. To make an omelette, one always had to break some eggs.

He and his men needed the uniforms, just as they needed the BTR-70 armored personnel carrier that the troops had been riding in when they'd been summoned, in flawless Farsi, by radio to a remote spot where Barak's commandos had set up a crude but effective rock trap designed to immobilize the vehicle without damaging it too much.

The rock trap was one used a lot by the Afghan guerrillas in their brief but bloody war against the Soviets during the 1980s, and it was a trap they had developed to perfection. As soon as the armored BTR had plowed across a trip wire invisibly strung across the road, tons of boulders perched atop a desert promontory tumbled onto the APC, trapping it like a huge, steel-plated rhinoceros beetle.

Before the shocked crew could react, flashbang grenades were shoved through the BTR's gunports at front and rear, immobilizing the troops inside, who were killed by the application of automatic nine-mm Uzi fire through the same gunports. With the bodies of the Iranians joining the boulders cleared from the BTR at the bottom of the wadi below the roadbed, Barak's crew changed uniforms and climbed into the carrier.

Barak now had fresh orders, which had just come in via secure satellite communications direct from Tel Aviv. His orders came straight from the prime minister, by way of a now somewhat more contrite Assaf Gilad. His team was to make contact with the U.S.-Russian fusion cell. The cell was pinned down some distance away at a caravansary. Barak's force was to assist it as a unit in reserve.

Under no circumstances were the Egoz to intervene directly or to do anything to the downed stealth aircraft. They were only to offer assistance, and then pull out. That was all. Assist and withdraw, but under no circumstances become embroiled in the worsening international conflict.

Barak acknowledged these orders. Then he promptly forgot about them and invented new ones of his own. In his rule book, orders were among the many things in the world that were made to be broken.

"Flash just came over VLF, sir."

"Let's have it," Gustavsen said back, his eyes on the map on the table in front of him.

The *Teaneck*'s communications officer handed the captain the sheet of paper that had just come off the secure satcom teleprinter. Normally, transmissions to the Los Angeles–class nuclear attack submarine were received at periscope depth during scheduled surfacings along its patrol route. An array of antennas on the fairwater would be raised to receive satcom, ground station, and airborne radio signals. Then the sub would resurface and be on its way.

Flash-coded messages were transmitted using very low-frequency radio waves or VLF, which penetrated the water and could be picked up by the nuclear boat's towed sensor array. Using the new HAARP antenna farm in Alaska, however, VLF signals could now travel across even greater distances, and over the earth's horizon. These could pass through water and be received below periscope depth, but were reserved for high-priority messages due to their relative slowness, bandwidth limitations, and the need to trail a long wire antenna behind the cruising submarine.

Gustavsen scanned the transmission sheet. The message, which had been decrypted by the sub's computers before being printed, read:

FLASH
FROM: CINCLANTFLT ELMSWORTH ADM

TO: SSBN 1889-YYN TEANECK// J3 NMCC//
AIG 931
  TOP SECRET U M B R A
  FG0284//OPREP-3 PINNACLE COMMAND ASSESSMENT//
  001//021950Z MAR 21 02//

(TS/SI) ALL EVIDENCE IS THAT IRANIAN MRBMS LO-
CATED AT AGHA JARI HAVE BEEN BROUGHT TO STATE
OF LAUNCH READINESS. MISSILES ARE THOUGHT TO
BE TARGETED ON STRATEGIC NATO TARGETS IN
SOUTHERN EUROPE. YOU ARE TO SET COURSE FOR
GRID COORDINATES 0027BF-96W61 AND REACH THIS
POSITION BY 0600 HOURS TOMORROW. AT THAT TIME
YOU WILL RECEIVE GO/NO-GO CONFIRMATION FOR
TLAM STRIKE ON MISSILE TARGETS IN IRAN VIA SAT-
COM.

END MESSAGE.

"What's up, Skipper?" asked Gustavsen's exec, who
had seen the look on his face as he scanned the message.
Gustavsen wordlessly handed him the sheet. The exec
nodded and handed it back.

"Gonna be a bitch," he told the captain.

"Tell me about it, Danny."

Gustavsen fed the orders to the shredder beneath his
desk. While it consumed its snack with a low growl of
meshing corkscrew gears, Gustavsen picked up the handset beside him and punched in the exchange number of
the boat's navigator. While relaying his instructions for a
new course plot, Gustavsen was already scanning one of
the bathymetric charts that his exec had brought over.

The chart showed that the coordinates related to a spot
in the Mideast a few nautical miles from the mouth of the
Gulf of Oman.

The exec then drew a grease-pencil plotline across a
clear acetate plotting sheet.

Where he made a circle was where the sub had to be
in a day's time. From the sub's present position in the

Indian Ocean, that was more than eight hundred nautical miles—a long haul at the sub's maximum thirty-knot sub- merged cruising speed. But, hell, thought Gustavsen. This was the Navy, wasn't it? Same business, different day.

Twenty
Dogs in the Manger

Nominally, the Hawkman worked for DARO, which made him a civilian employee of DARPA, which in turn made him an employee of DARPA's controlling organization, the Department of Defense or DOD. This was technically true but not, as they say, completely true. Although the Hawkman did in fact technically work for DOD, he really worked for NSA, an acronym that stood for the supersecret intelligence organization officially called the National Security Agency, and less officially called No Such Agency or Never Say Anything by many in government and politics familiar with its superclandestine methods of operation.

Since NSA is, according to the U.S. Government Manual, part of the Department of Defense, the partial truth was given some shred of credibility and the Hawkman's cover as a technical engineer with a high security clearance employed by DARPA was able to hold up under scrutiny. If anyone was interested in checking the Hawkman out more thoroughly, they could contact the appropriate offices at DOD and pull his file jacket, which described him as a skilled expert in computers and robotic systems who had worked on government projects at IBM, McDonnell Douglas, and various other major defense contractors.

Personal data on the Hawkman would include information on his age, educational background, personal habits, marital status, and finances, all of which would depict him as a highly competent if slightly eccentric and belligerent whiz kid who enjoyed playing with high-tech toys for his Uncle Sam, and being well paid for it in the bargain. He had even written a few paperback spy and military novels for Berkley books and other publishers. Some of these even sold.

All of this would be convincing, but it would also be a complete fabrication and a carefully stage-managed lie devised to conceal the real truth concerning who and what the Hawkman actually was, because these truths were bound up with the covert history of America in the years since the Korean War and covert history and true nature of the NSA itself.

The NSA was formed in 1952 by executive order of President Harry S. Truman, an order so secret that it remained classified for over thirty years; even today its text has never been publicly divulged.

Unlike the CIA, which was created by act of Congress, the NSA has never openly revealed its exact nature, the identities of its staff, or precisely what it is empowered to do, only that it has something to do with a vaguely defined state of affairs dubbed "national security."

In fact, it's believed by some that the CIA is no more than a front for the NSA, and that the operations of the CIA are often little better than a cover for the much deeper and blacker operations conducted by the NSA. It has been estimated that the director of central intelligence controls less than 10 percent of the combined national and tactical intelligence efforts of the United States; the NSA controls the other 90 percent.

Even the Hawkman, who had worked for the NSA since the secret wars in Laos and Cambodia at the close of the Vietnam era, and possessed a coveted NSA security clearance of top-secret Category Three, Cryptographic Code Word Two, did not have a handle on the big picture. The NSA is obsessed with the concept of need-to-know.

The organization's stock-in-trade is information, which to its nameless, faceless personnel, is the very essence of power. Every scrap of information is compartmentalized and controlled through codes, as identities are controlled through aliases and code names. Within the agency, power and rank are denoted solely by security clearances and the codes a person has the ability to read and understand. Within the pyramidal structure of the NSA, access to information leads to promotion and power, lack of access leads to failure and ostracism.

The Hawkman's orders were passed on to him in a secure area within a deep underground facility outside of Washington, D.C., known as a Space-Three facility. He never came within miles of the NSA's supposed headquarters at Fort George G. Meade, as these so-called headquarters are actually a vast computer farm and a control center for the less covert satellites that the NSA orbits around the earth. Contrary to well-cultivated popular belief, the true nerve centers of the NSA lie deep within the earth, in a series of ultrasecret facilities. These are easily the most secure areas on the planet, impregnable even to a nuclear strike at ground zero and capable of sustaining the lives of occupants for up to a year.

After passing through an elaborate security screen and several cipher-locked guillotine gates, where his identity was checked and verified at each point, the Hawkman had entered Space Three. There he met an NSA briefer who gave him his orders.

The briefer, whom the Hawkman had never met before and would never meet again, did not understand the words he spoke to the operative whom he was briefing. Most of the words were in arcane codes, and the briefer merely passed these on to others in the chain of command. The

Hawkman, cleared for the codes, understood the meaning fully. The briefer comprehended nothing.

On completion, the Hawkman left and began his mission. He would return to be debriefed in the same Space Three facility, and repeat the process in reverse, passing on a string of incomprehensible code words that would in turn be passed on by his debriefer until they reached someone in the NSA hierarchy who possessed enough clearance to understand their meaning.

The Hawkman's real name was no longer real to him, so he never used it. It had been lost, with his original identity, in the disarray of the Indochina misadventure. After that, his name became whatever name the mission demanded; his identity became the self that the job called for to get done. Those names, identities, and jobs had varied with the years between his loss of operational virginity and the present day. In the beginning they had comprised a string of covert rescue-and-assassination missions inside the triple-canopy jungles of Southeast Asia. After that, the focus of the Hawkman's efforts had shifted to Eastern Europe, then Latin America, and then into Russia and the Balkans before, during, and after the Soviet breakup.

Throughout his career, the Hawkman's genius for remote weaponry and robotics had involved him with cutting-edge operations. He had been the architect of several of the most ambitious ever attempted, including the secret mission to fly a refurbished SR-71 spy plane over the Soviet Union following the mysterious blinding of United States surveillance satellites almost a decade before and an attempt by a cabal of rogue military officers to provoke a limited nuclear war between East and West.

It had been on the Hawkman's orders that veteran SR-71 Blackbird pilot Dan Cox had been selected to fly the mission. The Hawkman had known Cox in his early Indochina days and had been behind the CIA's ferreting him out to fly the once mothballed SR-71. Cox's mission had averted a nuclear exchange between the superpowers and had paved the way for the shaky but so far unbroken peace that was to follow. The Hawkman, using a pen name, had written the story as fiction and published it under the title *Bandit*.

But this peace was only a by-product, a reflection in the real world of politics and people of the hidden world in which he was a player. In the true world of intelligence, the only thing that counted was the game; playing it, staying in it, winning a round as often as possible. The highest aspiration for winning was this and this only: you got to play again.

The Hawkman was playing another game today.

As usual, unlike the majority of the other players, he was one of the few who knew it.

Twenty minutes before, a powerful rocket engine had executed a multisecond booster burn, propelling Global Hawk into an angular climb to twenty thousand feet above the barbecue-hot sands of southern Nevada. The ascent of Global Hawk was visible to anyone peering from the window of one of the high-rise casinos on the Vegas strip, but there were so many flights out of Nellis every day that few—even the sober ones—would have noticed.

Once the UAV had reached its ceiling, the now useless booster rocket engine was jettisoned and the vehicle's single jet turbofan ignited. The specially built ramjet engine would carry Tier III Minus to its destination and back again, consuming the minimum amounts of fuel to keep the bird aloft and enable it to perform its intelligence-gathering routines from high- and low-altitude surveillance envelopes.

In the control center in the cordoned-off area of 11th Recon's ultrasecure hangar at Nellis, the Hawkman was monitoring the progress of the UAV from his instrumentation console. A large, fifty-inch, flat-panel display screen showed near-real-time imagery from Global Hawk's array of cameras and sensors of various kinds: the god screen.

At a mouse click, the god screen could switch from a single zoom view from any one of the UAV's cameras or sensors to display multiple windows from some or all of the drone's imaging suite. There were backup screens that showed real-time satellite imagery from orbiting Keyhole satellites so the UAV itself could be kept in direct view at all times.

Beside the keyboard, there was an elaborate joystick that could be used to control the bird while in flight, aim its imaging sensors, or activate its autodestruct mechanisms in case the mission had to be aborted. As the Hawkman chewed on the crust of a double-cheese pepperoni pizza his staff had brought from the surprisingly well-stocked Nellis canteen, and listened to the Cream's "White Room" on the nearby stereo system, he used his free right hand to pilot the UAV on the first leg of its long flight, which took it on an easterly course across the lower third of the continental U.S. and then out to sea.

At the moment the Hawkman's interest was in checking out the way the drone handled and running a few in-flight diagnostics. In a few minutes, he would put the UAV on autopilot and kick back and just keep a weather eye on the god screen. There would be another ten hours of flight time until the drone reached its operational envelope, and then things would start getting hairy. Until then, he could relax, listen to the music, and watch the in-flight movie that only Zeus normally gets to scope.

Colonel Ghazbanpour waited tensely for the report from the field. He needed results. The rear-echelon generals in Tehran were frantic. First the damned stealth plane disappears, then a foreign commando unit operating in Iranian territory can't be found—vanishes right off the goddamned map. Finally, an Iranian patrol has gone missing, complete with APC, weapons, and radio. Something had better be done, and quickly, they had told him, or he would be held responsible.

Ghazbanpour received a report that a helicopter crew had noticed signs of suspicious activity in the northeastern quadrant of the desert. This was in Sector Hamadi, one of six sectors into which his staff had divided the overall search area. This new sighting was far from where the last reports of the commando force had put the likely position of the American special-forces unit, but that did not necessarily mean the sighting was in error. Ghazbanpour had ordered a mobile detachment to encircle the area and be prepared to attack if necessary.

Many kilometers away from Ghazbanpour's desk, two companies of Iranian regulars, with APC and helicopter support, were closing in on a group of men in a desolate region of decaying ruins. The men within the enclave did not see the troops approach. Their orders had been to take the commando force alive, if possible. But then automatic fire had started up, and the assault force responded with every available gun. The helicopters targeted their missiles on the ruins and fired salvo after salvo of high-explosive rounds down into the rubble.

Minutes later nothing moved within the smoking bomb crater gouged from the earth. The attacking force sent a detachment into the blasted ruins with rifles at the ready and bayonets fixed. As they mounted the heaps of shattered rubble through clouds of acrid cordite smoke that stung their eyes, nothing moved. The only sign of human presence was the scattered body parts of those who had sheltered within. The denizens of the ruins had been blown to pieces by the sustained barrage of bullets and explosives. None still lived.

The company's leader, a Captain Hammoudi, immediately debriefed the detachment and radioed back to the colonel. Ghazbanpour tensed as he heard the news and hung up the telephone, clenching his fists.

Hashish smugglers! The U.S. commando assault force was still at large, and each day brought his career closer to a halt.

Sergeant Wayne Tollier hunched over the militarized TRAVLER unit, the laptop's shockproof metal case perched atop a small, flat-topped boulder that served as his desk. Tollier had gotten to kind of like it by now. For a rock, it made a neat desk. He had been attempting to install the upgrade package he had just downloaded via high-speed satcom transmission, but the OS or operating system of the wireless adaptive mobile information system or WAMIS node continued to reject the new program. Without the upgrade, TRAVLER would not be able to receive telemetry from the unmanned aerial vehicle whose ETA put it at less than an hour from the edge of its performance envelope.

Due to issues of fuel consumption, the time that Tier III Minus could loiter overhead was limited, and every spare minute counted for two. Tollier, the fusion cell's communications specialist, had been on the team's Hammer Lane secure satcom link to Nellis, where a DARO computer systems specialist was talking him through the install, so far without success. The OS was telling him the drivers were loaded, but when he restarted TRAVLER, they vanished back into the electronic ether. Tollier was pissed. This was one fuckup you couldn't blame on Bill Gates.

While Tollier worked to establish a reliable downlink to the arriving Tier III Minus, the three-man patrol that Mitchell had dispatched to conduct a recon mission reported in via secure SINCGARS radio transmission. The position of the U.S.-Russian team was pinpointed on a TRAVLER map display of the region. Hanes, Judson, Vishinsky, and Nazarov had been conducting a long-range patrol that had taken them in a fifty-kilometer arc to the southwest of the base. They had moved by night only in their FAVs, holing up during the hours of daylight in shallow wadis deepened with entrenchment tools.

So far they had spotted a few patrols and some itinerant groups of desert Bedouin, but the Iranians didn't seem to have a clue to the cell's whereabouts. The patrol had reported that they had quit the ruins of a desert outpost only a few hours before, when they soon heard the sounds of firing. Reconnoitering from the vantage point of a desert promontory, they saw that the outpost was under fierce attack by Iranian ground forces backed up by heavily armed Hip attack helicopters. The "black bottoms" were gunning for bear.

Mitchell ordered the patrol to immediately return to the caravansary. He knew the team could not remain there for longer than a dozen hours or so. They would have to move soon or risk an unevenly matched confrontation.

"Got it!" Mitchell suddenly heard Tollier say behind him as the program finally loaded, and this time stuck. The next fifteen minutes were spent waiting for the UAV to come within range, at least three of them on a round robin of high fives. Tollier even kissed his rock.

The Hawkman slipped an old Guns N' Roses CD into the changer and pulled on a special pair of gloves. This phase of the operation called for detailed work and he needed the right music for the job. The gloves, which were fastened around his wrists with Velcro quick-tabs, were wired and pumped full of air. Tiny sensors embedded in the spun nylon fabric were capable of detecting even the most subtle movements and pressures of his fingers.

The force-feedback gloves, as they were called, were linked to the high-speed computer processing system that controlled Global Hawk, which had now reached a point thirty thousand feet above the surface of the earth and more than three thousand miles from where the Hawkman sat. Before putting on the gloves, the Hawkman had strapped on a compact and lightweight head-mounted display or HMD.

The HMD design had come a long way since the first VCASS helmet was introduced in the early eighties. The VCASS, which quickly became known as the "Darth Vader" because it wrapped around the head like a strange, bug-eyed metal mask, used a primitive head-tracking system and arrays of cathode-ray tubes or CRTs to beam its imagery at the wearer's eyeballs. Although they were marvels of miniaturization for the era, the CRTs were huge, energy-intensive, and contributed to the sense of disorientating "simulator sickness" that testers of the Darth Vader reported after sessions.

By contrast, the HMD that the Hawkman wore as he listened to the opening guitar chords of "Welcome to the

Jungle" was about the same size and weight as a pair of safety goggles and flashed its imagery onto the human retina by means of a flat, semitransparant display film that gave a sharp, realistic wraparound view. The head tracker unit was no larger than a silicon chip, and as sensitive to movements of the Hawkman's head as the datagloves were to those of his hands. The ultra-fast computer processor and software suite insured that he maintained real-time control of the UAV.

What the Hawkman now saw in his visual field was the view he would have had if he were actually ensconced inside the cockpit of Global Hawk instead of thousands of miles away. There was a bank of virtual display screens in front of him, keyed to the various image sensors that studded the UAV's bottom and sides, as well as computer-aided radar imaging.

Within reach of his "hands" was an aircraft-style steering yoke with additional controls mounted on its surface. He could use the yoke to control the flight path of the drone in any direction he wanted. None of this was real. It was all computer-generated imagery, including the life-like firmness of the yoke in the Hawkman's fists. He would be piloting Global Hawk in cyberspace.

We got fun and games, he thought as the music played.

Mitchell and Tollier studied the screen of the TRAVLER field unit in front of them. The ruggedized laptop's ten-by-twelve-inch flat-panel display gave them a view of the op zone from twenty thousand feet in the air, downlinked from the several electro-optical sensors embedded in Global Hawk's sleek airframe.

With their multiband communications links to the UAV now securely established, the cell was able to see what the Hawkman saw on the god screen back at Nellis. Although the fusion cell had no direct control over Tier III Minus, they were now able to act as backseat Hawk drivers, telling the Hawkman about terrain features at which they wanted a better look.

Hours had passed already, and although the remote,

low-altitude reconnaissance of the desert had been thorough, it had also proven to be monotonous—and ultimately fruitless—going. So far the search hadn't turned up any solid leads regarding the location of the downed stealth plane.

"Wait one." It was Tollier who piped up.

He had noticed what looked like a possible man-made object at the bottom of a dry canal or culvert. *A wing section, maybe?* he thought.

No, he corrected himself, it was the *shadow* of a wing assembly's leading edge. No mistaking the object's angular contours. He'd been over this culvert area earlier, too, remembering the lessons from Iraq, but the sun's angle had been too high then. Now, though . . .

"What's your take on this, boss?" he asked Mitchell over his shoulder. "Think it's maybe our missing stealth plane?"

"Could be," Mitchell said back, watching the screen and drawing the same conclusion as Tollier. "Get in closer."

"Good to go, boss."

Tollier clicked the magnification factor up to 200, then 300, then 500 percent. This time he thought he also saw the trailing edge of an actual wing that protruded from just beyond the overhang of a road bridge spanning the culvert.

"Hawk One, please swing your bird around for another look," he said into the lip mike of the headset he wore. Consulting the search grid he'd clicked over the real-time active matrix display, Tollier continued, "Make altitude ten thousand feet and heading thirty-point-six degrees north-northeast."

"Your wish be my command, dude," said the Hawkman's voice in his ear, adjusting course and altitude and pointing the nose of his Hawk down toward the line of highway that stretched toward a culvert system that bordered a line of high-tension cables.

As he did, the Hawkman punched up a moving map display on one of the virtual screens in his HMD field of view. The map showed that this was an oil-producing region called Gur Qudair, a foul-smelling wasteland of pipes, vats, bubbling tar pits, and humming, crackling electrical power cables lying between the southern industrial centers and Tehran many klicks farther to the north.

Now the Hawkman could see what Tollier had been pointing at.

There, down below, was a black rectangular patch that he had at first mistaken for a shadow cast by one of the tall, pointed pyramidal structures that supported the elevated high-tension cables that ran across the desert floor and disappeared over the horizon. The Hawkman sharpened the image resolution and was left with no doubt that what was being looked at was a man-made object.

"Eenie meenie meinie mo. Gonna see how low this sucker can go," he told Tollier, and executed a ninety-degree turn, aiming the nose camera of the Hawk down from another angle, one that pointed away from the disk of the afternoon sun.

Minutes later, as the UAV returned for another overflight at fifty thousand feet, its cameras picked up the characteristic swallowtail rudder assembly of the Russian stealth plane. No other aircraft, save the F-117A that it had been cloned from, could produce that telltale design signature. The computer agreed, matching the imagery with a profile stored on disk.

The cell had found its thus-far-elusive quarry, and not a moment too soon—a virtual fuel gauge and warning icon had popped up on the god screen, showing that Global Hawk was now flying on its reserves. The UAV could not loiter over the area any longer.

"Gotta hop back into my magic lamp now, guys," the Hawkman told Tollier and Mitchell. "But—to quote the immortal Arnold—I'll be back."

The Hawkman wasted no time in turning the bird around, ascending the UAV to its SAM-resistant high-altitude flight ceiling, and plotting a return course.

Twenty-One
Zero-Sum

Even the flattest of deserts—and the Dasht is among the world's flattest—has subtle depressions and elevations, rifts and hollows, folds and inclines, into which men and vehicles can disappear and from which they can unexpectedly emerge to evade or engage enemy forces.

Desert warriors speak of needing to develop a so-called feel for the desert in order to operate successfully in its stark environs, in acquiring the habit of memorizing the location of every wadi, rock formation, and thornbush they encounter, in interpreting the sights, sounds, and smells that might warn of danger or herald safety from attack, and in honing the instincts necessary to survive and thrive in one of the planet's most forbidding natural environments.

The Israelis are no exception to this iron law of necessity; in fact, they are pioneers in this particular sphere of land warfare. Developing a feel for the desert is an essential facet of Israel's military doctrine and especially applies to commando troops, who are trained in the fine art of SERE—search, evasion, rescue, and escape—as it relates to the intricacies of desert combat.

For days, Barak's team had been using the desert topography to their advantage, as part of their *taboula*, Hebrew for "battle strategy" back in Joshua's day, as now. Although the commandeered Iranian APC was roughly the size of two pachyderms yoked in tandem, Barak's team exploited wadis, roadbeds, rises, and hollows in the landscape, and other natural terrain features, to keep itself well hidden from view.

This was the same basic strategy described in what the IDF calls Plan Ashdod. This secret contingency plan, prepared in the event that Israel should ever find herself faced with waging another ground war against her Arab neighbors to east, south, and north, calls for Egoz forces to stage wasting actions against the flanks and rear of Syrian and/or Egyptian armor while air and ground elements conduct a more conventional military campaign.

During the reign of the shah, Israel had conducted secret liaison exercises in the Iranian desert, where a core group of experts on special warfare in the Dasht had been formed. Barak had been one of these experts. Such were the intricacies of Middle Eastern power politics that even after the ascent of the Ayatollah Khomeini in 1979, and the turbulent wave of extremist Islamic fundamentalism that followed, the Israel-Iran special relationship continued. Later on, as relations thawed, Israeli agents could again be infiltrated into the remote fastnesses of the Iranian sand desert, to study and familiarize themselves with its unique ground truths.

Most of Barak's commando team possessed firsthand experience with the complexities of land navigation and land combat in the Dasht-e-Kavir. By this time Barak knew the desert almost as well as the Bedouin Arabs, Kurds, and other nomadic tribesmen, or *mohajer* in Farsi, who plied its arid wastes.

This knowledge of the desert was far more intimate and complete than anything that American high technology could duplicate, try as it might. No matter how good Global Hawk's sensor imaging suite, or how adept at interpreting the data was the crew at Nellis or the Deltas in Iran, the Israeli team knew the Dasht's secrets better than any Westerners without hands-on knowledge could ever hope to equal, even on their best day.

And so it was that as Barak's crew monitored wireless communications frequencies using their land-mobile radio equipment, they discovered a vital clue to the location of the missing stealth. On a civil band channel they heard a police report in Farsi concerning the unexplained disappearance of a heavy trailer truck in the Gur Qudair region. The truck, and its driver, had disappeared without leaving so much as a tire track behind. Something about the report rang a bell in Barak's mind. Particularly something about Gur Qudair. But what, exactly?

Asking one of his men to fetch him a map, Barak laid it out on the sand and propped its edges with a few rocks to keep it flat against the cold, steady wind. Crouching on the balls of his feet, he studied the empty terrain of the Gur. As soon as his eyes fixed on the culvert, he smelled pay dirt.

Barak mentally went over the image of the culvert, which had been built during the last year of the shah's reign with the help of the Israeli army engineer corps. He had chanced to have an opportunity to visit the building site near its completion in 1978 as part of Assaf Gilad's entourage. As he recalled, the plan had been to divert the course of an underground river that flowed beneath the northwestern part of the Dasht and spanned the major wadis, a project requiring the emplacement of a network of massive siphons and culverts of poured concrete. Would one such culvert be large enough to hide a stealth fighter with the rough dimensions of an American F-117A?

Assuming the plane could somehow be gotten down into the place, yes, definitely. Though it was unlikely that one battered pilot, acting on his own, could accomplish this feat, Barak had to admit it was technically possible. There was one other thing, too, that Barak noticed as he scanned the map—the location of the culvert put it athwart the flight path that Shadow One was projected to have flown to its initial ordnance release point, according to his premission briefing by AMAN personnel.

"Piss call is over," Barak shouted as he rolled up the map and stood erect. "We're moving out."

"Where?" asked one of his men as he flung a cigarette into the sand.

"You'll see," Barak said, and climbed in beside the APC's driver.

The plane sat there on the trailer, baking in the cold desert sun. Petrov was baking, too, the sun sucking the moisture out of his body. Odd how it could do this even in the cool of winter, but the place was so damned dry . . .

Petrov didn't finish the thought. It didn't matter. The point was that neither he nor the aircraft could remain here much longer. Neither was designed for these conditions. The plane needed a hangar and regular maintenance. Even exposure to the extremely fine particles of windblown desert dust for any length of time could damage its avionics and propulsion systems—a few stray particles in the wrong places and the engines would not even start.

He'd covered the engine intake ducts and other avenues of ingress as best he could, but who could be sure? Petrov was tired, cold, hungry, thirsty, lost, and alone. He estimated that he could hold out here for another twenty-four hours—at the very most. Then he would have to break cover or begin to starve; his rations would be gone.

Petrov's only hope lay in flying Shadow One out and back across the border, and he had been working on this option ever since it had gotten light enough for him to see. Shivering in the early-morning chill, refreshing himself as best he could by drinking brackish water that he had scooped in the hollow of his palm from the muddy bottom of the culvert, the pilot struggled to make repairs to the MFI's critical flight systems.

The most critical of all these had been the plane's INS or inertial navigation system, and here he had gotten lucky. He had believed that the Iranian techs had tampered with the VHSIC modules that comprised INS, and since he had no spares, this would have meant he could not reliably get the plane airborne again.

But, as Petrov carefully removed each module and inspected the ICs that were socketed on the printed circuit boards, he discovered that nothing was missing, every chip, circuit trace, and pin jumper was where it should normally be found. After detaching and reinserting each of the four VHSIC modules, Petrov started up the Shadow's avionics from the cockpit and ran through diagnostics again. In the absence of a sweep oscilloscope and other diagnostic tools, merely repositioning components on a board was a crude fix, but it often worked.

To his immense relief, Shadow One's systems now reported that INS was performing perfectly, even after running diagnostics again and again to confirm their integrity. Petrov surmised that one of two things had happened. The first was that something foreign, maybe even something as small as a few dust-fine sand particles, had shorted a passive backplane connection and screwed up his system—not an uncommon occurrence where high-technology military systems meet the ancient, windblown Mideastern deserts. The second was that the Iranians had pulled some of the modules just as he'd done but had not reinserted them just right, which might have had the same net effect. Then, too, there had been the multiple shocks of the initial landing and his recent narrow escape.

After several hours of work, Petrov was sure that Shadow One was flight capable. Now it was time to grab whatever sleep he could, because once night fell he would have to roll the HET back up onto the highway, single-handedly winch the stealth back off the end of the huge flatbed, and take off, using the highway as a runway.

Making himself as comfortable as possible beneath the flat underbelly of the plane—there was no room beneath the low-slung HET trailer itself—Petrov closed his eyes, thinking about how to block oncoming traffic later that night in place of counting sheep. Soon he slept fitfully, though deeply enough not to notice the tread of eight tiny feet.

These belonged to the scorpion that was slowly making its way up along his arm and inching toward his face, as the tip of its tail stinger gleamed with a clear drop of poison.

Skimming low across the arid, lunar surface, its mantis shadow stretching and twisting like elastic smoke as it passed across the high and low places in the desert crust, the Mi-8AMTSh variant of the Hip-H attack/transport helicopter hunted the night for an elusive prey.

The Hip's A suffix stood for *ataka,* indicating that it was equipped for automatic gun and rocket attack on ground targets, and its MT designation, standing for *modifitsirovanye transportnoi,* indicated that it could ferry a platoon of troops to any battle zone within its four-hundred-kilometer combat radius.

Colonel Ghazbanpour had both increased mobile ground patrols and aerial search missions as well as placed all his forces on round-the-clock alert status. He was under increasing pressure to locate and destroy the commando cell that had infiltrated the desert. He needed to locate the missing aircraft before they reached it and destroyed it, for such was surely their mission. Another twenty-four hours without results and Ghazbanpour would be relieved of command, of this he had been assured.

Yet it was pure luck that accounted for the first success against the invaders that Ghazbanpour could boast so far. The Mi-8's pilot had made a chance sighting of one of the cell's patrols as it was returning to the caravansary just before first light on the final day of the mission.

Flying conditions were excellent, and this was the primary reason for the break in Ghazbanpour's long streak of bad luck. The darkness was pellucidly clear, the moon not quite full, yet bright enough to blanket the barren desert expanse far below with a milk-white lunar radiance. Here and there the landscape glistened where dew had frozen into fragile patches of thin ice, and a mild night wind swept across the moonlit sands.

The chopper crew was about to swing back for base, when suddenly, in the distance, off to the west in an area that the helo's crew had not yet searched, something seemed to move against the hairline blue glow of the far horizon, making a band of stars low on the inverted bowl of the sky wink on and off in a straight line.

"Did you see that, Massoud?" the pilot asked his copilot via helmet commo.

"Yes, Adnan. Think it's anything?"

"Try to put it on TI," the pilot suggested.

There was nothing on the thermal imagining screen except open desert and the forms of night predators. Their fuel reserves precariously low, the Hip crew decided that they'd seen a mirage and proceeded to turn again, when suddenly the dust trail raised by a small, highly mobile vehicle crossing the desert was caught on the thermal scope.

Normally, such dust trails are dead giveaways, and during daylight hours are visible for miles around, which is one reason why the fusion cell's patrols moved only at night.

"Zoom to highest resolution factor," the pilot ordered, his voice now tense and without any trace of his former casualness.

The copilot punched buttons and there it was—the scout patrol's FAV caught rolling across the open desert. The pilot smiled triumphantly. He knew he had them now. If he watched his fuel gauge carefully, he would be able to make it back all right. Dropping low to mask the chopper behind terrain features, the pilot vectored in for the kill.

The two FAVs composing the long-range scout detachment were on their way back to the caravansary. They had little more than another six kilometers to cross before they reached the relative safety of the ruins. They were not to make it.

The Mi-8 Hip loomed up from behind the rise they were about to cross, cutting into the face of the moon like an apparition sprouting from the grave. The Hip driver was slick. He had positioned the chopper just beneath the lip of a deep wadi, unmasking the helo at exactly the right moment. To the patrol, it seemed to have popped right out of the earth like a jack-in-the-box.

The crew of the first FAV opened up immediately with automatic fire from the fifty-caliber MAG heavy machine guns mounted atop the roll bars of the vehicles. At the same time Sergeant Munnion Higgs, team leader, keyed his lip mike and got off an alert to Blue Corner.

"We're taking fire," he reported to the main body of the force at the caravansary.

"I copy that, White Corner. We are making arrangements." The communications watch officer consulted the orbital imaging from an Iridium satellite equipped for infrared photoimaging of the earth below it. "I have one helo on you. Repeat, only one helo."

"Affirmative," Higgs replied. "One—"

The transmission was abruptly cut off.

The satellite imaging was technically real-time, but in fact it was near real-time; there was a two-to-three-second delay in the video feed.

Two seconds after Higgs's voice stopped in midsentence, the watch officer saw a bright flash of light and a boiling fireball that ballooned high off the desert floor, all of it captured in the blacks, whites, and grayscales of thermal imaging sensors. The FAV was gone from view. It had been disintegrated by a rocket strike from the Hip.

Fragments of the disintegrated vehicle and the mangled human remains of the patrol lay burning in scattered heaps across a fifty-foot blast radius. Above the shattered, incinerated flesh and metal hovered the Mi-8. The watch officer stared in helpless shock into the screen showing satellite imaging as the helo rose and darted off toward the west, leaving the zone of destruction devoid of any living thing.

"Goddammit," Mitchell cursed as Arbatov looked on

and shook his head. Those men had been friends and comrades, closer in many ways even than family. Now they were gone, their lives snuffed out in an instant of contact with the remorseless certainties of pushbutton warfare.

Mitchell heard a beep in his communicator headset. The Hawkman's face appeared in a window of the global-mobile field unit's LCD screen. By now the team had nicknamed him "God" from the way he kept watch on them all this time.

"I saw what happened on satellite feed, and I'm sorry about it," the Hawkman said, "but there's more shit on the way. Take a look."

Back at 11th Recon, the Hawkman moved a mouse cursor and clicked on one of the radio buttons above his windowed screen, duplicating the image on the remote unit several thousand kilometers away in the Iranian Dasht. The window that popped into being depicted a radar image from a Rhyolite satellite in low earth orbit. The Rhyolite had only minutes before reached an orbital trajectory that put it over most of northern Iran.

The Rhyolite's synthetic aperture radar or SAR is of photographic quality. Mitchell and Arbatov could clearly discern the wing of heavily armed Hips flying out from al-Munir Airbase about two hundred klicks southward, while armor and infantry was mobilized from local garrisons in the desert. Waves of hunters were spreading out toward them, and contact was inevitable.

"Wait one," Mitchell told the Hawkman as the Russian communications officer gestured for him and Arbatov to come over to his position. With Arbatov translating for Mitchell, the comms operator informed them that the Antonov An-72 "Coaler" medium-range STOL—or short takeoff and landing—transport was at an estimated range from their position of 620 kilometers, which would give it an ETA of two A.M. local time, depending on the RV zone selected.

The fusion cell's two leaders consulted their tactical maps and checked their watches. A single rendezvous point, given any chance of taking down the aircraft at the culvert with enough time to spare for a getaway, presented itself. The two-lane blacktop highway adjacent to the culvert could also be used as a landing zone for the cell's Antonov transport back into C.I.S. airspace. Alternatively, the Antonov could also land on the flat desert, if the terrain were properly cleared and marked with chemlights. The aircraft was built for rough-field capability and short takeoffs that other planes in its class, including the American C-135 Galaxy, would have a hard time handling.

Arbatov relayed the RV point's map grid coordinates to the comms operator and he transmitted it to the Antonov's crew. The decision whether to use the highway or the desert as a landing site would be put off until a few minutes before landing and depend on the tactical picture at that time. Otherwise, the plane was on schedule.

The cell's travel arrangements out of Iran having been taken care of, Mitchell turned back to TRAVLER's display screen, where the Hawkman was waiting for his feedback.

"While you were away . . . I worked up a rough plan for getting to the MFI," the Hawkman said. "Check it out."

The screen now displayed a color map of the surrounding terrain with a projected line of advance toward the Antonov's landing zone boxed in green. The threat envelopes of helos and Iranian ground forces were represented by icons of varying shapes denoting aircraft and ground vehicles. The path to the LZ wound and snaked between the threat balloons, changing position as the balloons marched across the desert terrain.

"As you can see, I project about an hour's ETA to the culvert if you move out now," the Hawkman summed up. "But I mean *now* like in *yesterday, capisce?*"

Mitchell and Arbatov studied the picture. What could they say? God had spoken.

Twenty-Two
Introductions Are Made

Gustavsen had done it with time to spare.

At five hundred forty hours, zulu, SSBN *Teaneck* reached her assigned station coordinates, having completed the more than thousand-kilometer passage in just under twenty-three hours. Maybe not a record for the Navy, but a record for Gustavsen's boat for sure.

Cruising at periscope depth, *Teaneck* was now making a leisurely seven knots. Before surfacing, its skipper and crew had run through a precautionary checklist of procedures to scan for hostile, and potentially hostile, underwater and surface sonar contacts. Even commercial vessels posed grave dangers. Since the sub had little positive buoyancy, being rammed by a large surface ship could break her up and quickly send her to the bottom.

In her combat information center or CIC, the electronic environment in the air above the sub was scanned for traffic that might present a threat. Then Gustavsen raised the periscope mast and made a sweep of the surface. Only after the skipper had visual confirmation of the absence of surface threats from three full periscope circuits, did he give the order to surface.

While the sub proceeded on its course, encrypted satcom transmissions from one of the array of FLTSATCOM satellites in geosynchronous earth orbit was beaming telemetry into the *Teaneck*'s BSY-1 weapons control system. Under the watchful eye of the boat's chief torpedoman, the coded signals were downloading updated targeting data into the electronic guidance systems of six of the twelve Tomahawk Block III cruise missiles that the *Teaneck* carried in vertical launch tubes arrayed along its hull.

BSY-1's decryption processors decoded the telemetry into trajectory information that would enable the Tomahawks to fly stealthy overland routes into Iran to destroy the missiles on their launchers. The missiles would rely on their TERCOM and DSMAC navigational systems to reach their destinations. Using high-speed digital communications, the entire update would require less than fifteen minutes at periscope depth, yet Gustavsen counted every minute that passed.

He knew how vulnerable his boat was near the surface, and how little it would take to sink her. The Iranian navy, or IRIN, was perhaps the best equipped in the Gulf, and his latest situation reports had shown that IRIN surface vessels and subs were heavily patrolling the sea lanes.

Gustavsen's worst worry were the Kilo-class diesel-electric boats that the Iranians had bought from the C.I.S. The subs were arguably the best nonnuclear boats in the world. They were fast, stealthy (their hulls were lined with sonar-absorbent anechoic rubber tiles), and formidably armed. They had damn good sonar, too. Gustavsen knew he would have to be ready to deal with them once inside the Gulf—evade them if he could, kill them if that's what it came to.

Mounted on five surviving FAVs, the Delta-Spetsnaz fusion cell made for its rally point through the cold desert night. To preserve stealth, the headlights of the FAVs were damped and none but essential communications between crew personnel were permitted.

All instrumentation controls, including buttons, switches, and dials, were lit by a dim blue-green electro-luminescent glow. Invisible to distant observers, it was readily seen by passengers wearing night-vision goggles or NVGs. All members of the fusion cell were equipped with NVGs using advanced GEN-III light-amplification tubes.

A TRAVLER mobile terminal secured to each vehicle was uplinked to an array of satellites that constantly updated navigational data. These data were fused in a multispectral display that showed the team's projected safe route toward the RV point superimposed over a moving map display.

Along the line of advance, which shifted somewhat as TRAVLER updated the route with minor course corrections, line-of-sight data, such as GPS waypoints, elapsed time to RV, and time till daybreak, were also displayed in the form of numerical readouts.

The scheduled route was navigated without incident. A little before daybreak, the fusion cell had reached its rally point at Gur Qudair and was within unaided visual range of the culvert.

A high-low warble preceded the Hawkman's voice in Mitchell's earbud.

"I have the plane on my screen again," he said. "I can see a piece of the tail assembly jutting out from beneath one of the overpasses about a half klick to your left. The walls are steep, but if you jog right a tad, you'll reach some kind of access or maintenance ramp."

The Hawkman threw the revised projected path on the TRAVLER display in red, to overlay the green wire-grid diagram of the original route of advance.

"Roger, I copy that," Mitchell said back. He informed his men via the lightweight headsets the team wore that they were following the course update.

Under fifteen minutes later the cell reached the access gradient that sloped away from the desert roadbed. This was a ramp that graded down to the poured concrete floor of the culvert. Mitchell's FAV took the point, with three of the other five dune buggies rolling down the incline after it. A perimeter security detail was left on the flanks of the culvert to scout for trouble.

As the lead vehicle rolled slowly down the wet, muddy centerline of the concrete-walled ditch, they quickly spotted the HET with the aircraft strapped to its back. The cell quickly dismounted its vehicles and fanned out across the middle of the trough, weapons kept at the ready, eyes alert.

"Maggard, sitrep." Mitchell asked the scout team leader over headset comms. "Any action up top?"

"Negative. Lizards are fucking the snakes. That's all."

"Don't ever teach biology, Maggard," Mitchell told the sergeant. "Sitrep in five."

"Gotcha, boss."

The cell element at the bottom immediately got to work checking out the aircraft and searching for the pilot, who hadn't put in an appearance and was nowhere to be seen.

"Over here," Mitchell heard in his headphone while Arbatov heard the same in Russian from one of his Spetsnaz.

They ran toward a corner of the culvert where the cell's Russian medical officer was ministering to a prone man. Mitchell listened to the byplay in Russian between the doctor—he was a fully trained physician, not a corpsman—and the man on the culvert floor.

"This our pilot?" asked Mitchell.

"Yes," said the doctor, switching to English. "His name is Petrov."

Mitchell looked down at the injured Russian, and then at the HET with its ungainly cargo.

"He loaded the plane on that flatbed and got it down here all by himself?" Mitchell asked.

"Yes," translated the doctor. "And he says he would have tried to fly it out, too, had he not been poisoned by the scorpion's sting while he slept."

"Tell him he's nuts, but he's a hero," Mitchell said, adding, "and that we'll be taking him out with us."

"He's also lucky the scorpions in this desert have weak venom," the doctor added. "A North African scorpion would have finished him."

Mitchell left the doctor to his patient and walked over to the HET, where Arbatov was supervising the demolition of the aircraft. Plastic explosive, det cord, and electronic timers were being unshipped by cell personnel working all around the HET.

"Maggard, sitrep," Mitchell said into his lipmike.

"All is cool, boss. Was just about to call you."

"In five, Maggard."

"Yo, boss. Five."

Arbatov hailed Mitchell over.

"We can have the plane done in ten minutes. We'll set it for remote detonation. We can blow it up as the Antonovs land, with a five-minute delay as a fail-safe in case it doesn't take."

Mitchell regarded the stealth fighter and the large flatbed truck.

"That'll about do it," he agreed.

"Boss, the pilot wants to tell you something," one of the American personnel said in Mitchell's earbud.

"Be right there."

Arbatov came along, too. It turned out that Petrov was better now. Moreover, he felt well enough to finish what he had come to the culvert to do in the first place.

"I can fly this plane out of here," he told them. "It's got enough fuel to make the trip back. I'm well enough."

Petrov explained that he had checked the plane out. There had been problems with the inertial navigation system that he'd first attributed to tampering by the Iranians, but later discovered were due only to a loose integrated circuit chip on one of the controller boards. The plane worked perfectly. He could make it.

"No can do," Mitchell said. "We can't take the risk. That plane's a shit magnet."

Arbatov agreed. It was better to blow the stealth aircraft

on the ground than risk an attempt at flying it out. Too much bad luck had attended the flight of this particular plane, and soldiers could be superstitious, especially of any man, unit, or piece of equipment that seemed to have acted as a lightning rod for trouble. To the cell's leaders, if not Petrov, this plane had brought trouble in spades. Besides, they had their orders—blow the plane and get out.

The demolition prep work continued.

Barak's team spotted the cell's security detail on the perimeter of the culvert long before they were aware of the Israeli commando unit's presence. In part, it was because luck happened to be on Barak's side.

The Rhyolite had since moved out of position and they were in a transmission gap between it and the Keyhole that was moving into an overhead surveillance window as they approached. Trained to move soundlessly across the desert's surface, a detachment left the BTR with orders to kill only if necessary and to disarm if possible.

The watch detail's first intimation that they were in trouble came when they felt the barrels of captured Iranian AKS autorifles jammed against the sides of their heads. The detachment was quickly subdued with cable ties and made to lie facedown on the ground under armed guard.

With the cell's ground-level security screen down, the main body of the Israeli team rappelled down the sides of the culvert, avoiding the ramp that they suspected the fusion cell had used, and possibly mined with claymores. They reached their target just as the demo charges around Shadow One were being armed.

Barak, preparing to follow them to the channel floor, took the headset from one of the captured cell members. He heard a voice speak faintly from it.

"Maggard, sitrep," Barak now heard the voice say clearly, as he placed it over his head.

The double click over Barak's handheld radio transceiver was the signal for the BTR crew to turn its powerful hundred-kilowatt spotlight down into the culvert. Caught unaware, the light blinded the fusion-cell personnel, who were quickly herded into a compact unit by Barak's crew already inside the culvert. Most were no longer wearing NVGs, but those who did experienced severe blooming effects when the light came on. By the time their vision had adjusted, the surprised soldiers were prisoners, and Barak's technical people were going over the aircraft.

"Let me introduce myself," Barak announced, and proceeded to do just that, informing his captives of how he had been fully briefed on their mission and instructed by the Israeli prime minister on behalf of the U.S. and C.I.S. to offer the fusion cell every assistance possible.

"But," Barak added, a harlequin's smile contorting his damaged face as he lit a cigarette and swept his eyes across the faces of the cell members, "I don't give a crap about the prime minister or anybody else, including the great nations you represent. I care only about number one." He jabbed a thumb at his chest. "And I mean to have this plane if I can, gentlemen. It will make me rich."

Barak called out to his technical crew.

"What's her condition?"

"She's flyable," he was told. "All systems check out. All we have to do is drive this HET onto the roadbed, winch the stealth onto the highway, and take off. There's enough fuel to cross the border."

Barak nodded, understanding the reference to crossing the border to mean the Israeli border, with the added implication that there would be sufficient fuel reserves to enable the aircraft to land on the many kilometers of fenced-off Negev land owned by Assaf Gilad.

Barak still had the long-range burst transmitter that Gilad had given him. He could send a satcom message with reasonable security once the plane was airborne. Gilad would have an airstrip lit by infrared landing lights ready. It could be done.

"Chayim," Barak called out to another of his technical officers, who was punching the keys on one of the mobile

TRAVLER terminals, "what can you tell me about this contraption?"

"I would call this device a high-bit-rate, point-to-point, wireless multibandwidth link with multihop capability," the team's technical officer answered.

"You would call it that, eh?"

"Yes, I would," Chayim affirmed smugly.

"Then I would call you a putz with an enlarged vocabulary," Barak answered. "In plain Hebrew, what is this fucking thing?"

"It's a sophisticated communications and navigational computer," a chastened Chayim answered. "We're working on something like it."

"And what does this contraption tell you?"

"Something is on the way," Chayim reported, working TRAVLER's integrated mouse and clicking at the keys, his eyes on the screen. "I think . . . yes, it's a transport, a Russian transport . . . ETA less than one half hour."

"Then we'd better move fast," Barak declared.

"You're the one who gives the orders," Chayim replied testily.

Barak turned. He issued instructions to his crew to dismantle the demo charges around Shadow One and roll the HET up the ramp to the highway above.

Twenty-Three
A Takeoff Run

A warble in the earphone of the Antonov pilot's helmet radio preceded a secure transmission from the operation's command post in Kuwait.

"One-Zero-Foxtail to Big Bear. Do you copy?"

"Affirmative, One-Zero-Foxtail. What can I do for you?"

"There has been a change in plans. Your LZ has been moved to map references seven-zero-three-dash-four-zero,-slash-zero-niner-zero-dash-five-zero-six. That is a section of Highway 32 running north-south about thirty kilometers from your original LZ."

"Wait one, please," the pilot said into his helmet mike.

The Antonov's navigator had already entered the map reference coordinates into the aircraft's navigational computer and was now consulting a printed map of northern Iran that was propped open in front of him.

"I have it," he told the pilot over the aircraft interphone. "A level stretch of roadway. Straight as a damned ruler."

"Can we land on it?"

"I suppose we'll be finding out, Fedor."

The pilot keyed his throat mike and said back to the distant command post, "That's affirm on the revised LZ. We copy the nav update. Estimate time to the LZ at approximately fifteen minutes. Advise that traffic on the highway could present a problem on landing."

"Affirmative. Forces on the ground will be advised. Good luck."

The pilot broke squelch and executed a thirty-degree turn. The new heading put the Antonov on a course for the revised LZ.

"What do you make of that?" he asked the copilot.

"What do I make of it?" he repeated. "I suppose we'll find out soon enough, Fedor."

"Is that all you can say, Nikolai?" asked the pilot.

"What, Fedor?"

"Never mind, Nikolai," the pilot replied, and flew his new black line.

A numerical readout showing zulu, or Greenwich Mean Time, flashed across the bottom of the god screen set up at 11th Recon. The view was downward, from a geostationary Keyhole satellite positioned over the Persian Gulf. Resolution was at a medium zoom factor, looking down through the thin, striated clouds meteorologists call nimbostratus, showing a three-hundred-mile swath of the earth's blue-green surface, with the Gulf glittering off to the extreme left and the Iranian coastal regions occupying the center of the picture.

The Hawkman's gray eyes were fixed on the god screen as he munched honey-roasted peanuts from a cellophane bag and sipped at a Diet Pepsi through a striped plastic straw.

"Bingo," he said. "Make that mah-jongg."

Suddenly the bulbous forward assembly of Tier III Plus popped into view from high on the left, soon followed by the razor-shaped, swept-back wings, and aft section of the reconnaissance drone. The second, armed version of Global Hawk that had lifted off some ten hours before had just been acquired by the overhead surveillance platform.

Craning back in his chair, the Hawkman emptied the last of his peanuts into his mouth and chucked the balled-up bag into a nearby trash receptacle, one that had been steadily gathering an assortment of other junk-food packaging and dented aluminum soda cans over the last several hours. He then proceeded to keystroke data into the keyboard resting on his lap as he propped his sneakered feet up on the edge of the trestle table piled with equipment. The commands he'd entered had just told the Keyhole to begin tracking Tier III Plus and change to a higher magnification setting.

The computer had calculated an estimated time of arrival to the attack coordinates of about twenty minutes. While Global Hawk was en route, the Hawkman deflowered another bag of honey-roasted nuts and ran a diagnostic check on the flying arsenal's weapons systems. It never hurt to be careful. And how come you never got a flex-o-straw with a can of soda anymore?

They had rolled the HET onto the tarmac, parked the lumbering metal brontosaur, and extended the four stabilizing pylons on the vehicle's sides to keep it steady during the off-loading process. Barak supervised the work crew, looking on and issuing orders while Shadow One was stripped of its tarp coverings and its tie-downs, then slowly and carefully winched off the back end of the low-rise flatbed.

After all three landing gear were secure on the tarmac, the HET was driven a few meters down the highway and ditched on the side of the road. The MFI now stood on its own like a newborn black monster insect, drinking in the darkness that was its natural element. The Israelis had cheered spontaneously, and Barak had permitted them a moment of jubilation, despite the fact that sound carried far and clearly in the desert, and Iranian forces might be in the vicinity. Yet, if ever there was a moment to break the rules, this was it.

By the spectral light cast by vehicle-mounted spotlights and headlamps, Barak watched the ground crew maneuver the aircraft onto the blacktop and disengage the HET's motorized winch cable from the tie-downs that made the tarp fast around the plane. Once these were gone, Barak studied the plane for a moment, drinking in the stark black beauty of its angular airframe.

A great prize had come into their possession, of this there was no doubt. Barak's cut of the plane's realized value, once it was safely back in Israel and in the hands of Gilad's affiliates in the defense industry, would amount to millions of dollars. He could retire for life on the proceeds of this one deal alone.

Each of the plane's subsystems was, almost literally, worth its weight in gold. The advanced stealth and avionics technologies could be back-engineered and repackaged in a variety of new ways, then sold to various global clients for a huge return on the original investment. For Raful Barak, the term "black gold" had just taken on an entirely new meaning.

The Old Man in the Negev would fix the political end of things. He'd always managed to succeed at this in the past.

Gilad was a survivor of three regional wars and scores of political battles. He had come through the War for Independence, the Six Day War, and the war in Lebanon with few physical injuries. His worst defeat was at the hands of his friend and political mentor Menachem Begin, who had been in on the frame for the Sabra and Shatilla massacres that had blackened Gilad's name.

But the wily old campaigner had outlived Begin, as he had survived so much else. Barak had no doubt that Gilad would find creative ways to turn this operation into something that had never happened.

"Zamir," Barak called out as his thoughts returned to the present. He gestured at one of his men who had climbed into Petrov's flight suit on Barak's orders while the stealth was being off-loaded from the HET.

"Can you do this?" Barak asked, his eyes on the plane as the soldier came over.

"*Magneev*—no problem," Zamir told him. "Stop worrying, Raful. I've already told you three times I can handle this aircraft." He clapped his hand on Barak's shoulder.

"If I don't worry, who will?" Barak shot back.

"My mother in Tel Aviv," Zamir said. "She worries enough for all of us."

Despite the tension, both men laughed at the crack.

The Israeli pilot was the veteran of numerous air combat missions, overt and covert. He had participated in the air war over Lebanon, which so far holds the record for the biggest aerial dogfight in air-warfare history.

"I've talked with the Russian pilot," Zamir explained. "It will be simple. There should by rights be an auxiliary-power supply unit hooked up to the aircraft prior to takeoff, but this can be done without. The electrical system seems fully stoked."

Zamir Amroni had retired with an Israeli air-force colonel's full pension, but it had not been enough to pay his gambling debts, alimony, and the lavish lifestyle to which he had become addicted during his years at the top.

"Let me know when you're ready to take off," Barak told him.

Amroni nodded and loped off toward the plane. Moments later he had undogged the canopy and climbed into the cockpit, which was soon illuminated by the soft blue glow of the instrumentation console. Barak smoked a Marlboro and watched Amroni as he began running down a preflight checklist of all systems. The whine of electrical systems and turbines was soon bansheeing through the desert night. *Not good, all that noise,* Barak thought. *But it can't be helped.*

Barak turned away from the plane and flicked his cigarette into the darkness amid a brief spray of orange sparks. His glance now fell on the captive members of the U.S.–Soviet fusion cell.

Now to other matters, he thought. His lighter flared, and he soon dragged hard on a fresh smoke.

Colonel Ghazbanpour removed his glasses and rubbed his burning eyes and the pinched bridge of his aquiline Persian nose. He glanced at his wristwatch. It was one hundred twenty hours—again. He had been awake for almost four straight days, grabbing fitful snatches of sleep on the wobbly cot in his cramped office. He couldn't go on this way much longer. He would need a few hours of real sleep, in a real bed soon, or he would be incapable of thinking clearly.

But he could not yet afford himself this luxury. As long as the plane remained out there—Ghazbanpour replaced his glasses and stared at the wall map—likely somewhere in the Dasht, he had to remain awake, had to stay in constant touch with his forces on the ground. The troops were well trained and many were dedicated, but he had no illusions about their capabilities, especially in the face of a new commando offensive to retake the plane.

Where had it gone? Where? The desert was a big place, true. Yet the aircraft had simply disappeared, as thoroughly as if the ground had opened up and swallowed it. It had never crossed the border. Even a stealth could not have slipped past the alert following the Russian's escape. Of course, he thought, there was the story of a derailed diesel locomotive that had been buried in the Dasht, hidden from the eyes of the shah, who was arriving for an inspection tour of a new railway line. But it had taken a full crew with a backhoe to accomplish this feat.

Ghazbanpour turned from the map and reached for the pitcher of ice water on his desk. Suddenly his mind fell into sync, and he saw a connection that had escaped him before. His head jerked back to the map. This time the dead eyes were alive, the sleep-hungering mind keen and alert from a quickening rush of adrenaline.

He stared at the water, and then at the map.

"As if the earth had swallowed it . . . *swallowed* it . . ." he muttered.

Yes, of course. That was it. Had to be. Everything had suddenly crystallized and become whole, where before there were only pieces. Amazing how that happened under pressure sometimes.

The culvert system. Large and deep enough and . . . what else? Something in the back of his mind still gnawed at him.

Setting down the pitcher, Ghazbanpour was rifling through sheaves of intelligence reports strewing his desk, and—yes! There it was. He pulled a page from the stack of Teletypes and faxes that had come in since the night the plane had been retaken by the escaped Russian pilot.

The report cited a missing trailer truck, one used to haul heavy equipment over great distances. In this case it had been a construction crane that had gone to a building site in Tehran. Again Ghazbanpour consulted his wall map. He saw that the truck could indeed have passed close to the culvert on its route through the Gur Qudair. Any truck that could have hauled such a huge piece of equipment could also easily accommodate a fighter plane.

But the Gur Qudair was no-man's-land. The last place on earth anyone would willingly venture. Yet such a place was the perfect earth for foxes. And this pilot had been a fox, hadn't he? One being chased by hounds, in fact.

Ghazbanpour stared into the blackness outside the window of his office. The full moon shone with a limpid light, but it had sunk lower in the sky since he had last looked. Time was fast running out. The colonel picked up the phone and dialed his adjutant, ordering a helicopter readied for immediate dust-off. This time he would personally lead the operation. There would be no more foul-ups. The plane was hidden in that culvert. He would stake his life on it!

The second Global Hawk variant, Tier III Plus, had reached its operational envelope sixty thousand feet above the northeastern desert of Iran. Its onboard processor activated the array of imaging sensors located on the underside of its forward fuselage, and these shifted into spot scanning mode. Within a matter of seconds the imaging array had detected the movement of an Iranian armored column in the direction of the culvert.

The Hawkman had by now donned his HMD and force-feedback gloves and was in control of the second Hawk. Minutes later the robot aircraft was within sensor range of the culvert and the Hawkman had a good picture of what was taking place on the ground.

He could clearly see the stealth plane being prepared for takeoff. Its hot engines, cowled and baffled as they were, gave off a telltale IR signature and its avionic systems were emitting tempest energies, the leakage of radio emissions from energized electronic circuitry that produced a signature as distinct as that of other forms of radiant energy, such as heat or light.

The Hawkman could also see something still more disquieting. The fusion cell was being held captive by an armed commando force. He would have to do something about that. Moving his hands across a virtual control panel that occupied a corner of his visual field, the Hawkman dragged the gun-shaped icon across the screen, activating the weapons package of the Hawk.

Barak faced Mitchell and Arbatov across the tarmac. They, along with the plane, had been brought from the culvert to the level of the highway above. In a pool of light cast by magnesium arc lamps mounted on the captured FAVs, he sized up both men, pondering their fates. There was, of course, only one way to end this, and no reason whatever to hesitate.

The two commando leaders had to be taken out. This went for the entire fusion cell, for that matter. It would not do to have any witnesses to what was about to take place.

"We seem to have come to the end of the road, literally and figuratively," Barak told the American and the Russian. "The plane is in my hands and my pilot is about to fly it out to safety. Your involvement leaves me with a problem. But also, I think, with an opportunity."

The short-barreled AKS assault rifle in the Israeli's grip was locked and loaded with a thirty-round magazine jacked into its receiver. Barak held the rifle casually in his right hand, its muzzle pointing at the ground. But his index finger was lightly curled around the trigger, and when he brought the AKS up and into play, he could squeeze off a burst in a fraction of a second.

"You see," he went on, "a few American and Russian corpses left behind after the plane takes off could prove advantageous. They might divert attention from the involvement of, shall we say, a 'third force.'"

Barak paused and studied the faces of the men he was about to shoot down at point-blank range. "Yes, that's how we'll do it."

He jerked the rifle up from his hip, leveling its business end at his captives. As always, Barak wore a sardonic smile frozen on his face. This time, though, the graveyard grin was genuine.

"Like, extreme close-up!"

The Hawkman zoomed in the video on three figures near the fringes of the activity on the road. At a magnification factor of three hundred, the image resolved into a man in Pasdaran-issue olive-drab fatigues and red beret facing two other men in NATO chocolate-chips BDUs. The man in ODs held a baby Kalashnikov. The other two were unarmed.

"Got a bad moon rising here," the Hawkman said, enlarging the image still further so he could get a clear shot of their faces.

Once he had them, the Hawkman used a scissor tool to outline each face and dragged the images into the database icon on the floating palette bar. Seconds later the computer gave him two matches out of three: the dude with the rifle was unknown, but the other two were the fusion-cell commanders, Mitchell and Arbatov.

Suddenly the unidentified man in the Iranian ODs raised his weapon. The Hawkman knew he'd fire in a split instant.

"Bummer," he said to himself, pushing a mouse cursor across the display.

The men stood too close together to target any of them accurately by one of the kinetic energy rounds that the Hawk fired, but the Hawkman could come pretty close. He had already put Tier III Plus into a steep dive with its thermal gun cameras trained on the area in focus. Before the shooter had a chance to pop some caps, the Hawkman triggered a salvo of kinetic-energy fléchettes from the swooping Hawk's electromagnetic coil gun.

The burst struck the edge of the blacktop close to the APC. The three-inch darts of depleted uranium alloyed with tungsten contained no explosive, but the sheer velocity released tremendous energies on impact. The fléchettes tore sizable chunks out of the roadbed and produced a sound similar to that of a mortar round hitting.

"Yeah, we bad," shouted the Hawkman. "We baddddd!"

Tier III Plus now swung around for a second attack run, this time tearing into the machine gunner atop the APC and ripping off half the top of the vehicle, which quickly exploded and burst into a fireball.

The Hawkman circled his bird around one more time and came in for another final strafing run. Then he got the hell out of there. He had other things to do. A high-low warble had sounded in his ear. The Antonov was getting in touch. The transport was about to commence its approach and landing on the highway.

Teaneck was less than three nautical miles to her Tomahawk launch coordinates when she caught a whiff of trouble.

"Skipper, I have two transient contacts at bearing zero-seven-six-zero and zero-seven-eight-five," the chief sonarman called out to the helm. "Cavitation noises . . . I make them Kilo boats. Textbook sonar signatures."

Gustavsen didn't want a fight, and though he could outrun the Kilos, he could well find himself flying into the teeth of the Iranian navy by doing so.

If possible, he would opt to hide from the Kilos. Their sonar suite was good, he knew, but not as good as all that, and the *Teaneck* had a lot of stealth technology—including sonar-absorbent anechoic tiles that lined her hull—built into her design. Plus, his charts told him that the thermal makeup of the Gulf waters and the topography of its floor would help to conceal his boat from sonar detection if he played his cards right.

"Full stop," Gustavsen said to his exec, who relayed the orders to the chief diving officer, who in turn commanded his planesmen. The crisp, clear chain of spoken commands left no room for misinterpretation during combat. The *Teaneck* stopped dead in the water, her propeller still.

The crew in the control room was silent. Minutes ticked by as the sonarmen listened through their headphones and intently monitored the waterfall displays linked by high-speed computers to the sensitive hydrophones at bow and stern, including the new BQR-24 conformal array of hundreds of three-inch sensors that made up the sub's passive sonar sensor system.

"Contacts are moving off," the chief sonar operator reported after several minutes had passed. "I don't think they've seen us. Distance is increasing. Contacts have now passed beyond passive sonar range. We've lost them, Skipper."

Gustavsen hoped the sonar operator was right. He waited an extra five minutes to make sure neither of the Kilos had doubled back, then resumed *Teaneck*'s course to her missile launch point off the coast of Iran.

Twenty-Four
Outbreak of Peace

Mitchell prepared himself. He knew he was about to take a burst in the heart. There would be a moment of pain, then some drifting, then a forever of nothing. He'd never let the idea that he might die in combat trouble him. It went with the territory. Mitchell was ready for it, when and if it came. He was ready for it now.

But when the explosions struck, it was not the cycling of automatic fire that Mitchell heard. It was the lightning crack of high explosive. Gouts of rock fragments, geysers of sand, and spouts of upflung asphalt rubble erupted in all directions. It seemed like somebody was dropping mortar rounds on his position, but that wasn't exactly right, either.

They definitely weren't being shelled. There was no telltale ripping-silk sound of inbound mortar or artillery rounds, no acrid stink of cordite. They had certainly come under attack. But from where? And from what?

Barak had turned, too, as alarmed and as perplexed as

Mitchell and Arbatov beside him. Barak also asked himself the same questions as Mitchell. More important from Mitchell's standpoint was that the barrel of the Israeli's AKS was now temporarily turned away from himself and the Russian.

Without hesitation both men jumped Barak, but the Israeli was fast on his feet. He reacted like a cornered cougar, lashing out savagely with the weapon. A side slash of the AKS's buttstock to the side of Arbatov's head knocked him over, felling him like an axed tree. Barak spun on the follow-through and went for Mitchell, but before he could connect, Mitchell sidekicked him with a spinning geri that ripped the rifle from Barak's hands and sent it clattering to the sands.

The Israeli recovered quickly from the lightning foot blow. Now unarmed, he whipped around and delivered a flurry of karate-style front kicks that sent Mitchell dodging and ducking to avoid being tagged. The Egoz was a good fighter, strong and fast, sharp and cool. He would not go down easy, if at all, Mitchell knew. Closing with Barak, Mitchell blocked another flurry of kicks, and lunged at Barak with a series of hand blows using fists and elbows to the face and upper chest.

Both men were aware of more nearby explosions and the clamor of shouting and sporadic small arms fire. Glimpsed scenes of the firefight now taking place all around them reached them in a detached, abstract way as each man fought for survival. Mitchell and Barak were locked together in a death struggle, in a tunnel where time moved like burning magma. Neither had a decisive edge over his opponent, and a moment's lapse in concentration could translate into sudden death for either one of them.

Mitchell parried a series of kicks and closed-fist blows delivered by Barak with a flurry of blocks and kicks of his own, which sent the other man whirling backward. Then Barak's foot struck a rock and he lost his balance. Barak pitched sideways. A second later his own momentum had brought him down, and he hit the sand, sliding on his face. His head struck a sharp stone and blood spurted from a cut above his left eye.

Barak felt himself start to black out, but the dull glint of moonlight on gunmetal brought him back to his senses with a sudden rush of adrenaline. His dropped rifle, he saw, was only inches from his outstretched hand. A desperate lunge, and the gun was in his grasp once again.

Before Mitchell could rush him, Barak was back up on his feet, leveling the weapon into firing position from a half crouch.

Barak was breathing hard and blood streamed down his face from the deep cut above his left eye. But before pulling the trigger, he permitted himself a grin. All that mattered in the end was who came out on top. To a soldier, it was one of battle's timeless truths.

"You lose," Barak said, and pulled the bullpup's trigger, wasting no more time on banter. The air was suddenly rent by an earsplitting report.

The stricken man felt a hammer blow in his upper torso, was lifted off his feet, and fell to earth in a bloody sprawl. Half his right chest was suddenly gone, and in its place was a raw mass of butchered organ matter and gore-streaked blood.

Mitchell rose from the dust and ran over to where Barak lay in the shell hole blown by the Iranian mortar round that had landed within inches of the Israeli commando. Both men had heard the telltale whistling of the incoming round and Mitchell had dropped prone in a fast hunker. Nothing Barak could have done would have saved him. The round had had his name written on it. It had been almost a direct hit, with Barak standing right on the bull's-eye.

Amazingly, Barak was still alive, though Mitchell didn't need a medic to tell him that he wouldn't be for long. The Israeli's life was draining away, soaking into the dark, cold sands on which he'd fallen. Mitchell crouched beside the dying man, feeling bloody fingers pulling at his arm with demonic power.

Barak wanted to tell him something. His hand closed

on Mitchell's arm and gripped it with amazing pressure and force. Mitchell was irresistibly drawn down toward the face that was already somehow skeletal, as a death pallor spread across the gaunt features. Barak's thin lips moved and he tried to croak out his final words. He struggled with every last ounce of strength he possessed to mouth them . . . and ultimately he succeeded.

"Tizdayen . . ." was all Barak said.

Then he expired, his macabre harlequin smile still frozen on his cadaverous face. Peace, who didn't know Barak's native language, heard something that sounded like " 'tis dyin' " and wondered what the Israeli had meant. Some philosophical statement about death, maybe? Who knew?

But Mitchell had no time to reflect on this. He struggled to pry loose the fingers of the corpse that were locked like a vise of muscle and bone around his arm. He finally worked them loose and struggled to his feet, Barak's dropped AKS cradled in a combat grip.

Standing, Peace tried to reorient himself to his immediate surroundings. How much time had passed since the moment before his imminent execution? It seemed like hours, but time telescopes in a fight.

Where was Arbatov? Mitchell caught sight of the Russian over by the stealth. He then recognized his exec, Sergeant Martinez, and called him over. Just then a mortar round came whistling in—this time it was unmistakable— and Mitchell went prone, crabbing in the sand. When he came back up, amid acrid cordite clouds and a fog of airborne dust particles lit by explosive flashes, Martinez was at his side.

"Taking mortar fire, boss, in case you didn't just figure that out yourself," Martinez explained. "An Iranian column's on the way in. We got aerial surveillance again, by the way."

"What about the Antonov?"

"ETA ten minutes, maybe less," Martinez answered. "Even money whether the Iranians beat the plane into the

LZ or whether it can't land because of the shelling. We're standing by, either way."

"What about the stealth?"

"Change of plan, boss," Martinez replied. "Arbatov wants to brief you. He's over by the aircraft right now."

Martinez added that "God" was back on the screen. He had sent down some thunderbolts in the nick of time. That had been the first "attack." The fléchettes explained what Mitchell had originally thought was a mortar strike. Using the diversion, the fusion cell had turned the tables on the rogue Israelis and a brief but intense firefight had ensued. The four Israeli survivors were now prisoners, but it had cost. There had been casualties on both sides.

Pausing to take cover as another Iranian mortar round whistled in and exploded with a loud *crump!* in a geyser of flame, noise, cordite stink, and choking desert dust, Mitchell made his way across the highway blacktop to where the Spetsnaz commander was speaking to a pilot wearing a flight suit.

This time it wasn't the Israeli pilot, but Vassily Petrov, who was suited up and ready to climb into the MFI's cockpit.

"Change in plans, my friend," Arbatov told Mitchell as soon as he was in earshot. "Petrov flies her out."

"Why not blow her up?" Petrov noted that Arbatov's head was bandaged and taped on one side, the gauze caked with dried blood. Barak had landed a solid shot.

"Too risky now," Arbatov answered with a shake of his head. "We have no time to guarantee that the charges will be properly placed. The Antonov is now minutes away. What happens if there's a foul-up?"

"Yeah, this has been one goat rope after another."

"*Da.* A real *pizdetz,* as we say; a flaming fuckup."

"What about the Hawk?"

"Our friend 'God' says he's out of lightning bolts for the moment," Arbatov replied. "Check for yourself if you've any doubts."

Arbatov nodded at one of his men, who handed Mitchell a wireless headset keyed to the TRAVLER ground station. A brief conversation with the Hawkman settled Mitchell's residual doubts. Mitchell signed off and turned back to Arbatov.

"You're right about that. He used up his ammo reserves pulling our asses out of a sling before."

"It doesn't matter," said Arbatov. "The Iranians seem to have loaded two new Addax missiles from their inventory in the stealth's missile bay. Petrov thinks they were about to make a test flight using live ordnance. We can use our newfound plane on our way out of this mess to ride the stagecoach, as you say."

"Ride shotgun," Mitchell corrected. "We'll have to—"

An earsplitting din drowned out his words. This time it wasn't another incoming mortar salvo. The roar belonged to the immense wing-mounted turbofans of the AN-72 Coaler as the huge transport plane appeared out of thin air like a flying mountain and approached for a landing, its mammoth engines whipping up a minisandstorm in the process.

The transport had its landing gear extended, but before the plane touched down, another mechanical scream split the night. This one was the sound of Shadow One's engines firing up to full power. Mitchell and virtually everyone else in the vicinity watched the black stealth plane begin to roll along the highway—which had been turned into a makeshift illuminated runway by the placement of chemlights along its flanks—picking up speed until it began to lift into the air. The stealth finally nosed up and disappeared into the night, its rectangular exhausts glowing with yellow-blue flame.

Once the plane was out of sight, the crew on the ground sprang into action. FAVs were driven off the roadbed, which was a simple task since the highway was no more than a layer of asphalt steamrolled across the flat pancake crust of the Dasht. The commandeered Iranian BTR was trundled out of the way while the HET was driven off the shoulder and onto the desert.

Now the Antonov touched down, its immense girth filling the highway as its outsized nose gear bit into the tarmac with a deafening screech. Then its rear landing gear and tail assembly descended to earth. The screaming engines changed pitch suddenly as the pilot applied reverse thrust, and the plane began rolling to a full stop. The aircraft was stationary no longer than a few seconds when the top of its rear fuselage canted upward on pneumatic actuators, exposing its yawning cargo bay to the night, wind, and clouds of blowing sand.

As the plane continued to roll slowly along the highway, the FAVs and men were hustled into the rear of the cargo area. The AN-72's pilots kept the plane's engines hot as more mortar rounds came whistling in and exploded with an earsplitting tumult, coming thicker and faster as the Iranian mechanized column advanced.

In a matter of minutes all personnel and vehicles were onboard the Antonov, and the pilot reapplied thrust, rolling forward along the blacktop with gathering speed. The assault transport aircraft was quickly airborne again, and flying eastward at its maximum speed and ceiling. By the time the advancing Iranian armored column reached the rally point, the LZ was stone-cold.

The MiG-29 Fulcrums were first-line fighters, and the best planes the Iranian air force had in its inventory. The Fulcrums' pilots were the cream of the Iranian top-gun academy. A sortie of two planes was scrambled and ordered to intercept the Antonov. They already had its rough heading and position punched into the MiGs' navigation computers.

Much faster than the transport, the agile, powerful fighter aircraft closed with the lumbering jet heavy-lifter before it had gone very far on its transit to the border.

"There she is." The flight leader heard his wingman's voice in his headset. "I have radar contact with the transport."

"I copy that," the flight leader said. "This should be child's play, but be careful—we don't know what we're up against. Missiles from standoff range."

"Come on, Nabil"—the wingman's voice came back in

his helmet radio—"we don't have to do that. Let's have some fun with that fucking dinosaur of a plane. We can fill her full of holes with our nose cannons and watch her break apart. With a missile kill it's a fireball and then— *poof!* That's it."

The flight leader considered a moment. He had not received any orders that would preclude simply strafing the transport. The Antonov was armed, of course, and it was equipped with antimissile countermeasures, but that would only put some more sport into the game.

Hell, why not? he thought. It would be good for his pilots' morale, instill more of a thirst for blood in them that might come in handy during a real dogfight, say with the Israelis or Americans one fine day.

"Okay, Ibrahim," he answered after a pause, "we'll have it your way. Gun cannons it is. But if there's any trouble, we'll finish her with missiles."

"Affirmative," the wingman answered, the relish in his voice plain to hear.

"Tracking radar emissions," the copilot of the Antonov announced as he scanned the symbols on his scope. "MiG-29 tracking radars. Six hundred meters and closing."

Now the pilot saw the threat symbols appear on his main scope. The Antonov's avionics suite came equipped with the best radars and antijamming and electronic countermeasures the Russians had available. The bogies were identified as MiG-29 fighters.

"Activate ECM," the pilot ordered.

"Activating countermeasures," he heard the copilot say.

Switches were flipped and dials turned on rack-mounted ECM black boxes. Podded transmitters on the underside of the plane emitted intense signal noise across multiple bandwidths, returning false radar echoes to the search and tracking modulators aboard the MiGs.

The countermeasures worked, but only temporarily.

"They're burning through our jamming," the copilot warned after a few minutes and several score more kilometers had passed.

"I'll try to ditch the bogies," the pilot said, and put the large plane through a series of jinks, dives, and S-turns in an effort to throw off the Fulcrums' tracking radars.

"Still closing, closing. Five hundred meters. Continuing to close," the copilot declared in stages. "Less than two hundred meters now . . . one hundred meters . . . still closing . . ."

"Why haven't they launched a bird?" the pilot wondered out loud.

"I don't know," the copilot replied. "There's nothing so far. No missile homing radar. No indication of a launch signature."

"Check your—"

A MiG suddenly burst into view from below, crossing directly in front of the AN-72's flight deck. The warplane did not fire, but the larger, slower transport aircraft was buffeted by a sudden, fierce shock wave. In a heartbeat, another MiG passed beneath the Antonov's underfuselage, so close to the plane's underside that the shock front of compressed air it generated at Mach one velocity almost sent the Antonov into a flameout.

"*Ebat-kopat!* The bastards are toying with us like cats with a fat mouse," the copilot cursed.

Suddenly another MiG appeared. For a fraction of an instant before they heard the telltale stuttering of the thirty-mm nose cannon, the Antonov crew saw the rotoring belches of yellow-white flame that indicated they were taking cannon fire. A heartbeat later they felt the thud of the armor-piercing rounds punching through the aircraft's thin metal skin.

Fire licked and smoke belched from the Antonov's control panel and bulkheads. The copilot jumped up and unclipped a fire extinguisher from one of the racks, spraying the panel where a section of gauges had shorted and burst into flame.

Suddenly the pilot noticed he'd been hit. Blood welled from his arm and his flight suit had begun to sop with it. The pilot called for a medic, and the cell's doctor rushed forward from the aft cabin with his first-aid kit and began to apply a sterile dressing. Suddenly another MiG appeared athwart the Antonov, and more bullets rotored out, stitching a line across the plane's underfuselage.

Now the AN-72's left engine was trailing smoke, and flames sporadically erupted from the damaged turbine nacelle. The system diagnostics readouts were flashing on the plane's instrument console, dire warnings appeared on all of the displays and readouts. It was clear to the aircrew that after another such salvo they would likely break apart.

But neither the crew of the Antonov, nor the sortie of MiGs that attacked the transport, was aware that twelve thousand feet above them, Shadow One's fire-control system had already made its final calculations on a solution for the two Addax air-to-air missiles the stealth carried, or that Petrov had opened the conformal ordnance bay to lower the missiles into firing position from beneath the belly of the stealth.

Roughly equivalent to the AIM-190X AMRAAM of the U.S. inventory, the Addaxes were heat-seeking missiles that were resistant to countermeasures, including flare and chaff clouds. Shadow One's fire-control system was capable of tracking nine targets simultaneously and plotting firing solutions on four of them.

The MiGs could not see the stealth on their radars, but scope icons had popped up telling them that they had been acquired by an unidentified aircraft. Petrov already had a firing solution on both Iranian fighters, but the planes were spaced too close to the Antonov to risk Shadow One's missiles breaking lock and striking the transport instead in error. Petrov kept his eyes on his scopes, waiting for his chance.

The minutes ticked by. And then his patience paid off. Petrov saw the transport begin to pull away from her attackers, yet the MiGs did not pursue. Petrov knew what was about to happen. The flight leader had called for missile strikes against the transport to finish her off. They had grown tired of their cat-and-mouse game and were about to loose the killing stroke. First the MiGs would deploy to standoff range. Then they would fire.

Petrov calculated the maximum time he could wait to launch his own birds against the distance the Antonov had gained on the MiGs, and watched the gap between the MiGs and the Antonov continue to widen. At the last possible moment before he judged the MiGs would fire, he pickled off the Addaxes, feeling the MFI shudder and restabilize as the missiles left their conformal racks and sped forward, their glowing exhausts shrinking to pinpricks in the night.

As the rounds disappeared, Petrov switched to his remote nose-camera scope that relayed real-time data from the missiles' warhead assemblies. The missiles could be set to auto or manually overridden. He had programmed them for auto but had flipped the protective shrouds off the lighted manual detonation buttons for each round. As his eyes scanned the realtime gun-camera feed, he was ready to press the buttons at any moment.

Petrov continued monitoring the video feed. The cluster of MiGs grew in his scope until they seemed to be right on top of him. By this time the two Iranian fighters' own threat radars had picked up the incoming missile rounds. But it was now too late.

At the instant the MiGs took evasive action, Petrov pushed the remote detonate button to the side of the main scope and a bright flash filled the thermal imaging window on the stealth's console display. Outside Shadow One's cockpit canopy window, multiple detonations pulsed in the heavens, lighting up the black sky for microinstants with throbbing, booming fireballs and pinwheels as the sortie of MiG-29 Fulcrums exploded into supernovas of vaporized metal, spinning debris, and burning fuel.

Moments later the night sky was cleared of MiGs. Petrov applied full thrust and shot ahead of the Antonov. As he passed it, letting it have a taste of his own pressure wave, he jinked Shadow One's wings back and forth in a farewell salute.

The AN-72's pilot and copilot saw the MFI through their flight-deck windows, and then the stealth plane was gone, becoming invisible to their eyes and their radars. This time, Petrov told himself, there would be no more mishaps. If nothing else, God and the dues he had paid would see to that. He would return to Vladivostok again, he knew this in his marrow. His dream had not lied. He would fly to freedom, just as it had foretold.

Petrov didn't know it, but "God" was watching him. The Hawkman had been cruising his bird high above the action. At seventy thousand feet, he had a good view not only of the situation in the air, but of the situation on the ground as well.

He had loitered the Hawk until the Antonov had gotten clear of Dasht airspace and was flying over the eastern mountain range, making fast for the border, satisfied that nothing else was in the air that could find it or harm it on its way back into the Caucasus.

On his own way home, the Hawkman couldn't resist dropping down to fifty thousand feet and getting some close-up imagery of the Iranian armor on the ground. Apparently there was some new stuff in the mix of tanks and APCs that the Pentagon would want to know about— looked Chinese, but the analysts would figure out the nuts and bolts. Now the Hawk was at the top of its envelope, cruising westward at its flight ceiling of eighty thousand feet. The Hawkman slipped off his HMD and pulled off his force-feedback gloves. Autopilot could take his bird the rest of the way.

It was time to change the music.

"Hendrix at Woodstock," he called out. As he reached for the last cold soda can in the cooler nearby, the strains of an electrified fuzz guitar playing "The Star-Spangled Banner" began to blare from the boombox.

"Louder, man," he said, taking a slug and working the stereo remote.

"Much louder."

Tomahawk launch depth was fifteen meters, a little below periscope depth. With the sub stopped dead, Gustavsen scanned his final orders from CINCLANTFLT. The launch order was still a go. It was time the fat lady sang.

"BSY-1 systems report full readiness. Targeting data are loaded. Ready for missile launch on your command," was the status report from the torpedo room.

"Open launch-capsule hatches one through six," Gustavsen said to his exec, who echoed the order to the torp room over the boat's interphone circuit.

"Launch-capsule hatches are open," the exec said back less than a minute later.

Now only a thin plastic membrane separated the missiles from the surrounding seawater, the pressurized atmosphere in the launch capsules preventing water pressure from flooding the tubes.

"Launch on my mark," Gustavsen said back to his exec. "Three, two, one—mark!"

"Launch the birds. Now, now, now!" the exec echoed to the chief torpedoman.

At the bottom of capsule one, an explosive charge detonated, thrusting the first Tomahawk through the membrane and catapulting it away from the launch tube. Under a second later, at approximately eight meters from the *Teaneck*'s hull, the missile's booster stage ignited, shotgunning it up through the surface and into the air, where its tail fins popped out to stabilize its upward flight.

The Tomahawk climbed to a 304-meter altitude, where its booster burned out and dropped away, and then the missile began its transition to level flight. Stub wings slid from grooves in the fuselage and a rear air scoop deployed, forcing air into the missile's turbofan engine, which spooled up and began to deliver thrust as the round went horizontal and began flying its programmed track.

Before the first Tomahawk had leveled off, the second cruise missile was repeating the initial phase of the firing sequence, roiling the water around *Teaneck* as it streaked toward the surface. In a blur of sound and fury, fire and steam, the sea above the submarine would erupt four more times, as *Teaneck* launched the rest of her missile load at her land-based targets.

As far as her skipper was concerned, he had just tele-graphed the boat's position to the entire Iranian navy. He would need all his skill and a mortgage on his luck to make it to the safety of the Arabian Sea, where the carrier battlegroup *Strickland* had steamed at flank speed to fore-stall action by the Iranian navy. Gustavsen made his chances as one in three of his crew surviving the next hour in the water. But anything was better than staying where he was currently.

"Diving Officer, make my depth sixty-five feet. Prepare to dive," Gustavsen ordered, and the command was ech-oed down the line.

Though their targets were a group of launchers clustered together, the Tomahawks did not fly identical tracks to reach them. To maximize their chances of survivability, and to confuse the tracking radars of Iranian early warning and SAM installations, each cruise was programmed to fly a slightly different, looping, snaking track to the target zone and to detonate at varying altitudes once there.

Guided to the shoreline by their inertial navigation sys-tems, the missiles switched on their TERCOM maps once they'd crossed the sea-land boundary of the Iranian lit-toral. Radar returns of the terrain below were digitized by onboard altimeters and compared against digital terrain maps stored in memory that were composed of grids of contoured squares.

From this first TERCOM map, the Tomahawks took their preliminary course readings and made initial correc-tions. Farther inland, TERCOM switched on to repeat this process over a series of increasingly smaller grids as the missiles flew their tracks, until each Tomahawk had ad-vanced to within a few kilometers of its designated target. At this point the DSMAC system switched to active mode to provide terminal guidance via infrared imaging of the terrain and landmarks below.

With a CEP or circular error probability assured to less than ten feet, all six Tomahawks reached their impact points within minutes of launch. Some missiles popped up from low-trajectory flight paths to explode in airbursts that hammered their target sets with concussive wavefronts and gouts of broiling flame. Others plowed straight into the missile launchers, detonating at the moment of impact. The net result was a firestorm so intense, as it fused metal and incinerated fissionable warhead materials, that the light could be seen and the sound could be heard as far inland as Tehran.

This time, nothing humanly possible had been left to chance.

Onboard the AN-72 Coaler, Mitchell went across to where one of his men stood guard over the sullen group of captive Israeli commandos. Mitchell suspected their ultimate fate would be repatriation to Israel, where they would either be put on trial to draw heat off other guilty parties too politically well connected to touch, or to simply fade into the woodwork. Right now, though, he had a question to ask of them. Peace had been turning over the words Barak had uttered just before he'd expired. Mitchell wondered what " 'tis dyin' " meant. With the fighting over, Barak's last words gnawed at him.

Mitchell could not get the look in the doomed man's eyes out of his mind. Could he have been asking him to pray for his eternal soul? he wondered. Barak had been an enemy. Yet Mitchell would still not feel right about denying him his last rites. Barak had been a soldier, and a brave one. Despite his twisted value system, there was a shared commonalty between them.

Since all of the Israelis spoke fairly good English, Mitchell had no trouble learning the answer. In fact, they were all too eager to tell him what he wanted to know.

"Tizdayen?" one of the prisoners replied, dragging on a cigarette, the price of his knowledge, and glancing over to the pile of zippered mortuary bags lashed down in a corner of the plane that contained their leader's mortal remains. "Ah yes, a very good Hebrew word.

"It's very simple, my American friend," he went on as smoke curled from his nostrils. "With his last breath, Raful was telling you something in Hebrew. He was telling you—*to go fuck yourself.*"

Gouts of pent-up laughter erupted from the throats of the captive Israelis. Somewhere, they all felt, Barak was laughing, too. To the surprise of all, the laughter proved infectious, and Mitchell, too, got caught up in it. Soon it had spread to the entire plane. The psychs had a name for it. They called it postcombat euphoria and both Mitchell and Arbatov knew what was happening.

But fuck it, they thought.

It was a gift.

"Bradley, are you there?"

"Yes, Scott."

"Bradley, can you still see the fires in the distance?"

"Scott, I can not only still see them, but I can still hear some secondary explosions, which, they tell me, are the result of ammunition depots blowing up in the wake of what was apparently a preemptive air strike by Tomahawk missiles on Iranian missile targets."

"Now, for the benefit of viewers who have recently tuned in, these are suspected to have been nuclear-tipped missiles, weren't they?"

"That's right, Scott. Pentagon spokesmen claim that a preemptive strike was launched just an hour ago to prevent Iran from firing those missiles on targets as far away as Turkey or Greece."

"Both members of NATO."

"That's right, Scott. The Iranians confirm that missile installations were hit, but deny that any of the missiles had nuclear capability or for that matter anything like the range which the Pentagon claims. They insist the missiles are for defense only."

"Okay, Bradley. We need to pause for a commercial break right now, but we'll return to you shortly, so please stay with us." The split screen dissolved and the camera pulled in close on the newsanchor's familiar, craggy face. "Again, for the benefit of those who have just tuned in, U.S. missiles have hit what are claimed to have been nu-

clear missile sites in Iran. All Iranian missiles are report-
edly destroyed. More when we come back in just a few
minutes with up-to-the-minute reporting on this breaking
news story."

The newsanchor held his expression steady as the camera stayed tight on his face. Two seconds later the television screens of millions of dinnertime viewers switched
to a multicolor animated logo that read TENSION IN THE
GULF. Drumrolls and brassy horns sounded in the background. Then a commercial for a new luxury sedan filled
the airwaves. For a few minutes more the world was safe
again, and business went on as usual.

If you enjoyed
SHADOW DOWN
then don't miss . . .

INVASION

by Eric L. Harry

*Available in paperback from Berkley Books.
Here is a sample of this explosive new novel . . .*

Prologue

How did it ever come to this? thought eighteen-year-old Pvt. Stephanie Roberts as she stared at the dusty roadblock that marked the new boundary carved into America.

Stephie, the youngest infantryman in the squad of nine and one of only two women, climbed aboard the truck. "I don't trust you," the hulking Animal said to her. At five-seven and 125 pounds, Stephie and her rifle were security for the lone machine gun attached to her squad. Attached to the machine gun was a 250-pound asshole who sank onto the bench seat beside Stephie. The white, former junior college football lineman was nineteen, but he had an emotional age of six. "I don't trust split tails," he whispered with breath that made Stephie wince, "so just stay the hell outa the way of my gun, or I might have to kill you to kill Chinese." Her squadmates ignored her clash.

"Suits me fine," Stephie replied. "And you stink."

It was a hot day. Throngs of refugees crowded the border of the Exclusion Zone two hundred miles north of the

Alabama Gulf Coast. Two hundred miles north of her home. On the northern side, all seemed normal. Laundry hung on clotheslines within a stone's throw of the sand-bagged guard post. Stores were open. Towns were busy. People went about their lives. Had it not been for the concealed machine guns, tanks, and missile batteries, the casual eye wouldn't have detected much change. Even the evacuee relocation center—tents pitched amid motor homes and barbeques—looked like a national park campground in summer.

The mixed team of MPs and state highway patrolmen raised the barrier and waved the dozen-vehicle convoy through. The diesels growled and belched noxious fumes, but Stephie was glad even for that breeze on the sweltering day. Their truck passed the sentries, and Stephie got the distinct impression that they were leaving America.

The sandbagged walls that rose up the road's shoulders parted, and the pavement began to flash by. They were in disputed territory. The no-man's-land between two great armies. Barren of life. Still and quiet and empty as if braced for the violence to come.

No maps had been redrawn to show the dashed lines that now carved into the southeastern United States, but the CO had shown everybody in their infantry company maps, stained with blood, that had been captured from Chinese reconnaissance teams. The American teenagers had passed them around in silence while seated on helmets and packs at the end of a week-long field-training exercise. They were 110 brand-new infantrymen—only one month removed from the shocking rigors of boot camp, and four from cocoons of middle-class comfort. All now were grimy, sunburned, sweaty, mosquito-bitten, scraped, and bruised. Exhaustion was evident in their slumped reposes.

But as the maps were handed from soldier to soldier, anger crackled. It burned in squinted eyes. It swelled from rhythmically clenching jaws. The maps had made the circuit by the time the trucks had arrived to return them to their makeshift barracks in a nearby Holiday Inn, but no one rose from the big circle in which they sat. The rides meant back to a semiprivate room shared with nineteen-year-old Becky Marsh from Oregon, the other woman in Stephie's squad. It meant showers, air conditioning, soft beds. But the bone-weary teenagers refused to leave the field. Lieutenant Ackerman, their platoon leader, feigned annoyance while hiding a grin. Staff Sergeant Kurth, their platoon sergeant, and his noncoms never smiled.

That day, troops led their officers back into the woods. They spent another week digging holes, chopping brush, firing at trees, and assaulting a charred hump of dirt. The names of the Alabama towns that were shown on the captured enemy maps were already printed in Chinese.

"Lock 'n load," Sergeant Collins, their squad leader, barked as the trucks picked up speed. The first deployment of their newly-formed unit was a combat patrol of the exposed Gulf Coast beaches. Metallic clacks of magazines and snaps of breech covers pierced the steady *whoosh* of the wind of the road. They had cinched up the truck's canvas sides to get a breeze, and Stephie began to point out the familiar landmarks of her native state. She knew the cracked two-lane highway like the back from her hand. They passed the Stuckeys where Stephie's stepfather had always stopped for peanut brittle on the way home from football games in Tuscaloosa. She recognized the service station where they had waited one long, hot day for their leaking radiator to be repaired. And there was the stand that her mom had always insisted carried the freshest watermelons of any place on earth. All were now boarded up. Abandoned. Forlorn.

Her squadmates, for their parts, pointed out the road's new attractions. A billboard with the image of a famous actress, who always played the high school slut in the slasher flicks, pressing her index finger to ruby red lips. The seductive image drew lewd comments and gestures from the boys, who overlooked entirely the point of the message. "Loose Lips Sink Ships," read the legend at the top. Stephie wondered at how bad the actress's career must have turned.

Concrete bunkers with periscopes and electronics mast-heads—facing south—had been dug out of the banked earth of highway overpasses. Bridges had been marked with orange signs that read, "Warning! Wired for demo-lition!" In the distance, open farm land—potential landing zones if aircraft suicidally flew at their missile defenses—had been pitted with black craters by preregistered artil-lery. And along the side of the road, ubiquitous triangular markers lined the roadside warning not to stray from the pavement onto shoulders already dotted with landmines. The regularly spaced triangles—black skulls and cross-bones on yellow signs—flashed by as the convoy drew ever nearer the dangerous sea.

Every so often they passed small towns still being stripped by engineers. Tractor trailers were being loaded with everything militarily useful: portable generators, back-hoes, transformers, propane tanks. What the engineers couldn't move, they destroyed. Columns of black smoke rose from all points of the compass. The convoy was stop-ped periodically by the demolition. Hoops and hollers rose from the parked convoy as charges toppled a metal water tower. Painted on the falling tank's side was a weathered, "Go Wildcats! Division II Basketball Champs 2001–02." After the great crash, the agitated male and female infan-trymen reenacted the stupendous sight with hand gestures and special effects sounds. All were on their feet, agitated. Excited. *Scared out of their fucking skins*, Stephie thought with a quiver as if cold on the hot, hot day.

Over the next half hour, the thunderous booms that rolled across the landscape from unseen engineers near and far eventually had the opposite effect of that big steel crash. The thumps of high explosives on their bodies soon quieted the anxious chatter in the truck. War hadn't yet come to America, but the thudding jolts that rattled their insides frayed their nerves with portents of death. The teenagers looked inward. Peer pressure demanded it. No one contemplated what loomed ahead out loud, except Becky. Stephie's roommate spent two weeks at the Holiday Inn imagining doom to all hours of the morning despite Stephie's pleas for sleep.

The convoy resumed their journey toward the Gulf at about 0800 hours and soon plunged into a thick, low-hanging haze. Some covered their mouths and noses with handkerchiefs against the choking smell. Stephie remembered. The Canadian Rocky Mountains, summer vacation, when she was eight. Her first smell of a forest fire.

The conflagration that consumed the Alabama woods was nowhere in sight, but the trees that lined the highway were now nothing more than charred hulks, brittle limbs, and pointed black fingers. The Chinese would find no wood for shelter or for campfires when the nights grew cold. There would be no brush to provide concealment from killing American fire. They would find nothing but death and devastation, Stephie thought with boiling hatred. Her face twitched and she fought back tears. Anger always made her cry.

Only PFC John Burns, seated beside her, noticed. He glanced her way, cracked a half-smile from one side of his mouth, then closed his eyes to resume his slumber.

At first, he was the only one among the almost two dozen soldiers in the truck who seemed to be resting comfortably. The two squads and weapons teams were packed shoulder-to-shoulder. Everyone other than Burns stared out in sullen silence at the cloud-shrouded, desolate scenery. They clutched their weapons as if for psychological comfort.

One-by-one, however, they began to drift off. Soon—miraculously, Stephie thought as she looked all around—every last one of her comrades had fallen sound asleep, including Animal, the beef eater next to her, who slumped her way. The huge guy created quite a stir when he shouted after Stephie knocked his leaning machine gun back against his helmet. Animal's eyes opened wide. For a heartbeat that Animal clearly believed would be his last, he thought that he'd been hit. He was so happy to be alive that he grinned at Stephie instead of punching her, then went back to sleep in seconds.

Stephie felt the same pull toward slumber. The warm

breeze stifled conversation, forcing thoughts inward. The clicks from the tires as they crossed the regularly spaced seams in the aging concrete were almost hypnotic. The old truck's stiff suspension rocked steadily from side to side and front to back. But Stephie could never rest while on the road. She had never felt comfortable enough to relax in a moving vehicle.

John Burns flashed Stephie another encouraging smile before again closing his eyes and leaning his helmet back against the metal frame that held the canvas. Stephie had smiled back at the boy—the man, really, for the dark-haired Burns was a little older than the others in their platoon—out of a habit bred in high school. *High school,* she thought. *High school!* Four months earlier, she had walked across the stage and been handed her diploma. The night of the prom she and Conner Reilly, her boyfriend, on leave from his unit, had hopped until dawn from one party to the next in the rented limousine. *Four months ago.*

She felt depressed, on edge, dispirited, and suddenly totally unprepared. In the balmy silence of the late-summer morning, a single question dominated the eighteen-year-old's thoughts: *How did it ever come to this?*

Scenes of a distant war flickered across the television screen. Ten-year-old Stephie Roberts watched though her mother ignored the grainy pictures of combat on the nightly news. "The addition of Thai army forces to the war in Vietnam has done little to slow the advancing Chinese." When the news moved on to some boring ceremony in Korea, Stephie returned to her journal. "Sally H. said today that we'll look really hot when we get our braces off, but that Gloria W. needs a nose job. I told Judy, who told The Evil James Thurmond, who told Gloria, who got really, REALLY pissed at *me*," she underlined, "for some totally warped reason!" U.S. troops, the reporter explained, had been withdrawn as a condition to reunification of the North and South. On the eve of a nationwide free election, the North Korean government had collapsed as its leaders—fearing retribution—had fled the country. China and South Korea had both stepped into the void to quell the violence. Their armies had clashed, and China had occupied the entire Korean Peninsula: North and South. The Chinese-backed puppet government was now celebrating the long-awaited reunion. "Must destroy James Thurmond!" Stephie wrote as she muted the boring program. "Hey, hey!" her stepdad said, grabbing the remote. They listened to a report that affected the company where he worked. Despite falling defense appropriations, Congress was authorizing billions of dollars for an antimissile shield. Her stepdad was beaming. Her mother said, "Now, finally, maybe you'll get the guts to ask for a raise." Stephie went outside and took a walk down the beach barefoot in the fading Alabama sun, plotting the total social demise of The Evil One.

The blue water of the Gulf didn't look the same as it had in Stephie Roberts's youth. Nothing was the same as it had been before. "First Squad, *out!*" shouted Sergeant Collins. "Stay off the beach! It's mined! Look *alive!*" The six other men and two women of Stephie's squad climbed down from the green, canvas-covered truck with their weapons and combat loads. Tony Massera, a private from Philadelphia, stood on the pavement squinting into the midday sunshine before donning his army shades. "Is it *always* this fuckin' hot in Alabama, Roberts?"

"*Puh*-ssy," Animal coughed into his fist. His fit of faux hacking ended with, "Puh-, puh-, *pussy!*" and a smile at Massera to ensure that he'd heard it correctly. Had the insult come from anyone else, the wiry and tough Massera—Animal's assistant machine gunner—would clearly have faced the man down or pummeled him to the ground with a flurry of blows. But the hulking machine gunner they all called Animal—who was semi-permanently attached to their squad—was a would-be offensive lineman for Ohio State. He dwarfed everyone else. Massera let it drop. Animal cleared his throat. "Sorry. *Shit!* Must be comin' down with somethin' Antonio."

"Tony," Massera corrected for about the hundredth time since the crew-served weapons had been handed down to the platoons. No one else had anything to say.

By age twelve, Stephie was even less interested in world events. But she remembered the day her class was watching the big screen in the Internet Lab of her Mobile, Alabama middle school. A grown man—India's prime minister—stood crying on a dock in Bombay. The sight riveted the darkened room filled with seventh graders. All were still young enough to take their cues from distraught adults, but not yet old enough to fully understand the reason for their shared distress. Indian civilians and soldiers were hastily boarding an overcrowded gray destroyer. "Does anyone know why the Indian prime minister didn't get on that ship?" the hyperstrict teacher asked the class. When no one answered, she said, "With Pakistani and Chinese troops just outside the city?" Again, no one ventured a guess. "Because the ship is *British*," the teacher explained with a sigh. It was a class for the gifted and talented. Stephie felt they were letting her down. "He was too proud to leave his country on a foreign ship." Everybody stared at the crying man. Stephie raised her hand and, when called upon, politely asked what had happened to him. "He was executed," came the teacher's reply. "Shot." All Stephie could think to say was, "Thanks."

"Shut up and shoulder yer loads!" snapped their squad leader despite the fact that no one standing at the back of the truck was talking. At twenty, Sergeant Collins was the oldest among them, and he was nervous. "This is the *coast*, in case you morons missed it!"

No one *had* missed the fact, of course. The nearer their convoy had come to the water, the flatter the terrain had grown. The Corps of Engineers had over a month before completed its work on the ghost towns outside Mobile. Peter Scott had commented that the blackened rubble of hospitals, schools, and courthouses already looked like the aftermath of heavy fighting. But Stephie had scrutinized the pictures of war's total devastation on the covers of news magazines. The selective demolition of public buildings paled when compared to the moonscapes left in Yokohama, Singapore, and Bombay. *And Tel Aviv,* she thought with a shiver.

Their first sight of the Gulf had come as a shock. The azure horizon visible in gaps between the tall pines had caused Stephie's stomach to begin to turn flips. After they had taken the coast road, some of the soldiers had stared at the shore as if to confront their inner demons. Others had rested their helmets against the raised front sights of their army surplus M-16s, focusing instead on their boots.

At thirteen, Stephie's soccer team won the state championship. Stephie played all ninety minutes at midfield. Although she got no goals or assists in the one-nil victory, she ran her heart out from penalty area to penalty area, challenged every header, made crisp passes despite legs that ached from the week-long tournament. Her crowning achievement in life to that time came in the waning moments of the game when she cleanly tackled the ball away from their opponent's greatest scoring threat. When the whistle blew, the entire team slid on their bellies into a pile on the rain-soaked pitch and hugged, cheered, and cried in equally shared, maximum celebration. At the beginning of the season, the coach had promised them that if they won state—and they had a chance—they would go as a team to soccer camp the following summer . . . in the south of France! They had practiced five days a week. Played regular season games, then driven to faraway tournaments and played again later the same day. Before the quarterfinals in the statewide, all had agreed not to talk about the trip for fear of jinxing it. As they left the pitch after the semis, however, a muddy Sally Hampton into Stephie's ear, "We're going to *France!*"

And she was right. They had won the state championship.

Over the squeals of excitement, all heard their coach's voice. "Sorry, girls!" he shouted apologetically. They all looked up at him. "We're not going to be able to go." There were a couple of cries of "*What?*" but a half-dozen cries of "*Why?*" He replied that because of the war in the Indian Ocean, the French had canceled the soccer camp. "Can't we just go *anyway?*" objected Gloria Wilson, their goalkeeper. "Your parents don't think it's safe," replied their frowning coach. The girls, still lying prone rose to their cleats and descended upon the gathering of parents, employing every conceivable argument. "We're not going by boat, we're *flying* over!" tried one. "The war is, like, a thousand miles away!" came another attempt. "You *promised!*" was the last, plaintive gasp. Their coach held out his hands to quell the uprising. "Everybody's really sorry, girls, but after the battle Europe lost to China in the Indian Ocean, it's just not safe to go overseas any-more. Nobody really knows what's gonna happen next." The girls were crushed. Some of the holdouts cried and argued their way to the car. The only thing that prevented Stephie from doing the same was that she spotted her father—her real father—still sitting in the stands. Ste-phie's mother rolled her eyes on seeing him and seethed at his mere presence.

Stephie ran to him. He held out his arms and threw them around her, holding her tight. "I'm so proud of you!" he said into her hair as she grinned and pressed her face flat against his chest. "You ran so hard! You won so many headers! Your passes were all right on target! And that steal at the end from the other team's best player was what won the game!" Stephie raised her face to beam at him, but had to stifle the grin with lips that she curled over her teeth. "You can smile now, Stephie," her father said, gently grasping her chin and raising her face. "You're not wearing braces anymore. You have always been, and are now, the most beautiful thing in heaven or on earth." She laughed. He tenderly cupped her mud-flaked cheeks in his hands. "I love you with all my heart," he said. At the team cookout, Stephie's angry mother had groused incessantly about her ex-husband ruining Stephie's wonderful day, and her sul-len teammates had vented their ire on their parents about the canceled trip with a pre-agreed wall of silence. But behind her wall, Stephie had been euphoric. Absolutely euphoric. All was right with the world. Things were great.

Stephie backed up to her heavy field pack, which stood upright on the truck's tailgate. "You want me to carry some of your gear?" John Burns asked in a low voice. He was stooped forward under the weight of his own eighty-pound pack, and he wasn't even in Stephie's squad. Animal wagged his tongue obscenely up and down in the air. Her squadmates snickered at the machine gunner's crude mockery of John's offer. "I can handle it," Stephie said, hoisting the pack onto her back with a grunt. Her legs almost buckled but she clenched her teeth and tried to continue breathing while tightening the harness across her chest and stomach. She then grabbed her M-16, which came with an M-249. The 40-mm grenade launcher mounted underneath the barrel looked like a toy. The stubby, bullet-shaped projectiles bulged from sleeves on bandoliers crossed over her torso, making her look like some large-caliber *pistollero*.

Becky Marsh watched John join the ranks on the road without once offering her his assistance. She winced and grunted as she shouldered her own massive pack. "No, *I* don't need any help," she muttered sarcastically, "but thanks for fucking asking!" Becky glared at Stephie, who chose not to notice.

Third platoon consisted of thirty-one soldiers. Lieutenant Ackerman and his commo and Platoon Sergeant Kurth stood in front of four, nine-man squads of infantry, which formed ranks for inspection. Of the twenty-seven infantrymen in the four numbered squads, nineteen were men and eight were women. Each squad had two fire teams, and the eight women were evenly distributed: one in each fire team. The squad leaders—three buck sergeants and a corporal—stood at the far right with their squads stretched at arm's-length to their left. The soldiers in the formation raised their left arms for proper, parade-ground spacing. The formation extended longer than normal because of the four soldiers added to the end of each squad's rank. A two-man machine gun crew and a two-man all-threat missile crew from the company's weapons platoon had been attached to each squad. With the four medics from the battalion medical detachment in the rear, Third Platoon today fielded fifty.

At fourteen, Stephie became obsessed with the opposite sex. And the latest in a series of the-cutest-boys-she'd-*ever*-seen was at an interdenominational prayer service for the victims of the Second Jewish Holocaust. He looked to be older—sixteen—and had shiny black hair, dark eyes, and smooth skin as white as paper. *He must have dermatologists for parents,* she marveled. Then, all of the sudden, Stephie realized that he must be Jewish. As the prayers wore on—some familiar, others in Hebrew—an imagined romance blossomed in Stephie's mind until her stepdad leaned over and whispered, "They brought it on *themselves*, you know. China *warned* Israel not to use nukes." Stephie's mom crushed her stepdad's toe in embarrassment. When he hissed in pain, Stephie's imaginary boyfriend looked back and shocked Stephie straight to the core. Tears flowed from "radiant pools," she wrote in her journal, down the mysterious boy's porcelain skin. That night, Stephie got on the Internet and read news reports about Tel Aviv. It turned out that China *had* warned Israel against using nuclear weapons to try to stop their invasion. In retaliation, China had destroyed Tel Aviv with its population trapped inside. Stephie watched the video over and over. She couldn't read the Chinese characters in the lower righthand corner, but the countdown on the clock was universal. When the clock struck zero, half a dozen blinding flashes swallowed the city's skyline.

"First, second, and third squads and attached crews," the tall and angular Ackerman, newly commissioned officer and platoon leader, announced, "will come with me and Platoon Sergeant Kurth for a patrol of the beach! Fourth Squad will guard the trucks!"

"Knock it off!" Staff Sergeant Kurth boomed, although

Stephie had heard nothing from the troops. His stare men-aced fourth squad in the rank behind Stephie. The squad that had drawn easy duty.

"Everybody patrolling the beach, keep your eyes open!" continued Ackerman. "West Point" is what most called him behind his back. "If you see any tracks, call 'em out! This is a free-fire zone! Watch for mines on both sides of the road. The mines underneath the pavement are under positive control and are currently safed. Weapons loaded. Rounds chambered. Safeties *on*." There was a steady clacking of metal as men and women pointed their weapons away from their buddies and checked their se-lector switches. Stephie ejected a curved, thirty-round magazine. The brass cartridges shone from atop their dou-ble stack. She reloaded the full mag into her assault rifle and loaded a 40-mm fragmentation grenade into the breach of her launcher. She slid the launcher shut with a snap like a pump shotgun and confirmed that the selector switches on both weapons were on "safe."

"Pursuant to the Coastal Defense Act," Lieutenant Ack Ack announced officiously, "this area is under martial law! We have orders to arrest any civilians we come across, and we are authorized to use deadly force! If we come into con-tact with any Chinese forces, we are to report in, engage, and destroy! Single file! Corporal Higgins, you're wired for the point! Take the lead! Let's *move* out!"

Fifteen was a time of questioning for Stephie. "Why'd those people in New Zealand throw garbage at our ship?" With his mouth still full, her stepfather said they were un-grateful 'cause we didn't defend 'em. Stephie's mom cleared her throat at her husband's table manners. "Why didn't we defend them?" Stephie asked. 'Cause it wasn't worth World War Three, 'specially right before the new, second-generation missile shield's in place. "Who's stronger—us or the Chinese?" Us. "Then how come we let 'em rape Manila?" Don't use that *word*, her mom said. Ste-phie's stepfather replied that the Chinese had used Korean shipyards that previously had built super*tankers* to build their new super*carriers*. They're five times bigger than our carriers and hold three times as many planes. Some are transports that can carry twenty thousand troops at a time. "How big is their army?" Stephie asked. Thirty, forty million, give or take. "How big is *ours*?" Dunno. A few hundred thousand. "Then how can you say *we're* stronger than *them*?" 'Cause of the missile shield his company was helping build. "But aren't *they* building one, *too*? Isn't *everybody* building one?" Her stepfather grew tired of Stephie's incessant questions.

One by one the ranks headed down the highway parallel to the shore, straight toward Stephie's house. Her squad was third and last in line. With a ten-meter spread, the point man was over 300 meters ahead, but Stephie could see what Higgins saw from the point—an empty ribbon of road that swayed with the point man's every step—on a one-inch LCD screen suspended on a slender boom before her face. The old-style Kevlar helmets had been retrofitted with a strap-on electronics suite. It consisted of the screen and a microphone on the boom, headphones under the armored ear flaps, and a wire running to a battery and receiver on the shoulder of the webbing. To that ensemble, the point man added a tiny pen-sized camera and transmitter.

The electronics system of the newly raised 41st Infantry Division was, however, basically just a hodgepodge. It wasn't nearly as advanced as the equipment of the lower-numbered divisions of America's regular, standing army. The system used by the professionals was fully integrated into their newer and lighter ceramic helmets.

Stephie scanned the dunes on the left and beaches on the right, but saw nothing save the litter common to any roadside. Candy wrappers. Coke cans. Yellowed newspapers half buried in sand.

"Lookie *here*!" Stephon Johnson said from ahead. His voice broke in and out on her balky left earphone. Johnson—a corporal—was a grenadier from Washington, DC, and the leader of Stephie's fire team alpha. He kicked at a used condom with his combat boot. "Looks like you had yourself some good *times* down here on the Redneck Riviera, *Roberts*." Men laughed and commented in turn as they passed the wilted prophylactic.

"Cut the shit!" Sergeant Collins finally snapped. They marched on in silence, skirting a fresh crater in the cracked pavement that was half-filled with brackish green water. It must have been from a practice bombing run, Stephie thought, or an Air Force attack on a Chinese probe.

Stephie's thighs and lungs began to burn. Her lower back and shoulders grew to ache from the heavy "existence load." Sweat showed through the men's thick, woodlands-camouflage battle dress as they marched farther and farther from the trucks. Closer and closer to her house. The only contact they had with the outside world came in the form of an occasional crackle over the commo's audio/video gear, which carried on the ocean breeze from the middle of the formation where Ackerman and the commo were. Two other platoons in their company were on different stretches of the empty shoreline, and the company commander was with one of them. Although they weren't in range now, when they were within a four-mile radius of the transmitters, the CO could watch video from any of his four platoons.

Or so it was supposed to work. No one really had any idea what to expect. Their unit—the 41st Infantry Division—had first unfurled its colors at a ceremony at Fort Benning, Georgia, only one month earlier. The six hundred men and women of Stephie's 3rd of the 519th Infantry Regiment were in one of the division's fifteen infantry battalions. Charlie Company of the 3/519 had been given orders for this—their first mission—only the day before.

Stephie had wondered about the mission's real purpose ever since. During a semisleepless night, she had reasoned that they could reconnoiter the coast by air. But she knew they were sending units south every day. Maybe it was to give them tactical training on the theater's terrain. A chance to get a feel for the ground on which they would fight. Or maybe it was a purely symbolic act. Going down to the water's edge one last time to assert U.S. sovereignty over territory that would soon be the property of the Chinese. But even if symbolic, their combat patrol was dangerous. There were skirmishes practically every day. The coast was alive with Chinese scouts, pathfinders, patrols, and raiding parties. *But*, she decided, *we've gotta get blooded some time. Better now—against a recon team that we outnumber ten-to-one—than when we match up against the Chinese one-to-ten.*

Third platoon's Caucasians, Hispanics, African-Americans, and "Others" came from all parts of the country. There were practically no deferments from the draft, so they came from every socioeconomic class. But the representatives of their generation were more alike than any other soldiers that America had fielded in its history. In an interconnected world they had melded into a uniform blend. And one attribute shared by the forty-odd teenagers was that none had ever killed a living thing. There was not a single hunter or outdoorsman among the teenage urban-and suburbanites.

Stephie had her first beer and smoked her first pot on her sixteenth birthday. On a walk down the beach she ran into some juniors from her high school, who were drunk on the six-pack they'd bought at a nearby convenience store. Conner Reilly, the coolest of the cool, finally offered her a beer.

"You know they're out there," said Conner Reilly, nodding at the Gulf, as soundless coughs still wracked Stephie's chest. Conner was tanned and tall—on the basketball team—but had green eyes and long eyelashes like a fashion model. He also dated the best looking girl in school, Stephie reminded herself, who would crush Stephie, socially, if she perceived any threat, which she couldn't possibly. "Bullshit," replied Walter Ames. Walter's father was black, and his mother was white. Walter defined the word cool. Stephie felt cool just being around him, and she wondered if any of the boys would acknowledge her Monday when they went back to school.

"They're too busy invadin' Japan," Walter insisted, but Conner was unswayed. "China's got bases," he said, rocking forward in the circle and drawing a map in the sand, "on those islands up and down the coast of Africa!" Conner's islands looked like freckles on his hand-drawn sea. With her finger, she completed the sea's smiley face.

They marched about a mile down the beach before they came upon a body. It had washed up on the shore and was covered in seaweed. You couldn't tell much more than that from the road. They took a break as the LT checked his map showing minefields, then sent two men out onto the beach. The soldiers recoiled in disgust and returned to report to the LT, who called a report in to the CO. Word quickly spread that it was a U.S. sailor who'd been in the water a long, long time. Men returned to the corpse, sunk a piece of driftwood into the sand, and tied a white towel to the upright marker.

"Must've been from the Straits of Havana," Animal said. He was sweating profusely and rested his heavy, vintage M-60 in his lap as he mopped his face with a towel. He and Massera were from weapons platoon—not a numbered platoon—thus they, like the missile team, were outsiders.

The ultimate insider was Stephon Johnson, who knew everybody in every unit. He had advance word of just about everything important because of the network of contacts that he always touted. "I hear there was 30,000 squids 'n jarheads on those ships. That Chinese wolfpack had a hun'erd subs in it, just waitin'. Bodies been washin' up all the way over to Texas."

"And there are five million Chinese soldiers in Cuba," Stephie said in the low tones everyone else had assumed. Nobody said a word in reply.

PERSPECTIVES ON PSYCHIC CONVERSION

PERSPECTIVES ON PSYCHIC CONVERSION

Edited by

JOSEPH OGBONNAYA

MARQUETTE
UNIVERSITY

PRESS

Marquette Studies in Theology
No. 95
Lonergan Studies, International Institute for Method in Theology
Joseph Ogbonnaya, General Editor

© 2023
Marquette University Press
Milwaukee WI 53201-3141
All rights reserved.

Text design and composition by Rose Design

Library of Congress Cataloging-in-Publication Data

Names: Ogbonnaya, Joseph, 1968- editor.
Title: Perspectives on psychic conversion / edited by Joseph Ogbonnaya.
Description: Milwaukee, Wisconsin : Marquette University Press, [2023] |
  Series: Marquette studies in theology ; no. 95 | Includes
  bibliographical references and index. | Summary: "Central to empirical
  consciousness and the primary basis of human knowledge is the nexus
  between the body and the mind called the psyche. Healing for the
  dramatic bias is psychic conversion. The book provides the various
  approaches to the psyche and its relation to the two ways of knowing"--
  Provided by publisher.
Identifiers: LCCN 2023028811 | ISBN 9781626007284 (paperback)
Subjects: LCSH: Conversion--Christianity. | Spiritual life--Catholic
  Church. | Christian life.
Classification: LCC BV4916.3 .P47 2023 | DDC 248.2/4--dc23/eng/20230712
LC record available at https://lccn.loc.gov/2023028811

ASSOCIATION
of UNIVERSITY
PRESSES

Contents

Introduction

Conversion is central to Christian message. Jesus preached repentance as a key requirement to the establishment of God's reign. Conversion, in the sense of a deep turnaround, transformed Christianity from a movement within Judaism to a distinct religion with worldwide geographical reach when its foremost persecutor, Saul, after a vision on the road to Damascus, converted to Christianity and championed the spread of Christianity to the then known world. As a process towards authentic living, conversion is an ongoing process that affects the entirety of human existence. According to Bernard Lonergan, "Conversion as lived, affects all of a man's conscious and intentional operations. It directs his gaze, pervades his imagination, releases the symbols that penetrate to the depths of his psyche. It enriches his understanding, guides his judgments, reinforces his decisions."[1] Conversion, in a specifically religious sense, goes beyond changes in orientation, adoption of a new lifestyle, accepting new ideas, dropping previous convictions. It is a radical transformation that affects all aspects of one's life, commitment, values, purpose.

Even though not clearly set out in *Insight*, conversion is at the heart of the Lonergan project. It is treated extensively in *Method in Theology*, receiving over fifty entries in the index. It equally is mentioned in Lonergan's pre- and post-Method writings.[2] Conversion which Lonergan identified as a deep turnaround is intellectual, moral, and religious. In religious conversion, "a person receives God's

---

1. Bernard Lonergan, *Method in Theology*, CWL 14 edited by Robert M. Doran and John D. Dadosky (Toronto: University of Toronto Press, 2017), 126.

2. A look into the index of these writings is revealing. *The Philosophical and Theological Papers 1965–1980* (fifteen mentions), *Collection* (eight mentions), *The Third Collection* (ten mentions), *The Second Collection* (ten mentions), *Verbum, Word and Idea in Aquinas* (six mentions), to mention but a few.

love and then transvalues his life's values."[3] "Intellectual conversion is the abandonment of the myth that human knowing is essentially a type of conception. Moral conversion is the rejection of satisfaction and the acceptance of value as the motive for a person's actions."[4] Conversion, Lonergan stated, is a "modality of self-transcendence."[5] "Intellectual conversion is to truth attained by cognitional self-transcendence. Moral conversion is to values apprehended, affirmed, and realized by a real self-transcendence. Religious conversion is to a total being-in-love as the efficacious ground of all self-transcendence, whether in the pursuit of truth, or in the realization of human values, or in the orientation man adopts to the universe, its ground, and its goal."[6] Intellectual conversion is adopting the critical realist position that knowing is a compound of intentionality analysis, a unit of experiencing, understanding, judging, and deciding. Moral conversion is commitment to values rather than to satisfactions. Religious conversion is being in love with God. Intellectual conversion leads to moral conversion, moral self-transcendence ultimately leads to religious conversion. Yet this in no way means that conversion must first be intellectual, and moral, before being religious. On the contrary, according to Lonergan:

> Though religious conversion sublates moral, and moral conversion sublates intellectual, one is not to infer that intellectual comes first and then moral and finally religious. On the contrary, from a causal viewpoint, one would say that first there is God's gift of his love. Next, the eye of this love reveals values in their splendor, while the strength of this love brings about their realization, and that is moral conversion. Finally, among the values discerned by the eye of love is the value of believing the truths

---

3. William F. J. Ryan S.J. and Bernard J. Tyrrell, S.J., "Introduction," in William F. J. Ryan S.J. and Bernard J. Tyrrell, S.J., eds., Bernard Lonergan, *A Second Collection* (Toronto: University of Toronto Press, 1974), ix.

4. Ibid., ix–x.

5. *Method in Theology*, 226.

6. Ibid., 227.

taught by the religious tradition, and in such tradition and belief are the seeds of intellectual conversion.[7]

While conversion leads to progress, breakdown or absence of conversion leads to societies' decline as biases of common sense takes over the polity, wreaking havoc to all aspects of societal life.

Lonergan's interest in conversion is aimed at theological foundations especially of doctrines, systematics, and communications. The focus is the conversion of the human subject who does theology, who reflects on religion and who by cognitional, moral, and religious self-transcendence is at the center of contemporary theological method. He writes: "Foundational reality, as distinct from its expression, is conversion: religious, moral, and intellectual. Normally it is intellectual conversion as the fruit of both religious and moral conversion; it is moral conversion as the fruit of religious conversion; and it is religious conversion as the fruit of God's gift of his grace."[8] Lonergan's interest in conversion is informed by his desire for a theological method. As Michael Leonard Rende explains: "Lonergan's prolonged intellectual labor can be understood as a search for a contemporary theological method and one of the chief results of that search has been the establishment of the notion of conversion at the very heart of contemporary method."[9] Lonergan's aim at contemporary theological method becomes clearer in view of Robert M. Doran's inclusion of psychic conversion to Lonergan's three conversions.

Psychic Conversion

Doran's addition of the psyche to Lonergan's three level conversions: intellectual, moral, and religious, has received different reactions from

---

7. Ibid., 228–229.

8. Ibid., 251. See also "Theology in Its New Context," in *A Second Collection*, ed, William F. J, Ryan and Bernard J Tyrrell. (Philadelphia: The Westminster Press, 1974) p. 67.

9. Michael L. Rende, *Lonergan on Conversion: The Development of a Notion* (Lanham, New York: University Press of America, 1991), ix.

Lonergan scholars. But at the heart of Doran's conviction was the integral role of feeling to cognitional self-appropriation. Doran realized this through guided counselling:

> . . . that interiority is more than the operations of experiencing and inquiring and understanding and reflecting and judging and deliberating and deciding—it's all the feelings and the images and the symbols and the dreams. That's all part of the appropriation of interiority. It's not just reading *Insight* that will give you an appropriation of interiority. That gives you an appropriation of intentional interiority—it does. But there is a whole other psychic interiority that is distinct from but related to that, and it accompanies the intentional operations so that your feelings change when you perform certain operations. When you have an insight, you also feel differently from the way that you felt before you had that insight, and so there's the two things together.[10]

Doran was equally influenced by Heidegger's distinction of the two inseparable but distinct ways of being conscious or *Dasein*: *Verstehen*, which is cognitive, and *Befindlichkeit*, the affective. "They're equiprimordial constituent ways of being *Dasein*, and you if you're going to do appropriation, you've got to appropriate both of them and not just the intentional, the cognitive."[11]

Doran developed psychic conversion and shared it with Bernard Lonergan whom he said "had no problem with it. He bought it immediately. Immediately. And he never questioned it at all. Never."[12] Lonergan's endorsement of Doran's addition of psychic conversion to his is clear from Lonergan's response to the twenty-five theses Doran submitted to him on November 18, 1973.[13] In these theses, Doran

---

10. Robert M. Doran, *Conscious in Two Ways*, edited by Joseph Ogbonnaya, Jeremy W. Blackwood, and Gregory Lauzon (Milwaukee: Marquette University Press, 2021), 17–18.

11. Ibid, 18.

12. Ibid., 20.

13. Doran's Twenty-Five Methodological Theses is published as an appendix to Doran's *Conscious in Two Ways* edited by Joseph Ogbonnaya, Jeremy W. Blackwood, and Gregory Lauzon.

developed psychic conversion and explained its relevance to Lonergan's conversion. In the eleventh thesis, Doran writes: "Psychic conversion is to be joined to the religious, moral and intellectual conversions
specified by Lonergan as qualifying the authentic subjectivity which
is the foundational reality of theology."[14] Lonergan's response to Doran's theses is in the affirmative: "As far as I can see your account of my
position is accurate. In the same sense, I think your work is a needed
complement to my own."[15] Lonergan went ahead to encourage Doran:
"I suggest that you make this your magnum opus; take some definite
part of it for your doctoral dissertation."[16] Of course, Doran did and
wrote his doctoral dissertation on *Subject and Psyche*.[17] Reflecting on
his lifelong project incorporating psychic conversion to Lonergan's
intellectual, moral and religious conversion, Doran emphasized the
need for psychic conversion for all, especially for Lonergan scholars;

> So, on the psychic conversion thing—it's largely Lonerganians
> that need this conversion because they neglect the first level of
> consciousness. They need to be brought back to the Earth, you
> know. So, if there is a conversion involved, a lot of times it's peo-
> ple who are caught in what John Dadosky has called, and I called
> in an early article of mine, "intellectualist bias"—the position
> that, "The level of symbol, oh well you can forget about that,"
> and so on and so forth. A lot of people in the Lonergan camp—
> in those days, at least—were into that. So, if anybody needed the
> conversion, it's the people who thought I shouldn't be talking
> about this as a conversion, because they needed it because they
> were losing the ground under their feet.[18]

Doran reviewed criticisms against psychic conversion and nar-
rowed it down to people thinking of dialectics as only contradictory,

14. Doran, *Conscious in Two Ways*, 108

15. Ibid., 111.

16. Ibid., 112

17. Robert M. Doran, *Subject and Psyche* 2nd edition (Milwaukee: Marquette
University Press, 1994).

18. Doran, *Conscious in Two Ways*, 18–19

ignoring that dialectics could also be of contraries. These people, he observes, "set practicality over against intersubjectivity, as though you have to choose one and reject the other. That's wrong, you have to get the two working together, and psychic conversion will get the two working together, you know. So, I think it is a conversion. I think it's a conversion that people who have been raised in the technocratic or highly intellectual or technical atmosphere need to get back to reality."[19]

Psychic Conversion and Theological Foundations

Before I summarize the contents of this volume, I want to reflect briefly on the twenty-third thesis of Doran to Lonergan: "As foundational for theology, psychic conversion allows the derivation of theological categories, positions, poetic, aesthetic. The terms and relations of systematic theology are psychological, not only in terms of cognitional theory, but also in terms of the psychology of the imaginal."[20] My interest here is informed by the relatedness of Doran's position to Lonergan's on conversion as foundational for contemporary theological method.

One of the intriguing aspects of Doran's psychic conversion is not only on why he uses the word "conversion" but also his claim of psychic conversion as being foundational for theology in the light of the functional specialty *Foundations*. In fact, Doran is emphatic on his pursuit of theological method and foundations through his elaboration of psychic conversion. He confessed: ". . . I have worked out my notion of the psyche, and of its religious involvement, within the overall context of attempting to make a contribution to the questions of theological method, theological foundations, and theological responsibility for interdisciplinary collaboration, as these questions have been clarified by Lonergan."[21] The place of psychic conversion within theological

---

19. Ibid., 19.
20. Doran, *Conscious in Two Ways*, 108.
21. Doran, *Theological Foundations I*, 339–340.

foundation is less problematic once one understands the imperative of the conversion of the theologian as an existential subject for theology.[22] The theologian has a mind and uses it, Lonergan says of the importance of the transcendental method in the grounding of theology.[23] Thus, "the foundational reality of theology is the intellectually, morally, and religiously converted theologian."[24]

Doran opts for the word "conversion" to describe his suggestion of the inclusion of the psyche in intentionality analysis. His position is based on conversion being the foundation of theology which reflects on religion. He labors to explain the importance of the aesthetic stream of consciousness in Lonergan's invitation to bring the operations of intentional consciousness as intentional to bear upon these same operations as conscious. He is convinced that without the extension of the operations to the sensitive consciousness, theology and spirituality will be truncated and distorted, creating needless dualism not only in theology, but also in the human subject.[25] This is very important in view of the place of context for theological exigence as the questions set by theology are answered in the variety of contexts and in harmony with our constitution as human subjects. The relevance of Jung's psychology for theology thus lies in the role of that psychology in the individuality of the person foundational for theology.[26] It opens up the preconscious imagination and intelligence towards providing the requisite insights that enables us as humans to pass correct judgments and act rightly so as to make our lives a dramatic art.[27] Psychic conversion is foundational for theology in the sense of contributing to the full sense of the subject providing

---

22. Doran, *Theological Foundations I*, 76

23. Doran, *Theological Foundations I*, 367.

24. Doran, *Theological Foundations I*, 92.

25. Doran, *Theological Foundations I*, 341.

26. Doran, *Theological Foundations I*, 366

27. Doran defines psychic conversion as "the opening of the preconscious collaboration of imagination and intelligence to the imaginal materials issuing from the organism through the psyche to the spirit, enables this objectification by disclosing to the willing subject the symbolic representations of the affective component of the human search for direction in the movement of life." *Theological Foundations I*, 357.

the neural and psychic manifold required for the self-appropriation of intentionality. To quote Doran:

> Jungian psychology, it seems, can function for the theologian at the level of psychic self-appropriation in a manner analogous to the functioning of the intentionality analysis of Lonergan at the level of intellectual self-appropriation. As Lonergan's cognitional theory helps one to answer the question, What am I doing when I am knowing? so Jungian psychological analysis promotes the self-appropriation of what one has done and is doing to create a work of dramatic art out of the materials of one's life: a human story with a meaning, with a direction, and with the integrity that comes from heightening and expanding one's consciousness through negotiating the various complexes of affect and image that constitute one's sensitive participation in the historical drama of life, and in the dialectic of history itself. In each instance, with Lonergan as with Jung, there is a disclosure of the concreteness of individuality, and so an appropriation of a portion of the foundations of one's affirmations and systematic understanding as a theologian.[28]

Methodologically, in the light of Lonergan's intentionality analysis, Doran provides eight reasons why Jungian psychology is pertinent for theological foundation.[29] Central to Doran's arguments is the role of Jungian psychology in the individuality of the human subject who does theology and the contribution of Jungian psychology to transcendental method. This, Doran says, has far reaching implications for theological method. First, it grounds theology in one's religious experiences. Second, not only experience is granted a role as ground for theology, one's experiences will also be enriched when one opens oneself to one's dream symbols. Psychic conversion attunes one to one's feelings and hence to one's psychic energy, making it possible for one to tell one's own story, articulate one's spirituality as a story.[30]

---

28. Doran, *Theological Foundations I*, 364.

29. Doran, *Theological Foundations I*, 365.

30. Doran, *Theological Foundations I*, 409.

For this reason, it promotes not only growth in self-transcendence but also in self-knowledge. Third, as feelings are represented in symbols and as symbols evoke feelings, psychic conversion gifts the theologian with hermeneutic tools to interpret "the religious expressions of other men and women at other times and places and in other cultures, and a foundational framework for introducing into one's own theological systematics the use of categories that are unapologetically symbolic, poetic, aesthetic, and yet explanatory, because derived from thoroughgoing interior self-differentiation."[31]

Thus, two major reasons underlie Doran's thought on the relevance of psychic conversion for theological foundations. First, proximately, in the systematic theologian's appropriation of the results of the first phase of theology, the phase that mediates theology from the past into the present. For this, he devotes a whole chapter of *Theology and the Dialectics of History* to the treatment of the problem of hermeneutics. Second, the centrality of the subject for theology. The subject here refers to the theologian doing theology as well as other persons whose existence make up the various situations the theologian addresses. For this reason, he emphasizes integral dialectic of the subject, that is, the authentic subject who maintains the tension between limitation and transcendence. Such authenticity consists of the unity of consciousness, of intentionality and psyche as well as the objectification of conversion—religious, moral, intellectual, and psychic, associated with conscious intentionality.

> In what way do psychic conversion and psychic self-appropriation enter into the foundations of direct theological discourse? That is our question. Obviously, the situation that a systematic theology addresses consists in part of more or less distorted or integral dialectics of the subject, and the foundations for addressing that situation will lie in the self-appropriation of the constitutive elements of an integral dialectic of the subject. These same foundations will also ground the possibility of evoking an alternative situation.[32]

---

31. Doran, *Theological Foundations I*, 381.
32. Doran, *Theology and the Dialectics of History*, 139.

xvi   PERSPECTIVES ON PSYCHIC CONVERSION

Specifically, the foundations of direct theological discourse are dependent on appropriation of the tradition. This appropriation of tradition is based on the self-appropriation of the subject which emerges from interiorly and religiously differentiated consciousness. For this reason, the foundations of systematic theology must treat both forms of consciousness which also are objectification of conversions: religious, moral, intellectual, and psychic. "The self-appropriating and self-transcending subject in love with God is the ultimate arbiter of all direct theological discourse."[33] Any situation to be addressed by systematic theology must be some form of history, that is, of the analogy of dialectics: integral dialectic of the subject, community and culture and the relations within the scale of values: vital, social, cultural, personal and religious; and the way the scale of values relate to the analogy of dialectics—the integral scale of values. The dialectic of the subject is central to the foundation of theology. For this reason, the neural demand functions and the censorship by intelligence is very important for theological foundations.

Doran, just like Lonergan, grounds theology on the conversion of the theologian. This means that theologians be religiously, morally, intellectually and psychically converted; that they be persons of integrity. "The [foundational] reality[of theology] is the theologian as subject of the operations that intend theological objects: the theologian as a more or less authentic human person, as more or less a person of integrity."[34] However, this position is not popular in the academy and among some theologians who resist it personally and existentially. But Doran is convinced Lonergan is not engaged in the disclosing of the subject merely cognitively. Lonergan aims at self-transformation of the subject, religiously, morally, intellectually and, Doran adds, psychically. "On every page he is evoking a set of transformations that in his later work he calls religious, moral, and intellectual conversion. Self-appropriation, and so the modern turn to the subject, does not come to term in self-understanding alone,

---

33. Doran, *Theology and the Dialectics of History*, 143.
34. Doran, *Theology and the Dialectics of History*, 162.

but in the radical transformation of oneself as subject of the operations one has come to understand and affirm."[35]

Doran will thus relate psychic conversion to theology in the context of the dialectic of the subject. The conversions "constitute an organic whole of interrelated parts, a dynamic structure of personal value."[36] Foundations as a functional specialty is the objectification of the conversions fructifying in the becoming of a person of integrity following the full flowering of the inner laws of the human spirit. In other words, "the self-appropriation of the transcendental a priori initiates one into foundations. But conversion is the central category in that account."[37] Doran grounds psychic conversion to foundations by emphasizing how intellectual conversion (permeated aesthetically by psychic conversion) is awakened by religious and moral conversion. Conversion is made possible through the revelation by the transcendent being of the word which humans believe through the eye of love-faith. Theological truth is articulation of divine word as it is meaningful first elementally to the human subject.

> Thus manifestation, unveiling, *aletheia*, mystery, elemental meaning—these ground, precede, awaken, the cognitive process that leads to proclamation, judgment, word, objectified formal and full meaning. Seeing grounds and precedes saying; it awakens the process that attunes saying to what has been seen; seeing is engendered by what is seen; and so the profoundest depths of being do in fact proportion the cognitive subject to the objective of the desire to know, to being, in a more primordial fashion even than that exhibited in the reception of the word of tradition.[38]

Doran's concern with the intellectual integrity and dramatic artistry is also a concern with the religious ground of personal and intellectual integrity which ultimately, he interprets as the work of divine grace. The relation of psychic conversion to theological foundations is

---

35. Doran, *Theology and the Dialectics of History*, 159.
36. Doran, *Theology and the Dialectics of History*, 162.
37. Doran, *Theology and the Dialectics of History*, 162.
38. Doran, *Theology and the Dialectics of History*, 165.

indirectly a discussion of the religious development of the theologian who engages in intellectual collaboration aimed at cosmopolitan collaboration.[39] The ground lies in the religious value of charity which facilitates the willingness of the theologian to engage in the intellectual collaboration towards the emergence and restoration of critical culture.

Synopsis of the Chapters

The essays gathered in this volume (in four parts) addresses some questions surrounding psychic conversion, its appropriateness or not, its meaning and its relation to Lonergan's threefold conversion: intellectual, moral, religious. Accepting Doran's psychic conversion, some of the contributions apply it to various contexts: in trauma and psychopathology, in spirituality especially Ignatian spiritual exercises, in the healing of the wounds engendered by oppression that distorts the psyche: in colonial and post-colonial studies, in dehumanization brought about by racism, and in the reinvention of the self from the impacts of biases that inhibit appropriation of the authentic self.

PART ONE using concrete examples, explains psychic conversion: its meaning, relation to other conversions and to science of neuroplasticity. In Chapter One, M. Shawn Copeland introduces psychic conversion as therapeutic for social transformation of American society struggling with varieties of biases, gender issues and racism. In conversation with Kelly Brown Douglas *Stand Your Ground: Black Bodies and the Justice of God,* Copeland enumerating cases of marginalization, police brutality, and racism, suggests measures for the healing of the psyche of Americans to foster love and grace. Fearing the consequences of human development in racially biased culture, Copeland invokes the power of integrating grace. "What is at stake is our willingness to accept and to pay the price of integrating grace in our living. The just, good, beautiful America for which we long is nested in the minds and hearts, behavior and actions—the character formation

---

39. Doran, *Theology and the Dialectics of History,* 186.

of our children." Hence the need for appropriation of conversion: intellectual, moral, religious, and psychic conversion "if good will is to be effectively harnessed in the struggle for social transformation." In Chapter Two, Joseph Ogbonnaya argues that Doran's thinking on the functional specialties is indispensable for accessing Lonergan's cognitional theory, existential conversion and consequently, theological foundations. To make sense of psychic conversion, Ogbonnaya maintains that the recognition of the intrinsic connection between the psyche and the mind, in the fashioning of meaning and value is the pivot to Lonergan's intentionality analysis and the cognition theory. Since the psyche complements Lonergan's intentionality analysis, it provides what was lacking in *Insight*'s emphasis on consciousness. In Chapter Three, John Dadosky notes that the idea of conversion is a significant gateway to connecting Lonergan's thoughts to psychology and this has been demonstrated sufficiently in the works of Doran (Psychic conversion), Tyrell (Affectional conversion) and others, having applied the Occam's Razor. But the bigger question rests in the fact that success in this endeavor certainly lies in the extent to which Lonergan is, a) understood to be making this link, b) made the link and c) has come to be understood to be making this connection by other scholars in their understanding and appropriation of Lonergan. Dadosky accepts that the fourth level of conversion finds its basis in Lonergan's statement of "affective" conversion. Nonetheless, he argued that Doran's psychic conversion already makes the basic arguments that other candidates for other types of conversion make and enjoys the approval of Lonergan himself. In Chapter Four, Mary Josephine MacDonald asks at what point, and to what degree is the bodily component relevant in Lonergan's interiority and intentionality discourse of the human subject? McDonald's theological anthropology seeks to creatively establish the link between science, psychology and theology. It responds to Lonergan's call for creative collaboration between theology and science for the advancement of benefits in religion and the cultural context of the subject. McDonald brings the psychologist, Eugene Gendlin, into conversation with the science of Neuroplasticity and thus engenders a robust definition of psychic conversion.

PART TWO elaborates developments in the understanding of psychic conversion paying particular attention to bias, attentiveness and inattentiveness, implication of psychic conversion for foundations and systematicity. It equally engages Paul Ricoeur, Doran's conversation partner in the working out of psychic conversion. In Chapter Five, Elizabeth Murray in "Bias, Bigotry and Passion," contributes to the development of psychic conversion by demonstrating how group Bias ties to the reality of bigotry. She elaborates on how the passions in their flight from understanding, block or vitiate human development in terms of knowledge. This block, she maintains, can be remedied by way of psychic conversion as advanced by Robert Doran. Murray finds in resentment, an important dimension in the consideration of the impact of bias and the need for a psychic conversion. Jonathan Heaps in Chapter Six draws attention to what he calls terminological allergies, that is, the inattentiveness to the ways in which words have an effect on humans. He maintains that terminological allergies are an inflammatory reaction of consciousness to particular words or expression. Heaps' chapter therefore delineates these allergies, detailing different contexts, causes, dynamics, and aspects from a human consciousness data approach. He highlights these data in two categories—data of intentionality and data of the psyche. Heaps applies Doran's psychic conversion to the problem of terminological allergies.

In Chapter Seven, Ryan Hemmer draws attention to the distinctive contribution of speculative method to the universality and exclusivity of method. Hemmer argues that intellectual and psychic conversions must cooperate in generating the theorematic structure for speculative collaboration. Hemmer insists that we must look to the psyche if we are to understand the whence and the wither of the images required for insight. For in the psyche's repression and liberation lie the explanations both of understanding's foundering and its flight. He gives the reader some brief definitions of psychic conversion, from which he proceeds to strike the zenith chord of the chapter in arguing for the liberative transformation of the censor from repression to construction, insisting that to refuse insight is to refuse one's own development and to refuse one's own development is to embrace one's own decline. Hemmer asserts that psychic conversion is restorative because the constructive function of the censor in the existential subject is the natural and authentic form while repressive censorship is a distortion of that natural function to accept insight.

In Chapter Eight, Cody Sandschafer, traces the movement of Paul Ricoeur's thought, one of the thinkers who shaped Doran's thinking. According to Sandschafer, the transition from abstract thought in Ricoeur's *Freedom and Nature* to concrete philosophical anthropology in the *Fallible Man* brought about a change in methodology that eventually shapes the rest of Ricoeur's subsequent thoughts including the concretization of symbols to the universe of discourse important in Ricoeur's hermeneutics and textual analysis. While Ricoeur studied Freud and Jung, his preference for Freud over Jung could be because of lack of philosophical rigor in Jung. However, unlike Ricoeur, Doran prefers Jung's notion of the symbol and the imagination over Freud. Sandschafer argues that Doran while drawing a lot from Ricoeur, distanced himself from his naïve realism in preference for Lonergan's critical realism. Sandschafer compares Doran and Ricoeur and draws out other points of difference between them and argues that Doran advances Ricoeur while equally correcting Ricoeur's limitations.

PART THREE applies psychic conversion to spirituality, scripture, Ignatian spiritual exercises and to cases of trauma. In Chapter Nine, Danielle Nussberger relates psychic conversion to spiritual direction especially the relationship between the spiritual director with the directee through Tara Brach's development of the RAIN. Nussberger argues that RAIN "encourages an awakening of one's psychic dimension that is intimately interconnected with one's spiritual and physical well-being." "The acronym of RAIN that stands for recognize (what is happening), allow (life to be just as it is), investigate (with a gentle, curious attention) and nurture (with loving presence). Nussberger martials the importance of psychic conversion to overcoming ego's biases and prejudices and thus to establish the conditions necessary for communal and social transformation.

In Chapter Ten, Joseph K. Gordon presents Doran's psychic conversion as necessary if people must be healed from fear and wrongly
held notions about several biblical images. He calls for an application
of the transcendental precepts leading to psychic conversion and a
more profitable use of scriptural texts. Gordon clarifies that the psyche occupies a middle ground between organism and spirit and has
its finality in intellectual, moral, and ultimately religious self-transcendence. In psychic conversion, we are freed, to objectify, consider
and make fruitful use of those images in the flow of life in the work of
participating in and promoting the increasing self-transcendence that
comes from intellectual, moral, and religious conversion. Psychic conversion is the transformation of a preconscious psychic function. Gordon leads the reader through the three worlds of scripture: the world
behind the text, the world of the text and the world in front of the
text. He explains further that there are meanings that are lost due to
social and cultural malformation and stunted personal development.
This loss significantly shapes the dramatic pattern of the experiences
of individuals.

In Chapter Eleven, Gerard Whelan explains how closely the
notion of psychic conversion relates to themes found in *The Spiritual
Exercises of St. Ignatius*. Whelan engages an aspect of psychic conversion that opens the subject to the role of the supernatural in the realm
of self-appropriation, self-transcendence, and grace. He identifies in
Doran, the starting point of this nature-supernature correlation in
the censor related to the phenomenon of 'complexes' at the level of
the unconscious. As far as images go, Doran speaks of two sets of
data—of intentionality and of psyche—along two poles of "spirit"
and "psyche." It is within this duality that a vertical finality towards
participation in the line of the spirit emanates. These two poles operate in a dialectic of contraries where dreams, for example, proposes to
make possible a project and ensure that the project remains possible.
Whelan turns to a demonstration of Doran's exploration of the cross
as the most effective anagogic symbol. Whelan demonstrates precisely how Doran's psychic conversion bolsters an understanding and
practice of the spiritual exercises of St Ignatius of Loyola. One after

the other he strikingly demonstrates this connection with the themes of the cross and repentance for sin, Ignatian contemplation, Repetition and application of the scenes, and the theme of discernment and election. In Chapter Twelve, Randy Rosenberg's "The Spiritual Texture of Trauma" calls out the neglect of philosophers and theologians to the neural and psychic dimension of life which Doran has called attention to in his works. In establishing the link between Doran and the spiritual texture of trauma, Rosenberg employs the understanding of healing and trauma in Bessel van der Kolk and Doran's psychic conversion and self-transcendence as well as the integration of the role of imitation and mimetic desire in the later works of Doran. He identifies the damage and disintegration of the victim's fundamental human structure as consisting in a grave loss of trust in oneself, in others and in God. He demonstrates Doran's holistic vision of the human person as a salient entry point in attending to trauma in human experiences as it accounts for both self-acceptance and self-transcendence. Given its attention to the biological, neurological, and psychic dimensions of human experience, Rosenberg identifies Doran's approach as a psychology of orientation rather than a psychology of passional motivation—it is oriented towards self-acceptance and self-transcendence. He demonstrates how both von der Kolk (social dimension of trauma) and Girard (neurological/mimetic desire) can be harnessed to attend to the interrelated realms of organism, psyche, and spirit for the healing of victims of trauma. Psychic conversion is the meeting point that guarantees this transformation and healing of the psyche.

PART FOUR applies psychic conversion to the contemporary issues of racism, particularly Replacement Theory, Antiblackness, Decolonization, contemporary psychotherapeutic practices, and higher education. In Chapter Thirteen, Cyril Orji asks: If bias, understood as flight from insight, can be healed by the transformation of the censor from repressive to constructive agency, what then are the practical ways in which the healing potency of psychic conversion may be actualized in the practical experiences of the human society? Orji's chapter does justice to the question by establishing the replacement theory as a dramatic bias that psychic conversion must heal for the recovery of both the perpetrator and victim. It focuses on healing the perpetrator of this ill, presenting him/her also as being a victim of his own and society's machinations in the real sense. Orji acknowledges the difficulty in trying to change a long-held (false) notion, especially with the hold of *scotosis* that keeps the subject from corrective insights. But then psychic conversion, understood as a sublation of the three other moral, intellectual and religions forms of conversion hold the promise of transforming the repressive censor identified as the replacement theory in this case. The chapter therefore concludes that "it will require a psychic re-orientation for proponents and believers in Replacement theory to drop their misleading fears, errors, and ideologies with respect to immigrants and ethnic minorities . . . psychic conversion can turn the negative energy, fear, into a positive energy, love."

In Chapter Fourteen, Jeremy Blackwood takes on headlong, 'the plague of antiblackness that infects the social order, and cultural meaning and values of the United States.' Developed in two parts, Blackwood attempts to demonstrate the relevance of psychic conversion to Lonergan's understanding of redemption and the law of the cross. He describes antiblackness and its debilitating effects on the US society. The chapter concludes by arguing for psychic conversion as a workable solution in addressing the menace of antiblackness. Blackwood observes a move from the 'therapeutic' movement towards authenticity in all its dimensions of consciousness in early Doran to transformation of censorship into productive agency in later Doran. Blackwood sketches the implication of psychic conversion in addressing societal ills. He also makes a connection between Doran's psychic conversion and Girard's mimetic desires, showing how Girard's position not only reinforces Doran's and Lonergan's understanding of dramatic bias but also specifies and offers a great approach to psychic conversion. Blackwood thus problematizes antiblackness in the American society as a specific evil that an advanced understanding of psychic conversion, enhanced by mimetic desire can effectively address.

In Chapter Fifteen, Mark Obeten, focuses on ways in which theological engagement can contribute to the development of African nation states by enhancing a change or reorientation in approaches to development in the continent. It takes a cursory look at the relationship between colonialism and the poverty, bad governance, religious charlatanism, gross lack of infrastructure and a wide spectrum of less-than-perfect situations in Africa. In a historical overview, decolonization is approached in three stages or periods namely pre-independence, independence, and postcolonial efforts. It adopts a definition of decolonization as all efforts to challenge the continued dominance of the European or Western hegemony of knowledge and overall control in Africa. Obeten contributes to the decolonization discourse on two levels. First, he challenges the western powers to let Africa be truly independent in running her affairs and deciding structures of governance and economic policies that are best for its own peoples and realities. Secondly, he challenges the African leaders and people to be more intentional in breaking from dependence on western knowledge curriculum as they build policies and strategies for development in the continent. He insists that the contribution of theology must begin from within the religious arena ridding itself of the superficiality and misguidedness of prosperity gospel and magical divine interventions. In effect, he calls for a psychic conversion that will promote authenticity, self-transcendence and (psychic) conversion in the process of decolonization and hence development. In Chapter Sixteen Andrea Stapleton's Psychic Conversion and Catholic Higher Education seeks to evaluate and strengthen approaches to Catholic higher education in terms of psychic conversion. It illustrates how psychic conversion can affect students' overall human development with the right orientation of the need to attend to the psychic component of education, orienting students to the broader world. Given that the dialectic of history is such that the individual both influences society but is a product of it, she argues, attention must be paid to how institutions build individuals who will in turn develop an authentic society; care must be taken to see that evil or distortion of the good images do not get reinforced instead of the good. So, while individuals need to experience psychic conversion, society must produce true images and symbols to make the individual's psychic conversion achievable. This positive influence of the society is guaranteed by what Doran calls 'cultural integrity' and is true for both the broader society for which the students are being prepared and the Catholic institution that forms them. Catholic Higher Education must take headlong, the challenge of moderating meaning and reversing the cycle of decline in society by promoting a discipleship that would catalyze a global network of community who counter contemporary competing and escalating distortions in the society. Psychic conversion helps students towards authentic development by making judgments of value based on the genuine attention and response to one's true desire—autonomous decision making, sense of the common god and a grounding in the experiences of transcendent meaning. The author argues that in this way, psychic conversion can make for a method to approach religion and one's vocation in a more appealing and authentic fashion. Therefore, Stapleton concludes that CHE, as a faith-based organization can strengthen the mission of schools by the transcendental method projected by psychic conversion and its emphasis on self-transcendence and dialectic of history.

In Chapter Seventeen, Cecille Maldonado applies the Christian idea of God as Trinity of Persons in relation to the whole human person. She recommends healing of this whole person and creates awareness of the human imitation of Trinitarian life mirrored in contemporary psychotherapy. Thus, the Trinity remains relevant in all contexts particularly in health care. She connects Lonergan and Doran's Trinitarian theology with the practice of mindfulness connecting self-compassion to the psychological analogy of the Trinity.

ACKNOWLEDGEMENTS

presented the topics *Intellect, Affect and God: The Trinity, History and The Life of Grace*; and *Perspectives on Psychic Conversion as Robert M. Doran's Core Academic Contribution* to the Marquette University's College of Arts and Sciences Poster Session in 2020. The former which I edited with Gerard Whelan, SJ of Gregorian University Rome was published in 2021. I am happy this volume is seeing the light of day. I am also happy Robert M. Doran SJ knew of the volume. Since he died before its publication, I am dedicating it to him in praise of his contribution to the academic community and to the advancement of the Lonergan project.

I thank the various contributors for their patience as the project gradually came together in one piece. I worked closely with Mark Obeten, a PhD student at Marquette, who assembled the contributions and constructed the initial draft of the synopsis of the chapters. Special thanks are due to Marquette University, the Dean of the College of Arts and Sciences, Heidi Bostic, and to the Chair of Theology Department, Conor Kelly, whose continued support for the Lonergan Project, and the International Institute for Method in Theology keeps Lonergan studies afloat. Thanks also to the members of the Marquette Lonergan Society whose dogged efforts sustain interest in the Lonergan studies.

I am immensely grateful to the Marquette University Press and to Maureen Kondrick for publishing this volume. I especially recognize the sacrifices that go into the process and salute their effort to make Lonergan studies available to the reading public.

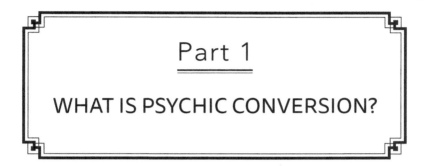

Part 1

WHAT IS PSYCHIC CONVERSION?

1

Societal Impasse and Social Grace

M. Shawn Copeland

Boston College

The fracture of national life provoked by the novel coronavirus and its mutants demoralized many of us Americans. Anxiety and isolation drove some of us to fantasy and indifference, others of us to rage and hostility, and still others of us to exhaustion and despair. Some of us wallowed in "willful blindness, scapegoating, and lies," others of us touted "conspiracy theories"[1] or hawked miracle cures. But when we watched Derek Chauvin press his knee into George Floyd's neck for more than nine minutes, *we the people*, or at least several hundred thousands of us, rose up in protest and sorrow, in fear and hope.

Indeed, many of us recognized, perhaps, for the first time, that we can no longer dodge our nation's historical, cultural, and social dilemmas: The uncritical surrender to neoliberalism's manipulation of the market economy with its resulting gross inequity and the mockery of the nation's political process; the criminalization of poverty and contempt for poor and working people;[2] disdain for those who are homeless;[3] arrogant and casual misogyny that has generated 'rape

---

1. George Packer, "We Are Living in a Failed State," https://mail.google.com/mail/u/0/#inbox/FMfcgxwHMsSvWfxhRQxKFbMBrShZvTTr

2. See Steven High and David W. Lewis, *Corporate Wasteland: The Landscape and Memory of Deindustrialization* (Ithaca/London: Cornell University Press, 2007).

3. See Matthew Desmond, *Evicted: Poverty and Profit in the American City* (New York: Penguin Random House, 2016), Deborah Padgett et al, *Housing First: Ending Homelessness, Transforming Systems, Changing Lives* (New York: Oxford, 2016).

culture';[4] disregard of Indigenous peoples;[5] anti-Semitic shootings and verbal assaults;[6] obliviousness to environmental racism,[7] condescension to differently-abled women and men,[8] capricious and for-profit incarceration of Black and brown men, youth, and women;[9] indifference at the deaths of Black and brown youth, men, and women while interacting with police or their agents;[10] hate-fueled crimes against LGBTQI persons;[11] nativism and bigoted treatment of immigrants

4. See Kate Harding, *Asking for It: The Alarming Rise of Rape Culture and What We Can Do about It* (Philadelphia: Perseus Press, 2015).

5. Ana Mari Cauce, "Ending Violence against Indigenous People Starts with Ending Silence around It," https://www.washington.edu/president/2022/05/04/mmip-awareness-day-2022/; see Roxanne Dunbar-Ortiz, *An Indigenous Peoples' History of the United States* (Boston: Beacon Press, 2015).

6. Campbell Robertson, Christopher Mele, Sabrina Tavernise, "11 Killed in Synagogue Massacre; Suspect Charged with 29 Counts," October 27, 2018, https://www.nytimes.com/2018/10/27/us/active-shooter-pittsburgh-synagogue-shooting.html / The Southern Poverty Law Center, "The Year in Hate and Extremism," documented 50 anti-Muslim groups active in the U. S. in 2021, https://www.splcenter.org/sites/default/files/splc-2021-year-in-hate-extremism-report.pdf/

7. Consider the Flint, Michigan, water crisis that began in 2014 when the city of Flint switched its water source from the Detroit Water and Sewage Department to the Flint River.

8. See Susan Burch and Michael Rembis, ed., *Disability Histories* (Urbana: University of Illinois Press, 2014).

9. See Michelle Alexander, *The New Jim Crow: Mass Incarceration in the Age of Colorblindness* (New York: The New Press, 2010), Bryan Stevenson, *Just Mercy: A Story of Justice and Redemption* (New York: Random House, 2015).

10. Consider these senseless racially-motivated killings—in 1998 James Byrd; in 2012 Trayvon Martin and Rekia Boyd; in 2013 Andy Lopez; in 2014 Michael Brown, Eric Garner, and Tamir Rice; in 2015, Freddie Gray, Jr., Sandra Bland, and in Charleston, South Carolina at Mother Emanuel AME Church: Sharonda Coleman-Singleton, DePayne Middleton Doctor, Cynthia Hurd, Susie Jackson, Ethel Lance, Clementa Pinckney, Tywanza Sanders, Daniel Simmons, and Myra Thompson; in 2016, Alton Sterling and Philando Castile.

11. Recall these senseless homophobically-motivated murders—in 1998 Matthew Shepherd; in 2003 Saskia Gunn, Shani Baraka and Rayshon Holmes; in 2008 Angie Zapata; in 2016 the 49 women and men in Orlando, Florida at the Pulse Night Club including Stanley Almodóvar, Amanda Alvear, Antonia Davon Brown, Luis Daniel Conde, Anthony Laureano Disla, Mercedez Marisol Flores, Eddie Justice, and Christopher Andrew Leinonen.

and asylum seekers;[12] increasing racial animus directed at Latino and Asian children, youth, women, and men.[13]

Only now are we beginning to reckon with the meanings, implications, and consequences of the underside of nation's history. We are undergoing 'something'—the air we breathe is thick with uncertainty, mistrust, and political volatility; shared cultural assumptions and civic mores are in upheaval, on the verge of breakdown and collapse; each night we lie down beside gnawing anxiety. We do not know what to do or how to do it. Perhaps, our long, languishing moment is redolent of what Christian spiritual tradition knows as 'dark night,' or what Carmelite theologian Constance FitzGerald identifies in the social domain as 'impasse,' 'the dark night' of our world.[14] The notion of impasse refers generally to a situation from which

> there is no way out of, no way around, no rational escape from, what imprisons [us]. . . . [E]very normal manner of acting is brought to a standstill, and ironically, impasse is experienced not only in the problem itself but also in any solution rationally attempted. Every logical solution remains unsatisfying, at the very least. . . . Any movement out, any next step, is canceled and the most dangerous temptation is to give up, to quit, to

---

12. Esther Yu His Lee, "Poll: Americans' Anti-Immigrant Attitudes Are Fueled by Racism," *Think Progress*, July 7, 2016, http://www.thinkprogress.org/poll-americans-anti-immigrant-attitudes-are-fueled-by-racism-30968b83a908/.

13. Recall that on February 19, 1942, President Franklin D. Roosevelt signed Executive Order 9066 authorizing the Secretary of War to identify and secure certain areas of the country as military zones and, thus, incarcerate Japanese Americans; see Yoshiko Uchida, *Desert Exile: The Uprooting of a Japanese American Family* (Seattle: University of Washington Press, 1982); Jaweed Kaleem, Kurtis Lee, Melissa Etehad, "Anti-Asian Hate Crimes and Harassment Rise to Historic Levels during COVID-19 Pandemic," *The LA Times*, March 5, 2021, https://www.latimes.com/world-nation/story/2021-03-05/anti-asian-crimes-harassment

14. Constance FitzGerald, "Impasse and Dark Night," 77, in *Desire, Darkness, and Hope: Theology in a Time of Impasse, Engaging the Thought of Constance FitzGerald, OCD*, ed., Laurie Cassidy and M. Shawn Copeland (Collegeville, MN: Liturgical Press, 2021).

surrender to cynicism and despair, in the face of the disappointment, disenchantment, hopelessness, and loss of meaning.[15]

The more we thrash about in attempts to escape our situation by avoiding it or ignoring it or blaming it on someone or something else--the worse it becomes. Thoroughgoing impasse, Sister FitzGerald writes, puts an end to our habitual ways of acting and thinking; neither reason nor logic, neither careful analysis nor meticulous planning can resolve the matter or lead to solutions. Rather, we must acknowledge [our] powerlessness and engage practices of openness, of waiting, and Dorothee Soelle called "revolutionary patience" for what cannot be demanded.[16] The unexpected, the new vision lies just beyond conscious efforts at rational analysis, receding at every attempt to wrest control.[17] *Impasse*: the strange and discomfiting societal situation that we ourselves have made through our refusals *to live mindfully—to live reasonably, responsibly, and lovingly* in relation to the Divine and the entire created order.

Robert Doran in his article "Social Grace" raises the basic issue with which I am concerned. Namely, that "theology [ought to] elevate 'collective responsibility,' in the concrete dispensation that is ours, into something like "social and cultural grace.""[18] In order to sharpen and focus reflection on social and cultural grace, this chapter analyzes an event recounted by Kelly Brown Douglas in her *Stand Your Ground: Black Bodies and the Justice of God*.[19] First, I relate the anecdote and ask what is at stake in this event; then, consider racism as a systemic or structured result of bias; third, interrogate human development in a

---

15. FitzGerald, "Impasse and Dark Night," in *Desire, Darkness, and Hope*, 78–79.

16. Cited in FitzGerald, "Impasse and Dark Night," 102, in *Desire, Darkness, and Hope*. FitzGerald writes that Dorothee Soelle understands contemplation as "revolutionary patience" and [it] is "the epitome of passionate desire, activity, self-direction, autonomy, and bondedness;" see Dorothee Soelle, *Revolutionary Patience* (Maryknoll, N.Y.: Orbis Books, 1977).

17. FitzGerald, "Impasse and Dark Night," 96, in *Desire, Darkness, and Hope*.

18. Robert M. Doran, "Social Grace," *Method, Journal of Lonergan Studies* 2, 2 (2011): 131–142, at 132.

19. Kelly Brown Douglas, *Stand Your Ground: Black Bodies and the Justice of God* (Maryknoll, N.Y.: Orbis Books, 2015).

racially biased culture; and finally, say something about social grace—
integrating grace in the social order.

The Anecdote and What is at Stake

In *Stand Your Ground*, Kelly Brown Douglas, a brilliant systematic theologian and Episcopal priest, recalls an incident that occurred many years
ago, when one morning she took her then two-year-old son to play in
a park. After their arrival, the two-year-old soon settled in and played
at driving a toy car. A short time later, a group of what appeared to be
first or second grade students from a nearby elementary school recessed
into the park's playground. Two little White boys, one blond-haired, the
other red-haired purposefully ran toward the car in which Douglas's son
was playing; when he saw the other boys running toward the car, the
two-year-old jumped out and moved away. But, almost immediately the
two White boys stopped running and began to fight with each other:
Who would be first in the car. Then, the little red-haired boy noticed
the little Black boy looking. He stopped fighting, pointed a finger at
Douglas's son, and said: "You better stop looking at us, before I put you
in jail where you belong."[20] Before Douglas could react, a White female
teacher, standing within earshot, approached. Douglas writes that she
expected the woman to admonish the little White boy and direct him to
apologize. Instead, she states, the teacher "looked at my two-year-old son
as if he were the perpetrator of some crime and said to the other two little boys, 'Come on with me, before there is trouble.'"[21] Quietly seething
with anger, Douglas took her son, left the park, and drove home in tears.
"I felt," she recalled, "an unspeakable sadness and pain."

> At two years old my son was already viewed as a criminal. At
> seven or eight years old the link between a black body and a crim-
> inal had already been forged in the mind of a little white boy. If
> at two years old my son was regarded as guilty of something by

20. Kelly Brown Douglas, *Stand Your Ground: Black Bodies and the Justice of God*
(Maryknoll, N.Y.: Orbis Books, 2015), 86–87.

21. Douglas, *Stand Your Ground: Black Bodies and the Justice of God* , 87.

the white teacher, I feared what his future would bring as he got older.[22]

What is at stake in this anecdote: Certainly, the long, compound-complex, and fragile work of character formation *in* and *for* each of these three little human beings, their growth and maturity into personhood. The little White red-haired boy is angry; perhaps, he has played with the toy car frequently and just as frequently raced against the little White blond-haired boy to take the prize. But, now a little Black boy, although younger and smaller, has intruded into *his* space. The little White red-haired boy does not like the little stranger looking at him. He lashes out, repeating words he has heard, perhaps, from a parent or relative, a television commentator. An adult, relevant, perhaps, even significant to the formation of his character, affirms his anger and reaffirms his feeling that Black bodies are dangerous, even criminal, and should be punished and jailed.

The little Black boy sees the bigger boys coming, jumps out of the car, and watches intently. The sudden angry outburst directed at him, more than likely hurts and confuses. Perhaps, he experiences a confused, inchoate sense that something is wrong; perhaps, he feels uncomfortable; certainly, he has been made to feel unwelcome in public space. Perhaps, the little Black boy may even experience anxiety about his body, about his race. His mother, so significant to the formation of his character, removes him from this awkward space and wrestles with the disconcerting knowledge that quite likely her son will have such encounters again.

What is at stake in this anecdote is the character formation of three little human beings, but not *their* individual formation only or merely. We humans are social beings embedded in "biological, genetic, neurological, and psychic sets of schemes of recurrence relating us unconsciously and consciously to others."[23] What is at stake in

---

22. Douglas, *Stand Your Ground: Black Bodies and the Justice of God*, 87.

23. Matthew Lamb, "The Social and Political Dimensions of Lonergan's Theology," 260, in *The Desires of the Human Heart: An Introduction to the Theology of Bernard Lonergan*. Vernon Gregson, ed. (New York: Paulist Press, 1988).

this brief narrative is our human capacity for recognition and acknowledgment, correction and self-correction, humble and determined efforts to face up to and eradicate bias in our personal, interpersonal, and communal living. What is at stake here is our shared civic culture, our national character as a moral community. What is at stake is *realization of the human good* with its dependence on the genuineness of human persons; on human attention, intelligence, judgment, responsibility, appropriate and adequate action (self-appropriation); on the quality, verve, and authenticity of human relationships.

Bias and Racism

Lonergan deploys the term bias quite precisely to denote aberrations of human understanding or affect that exclude and repress insights and the further questions they may generate. Bias stems from the flight from insight; it is the more or less conscious and deliberate choice to be incorrect, to repress or to deny the surfacing of further questions or insights; the refusal to think, to act, and to live attentively, intelligently, rationally and responsibly.[24]

All human beings are susceptible to bias as it distorts and inhibits our conscious performance in everyday living by blinding our understanding, stunting affective growth, and damaging the achievement or realization of community. Bias may occur in any of four principal ways—dramatic, individual, group, and general bias. Dramatic bias takes the form of the denial of painful affect in the day-to-day living out of our lives; this may be brought to light by psychology. Individual bias expresses itself in egoism, in self-regarding self-regard. Group bias expresses itself in singular regard and safeguarding the exclusivity of privileges and prerogatives that ensure the prominence and dominance of 'my' particular group or association or social class or race at the expense of the common human good. Finally, through general bias, common sense smugly considers itself

---

24. Bernard Lonergan, *Insight: A Study of Human Understanding* (New York: Philosophical Library, 1957), especially, Chs. 6, 7, 18–20.

omni-competent, jousting against science or technical specialization, theory or philosophy. This last form of bias exerts a distinctive role in constricting and distorting insights for the practical, intelligent, imaginative ordering of the human good, for healing and creating in society and in history. Individual, group, and the general bias function as alienations of empirical, intellectual, rational, and responsible consciousness.

The most concise definition of *racism* is *prejudice + power*. Prejudice literally conveys pre-judging, that is, coming to judgment about something or someone prior to experience or knowledge of or encounter with. Because prejudice stems from ignorance, it may be corrected and judgments revised; but the refusal to accept correction, to revise judgments, to incorporate corrected information and new judgments into one's repertoire is bias.

Racism is the spoiled fruit of bias; it links attitudes or feelings of superiority to putatively legitimate exercises of power. A comprehensive definition of racism comes from the work of James Lee Boggs:

> Racism is systematized oppression of one race of another. In other words, the various forms of oppression within every sphere of social relations—economic exploitation, military subjugation, political subordination, cultural devaluation, psychological violation, sexual degradation, verbal abuse, etc.—together make up a whole of interacting and developing processes which operate so normally and naturally and are so much a part of the existing institutions of society that the individuals involved are barely conscious of their operation.[25]

Racism does not rely on the choices or actions of a few lone or even so-called 'rogue' individuals; rather it is structured or institutionalized; indeed, racism as bias is woven into the fabric of our daily human living. If we define culture as the various sets of meanings and values that inform the way we live, then racism has infiltrated those meanings—shaping

---

25. James Lee Boggs, *Racism and the Class Struggle* (New York: Monthly Review Press, 1970), 147–148.

our ideas, attitudes, and dispositions; directing our norms, rules, and expectations; guiding our linguistic, literary, artistic, media representations and socio-cultural practices.

In short, we generate and sustain, live and love, work and worship within a racist culture.[26] Group bias as expressed in racism, sexism, homophobia, exploitation, violence, anti-Semitism, Islamophobia, anti-Asian hate are not *out there*, they are *in* us. They are sedimented in our consciousness, they suffuse all our decisions about the concrete human set-up, they penetrate all our relations, and they are involved in the mediation of those meanings and values that constitute our culture. Indeed, bias so structures our worldview, that to behave otherwise is deemed abnormal.

Human Development in a Racially Biased Culture

The sad encounter between two little boys—one white, one black—exposes the potential for dramatic and individual bias as well as for *ressentiment*[27] to take root in the human mind and heart. This encounter also illustrates graphically the intimate connection between what we know, what and how we feel, and how we behave toward ourselves and toward others.[28] Human development is no simple negotiation: Early childhood calls for the development of motor and cognitive skills of every sort. These must be modeled or taught, grasped and tried, practiced and mastered. Consider some of the shifts in affective life or feelings or emotions that a school-age child must effect. The young

---

26. David Theo Goldberg, *Racist Culture: Philosophy and the Politics of Meaning* (Oxford: Blackwell Publishers, 1993), 8.

27. To illustrate the enervating power of aberrant feeling particularly in the social pattern of experience, Lonergan introduces Max Scheler's reformulation of *ressentiment*, a French loan-word introduced into philosophy by Friedrich Nietzsche (Max Scheler, *Ressentiment*, trans., William W. Holdheim (1912; 1915; New York: The Free Press of Glencoe, 1961) and Manfred Frings, *Max Scheler* (Pittsburgh, PA: Duquesne University Press; Louvain: Editions E. Nauwelaerts, 1965).

28. Walter Conn, *Conscience: Development and Self-Transcendence* (Birmingham, Alabama: Religious Education Press, 1981), 86; see also, Conn, "Passionate Commitment: The Dynamics of Affective Conversion," *Cross Currents* (Fall 1984): 329–336.

child's "unilateral respect" for parents or other adults leads him or her to a morality of obedience or heteronomy; but growth and deepening calls for further development. When children cooperate among themselves a new social life emerges, so too do new feelings of "mutual respect" for others. But, the most significant and distinctive stage of emotional or affective development, Jean Piaget argues, is the emergence of a more or less organized cluster of values and of the will.[29] "Mutual respect and cooperation, which recognize the relative autonomy of individual conscience, lead to an organized system or scale of personal values—honesty, a sense of justice, reciprocity."[30] Yet, moral educators like Walter Conn and developmental psychologists such as Lawrence Kohlberg point out that as "this sense of justice develops . . . it reinforces respect for authority and for the rules of adult society" even if it may not overlook more informal peer norms.[31]

Given this psychological sketch of affective development among school-age children, what happens to such development in a racially biased cultural setting? To explore this question, let's revisit Douglas' anecdote. The red-haired boy is on the cusp of the shift from heteronomy to autonomy; heretofore, his cognitive and affective behavior has been shaped by unilateral respect for parents and adults. Perhaps, in spite of fighting with the little blond boy, he has begun to feel respect for him and for his other classmates; perhaps, he even yearns to cooperate with them. Perhaps, he has begun to think about what is fair (*not yet justice*), about sharing. But on this particular morning, it seems as if he is unable to risk a further step.

For whatever unintentional feeling, for whatever reason the presence of the little Black boy unsettles and aggravates him. He speaks

---

29. Conn, *Conscience: Development and Self-Transcendence* (Birmingham, Alabama: Religious Education Press, 1981), 61; see Jean Piaget, *Six Psychological Studies*, 55, cited in Conn, *Conscience: Development and Self-Transcendence* (Birmingham, Alabama: Religious Education Press, 1981), 61

30. Piaget, *Six Psychological Studies*, 58–59, cited in Conn, *Conscience: Development and Self-Transcendence* (Birmingham, Alabama: Religious Education Press, 1981), 61.

31. Conn, *Conscience: Development and Self-Transcendence* (Birmingham, Alabama: Religious Education Press, 1981), 65.

in an imperative (even imperious) tone: *"You better stop looking at us, before I put you in jail where you belong."* The sentence carries the force of a command, a threat with well-defined consequences. It resonates with surety, control, authority: *"I [can] put you in jail."* The sentence is inflected with racial recognition and racial stereotypes that shape not only how he/we are taught to see and, too often, do see Black people, but how we interpret their behavior, their actions, or facts about them.[32] Further this utterance warns of a boundary—*"stopping looking at us."* The fight is finished: now, it's *us* and *you*, insider and outsider, free and controlling, restricted and controlled. The little boy is only seven or eight; he repeats or says what he has heard, picked up. In this event, he remains on the cusp of autonomy, he clings to the familiarity of what he has heard or learned and repeats it.

The teacher's (mistaken) affirmation encourages both little White boys to develop an idealized picture of themselves as in control, sure, and authoritative, perhaps, even to hold themselves aloof and apart from 'others' who may be different—not only in race, but ethnic heritage or gender or social class. Certainly, intersubjectivity, the basic component of our humanity within which affective and cognitive development may occur, is disrupted. Three little boys are left with varying sets of distorted experiences and impressions as well as emotions that could become the foundation for distorted understandings of and affect toward others.

That the little Black boy jumps out of the car as the two White boys approach intimates he already has imbibed something of what might mean to be 'other.' He is insulted and excluded, made to feel an outsider and unwelcome; he does not belong. Indeed, in the presence of one of the two most important adults in his life, he has been threatened—for looking. An adult considers that he is a putative (potential) troublemaker, a putative (potential) criminal. He is the object of instructions from others, the object of this incident, not its subject. He well may remember this day, mull it over, use it

---

32. Cheryl I. Harris, "Whitewashing Race: Scapegoating Culture," *California Law Review* 94, 3 (2006): 907–943 at 934.

as a reference point, or he may come to suffer *ressentiment*—that powerful, intentional, reactionary emotion welling up in persons who have been emotionally hurt or injured and who are prompted by reactionary resistance to those wounds. We may discern *ressentiment* among persons and groups who experience suppression or social domination or oppression. Should the two-year-old repeatedly *re-live* and *re-feel* the hurt or shame, he well might experience "psychic self-poisoning."[33] We also may discern *ressentiment* among persons and groups who are tricked into believing that their 'place' in the order of things has been claimed, usurped by outsiders, others. Should these little boys repeatedly re-live and re-feel the power to thwart others, to deny, to bully, another form of 'psychic self-poisoning' eats its way into their minds and heart. The little White boy who racially bullied and threatened the little Black boy might well grow up to be or be like Dylann Roof. Or that little boy could well have been a young white college student who hurls vicious epithets at African American or Asian college students. Or that little boy could well have been the students who hung a banner outside their dorm, "Let's finish what Katrina started."

Douglas removes her son from what has become a psychically dangerous space as quickly as she can; they go home. For most human beings, self-esteem remains a fragile achievement, for persons who experience social oppression it is even more tenuous. As a priest and a theologian, Douglas has the resources to comfort his bruised spirit and to bolster and challenge him to authentic emotional and affective growth, but she possesses neither the resources nor the social power to adequately protect him from biased authorities, who in fear and panic, might end his life.

Three little boys are left with sets of distorted experiences and impressions as well as emotions that may become the foundation for distorted understandings of and affect toward others. The incident illustrates the ability of racism to disrupt basic intersubjective spontaneity which is the primordial basis of human community. Yet,

---

33. Frings, *Max Scheler*, 83.

inasmuch as the account of bias is compatible with Lonergan's cognitional theory, the biases are correctable.[34] Conversion or transformation of mind and heart, behavior and action are possible; conversion or transformation of human persons, their cultures and societies is possible. Such conversion or transformation is costly, but possible.

Integrating Grace

In our concrete universe of being, the order of grace is distinct, but it is not sealed off and separate from the order of reason and the order of nature. Jean-Marc LaPorte reminds us that the "universality of grace . . . ranges beyond the ecclesial and sacramental and enters into the secular and the day by day realities of life, even when they lack explicit Christian or religious motivation."[35] For grace floods human hearts through the gift of the Holy Spirit given to us (*Romans* 5:5) and is poured out in Divine love on the whole of creation.

What is at stake is our willingness to accept and to pay the price of integrating grace in our living. The just, good, beautiful America for which we long is nested in the minds and hearts, behavior and actions—the character formation of our children. And, the conditions for that formation depend upon our attention, intelligence, judgment, responsibility, and action. We must be willing to incarnate what Australian theologian Kathleen Williams calls that "friendly authenticity"[36] through which we seek another's well-being. Her concern dovetails with Lonergan's insistence that the key to achieving the human good is located in personal relationships—in relationships between and among persons.

---

34. In his *Solidarity with Victims, Toward a Theology of Social Transformation* (New York: The Crossroad Publishing Company, 1982), Matthew Lamb argues Lonergan's cognitional theory as "radical cognitive therapy," 85.

35. Jean-Marc LaPorte, *Patience and Power: Grace for the First World* (Mahwah, NJ: Paulist Press, 1988), 41.

36. Kathleen M. Williams, RSM, "Friendly Authenticity in a Fractured World: On the Way to Peace," Paper read at the Lonergan Workshop, Boston College, Chestnut Hill, Massachusetts, June 2004.

We model "friendly authenticity" for those three little boys in Douglas' anecdote by reaching out and breaking down barriers; by patiently, consistently, and gently refusing to indulge hostility and calculated misunderstanding. We model such behavior for them–and all our children when we meet one another as "unique treasures rather than as threats," for grace affirms rather than suppresses difference.[37] We model such friendly authenticity by gently coaxing forward the wonder, affectivity, and psychic growth of our youngsters, even as we scrutinize ourselves. For many of us have experienced and know the delight of casual encounters deepening into rich and authentic friendships; many of us have experienced and cherish the bloom of encounter into marriage and intimate love, into family.

Could the adults in the anecdote have responded differently? Perhaps, the teacher could have reached out—not to affirm or brush away the little boy's comments, but to correct them. Perhaps, Douglas could have reached out—not in exasperation, but in expectation that in such a moment of adversity something 'new' might emerge. Both adults have capacity for what Christian tradition names *kenosis*, for meeting the negative or destructive creatively. Perhaps, it is too much to ask the White teacher to respond to a child's churlish behavior in a way that makes space for all children. Perhaps, it is too much to ask the Black mother not to defend her child, but Black mothers have been forced to do this in the most extreme circumstances for centuries. This is a moment of *impasse*: Nothing logical will suffice, the encounter is clash; it is racially charged; emotions or feelings are running high, placing heavy burdens on rational and psychic consciousness, on intellectual, psychic, and moral conversion. It is not a time to surrender to cynicism and despair and disenchantment. The children and the women involved are caught in reinscription of a centuries old and traumatic dilemma. Doran has rightly and ever so helpfully emphasized the importance of psychic conversion, "if good will is to be effectively harnessed in the struggle for social transformation."[38]

---

37. LaPorte, *Patience and Power*, 272.
38. Doran, *Psychic Conversion*.

Through the gift of grace accepted and actuated in human lives and hearts, our values and practices can meet the effects of racism that vitiate our social order. The realization of justice, friendship, and beauty within that social order depends upon the critical and humble appropriation of one's own subjectivity in religious, moral, and intellectual conversion; upon the critical and conscientious scrutiny of that complex of relations which shape the social and cultural ordering of our human situation; and upon those judgments of value realized in human practice. We women and men are instances of incarnate moral and ethical choice in a world under the influence of sin, yet we stand in relation to a field of grace.[39] To promote the human development and flourishing of those three little boys in that park and in all our parks and places, we must emphasize and engage humanity's essential humanness. Our resistance to racism must be rooted not in arrogant triumph over evil, but in humble love of human persons. Only love can bridge the impasse, the interpersonal abyss that racism generates. That love must acknowledge and witness to the oneness of human creatures and honor the richness of human diversity as a most basic feature of our human unity at the same time situating human creatures within the beauty of the order of God's creation.

---

39. Lonergan, *Insight, A Study of Human Understanding*, 422; Idem., "Finality, Love, Marriage," 16–53, in *Collection: Papers by Bernard Lonergan, S. J.*, ed. Frederick E. Crowe (Montreal: Palm Publishers, 1967).

2

Making Sense of Doran's Psychic Conversion

Joseph Ogbonnaya
Marquette University

While Lonergan is engaged with human consciousness, Doran introduces the important engagement with the imagination and disposition.[1] "Any human subject whose world is mediated and constituted by meaning is primordially in a condition of immediacy to oneself as cognitional and dispositional in that world: an immediacy to 'understanding,' that is to cognitional process, and an immediacy to mood."[2] The introduction of the psyche advances Lonergan's emphasis on the existential subject responsible for bringing about the good by acting on what one affirms as true because one understands, and one has experiences leading to such knowing. The notion of the psyche does not therefore exclude questions of cognitional theory, epistemology and metaphysics. If anything, it is built on them by the previous level of consciousness in what Lonergan describes as the process of sublation. So, the alternative to the neglected or truncated or immanentist or alienated subject (Lonergan listed in his 1965 paper "The Subject"),[3]

---

1. Robert M. Doran, *Subject and Psyche* 2nd edition (Milwaukee: Marquette University Press, 1994), 28.

2. Robert M. Doran, *Theological Foundations I: Intentionality and Psyche* (Milwaukee: Marquette University Press, 1995), 30.

3. Bernard Lonergan, "The Subject," in *A Second Collection: Papers by Bernard J.F. Lonergan, S.J.*, edited by William F.J. Ryan, S.J. and Bernard J. Tyrrell, S.J. (Toronto: University of Toronto Press, 1974).

Doran says, "lies in cognitional and existential self-appropriation."[4] To this he adds psychic self-appropriation which takes place within this existential self-appropriation; thus, extending Lonergan's interiority analysis to the level of the psyche. He asks: "But is the dramatic differentiation that existential self-appropriation is intrinsically linked to, even dependent upon, not itself in need of a conversion if it is to succeed? This is what I have argued in speaking of psychic conversion."[5] This chapter aims at exploring Doran's notion of the psyche, his expansion of Lonergan's three level conversion—intellectual, moral, and religious, with the inclusion of psychic conversion and its implication for theological foundation. It problematizes Doran's thinking in the functional specialty Foundations and argues for its indispensability both for Lonergan's cognitional theory as well as existential conversion and hence theological foundations. Because Doran's psychic conversion draws from Carl Jung's notion of the psyche, I will briefly expose Jung's psychology especially as it relates to the psyche. Also, as Doran's appropriation "heuristically integrates Jung's incredible familiarity with the human psyche with Lonergan's masterful treatment of intentionality,"[6] the psyche will be correlated to Lonergan's intentionality analysis.

The Importance of the Psyche in Jungian Psychology

In his autobiography, *Memories, Dreams, Reflections*,[7] Jung considers the inner life, the unconscious, the psyche, as the stone upon which external life is founded. It is the rock holding physical life, the imperishable world responsible for order in the transitory perishable world of human existence. For this reason, Jung is more concerned with it than anything else. "Outward circumstances are no substitute for inner

---

4. Doran, *Subject and Psyche*, 52.

5. Doran, *Theological Foundations I*, 245.

6. Doran, *Theological Foundations I*, 292.

7. C. G. Jung, *Memories, Dreams, Reflections* edited by Aniela Jaffe, trans. Richard and Clara Winston (New York: Vintage Books, 1989), 4.

experience . . . I can understand myself only in the light of inner happenings. It is these that make up the singularity of my life, and with these my autobiography deals."[8] Jung warns against considering the psyche "as a merely personal affair and to explain it from a personal point of view."[9] On the contrary, it is better to think of it as an autonomous power separate from human conscious personality. In other words, the psyche is separate from the conscious powers of human consciousness. It is the unconscious aspect that together with consciousness constitute human powers and ability to know and to create and to appropriate insight. The psyche is indispensable for knowledge and insight. "Without the psyche there would be neither knowledge nor insight."[10]

It (the psyche) determines all aspects of human life and controls the mechanism of societal life.[11] The development of the human person is dependent on the expansiveness of the psyche, when the psyche can grow and expand beyond the merely material but into the spiritual, with enriched inner experience. Jung uses the male and female aspects of human personality (*anima* and *animus* respectively) to describe the unconscious. The *anima* and *animus* represent the feminine element in men and the masculine element in women. They play typical role in the unconscious of human beings. They also have positive and negative aspects. The *anima* as the "mouthpiece of the unconscious"[12] on its own, independent of the conscious, can destroy a man. So, the *anima* always needs the conscious which can understand the unconscious and take a position toward them. Positively, the *anima* communicates the images of the unconscious to the conscious mind. For this reason, it is clear, the psyche complements the conscious aspects of human mental states. Together they constitute the human mind; separated, the intellect, stifled of feeling, suffers from neurosis.

---

8. Jung, *Memories, Dreams, Reflections*, 5.
9. Jung, *Psychology and Religion*, 16.
10. Jung, *Memories, Dreams, Reflections*, 98.
11. Jung, *Psychology and Religion,* 102.
12. Jung, *Memories, Dreams, Reflections*, 187.

Jung discovered the goal of psychic development to be the self. "I know that in finding the mandala as an expression of the self I had attained what was for me the ultimate."[13] Thus, he recommends not only allowing the images of the unconscious to rise, but also that humans take the trouble to understand them and draw ethical conclusions from them. "The images of the unconscious place a great responsibility upon a man. Failure to understand them, or a shirking of ethical responsibility, deprives him of his wholeness and imposes a painful fragmentariness on his life."[14]

Erich Neumann, a Jungian analytical psychologist whose book *The Origins and History of Consciousness*[15] Jung acknowledged as continuing and expanding his work,[16] endorsed and further explains Jung's emphasis on the psyche as the original ground of human consciousness. Neumann's position is to the effect that the unconscious preexisted the conscious (the ego). The emergence of the ego, of the self, from the psyche is the beginning of consciousness, of history. And this was done through cosmogonic myths.[17] The unconscious being prior to the conscious mind surrounds the object to be explained with concentric grouping of symbols able together to describe the unknown from many sides. The stories of creation are examples of such symbols. One symbol by which the psyche provides answer to the question of the whence of human origin, the origin of the cosmos and of consciousness is the symbol of the circle, the egg and the *rotundum*-the "round."[18] This is the symbol of the perfect, of the complete, of the self-contained, perfect fullness. Such self-contained circle in ancient cosmogony is the uroboros, the heavenly serpent, which in hermaphroditic representation is both male

---

13. Jung, *Memories, Dreams, Reflections*, 197.

14. Jung, *Memories, Dreams, Reflections*, 193.

15. Erich Neumann, *The Origins and History of Consciousness Vol 1*, trans. R. F. C. Hull (New York: Harper and Brothers, 1954).

16. C. G. Jung, "Foreword," Erich Neumann, *The Origins and History of Consciousness Vol 1*, xiii–xiv.

17. Neumann, *The Origins and History of Consciousness Vol 1*, 6.

18. Neumann, *The Origins and History of Consciousness Vol 1*, 8.

and female.[19] The Uroboros is the symbol of the human psyche, the pre-ego stage of humanity. As symbols like the mandala indicates, the ego gradually moves toward the self, consciousness. The goal of life is to make oneself independent, to stand by oneself, to free oneself from one's mothers apron strings, freedom from the world and all its constraints in the attainment of one's individuation, self-formation or "centroversion."[20] One realizes oneself by remaining in the tension of the opposites of the unconscious and the conscious. The point of emphasis here is the perfect harmony, the unity and the oneness of this symbol representing what later should be understood as the unity of consciousness, that is, the unity of the psyche and intentionality, of the unconscious and the conscious.[21] The nature of the creative force being represented in the symbol of the uroboros should also be an indication of the unity of human consciousness, of human knowing, of the psyche and intentionality. According to Doran: "What Lonergan has captured in his articulation of intellectual conversion is, in part, a cognitional thematizing of the psychically necessary victory of the knower over the uroboric dragon of myth, of the desire to know over the desire not to know, of the intention of being over the flight from understanding.[22] But unfortunately, the emergence or the development of ego consciousness often results to the neglect or forgetfulness of the unconscious. This leads to disintegration of the original and necessary wholeness required for human personality. "Ego formation can only proceed by way of distinction from the nonego and consciousness only emerge where it detaches itself from what is unconscious; and the individual only arrives at individuation when he marks himself off from

---

19. Neumann, *The Origins and History of Consciousness Vol 1*, 10.

20. Neumann, *The Origins and History of Consciousness Vol 1*, 37.

21. It is important to note, however, the limitation of Jung's notion of the spirit as it is limited to the cosmological realm, revolving around nature and not geared toward self-transcendence. Doran will later remark on this in his analysis of Jungian psychology and his quest for the reorientation of depth psychology. See Robert M. Doran, *Theology and the Dialectics of History* (Toronto: University of Toronto Press, 1990), 296–97.

22. Doran, *Theological Foundations I*, 37.

the anonymous collective."[23] The consequence of this disconnection of the ego from the nonego, of the conscious from the unconscious in Western thought is scary enough manifest in the modern decay of values; the integration, i.e., "the achievement of wholeness"[24] of the two systems of the conscious mind and the unconscious has to be speedily realized.

One of the avenues human natures seeks to maintain the unity of the unconscious and the conscious is through dream symbols as ways the unconscious makes entry into human consciousness. Jung shared Freud's dream interpretation and its relation to repression mechanism. However, while for Freud dreams are meanings already known but hidden from consciousness, for Jung, dreams are natural, and direct exponents of the unconscious. Dreams are not ridiculous nonsense but can form part of the inner experience by which one can get messages arising from the inner experience. For this reason, in his psychiatric activities Jung attends to his dream and to the dream of his patients. This provides the window into the psyche of his patients. His cure also revolves around open discussion of such dreams and their interpretation to his patients. It probes the depths of the psyche which is often hidden from the conscious aspects of human existence. In fact, dreams, Jung notes, "reveal the unknown inner facts of the psyche and of what these facts consist."[25] Dreams can be understood succinctly as "reflecting the spontaneous and autonomous activity of the objective psyche, the unconscious."[26]

Doran's Psychic Self-Appropriation

Doran's early appropriation and foundational use of Jung's emphasis of the psyche is in his doctoral dissertation published as *Subject and*

---

23. Neumann, *The Origins and History of Consciousness Vol 1*, 122.

24. Erich Neumann, *Depth Psychology and A New Ethic*, trans. Eugene Rolfe (Colorado: Shambhala Publications Inc. 1990), 102.

25. Jung, *Psychology and Religion*, 26.

26. Jung, *Psychology and Religion*, 57. Jung departed from Freud with the publication of his *Psychology of the Unconscious* (1912).

Psyche. In the book, Doran is engaged neither directly with Jungian psychotherapy nor in the analysis and updating of Jung's work but with theological method and foundations made possible through appropriation of the existential subject in the light of the psyche. The self-appropriation Doran is engaged here is akin to Jung's notion of individuation "as a cumulative process of the reconciliation of opposites under the guidance of responsible consciousness and with the aid of a professional guide."[27] Jung's psyche is limited by its Kantian bent and thence his non-recognition of the tending of the psyche to the transcendence which it is open to. Doran thus accuses Jung of "psychological immanentism"[28] which severely limited the scope of the reach of the psyche for him. This is because of Jung's inability to conceive of the self-transcendence of the unconscious into the conscious, from darkness to light. He asserts: "The only adequate horizon for understanding psychic data seems to demand not only the sublation of depth psychology by intentionality analysis but also the sublation of both psychology and method by the process of the discernment of spirit."[29]

Doran sets the immediate context for the discussion of the psyche within the existential context of the subject and hence of Lonergan's cognitional theory: those of moral and religious conversion.[30] Lonergan's advancement of morality in *Method in Theology* with his recognition of the good as a distinct notion brings to the fore the importance of feeling and hence of their integration for authenticity of moral self-transcendent existence, fidelity to the transcendental notions of attentiveness, intelligence, reasonableness and responsibility. In other words, taking cognizance of one's feelings help uncover the reasons for one's inauthenticity and thus assist in overcoming them in the future. It is within the context of value then that Lonergan mentions the role of the psyche, of psychotherapy as appropriating one's feelings just as one does one's attending, inquiring, understanding, conceiving and

---

27. Doran, *Theological Foundations I*, 88.
28. Doran, *Subject and Psyche*, 34.
29. Doran, *Theological Foundations, I*, 165.
30. Doran, *Subject and Psyche*, 53.

affirming.[31] This, Lonergan explains, is because "our apprehension of values occur in intentional responses, in feelings" through symbols.[32] Based on this correlation between psychic wholeness and cognitional authenticity, Doran concludes psychotherapy resembles Lonergan's moral conversion.[33] He argues that psychic self-appropriation complements the self-appropriation of intentional consciousness and further refines the self-knowledge of the existential subject.[34] "What Lonergan hints at is that the deliberating, evaluating, deciding, existential subject is also the aesthetic subject."[35]

In actual fact, cognitional self-transcendence without psychic self-appropriation leaves the subject isolated, "cut off from his or her roots in the rhythms and processes of nature, separated from his or her psychic ground, alienated from the original darkness which nourished one at the same time as it threatened to smother one, guilty over the primal murder of an ambiguously lifegiving power."[36] Doran observes that while Jung sees a human being through the prism of the psyche, Lonergan's distinction of the intentionality and the psyche better expresses human cognitional structure. The psyche complements Lonergan's intentionality analysis because it provides what is neglected in *Insight*'s emphasis of consciousness by supplying the unconscious element equally important in human knowing. Cognitive wholeness will demand appropriation of the psyche just as psychic wholeness will demand differentiation also of the thinking function.

> Insight, judgment, and decision have their home in the movement of life, in the aggregates of aggregates of aggregates of physical, chemical, botanical, and zoological conjugates that find their higher integration in psychic sensitivity. Through insight, judgment, and decision, we find direction in that movement. By

31. Doran, *Subject and Psyche*, 65.
32. Bernard Lonergan, *Method in Theology*, CWL 14,) 64–65.
33. Doran, *Subject and Psyche*, 67.
34. Doran, *Subject and Psyche*, 95.
35. Doran, *Theological Foundations I*, 124.
36. Doran, *Theological Foundations I*, 37–38.

finding and following the direction disclosed by insight, reasonable judgment, moral decision, and religious love, we mold the aggregates of aggregates of aggregates of lower order conjugates into a work of art. We make the movement of life a work of art. By neglecting insight, rational judgment, and authentic existential response we distort and corrupt the aggregates of aggregates of lower order conjugates. We make the movement of life into a series of disassociated and nonconsequential complexes.[37]

In a related sense then psychotherapy could be considered as "soul making," a way the twentieth century began to make amends for its neglect of the sensitive psyche.[38]

In other words, psychic conversion critically grounds intentionality analysis as Lonergan emphasizes intellectual, moral, and religious conversion. Doran focuses on finding a complementary understanding of psychic evolution in terms of the relations between intentionality and the psyche. It engages the psychic bases of human experience. *Subject and Psyche* is limited to the one task of correcting Jung's understanding of intentionality by presenting what Doran believes is a more adequate methodological framework of such depth-psychological articulation.[39] Psychic conversion is the gaining of psychic harmony, ability to integrate the three systems emphasized by Jung as constituting what Lonergan might call the unity of consciousness: instinct, psyche, and spirit. Doran toes the lines laid down by Jung in articulating the dialectics of the psyche: instinct (organism), psyche and the spirit. Consciousness is the integrator of the dialectics.

Doran appropriated, and corrected Jung's *animus* understood merely sexually into idea, word, spirit, intellect, principle, meaning, abstract. In this sense, he recommends appropriation of the *animus* as a good starting point of the appropriation of interiority leading towards the emergence of the authentic existential subject in Lonergan's sense.

---

37. Robert M. Doran, *Psychic Conversion and Theological Foundations: Toward A Reorientation of the Human Sciences* (California: Scholars Press, 1981), 158–159.

38. Doran, *Psychic Conversion and Theological Foundations*, 159.

39. Doran, *Subject and Psyche*, 102–3.

"As *animus* needs *anima*, so intentionality analysis needs psychic analysis. The discrimination of spirit must be complemented by the cultivation of soul and finally by the surrender of both spirit and soul in authentic religion."[40] Psychic conversion could be likened to a retrieval of the imaginal, the symbolic, the images, myths, feeling, nature, rhythm, etc. left behind as the Western mind opted for the *ratio*, for idea, abstraction, intellect, etc. Put differently, psychic conversion is an invitation to the Western mind to acknowledge feeling, symbol, love, the heart.[41] It is also an invitation of the non-Western mind to acknowledge and adopt the Western emphasis on reason, logic, idea, abstraction, etc. It is nothing but the recognition of the intrinsic connection between the psyche and the mind, in the fashioning of meaning and value.

Doran employs the methodological categories of the concept of "primordial immediacy," "second immediacy," "dispositional immediacy," to understand psychic self-appropriation in the light of Lonergan's intentionality analysis. "Primordial immediacy," understood as the primordial infrastructure of human consciousness is akin to Lonergan's unity of consciousness which comprises intentionality and the psyche, the cognitional and dispositional aspects which are inseparable. "Second immediacy" is the recovery of primordial immediacy through method.[42] It consists of three stages: intentional self-appropriation, psychic self-appropriation, and religious self-appropriation.[43] "Dispositional immediacy" is the expression used to describe what is recovered in the second immediacy through method. It is akin to Heidegger's *Befindlichkeit* which go together with *Verstehen* (understanding) as "constitutive ways of being the "there" of Being."[44] Doran uses this term in place of "feeling" because feeling has specific meaning in Jungian psychotherapy which does not exhaust what the notion

---

40. Doran, *Subject and Psyche*, 105–6

41. Doran, *Subject and Psyche*, 107.

42. Doran, *Psychic Conversion and Theological Foundations*, 162.

43. Doran, *Theological Foundations I*, 31.

44. Robert M. Doran, *Psychic Conversion and Theological Foundations: Toward a Reorientation of the Human Sciences* (California: Scholars Press, 1981) 157.

dispositional immediacy mediated by meaning would seek to imply. Dispositional immediacy could be expressed in the simple question we ask one another, "how are you doing?"[45]

> The mediation of primordial immediacy in its fullness involves the discrimination of spirit or intentionality, the cultivation of soul and psyche, and the surrender of both spirit and soul to the action of God's love in the world. Second immediacy would be enjoyed by one who has labored to achieve a self-conscious integration of intentionality and psyche or who has learned to live attentively, intelligently, reasonably, responsibly, lovingly, with their customary tension.[46]

Psychic self-appropriation (dispositional immediacy) and conscious intentionality (through method) is integrated through the sublation that surpasses what went before without destroying it in the process of advancement to the next level of consciousness. Failure to achieve individuation results to the loss of the spontaneous relationship that should ordinarily exist between the psyche and intentionality, between the conscious and the unconscious aspects of the mind.

The Self and Individuation Process

Doran's engagement with Jung's process of individuation ("development toward wholeness")[47] is in the light of Lonergan's generalized empirical method. Individuation is not just a reconciliation of opposites of matter and spirit, of good and evil, but a transcending process achieved through sublation. It "is a process of discovering, exploring, attending to that dimension of our being that is properly called psychic. Through this exploration, one comes to, one becomes, oneself, and one does so precisely by discovering a superabundance of meaning, beyond rational comprehension, that enables one to live what

---

45. Doran, *Theological Foundations I*, 30.
46. Doran, *Subject and Psyche*, 123–124.
47. Doran, *Theological Foundations I*, 266.

Jung called the 'just-so' life."[48] The summit of individuation is the self, understood as the subject, as the complex of the conscious and the unconscious dimensions with the unconscious entering the conscious through the dream symbols. Doran offers a corrective to the self-limiting dynamic of Jung's notion of the self, incapable of self-transcendence because of its inability to recognize the existential subject attentive, intelligent, reasonable, and responsible. This corrective which also is what he recommends for the reorientation of depth psychology presents a much more wholistic notion of the self. "Jung fails to appreciate how significant it is to the process of becoming, or living our way into the self, that the self is an intentional self, intent on and capable of affirming true meanings and making good decisions - where 'true' and 'good' denote self-transcendence as the criterion of one's genuineness as a knower and as a moral agent."[49]

Doran appropriates Jung's approach to dreams, but in terms of psychic energy. Doran's distinction makes sense because the unconscious is the sum of all energies in the universe that is not present to itself. In dream, these energies become conscious and so is called psychic energy.[50] Doran also differentiates with Jung the ego (he calls differentiated consciousness) and the self (totality of subjectivity). The self is a compound of the differentiated consciousness, the conscious but not objectified, and the strictly unconscious energy of neural-physiological process.[51] He distinguishes three forms of psychic energy in dreams: the personal (neural-physiological), the archetypal, collective unconscious for Jung, (reflecting nature as their content is on life, death, and rebirth) and the anagogic (transcendent and divine). A portion of the strictly unconscious enters the conscious realm when neural-physiological energy enters consciousness in the dream. While this dream symbol could be personal and hence could be permeated with intelligence, other dreams are archetypal (taken from and imitate nature) and "reflect more universal and generalizable motifs of personal

---

48. Doran, *Theological Foundations I*, 416.
49. Doran, *Theological Foundations, I*, 218–219.
50. Doran, *Theological Foundations I*, 322.
51. Doran, *Theological Foundations, I*, 162.

development and decline."[52] Anagogic dream symbols recorded in most religions originate from the transcendent being and is often associated with vocations and divine revelation. It is expression of mystery and human finality and foundational of history. And so, from existential point of view, Doran suggests there could be seven kinds of dreams: 1. Dreams of the night, that represent mere physiological states or conditions, often with little significance for the ordering of one's life; we hardly remember them. The rest are dreams of the morning. 2. Personal existential dreams which could be literal or symbolic. When literal, they come with scenes taken from one's acquaintances and localities one is familiar with. Symbolic personal dream represents complexes of one's psychological interiority. 4. Dreams with archetypal significance with scenes and figures taken from nature "assume a more universal and usually mysterious significance permeated with a deeply resonant emotion."[53] 5. Anagogic dreams although taken from nature often has supernatural meaning. 6. Prophetic dreams whose symbols could be either literal or symbolic, and the symbolism may be personal, archetypal, or anagogic, foretell a future event. 7. Synchronistic dreams which may also be literal or symbolic are of events occurring as they are being dreamt.[54]

Dream symbols are the operators effecting the sublation of the neural and psychic process into recognition in much the same way "as questions are operators promoting successive levels of intentional consciousness"[55] and as such are the foremost signals of the existential subject in the world. "Dream symbols are operators effecting the internal communication of organism, psyche, and mind."[56] The psyche through dreams releases to the subject the present status of the drama of life for "what discloses itself in dreams is the status of our desire"[57] and it is aimed at leading the subject to self-transcendence. When one

---

52. Doran, *Theological Foundations, I,* 163.

53. Doran, *Theological Foundations I,* 324.

54. Doran, *Theological Foundations I,* 299, 323–325.

55. Doran, *Theological Foundations I,* 82.

56. Doran, *Theological Foundations I,* 321.

57. Doran, *Theological Foundations I,* 195.

attends to the dream symbols, and the feelings associated with them and correctly interprets them, one enters a new world, one's own world. Primordial immediacy becomes articulate in dreams which tells its story.

> The dream thus discloses in sensitive consciousness a complex of underlying physiological transformations. It integrates these transformations by granting them psychic representation in the form of elemental symbols. These symbols then can find their own higher integration as they are sublated into waking consciousness through memory, into intelligent consciousness by insight, into truthful consciousness by reflective understanding of the adequacy of one's insight, and into responsible consciousness by decisions which in turn will operate further transformations of the underlying sensitive manifold. Dream symbols thus provide materials for one's work of dramatic art.[58]

From experience of his own dreams, Doran testifies to the efficacy of dreams and the correctness of Jung's position opposed to Freud's that dream is a true story of precisely what is going on. "It is to the realm of the dream that one can often turn for the elemental symbols that narrate the drama, the psychic experience, of one's various human desires, and that, for the existential adult, portray one's engagement in the ground theme of every mature story."[59]

While dream images can be conscripted to assist in authentic self-transcendence, they must be intelligent, reasonable, and decisive conscription without which the psyche runs wild and inhibits the cognitional process. Doran, therefore, warns dreams must not be construed to be an explanation of the actual situation, even though there could be exceptions (like synchronistic dreams).[60] Professional guide familiar with the vagaries of dream consciousness is indispensable for fruitful dream analysis as the language of dream is different from that

---

58. Doran, *Theological Foundations I*, 322.

59. Doran, *Theological Foundations I*, 347

60. Doran, *Subject and Psyche*, 211.

of waking conscious language. The dream is very important for psychic conversion, for gaining the capacity to negotiate the images vital to the existential subject. For in the dream of the authentic subject making of his or her life a dramatic art, the neural demand functions enter consciousness in the way it should, and images are not repressed enabling the imaginative schemata to generate the much-needed insights.[61] Thus, even though dreams should not be taken literally, we must attend to them as they serve as the window into the world:

> The universe can become love in human consciousness, and its entrance into this capacity, its expression of this finality, occurs in the dream. The universe is at the mercy here of the human subject, for everything depends on what one does with one's dreams. I can be completely oblivious of them, as most white Westerners are. I can reject them as insignificant. I can interpret them naively or superstitiously or protectively. Or I can live the dream forward intelligently, truthfully, deliberately, erotically, agapically. Then the universe is promoted to a higher integration, to a fuller being. But if the dream is forgotten or rejected, ridiculed or denied, an evolutionary blind alley or false start or even complete breakdown and collapse has been suffered. The universe depends on the subject to promote its upwardly but indeterminately directed dynamism, its finality.[62]

Development in *Theology and the Dialectics of History*

Theology and the Dialectics of History is the hallmark of Doran's writing that clarifies better his notion of psychic conversion.[63] In this book,

---

61. Doran, *Theological Foundations I*, 248.

62. Doran, *Theological Foundations I*, 291.

63. Robert M. Doran, *Theology and the Dialectics of History* (Toronto: University of Toronto Press, 1990) devotes six chapters (2, 6, 8, 9, 10, and 20) to psychic conversion. The rest of the chapters including the introduction in one way or the other discusses psychic conversion. For instance, in Chapter Three, the role of psychic conversion grounds the notion of dialectic.

Doran explains his notion of psychic conversion came about from his reflection on Lonergan's discussion of symbols in *Method in Theology* and the brief remarks he made there about dreams.[64] Doran strongly affirms his position in the earlier writings we have examined above, giving rationale for his notion of psychic conversion. He is forthright in his explanation. Attention to sensitive psyche is aimed at improving self-development (or self-appropriation). The science of depth psychology as developed by its giants Freud and Jung which upheld the view that the psyche alone can supply the data for self-development is inadequate. For this reason, depth psychology ought to be supplemented or reoriented in the light of Lonergan's intentionality analysis. The reason for this is not far-fetched: there is duality in consciousness: intentionality and psyche. "There are two sets of data of consciousness, the data of intentionality and the data of the psyche."[65] Both provide the cognitive therapy and the psychological therapy humans need not only to experience the movement of life but also to perform acts through which we find direction in that movement.

The psyche refers to the sensitive flow of consciousness[66] and is oriented to transcendence (its vertical finality) achieved through successful integration with intentional consciousness.[67] In the levels of intentional consciousness, the psyche is the empirical level distinct from but with other intentional operations (reflection, judgment, and deliberation) constitutes dimensions of consciousness or intentionality. The various operations of intentional consciousness also are levels of self-transcendence and meaning through which humans achieve authenticity. Because sensitive consciousness underscores the importance of feelings for human authenticity, we must attend not only to the operations of intentional consciousness but also to our sensitive psyche. The point being made is clear "that the realm of the psyche, and especially of feelings, is of particular relevance to the constitution

64. Doran, *Theology and the Dialectics of History*, 45.
65. Doran, *Theology and the Dialectics of History*, 46.
66. Doran, *Theology and the Dialectics of History*, 46.
67. Doran, *Theology and the Dialectics of History*, 48.

of the self as the psyche is sublated at the fourth level of intentional consciousness."[68] Furthermore, as feeling is the intermediate term between symbols and values, the elemental symbols of our psyche like the dreams manifest our existential constitution as humans and our self-transcendence.

Doran keeps using affective integrity, affective transcendence in explaining his notion of psychic conversion. One is curious to discover the difference between Lonergan's affective conversion and Doran's psychic conversion. Are they the same thing? If they are, does calling it psychic conversion add anything to the same notion and why is it necessary to change the name in the first place? Doran is convinced they are not the same.

> Psychic conversion is not the same as what Lonergan calls affective conversion. It is not the achievement of an affectivity that is of a single piece because one loves God with all one's heart and soul and mind and strength. Such unrestricted love is the goal of a complete conversion process involving the four distinct but related dimensions of religious, moral, intellectual and psychic conversions . . . Psychic conversion is a transformation of the psychic component of what Freud calls "the censor" from a repressive to a constructive agency in a person's development.[69]

Doran understands Lonergan's affective conversion in the religious sense of a deep turnaround of one's whole life, a recommitment to love of God that includes all the levels of consciousness and their corresponding conversions—psychic, intellectual, moral, and religious. Psychic conversion on the other hand, refers rather to self-appropriation, that is, the natural process of the entrance of affect-laden images of the psyche needed for insight into consciousness. "The habitual orientation of our intelligence and affectivity exercises a censorship over the emergence into consciousness of the images that are the psychic representation and conscious integration of an underlying

---

68. Doran, *Theology and the Dialectics of History*, 57.
69. Doran, *Theology and the Dialectics of History*, 59.

neural manifold."[70] The censorship could be constructive or repressive depending on whether its images are oriented towards insight, reasonable judgment, responsible decision, and love or not. Psychic conversion is "the conversion of the psychic dimension of a repressive censorship to a constructive role."[71]

The Healing of the Psyche

While the complex of psychic energy can be quite positive in their effects lending their energy in the fulfilment of the search for direction in the movement of life by supporting the dynamics of human intentionality, our psychic energy can be blocked thus inhibiting the functioning of the creative vector of consciousness from self-transcendent participation in the quest for intelligibility, truth and the human good. Psychic disorder inhibiting psychic spontaneity could be caused by external factors arising from distorted dialectic of community resulting to violence to one's psyche. It could also be because of one's own self-destructiveness caused by distorted dialectic of the subject. "The point" according to Doran, "is that *psychic spontaneity as such is not morally responsible for its own disorder.* The psyche's order and disorder are a consequence of action that affects it from beyond itself, whether that action be that of others or of oneself. Disordered complexes are the victim of history; of significant others, of social situations emergent from the distorted dialectic of history, of derailed cultural values, of one's own freedom, or of some combination of these various sources."[72] Doran understands these psychic blocks heuristically in the light of Lonergan's four varieties of bias: dramatic, individual, group, and general. Dramatic bias is more a consequence of those complexes beyond one's control than egoistic and general bias which result from one's self-destructiveness and of moral and intellectual distortion respectively. But we must note that an exhaustive account of

---

70. Doran, *Theology and the Dialectics of History*, 59–60.

71. Doran, *Theology and the Dialectics of History*, 185.

72. Doran, *Theology and the Dialectics of History*, 232.

the victimization of the psyche cannot be given by general or exclusive account. "The genesis and constitution of affective disorder will vary from person to person."[73]

The impact of the psychic darkness consequent upon the victimization of the disordered complexes could in some instances lead to repression of the complexes. Unfortunately, instead of leading to a cure which it is not, repression by constricting the emotional energy eventually proves explosive. This could lead to moral renunciation expressed in various forms of rationalization as such people begin to act out their disorder. Since these lead not to integration but further psychic pathology, Doran suggests detour through affective freedom from those complexes inhibiting the provision of images needed for insight and creative ways of responding to the riddles of life. This affective development enables the psyche to participate in the objectives of intentional consciousness, in the objectives of the creative vector. This is genuine psychotherapy, the healing of the psyche.[74] From theological perspective, Doran recommends participating in compassion of redemptive love. This consists first in recognizing that "the complex is a victim, whether of oneself or of history, and one can stop hating oneself for what one feels. Next, one can adopt an attitude of compassion in its regard. And finally, one can allow there to emerge from the recognition and the compassion a willingness to cooperate with whatever redemptive forces are available to heal the disorder of darkness and to transform the contorted energies, even to the point of consolidating them into the self-transcendent quest for direction in the movement of life."[75]

However, on account of moral impotence that makes it difficult for disordered complex to recognize the self-transcendent quality of participating in compassion of redemptive love, the healing vector, Doran holds, is a work of grace, of the healing from above beyond the creative consciousness. It effects conversion, a willingness to embrace the compassion of divine love, charity. "Psychic conversion is the

---

73. Doran, *Theology and the Dialectics of History*, 236.

74. Doran, *Theology and the Dialectics of History*, 231.

75. Doran, *Theology and the Dialectics of History*, 239.

transformation to such willingness of the psychic component of one's orientation in the world."[76] One chooses not satisfactions but values, and moves from affective victimization to affective freedom, moving from a low level of personality integration to the choice of self-transcendence as a criterion of world-constitution and self-constitution.[77] The conversion in question is not only religious but moral and intellectual as well and gradually moves the human subject to lives of virtue and commitment to self-transcendence.[78] Such openness to truth about oneself leading to openness to insights required for truth to emerge Doran writes, is psychic conversion, "the repressive censorship vis-à-vis neural demands begins to be transformed into a constructive censorship."[79] And so the complementarity of the creative and healing vectors constitutes "integral interiority."[80]

Reorientation of Depth Psychology

As a systematic theologian, Doran recognizes the inadequacies of depth psychology and seeks to reorient the discipline, so that it plays a role in theological foundations akin to that of Lonergan's intentionality analysis. As mentioned earlier, Doran wishes to ground the science of the psyche in Lonergan's cognitional theory in view of the complementarity of the psyche and intentionality. The reorientation of depth psychology is because the discipline is unable to work out the foundation of what constitutes human flourishing. Depth psychology has always concentrated on neurosis, on the sickness of the human psyche without facing the question of what constitutes human flourishing. Lonergan's intentionality analysis integrated to the psyche together answers the question of what makes for human flourishing. Doran clarifies his intention thus:

---

76. Doran, *Theology and the Dialectics of History*, 247.
77. Doran, *Theology and the Dialectics of History*, 249.
78. Doran, *Theology and the Dialectics of History*, 250.
79. Doran, *Theology and the Dialectics of History*, 250.
80. Doran, *Theology and the Dialectics of History*, 252.

I want to ground depth psychology in the normative order of the search for direction in the movement of life as this order has been disengaged by Lonergan. I want to enable this psychology to take its place in theological foundations in the same way Lonergan has established a place there for cognitional theory. And I want to fulfil both of these responsibilities within the context provided by our analysis of the situations to be addressed and evoked by a contemporary Christian systematic theology.[81]

The reorientation will consist in the elucidation of those operations of the sensitive psyche that collaborates with conscious intentionality and grounds the process of self-transcendence. As already mentioned, the operations of the sensitive psyche take place through processes Doran describes in the following terms. "Mediation of Immediacy," "Primordial Immediacy" and "Second Immediacy." Mediation of Immediacy refers to the process of the self-appropriation of the cognitional and existential subject by the meaning that constitutes interiorly differentiated consciousness. Primordial Immediacy is the subject as subject; "the spontaneously operative dialectic of the subject within the dialectic of culture and community."[82] Second Immediacy is one living habitually through the mediation of self-appropriation (of cognitional and existential subject), all the characteristics associated with interiorly differentiated consciousness: perception, insight, judgment and decision.[83] An understanding of primordial immediacy as both intentional and psychic, Doran holds, permits the reconstruction of the notions Sigmund Freud expressed in *The Interpretation of Dreams* in terms of Lonergan's intentionality analysis, especially his notions of primary and secondary process. Primordial immediacy as the movement of life is primary process and secondary process as the objectification of primary process heads toward the second immediacy. Primordial immediacy or primary process is characterized by intentionality and psyche. "Secondary process heads towards the second immediacy of the person

81. Doran, *Theology and the Dialectics of History*, 256–7.
82. Doran, *Theology and the Dialectics of History*, 264.
83. Doran, *Theology and the Dialectics of History*, 264.

of interiorly differentiated consciousness."[84] In order to head towards human flourishing, the reorientation of depth psychology must begin by relating the existential level of consciousness with the sensitive psyche. That is, relating feelings and values with feelings and symbols particularly dream symbols and linking them to the existential concerns of the world and the self.[85] As higher synthesis of neural processes, dreams facilitate the internal communication between intentionality and neural demands.

The reorientation Doran envisions is supposed to be beneficial to theological foundations by adding the psychic component to intentionality analysis, thus grounding theological foundations solidly in personal integrity. It is also beneficial to sensitive psychology by transforming depth psychological tradition from the hegemonic control of what Eric Voegelin calls the psychology of passional motivations to a psychology of orientations.[86] Psychology of passional motivations and psychology of orientations were used by Eric Voegelin to distinguish the science of distorted psyche ordered by a balance of motivations from the science of a healthy psyche "in which the order of the soul is created by transcendental orientations."[87] Psychology of passional motivations regard the human person merely biologically. As such, individuation is striving towards wholeness and self-fulfillment rather than towards self-transcendence which is the concern of the psychology of orientations.[88]

The major difficulty and the almost insurmountable obstacle of most depth psychologies is the radical duality of organism and the spirit upon which they operate. This inhibits them from recognizing the human orientation towards self-transcendence. The body is often set against the whole of consciousness and considered as hindering the progress of the self. Little wonder Doran emphasizes the triple constitution of the human person as compound of bodily organism,

---

84. Doran, *Theology and the Dialectics of History*, 265.

85. Doran, *Theology and the Dialectics of History*, 262.

86. Doran, *Theology and the Dialectics of History*, 257.

87. Eric Voegelin, *The New Science of Politics* (Chicago: University of Chicago Press, 1952), 186.

88. Doran, *Theology and the Dialectics of History*, 282.

sensitive psyche, and spiritual intentionality. The advantage of recognizing this threefold compound of human constitution is not only the recognition of the distinctness of each of the systems with its own sets of schemes of recurrence, but also their relatedness by obedience to the laws of human development—emergence and correspondence: "psychic events emerge from organic and neural process, and intentional operations from psychic images."[89] The issue is not whether Jung grasped the mediatory role of the psyche between bodily organism and the spirit, but his limitation of the self to the cyclical nature of cosmos. Thus, according to Doran, the core of the reorientation of depth psychology is the recognition of the finality of the psyche and its participation in the life of the spirit.

> While Jung grasped the mediate position of the psyche between organism and spirit, Kantian and perhaps even Nietzschean presuppositions prevented him from accurately understanding the spirit pole of the dialectic of the subject. That pole is clarified in Lonergan's intentionality analysis, which also serves to specify more concretely than Jung's psychic wholeness wherein lies the objective of psychic teleology. The psyche's finality is an upwardly directed dynamism to sensitive participation in the operations of inquiry and understanding, reflection and judgment, deliberation and decision, and in the dynamic state of being in love in intimacy, in the community, and with God . . . The psyche is to be understood in the context of self-appropriation established by Lonergan's intentionality analysis. The changes of psychic experience with various intentional operations manifest that the psyche is endowed with a vertical finality to participation in the life of the spirit.[90]

Crucial to the reorientation of depth psychology Doran is proposing is his notion of dialectic according to which improving Lonergan's notion of dialectic, the linked but opposed principles of change

---

89. Doran, *Theology and the Dialectics of History*, 282.
90. Doran, *Theology and the Dialectics of History*, 302.

constitutive of dialectic can be not only of contradictories but also of contraries. The relation of the psyche and the spirit is not of contradictories, as they are not opposed to each other. Rather, it is one of contraries, of complementing one another. While distinct, yet they are related. Dialectic of contraries maintains the integral unity in tension of the dialectic of the subject, of psychic sensitivity and inquiring intentionality. Dialectic of contradictories would be choosing either of the principles of the dialectic. This does not happen in the integral dialectic of the subject or else the dialectic of the subject will be distorted resulting either to neurosis or psychosis.[91] Doran asserts:

> The position in Jung's work can be advanced, and the counter position reversed, by building on the insight that there are two quite distinct forms of the single but complex notion of dialectic. Among the dialectics of contraries are the basic dialectic of the subject between consciousness and the unconscious and the derived dialectic of the subject between conscious spirit and conscious psyche. Among the dialectics of contradictories is the dialectic of good and evil. Jung collapses the dialectic of good and evil into a dialectic of contraries. He judges that it can reach an integrity beyond the opposites. The ambition to resolve this dialectic in this way is precisely Jung's choice of the demonic. It takes the form of choosing constant rotation in the order of nature when invited to acquiesce in the movement operated by grace to 'the apocalyptic world above.' . . . Jung's work can be reoriented by accepting his contribution to what is good and by introducing the distinctions needed to transform his contribution to what is evil and what is demonic.[92]

Conclusion

Doran advances Lonergan studies by advocating for psychic conversion as an addition to Lonergan's intellectual, moral, and religious

91. Doran, *Theology and the Dialectics of History*, 304.
92. Doran, *Theology and the Dialectics of History*, 297–98.

conversion. His hypothesis draws from an in-depth study of Carl Jung's conception of the unconscious. Jung's hypothesis based on his dialectical theory of opposites (of the conscious and the unconscious) aimed at the emergence of the Self prioritizes the unconscious, the various movements of psychic energy, analyzing the psychic processes underlying them, which leads either to progress or retrogression of the psyche, over the conscious element of human intentionality. Doran's significant contribution through appropriation of Jung's notion of the psyche is reorienting depth psychology through Lonergan's intentionality analysis. He argued for the unity of consciousness which consists in recognizing the complementarity of intentionality and psyche not only for knowledge but for the successful navigation of the search for movement of life, a search that can be either gained or lost. Human authenticity consists in remaining in the dialectical tension of opposites of intentionality and the psyche. Both Lonergan and Jungian studies benefit as there are two ways of being conscious: sensitivity and intentionality.

Psychic conversion demands attention to the unconscious elements which underlie consciousness. Consciousness makes sense only in relation to the various layers of the unconscious. "In other words, just as the process of bringing psychic contents to consciousness involves a sharpening and clarifying of the ambiguities of the unconscious, so the individual emerges out of society by a process of differentiation and individuation."[93] Doran, however, does not endorse this sole concentration on the psyche characteristic of Jung's psychology. Instead, in the light of Lonergan's intentionality analysis, he posits an integrated study of the human person leading to authenticity with attention paid to both the biological, emotional aspects as well as the cognitive abilities of humans. Such psychic elements that form part of the human being like the symbols of dream should not be discarded. At the same time, they should not be accepted naively without proper interpretation by the specialist trained psychiatrist. Psychic conversion is recognition of the role of the psyche in human cognition and the emergence of human personality.

---

93. Ira Progroff, *Jung's Psychology and Its Social Meaning*, 164.

3

Healing the Psychological Subject: Towards a Fourfold Notion of Conversion?[1]

John D. Dadosky

ABSTRACT

This paper addresses some of the developments in the theoretical reflection on conversion following Lonergan's threefold differentiation of conversion as intellectual, moral, and religious, and it also addresses the issues arising from this development. Specifically, the paper begins by focusing on the contributions of Robert Doran (psychic conversion) and Bernard Tyrrell (affectional conversion). Each has made significant contributions to integrate further Lonergan's theories into psychology. There follows an attempt to situate these developments in light of Lonergan's comments concerning "affective" conversion in an attempt to bring some clarity and succinctness to the discussion.

---

1. This article originally appeared as "Healing the Psychological Subject: Towards a Fourfold Notion of Conversion?" *Theoforum*, 35/1 (2004): 73–91. With the exception of some minor editorial changes, insertion of leading quotes, and the updating of some bibliographical references, the work appears in its original form. The purpose of the article was to: 1) argue for four conversions (psychological, moral, intellectual, religious); 2) clarify that conversion heals blocks in development; 3) argue for a synthetic view of psychological self-appropriation, a psychological conversion and 4) argue for limiting conversion, as Lonergan understands it, to four types.

"I used to believe there were three [conversions] but my friend from Marquette, Robert Doran, has convinced me there is a fourth."

—*Bernard Lonergan* (*Lonergan Workshop, Boston, 1978*)

"There is the bias of unconscious motivation brought to light by depth psychology."

—*Bernard Lonergan* (Method in Theology, *217*)

I. INTRODUCTION

In contemporary theological reflection, theologians continue to come to terms with the complexities involved in understanding the human subject brought about by the advancements in the natural, human, and social sciences.[2] In light of this new context, our understanding of *conversion*, among other things, must continue to be transposed in light of the developments in these various disciplines.

Contemporary scholarship on conversion continues to identify and clarify the various aspects of personal transformation. One can distinguish between, on the one hand, the aspect of conversion that pertains to the interior transformation of the subject, and, on the other hand, the understanding of conversion in nominal terms as it pertains to a change in one's explicit religious affiliation or religious status. The interior transformation of the subject is reflected in biblical theology as *metanoia* to connote a dramatic "about face" or "turn around" which is more than just repenting for one's sins. Rather, it is as Dom Marc-Francois Lacan states, "an interior transformation which blossoms out in a change of conduct, in a new orientation of life."[3]

---

2. See Bernard Lonergan, "Theology in its New Context," in *A Second Collection*, Collected Works of Lonergan, vol. 13, eds. R. M. Doran and J. D. Dadosky (Toronto, University of Toronto Press, 2016), pp. 48–59; A version of "New Context" was originally intended as chapter 1 of Lonergan's *Method in Theology*. That version is available as Appendix 1 of the Collected Works version. See "Appendix 1: Theology in its New Context," Bernard Lonergan, *Method in Theology*, Collected Works of Lonergan, vol. 14, eds. R. M. Doran and J. D. Dadosky (Toronto: University of Toronto Press, 2017), pp. 341–78.

3. Dom Marc-Francois Lacan, "Conversion and Kingdom in the Synoptic Gospels," in W. E. Conn, (ed.), *Conversion: Perspectives on Personal and Social Transformation* (New York: Alba House, 1978), 100.

Conversion can also refer to the transition from one belief system or institution to another belief system or institution. Religious scholars refer to such changes in the outward expression of religious identity as *tradition*, *transition*, and *institutional transition*.[4] When speaking of conversion strictly in these latter terms, some scholars have ceased to use the term *conversion* at all in favor of terminology that more accurately expresses the historical-social dimension of religious affiliation and identity. For example, in his text *The Germanization of Early Medieval Christianity*, James Russell refers to the mass transition of the Germanic people to institutional Christianity as *christianization* rather than "conversion."[5] Russell's work identifies the need for a terminology that will help clarify the distinction between the sociological aspect of conversion that includes the explicit religious identity and institutional affiliation, on the one hand, and the inner process of conversion as it pertains to the subject's interiority in striving for authenticity and self-transcendence, on the other hand. However, suggesting a distinction between "inner" and "outer" conversion is not to bifurcate the two aspects but rather to clarify the various aspects of conversion. Obviously, one can undergo a conversion without changing one's religious affiliation.

To invoke an idea from Eric Voegelin, the shift in our understanding of conversion has gone from one of *compactness* to a more differentiated notion, that is, one that considers the personal, moral, religious, social, and psychological aspects of conversion. However, *compactness* implies that these latter differentiations of conversion are at least to some extent implicit in earlier notions. Bernard Lonergan's threefold differentiation of conversion as *intellectual*, *moral*, and *religious* represents a provocative contribution towards a contemporary

---

4. John S. Strong, "Conversion: Perspectives on Personal and Social Transformation" in Mircea Eliade (ed.), *Encyclopedia of Religion*, Vol 14 (New York: Macmillan, 1987), p. 74. Obviously, it goes without saying that one can undergo a conversion without changing one's explicit religious identity or religious affiliation.

5. See James C. Russell, *The Germanization of Early Medieval Christianity* (Oxford/New York: Oxford University Press, 1994), especially chap 2: "Conversion, Christianization, and Germanization."

understanding of conversion.[6] His explication of a threefold notion of conversion constitutes a development in our understanding of conversion from a more compact notion to one differentiated in terms of its moral, intellectual, and religious aspects. One can apply the threefold distinction as a hermeneutic tool that can enrich our understanding of various aspects of personal transformation as exemplified, for example, in Augustine's *Confessions*.[7]

In addition to Lonergan's formulations of intellectual, moral, and religious conversion, the exigencies of our modern context call for an integration of the theological and the psychological aspects of conversion. An integral theological and psychological understanding of conversion offers the promise of preserving psychology from the blind alleys of reductionism while simultaneously challenging theologians and philosophers to "wrestle with their own demons" which can flow from the fourfold bias: dramatic, egoistic, group, or general.[8] Following

---

6. *Intellectual conversion* involves a "radical clarification" regarding knowledge and reality. Specifically, this necessitates the elimination of a false assumption that knowing involves "taking a good look." This involves the fuller realization that human knowing entails the compound of operations of experience, understanding, and judgment—that the content of these operations constitutes the world mediated by meaning. *Moral conversion* "changes the criterion of one's decisions and choices from satisfactions to values." This conversion occurs to the extent that one is able to choose the "truly good" over immediate gratification, or sensitive satisfaction, especially when value and satisfaction conflict. *Religious conversion* concerns a transformation such that one's being becomes a dynamic state of being-in-love with the Ultimate being or God. There follows a desire to surrender and commit to that love which has content but no apprehended object. Lonergan, *Method in Theology*, pp. 224–26.

7. Walter Conn applies Lonergan's threefold notion of conversion to the life of Thomas Merton, which he believes offers concrete examples of religious and moral conversion. See his *Christian Conversion* (Mahwah, NJ: Paulist Press, 1986), esp. Chapters 5 and 6. In a more summary fashion see his *The Desiring Self: Rooting Pastoral Counseling and Spiritual Direction in Self-Transcendence* (Mahwah, NJ: Paulist Press, 1998), Chapter 7. Similarly, Elena Malits, C.S.C. applies Lonergan's threefold notion of conversion to a study of the life of Thomas Merton. See *Journey Into the Unknown: Thomas Merton's Continuing Conversion*, Fordham University Ph.D. dissertation (Ann Arbor: MI: University Microfilms, 1976).

8. In *dramatic bias*, the flight from understanding is rooted in a psychic wound of the subject, and results in irrational behaviors that can be attributed to the psychic wound. *Egoistic bias* is rooted in one's self-centeredness; it results in one's criteria for

Lonergan's developments, scholars have attempted to develop his ideas by integrating them with insights from modern psychology. In turn, this has led to the positing of additional differentiations or notions of conversions by various scholars. Undoubtedly, operative in the background of their reflections are the few and brief comments that Lonergan made regarding, *affective conversion*.[9] These statements about affective conversion suggested the possibility of additional notions of conversions and led to multiple, nuanced interpretations of what Lonergan meant by *affective conversion*.[10]

Nearly two decades after Lonergan's death, there remains little consensus among scholars concerning the psychological and affective dimensions of conversion. While several scholars have made significant contributions to developing Lonergan's notion of conversion along these lines, the multiplication of various notions of conversions that often results threatens to cloud rather than to clarify the issue. This lack of clarity prompts one to ask: To what extent is the development of additional notions of conversion even necessary?

The questions these issues raise are complex, and so I limit this paper to the contributions of two scholars who write specifically on the subject of healing of the psychological subject. First, I will summarize

---

knowing and choosing being limited to one's own selfish outcomes. One could call *group bias* a collective egoistic bias in that it favors what is best for the group at the expense of others outside of the group. *General bias* resists theoretical knowledge and is content to live in the concrete world; it refuses to permit questions that might lead to theory. On bias see Lonergan, *Insight*, pp. 214–15 and 244–251.

9. Bernard Lonergan, "Natural Right and Historical Mindedness," in *A Third Collection*, Collected Works of Lonergan, vol 16, eds. R. M. Doran and J. D. Dadosky (Toronto: University of Toronto Press, 2017), pp. 163–76.

10. See Walter Conn, "Affective Conversion: The Transformation of Desire," in T. P. O'Fallon, and P. B. Riley, (eds.), *Religion and Culture: Essays in Honor of Bernard Lonergan* (Albany: State University of New York Press, 1987), pp. 216–226. Robert Doran, *Theology and the Dialectics of History* (Toronto: University of Toronto Press, 1990), especially chap. 6; henceforth this text is cited parenthetically as *TDH*. Donald Gelpi, *Experiencing God* (New York: Paulist Press, 1978), pp. 179–81. Bernard Tyrrell, "Affectional Conversion: A Distinct Conversion or Potential Differentiation in the Spheres of Sensitive Psychic and/or Affective Conversion?" *Method: Journal of Lonergan Studies,* 14 (1996): pp. 1–35; henceforth cited parenthetically as *AC*.

and compare the work of Robert Doran on *psychic conversion*, and Bernard Tyrrell on *affectional conversion* (not to be confused with Lonergan's use of *affective conversion*) and inquire as to whether or not these two conversions are distinct from each other and to what extent they might be complementary. In view of this, I suggest further that what may be moving forward in both of their developments is a fuller, synthetic account of the psychological aspects of conversion. Secondly, in light of the possibility of the latter, I inquire as to the feasibility of limiting the number of conversions. The use of an Occam's Razor in the subsequent reflection on conversion may help to prevent the unnecessary multiplication of other notions and hence bring more clarity to this ongoing reflection.[11]

II. PSYCHIC CONVERSION
AND AFFECTIONAL CONVERSION

Before proceeding, it will be helpful to summarize briefly Lonergan's theory of intentional consciousness.

There are four levels of *intentional* consciousness in Lonergan's cognitional theory: *experience, understanding, judgment* and *decision*.[12] *Knowing*, in the strict sense, occurs to the extent that one is attentive to one's experience, intelligent in one's understanding and reasonable in one's judgment—to the extent that one answers all the relevant questions to a specific inquiry through these operations. In turn, a question of value arises, which one would hope, prompts a person, to make responsible decisions based on those values. To the extent that

---

11. Admittedly, however, the number of conversions is ultimately an empirical question and so my preference to limit the number to four remains at this point a working hypothesis.

12. The philosophical foundations for Lonergan's theory of consciousness are expounded in detail in his text, *Insight*. For a more concise overview of his theory of consciousness see his articles: "Cognitional Structure," in *Collection*, Collected Works, Vol. 4, eds. F. E. Crowe and R. M. Doran (Toronto: University of Toronto Press, 1988), pp. 205–22; "The Subject," in *A Second Collection* 60–74; and chap. 1 of *Method in Theology*. Lonergan of course, uses the term "level" in a metaphorical sense, see "The Subject," in *A Second Collection*, p. 70.

this pattern of operations is allowed to unfold properly in the subject without the distortion of human bias, then one can say with Lonergan that: "Genuine objectivity is the fruit of authentic subjectivity. It is to be attained only by attaining authentic subjectivity."[13]

The "distortion of human bias" that may block a person's intellectual, moral, psychological, social, or spiritual development can signal the need for conversion. In this way, conversion for Lonergan "is not merely a change or even a development; rather, it is a radical transformation on which follows, on all levels of living, an interlocked series of changes and developments."[14] He emphasizes that conversion can occur in dramatic moments, as in the case of Saint Paul on the road to Damascus, or it may be more gradual, that is, "extended over the slow maturing process of a lifetime."[15]

Psychic Conversion

As stated above, Lonergan put forth the notions of religious, moral, and intellectual conversion. Robert Doran, however, seeks to integrate Lonergan's threefold notion of conversion into depth psychology and he calls this formulation *psychic conversion*. The latter fits within the context of Lonergan's other conversions as follows:

> Religious conversion [. . .] affects proximately a dimension of consciousness—at times Lonergan called it a fifth level—where we are pure openness to the reception of grace; moral conversion affects the fourth level; intellectual conversion affects the second and third levels; and psychic conversion affects the first level (*TDH*, 42).[16]

---

13. Lonergan, *Method in Theology*, p. 273. Of course, not all knowledge is immanently generated; there is being-in-love in an unrestricted manner, which for Lonergan is the foundation of faith.

14. Lonergan, "Theology in its New Context," in *A Second Collection*, p. 57.

15. Lonergan, "Theology in its New Context," in *A Second Collection*, p. 58.

16. Lonergan's use of the term *fifth level* of consciousness refers to non-intentional consciousness in the sense that there is no object intended in consciousness. Religious conversion culminates in a person being-in-love in an unrestricted manner. Hence,

Psychic conversion pertains to the first level *experience* and helps to heal the dramatic bias which prevents someone from attending to relevant data in one's experience.

There is significant evidence to suggest that Lonergan not only endorsed Doran's notion of psychic conversion but he saw it as an extension of his threefold notion of conversion. Lonergan states, in a letter to a publisher,

> Intellectual, Moral, and Religious conversion of the theologian are foundational in my book on method in theology. To these Doran has added a psychic conversion in his book on *Psychic Conversion and Theological Foundations*. He has thought the matter through very thoroughly and it fits very adroitly and snugly into my own efforts.[17]

Simply stated psychic conversion "is a transformation of the psychic component of what Freud calls 'the censor' from a repressive to a constructive agency in a person's development" (*TDH*, 59). The censor, according to Lonergan, is a "law or rule of interrelations between successive levels of integration."[18] When the censor operates constructively, it sorts through irrelevant data and allows us to receive the necessary images needed for insights (*TDH*, 184). When the censor is repressive, it does not allow access to images that would allow needed insights. As a result, one may experience blocks in one's psychological development.

---

that with which one is in love remains uncomprehended—it is mystery. For summary of this problem and the fifth level, see Jeremy Blackwood, *And Hope Does Not Disappoint: Love, Grace, and Subjectivity in the Work of Bernard J.F. Lonergan, S.J.*, Marquette Studies in Theology, No. 88, Andrew Tallon, Series Editor (Milwaukee, WI: Marquette University Press, 2017).

17. Lonergan's Recommendation to publisher in support of a book proposal by Robert Doran, A2280 (File 490.1/6), Archives, Lonergan Research Institute of Regis College, Toronto. Similarly in a letter to Fr. Edward Braxton (February 12, 1975) Lonergan wrote: "I agree with Robert Doran on psychic conversion and his combining it with intellectual, moral, and religious conversion." File 132, p. 1, also from the Lonergan Archives. I am grateful to the Trustees of the Lonergan Estate to cite from this unpublished material [2003].

18. Lonergan, *Insight*, 482.

This process pertains to the dramatic pattern of experience and usually results from a psychological wound due to victimization or abuse. For Doran, repression is primarily of *images* rather than *insights*, and these images are "concomitant" with feelings. As a result, feelings may become disassociated from the repressed images and, in turn, become concomitant with other "incongruous images" (*TDH*, 60). For example, a child who has a violent fear of dogs may be responding to trauma from a prior animal attack. She may not remember the actual incident, but the presence of *any* dog quickly arouses her horror. Furthermore, it is also possible for feelings to be repressed insofar as they are coupled with the repressed images (*TDH*, 184). For example, the child, despite her fear of dogs, may also harbor repressed feelings of rage towards them.

Again, often the repressive functioning of the censor is the result of victimization or abuse. A psychic wound or dramatic bias develops which causes the censor to repress the painful images and, in this way, it functions as a form of psychic defense. However, during sleep the censor can be relaxed and thus may allow the repressed images to surface into one's consciousness (*TDH*, 60). Dream interpretation as such, in the context of psychotherapy, may facilitate psychic conversion and likewise assist in eventually bringing about psychological healing.

Doran calls for a re-orientation of depth psychology (especially with certain insights from Jungian psychology) through Lonergan's theory of intentional consciousness. He believes that this in turn will provide a point of theological integration between depth psychology and theology (*TDH*, 304).

Affectional Conversion

Bernard Tyrrell addresses the healing of psychological neurosis in terms of *affectional conversion*. Specifically, he distinguishes between *deprivation* neurosis and *repressive* neurosis. The former refers to a neurosis resulting from a person's inner feelings of worthlessness and unlovableness. The latter refers to the "severe repression" neurosis that may result in destructive expressions to self or others. His notion of affectional conversion addresses, for the most part, the healing of deprivation neurosis (*AC*, 2 n. 5). However, he admits that deprivation neurosis can be severe enough to cause a repressive neurosis: "I think one can legitimately draw a certain analogy between degrees of severity or pathology involved in the stages of felt unlovableness and worthlessness and the degrees of severity at work in repressive psychic disorders" (*AC*, 16).

Furthermore, Tyrrell distinguishes two types of affectional conversions: *primal affectional conversion* and *upper level conversion*.

> Primal affectional conversion consists in a shift on the level of sensitive awareness from the felt sense of frustration of the pleasure/love/desire/ appetite to a felt sense of fulfillment of this appetite. It is a shift from a felt sense of affectional deprivation to a felt sense of affectional acceptance and fulfillment. Primal affectional conversion occurs on the first level of consciousness, which Lonergan designates as the level of experiencing. Upper level affectional conversion consists in a healing transformation of a consolidated, ongoing affective-deprivation insofar as this deprivation is at work and negatively impacting the individual on the levels of understanding, judging, deciding, loving in Lonergan's model of consciousness (*AC*, 18).

In short, my understanding of Tyrrell's distinction of the two types of affectional conversion is that primal affectional conversion refers to the healing of psychic wounds inflicted on individuals as a result of pathological affectional neglect, and, like psychic conversion, it is proximate with the first level of operations in Lonergan's theory of consciousness—*experience*. On the other hand, upper level affectional conversion refers to the extent that those in need of this type of affectional healing make harsh self-judgments and self-destructive decisions out of their own inner feelings/beliefs of self-worthlessness. Tyrrell states, "two affectional conversions are really distinct to the extent that they can be related to transformations on distinct levels of consciousness." Together, affectional healing as primal and upper level affects all levels of consciousness (*AC*, 18).

Tyrrell distinguishes affectional conversion, specifically primal affectional conversion, from Doran's psychic conversion. He sees the "essential difference" as follows:

> As I understand it, in the case of psychic conversion the focus is on the *data of the psyche that pertain to repression* as it is at work on the sensitive psychic level and to the transformation of the "censor" from a repressive to a constructive agency in a person's development, on the other hand in the case of primal affectional conversion the focus is on the *data of sensitive consciousness that pertain to the frustration of the pleasure/love appetite* in an individual and the transformative process results in the fulfillment of the sensitive love-desire (*AC*, 21, emphasis added).

Like psychic conversion, primal affectional deprivation can result in a repression of feelings as well (*AC*, 21–22). Still, despite Tyrrell's clarification it remains unclear as to how distinct primal affective conversion is from psychic conversion. One could argue that primal affectional conversion is a result of psychic conversion.

Doran and Tyrrell have each labored significantly to integrate the insights of modern psychology with Lonergan's threefold notion of conversion. Both thinkers posit their conversions as being proximate with the first level of experience (primal affectional conversion for Tyrrell) and both acknowledge the role of love in bringing about the psychological healing of the subject. Both claim that their respective notions of conversion are distinct from what Lonergan referred to as *affective conversion*. Nevertheless, the question arises as to what extent their respective formulations overlap and to what extent they differ. Might there be a potential synthesis going forward in both of these formulations?

I return to the distinction that Tyrrell makes between *deprivation* neurosis and *repressive* neurosis.[19] Perhaps a complementary

---

19. Perhaps we are all in need to some degree of psychic and/or affectional conversion. For the purpose of this discussion, I will prescind from using examples of "healthy" or "normal" people. I will focus instead on the extreme neurotic forms that call for dramatic psychic healing.

understanding between psychic and upper level affectional conversion (not primal affectional conversion) lies in the fact that the latter addresses deprivation neurosis while psychic conversion addresses the healing of repressive neurosis.

In this way, it would seem that, in the more severe cases of abuse, the healing of the wounded psyche would involve both conversions. That is, psychic conversion would account for the bringing forth of the materials from the unconscious (for instance, memories) that the censor represses. In turn, affectional conversion would treat the inner feelings and beliefs of worthlessness that result from the effects of severe physical, mental, and psychological abuse of individuals. In this fashion it would seem that psychic and affectional conversions could operate in a complementary fashion to bring about a fuller healing of the psychological subject—each emphasizing different aspects of the complex healing process.

Doran suggests that psychic conversion already includes the healing of affective wounds and habits (*TDH*, 62), and, to the extent that this is true, then Tyrrell's work may overlap on this point. Tyrrell does speak about affectional deprivation neurosis being severe enough to cause repression, and, insofar as he presupposes that affectional conversion can heal this type of neurosis, then I think his notion does overlap with Doran's psychic conversion. That is, it would seem that once the censor is operating to repress material needed for psychic integration, there is a need for psychic conversion. In other words, where there is repression involved, and where the healing is linked to that repressed material, then I think that Doran's psychic conversion has already covered this ground quite adequately. However, this is not to say that Tyrrell's formulation of affectional conversion does not make a contribution to understanding the healing of the fuller psychological subject. I think that the strength of Tyrrell's formulation of affectional conversion, specifically upper level affectional conversion, is that he elaborates more fully than Doran on how the healing of the wounded psyche is affected on the subsequent levels of intentional consciousness, that is, understanding, judgment, decision. I also think that Tyrrell has sought to integrate a broader range of psychological theories beyond that of depth psychology, which is Doran's primary concentration.

Doran and Tyrrell have laboured to flesh out the details of conversion with respect to the healing of the psychological subject that remained undeveloped in Lonergan's thought. I have attempted to point out in a succinct way where their respective developments differ and where they overlap. In view of this brief analysis I would further suggest that what is perhaps going forward in both of these developments is an emerging systematic synthesis that draws upon the insights of the broader field of psychology (as opposed to just depth psychology), and that this would further complement Lonergan's other three conversions. In this way I would borrow a term from Tyrrell and call this emerging synthesis *psychological conversion*.[20] Hence, one could speak of conversion as fourfold: religious, moral, intellectual, and psychological. The latter would include Doran's formulation of psychic conversion filled out with aspects of Tyrrell's formulation of affectional conversion. What is going forward in both of their formulations, then, is really one conversion (psychological) that concentrates on healing the wounded psyche and the healing of the ramifications of this woundedness on each of the levels of intentional consciousness. Admittedly, I find the succinctness of this formula provocative; however, whether it is adequate remains a further question.

III. TOWARDS A FOURFOLD CONVERSION?

The foregoing analysis raises an interesting and ongoing question: Did Lonergan ever acknowledge a limited number of notions of conversion beyond his threefold distinction? We have noted that he accepted Doran's psychic conversion as a legitimate extension of his theory.

---

20. Bernard Tyrrell, "Passages and Conversion." In Matthew Lamb, (ed.), *Creativity and Method: Essays in Honor of Bernard Lonergan, S.J.* (Milwaukee, WI: Marquette University Press, 1981), p. 24. *Psychological conversion* is an early notion of Tyrrell's that, as far as I can tell, he has moved beyond and incorporated into affectional conversion. I am simply borrowing the term, not the notion itself.

Furthermore, when asked directly if Lonergan "envisioned a limited number of conversions," he answered, "Yes. I used to believe there were three but my friend from Marquette Robert Doran has convinced me there is a fourth."[21] Lonergan goes on to reiterate his initial response to the same question, "Yes, four: intellectual, moral, religious and aesthetic, or psychic or whatever you want to call it."[22]

Prima facie, these comments indicate that Lonergan was open to a fourth formulation of conversion and endorsed Doran's notion of psychic conversion as constituting the key development in this area. However, his comments also suggest some tentativeness regarding what exactly this fourth conversion entails, that is, "aesthetic, or psychic or whatever you want to call it".

However, it must be admitted that Lonergan's comments are spontaneous, and one cannot be certain to what extent they reflect his own position accurately had he worked it out more extensively. Moreover, even assuming that Lonergan does limit the number of conversions to four, one cannot be certain that he would not have changed his mind and been open to the possibility of other notions of conversions. Hence, I may be skating on thin ice in attempting to limit the formulations of conversion to just four. Nevertheless, it may be that Lonergan's response gives us a glimpse of the direction he was moving with respect to the issue of additional notions of conversions.

There remains, however, a further complication. Let us assume that Lonergan favors limiting the number of conversions to four: the question then arises, "What sense do we make of his mention of *affective conversion*?" Could it be that perhaps scholars have read too much into Lonergan's use of the term '*affective conversion*' in "Natural Right and Historical Mindedness" by regarding it as evidence that he was positing an additional conversion?

Doran and Tyrrell have each dealt with the affectivity involved in healing the psychological subject. It seems that Tyrrell, following

---

21. Verbatim transcripts of question-and-answer session from the 1978 Lonergan Workshop, Boston College, File #885 Archive, Lonergan Research Institute of Regis College, Toronto, p. 8.

22. File #885, p. 9.

Lonergan's suggestion of affective conversion, went on to develop his own notion of *affectional conversion*. Doran, on the other hand, incorporated affective conversion into his theory of psychic conversion. He suggests that affective conversion is the *fruit* (in part) of psychic conversion (*TDH*, 9). Doran may be closer to what Lonergan had in mind if one considers that Lonergan does seem to link explicitly the notion of affective conversion to his understanding of "psychic" conversion. That is, in the same response to the question mentioned above, Lonergan specifies his own understanding of "psychic conversion." He states: "It is a conversion of one's affectivity. One's affectivity can have things go wrong with it, and they go wrong with it before you even know what affectivity is, and it keeps getting worse. There is an affective conversion and there is affective liberation."[23]

Again, these comments from Lonergan are spontaneous, and we cannot be certain whether what he means by "conversion of one's affectivity" is in fact the same as what he means by affective conversion in "Natural Right and Historical Mindedness," and if so, to what extent these comments are related to his suggestion of affective conversion in "Natural Right and Historical Mindedness." Moreover, we cannot be certain what he means by the phrase "there is an affective conversion and there is affective liberation", that is, whether affective conversion and affective liberation are distinct in his mind, and if so to what extent each pertains to psychic conversion. Nevertheless, *prima facie*, Lonergan's comments seem to corroborate Doran's suggestion that affective conversion is the fruit of psychic conversion, that is, at least insofar as psychic conversion facilitates affective conversion/liberation.[24]

Moreover, there is a further complication, and it concerns a point that is often overlooked in Lonergan's mention of affective conversion in "Natural Right." Specifically, he does not use the term (at least directly) in reference to the healing of the psychological subject. Walter Conn speaks of affective conversion as "a radical reorientation of

---

23. File #885, p. 9.

24. For Doran, the healing of the censor from a repressive to a constructive agency in the subject may enable a person to recover those "affect-laden images of the psyche" (*TDH*, 61).

our passionate desires from obsession with self-needs to concern for the needs of others. . . ."[25] I agree with his emphasis, but I would view affective conversion as essentially an aspect of moral conversion (as Lonergan defines it) and not as a distinct conversion because it involves essentially the conversion from selfishness/self-centeredness to a commitment to the other (family, community, God). That is, affective conversion entails a shift in the criterion of one's decisions from satisfaction to value, wherein decisions based on satisfaction reflect decisions based on selfishness/self-centredness while the transformation of that desire leads to a commitment to one's family, community, and God which are all fundamentally choices of value. Viewed in this way, affective conversion is basically a moral conversion but with an emphasis on the conversion from selfishness/self-centredness. However, I am not convinced that it is feasible to speak of affective conversion as a distinct and unique conversion at least as Lonergan invokes the term in "Natural Right." That is, if one looks closely at Lonergan's use of the term *affective conversion* in "Natural Right," one finds that it is used in the context of being-in-love with one's family, being-in-love with one's neighbor (community), and being-in-love with God.[26] Lonergan uses these same three examples of *being-in-love* in the chapter on religion in *Method in Theology* but he discusses them specifically in light of religious conversion. His reference, for example, to the love of husband and wife is used as an analogy of the "other-wordly" being-in-love with God. Religious conversion culminates in the fulfillment of one's conscious intentionality which accompanies being-in-love in an unrestricted manner.[27]

In the context of his comments in "Natural Right," affective conversion promotes a threefold commitment to love through being-in-love with one's family, through being-in-love with humanity, and "faith in the

---

25. Conn, "Affective Conversion," in O' Fallon & Riley, Religion and Culture, p. 270.

26. Lonergan, "Natural Right," in *A Third Collection*, p. 173.

27. Lonergan writes *in Method in Theology*: "Being-in-love is of different kinds. There is love of intimacy, of husband and wife, of parents and children. There is the love of one's fellow men with its fruit in the achievement of human welfare. There is the love of God with one's whole heart and whole soul, with all one's mind and all one's strength (Mk. 12, 30)," (p. 101).

destiny" of humanity.[28] In this sense, Lonergan's use of the term *affective conversion* suggests that the notion incorporates *all* forms of being-in-love. Being-in-love with God (or religious conversion), then, would be a subdivision of affective conversion.[29] Moreover, he does not link affective conversion directly to the healing of the psychological subject although one could infer it indirectly to the extent that dramatic bias may prevent one from being-in-love in either of these three ways.

Finally, it is quite possible that in Lonergan's reference to affective conversion in "Natural Right," he was referring to his own notion of religious conversion and simply substituted the term "affective conversion" in that instance out of consideration of his audience.[30] However, even if this was the case, this does not eliminate the need to address the psychological and affective dimensions of conversion in Lonergan's theory of conversion.

A further point to consider: perhaps part of the confusion surrounding Lonergan's few comments concerning affective conversion is that there has not been an adequate treatment of the structure of affectivity within Lonergan's overall theory of consciousness. That is, in *Insight*, Lonergan outlines a precise structure of the intellectual pattern of operations involved in human knowing, but he does not outline the structure of affectivity in human knowing. Nor should this be expected, since it was not his primary concern at the time. However, he does treat the topic of affectivity in the chapter titled "The Human Good" in *Method in Theology*. His treatment, though, is far from exhaustive and he deals specifically with ethics and the human good, emphasizing the inextricable relationship between values and feelings.

There are implicit references to feelings and affectivity throughout Lonergan's theory of consciousness, but the fuller structure remains to

---

28. Lonergan, "Natural Right," in *A Third Collection*, p. 173. [2021 note: I removed "being in love with God" from the original publication because it was not completely accurate to what Lonergan was saying in "Natural Right".]

29. I am grateful to my conversations with Daniel Monsour, for helping me to clarify this point.

30. I am grateful to Robert M. Doran for this hypothesis. [2021 note: Lonergan's audience for "Natural Right" was philosophical so he may have prescinded from speaking of religious conversion and other theological topics.]

be fleshed out. For example, Lonergan begins his work in *Insight* with a reference to Archimedes and the famous scenario where, upon discovering the solution to the problem that plagued him, he ran naked through the streets shouting "Eureka!"[31] Archimedes' shout for joy illustrates the inextricable relationship between affectivity and the intellectual *desire to know* and the joy that can accompany the fruit of successful inquiry. There are also other implicit treatments of affectivity throughout various aspects of Lonergan's thought; but again, these remain aspects to be fleshed out and made more explicit.[32]

A handful of scholars have attempted to develop the role of affectivity in Lonergan's theory of consciousness. However, the bulk of this scholarship deals solely with the affective dimension as it pertains to the fourth level of operations and specifically concerns ethical/moral decision-making.[33] There remains a need to clarify and flesh

31. See Lonergan, *Insight*, pp. 27–28.

32. Some examples include: Lonergan speaks of the aesthetic pattern of experience and later derives a definition of art from his reading of Susanne K. Langer's *Feeling and Form* (New York: Charles Scribner's Sons, 1953). See Bernard Lonergan, *Topics in Education: The Cincinnati Lectures of 1959 on the Philosophy of Education*, in *Collected Works*, Vol 10, ed. by R M. Doran and F. E. Crowe (Toronto: University of Toronto Press, 1993), p. 211. Lonergan refers to "transcendental feelings" which he takes from the Introduction of J. A. Stewart's *The Myths of Plato*. Michael Vertin cites his own unpublished interview with Lonergan. See Michael Vertin, "Judgments of Value in the Later Lonergan," *Method: Journal of Lonergan Studies,* 13 (1995): p. 235 f.46. Lonergan also infers the role of affectivity in chap 17 of *Insight* when he refers to the unplumbed depths of the known unknown. See Lonergan, *Insight*, p. 555.

33. See, Elizabeth A. Morelli, *Anxiety: A Study of Affectivity of Moral Consciousness* (Lanham, NY: University of America Press, 1985); Mark Doorley, *The Place of the Heart in Lonergan's Ethics: The Role of Feelings in the Ethical Intentionality Analysis of Bernard Lonergan* (Lanham, MA: University of America Press, 1996); William Sullivan, *The Role of Affect in Evaluations According to Bernard Lonergan: Ramifications for the Euthanasia Debate* (University of Toronto, Dissertation. 1998). Jason Edward King, *The Role of Feelings in Decision-making According to Bernard Lonergan* (Ph.D. Thesis, The Catholic University of America, 2001); Hazel Markwell, *The Role of Feelings in Informed Consent: An Application of Bernard Lonergan's Work on Feelings* (Ph.D. Thesis, 2001); Walter Conn fleshes out the close relationship between affective conversion and moral self-transcendence (moral conversion). See his *Christian Conversion* (Mahwah, NJ: Paulist Press, 1986), 153.

out in a more comprehensive way, the relationship between affectivity and the operations of intentional consciousness, taking into account Lonergan's full theory of consciousness.[34] This is a tall order. In order to explicate fully the structure of affectivity throughout Lonergan's theory of consciousness, one would need to distinguish between the affectivity involved in each of the specific levels of operations of consciousness (experience, understanding, judgment, and decision) as well as in each of the transformations of consciousness (conversions).[35] Such a project would include clarifying the role of affectivity as it functions in each of the various transformations of consciousness, that is, as it functions distinctly in *intellectual conversion*, as it functions distinctly in *moral conversion*, as it functions distinctly in *religious conversion*, and as it functions distinctly in the *psychological healing* of the subject. This project obviously lies beyond the scope of this paper. The problem is worth mentioning, however, because this lacuna in Lonergan's theory of consciousness has undoubtedly contributed to the confusion and lack of clarity surrounding subsequent attempts to understand what Lonergan may have meant by affective conversion.

I believe that the fact that Lonergan himself never fully develops the psychological dimensions of conversion, coupled with the fact that he never explicated the structure of affectivity in his theory of consciousness, has prompted scholars to draw upon his use of the term "affective conversion" in order to fill out in part these aspects lacking in Lonergan's theory of intentional consciousness.

34.Written in 2003, this statement concurs with a more recent one by Patrick Byrne when he writes: "Feelings as intentional responses are always operative throughout the entire dynamic structure of human consciousness." Patrick Byrne, *The Ethics of Discernment: Lonergan's Foundations for Ethics* (Toronto: University of Toronto Press, 2016), 98. His work, as well, pertains to the affectivity in ethical deliberation.

35. Andrew Tallon's work, although not explicitly in line with this approach, is an attempt to integrate the affective and cognitive dimensions of human consciousness. See his *Head and Heart: Affection, Cognition, Volition as Triune Consciousness* (New York: Fordham University, 1997), See especially pp. 208–11.

IV. THE NEED FOR THE APPLICATION
OF OCCAM'S RAZOR?

We have noted that the question remains unanswered regarding what Lonergan actually meant by affective conversion and whether or not he actually was speaking of a distinct conversion. We have noted as well that there is a lacuna that remains in Lonergan's theory of consciousness concerning the explicit structure of affectivity. These two conditions, along with the need we have suggested for an integrated notion of the psychological aspects of conversion, have led some developers of Lonergan's thought to multiply unnecessarily the various notions of conversion. Hence, there may be a precedent for applying an Occam's Razor to this type of reflection. This could be done in such a way as to restrict the multiplication of notions of conversions to no more than absolutely necessary. Let us look at some examples.

Lonergan spoke of religious, moral, and intellectual conversion, with a few remarks about affective conversion (although he accepted psychic conversion). Doran speaks of religious, moral, intellectual, and psychic conversion, wherein affective conversion is the fruit of psychic conversion. Donald Gelpi presupposes the existence of Lonergan's threefold conversion but develops this by a more precise treatment of moral conversion. In turn, Gelpi distinguishes two types of moral conversion: *personal* and *sociopolitical*. He acknowledges Doran's contribution of psychic conversion but prefers to keep the term affective conversion. For Gelpi, the fruit of the latter conversion allows full access to one's emotional, imaginative, and aesthetic sensibilities.[36] Bernard Tyrrell, as we have seen, affirms the above conversions of Lonergan and Doran but develops his understanding of Lonergan's affective conversion in terms of the twofold distinct aspects of affectional conversion (upper level and primal affectional). Tyrrell has also pondered the question of the possibility of *aesthetic conversion* (*AC*, 31). In his earlier work he pondered the notion of *conversion from addiction*.[37]

---

36. Donald Gelpi, S. J., "The Authentication of Doctrines: Hints from C. S. Pierce," in *Theological Studies*, 60 (1999): pp. 272–73.

37. B. Tyrrell, "Passages and Conversions," in Lamb, *Creativity and Method*, pp. 24 ff., 31 ff.

In a recent study on modern spiritual autobiography, David Leigh uses some categories from Lonergan that he obtains from Walter Conn's *Christian Conversion*. Among these Leigh invokes affective, religious, intellectual and moral conversion. In addition, he adds his own formulation that he calls *imaginative conversion*.[38] This does not necessarily exhaust the list and there will probably be more developments and formulations of conversion to follow.[39]

In the first section of this paper, it could be said that I was applying Occam's Razor when I suggested that what might be going forward in the formulations of psychic and affectional conversions is a fuller understanding of the healing of the psychological subject. I borrowed a term from Tyrell to call this emerging development *psychological conversion*.

Perhaps there is a sense in which the multiplication of various notions of conversions reflects the complex polymorphic structure of human consciousness. However, it seems more prudent to try to be more concise and move towards synthesis of these notions of conversions where feasible. After all, it seems redundant to speak of a sociopolitical conversion, for example, when it would appear that the transformation of social, economic, and political structures follows from the cumulative effects of the intellectual, moral, religious, and psychological conversions of individuals who participate and play a constitutive role in those structures.[40]

Similarly, it seems redundant to speak of conversion from addiction, for example, when in Lonergan's schema, such a conversion would

---

38. David Leigh, *Circuitous Journeys: Modern Spiritual Autobiography*, (New York: Fordham University Press, 2000), p. 15. He defines *imaginative conversion* as "the discovery and transformation of one's directional images, which lead one beyond the self toward a search for ultimate meaning through a lifetime" (p. 15). As defined, this notion is dealt with by Doran insofar as *psychic conversion* allows one access to one's own symbolic system (*TDH*, 61).

39. For example, Dr. Miguel Bedolla proposed the notion of a somatic conversion but as far as I am aware he has not developed the notion further. "The Notion of Somatic Conversion." Unpublished paper distributed at the Lonergan Workshop, Boston College, 1989.

40. Walter Conn suggests that "social commitment," that is, commitment to social justice, is one of the fruits of affective and moral conversion. See *Christian Conversion*, pp. 153–57.

fall under the rubric *of moral conversion*. This is not to say that addiction is a moral problem *per se*, although it certainly affects one's moral behavior. However, in terms of Lonergan's definition of moral conversion as the transformation of the criterion for one's choosing from *satisfactions* to *values*, it could be argued that this definition includes the healing of addiction.[41] That is, insofar as addicted people do not have the ability to resist the satisfactions (that is, immediate gratification) of their "drug of choice," the addictive cycle progresses, and their ability to choose *value* over *satisfaction* is increasingly compromised through a progressive, uncontrollable pattern of self-destructive behavior.

Applying Occam's Razor further to the ongoing reflection on conversion, one wonders if it is necessary to speak of an *aesthetic conversion* as a distinct, additional conversion. Might it not be better to speak of the effects of the so-called aesthetic conversion as included as the fruit of psychic conversion? For Doran, psychic conversion allows one access to one's own symbolic system and, further, he also suggests that there is a link between psychic conversion and the transcendental *beauty*.[42] Or, perhaps it might be better to drop the idea of an aesthetic conversion altogether and speak instead of an aesthetic differentiation of consciousness as exemplified by the artist and which is developed to greater and lesser degrees in other people. This raises the questions concerning the relationship between conversion and differentiations of consciousness, which is beyond the scope of this paper.

Finally, we have noted that Lonergan seemed to suggest that there were four conversions. My preference is to consider this suggestion as a precedent for applying *Occam's Razor*. That is, since there are four levels of operations in Lonergan's theory of intentional consciousness (experience, understanding, judgment, and decision), why not try to

---

41. Consider this quote from one of the primary texts of Alcoholics Anonymous concerning the alcoholic prior to sobriety in that program: "We had lacked the perspective to see that character-building and spiritual values had to come first, and that material satisfactions were not the purpose of living." *Twelve Steps and Twelve Traditions* (New York: Alcoholics World Services Inc., 1953), p. 71. Accordingly, Pope Francis call for an ecological conversion pertains to moral conversion since it involves a healing of the block in our inability to see creation for its intrinsic value.

42. On symbolism, see *TDH*, 286–288; on beauty, see *TDH*, pp. 161–69.

limit this type of reflection to four conversions: intellectual, moral, religious and psychological? Certainly, I am not suggesting that each of the conversions matches neatly with each of the levels of intentional consciousness respectively. Nor am I suggesting that limiting the number of formulations of conversions to four should be held to rigidly; it would certainly have to be modified in light of future empirical data. Nevertheless, I think Lonergan's comments concerning a limit of four conversions is provocative enough to warrant further testing of this hypothesis. If nothing else, it promises: 1) to promote a critical appraisal of subsequent formulations on conversion, following Lonergan's threefold development; 2) to bring more rigour to this type of reflection so as to avoid unnecessary formulations; and 3) hopefully, to bring more clarity to this reflection.

4

Body-Psyche-Mind in the Self-Appropriation of the Subject: Complexifying Lonergan's Account of Nature and Supernature

MARY JOSEPHINE MCDONALD THD

n the opening page of *Method in Theology,* Bernard Lonergan expresses a concern that theology would understand its role at this important juncture in history—a time when the modern world enters a new realm of meaning, one that represents a shift from classicism to interiority. In order to fulfill its task of mediating "between a cultural matrix and the significance and role of a religion in that matrix,"[1] Lonergan states that theology must understand that it is no longer a "permanent achievement," but rather "an ongoing process."[2] In proceeding, therefore, theology must become acquainted with the "framework for collaborative creativity" in the "ongoing process" that Lonergan calls method.[3] In addition, Lonergan emphasizes that "a contemporary method would conceive those tasks in the context of modern science, modern scholarship, modern philosophy. . . ."[4]

---

1. Bernard Lonergan, S.J., *Method in Theology* (Toronto: University of Toronto Press, 2003), xi.

2. Ibid.

3. Ibid.

4. Ibid.

This paper seeks to "collaborate creatively" with "modern science" in order that both theology and the cultural context might be mutually enriched. By drawing on the insights of the science of neuroplasticity, along with those of the psychologist, Eugene Gendlin, this paper undertakes the task of developing an understanding of the bodily aspect of the human person in an interiority analysis. The primary goal of this work is the development of a theological anthropology.

Lonergan's question, "What in terms of human consciousness is the transition from the natural to the supernatural?" in "Mission and the Spirit,"[5] along with his articulation of the body-psyche-mind relations in his principle of correspondence in *Insight*,[6] provide the framework for this development. A developed understanding of the body's role in the transition from the natural to the supernatural furthers Doran's work on psychic conversion by including "body data" in the self-appropriation of the unconscious. Such an integration of the organic and psychic spontaneities with conscious operations increases the probability of authentic agency in the unfolding of the Reign of God.

The argument for developing a theological anthropology that includes "body data" proceeds in the following way: first by introducing Eugene Gendlin's notion of body knowledge, then transposing his descriptive categories into the explanatory categories of interiority, offering a developed understanding of psychic conversion by including the self-appropriation of body data and finally bringing neuroscience into a depiction of the body in a theological anthropology.

Gendlin's Description of Body Knowledge

As a psychologist, Eugene Gendlin offers a unique approach to an understanding of the body. As a philosopher, he appears to be

---

5. Bernard Lonergan, S.J., "Mission and the Spirit," in *A Third Collection*, ed. Frederick E. Crowe (Mahwah, NJ: Paulist Press, 1985), 23.

6. Bernard Lonergan, S.J., *Insight: A Study of Human Understanding*, vol. 3, *Collected Works of Bernard Lonergan*, ed. Frederick E. Crowe and Robert M. Doran (Toronto: University of Toronto Press, 1992), 555.

struggling within the confines of theoretical meaning in search, but not yet aware, of the categories of interiority needed to explain his therapeutic experience of the body. The task at hand entails drawing on his therapeutic insights on the human body for the purpose of further differentiating Lonergan's categories of interiority.

Through his observations as a therapist, Gendlin became aware of the body's role in healing psychic disturbances or blocks. Resolving repressed images, Gendlin determines, must come from the unconscious or body itself, and not by way of the intellect concerned with theoretical analysis. He observed that one needs only to pay attention, to focus on the felt sense[7] in the body during any given situation. As one gently probes the felt sense with questions, much like teasing out threads from a knot in one's sewing, the body responds. The once unclear bodily sense gives way to an ever-increasing clarity in the felt sense, finally culminating in the release of an image into consciousness. A concomitant release of energy accompanies this final step. Gendlin calls this moment of energy release a "felt shift." It is this "felt shift" that verifies the viability of the process.

Gendlin's work offers two main insights into an understanding of the human body. First, Gendlin shows that the body is inherently dynamic, ever seeking higher forms. Secondly, within this dynamism there is an intelligibility, a meaning that is more than the human person can know rationally. Both points will be explored together in a manner that develops an understanding of their interrelations. Gendlin contends that

there is meaning before and also beyond language. Living bodies *imply* (they mean) their further environmental interactions. With a broad bodily process (including its muscles, nerves,

---

7. "A felt sense is not a mental experience but a physical one. A bodily awareness of a situation or person or event. An internal aura that encompasses everything you feel and know about the given subject at a given time—encompasses it and communicates it to you all at once rather than detail by detail. . . . A felt sense doesn't come to you in the form of thoughts or words or other separate units, but as a single (though often puzzling and very complex) bodily feeling." Eugene Gendlin, *Focusing*, 2nd ed. (New York: Bantam Books, 1981), 32.

gland, and circulation) the body *implies* its continuation, and thereby also the objects, things, words, involved in this next step.[8]

Insisting, furthermore, that the body possesses meaning prior to a person's ability to think and reason, Gendlin argues,

> I begin by rejecting a certain assumption: It is currently assumed that human behavior is organized only by externally imposed forms or patterns. . . . We seem to miss the point that our social training has already formed us by the time we ask and think.[9]

What is this prior meaning or intelligibility "before and beyond language," this knowledge that Gendlin contends that the body possesses? According to Gendlin, the "felt sense" of any given situation constitutes the entire, myriad encounters stored over the years that "come to you all at once, as a single great aura sensed in your body."[10] In short, the body operates in an ongoing interaction with its environment, and, as such, acts as the "warehouse," the storage facility that houses all human experience.[11]

> The body is a biological computer, generating these enormous collections of data and delivering them to you instantaneously when you call them up or when they are called up by some external event. Your thinking isn't capable of holding all those items of knowledge, nor of delivering them with such speed.[12]

---

8. Eugene Gendlin, "Meaning Prior to the Separation of the Five Senses, in *Current Advances in Semantic Theory*, ed. M. Stamenov (Amsterdam/ Philadelphia: John Benjamins, 1992," 9.

9. Ibid., 1.

10. For example, when greeting a friend, "The sense of 'all about your friend' comes to you in . . . a huge file of data: what he looks like, how he speaks, how you and he first met, what you need from him, what he said yesterday, and what you said in return. The amount of information is staggering—yet somehow, when you think of [your friend], all the relevant facts and feelings come to you at once." *Focusing*, 33–34.

11. The argument presented in this paper offers the explanation that human experience is stored in the very manner that it shapes the nervous system.

12. Ibid., 34 A good example of this may be observed on the occasions when a person finds herself in danger. The awareness of danger comes first from the body's response

Yet, the stored material exists not merely as random bits of data but rather as an intelligibility, a patterned meaning that is oriented toward, or *implies,* a higher form of meaning in conscious image and knowing. Given its possession of intelligible meaning from prior interactions with its environment, the body guides human behaviour. By way of its "bodily sense" of a situation, the body provides the necessary data needed to interpret a new situation.[13]

> We do not speak to ourselves about each facet of a situation—if we did, we could not handle any situation at all. To do any simple thing, we must "know" what led up to the situation, what we are trying to bring about or avoid, who the people present are, how to walk, sit, speak, and countless other facets. We can think only very few of these explicitly. All the rest are "known" in a rich, holistic feeling of the whole context, which we can have only in a bodily concrete way.[14]

As a complex interactional system, Gendlin argues, the body's intelligibility not only guides conscious living but also seeks higher integration, both in the release of images to consciousness and by producing the "story" of its complex daily interaction every night in one's dreams. This dynamism, this orientation of the body's intelligibility to seek higher forms or to *imply* its continuation in the human person constitutes what Gendlin argues is "body knowledge."

---

to the situation. It is the "hair raising," adrenaline rush, vague gut sense of discomfort that alerts consciousness to the presence of danger. The body has already interpreted the present situation based on the meaning internalized from its prior experiences (and from other instinctual reflexes).

13. It is important to clarify that the process of interpreting a new situation does not occur in the body, but rather in the higher functioning of conscious thought. However, the meaning of the new, reinterpreted situation is retained as a "felt experience" in the body.

14. Eugene Gendlin, "Imagery is More Powerful with Focusing: Theory and Practice," in *Imagery—Its Many Dimensions and Applications,* ed. Joseph E. Shorr, Gail E. Sobel, Pennee Robin, and Jack A. Conella (New York and London: Plenum Press, 1980), 1. It is the manner in which meaning is stored from the body's previous interactions and thus made available to guide further interactions that appears to find synchrony with Lonergan's statement that somehow past judgments remain with us.

Situating Gendlin's Work in Interiority: Body Knowledge and Received Meaning

Gendlin's notion of "body knowledge" provides a further descriptive context to Doran's articulation of the dynamics that are operative within intentional consciousness "from above," the "sedimented communal meanings and values" or the elemental, received meanings that emerge into consciousness "already patterned, and the pattern is already charged emotionally and conatively."[15] At the same time, Doran's work on "received meaning" aids in the task of situating Gendlin's understanding of the body within the categories of interiority. Recalling Lonergan's point regarding the relative dominance of the community over the subject,[16] Doran has further clarified how the dominance of community over the subject points to an understanding of "received meaning."

> This relative dominance means that the horizon of the subject in his or her world, a horizon constituted by meaning, along with the world that is correlative to that horizon, are, prior to critical reflection on the part of the subject, largely a function of . . . "being thrown into existence in the world at this particular time and with these particular people, with their own horizons similarly determined for them by historical dialectics over which at the outset they have no control." All of this "gives rise to the situation that stimulates neural demands, and it molds the orientation of intelligence that preconsciously exercises the censorship," so that the very reception of data that are also invested with meaning is itself constitutive of the subject's horizon.[17]

---

15. See Doran in dialogue with Lonergan on the topic of received meaning in *What Is Systematic Theology?* Toronto: University of Toronto Press, 2005, 126.

16. Doran adds the further dominance of one's culture, as well. See Ibid., 137.

17. Ibid. Lonergan notes that the dramatic pattern plays a key role in the orientation of intelligence. He is clear that, because the dramatic subject is always "in the presence of others," "who are also actors in the primordial drama," human dramatic development is always "inspired by example and emulation, confirmed by admiration and approval, sustained by respect and affection." (*Insight,* 107). The principal point

With this understanding of the reception of meaning "from above," Doran proposes that Lonergan's statement that "past judgments somehow remain with us" can be viewed in a new light. The past judgments that somehow remain with a person concern not only one's own judgments but also encompass the judgments and values of the community into which one was born. This relationship of the present to the past connects to Lonergan's term "ordinary meaningfulness," while the relations within the present and those of the present to the future concern the cognitive and evaluative processes of one's own "original meaningfulness."[18]

While Gendlin has not specifically distinguished between the two types of ordinary and original meaningfulness in his work, he has alluded to both respectively in his assertions, "[O]ur social training has already formed us by the time we ask and think,"[19] and "[T]he body *implies* its continuation, and thereby also the objects, things, words, involved in this next step."[20] In addition, Gendlin emphasizes the importance of acknowledging that the meaning of both is held within

---

is that the dramatic actor is molded by the drama in his or her own environment, or is socialized into habitual ways of behaving in a manner that is pre-reflective. From this pre-reflective functioning of the dramatic pattern, the human person achieves an ability to anticipate possible ways of behaving, and these ways of behaving are already invested not only with feelings but also with meaning, the meaning and values that constitute the drama itself. It is this understanding of how a community of meaning occupies a dominant role in the shaping of one's dramatic pattern that leads to the position taken here, that is, that Doran's notion of received meaning furthers an understanding of Lonergan's portrayal of the dramatic pattern.

18. "That ordinary meaningfulness may be more or less sinful, more or less under the influence of grace." Ibid., 138–9. "And the received intelligibility that I am suggesting is also the historical product of the original meaningfulness of the insights, judgments, and decisions of others who have preceded us, or of their biases, their failures to be intelligent, reasonable, and responsible, or of some combination of intelligence and bias." Ibid., 130.

19. Eugene Gendlin, "Meaning Prior to the Separation of the Five Senses." In *Current Advances in Semantic Theory*, edited by Maxim I. Stamenov, 31–53. Amsterdam/ Philadelphia: John Benjamins, 1992. http://www.focusing.org/gendlin/docs/gol_2111.html, accessed February 3, 2011, 1.

20. Ibid., 9.

the body that continually seeks higher forms of consciousness. This emphasis serves to highlight Doran's insistence that this level of meaning needs to be brought into the light of conscious awareness. At the same time, Doran's work on received meaning has provided Gendlin's therapeutic descriptive categories the necessary grounding in interiority, thereby serving a needed explanatory function.

The Transcendental Precept to Be Attentive: Focusing Fills Out Doran's Understanding of Psychic Self-Appropriation

Bringing the body into a developed understanding of Doran's notion of psychic conversion involves but a small step. Doran has already brought the organic aspect of the person into his discussion of interiorly differentiated consciousness and the further need for psychic self-appropriation.

> But I have argued that the process [of interiorly differentiated consciousness] can and must be further extended to include the self-appropriation of those dimensions of consciousness that are properly psychic: in effect, an appropriation (1) of the first, empirical level of consciousness (the psyche) that consists in the sensitive flow of sensations, memories, images, conations, emotions, associations, spontaneous inter-subjective responses, bodily movements, and received meanings and values, and . . . , (2) *of the potential openness of intentional consciousness to an underpinning transition from the neural to the organic to the psychic.*[21]

Having argued that Doran's work on received meaning has provided Gendlin's therapeutic descriptive categories on the body the necessary grounding in interiority, the further step at this juncture

---

21. Doran, *What Is Systematic Theology?*, 111. Italics added. "I have addressed dramatic bias and scotosis, and acknowledged the need to extend this discussion to the organic." Ibid., 139.

articulates the manner in which the self-appropriation of the interiorly differentiated terms and relations at the level of the organism might be brought to consciousness. In short, this further step provides a development in the understanding of Doran's notion of psychic conversion.

Developing an understanding of psychic conversion emphasizes the distortions in the relations between the body and the psyche—how the body or the organic aspect of the human person is involved in scotosis or dramatic bias.[22] From this perspective that explains the need for healing at the organic level, Gendlin's focusing technique will provide a means to discuss self-appropriation at this level. The basic premise from which this discussion proceeds is that scotosis affects the organism. The distorted effects of scotosis on the organism can be objectified in the immediacy of a felt sense through focusing. Focusing acts as a means for the unconscious organism to circumvent the repressive censor responsible for the scotosis. Viewed in light of this premise, an expanded understanding of psychic conversion involves acknowledging the need to be attentive to the organic level of one's being, to the felt sense in a given situation.

The task outlined in this section, involves identifying the complex relations between the organism and the psyche. On the one pole of the "unity in tension" in the human person are the vital spontaneities of neural processes, "sensations, memories, images, emotions, conations" and received meanings and values, and, on the other pole of the "unity in tension, is the censorship, functioning as the collaboration of dramatically patterned intelligence with imagination in the control and selection of the neural demands. The upward, dynamic vertical finality of human development occurs within the taut balance of these two poles.

---

22. Unlike group, individual and general biases, which involve an ever-increasing element of "personal default on the part of the spirit, for which the individual is somehow to be held accountable . . . [d]ramatic bias . . . is a function of an affective disturbance resulting primarily from the victimization of our psyches by others in a way that was originally beyond our control." Doran, *Theology and the Dialectics of History*. Toronto: University of Toronto Press, 1990, 2001, 234. Due to its effects prior to consciousness, dramatic bias occupies the concerns of the present discussion.

Delineating the two poles of the "unity in tension" in terms of neural demand functions and censorship provides an explanatory basis for the second stage in the process of developing an understanding of psychic conversion. The two principles of change, the spontaneous drive to psychic integration by neural demands and the exigence of the neural manifold for appropriate integration by the censor, operate not only in harmony but also in opposition. How, then, is the body involved in the dialectical distortions between these two ordering principles manifest in what Lonergan calls dramatic bias?[23] Dramatic bias is a distortion in the constructive activity of the censorship. As constructive, the censorship meets the demands of the neural processes for appropriate psychic integration in a manner that would give rise to an insight. The negative aspect of this positive, constructive activity is one of leaving behind the psychic materials not required for the insight.[24] Lonergan notes that this negative activity by the constructive censorship "does *not* introduce any arrangement or perspective into the unconscious demand functions of neural patterns and processes. other than what is needed for an insight?"[25] In contrast, however, dramatic bias constitutes an aberration of the censorship that is repressive. As repressive, the positive activity of the censorship is to "prevent the emergence into consciousness of perspectives that would give rise to unwanted insights."[26] Unlike the negative activity of a constructive censorship that leaves behind irrelevant psychic material, this repressive activity of a distorted censorship

> *introduces*, so to speak, the exclusion of arrangements into the field of the unconscious; it dictates the manner in which neural

---

23. Dramatic bias holds a more prominent influence over the psychic dimension than do general and egoistic biases. On this subject Doran explains, "Dramatic bias . . . functions as a dimension of an already established dialectic of the subject. It is a function of an affective disturbance resulting primarily from the victimization of our psyches by others in a way that was originally beyond our control." Ibid., 234.

24. Lonergan, *Insight*, 216.

25. Italics mine. Ibid.

26. Ibid. "Insights are unwanted, not because they confirm our current viewpoints and behavior, but because they lead to their correction and revision." Ibid., 217.

demand functions are not to be met; and the negative aspect of its positive activity is the admission to consciousness of any materials in any other arrangement or perspective.[27]

It is this habitual *introduction* of repressing arrangements into the unconscious that sheds light on how dramatic bias affects the relationship between the organism and the psyche. Indeed, by examining the effects of dramatic bias on the organism specifically, the foundation will be laid to argue that focusing represents a needed complement to the present understanding of psychic conversion.

What happens to the energy from the universe at the entry point of the human organism when there is a repressing censor at work?[28] Clearly, the anguish of abnormality representative of the distorted relations between the organism and the psyche must manifest itself not only on the psychic level but also on the organic level, as well. Long-term, habitual repression *introduces* an arrangement into one's neural demand functions that inhibits the performance of the dramatic artistry of the human person. Lonergan writes,

> Apprehension and affect are for operations, but as one would expect, the complex consequences of the scotosis tend to defeat the efforts of the dramatic actor to offer a smooth performance. . . . [T]he division of conscious living between the two patterns of the ego and persona can hamper attention to the higher-level controls and allow the sentiments of the ego or shadow to slip into the performance of the persona. . . . In a systematization of Jung's terminology, the conscious ego is

---

27. Italics mine. Ibid. In the extreme, the repression of neural processes will operate as a force or principle that warps the rest of a person's life of experience, insights, judgments and decisions causing blind spots or scotomas. Dramatic bias ultimately manifests itself as a principle of social and historical decline, operating in opposition to the drive of vertical finality. Ibid, 214–22

28. While the term "energy" may not be a commonly used category in the Lonergan community, nevertheless, the position here represents agreement with that of Doran, who interprets psychic energy "on the basis of Lonergan's understanding of genera and species and of the emergent probability of universal process." *Theology and the Dialectics of History*, (see n.11), 686.

matched with an inverse nonconscious shadow, and the conscious persona is matched with an inverse nonconscious anima.[29]

In other words, the repressing arrangements that are introduced into one's neural demand functions by a repressive censor have long-term and complex results. Lonergan's quote suggests that the scotosis or repressing arrangements participate in the covert activity associated with what, in Jungian terminology, constitutes the nonconscious shadow and nonconscious anima.[30] These repressing arrangements, which Jung terms negative complexes,[31] inhabit the shadowland of the human organism.[32] Over time as the scotosis becomes more deeply entrenched into one's habitual way of being, a point is reached where the neural demands are so loaded with inhibitions that affects become disassociated from their congruent objects. At this point, the stream of consciousness is no longer capable of functioning in its role of providing psychic representation and conscious integration for the neural demands. Then the "anguish of abnormality" of the distorted neural demands "assert themselves in waking consciousness through inadequacies, compulsions, pains, and anxieties of the psychoneuroses."[33] Yet, the point being made here is that the "anguish

---

29. Lonergan, *Insight*, 217.

30. On a further note, the shadow includes not only repressed psychic material but also aspects of the human person that are under-developed.

31. Doran draws on Jung for the notion of psychic energy as "bound up" in a negative complex. "[Healing] would be a matter of freeing the psychic energy bound up in what Jung called negative complexes, so that it is free to cooperate rather than interfere with the operations of meaning and love through which direction is found in the movement of life." *Theology and the Dialectics of History*, 53.

32. Doran notes that Jung depicts all psychic energy as being distributed into complexes. Not all are negative. "Some of these, formed by the development of habits, support and aid . . . the creative vector in consciousness, while other [negative complexes] interfere with, subvert, block, derail this quest." Ibid., 229.

33. Ibid., 221. Doran details the effects of the repressive arrangements as psychic disturbances. "Our psychic energy can be blocked, fixed in inflexible patterns, driven by compulsions, plagued by obsessions, weighed down by general anxiety or specific fears, resistant to insight, true judgment and responsible action. . . . The person must detour through the disturbing set of complexes and release the inhibiting energy that is blocking the flourishing unfolding of creative operations." Ibid.

of abnormality" of the distorted neural demands is also manifest in a "felt sense" in the body. In short, the effects of a repressing censor will, over time, become manifest on both "poles" in the relations between the psyche and the organism.[34]

The body, as integrator of energy from the universe and operator of its higher integration in psychic material, manifests the distortion of this integral relationship both on the psychic level, as "arrangements other than that which is needed for an insight," as well as on the organic level, as the "felt experience" concomitant with the introduction of excluding arrangements into the unconscious or body. Clearly, attention must be paid to such bodily manifestations of distortion that inhibit the unfolding of the creative finality of the human person. The development of an understanding of psychic conversion, therefore, would need to include the data of consciousness related to the organism along with that of the psyche.

Finally, to conclude the task of developing an understanding of psychic conversion, this stage begins by providing empirical data to support Gendlin's claim that a "felt shift," experienced as the release of energy facilitated by the focusing technique, verifies the integrity of the concomitant images released into consciousness and, subsequently, verifies the integrity of the body-psyche relation.[35] It establishes how focusing functions in addition to dream analysis in the self-appropriation of psychic material.[36] Furthermore, in arriving at a

---

34. The manner in which "repressive arrangements" are introduced into the unconscious organism over time becomes a habit. In the following section, this "habit" will be discussed in terms of neurophysiology.

35. The following section of this paper provides the further empirical data necessary to ground Gendlin's work by drawing on neuroscience to explain "body knowledge." In view of the present task involved in expanding an understanding of psychic conversion, the empirical data offered in this section will be restricted to explicitly supporting Gendlin's notion of the "felt shift."

36. In the opinion of the writer, the focusing technique offers an "intentional" component that other "body work" techniques do not. The "body scan," for example, introduced by Jon Kabat-Zinn appears to be a meditative practice that aids in calming obsessive thought processes. As such, it may provide the necessary condition for the release of the natural spontaneity of the body in the upwardly directed finality of human self-transcendence. However, it does not appear to facilitate the release of repressed

position that acknowledges focusing as a needed complement to psychic self-appropriation, there is also established a broadened understanding of the transcendental that prompts "attentiveness" at the level of experience. Authenticity requires attentiveness, not only to empirical consciousness and dreaming consciousness, but also to bodily consciousness.

What is a felt shift? Recall that Gendlin describes the body, not in static terms, but rather in terms of a dynamic process, constantly engaged in interactions with its environment. The body's "felt sense" of any given situation refers to the meaning held within the body from past interactions. Since the body's meaning also seeks or implies its continuation in the higher form of images, once one has focused on the "felt sense" of the body's meaning, one discovers a new awareness as images begin to spontaneously form in one's consciousness. A "felt shift," experienced as a bodily release of energy, accompanies the release of an image into consciousness. Thus begins the further "higher" process of engaging the intellect to name and interpret the images. Focusing, then, provides access to the vast measure of elemental meaning held within the body that intelligence can only know in increments.

It must be noted that the body's "felt sense" and, to a certain extent, the practice of focusing, as articulated by Gendlin, are common, everyday human experiences.[37] Implicit in his articulation is the invitation to discover the process within oneself, especially observable when engaged in a creative pursuit. First, one may observe a bodily sense of a situation, problem or artistic endeavor without as yet having any words, body movements or symbols with which to give it expression. As one intentionally seeks an answer, one may experience a shift in the felt sense of the situation. This might be the experience of a dancer waiting for images to portray the next steps in her choreography, or a

---

psychic material in the conscious and intentional way that the focusing technique operates. For more on the body scan technique see Jon Kabat-Zinn, *Full Catastrophe Living: Using the Wisdom of Your Body and Mind to Face Stress, Pain, and Illness* (New York: Dell Publishing), 1990, 75–93.

37. The technique of focusing, in effect, exaggerates the normal practice that occurs when searching out an answer to a problem. The exaggeration or intentionality of the technique serves to overcome the effects of repression in the body.

mathematician pursuing an implicit sense of the answer to a problem. In each case, one could readily observe a bodily "felt shift" or release of energy accompanying the "eureka" moment of new insight that follows upon the release of a needed image into consciousness. One may also observe that there is a quality of resonance that one's body has with the new image as though the body says, "Yes, that is right!" It is this bodily shift or release of energy that provides the assurance that one's insight is correct: "That's it!" When repression inhibits this spontaneous dynamism within the body, Gendlin's focusing technique proposes an intentional method of facilitating the release of the "repressing arrangements" that have blocked certain images and affects from arising into consciousness. Yet, can it be shown empirically that the body's indication of "that's it" is, indeed, correct? What empirical evidence grounds Gendlin's notion of the viability of the "felt shift"?

Drawing on a model proposed by W. T. Powers,[38] Norman S. Don, a biologist, explained the "felt shift" as the "reorganization" by the organism that occurs as a result of a "sensed intrinsic error" by the central nervous system.[39]

> The central nervous system is modeled as a hierarchy of such feedback controlled loops. Level one deals with the control of musculoskeletal intensity through the spinal reflex loops. Succeeding levels control higher functions: sensations, configuration . . . patterned "logical" processes. . . . This hierarchy of feedback controlled functions controls its own lower levels of the hierarchy by establishing "reference levels" or signals at which they are to operate. . . . [E]ach intrinsic quality [in the hierarchy] has a genetically preferred state. . . . When there is a difference between the biologically determined intrinsic reference signal and the sensed intrinsic state of the organism an

---

38. W. T. Powers, *Behavior: The Control of Perception* (Chicago: Aldine, 1973). Power's theory provided a model by which to understand behaviour within living organisms.

39. Norman S. Don, Ph.D., "The Transformation of Conscious Experience and its EEG Correlates," *Journal of Altered States of Consciousness* 3 no. 2 (1977–78): 147–168.

intrinsic error signal is issued to the behavioural, learned hierarchy which undergoes perceptual/behavioural reorganization until the intrinsic error signal is reduced to zero. This is how learning is posited to occur. Thus, sensed intrinsic error drives reorganization. And that is how the reorganization of conscious experience occurs.[40]

Don concluded that Gendlin's term "felt sense" can be understood as one's sense of intrinsic error in the body, and that focusing drives the process of reorganization; the resultant, *newly reorganized state coincides with the experience of the "felt shift."*[41]

Several relevant points come to light in this empirical grounding of Gendlin's work. First, the body has an internal mechanism for maintaining the integrity of its internal and external relations. This point justifies Gendlin's claim that focusing serves as a means to facilitate the body's natural orientation to "imply its continuation" forward to imaginal form. Don's study, which depicted EEG correlates during focusing, illustrated how focusing facilitates this regulation. The alpha waves on the EEG during focusing showed that focusing induces an "inner attentive" state of consciousness that further deepens into a high theta state during which a person is more prone to experience "eidetic-like imagery." Thus, through focusing a person can gain access to images previously blocked from consciousness by a repressive censor. Second, the body's ability to alert one to an "intrinsic error" in its relations calls for a responsible stewardship that involves being "attentive" to the "felt

---

40. Ibid. Italics mine. The ability of the body to maintain the integrity of hierarchy of "controlled loops" by indicating an "intrinsic error" in the system appears to be a detailed representation of the relations that Lonergan holds in the principle of correspondence.

41. "Thus, it may be that the process of attention and reorganization that occurs during Focusing and especially during the felt shift, involves the deep experiential absorption in the object of attention. This leads to a stabilization of neuronal activity and the consequent slowing and synchronization of the EEG during these moments of complete absorption. In the case of Focusing, complete absorption would involve enhanced experiencing of intrinsic error, i.e., the felt sense. . . . The brain rhythms we have found during reorganization may be directly related to a well-known property of feedback-controlled hierarchies." Ibid., 163.

experience" of that "intrinsic error."[42] And finally, since self-transcendence provides the criteria for authenticity, a "felt shift" and its imaginal counterpart are verifiable to the extent that they lead one forward in that transformative process. The recognition of the body's ability to facilitate self-transcendence calls for a broadened understanding of psychic conversion.

The Explanatory Relevance of the Science of Brain Plasticity: A Developed Understanding of the "Upward" Movement—The Transition from Nature to Supernature

The final task now turns to drawing out the implications of this developed understanding of the body for a philosophical anthropology. That task will be accomplished by bringing the new data offered by neuroplasticity to a reinterpretation of Lonergan's question on the transition from the natural to the supernatural. The first step begins with a discussion concerning how neuroscience helps to develop our understanding of human nature in its "upward" vertical finality to the supernatural. The second step in reinterpreting Lonergan's question in light of the new data offered by neuroscience involves the "downward" movement of grace in the relation of the natural to the supernatural. The reinterpretation explains the twofold mission of the Son and Spirit as the work of grace operating at this very basic neurophysiological level.

A reinterpretation of Lonergan's question concerning the "upward" transition from the natural to the supernatural presents the human in his or her neurophysiological aspect at the forefront of the evolutionary process as it enters the realm of human meaning. Therefore, the task of reinterpretation generates a fuller account of the dynamic

---

42. Don did not specify the nature of the "felt experience" on which the candidates were focusing. It was not clear whether or not the focusing candidates were attempting to facilitate a learning process or to resolve a psychic disturbance caused by a repressive censor. "Intrinsic error" in this context, therefore, may be associated with the internal tension created by both situations.

relationship in the body-psyche-mind correspondence, and, in so doing, furthers our understanding of the transition from the natural to the supernatural.

Robert Doran's articulation of the dynamic relationship of the body to the psychic and mind aspects, in terms of a dialectic of contraries, provided the basis by which to examine how both a constructive and distorted censor affect the body's relation to the psyche and mind. Concerning a distorted censor, the body was shown to "hold" the repressive arrangements introduced into the unconsciousness as arrangements other than that which is needed for an insight. Neuroscience explains how the body "holds" these repressive arrangements in terms of the neurophysiological processes associated with trauma or stress.[43] The types of memories repressed by early childhood trauma, for example, are of the procedural types.[44] The neurons encoding the memory of a childhood trauma, such as the loss of a significant caregiver, become wired together in this early stage of development. Throughout the child's lifetime, other events that may be loosely associated with that early loss are often also repressed in order to block access to the original trauma. It is the pattern inherent in this particular neurological encoding of a traumatic memory that constitutes the manner in which a repressive arrangement is held in the body. In addition, neuroscience also explained how the stress response related to trauma remains throughout adulthood as a patterned style of attachment to others.[45] In both cases, the results of

---

43. The explanation offered here is not exhaustive, but merely an attempt to draw attention to some recent discoveries in neuroscience.

44. "Procedural memory functions when we learn a procedure or group of automatic actions, occurring outside our focused attention, in which words are generally not required. Our nonverbal interactions with people and many of our emotional memories are part of our procedural memory system. . . . 'During the first 2–3 years of life . . . the infant relies primarily on its procedural memory systems.' Procedural memories are generally unconscious." Norman Doidge, M.D., *The Brain that Changes Itself.* New York: Penguin Group, 2007, 228.

45. Attachment theory was created by a British psychiatrist by the name of John Bowlby in the mid-twentieth century in an attempt to explore the early childhood roots of adult chronic unhappiness, anxiety, anger and delinquency. "[Attachment theory]

these early childhood experiences can be linked to neurophysiological patterns in the body.

A constructive censor facilitates the authentic evolutionary unfolding of the person in his or her vertical finality to God. Lonergan's portrayal of the graced evolutionary unfolding of the self-transcending human person functioned on the basis of both classical and statistical laws.[46] How does neuroplasticity aid in this portrayal of the bodily aspect of this unfolding on the basis of both classical and statistical laws?

Recall Lonergan's use of the term, "scheme of recurrence," in his discussion of the vertical finality of the human person (and of the world).

> It remains that a word be said on total development in man. Organic, psychic, and intellectual development are not three independent processes. They are interlocked, with the intellectual providing a higher integration of the psychic and the psychic providing a higher integration of the organic. Each level involves its own laws, its flexible circle of schemes of recurrence, its interlocked set of conjugate forms. Each set of forms stands in an emergent correspondence to otherwise coincidental manifolds on the lower levels. [47]

Schemes of recurrence refer to "assemblies of interdependent and mutually supporting factors."[48] Each assembly constitutes an environment

---

focuses on the sense of emotional security or insecurity a child develops in the first years of life. Simply put, some children come to feel that the person who takes care of them is a reliable source of safety and comfort; other children find that this person is either an unpredictable harbor who is sometimes there to comfort them and sometimes missing in action, or is outright rejecting." According to attachment theory, there are three types of attachment styles, that is, the way that people form relationships: secure, avoidant and anxious. Sharon Begley, *Train Your Mind Change Your Brain: How a New Science Reveals Our Extraordinary Potential to Transform Ourselves*, New York: Ballantine Books, 2007, 186.

46. Lonergan, "Mission and the Spirit," 24–25.

47. Lonergan, *Insight*, 494.

48. "First, then, at any stage one is an individual, existing unity differentiated by physical, chemical, organic, psychic, and intellectual conjugates. The last three exhibit respective flexible circles of ranges of schemes of recurrence exhibited in one's spontaneous and effective behavior, bodily movements, dealings with persons and things,

that functions on the basis of classical laws and would continue to function until a disruption of its interdependent and mutually supporting factors occurred, the result of either an internal deterioration or an external interference. Each element in the cumulative sequence of interdependent and mutually supporting factors has its probability of emergence and its probability of survival. Statistical laws come into play as the schedules of probabilities of elements "link the emergence of successive assemblies of interdependent and mutually supporting factors."[49] In this way, the understanding of vertical finality as operating in accord with both classical and statistical laws depicts how the lower schemes of recurrence, as subordinate, are brought up and incorporated into the functioning of the higher schemes of recurrence. Lonergan calls this process "sublimation."[50]

The plastic brain functions in accord with the evolutionary process of sublimation. Prior to the recent discovery that the human brain can change itself, mainstream medical science believed that the brain's anatomy was predetermined by one's DNA and, therefore, was unchangeable. In other words, scientific and medical knowledge of how the brain functioned previously presented human neurophysiology in terms of the predictability of classical laws.[51] The basic structure of the brain, (the brain map), set in place according to the dictates of DNA, operates in accordance with classical laws as schemes

---

the content of one's speech and writing. . . . Secondly, man develops. Whatever he is at present, he was not always so, and generally speaking he need not remain so. The flexible circles of ranges of schemes of recurrence shift and expand, for neural, psychic, and intellectual conjugates pertain to systems on the move. The functioning of the higher integration involves changes in the underlying manifold, and the changing manifold evokes a modified higher integration." Ibid., 495.

49. Lonergan, "Mission and the Spirit," 25.

50. Lonergan, *Insight*, 479.

51. "Conventional wisdom in neuroscience held that the adult mammalian brain is fixed in two respects: no new neurons are born in it, and the function of the structures that make it up are immutable, so that if genes and development dictate that *this* cluster of neurons will process signals from the eye, and *this* cluster will move the fingers of the right hand, then by god they'll do that and nothing else come hell or high water." Begley, *Train Your Mind Change Your Brain: How a New Science Reveals Our Extraordinary Potential To Transform Ourselves*, 6.

of recurrence. The discovery of brain plasticity introduces the notion that statistical laws are also at work in human neurophysiology.[52] With this discovery, the understanding of a static and immutable brain has been dismantled.

The new understanding of the brain as plastic incorporates statistical laws. The most important finding uncovered by neuroscientists in the discovery of neuroplasticity is that neurons compete. That competition—which neural pathways develop stronger pathways than other neural pathways—operates in accord with human intention. Statistical laws, the probabilities associated with the emergence and survival of a new scheme of recurrence (the mutually conditioning and supporting factors involved in the linking of different neuronal groups and modules in new ways), function when a person pays attention to, and desires to, learn a new skill or habit.[53] The desire to learn a new skill, through practice, increases the statistical probability of its emergence or development; repeated, disciplined practice of the skill increases the probabilities of its survival in the form of a habit; habits manifest neurophysiologically as well-established neural pathways. The sublimation process can be identified in this example of learning, as follows.

> When two modules are linked in a new way in a cultural activity—as when reading links visual and auditory modules as never before—the modules for both functions are changed by the interaction, creating a new whole, greater than the sum of the parts. ". . . But as these parts connect with each other in larger and larger aggregates, their functions tend to become integrated, yielding new functions that depend on such higher order integrations."[54]

---

52. This shift in the understanding of the brain serves as a prime example of the modern shift away from classicism, which understood the world solely in terms of classical laws, to historical consciousness in which both classical and statistical laws together interpret the world.

53. Environmental factors, such as the necessary financial funds, or access to needed resources, and the cooperation of others also constitute the conditions of possibility.

54. Ibid., 295.

An evolutionary portrayal of the body's participation in the "upward" movement in the transition from the natural to the supernatural depicts a process of sublimation in which lower schemes of brain function can literally become wired together to form new wholes.[55] This process is particularly evident culturally in the civilizing of humanity's more basic instincts for survival, sex and security into the "higher" forms of community, marriage and politics, respectively.

Lonergan's principle of correspondence has provided the template for the discussion on the series of developments in an understanding of the relations of the body to the psyche and the mind in the process of higher integration or sublimation. Neuroplasticity furthers the development in an understanding of these relations. Recall that he wrote,

> higher integrations of the organic, psychic, and intellectual levels are not static but dynamic systems; they are systems on the move; the higher integration is not only an integrator but also an operator; and if its developments on different levels are not to conflict, there has to be a correspondence between their respective operators.[56]

Neuroplasticity contributes to the understanding of two points made in this quote. The first has to do with Lonergan's acknowledgment that, as a level, the body is both an operator and an integrator. As an operator, its dynamism promotes activity to ever-higher levels of its

---

55. An illustration of what Lonergan calls "defensive schemes" might be how new modules combine to function in a compensatory way in response to the injury or loss of one of one's senses. Those modules or recurring schemes conditioned by the strongest defensive schemes would be under the strongest genetic control, and therefore the most difficult to change. The reverse is also true. In her work with dyslexic children, Neville noted that there are "two sides to neuroplasticity. Systems and structures that display the greatest plasticity are those under the weakest genetic control and most subject to the whims of experience and the environment. That can be beneficial [as seen with the auditory cortex aiding the peripheral vision of the deaf]. . . . But it is also a risky way to make a brain. The same systems that display the greatest plasticity and are enhanced in the deaf are more vulnerable in development and will display the greatest deficits in developmental disorders such as dyslexia. . . ." Begley, *Train Your Mind Change Your Brain*, 102–03.

56. Lonergan, *Insight*, 555.

neural-physiological process—from the chemical, to the biological and further to the neurological schemes of recurrence. As an integrator, the body manifests a higher form of energy from the universe.[57] The basis for the discovery of neuroplasticity was founded on the observation that there exists a basic spontaneity within the neural pathways of the brain and within neurogenesis. Newly born neurons are easily prompted to become encoded into whatever function is most in demand; unused cortices quickly respond to different types of sensory stimulus; and neural pathways can become more or less dense depending on use. The fact that neurons can be recruited to participate in different functions and structures of the brain—that they are not "hard-wired" to a genetically determined function or structure—illustrates how the level of the organism functions as both an integrator and an operator. As with Doran's identification of a "symbolic operator" that undergirds consciousness, the identification of a "body operator" must be distinguished from the conscious operators. Conscious operators are questions for intelligence, questions for reflections and questions for deliberation.[58] The point here is to distinguish the fact that there are unconscious operators at work in the human person. Unconscious operators promote activity from one level to the next; however, they are not prompted by questions. The *a priori* anticipation appears to be the basic dynamism of life—"the potential of the universe to become," or the emergent probability of the universe as it takes on human form.

Secondly, the principle of correspondence identifies the human organism, not as a static system, but rather as a dynamic one seeking

---

57. Recall Doran's account of the unconscious. "In principle, at least, the unconscious is all energy in the universe save that which becomes present to itself as psychic energy in animal and human consciousness. Proximately, it is neural-physiological process in the human organism. Remotely, it is the world." Robert Doran, *Theological Foundations,* vol. 1, *Intentionality and Psyche,* 289. As a distinct level, the body's operator prompts the fertilization and gestation process where the "potential of the universe to become" takes on human form. As integrator, the neural-physiological make up of the human body seeks higher integration in imaginable form in the psyche.

58. Lonergan, "Mission and the Spirit," 28–29.

higher integration in the psyche and in the intellect.[59] Additionally, the phrase, the "correspondence between their respective operators," depicts the mutually conditioning nature of the relations between the higher and lower forms. Neuroplasticity demonstrates the mutually conditioning relationship between the psyche and neural processes through discoveries not only about how neural processes seek higher representation in dream images but also about how the higher form of dreams affects the lower form of neuronal "health." During a series of therapeutic interventions, corresponding serial dream interpretations provide symbolic evidence of the brain in the process of plastic change as "neural networks must unlearn certain associations . . . and change existing synaptic connections [that represent the trauma] to make way for new learning."[60] In this way, a change in the higher form of dream symbols expresses changes in the lower form of neural networks. The higher form of dreams, however, also conditions the lower, neural forms. A correlation has been drawn between the amount of rapid-eye-movement (REM) sleep (the stage where most dreaming occurs) and the occurrence of plastic change in the brain. "REM sleep seems necessary for neurons to grow normally."[61]

In short, neuroplasticity has contributed to an understanding of the body-psyche-mind relations in the human person, in its "upward" movement, by bringing to light the following points. The neural-physiological process is not static, but is instead dynamic, operating within the bounds of both classical and statistical laws. The body, therefore, "emerges" in the form of neuroplastic changes; elemental meaning exists in bodily form as both genetically and intentionally

---

59. In several places in *Insight*, Lonergan refers to the body's dynamic, mutually conditioning relationship to the psyche and intellect: "Not only have nerves their physical and chemical basis but also they contain dynamic patterns that can be restored to an easy equilibrium only through the offices of psychic representations and interplay" (218). "But the unconscious neural basis is an upwardly directed dynamism seeking fuller realization, first, on the proximate sensitive level, and secondly, beyond its limitations, on higher artistic, dramatic, philosophic, cultural, and religious levels" (482).

60. Doidge, *The Brain that Changes Itself*, 238.

61. Ibid., 239. Kittens deprived of REM sleep had smaller than normal neurons in their visual cortex. Ibid.

determined neural patterning. This elemental, body meaning exists prior to that which exists symbolically in the psyche as dreams.[62] While neuroplasticity does not "prove" Gendlin's claim that one can experience the immediacy of this intelligibility as a "felt sense," nevertheless, neuroplasticity does support Gendlin's claim that there is an intelligibility or "knowledge" in the body, and that it has an inherent dynamism toward seeking higher forms. Finally, neuroplasticity has provided explanatory grounding for the purpose of this paper—that, as a distinct level, the elemental meaning held within the unconscious neurophysiological aspect of the human person, or body, is available for self-appropriation. As such, the basis for an intentionality analysis has been expanded.

The Explanatory Relevance of the Science of Brain Plasticity: A Developed Understanding of the Graced, "Downward" Movement— Its Transition from Nature to Supernature

The second step in reinterpreting Lonergan's question in light of the new data offered by neuroscience involves the "downward" movement of grace in the relation of the natural to the supernatural. The reinterpretation explains the twofold mission of the Son and Spirit as the work of grace operating at this very basic neurophysiological level.

Neuroplastic evidence portrays the first "hearing" of the mission of the Son as "Word" (which mounts upward in human consciousness) as the pre-patterning or shaping of one's neurophysiology that occurs

---

62. Elemental meaning resides in the distinct patterning of each person's brain as characteristic of his or her interests, desires and life experiences. "In response to the actions and experiences of its owner, a brain forges stronger connections in circuits that underlie one behavior or thought and weakens the connections in others. Most of this happens because of what we do and what we experience of the outside world. In this sense, the very structure of our brain—the relative size of different regions, the strength of connections between one area and another—reflects the lives we have led. Like sand on a beach, the brain bears the footprints of the decisions we have made, the skills we have learned, the actions we have taken. . . . [T]he brain can [also] change as a result of the thoughts we have thought." Begley, *Train Your Mind Change Your Brain*, 8–9.

in one's early years through interpersonal relationships and interactions. Doran calls this "received meaning." A parallel was also drawn between "received meaning" and the dramatic pattern. In collaboration with imagination, the dramatic pattern's role in the censor functions as organizing unconscious material in a manner that is already pre-patterned. Doran claims that "received meaning" constitutes the "ordinary meaningfulness" of community, which "may be more or less sinful, more or less under the influence of grace."[63] Neuroplastic evidence explains "received meaning," as it is more or less sinful or under the influence of grace, by demonstrating that the familial, social and cultural environments can shape the attachment styles of the next generation and even alter the chemistry of their genes.

Regarding the second mission, the downward action of grace in human consciousness, a reinterpretation focuses on the healing and elevating effects of grace in the human body. One of the particularly interesting developments in neuroplasticity was the observation that the experience of love facilitates massive unlearning or the dissolving of certain neuronal networks. When a person commits himself in love, the brain undergoes a large-scale reorganization, far more massive than in the normal process of unlearning and relearning.[64] At such times, "the brain neuromodulater oxytocin is released, allowing existing neuronal connections to melt away so that changes on a large scale can follow."[65] In this way, when a person falls in love with God, or with one's spouse and children, the release of oxytocin "melts down existing neuronal connections that underlie existing attachments, so new attachments can be formed. . . . [I]t makes it possible for them to learn new patterns [related to the ways of being of the beloved—thinking, feeling, valuing and loving)."[66] This neurophysiological finding

---

63. Robert Doran, *What Is Systematic Theology?*, 138–39.

64. Norman Doidge, M.D., *The Brain that Changes Itself*, 118–19.

65. Ibid. "Neuromodulators are different from neurotransmitters. While neurotransmitters are released in the synapses to excite or inhibit neurons, neuromodulators enhance or diminish the *overall* effectiveness of the synaptic connections and bring about enduring change." Ibid., 118.

66. Ibid., 120.

gives new meaning to the understanding of the mutual-self-mediation that occurs within the state of grace.

Concerning the state of grace, recall that Lonergan describes the "just" as signifying the community, and by implication, further signifies the "state" of divine subjects in relationship with a community of human subjects. Lonergan wrote, "[B]y reason of this state the divine persons and the just are within one another as those who are known are within those who know them and those who are loved are within those who love them."[67] Neuroplasticity reveals that the way in which divine persons and the just are within one another constitutes a shared horizon of knowledge, values and love, first made possible by a massive brain restructuring. Lovers, therefore, not only share knowledge, value and love but also the neural patterns upon which the shared horizon of being has been established.

Conceiving the possibility of redemption as the reception of the original meaningfulness of divine meaning into the fabric of the ordinary meaningfulness of community now entails including an understanding of that reception in terms of neuroplastic changes. Divine love triggers the massive unlearning of destructive patterns in thinking, feeling and loving (biases and sin), and dissolves those existing neuronal networks so that, in forming the new attachment with God or with those from whom Divine love has been mediated, the person is enabled to relearn new habits or a new way of being. In this way, the neurophysiological changes in the brain associated with healing and learning a new way of being represent the emergence of the Reign of God into the world of human meaning. These changes at the neurophysiological level provide some of the conditions of possibility for the ongoing healing and creative processes that incrementally become constitutive of a community's meaning.[68]

---

67. Doran, *What Is Systematic Theology?*, 138.

68. Using terms associated with an emergent world view, recall that Doran portrayed the healing and elevating activity of divine meaning in the following manner. "God's entrance into the human world of meaning shifts the probabilities in favour of graced ordinary meaningfulness. And that shift in probabilities affects the reception, or better, the receptive potential, of subjects in community to the divine meaning intended by God when God enters our world of meaning." Ibid., 139.

Conclusion

Fundamentally, the discovery of brain plasticity depicts the human body in a much more dynamic relationship to the further aspects of the human as a knower and as an existential subject. It was shown that human intention provides the stimulus for changes in the brain. At the same time, neuroplasticity also portrays a basic spontaneity within neural processes—a demand for higher integration—that constitutes a neuron's inherent plasticity. These acknowledgements have provided the basis for an understanding of the dialectical relations of the body to the other aspects of the human person in an interiority analysis. Furthermore, by situating the body within an interiority analysis, further data has been provided for the authentic appropriation of Divine meaning.

As an originator of meaning in the creative unfolding of the Reign of God, this further data on the body sets in place a broadened understanding of authentic agency in the world. Under the influence of grace, human persons are responsible not only for the self-appropriation that would help them to be attentive, intelligent, reasonable and loving, but also for the self-appropriation that would help them to change their brain. From this viewpoint, the implementation of proportionate being by the existential subject involves the decision to live under the guidance of the norms immanent and operative on the levels of waking consciousness and dreaming consciousness, as well as on the level of the unconscious. In other words, authenticity involves the awareness that, within the organism, there is an intelligibility or "body knowledge" seeking higher integration. Attending to the "felt sense" frees the body from repressive arrangements introduced by a repressive censor that would inhibit the vertical finality operating in the body. In short, transformation and conversion occur at every level or aspect of the human being. The once static or mechanistic portrayal of the human body as merely "matter" gives way to an understanding of the body as dynamic, operating under the norms of both classical and statistical laws in the graced transition from the natural to the supernatural.

Part 2

DEVELOPMENT IN PSYCHIC CONVERSION

5

Bias, Bigotry, and Passion

Elizabeth Murray
Loyola Marymount University, Los Angeles

n his major work Insight, Bernard Lonergan differentiates four basic forms of bias: dramatic, individual, group, and general. These four differ in their noematic content and in the degree of consciousness of the subject. The key element common to all four forms of bias is the flight from understanding, which Lonergan explains is the root of all biases.

> Just as insight can be desired, so too it can be unwanted. Besides the love of light, there can be a love of darkness. If prepossessions and prejudices notoriously vitiate theoretical investigations, much more easily can elementary passions bias understanding in practical and personal matters.[1]

The first form, dramatic bias is largely unconscious, apart from general feelings of discontent and discomfort, and the occasional inexplicable Freudian slips and other parapraxes. The flight from understanding in this case is the unconscious censoring of images that would provide the subject with unwanted insights. The second form, individual bias or egoism, in the bad Aristotelian sense of the term, is largely conscious, although as habitual, it can become second nature and spontaneous. Lonergan writes:

> Nor is the egoist totally unaware of his self-deception . . . it is not by sheer inadvertence but also by a conscious self-orientation

---

1. Bernard Lonergan, S. J., *Insight: A Study of Human Understanding* [1957], CWL Volume 3 (Toronto: University of Toronto Press, 1988) p. 214.

that he devotes his energies to sizing up the social situation, ferreting out its weak points and its loopholes, and discovering devices that give access to its rewards.[2]

The avoidance of understanding is accomplished through deliberate obfuscation, brushing aside of relevant questions, and simple refusal to consider facts or opinions that might upset the egoist's narcissistic worldview. The third form, group bias, similarly, is conscious in its refusal to consider facts that would force one to alter one's opinion of one's own group and that of the other. Group bias, for Lonergan, is the bias that pertains to class conflict. Both individual and group bias interfere with the development of practical common sense, by excluding questions and ideas that would upend one's interests or the interests of one's group. The fourth form, general bias is the all-too familiar, commonsense presumption that sets the so-called 'real world' of quotidian, dramatic-practical concerns against the ivory tower pursuits of science and philosophy. It too is conscious, if unfortunately, habitually presupposed, as firmly set attitudes, opinions, and judgments. An example of general bias is the firmly entrenched anti-intellectualism characteristic of U.S. common sense.

Of the four biases, the one that seems to be the closest to underlying the phenomenon of bigotry is group bias. Lonergan's account of group bias is focused on class and economic conflict. He writes:

> Classes become distinguished, not merely by social function, but also by social success; and the new differentiation finds expression not only in conceptual labels but also in deep feelings of frustration, resentment, bitterness, and hatred.[3]

Here Lonergan seems to be describing the feelings and states of mind of the oppressed, but there can also be feelings of disdain, revulsion, and hatred on the part of those of the upper class towards the lower class, and increasingly on the part of countrymen towards immigrants.

---

2. Ibid, 245.
3. Ibid, 249.

In Chapter 2 of *Method in Theology* in the section headed 'Beliefs,' Lonergan expands somewhat on his account of group bias:

> Besides the egoism of the individual there is the egoism of the group. . . . Group egoism not merely directs development to its own aggrandizement but also provides a market for opinions, doctrines, theories that will justify its ways and, at the same time, reveal the misfortunes of other groups to be due to their depravity.[4]

The account of group bias as primarily economic, as that of class conflict may be too narrow. The concept of group bias could be broadened to include the range of phenomena described earlier, bias against political, ethnic, racial, religious groups, against women, the LGBTQ, and against individuals such as the Pope or the President. The noematic object of bias can be a group or an individual representing a group or groups. What makes group bias group bias and not individual bias is that it is an attitude, a set of opinions and judgments, held by the subject in community with others. The subject feels himself or herself to be a part of a group in opposition to the despised other.

As individual bias is largely conscious, so is group bias, but Lonergan adds, "the sins of group bias may be secret and almost unconscious."[5] He does not elaborate the subterranean life of these sins in *Insight*, but in *Method in Theology* he discusses the complex phenomenon of *ressentiment*.[6]

Nietzsche was the first to describe this affective aberration. In *On the Genealogy of Morals*, he recounts how the Jews during the time of the Roman occupation of ancient Palestine were oppressed and stripped of all political and priestly power.[7] Their resentment and hatred of the Romans was intensified by their impotence to affect any

---

4. Ibid, 54.

5. Ibid, 250.

6. Bernard Lonergan, S. J., *Method in Theology* [1972] (Toronto: University of Toronto Press, 1990), 33, 273.

7. Friedrich Nietzsche, *On the Genealogy of Morals*, trans. Maudemarie Clark and Alan J. Swensen (Indianapolis: Hackett Publishing Company, Inc., 1998) pp. 16–21.

redress for harms inflicted against them. Added to the resentment and feeling of impotence was a feeling of self-righteousness, which intensified the rage against the injustices they suffered. This broiling combination of resentment, impotence, and sense of injustice could barely be endured or contained. It gave rise to a revaluation of values, a desperate machination of self-deception by which the noble Greco-Roman values of honor, mastery, vigor, and wealth were devalued and deemed evil; and in their place meekness, forgiveness, turning of the other cheek, humility and poverty were elevated to the status of the holy. For Nietzsche, Christianity arose as a slave revolt in morality, and its flower was *ressentiment*:

> The slave revolt in morality begins when *ressentiment* itself becomes creative and gives birth to values: the *ressentiment* of beings denied the true reaction, that of the deed, who recover their losses only through imaginary revenge.[8]

Scheler, considered to be the Catholic Nietzsche, presents in his book *Ressentiment* a nuanced phenomenology of this affective complex.[9] He distinguishes essential elements of the phenomenon of *ressentiment*, the first of which is a negative feeling, such as, resentment, envy, jealousy, or spite. He then takes envy as a prime example and describes how relatively simple envy can devolve into *ressentiment*. The complex affective state of envy consists of: (1) a positive response to a value carried by another or by a group, for example, talent or beauty; (2) a desire for that value; (3) a feeling of impotence to attain that value; (4) a sense that by right I ought to have that value—that is, a sense of what is just and fair; (5) anger turning to rage that one does not and cannot attain that value; and [6] as the complex circles back, intensified desire that turns into obsession. The state of envy is a vicious circle that feeds upon and potentiates itself. At this point the envious subject can lash out and commit a violent act against the bearer of the value or against

---

8. Nietzsche, Ibid, 19.

9. Max Scheler, *Ressentiment* [1912], trans. William W. Holdeim (New York: Schocken Books, 1972).

society, resign himself or herself to never attaining the value, or allow the envy to persist and develop into *ressentiment*. The addition of three more components—mendacity, inversion of values, and repression, transform envy into *ressentiment*. The subject engages in the self-deception through which he is convinced that the unattainable value is not valuable after all, and thus is not desired. This sour-grapes conviction devalues the desired value and leads to the corruption of one's entire hierarchy of value-preferences. One convinces oneself that one does not want that value, but the conviction is only superficial. One's true longing for that value is repressed and continues to distort the psyche unconsciously. When the repression is thorough and fixed, the person of *ressentiment* even pities the poor soul that bears the value with a charity tinged with spite.

In Lonergan's discussion of ressentiment in *Method in Theology*, he acknowledges Nietzsche and summarizes Scheler's account. *Ressentiment*, Lonergan writes, is a "re-feeling of a specific clash with someone else's value-qualities. The someone else is one's superior physically or intellectually or morally or spiritually."[10] The feeling of hostility, anger, indignation that is neither repudiated nor directly expressed, may be lived out over a lifetime. It involves the continuous belittling of the value in question. Lonergan concludes that perhaps the worst feature of *ressentiment* is that "its rejection of one value involves a distortion of the whole scale of values and that this distortion can spread through a whole social class, a whole people, a whole epoch."[11]

At this point, we have numerous subjective elements that may underlie and contribute to bigotry. There are individual and group biases which are at base a flight from understanding fueled by elementary passions. Inasmuch as these passions and feelings lie in "the twilight of what is conscious but not objectified" they may be constituents of unobjectified *ressentiment*. But is it not also possible for someone to express bigotry, such as racism and antisemitism, and fully acknowledge and embrace one's hatred?

---

10. Lonergan, *Method in Theology*, 33.
11. Ibid.

For insight into freely chosen and passionately embraced hatred of a group let us turn to Sartre's phenomenological study, "Portrait of the Antisemite."[12] The elements of anti-Semitism that Sartre parses are found equally in other forms of bigotry; he writes: "The Jew is only a pretext [for the hateful coward]: elsewhere it will be the Negro, the yellow race [and so on]."[13] Sartre's phenomenology of anti-Semitism yields the eidetic features of bigotry in general.

Sartre understands anti-Semitism to be a condition of the whole man: "It is an attitude totally and freely self-chosen . . . it is a passion and at the same time a concept of the world . . . it is [a] syncretic totality."[14] As such, it has volitional, cognitive, affective, and even physiological dimensions. He interweaves these various aspects in this work but let us highlight the cognitive dimension. He characterizes the mode of thinking of the anti-Semite as 'emotional reasoning,' which selects and reinforces ideas, opinions, judgments, and creates monoideism. It involves the choice to reason falsely. But, Sartre asks, how can one choose to reason falsely? The anti-Semite, Sartre explains, feels the "nostalgia of impermeability."

> The rational man seeks truth gropingly, he knows that his reasoning is only probable . . . he is "open," he may even appear hesitant. But there are people who are attracted by the durability of stone. They want to be massive and impenetrable; they do not want to change. . . . This is an original fear of oneself and a fear of the true.[15]

Sartre further explains that if the anti-Semite is "impervious, as everyone has been able to observe, to reason and experience, it is not because his conviction is so strong, but rather his conviction is strong because he has chosen to be impervious."[16] Sartre proceeds to characterize the distorted rhetoric of anti-Semites:

---

12. Jean Paul Sartre, "Portrait of the Antisemite," [1946] in *Existentialism from Dostoevsky to Sartre*, ed. Walter Kaufmann (New York: Meridian, 1989), 329–345.

13. Ibid, 345.

14. Ibid, 332.

15. Ibid, 333.

16. Ibid, 334.

They know that their statements are empty and contestable, but
it amuses them to make such statements. . . . They have a right
to play with speech because by putting forth ridiculous reasons,
they discredit the seriousness of their interlocutor . . . it is not
a question of persuading by good argument but by intimidating
and disorienting the other.[17]

This account of the machinations of emotional reasoning is rem-
iniscent of Lonergan's notion of the flight from understanding.
Sartre does not specify a flight from understanding per se, but a general disregard for the laws of reason and the search for truth. The
bigot is unabashed by blatant self-contradiction. Sartre suggests
that ultimately the anti-Semite is engaged in a flight from inwardness: "He has chosen to be all outside, never to examine his conscience . . . he is running away from the intimate awareness that
he has of himself even more than from Reason."[18] The anti-Semite
is afraid of any kind of solitude; he chooses to be immersed in the
group thinking of the mob rather than "finding himself face to face
with himself."[19]

Sartre understands fear to be at the base of emotional reasoning
and its flight from inwardness. He also discusses hatred and anger
as central to the constitution of anti-Semitism. We saw how Scheler
includes 'negative emotions' as an essential principle of ressentiment.
Lonergan in *Insight*, similarly, writes of elementary passions and deep
feelings of frustration, resentment, bitterness, and hatred as at the base
of the biases, especially, group bias. And, in *Method in Theology* he
explicitly employs Scheler's notion of emotional responses to value and
disvalue, and their transformation and distortion of the value hierarchy in the case of *ressentiment*. Sartre concurs with both Lonergan and
Scheler on this point, but his account introduces a new dimension to
the phenomenology of bigotry, and more generally to the phenomenology of emotion.

---

17. Ibid.
18. Ibid.
19. Ibid, 335.

Sartre wrote "Portrait of the Antisemite" three years after completing his major work *Being and Nothingness*. He does not mention Scheler or the notion of *ressentiment* in his analysis of anti-Semitism, but he had discussed Scheler's phenomenology of emotional responses to value in Being and Nothingness. There are at least three significant departures from Scheler's account of emotion, which Sartre makes, and which may account for his omission of any talk of ressentiment in his essay on anti-Semitism. These contributions of Sartre are notable for those of us also interested in Lonergan's account of feelings in general.

Sartre characteristically places great emphasis on the role of human freedom, and in this context the role of decision in the very formation, continuation, and intensification of emotion. He writes that ordinarily we think of hatred and anger as being provoked, for example, "I hate the person who has made me suffer, the person who scorns or insults me."[20] In other words, we think of emotion as an intentional response to some value or disvalue. But Sartre sees in the anti-Semite a passion that "precedes the facts which should arouse it, it seeks them out to feed upon, it must interpret them in its own way in order to render them offensive."[21] Similarly, he describes anger as constituted by one's consent to anger: "We must consent to anger before it can manifest itself . . . we grow angry."[22] In brief, fear and anger and hatred are states that are constituted freely by the subject. One may feel a momentary and spontaneous revulsion but to sustain isolated feelings of revulsion or irritation and convert them into a permanent state requires self-reflective awareness and consent to the hatred.[23] Sartre agrees with Scheler that emotions are intentional, but he adds two important points: first, the critical point that such emotions are not simply reactive or given, they are constituted by the subject; and secondly, that this constitution is a matter of free consent and deliberate

---

20. Ibid, 332.

21. Ibid.

22. Ibid, 332.

23. Jean Paul Sartre, *The Transcendence of the Ego*, trans. Forest Williams and Robert Kirkpatrick (New York: Farrar, Straus and Giroux, 1957), 61–68.

fostering. Lonergan also writes of a volitional element in the formation of feelings:

> It is true, of course, that fundamentally feelings are spontaneous. They do not lie under the command of decision . . . But, once they have arisen, they may be reinforced by advertence and approval, and they may be curtailed by disapproval and distraction.[24]

While Sartre has a radical view of the role of decision in the very constitution of emotional states, Lonergan clearly acknowledges the role of decision in the development of emotions.

A third divergence from others in Sartre's phenomenology of emotion regards the matter of repression and the possibility of deep feelings persisting in the unconscious. In *Being and Nothingness*, Sartre provides a scathing critique of Freud's notion of the unconscious and the role of the censor in repression. Lonergan's clarifying formulation in Method in Theology of 'what is conscious but not objectified' as a more accurate characterization of what is commonly called 'the unconscious' helps to dispel the controversy over the unconscious.[25] Still, Sartre's rejection of repression and unconscious emotions, may account for his omission of any talk of ressentiment in his analysis of antisemitism. For, as we have seen, for both Nietzsche and Scheler, repression is an essential ingredient in ressentiment.

In our treatment of the subjective elements of bigotry, we have discussed cognitive, volitional, and affective dimensions. All three are found in Lonergan's analysis of bias, the affective is the focus of Scheler's analysis of ressentiment, and all three dimensions are at play in Sartre's account of anti-Semitism.

In an analysis of the phenomenon of bigotry we can refer generally to the role of the affective, but there is one aspect of the affective dimension that warrants special attention—passion. Could passion be

---

24. Lonergan, *Method in Theology*, 32.
25. Ibid, 34.

the affective force that integrates the subjective totality underlying bigotry? Each of the thinkers we have drawn upon mentions or discusses passion. Let us focus on a few salient features.

Lonergan in his introductory comments on bias, describes "elementary passions" which can bias understanding in practical and personal matters.[26] In Method, he describes positively the influence of deep-seated emotions on the whole personality:

> There are in full consciousness feelings so deep and strong, especially when deliberately reinforced, that they channel attention, shape one's horizon, direct one's life.[27]

Lonergan proceeds to identify love as the supreme instance of such passion.

In Scheler's major work Formalism in Ethics and Non-Formal Ethics of Value [1916], he provides a typology of feelings ranging from sensory sensations, which correspond to the basic somatic ego, to profound passions, which correspond to the ego as person, the self at the highest level of values. He identifies both love and hate as examples of such passion. The entire self can be permeated, driven, and overwhelmed by the passion of love or by the passion of hate.

Sartre describes anti-Semitism as not simply an ideology, a set of beliefs and opinions, but rather as "first and foremost a passion."[28] In addition to identifying the fundamental role of passion in anti-Semitism, Sartre characterizes the specific nature of such passion. The anti-Semite chooses to live on the 'passional' level. While ordinarily one loves the objects of one's passion—wealth, glory, power, the anti-Semite loves the emotional state itself. The object of his passion is the very feeling of hatred, anger, or spite.[29] Thus, the anti-Semite's passion is directed back at the self; it is the self-fueling and self-consuming love of one's own intense emotions.

---

26. Lonergan, *Insight,* 214.
27. Lonergan, *Method in Theology,* 32.
28. Sartre, *Portrait,* 330.
29. Ibid, 332.

Are negative feelings such as hatred, envy, resentment, and spite true passions like love? Stephan Strasser, Husserl's assistant at Freiburg, in his work Phenomenology of Feeling [1956] articulates four essential marks of passionate comportment, and thereby provides criteria for what counts as a passion:

1. Passion as a mode of readiness, ever latent and ever present: "Here disposition apparently consists in a heightened susceptibility and capacity for abandonment in reference to the valuable as such."[30] This explains the phenomenon of being overpowered, which makes up the passivity of passion.

2. The organizing power of passion: "There is a polarization of the present structures manifested in the behavior of the passionate man." Passion "exercises a concentrating influence upon the human existent." The passionate man is "disciplined in many respects in order to dedicate himself all the more unreservedly to a single thing."[31]

3. The ethical nature of passion: Passion always has as its object a definite region of value. The consequence of passion is "an increase in power which is expressed in the strength of desire, in the intensity of willing, of preparedness for sacrifice, of the gift of sensitivity for the discovery of means, and, in general, the productivity of the heart."[32]

4. Passion as a drive to self-transcendence: "Passion is rooted in an experience of a drive toward that which is beyond oneself."[33]

The first three of these four characteristics of passion can be found in profound hatred, and in the perversely introverted phenomenon described by Sartre—the 'love' of one's own negative emotional states.

---

30. Stephan Strasser, *Phenomenology of Feeling*, trans. Robert E. Wood (Pittsburgh: Duquesne University Press, 1977), 294.

31. Ibid, 295.

32. Ibid.

33. Ibid.

Intense hatred, fear, or rage is an ever-present disposition to being swept away by the ecstasy of the emotion. Profound hatred has an organizing effect on the whole self—one's imagination, thoughts, opinions, arguments, expressions, actions are infected and skewed by one's hatred. The third characteristic, that passion has as its object some range of values and thus is ethical, is also a mark of hateful states. These feelings are directed towards values in a desire to belittle or destroy them, or they are directed towards disvalues, such as humiliation and degradation, in order to multiply them. The fourth characteristic, however, is not found in the emotions underlying the hateful attitudes, speech, and actions of the bigot. No matter how intense and all consuming, the hatred and the rage, these emotions are not self-transcending.

Thus, the self-referential love of one's own hate or rage is not true passion; it is an inverted passion, which can be an extremely powerful force, nevertheless. Strasser uses the term 'antinomy of passion' and defines it as the condition when the self-transcending element is missing:

> Man encloses himself in a finite region of value and meaning. He flees from God to his god, from the Truth to his truth, from the Good to a good, which pleases him. A finite mode of pleasure, possession, exercise of power . . . and so forth, becomes 'All' for him.[34]

On the other hand, Lonergan's identification of love as the primary example of passion concurs exactly with Strasser's account. Love bears all four of the essential marks of passion: ready willingness, organizing power, ethical intention of values, and most importantly self-transcendence.

In summary, Sartre proposes that the heart of anti-Semitism and all forms of bigotry is passion, specifically the passion of hatred; and that this passion is freely chosen at every moment that it persists. Lonergan finds the root of all bias including the group bias characteristic of bigots to be the flight from understanding. The nature of

---

34. Ibid, 296.

the ersatz, inverted passion of the bigot, hatred, is primarily a refusal of self-transcendence. The term 'flight from understanding' can be understood in the context of cognitional theory as the blocking of the pure desire to know, or it can be understood more broadly as the deliberate refusal to respond to the exigence for self-transcendence. A refusal of self-transcendence is the blocking or thwarting of the transcendental notion at the core of the self, the fundamental intention of being. Considered in this way, the bigot of Lonergan's account of group bias and the bigot of Sartre's portrait of the anti-Semite are both engaged in a refusal of self-transcendence, which is sustained by passion, an ersatz, self-consuming passion.

6

Terminological Allergies

Jonathan Heaps
St. Edward's University, Austin, TX

Words are images. Like all images, they are potentially meaningful. But images may be meaningful in at least two ways. Their meaning may be immanent (as in a mathematical diagram) or it may be referential, such that it resides in another reality which the image mediates. Words are this latter kind of image. However, we commonly misconstrue the character of verbal mediation. For words do not primarily mean the realities about which we discourse, but first they mean what St. Thomas called an "inner word," a *verbum mentis* or *verbum cordis*.[1] These "inner words" are also a kind of image, though not in the sense of a "representation." They are, rather, an intellectually meaningful quality of self-presence. They are an embodied, diachronic, global experiencing of oneself that makes available for further reflection that intelligibility which has been spiritually, synchronically, and immediately grasped in and by an act of understanding. All of which is to say that words—whether spoken, written, or signed—are meaningful by reference to the intelligibility immanent in the experience of our intellectual consciousness.[2]

---

1. "The inner word is an efficient cause of the outer; and the inner word is what is meant immediately by the outer," Bernard Lonergan, *Verbum: Word and Idea in Aquinas*, eds. Frederick E. Crowe and Robert M. Doran, CWL 2 (Toronto: University of Toronto Press, 1997), 14. In St. Thomas, see especially *Summa contra Gentiles*, 4, c. 11, §6 and *Summa Theologica* I q. 27, a. 1.

2. For a detailed exploration of the various symbolizing functions outer words may play with regard to inner words, see Eugene Gendlin, *Experiencing and the Creation of Meaning: A Philosophical and Psychological Approach to the Subjective* (Evanston, IL: Northwestern University Press, 1997).

But we do not only relate to images intellectually nor are we always conscious in a predominantly intellectual fashion. Before we interrogate images, they affect us. Certainly, they affect our senses, for if they did not, they would not be images at all. They also affect our feelings, our mood, our conscious states and trends. We may more readily recognize this being-affected with regard to the aesthetic quality of a natural or built environment, a work of art, or even the nonverbal aspects of interpersonal communication. We do not seem as inclined to notice this affective moment in our experience of words. Admittedly, we may reflect on rhetorical style, on the rhythm, metrics, associations, and conjunctions of words in poem, prose, and speech. We may further bicker about the aptness of word choice. Still, I fear we give insufficient attention to the being-affected that accompanies hearing, seeing, or feeling words *qua* words—that is, on the experiential quality of their uniquely intellectual character. In turn, we may give insufficient attention to how being-affected by them affects what they can mean to us. I could treat this relatively specific topic in a number of ways, but I want to direct our attention to one particular phenomenon. I call it "terminological allergies" and they seem, from my observations anyway, to plague intellectual communication by means of words.

Terminological allergies are an inflammatory reaction of consciousness to particular words or expressions. This reaction commonly inclines one to reject the argument or discourse in which the words or expressions are embedded and/or the subject propounding them. In what follows I will delineate a number of different contexts, causes, dynamics, and aspects of terminological allergies, approaching them as embedded in two distinct, but inseparable sets of data on human consciousness. The first set are the data of intentionality that accompany intellectual, moral, and religious differentiations of consciousness. The second and more central set are what Fr. Robert Doran called the data of the psyche and they pertain to the pulsing flow of life, the passionateness of being that lend to our intentional consciousness their mass and momentum.[3] Terminological allergies are not solely an affliction

---

3. Robert M. Doran, *Theology and the Dialectics of History* (Toronto: University of Toronto Press, 1990), 43.

of the academic, but they do pose a particularly intense challenge to the life of the mind. Consequently, my primary focus will be on their deleterious effects upon intellectual cooperation in scholarship. Nonetheless, my remarks can be generalized to the wider world mediated and constituted by meaning. Finally, we will look at Doran's notion of psychic conversion applied specifically to the problem of terminological allergies and how it can open up airways in discourse closed off by their inflammatory effects on human consciousness.

Jargon and General Bias

Perhaps the most common and familiar form of terminological allergy is a negative reaction to so-called "jargon." It is certainly true that technical language in specialized discourse can become a body of hollow shibboleths. It is likewise the case that theoretical discourse necessarily generates terminology distinctive to its matrix of meaning. It shifts away from the common sense connotations of descriptive terms to the tighter controls of implicit definition and this shift is the source of properly technical terminology. Consequently, an aversion to jargon *might* be a justified distaste for turgid writing but it also might be a case of terminological allergies. In the latter case, one's inflammatory response to refined, technical, and/or so-called "abstract" language can be a symptom of what Bernard Lonergan characterized as 'general bias.'[4]

General bias, for Lonergan, is a restriction of intellectual interest to the concrete and practical, and so an aversion to the aloof disinterestedness of theory. It refuses to admit that theoretical questions, let alone theoretical answers are of any use because they do not obviously and immediately meet the present demands of common sense living. In foreclosing the second and third order lines of inquiry that generate theoretical accounts, general bias *a priori* excludes possibly relevant ideas from a situation on the canard that present pressures (especially time constraints) obviate their necessity. The long-term view available to theoretical approaches is

---

4. Bernard Lonergan, *Insight: A Study of Human Understanding*, eds. Frederick E. Crowe and Robert M. Doran, CWL 3 (Toronto: University of Toronto Press, 1992), 250–267.

especially likely to be excised by general bias, setting the practical situation it claims to be concerned with on a slow, but ineluctable downward spiral into ever-greater incoherence and intractability.

Jargon, then, can trigger terminological allergies as a *symptom* of an underlying general bias. Jargon's unfamiliarity, its awkwardness relative to the discourse of common sense can render jargon spontaneously distasteful to readers, listeners, and viewers. The need to devote precious time and energy to appropriating the theoretical horizon in which they have their significance can be prejudged as an unjustifiable waste. Jargon becomes a sign that the conversation has wandered off into a realm irrelevant at best and pernicious ideology at worst—no more than, as Wittgenstein had it, "language gone on holiday."[5] One may react with annoyance and even disgust in the presence of jargon and these feelings can serve as evidence that one's pre-existing bias against theory for the sake of common sense has (*ex post facto*) justification. In this way, terminological allergies against jargon can function as a kind of imitation inverse insight, an intuition that there isn't any "there" there.[6] Except this knock-off inverse insight does not spur one up to the heights of a higher integration. Rather, it invites one's gaze to descend to the workaday. It might allow one to dodge open wells at the expense of contemplating the heavens, but it can also produce deadly obliviousness to a storm brewing on the horizon.

Adjectives and Scholarly Group Bias

Scholars may, of course, develop both a principled aversion to jargon while still appreciating the essential function played by technical terminology in expressing academic insights and judgments. Indeed, scholars may find themselves on the defensive, making the case—against accusations of "jargonizing"—that technical terminology in their field

---

5. Ludwig Wittgenstein, *Philosophical Investigations*, ed. P. M. S. Hacker and Joachim Schulte, trans. G. E. M. Anscombe, P. M. S. Hacker, and Joachim Schulte, Fourth Edition (Malden, MA: Blackwell Publishing, 2009), §38.

6. On inverse insights, see Lonergan, *Insight: a Study of Human Understanding*, 43–50.

of specialization is "of the essence," expressing the refinement and precision of their conclusions with the necessary control. Still, scholars tend to sort into schools. Now, this too may have an appropriately intellectual justification, insofar as one may judge particular aggregate approaches to a subject matter more apt, fruitful, or even correct than others. It may well also have an appropriately practical justification, insofar as the modern scholarly task is so large as to demand a division of labor among complementary scholarly approaches that ask and answer parallel or converging questions.

Still, the sorting of our intellectual communities into schools can provide ample opportunity for the theoretician and scholar no less than the man or woman of common sense to fall victim to *group bias*. Even in the thin air of academic pursuits, common understandings and common commitment to a scholarly way of proceeding can generate robust bonds of community and fellow feeling. While this tendency is not of itself deleterious and indeed even situates the life of the mind in an atmosphere of mutual encouragement and support, it comes with a liability.[7] Differing approaches embodied in differing schools can and often do slide into mutual suspicion, mutual enmity. The ideas of another intellectual community, which might have provided parallel corroboration, complementary insight, or even just helpful contrast, can come to be seen not just as someone else's project, nor merely inapt or mistaken, but as an active threat, an insidious contagion endangering one's beloved academic camp. These ideas "must" be excluded, refuted, denigrated, and, in the limit, suppressed and their proponents, if not destroyed, then at least marginalized.[8]

---

7. See Lonergan on the "dialectic of community," in Lonergan, *Insight*, 242–44; See also Doran's expansion, extensions, and application of the notion in Doran, *Dialectics of History*, Part III, 355–472.

8. While Lonergan abbreviates group bias to "the egoism of the group" in *Method in Theology*, the more fulsome treatment in *Insight* is, for my money, the more illuminating. New ideas are excluded not just because they do not benefit the narrow interest of the group, as in Individual Bias, but rather because they threaten to loosen the bonds of fellow feeling in the group that are associated with the meanings and values that organize their common way of life. See Bernard Lonergan, *Method in Theology*, eds. Robert M. Doran and John D. Dadosky, CWL 14 (Toronto: University of Toronto Press, 2017), 53 and *Insight*, 247–50.

Scholars also commonly deploy adjectives as a way of abbreviating their discussions of a thinker or school's approach to the material. Whether we speak of an idea or figure or method as "Thomist," or "Kantian" or "Feminist" or "phenomenological," we engage in a kind of synecdoche, where a name or a label stands in for a whole network of insights and judgments. This kind of abbreviation is perfectly sensible, even necessary where delving into or repeating a detailed discussion would derail the flow of an argument or expand the length of a work beyond practicality or any other number of legitimate concerns that arise in the effort to say what one has come to understand about a topic to one's readers, listeners, or viewers. However, these abbreviations can become freighted with in-group/out-group connotations, such that they may be deployed not just as a means of brevity, but also to take advantage of the terminological allergies of others. These adjectival abbreviations function as "dog whistles" to the initiated about whether or not the subject under discussion is to be affirmed or denied, credited or suspect, praised or blamed. They cease to be primarily descriptive or efficient and become *mere* labels instead.

The tendency to abbreviate in this way can sometimes mix with those terminological allergies symptomatic of scholarly group bias and lead thinkers to argue by adjective. Putatively descriptive, for the in-group these verbal modifiers—"Jansenist," "Voluntarist," "Idealist"—function to signal intellectual and moral evaluations. They make terminological allergies into an epistemic virtue, granting eyes to see and ears to hear what "we" have always and everywhere agreed must be the case. In the process, of course, the baptism of a school's terminological allergies serves the underlying function of bias: the foreclosure of inquiry, the suppression of questions and answers. Argument-by-adjective plays on terminological allergies to effect this foreclosure and suppression, creating the rhetorical illusion that "we" already know the truth and the warrant for that belief is that "we" are "us."

Furthermore, a concomitant conceptualism can creep into one's reading habits, whereby one is on the lookout for watchwords that signal how an author and thinker sorts into aligned or opposing camps. If an author or presenter invokes "metaphysics" or "consciousness" or "participation" or "autonomy," then one may divine their school or their influences—and here I very much mean to invoke the magical thinking proper to divination à la the dowsing rod. The presence of certain words *by their mere presence* (never mind what the author means to convey by them) become evidence in support of *ad hoc*, speculative genealogies that excuse the reader from taking the discourse in which they are embedded seriously, from admitting the questions it raises or considering the answers it posits. These words, just by appearing, seem to constitute a residue of their malign origin and so reveal the discourse at hand as fruit of the poison tree, best left on the branch. One can become convinced that, as with medical allergies, the best strategy for managing one's terminological allergies is to avoid encountering allergens in the first place.

Fanciful Association and Individual Bias

If group bias restricts a community's spontaneous sense that certain words or expressions are relevant or admissible by prioritizing concern for the well-being of the group generally and its continuing bonds of fellow feeling specifically, individual bias constricts the horizon of concern even further. Individual bias only admits into consideration those questions and answers that might prove relevant to one's personal desires and fears, hopes and despairs, joys and sorrows. The world of such an egoist is a sad, small apartment of the universe rendered just barely livable by transforming every surface into a mirror in which he or she may create a sense of space and community while trapped alone with themselves. In a certain sense, there is not much to be said about it (even if this hardly stops the egoist from trying to fill the claustrophobic vacuum with incessant, self-aggrandizing chatter). His or her terminological allergies will be difficult to generalize about, because the verbal associations that occasion them will be so fanciful, so arbitrary, so coincidental as to frustrate the guesswork of just about anyone save perhaps their long-suffering psychotherapist. Discourse that does not converge on their private interest will bore them. Discourse that implies duties, obligations, responsibilities to others may not register at all. But they will turn out to be genuinely allergic only to those words evoking the sense that something, so to speak, may be coming between them and their dinner.

Conscious Inflammation and Terminological Allergies Proper

In the strictest possible terms, the above has not been considering terminological allergies directly, but rather as they may arise in the context of the intellectual aversions characteristic of those biases that afflict intentional consciousness. In each case, there exists a terminological *aversion*, but whether it manifests itself in the kind of inflammation of consciousness proper to terminological allergies *per se* depends probably on the circumstances and the individual. The havoc terminological aversion in general and terminological allergies specifically can play in the life of the mind merited considering them in the terms above, but it is necessary now to turn to consider the inflammatory effect directly.

I have spoken obliquely of a conscious inflammatory reaction. This reaction is spontaneous and can be characterized most generally as an uncomfortable quality of self-presence. Experiencing itself lacks ease and equipoise. The 'tone' of one's embodied consciousness may be 'high,' in a kind of buzzing, rattling, anxious activation. It may also be 'low' in a kind of dragging, smothering depression. Whether too high or too low, the discomfort consists in a tension manifesting a disintegration of conscious meanings, feelings, or both. Now, Eugene Gendlin had some success in popularizing his method of "focusing" as a kind of technique for therapeutically turning one's attention to the dis-ease in one's experiencing, asking after its significance, then identifying and symbolizing it iteratively.[9] This attentive, inquisitive, symbolizing process will be accompanied, Gendlin reports, by successive releases of tension and so reductions—to use my terminology—in the inflammation of one's consciousness. In other words, this release

---

9. Eugene Gendlin, *Focusing* (New York, NY: Bantam Books, 1981).

of tension is at the same time a transformation in the quality of one's self-presence.

But to respond to inflammation in one's consciousness with attentiveness, inquisitiveness, and deepening insight sublimates psychic tension within the directedness of intentional consciousness, transmuting it into the tension of inquiry, rendering it susceptible to progressive resolution. In Lonergan's metaphysical language, we might say that it elevates coincidental manifolds of feeling into the higher integration of intentional consciousness. Unfortunately, the very discomfort that accompanies the tension of conscious inflammation makes this integrating response unlikely. The sustained attention it requires demands tolerance of the very discomfort one is working to relieve. We are more apt to try to ignore the discomfort and avoid what aggravates it. Often enough conscious inflammation is produced endogenously by the clattering of neural demands, psychic materials, and/or maladaptive habits of mind. But such endogenous causes ultimately have their root in the self. We may consequently seek out ways to numb, distract, or otherwise alter our self-presence to withdraw from the discomfort. But, of course, wherever we go, there we are. The effort to withdraw from oneself devolves into the tragic, tightening circles of a cat or dog chased by their own tail.

My concern here, however, has been to illuminate those cases where, whatever endogenous antecedents exist, words or expressions function as exogenous causes of conscious inflammation. Similarly, whatever other exogenous sources of inflammation may exist and which we may have elucidated above, here I am concerned with the verbal ones, whether seen, heard, or touched. When approached phenomenologically (rather than in terms of causal reduction, as above), the eruption of conscious inflammation is primary. Whatever the occasioning word or expression, the discomfort and tension of self-presence washes over one's experiencing. In brief, the feeling is first. Moreover, the feeling is immediate. Even though it arrives in the encounter with a word or expression, it does not only color the objective experience of the offending term. Rather, it colors the quality of my self-presence. It becomes the quality of being-myself.

I do not think we give enough credence to the disruption caused by "inflammation of consciousness" in the life of a psycho-sensitive subject. It borders on the tautologous, but *I am myself*, and so to have the experience of being-myself become immediately uncomfortable means that I have become for myself an inescapable threat to the wellbeing of myself. Moreover, because the "site" of immediately experiencing being-myself is my body, the material substructures of this conscious experience are vital. This is to say that experienced threats to the wellbeing of myself sublate those biological and psycho-sensitive responses to life-threatening danger. Consequently, conscious inflammation is not just uncomfortable, but also—however unacknowledged—an experience of danger, even life-threatening danger.

Whatever the dynamics of intentional consciousness that terminological allergies bring into play, there are the more immediate dynamics of psychic consciousness at work in the mass and momentum proper to the world of feeling. When pain and danger are concerned, we may begin to speak of "fight, flight, or freeze" responses. Or we may note how, as I once heard a medical doctor put it, "pain in mammals produces aggression." Terminological allergies, then, consist in a latent propensity for aggression, avoidance, and/or paralysis. Again, the presence of certain words or expressions *by their mere presence* sets my conscious experiencing in a defensive crouch. The cool, detached, even vulnerable posture of inquisitive, intellectual consciousness has been precluded. Even if one continues to attend to the data, ask and answer questions for understanding, and raise reflective questions of correctness, the whole procedure has been placed on a different basis in conscious self-presence. Perhaps my reader will be able to recall those times when reading has become a battle with an enemy, listening a scrap with an opponent, watching a matter of gritted teeth.

Now, I do not mean to deny flippantly the manifest truth that another scholar's work may produce justified opposition, even rage in a reader. Inattentive, obtuse, irrational scholarly work is irresponsible, and a range of adverse feelings may evince our apprehension that a book or article or presentation is *bad*. Still, sometimes the reasons we give for our averse and even aggressive responses are rationalizations rather than genuine justifications. Sometimes our criticisms of a book, an article, a presentation, a post, or a Tweet are *ex post facto* "explanations" of what is in fact an arbitrary inflammatory response to words or expressions to which—for whatever reasons or no reasons at all—we have acquired a terminological allergy. As scholars, I fear we find ourselves in this mode of experiencing probably too often, though identifying it in any particular circumstance is a matter of personal discernment. I hope I have provided some sense of how we arrive there, but it remains to ask: how do we escape?

Psychic Conversion as Terminological Antihistamine

It has not always been appreciated, but on Lonergan's general notion, conversion is always also liberation. Religious conversion constitutes the most radical liberation from any constraint on one's willingness. The religiously converted person, from out of the bottomless depth of charity, would do anything for the beloved, where the beloved is primarily God and, through God, all that God loves. Moral conversion liberates from the narrow path of the pleasurable unto the wide highway of the genuinely worthwhile. Intellectual conversion liberates one from a habitat of the merely palpable into a universe of being mediated by human meaning and constituted by, at a minimum, divine meaning. These nesting liberations of intentional consciousness, Robert Doran saw, needed to be complimented by a corresponding liberation of psychic consciousness. This liberation he termed "psychic conversion."

For Doran, psychic conversion "is a transformation of the psychic component of what Freud called 'the censor' from a repressive to a constructive agency in a person's development."[10] While experiencing itself is immediate and global, still the constellation of our experiential acts is patterned in ways that, by the mediating function of that patterning, provides selection, focus, and direction to our consciousness. "The habitual orientation of our intelligence and our affectivity exercises a censorship over the emergence into consciousness of the images" that will be potentially meaningful to intentional consciousness going

---

10. Doran, *Dialectics of History*, 59.

forward. This patterning is constructive when "one wants a needed insight and so is open to the emergence of the images required" to occasion it. Conversely, "the censorship is repressive when one does not want the insight and so excludes from consciousness the images (needed)."[11]

It is important to note that, for Doran, a repressive patterning of experience suppresses not just images in their proto-intentional aspect, but also their "concomitant affects." My twofold treatment of terminological allergies above, under the aspect first of the deviations of intentional consciousness manifest in various biases and then under the psychical quality of conscious inflammation itself, anticipated this point. Terminological allergies short-circuit the process of self-transcendence both by projecting onto words in their intentional, imaginal aspect a faux significance that occludes the emergence of a meaning that might transform my world and my sense of self, but also by smothering beneath a painful edema of consciousness the symbolic significance those occluded meanings might have for the affective mass and momentum of my living. Terminological allergies, in other words, function as a repressive element in one's pattern of experience, introducing a "cumulative departure from coherence, a progressive fragmentation" at both the imaginal *and* affective origin point of authentic development. They prevent us both from coming to understand what we need to understand, but also from apprehending the values our feelings might bespeak were that understanding to find its needed place in our discernment of how to live. Our embodiment, instead of contributing to the integration of fully human living, becomes an instrument of distortion and alienation in the world mediated and constituted by meaning.

How, then, does psychic conversion transform the patterning of our consciousness from a repressive to a constructive function? As religious conversion consists in a transformation of one's living, moral conversion in a transformation of one's deciding, and intellectual conversion in a transformation of one's thinking, so psychic conversion consists in a transformation of one's attention. Indeed, the transformation involves granting attention to the nature, character, and qualities of that to which one habitually gives attention. Psychic conversion,

---

11. Ibid., 59–60.

then, *begins* in attention to one's self as one in fact is, under the aspect of one's relative attentiveness. It is a moment, therefore, in the pursuit of self-appropriation. "The point to psychic conversion," Doran writes, "as far as self-appropriation is concerned, is that it allows access to *one's own* symbolic system, and through that system to one's affective habits and one's spontaneous apprehensions of possible values."[12]

When it comes to our terminological allergies, then, psychic conversion can only serve as an effective terminological antihistamine to the extent that we first notice we have them. However, "since images are easier to repress" than feelings, one might be better served trying to notice the emotional quality that I have called "inflammation of consciousness" that accompanies one's allergic response to certain words or expressions. If one can notice the presence of that affective state and, moreover, if one can tolerate it sufficiently to make it into an object of attention (instead of avoidance), one may then begin to find its corresponding causes and occasions in intentional consciousness. Of course, I have already explored the psychic dynamics that militate against any willingness to face and tolerate one's inflammation of consciousness. Consequently, this initial turning toward one's terminological allergies will commonly result from the aid of God's grace. But with this initial help in psychic self-appropriation comes an invitation to cooperatively take up the task of discerning one's allergies, discerning their occasions, and so beginning to mention them (if only to one's self) as a way to begin to manage them. Self-appropriation, after all, is no less the appropriation *of* one's self than it is effected *by* one's self.

But because psychic conversion pertains to the "habitual orientation" of our patterned experience, the antihistamine effects of psychic conversion for one's terminological allergies will be the result of a sustained campaign of attention to their arrival and authentic response to their presence. Certain words or expression will continue, perhaps for a good long time, to set one's allergies off. Sustaining attention and inquiry into the discourse in which they are embedded will require a special effort in a set of running skirmishes with those biases which one finds have dug into him or herself defenses against unwanted

---

12. Ibid., 61 (emphasis in the original).

ideas. But Doran warns us not to conflate psychic conversion with "affective conversion." Psychic conversion is not yet "the achievement of an affectivity that is of a single piece because one loves God with all one's heart and soul and mind and strength." No, that perfected and unrestricted being-in-love "is the goal of a complete conversion process involving the four distinct but related dimensions of religious, moral, intellectual, and psychic conversions."[13]

Conclusion

The effort to ameliorate one's terminological allergies is just one element of one dimension of complete conversion, but it cannot be addressed unless it is named. Let us recall, then, in summary, how I have characterized terminological allergies. They are possible at all because words are a species of image and thus invite both intentional and psychic responses in human subjects. They are often a symptom of some bias, whether as an aversion to "jargon" arising from general bias, as an aversion to certain terms (especially adjectives) associated with the in-group/out-group dynamics of scholarly schools, or as an aversion rooted in the fanciful and idiosyncratic associations of the egoist. What makes such repressive avoidance of words or expressions properly "allergies," however, is the inflammatory response they provoke, which produces an uncomfortable tension in consciousness that, while it in principle *could* invite inquiry and so authentic engagement, more commonly and deleteriously produces the repressive aversion proper to bias. Finally, we noted that psychic conversion, insofar as it facilitates attention to repressive patterns of experience, furthermore, invites their reversal and, in the long run, can provide antihistamine relief to the inflammation of consciousness that terminological allergies produce. I hope that the foregoing, in rendering the dynamics of terminological allergies mentionable, has also helped to render them more manageable, especially for my fellow scholars and for others devoted to the life of the mind.

---

13. Ibid., 59.

7

Censorial Liberation and Speculative Method

Ryan Hemmer, Ph.D.
Editor-in-Chief, Fortress Press
Minneapolis, Minnesota, USA

Introduction

Theory aims toward universality and exclusivity. It explains a given nexus of terms and relations such that a single definition applies to all instances of that nexus and only to that nexus—independent of context or constraint, location or time. A circle, Lonergan reminds us, is a series of co-planar points equidistant from a center. Neither the weather of ancient China, nor the mountain ranges of medieval Spain, nor the urbanism of modern Kenya demand of that definition local adjustments. Circles are circles. Varied and various meanings may be attached to their visual representations in art, architecture, or religion, but as a mathematical object with a mathematical function, a circle is *always* a series of coplanar points equidistant from a center, and a series of coplanar points equidistant from a center is *only* a circle.

A twelve-year-old Alexander Grothendieck learned this definition from a fellow prisoner in a Vichy internment camp. It impressed him. It inspired him. And it led him to become one of the most influential mathematicians of the twentieth century.[1] But what did he learn when he learned the circle's definition? What did he now know that he

---

1. Rivka Galchen, "The Grothendieck Mystery," *The New Yorker* (May 16, 2022), 28.

didn't know before? To know "a circle" is to grasp and affirm the intelligibility expressed by its definition. And anywhere and anytime intelligence understands what is intelligible in that expression, it grasps one and the same intelligibility. But *how* intelligence grasps that intelligibility is contested.

Because mathematical objects are abstract, they lack the empirical residues of time and space. They are not individuated through union with matter. They exist only as intellectual expressions, only as the intelligible tension between necessity and impossibility. For this reason, Lonergan referred to mathematical examples to illuminate the pure process of the act of understanding. Because particularities and differences are irrelevant, one can more easily focus one's intelligence on the act itself. But as anyone who has tried to teach *Insight's* moving viewpoint can attest, starting with mathematics leaves in the student a lingering impression that mathematical insight is understanding's Platonic form, against whose measure the defective insights of natural science and common sense are so many flittering cave wall shadows. Theorists no less than students face the temptation to clumsily reduce all objects of inquiry to math's variables and values to claim for themselves the prestige of universal objectivity and thereby to avoid the more complex task of adapting their intelligences to concrete classes of intelligible objects.

Mathematical objects may be abstract, but mathematicians are not. As corporeal minds, even they need examples, diagrams, approximations, and models to understand what is intelligible but unimaginable in a circle's definition—lines, points, radii, planes. Mathematicians, in other words, are no angels. Yet, as Jane Jacobs reminds us, "Theories and other abstractions are powerful tools only in the limited sense that the Greek mythological giant Antaeus was powerful. When Antaeus was not in intimate contact with the earth, his strength rapidly ebbed."[2] Mathematics may offer us the sanitary conditions required for an initial insight into insight, but only in the hands of physicists, engineers, accountants, and craftsmen is the power of mathematics realized.

---

2. Jane Jacobs, *The Nature of Economies* (New York: The Modern Library, 2000), ix.

Mathematics is not the only realm of theory. Meanings are not only discovered. They are also made. The concrete, specific, often messy contexts of inquiry into meaning's constitutive function are such that neither the desire to understand nor the thing to be understood float free of cultural, intellectual, historical, and psycho-symbolic determinations. But rather than considering these expressions of finitude as evidence of defect in non-mathematic forms of inquiry, the determined theorist recognizes that inquiry itself has foundations in pre-intellectual processes and routines. Questions arise from interior depths, and so do the images upon which their answers depend. Such foundations undergird all inquiry, every attempt of intelligence and rationality to transcend sensibility and extroversion—from the practicalities of common sense to the abstractions of explanatory understanding and speculative method.

This latter relation, that of image to speculative insight, is the subject of the present investigation. The free flow of images, their constructive regulation, and their phantasmatic function in the act of understanding are the psychic foundations of speculative method. As intellectual conversion is the *sine qua non* for grasping "the relevant psychological facts" pertaining to the psychological analogy, so psychic conversion is the *sine qua non* for the emergence, regulation, and release of the images necessary for the phantasmatic pivot from the systematic exigence to speculative *intelligere* itself. And because these psycho-symbolic determinations include both archetypal and anagogic symbols, they function phantasmatically in a way that corresponds to the entitative distinction between speculative theology's theorematic domains, a distinction whose meaning is controlled by the theorem of the supernatural. Psychic conversion thus cooperates with intellectual conversion in generating the theorematic structure for speculative collaboration.

Psyche and Phantasm

Insight opens with an inscription: τὰ μὲν οὖν εἴδη τὸ νοητικὸν ἐν τοῖς φαντάσμασι νοεῖ—the thinker understands forms through images.[3]

---

3. Aristotle, *De Anima*, III, 7, 431b 2.

This matter-of-fact phrase from Aristotle's *De Anima* is at the heart of modern philosophy's dilemma. While sensibility senses immediately and passively, intellect actively understands through the mediation of phantasms. That activity, what Lonergan calls insight, thus depends upon the availability and adequacy of images. Both Aristotle and Aquinas appealed to universal human experience to insist that the intellect understands not through the intelligible species alone, but through images. Yet Lonergan notes that "to many profound minds, so brief a description seems to have been insufficient."[4] Platonists denied that the intelligible species subsists in individual things, thereby eliminating the need for images to relate universals to particulars.[5] Scotists denied the necessity of phantasms for actual understanding. Kant held to intuition's sensibility.[6] Against this philosophical legacy, Lonergan tried to recover the notion of *conversio ad phatasmata* not simply as a doctrine commanding devotion by the authority of its prophets, but as an expression of human experience—an articulation of what one discovers when they pay attention to their own successes in understanding anything at all.

But phantasms do more than occasion insight into abstractions. They also lay at the genesis of abstraction itself. Between the coplanar points of a circle and their equidistance center is the abstract idea of a radius, a line—a one dimensional and thus unimaginable object—connecting those points. As abstract, there can be no more than one radius. Yet, the definition of a circle only arises from an understanding of a series of radii, uniform in extension, resulting in uniform curvature. To hold each of these abstractions together in a single, synthetic intelligible unity requires some phantasmatic approximation to make of that unity an object for the possible intellect. An image is required to move the mind. "Human intellect," Lonergan writes, "needs phantasms as . . . proper objects."[7] Phantasmatic objects are necessary because "one cannot understand without understanding something;

---

4. Bernard Lonergan, *Verbum: Word and Idea in Aquinas*, Frederick E. Crowe and Robert M. Doran, eds., CWL 2 (Toronto: University of Toronto Press, 1997), 38.

5. Thomas Aquinas, *Summa Theologiae* I.84.7.

6. Lonergan, *Verbum*, CWL 2, 38–39.

7. Lonergan, *Verbum*, CWL 2, 41.

and the something understood, the something whose intelligibility is actuated, is the phantasm."[8]

While phantasmatic objectification is an insight into the universal formality of sensible particulars and not yet a definition of their abstract universal (the *verbum mentis* that proceeds from the understanding that phantasms make possible), no abstract universal could proceed from understanding without intellect's prior operation on the phantasmatic object. Before one can become a technician who grasps the terms and relations of explanatory theory, one must be a person of experience, whose understanding of the phantasms is the pivot between the sensible and the intelligible. Human beings are animals. They sense. But they are also rational. Sensing, they inquire.[9] But where do phantasms come from? How does Socrates know to draw approximations of geometric shapes in the sand? Why do those crude sketches occasion insight into the area of a square in the mind of Meno's slave? Plato credits *anamnesis*, but Aristotle, Thomas, and Lonergan see in the sand a phantasm and in Meno's slave a dramatic instance of *conversio ad phantasmata*.

For empirical consciousness, images can be no more than sensible, felt content. But for intellectual consciousness, images are symbols that link questions with as-yet undiscovered answers. They are signs that make possible the interpretation of the intelligible elements of experience.[10] But the genesis of images lies elsewhere. Their roots are deeper, stranger, and subject to structures and systems of regulation not at the command or control of the intellect. Images are the vital currency of the conscious operation of spirit, but they issue from the treasury of the subconscious operation of psyche. And so, we must look to the psyche if we are to understand the whence and wither of the images required for insight. For in the psyche's repression and liberation lie explanations both of understanding's foundering and its flight.

---

8. Lonergan, *Verbum*, CWL 2, 42.

9. Lonergan, *Verbum*, CWL 2, 45.

10. Bernard Lonergan, *Insight: A Study of Human Understanding*, Frederick E. Crowe and Robert M. Doran, eds., CWL 3 (Toronto: University of Toronto Press, 1992), 557.

Repression, Liberation, Construction

Conversion is both death and birth. Its about-face turns its back on one horizon and its countenance toward another. In *Method in Theology*, Lonergan refers to three such transformations: an intellectual conversion of one's criterion of the real, a moral conversion of one's notion of value, and a religious conversion of one's awareness of and before the absolute. These conversions, the need of which the functional specialty dialectics unearths and the functional specialty foundations meets, are the basis of the mediated phase of theology. From the conversions issue the generation of general and special theological categories, the personal appropriation of doctrines, the systematic understanding of the doctrinal nexus, and the communication of divine meanings and values in the human world. But if intellectual, moral, and religious conversions are necessary to secure the proper operation of theological functions, what of the images required for theological understanding itself? If spirit's intellectual, moral, and religious horizons require death and rebirth to enter the mediated phase of theology, what is required of the psyche to secure the adequacy of its images for this task?

Robert Doran termed this requirement "psychic conversion."[11] In his earliest exploration of the topic, Doran conceived of psychic conversion as a transformation of psychic energy that effectuates a sublation of the imaginal into the higher integrations of existential subjectivity. But in his later treatments, owing to his preoccupation with the dialectic of the subject and the theory of history, Doran defined psychic conversion more precisely as "the transformation of the psychic dimension of censorship . . . from a repressive to a constructive functioning in one's development,"[12] or "a transformation of the censorship exercised with respect to the entire field of what is received in empirical consciousness."[13]

---

11. Robert M. Doran, *Subject and Psyche*, Second Edition (Milwaukee: Marquette University Press, 1994), 217.

12. Doran, *Subject and Psyche*, 221n.15.

13. Robert M. Doran, *What Is Systematic Theology?* (Toronto: University of Toronto Press, 2005), 111.

While psychoanalysis in a Freudian key assigns this responsibility to "the censor," Lonergan and Doran insist that censorship is a complex phenomenon. "Censorship," Doran writes, "is exercised by dramatically patterned intentional consciousness, by the collaboration of one's habitual accumulation of insights, judgments, and moral spontaneities with one's imagination, by one's 'mentality' or mindset."[14] We can thus situate censorship as an operation belonging to the dynamic correspondence of spirit and psyche, of intentionality and imagination within the horizon of a mentality. But what is the object of this censorship? And what determines the quality of its operation? For Doran, censorial operation regulates "the sensitive flow of sensations, memories, images, conations, emotions, associations, spontaneous intersubjective responses, bodily movements, and received meanings and values."[15] And any successes at this regulation are measured by the emergence of questions, the selective release of regulated images, and the occurrence of insight into those images that answers those questions.

This nexus of sensitivity exists in a relation of sublation with the higher integrations of intellectual, rational, and existential consciousness. And while that integration may be self-assembling, it is not automatic. It is an achievement of the shared labor of psyche and spirit. Censorship is the function of this collaboration that either releases into intellectual consciousness relevant imaginal materials as phantasmatic objects for insight or represses them, prevents their emergence, and thus stymies understanding. Lonergan describes this habitual censorial repression as dramatic bias.[16] Dramatic bias is "the love of darkness" that "vitiate(s) theoretical investigations" and "bias(es) understanding in practical and personal matters."[17] The suppression of images and the consequent refusal of insights have cascading effects, for every answer to a question reveals still further questions, new domains of inquiry, new specifications of the notion of being. To refuse an insight is to

---

14. Doran, *What Is Systematic Theology?*, 111.
15. Doran, *What Is Systematic Theology?*, 111.
16. Lonergan, *Insight*, CWL 3, 214–231
17. Lonergan, *Insight*, CWL 3, 214.

refuse one's own development. And to refuse one's own development is to embrace one's own demise.

But censorship comes in constructive as well as repressive forms. In the absence of scotosis, of aberration, of repression, the psyche finds itself in dynamic collaboration with spirit in the development of a human subject. Constructive censorship selects for intelligence the images and schematic approximations necessary for insights and thus participates integrally and intimately in the self-correcting process of learning. Repressive censorship, as Freud discovered, is a diagnosis in search of a cure. The censorial liberation that restores constructive censorship is that cure. It is what the psychoanalyst works to elicit in the patient. It is what the authentic possess and the neurotic lack. It is the effective change in one's interiority brought about through psychic conversion that leads to self-transcendence. And for the theorist—if they are human—it is what is required for the insights proper to speculative method.

Symbols and Theorems

In the development of speculative method, the theorem of the supernatural was the instrument by which the intellectual difficulties associated with the doctrinal affirmations of grace and freedom were resolved. By its advent, properly speculative theology was born. Theology became a *scientia*. By positing "the validity of a line of reference termed nature," the theorem of the supernatural clarifies how theological and philosophical methods of inquiry can be distinguished according to their respective domains of terms.[18] Because the entitative disproportion between the natural and supernatural orders is an intelligible relation and not some already out there now real, its significance lies in thought, in the ordering of thinking, and in the coordination of thinking's term.

The theorem of the supernatural clarifies the formally disproportionate from the formally proportionate and organizes possible terms of inquiry into distinct theorematic domains. These domains are not ontological buckets, "tiers," or regions on a map. They are coordinates

---

18. Lonergan, *Grace and Freedom*, CWL 1, 17.

within thinking itself. Thus, those terms which are formally disproportionate to created natures and knowable solely on the basis of
divine revelation are distinguished intellectually from those terms that
belong to the natural line of reference, whose intelligibility belongs to
the universe of proportionate being.

Much of what is known through revelation does not belong to the
realm of technical, metaphysical language. Despite the utility the analogy of habit provided to the articulations of the theological virtues or
the notion of consubstantiality to the unity of *ad extra* operations, it
remains that many, even most of the contents of Christian belief lack a
metaphysical explanation, let alone an explanation that has moved from
a speculative hypothesis to a church doctrine. As Doran notes, "the element of mystery extends beyond what has been or perhaps ever will be
formulated in explicit dogmatic pronouncements. Systematic theological
understanding must find a way to include these elements."[19] But if the
theorem of the supernatural clarifies the domain of thinking in which
disproportionate terms of intelligible relations are given as revelations of
divine meaning in history, then the historical *ordo* of salvation, as given
and known, becomes not only a question for speculative theology, but
also a source of images, symbols, meaning, perhaps even analogies, which
might be brought to bear upon other speculative questions. If such symbols are to be analogical structures, then there must be ". . . some kind
of explanatory employment of symbols themselves through a further
immersion into the symbols that enables one *to grasp in their relations to
one another first the symbolic meanings, and through those meanings the elements of the drama that are affirmed precisely by employing these symbols.*"[20]

Part of the difficulty in admitting of explanatory methods of
symbolization in speculative theology is the fact that speculation's
hard-won and well-worn path to progress in theological understanding has been charted through metaphysical, technical, and "natural"
analogies. And one should not wager those gains lightly. Yet, we can—
and indeed should—ask with Doran, "must all systematic theological

---

19. Doran, *What is Systematic Theology?*, 23.
20. Doran, *What is Systematic Theology?*, 24.

construction eventually take a metaphysical turn?" If we answer in the negative, there is a consequent question, "where are the analogies to be found through whose help the mysteries of faith are understood?"[21] While Doran poses this question with an eye toward an aesthetic-dramatic modality of speculative analysis to be deployed in the explanation of the *pro nobis*, one can equally ask whether an aesthetic-dramatic modality of speculative analysis might employ the terms of the *pro nobis* itself in the speculative explanation of the *in se*. And it is precisely this kind of speculative bidirectionality that is opened when the theorem of the supernatural is allowed to both clarify its domains of inquiry, and to elucidate the relations between them.

Doran points to a little-noticed passage in the epilogue of Lonergan's *Insight* that is instructive. "[T]he theologian," writes Lonergan, "is under no necessity of reducing to the metaphysical elements, which suffice for an account of this world, such supernatural realities as the Incarnation, the indwelling of the Holy Spirit, and the beatific vision."[22] Consequently, ". . . there is nothing to prevent the analogies that would enable a properly theological understanding of at least some of these mysteries of faith from being aesthetic and dramatic analogies."[23] The contention here is that this "nothing to prevent" is a consequence of a properly generalized and methodically applied theorem of the supernatural. For not only does the theorem classify, organize, and correlate terms of inquiry into distinct theorematic domains, it also invites speculative interrogations to make use of those terms, and provides the regulative, dialectical means of controlling the fruits of their analogical deployment. For Doran, the possibility of an aesthetic-dramatic method of analogical predication must wrestle with a fundamental question, *"Whence the analogies that will render such technical discourse possible?"*[24] A generalized, repurposed theorem of the supernatural offers the beginnings of an answer: a theorematically controlled deployment of the symbols of revelation.

---

21. Doran, *What is Systematic Theology?*, 24.

22. Lonergan, *Insight*, CWL 3, 756. Cited in Doran, *What Is Systematic Theology?*, 25.

23. Doran, *What Is Systematic Theology?*, 25.

24. Doran, *What Is Systematic Theology?*, 26.

But the efficacy of any symbol depends upon the dynamic correspondence of psyche and spirit. It depends upon the release of the right images, the proper association of images with feelings, and the interpretation of images in intellectual consciousness. Symbols result from the integral dynamism of consciousness. If that dynamism is their source and the theorem of the supernatural is their control, it follows that there must be some disproportion between classes of symbols themselves. Some symbols belong to the line of reference termed nature, while others emerge from and interpret salvation history.

Doran posits just such a disproportion in his enrichment of Jungian depth psychology. For Doran, Jung's symbolic typology is both "too compact," and overdetermined by a naturalism that cannot admit of the possibility of world-transcendent meaning.[25] Beyond the personal symbols of the individual and the archetypal symbols that mediate affectivity trans-personally, Doran identifies anagogic symbols as a distinct class of trans-personal symbolic mediations. While archetypal symbols mediate the transpersonal conflicts connected with the dialectic of the subject and its poles of intentionality and neural demand functions (a dialectic of contraries), anagogic symbols reflect "the conflict between integral negotiation and disintegrated negotiation."[26] Such conflict finds resolution not in the balanced tension between limitation and transcendence associated with the law of genuineness, but rather in the negation of the negative pole of a contradiction. Good and evil have no higher integration. "Anagogic symbols," writes Doran, "reflect, not the participation of the *psyche* in the internal negotiation of spirit and matter, but the participation of the *person* in the conflict of good and evil."[27] Such conflicts hinge on choice, freedom, on the person as deliberative, and on that person's redemption from evil.[28]

If redemption is the hinge of anagogic symbolization, it is because such symbols, like redemption itself, have their origins not in the tensions of primordial psychic drama, but in "the orientation

---

25. Doran, *Theology and the Dialectics of History*, 270.
26. Doran, *Theology and the Dialectics of History*, 271.
27. Doran, *Theology and the Dialectics of History*, 272.
28. Doran, *Theology and the Dialectics of History*, 272.

to transcendent mystery," to grace, the created communication of the divine nature that is "the condition of the possibility of the resolution of the dialectic of good and evil."[29] Anagogic symbols, then, belong to the entitative order that Lonergan calls "the supernatural." Their theological deployment is controlled by the theorem of the supernatural and its elucidation of the disproportion between that order and the line of reference termed nature. When such symbols rise to intellectual consciousness, their deployment in speculative thought is evidence of and language for "the soteriological differentiation of consciousness that is the human side of the revelation that appears in Israel and Christianity."[30]

But that human side, as human, remains human. And thus, the archetypal symbols that belong to the natural line of reference retain their integrity as "natural," even as they are integrated into the soteriological differentiation of consciousness. The analogies that result from their speculative deployment remain "natural" analogies for supernatural realities. Archetypal symbols imitate nature even as they mediate supernatural realities. But anagogic symbols imitate the order of grace and the life of God. They express the inexpressible, and in so doing, make of the inexpressible a source of speculative understanding. Such expression serves not simply to expand a set of analogies for speculation, but also "to heighten that tension and release the psyche for cooperation with the divinely originated solution to the mystery of evil."[31] Thus, the theorematic differentiation of speculative domains by means of the theorem of the supernatural in the intellectual pattern of experience has as its psychic counterpart this soteriological differentiation of consciousness that distinguishes and relates proportionate and disproportionate classes of symbols. Such correlation points to the necessity of psychic conversion both to prepare the intellect for speculation and to provide the imaginal materials upon which the intellect operates in the course of its inquiry.

---

29. Doran, *Theology and the Dialectics of History*, 272.

30. Doran, *Theology and the Dialectics of History*, 272–273.

31. Doran, *Theology and the Dialectics of History*, 273.

Conclusion

In pursuing the psychic foundations of speculative method, this essay has restricted itself to the schematic and methodical features of the problem rather than concrete examples. This decision is, in part, born of a fear of saying too much and not enough, of moving too quickly through the hornet's nest of contested features of psychic integrity and spiritual operation. But slow and steady does not always win the race. It thus falls to other occasions to pursue the gestural elements of my thesis, the claims concerning speculative collaboration and pluralism that presume psychic conversion rather than arguing for it. Yet, Doran has already provided us with a proof of concept. His own speculative innovations put flesh on the schematic bones presented here and invite others to the unique boldness that intellectual community requires: an antecedent willingness to risk errors, to defer praise, to sacrifice material gain and recognition, and to offer oneself to others and to their questions.

Too much theology and philosophy is limited by the neuroses of theologians and philosophers. And too often such neuroticism is praised and admired. Some of us would rather be intuitionists than go to therapy, would rather be conceptualists than admit our ignorance, would rather deputize ourselves as vigilante inquisitors of the faithful than take speculative risks. But as Doran argues, ". . . the goal of psychotherapy or of any analogous journey to psychic self-appropriation is not self-fulfillment or wholeness, but self-transcendence: the dissolving of the energic obstacles to the performance of the operations whose normative order constitutes the authentic search for direction in the movement of life."[32] For some, that search for direction leads them to the systematic exigence, to speculative method, and to that unique *scientia* that is the science of God. Psychic preparation for that journey does not make success automatic (or make failure a heresy), but in its absence, speculative theology is little more than a ringing gong and a clanging cymbal.

---

32. Doran, *Theology and the Dialectics of History*, 276.

8

Linking Neural Demands to Finding Direction in the Movement of Life: Ricoeur's Contribution to Psychic Conversion

Cody Sandschafer

Marquette University

Ricoeur's study of Freud has affected my understanding of philosophy almost as much as has Lonergan's *Insight*.[1]

—*Robert M. Doran, Subject and Psyche*

As suggested by the epigraph, Paul Ricoeur's hermeneutics of the symbol profoundly influenced Doran's early work on psychic conversion. This is especially the case regarding Ricoeur's argument that there is a latent teleology within Freudian psychoanalysis as well as a latent archeology within phenomenologies of religious symbolism.[2] Building upon this position, Ricoeur argues that these teleological and archeological aspects operate through concrete symbols representing an archeological-teleological unity-in-tension. Consequently, the symbol becomes a privileged site of disclosure by revealing

---

1. Robert M. Doran, *Subject and Psyche,* 2nd ed (Milwaukee: Marquette University Press, 1994), 17.

2. Paul Ricoeur, *Freud and Philosophy: An Essay on Interpretation*, trans. Denis Savage, (New Haven: Yale University Press, 1970), 459–493.

the subject's past while directing the subject toward further development. The significance of this insight is that it bridges Lonergan's emergentist and teleological hermeneutic of psychic operations with the causal and archeological hermeneutic provided by psychoanalysis, especially Freud. In other words, Ricoeur's insights provide a means to understand the causal, archeological hermeneutic as complementary to and not in competition with an emergentist and teleological hermeneutic.

Despite this significant and early influence, Doran is not uncritical in his appropriation of Ricoeur and starkly diverges from him regarding his preference for Jung over Freud as the psychoanalyst best suited to explain the archeological-teleological unity-in-tension structure of the symbol.

Arguing for the benefit of Jung over Freud, Doran states the following:

> Perhaps, however, a more appropriate teleological counterpart to the Freudian archeology is to be found in Jung. For Jung treats the same dimensions of the subject as does Freud, and he finds there, not only the reference ever backwards of everything psychic, but also a forward-looking dynamism of the psyche constituting symbolic embodiments of an ever fuller elemental meaning. Especially since it is in a theory of symbol that Ricoeur would meet the Freudian archeology with a corresponding teleology, his argument would only have been strengthened by relying on Jung for the teleology.[3]

Notably, the criteria Doran uses to evaluate and judge Jung as the superior psychoanalyst is the exploratory dimension of the symbol to which Ricoeur also assents. Nonetheless, Ricoeur opts for Freud over Jung due to a separate set of criteria:

> This invitation to investigate psychoanalysis itself by confronting it with other points of view which seem to be diametrically opposed allows us to glimpse the real meaning of its

---

3. Doran, *Theology and The Dialectics of History*, 299.

limits. . . . Psychoanalysis is limited by the very thing which justifies it, namely its decision to know, in cultural phenomena, only that which falls under an economics of desire and resistances. I must say that it is this firmness and rigor which makes me prefer Freud to Jung. With Freud, I know where I am and where I am going; with Jung, everything (the psyche, the soul, the archetypes, the sacred) is in danger of becoming confused. It is precisely this limitation within the Freudian problematic which invites us first to contrast it with another explanatory point of view which seems to be more appropriate to the constitution of cultural objects as such and then to rediscover within psychoanalysis itself the reason why it has been surpassed.[4]

Ricoeur's criteria is the integrity of the psychoanalytic methodology. Unlike Jung, according to Ricoeur, Freud does not reach beyond the methodological limits of the discipline.[5] Thus, Freud presents psychoanalysis in a pure form whereby the limits and contribution of psychoanalytic methodology can be clearly obtained and set in opposition to other methodologies.

This essay will argue that the differences in criteria and preference for either Jung or Freud result from a more profound divergence between Doran and Ricoeur concerning the relationship between cognitive intentionality and sensibility. Moreover, understanding this divergence clarifies why Ricoeur is satisfied with Freud and fails to locate the teleological dimension of the symbol that anticipates new meanings in the psyche's spontaneous production of symbols, especially in dreams.[6] Clarifying this divergence will bring into focus Doran's innovation in placing the archaeological-teleological

---

4. Paul Ricoeur, "Art and Freudian Systematics," in *The Conflict of Interpretation: Essays in Hermeneutics,* ed. Don Ihde, trans. Willis Domingo, (Evanston, IL: Northwestern University Press, 2007), 208.

5. On a number of occasions, Doran does lament Jung's lack of philosophical rigor. This may be an additional reason why Ricoeur dismisses Jung. See Doran, *Subject and Psyche,* 153.

6. Paul Ricoeur, *Freud and Philosophy: An Essay on Interpretation,* trans. Denis Savage, (New Haven: Yale University Press, 1970), 505.

unity-in-tension in the psyche itself and the importance of this move for psychic conversion.

I. Ricoeur

> Perhaps one must have experienced the deception that accompanies the idea of a presuppositionless philosophy to enter sympathetically into the problematic we are going to evoke. In contrast to philosophies concerned with starting points, a mediation on symbols starts from the fullness of language and of meaning *already there*; it begins from within language which has *already taken place* and in which everything in a certain sense has *already been said;* it wants to be thought, not presuppositionless, but in and with all its presuppositions. Its first problem is not how to get started but, from the midst of speech, to recollect itself. (emphasis added).[7]

The epigraph above succinctly articulates Ricoeur's basic position and orientation. Weary of the various failed attempts to attain a universal, all-encompassing philosophical framework built up from *unquestionable* foundations, Ricoeur decides to start in the middle, in the midst of language, in what is *already* there, said, and has taken place. The unquestionable foundation Ricoeur has in mind is the modern, Cartesian project of securing knowledge through an appeal to the indubitable, intuitive understanding of consciousness summarized in Descartes' now infamous phrase *cogito ergo sum*.[8] What Descartes misses in this phrase is that consciousness is not a given but is always already mediated through culture. In other words, the I is only intelligible to itself through the values, beliefs, history, and language provided by a given cultural framework. Hence, to comprehend the *ego* of the *ego cogito*, the inquirer must arrive at the *ego* indirectly via reflection.[9] It is known as a "mirror

---

7. Ricoeur, "The Hermeneutics of Symbols and Philosophical Reflection: I," 287–8.

8. Paul Ricoeur, "The Hermeneutics of Symbols and Philosophical Reflection: II," in *The Conflict of Interpretation: Essays in Hermeneutics,* trans. Charles Fleilich, (Evanston, IL: Northwestern University Press, 2007), 326.

9. Ibid., 327.

of its objects, its works, and ultimately its acts."[10] Consequently, consciousness is not the first reality known but the last, for self-knowledge presupposes an 'other' already known through which the self can gain reflexive knowledge of itself.

A. Setting the Stage: Ricoeur's *Fallible Man*

Paul Ricoeur's early work *Fallible Man* represents a critical pivot in Ricoeur's thought. Here, Ricoeur transitions from working primarily within the pure phenomenological framework of Husserl to a phenomenological-hermeneutical approach. This transition represents an alternation in Ricoeur's questions that demand an alternation in methodology. Previously, Ricoeur was focused on the pure possibilities of volition given the embodied, involuntary situation out of which human volition emerges.[11] However, this abstract approach cannot capture the effects of evil and the occasional poetic triumph of the will that form the context for the concrete, historical person. Hence, the move towards a phenomenological-hermeneutical approach is an attempt to understand the person from within their historicity. This approach comes to full fruition in Ricoeur's linguistic turn represented by *The Symbolism of Evil* and *Freud and Philosophy: An Essay on Interpretation,* but prior to these works is *Fallible Man,* which outlines an anthropology linking Ricoeur's pure phenomenological work to these phenomenological-hermeneutical works. In this work, Ricoeur articulates the rudimentary theory of knowing, objectivity, action, and affectivity that form the background for his linguistic philosophy. Thus, to properly frame Ricoeur's work on the symbol and how it relates to the overall structure of cognition, *Fallible Man* is an indispensable work.

The methodological framework for *Fallible Man* starts from the position that the self is inherently a self-relation of finitude and infinitude.[12] To the extent that this relation is in conflict, the self experiences

---

10. Ibid.

11. Paul Ricoeur, *Freedom and Nature: The Voluntary and the Involuntary,* trans. Erazim V. Kohák, (Evanston, IL: Northwestern University Press, 2007).

12. Paul Ricoeur, *Fallible Man,* trans. Charles A. Kelbley, (New York: Fordham University Press, 1986),1–3.

fragility, whereas to the extent that the relation is in harmony, the self experiences solidity and unity. Ricoeur uses this position as a heuristic structure to investigate the activities of thought, action, and feeling by dividing these three activities into polarities representing the finitude and infinitude of the person. This section will only address the polarities within thought and the relationship between thought and feeling, for grasping the intradynamic relation between thought and feeling paves the way for understanding the relationship between the symbolic and conceptual.

B. Knowing, Feeling, and The Objectival

Thinking finds its intentional correlate in the thing or object.[13] Thinking can be investigated via reflection by working from the thing intentionally constituted. Notably, this indirect path to investigating thought differs from introspection insofar as consciousness and thinking are deemed not directly accessible but only accessible via the thing that consciousness constitutes. Hence, reflection starts from the concrete givenness of conscious activity constituting a thing other than the self to reconstruct the conditions of possibility for the formation of an object.[14]

Ricoeur asserts that reflection's primary operation is to analyze and divide the unified thing presented in consciousness into its different components.[15] That reflection's primary operation is to divide and, by implication, synthesize intentional content shows a hidden but operative presumption in Ricoeur's thought—namely, that discursive thought is separable from sensibility and operates upon it. As Ricoeur states:

> As soon as reflection comes on the scene it sunders man, for reflection is essentially dividing, sundering. . . . All progress in reflection is a progress of scission. We are going to devote ourselves first to this progression in scission, considering both parts of the divorce in succession.[16]

---

13. Ibid., 18.
14. Ibid.
15. Ibid., 19.
16. Ibid.

Regarding the object's constitution, reflection divides the object into the component parts of reception and determination, where reception correlates to the sensibility of the object through our embodiment, and determination correlates to the object's meaning via linguistic understanding.[17]

These two parts reflect the finite and infinite poles of the human person. That the object is received through our embodiment means that the object is always apprehended from a perspective. In other words, it is always limited by our point of view. However, the linguistic determination of the object always intends a meaning accessible from all points of view. For example, to determine this object as a tree is to intend all of the parts absent from this perspective, both temporally and spatially, that are part of the meaning 'tree.'

This analysis eventually leads Ricoeur to the position that the concrete object is received as expressible and is expressible because it has been received via embodiment. However, the difficulty is that neither the object's reception nor the object's linguistic determination can explain the other from their own categories. Therefore, there must be a third component that synthesizes these two opposing poles, knowable only through the thing.[18] Borrowing from Kant, this third component is labeled as the transcendental imagination synthesizing presence and meaning.[19]

Ricoeur is emphatic that the result of this reflective operation does not achieve knowledge pertaining to self-consciousness, but rather it only establishes the intentional correlate of consciousness as

---

17. Ibid., 19.

18. Ibid., 37.

19. Although Ricouer uses this Kantian term, he clearly points out how he differs from the Kantian understanding in the following: "The point where I differ from Kant is clear: the real *a priori* synthesis is not the one that is set forth in the 'principles,' i.e., in the judgments that would be prior to all the empirical propositions of the physical domain. . . . The real *a priori* synthesis does not appear even in first principles; it consists in the thing's objectival character (rather than objective, if objective means scientific), namely that property of being thrown before me, at once given to my point of view *and* capable of being communicated, in a language comprehensible by any rational being. The objectivity of the object consists in a certain expressibility adhering to the appearance of anything whatsoever." Ibid., 38–39.

constituted by a synthesis of appearance and meaning. This synthesis does not pertain to self-consciousness because the synthesis is in and of the thing, for "the objectivity of the object is by no means 'in' consciousness; it stands over against it as that to which it relates."[20] As a result, Ricoeur concludes that the objectival, the base for objectivity, always involves a displacement of the subject to bring about the synthetic operation that creates the object.

Ricoeur understands feeling to be coactualized in the operations of knowing through the intentionality of feeling being "felt *on* things, *on* persons, *on* the world."[21] However, unlike knowing, feeling also "reveals the way in which the self is inwardly affected."[22] This property of being inwardly affected manifests the subject's relation to and complicity within the world that is continually ruptured in the subject-predicate duality of thought. As Ricoeur states:

> Knowing, because it exteriorizes and poses its object in being, sets up a fundamental cleavage between the object and the subject. It detaches the object or opposes it to the I. In short, knowing constitutes the duality of subject and object. Feeling is understood, by contrast, as the manifestation of a relation to the world that constantly restores our complicity with it, our inherence and belonging in it, something more profound than all polarity and duality.[23]

Implied in this paragraph is that knowing and feeling, although coactualized, operate on two different irreconcilable planes. Feeling reveals a unified tripartite relationship between the self, world, and self's disposition, and this tripartite relationship can only be partially recaptured through the subject-object duality present in discursive rationality. For this reason, Ricoeur states that the feelings reveal something simultaneously pre-objective and hyper-objective.[24] Pre-objective because they

---

20. Ibid., 38.
21. Ibid., 84.
22. Ibid.
23. Ibid., 85.
24. Ibid.

are epistemically prior to any discursive thought reliant upon subject-object duality, and hyper-objective because they contain a surplus of meaning that cannot be fully recaptured through a subject-object proposition.[25] Therefore, they must be apprehended indirectly.[26] Consequently, if the tripartite relationship is to be cognized as a unity, then there must be a linguistic expression that possesses autonomy from propositions, even if they inchoately call for and are not fully comprehended until they come into propositional form. Furthermore, this linguistic term must relate indirectly to the tripartite unity, for any direct relationship would already be within the subject-object duality of discursive thought. This is precisely the role of the symbol, which Ricoeur famously says "gives rise to thought."[27]

The symbol, therefore, operates as a locus of potentiality for thought by already inchoately containing the actuality of the subject's primordial way of being-in-the-world. It possesses an overdetermination of meaningful content that is impoverished of meaning, and therefore content, to the extent that it undergoes interpretation, for the totality of the symbol cannot be cognized due to the objectification required for thought. However, the symbol also requires this objectification, i.e., interpretation, for it to be cognized at all. [28] Hence, Ricoeur conceives the symbol as always involved in the following tension: what is said about a symbol is always less than the symbol, but to conceive of the symbol requires propositional formulations of the symbol. This tension underlies Ricoeur's hermeneutic of the symbol. The skilled hermeneut grasps this tension and enters into a rhythmic movement between the objectifications of a symbol and thinking from the symbol.

---

25. Ibid.

26. Ibid.

27. Paul Ricoeur, *The Symbolism of Evil*, trans. Emerson Buchanan, (Boston: Beacon Press, 1969), 348.

28. Paul Ricoeur, "Structure and Hermeneutics," in *The Conflict of Interpretation: Essays in Hermeneutics*, trans. Kathleen McLaaughlin, (Evanston, IL: Northwestern University Press, 2007), 59.

C. Symbol

"The symbol gives rise to thought."[29] This succinct expression simultaneously communicates that the symbol's meaning is something given, not constructed, and this meaning provokes thought.[30] These two aspects of the symbol result from the symbol's analogical structure of double intentionality, which brings about a dual nature of possessing semantic and non-semantic content.[31]

Double intentionality refers to how a symbol leverages a primary meaning to grasp a secondary meaning. Notably, this secondary meaning is only obtainable via the primary meaning.[32] For instance, Ricoeur uses the example of a stain as a primary meaning that allows the person to apprehend how evil affects their existential state. The stain, primarily referring to how a foreign quality contaminates a particular material, communicates how evil is experienced as foreign, as something that should not be but merges with ourselves.[33] Notably, this primary meaning that refers to an external phenomenon cannot be removed after evil is apprehended through it, for it persists as a necessary condition for the secondary meaning even after the relationship between the two meanings is grasped.[34] Thus, it is not merely pedagogical. Moreover, the necessity of the stain, or a different symbol such as captivity, for the insight entails that we cannot directly name the phenomena of evil without leveraging an intersubjective meaning that mediates the perceptual field. This is the indirect mode of the symbol.

Beyond the symbol's indirect structure made possible by its double intentionality, it also demonstrates the surplus of meaning inchoately contained in the perceptual field. Continuing with the example of the stain, the stain has the primary, material meaning that can

---

29. Ricoeur, *The Symbolism of Evil,* 348.

30. Ricoeur, "The Hermeneutics of Symbols and Philosophical Reflection: I," 288.

31. Paul Ricoeur, "Metaphor and Symbol," in *Interpretation Theory: Discourse and the Surplus of Meaning,* trans. David Pellauer, (Fort Worth, TX: TCU Press, 1976), 53–54.

32. Ibid., 55–56.

33. Ricoeur, "The Hermeneutics of Symbols and Philosophical Reflection: I," 291.

34. Ricoeur, "Metaphor and Symbol," 56.

be transposed into communicating the subject's dispositional state within a world that inflicts evil on the self. This transposition entails that the meaning given through the stain exceeds the material definition, and this surplus of meaning within the symbol is why the symbol takes on the operative role of provoking thought.

The surplus of meaning within the symbol can be further analyzed by distinguishing between the semantic and non-semantic content inherent to the symbol. The symbol's semantic content allows for the symbol to be intelligibly apprehended via interpretation through other symbols, their position and function within mythic narratives, how meaning operates within metaphors, and conceptual elaboration.[35] The non-semantic content of the symbol, on the other hand, is because symbols always refer their semantic meaning to something else, whether that be hidden psychic conflicts, a vision of the world, or manifestations of the sacred.[36] In other words, the non-semantic content of the symbol represents the symbol's exploratory dimension that resists totalizing objectification, while the semantic content is the medium through which the exploration takes place.

The inability to bring the symbol into a totalizing objectification is because it communicates the pre-objective or hyper-objective experience previously referred to in the section on feelings. Consequently, any attempt to bring the symbol into the objectification necessary for thought will prescind from a meaningful aspect of the symbol. This is why, according to Ricoeur, there is a need to have a multiplicity of disciplines and methods to investigate the symbol. Ricoeur mentions three different methods of interpretation: psychoanalysis, poetry, and phenomenology of religion.[37] Each method fixates upon a particular referential aspect of the symbol and becomes bound to explicate that aspect.[38] The boundedness makes the symbol resist ever becoming a part of the purely discursive realm, i.e., purely within the conceptual realm.

---

35. Ibid., 54.
36. Ibid.
37. Ibid.
38. Ibid., 58.

The methods of psychoanalysis, poetry, and phenomenology of religion each bring to light a different possibility hidden within the opaque enigma that is the symbol. Psychoanalysis investigates the "boundary between desire and culture, which is itself a boundary between impulses and their delegated or affective representations."[39] In other words, psychoanalysis seeks to interpret the symbols as representative of a dynamism of psychic forces formed and developed through interpersonal relationships, the demands of reality, and the multilocular, often conflicting, pleasure drives. Poetry is directed "towards an interior, which is nothing other than the mood structured and expressed by a poem. Here a poem is like a work of music in that its mood is exactly coextensive with the internal order of symbols articulated by its language."[40] The poet finds herself in a system of ordinary language that fails to express the full range of possibilities for human living and the correlating mood expressing the subject's *Befindlichkeit*.[41] Finally, interpreting symbols as signs of the sacred is a mode of perceiving the items of the world as transparent signifiers of the beyond, ultimate, and Sacred.[42] This expresses itself in particular organizations of space and time that can be apprehended in rituals, architecture, and social and political organizations. These three modes of interpreting symbols are three modes of indirectly investigating the self as a being that is bound to materiality yet perpetually transcending materiality into a range of possibilities.

However, a difficulty arises in relating these various modes of exploring the semantic richness of the symbol. The interpretation of a symbol through a particular methodology prescinds from possible avenues of meaning yet still refers to the whole person. This is why Ricoeur states: "There is no way to distinguish the various hermeneutic perspectives with regard to their domain, for each one of them embraces the whole of man. If there is a limit . . . we must look for it

---

39. Ibid.
40. Ibid., 59.
41. Ibid., 60.
42. Ibid., 61.

not in the object but in its point of view."[43] Hence, separating the results of different methodologies into different ontological domains or synthesizing the results through a higher viewpoint only brings a false resolution. Both of these solutions are attempts to solve the tension through the mode of discursive reasoning that sundered the symbol in the first place. Thus, the resolution is accomplished by the inquirer finding their way back to the original surplus of meaning via a dialectical and deconstructive process. This process will show: (1) how both accounts are derived from the semantics of the symbol and (2) how both accounts implicitly presuppose the other account as formally operative even though neither account can be logically derived from other's conceptual system. Ricoeur speaks of these differing conceptual systems as different universes of discourse.

D. Universes of Discourse

Ricoeur uses the term 'universes of discourse' to refer to different conceptual schemas that create a systematic ordering of concepts resembling a closed system.[44] Hence, regarding the three dominant methods outlined in the former sections, each method leads to and works from a different universe of discourse.

Although in different respects, these universes of discourse are present within a singular symbol, symbolic economy, mythical employments, and conceptual schemes. Within a singular symbol, the universes of discourse are present as potential. For example, fire "warms, illuminates, purifies, burns, regenerates, consumes; it signifies concupiscence as well as the Holy Spirit."[45] This example displays that fire as a singular term and referent means nothing, in a certain respect, until it is brought into a system of reference, for some potential meanings are conceptually incompatible with other potential meanings. In other words, the hermeneut must prescind from some potential meanings in articulating others within a particular field of reference.

As the potential meaning for symbols becomes increasingly delimited into something definite and actual at the conceptual level, a gap is

---

43. Ricoeur, "The Hermeneutics of Symbols and Philosophical Reflection: II," 320.

44. Ricoeur, "The Hermeneutics of Symbols and Philosophical Reflection: I," 296.

45. Ricoeur, "Structure and Hermeneutics," 56–59.

wedged between different conceptual schemas that explain the same symbolic economy or mythical emplotment. In other words, through universes of discourse, symbols become actual rather than potential, thereby bringing clarity to the opaque enigma that is the symbol but at the expense of becoming conceptually disconnected from other avenues of meaning.

Ricoeur juxtaposes phenomenologies of religion and psychoanalytic interpretations of symbols to make this point. Ricoeur points to three ways phenomenologies of religion and psychoanalysis have contrary orientations leading to seemingly contradictory positions and interpretations. (1) Where phenomenological interpretations of religious symbols focus on describing the conscious, intentional state mediated through ritual, mythical speech, and mystical feeling, Freudian psychoanalysis interprets these intentional states through a dynamic, economic framework of energy.[46] (2) Phenomenological interpretations of religious symbols seek to understand the truth of religious intentionality upon the criteria of how the intentional actions become fulfilled in the Husserlian sense, whereas Freudian psychoanalysis interprets this fulfillment as an 'illusion.'[47] (3) Finally, phenomenological accounts operate from an ontological understanding of the symbol that is tethered to a pre-comprehension of Being, and this position is challenged by Freud's understanding of the 'return of the repressed.'[48] Of interest for this essay is not the details of this juxtaposition but rather Ricoeur's method and presuppositions for bringing these two juxtaposed accounts into a tense, unified account.

Recalling the points of the previous section, both methodologies intend the whole person, and therefore, the domain of both methodologies is equal in scope.[49] As a result, a synthetic account must avoid the temptation to divide Freudian psychoanalysis from phenomenological accounts of religion by separating them into different ontological

---

46. Ricoeur, "The Hermeneutics of Symbols and Philosophical Reflection: II," 318.

47. Ibid., 318–319.

48. Ibid., 319.

49. Ibid., 320.

regions as well as the temptation to synthesize the two at the conceptual level in a manner that abstracts the results from the method.[50]
This latter temptation is the temptation to which Jung succumbs in
this model. Therefore, the place to apply pressure is on the two method's point of view or horizon.[51]

Deconstructing the points of view via Ricoeur's method of reflection, Ricoeur arrives at the original tension within the symbol itself that
can be brought into objectification either archaeologically or teleolog-
ically.[52] The unifying glue between these two forms of objectification
is not a clear, transparent conceptual bridge but rather the categorical
assertion that self-consciousness is an achievement of interpreting the
opaque symbol rather than a clear intuition.[53] This achievement can
take the route of either a Hegelian path of understanding earlier stages
in light of later stages of consciousness or a psychoanalytic path of
understanding later stages of consciousness in light of anterior, functional psychic principles.

The decision to take up one point of view rather than the other
will determine the framework of reference intended to recapture the
whole. However, the point of view not chosen will remain operative
but unthematized, as is evidenced by Ricoeur's insight into the operative teleology within Freudian psychoanalysis and the operative
archeological dimension within religion.[54] Hence, the final criteria for
Ricoeur are ultimately the presuppositions of action, the objectification of which presupposes material from a different point of view that,
in some sense, must function as an unconscious support for the anti-
thetical objectification.[55]

---

50. Ibid.
51. Ibid.
52. Ibid., 318–322.
53. Ibid. 317.
54. Ibid., 333; Paul Ricoeur, *Freud and Philosophy*, X.
55. For another example of this process in Ricoeur's work see: *Time and Narrative, vol. 3* trans. Kathleen Blamey and David Pellauer, (Chicago: University of Chicago Press, 1988) 241–274. Here Ricoeur attempts to solve the aporia of temporality by showing how action presupposes juxtaposed positions.

Returning to the epigraph, Ricoeur operates on the presupposition that there is no secure, *unquestionable* content that can serve as an *a priori* for philosophical construction. This leads Ricoeur to look at the content *already* there as the place to begin understanding the self. However, this method overlooks the possibility of starting from questionable foundations that reveal the human subject as possessing an unrestricted desire to know as a foundation, for to question this foundation is to affirm it. Through this method, the inquirer does not need to start with dialectically relating content already-out-there-now, but can start from the fact that they are an inquirer. Furthermore, and of equal importance, by starting from Lonergan's cognitional theory rather than a Kantian division between sensibility and understanding, Doran can articulate why and how the symbol retains its integrity within objectivity and thereby provides a higher viewpoint that can conceptually harmonize the archeological-teleological content of the symbol.

II. Doran

> The task of philosophy has become, with the work of Lonergan, that of the mediation of immediacy through self-appropriation. This task is not fulfilled primarily by moving from an understanding of human objectifications in language, culture and action to an understanding of experience, no matter how dialectical, even no matter how accurate, the understanding of these objectifications may be. The essential movement is the other way around.[56]

This paragraph shows one of the occasions where Doran is explicitly distancing himself from Ricoeur's methodology and siding instead with the position and methodology of Lonergan. In juxtaposition to Ricoeur's insistence that consciousness must always be sought indirectly through something already-out-there-now, Doran holds the position with Lonergan that in addition to the data of sense, there is the data of consciousness: "To affirm consciousness is to affirm that

---

56. Doran, *Subject and Psyche*, 152.

cognitional process is not merely a procession of contents but also a succession of acts."[57] Hence, just as the contents of consciousness result from the mediation of sensible data through questions, so do the acts of consciousness become objectified through questions that mediate the data of consciousness. Therefore, to claim that there exists data of consciousness in addition to data of sense is not to claim that self-consciousness is accessible through some intuitive, inward look.[58] Moreover, true self-consciousness is a precarious attainment due to the effects of temporality and bias. Nonetheless, it is possible to bring the acts of consciousness into objectification through an inquiring and often therapeutic attention to the immediate data of consciousness.[59]

Two important differences pertinent to the hermeneutics of the symbol arise from this methodological difference. First, this objectification of conscious acts allows Doran to replace Ricoeur's negative concept of the pure imagination with Lonergan's positive concepts of insight and having experience for its own sake. This difference alters Doran's understanding of how the subject objectifies the symbol. Second, pervasive in Doran's anthropology is that the entire human person is oriented to the notion of being through the pure desire to know. Hence, every component of the person is oriented towards this finality. This normative orientation will subtly change the meaning of the inexhaustibility of the symbol. It is the combination of these two differences that help explain Doran's preference for Jung over Freud.

A. Insight: The Pivot Between the Imagination and the Concept

Between the imagination and the concept lies the conscious act of insight.[60] Insights are spontaneous, emergent acts that arise as solutions to the tensions within consciousness. These tensions arise within

---

57. Bernard Lonergan, *Insight: A Study of Human Understanding,* ed. Frederick E. Crowe and Robert M. Doran, (Toronto: University of Toronto Press, 1992), 345.

58. Ibid., 344.

59. Doran, *Theology and the Dialectics of History,* 264.

60. Lonergan, *Insight,* 35.

particular patterns of experience that organize the data of sense, either external or internal, through an interest that forms a conscious aim.[61] Hence, tension occurs when the data of sense fails to have an immediate coherence within the particular aim of a conscious subject. For instance, a person may be driving across town, but the GPS signals her to take a roundabout route to the destination. At first glance, this appears puzzling because the driver knows from previous trips that the fastest route is cutting straight through the center of town. Hence, the sense data is presented as a puzzle to be solved or ignored. Notably, even if it is ignored, what is ignored is a puzzle or aporia. The tension felt in the imagination is the rudimentary question with or without linguistic formulation, and questions need not be answered.

If the subject attempts to solve this puzzle, the following insights may emerge: maybe there is construction, heavy traffic, or an accident on the normal route, or maybe the GPS is malfunctioning. In each of the solutions, an additional relation and term is postulated to bring coherence to what was initially incoherent. Notably, in all of these cases, the solution is something that 'might be' the case. Therefore, further questions, actions, and sensible presentations are necessary to affirm or reject one or more of these possible solutions. Only when there are no further pertinent questions can the subject state with some degree of confidence what is the case. Objectivity is arrived at by answering these further pertinent questions.

Possessing the terms construction, traffic jam, accident, and GPS as possible missing terms and relations necessary for solving the aporia necessitates that the inquirer has inherited and thinks within a linguistic community. However, two points need to be noted that differentiate Lonergan's position, and therefore Doran's, from Ricoeur's. (1) The initial insight is not yet a linguistic formulation. It is merely the postulation of a missing term and relation that fixes the problematic sensible data into a coherent unity. Only through further insights does this initial insight approach and come into utterances, sentences, and

---

61. Ibid., 205.

paragraphs. (2) The missing terms, i.e., construction, heavy traffic, etc., are concepts that are themselves the product of insights bringing coherences through fixing other terms and relations. For example, heavy traffic involves relating vehicles and road capacity. It is not, first and foremost, a predicate of a subject but an intelligible relationship between terms where "the terms fix the relations, the relations fix the terms, and the insight fixes both."[62] Consequently, the concept is not the result of prescinding from the self's involvement by opposing an object to conscious intentionality that is already contained within a subject-predicate structure but is the work of insight. Moreover, insights are not limited to external data, for there can be an insight into insight that allows for the subject-as-subject to be apprehended as the subject-as-object.

B. Experience for its own sake and Symbols

Unlike the sensible experience of other sentient animals that experience data in reference to biological purposefulness, the human person experiences data as autonomous.[63] In other words, the data is not predetermined by instinctual responses to bodies already-out-there-now-real. Instead, human experience goes beyond biological purposiveness such that experience can occur for the sake of experiencing.[64] This autonomy is at the foundation of human potency and responsibility, for it means that human beings are capable of organizing elemental experience into artistic creations, can play with images in order to arrive at explanatory relationships between things, and can implement and are responsible for novel schemes of recurrence through social organizations, technology, artistic presentations, and language.

---

62. Ibid., 36.

63. There are some qualifications that need to be made to this statement. Lonergan notes that "kittens play and snakes are charmed" (*Insight*, 207), and this statement implies that there is some degree to which other animals are not completely bound to biological purposefulness. However, they are not yet at the point of organizing elemental experience into artistic forms. This implies that there is still a limit to how much the data of experience is experienced as autonomous from the biological pattern of experience.

64. Ibid., 208, 291.

The flip side of this potency is that the direction of life is something to be discovered through the sensitive flow of consciousness, giving rise to questions for intelligence and reflection. It is not something already-out-there-now-real as it is with animals dominated by biological purposefulness. Instead, by being freed from the dominant structure of biological purposefulness, the human subject encounters the world as a question within and through elemental experience. As Lonergan states:

> Prior to the neatly formulated questions of systematizing intelligence, there is a deep-set wonder in which all questions have their source and ground. As an expression of the subject, art would show forth that wonder in its elemental sweep. Again, as a twofold liberation of sense and of intelligence, art would exhibit the reality of the primary object for that wonder. For animals, safely sheathed in biological routines, are not questions to themselves. But man's artistry testifies to his freedom. As he can do, so he can be what he pleases. What is he to be? Why?[65]

This deep-set wonder is the pure desire to know that intends the notion of being. In this instance, being is not limited to known content that has already made its way through the cognitional structure but also includes all that is unknown. It is precisely because it includes all the content to be known that the human subject can go beyond the known content at its disposal and ask questions concerning what is unknown as well as come to the judgment that there are no further pertinent questions, and therefore, this is the real.

This pure desire to know, experienced as wonder by encountering the world as a question, underpins, penetrates, and constitutes all cognitional operations.[66] It selects and arranges sensible data for insights which are then brought to higher levels of consciousness through questions for reflection and deliberation. Entailed in this movement is the fact that the primary process or primordial immediacy of the subject-as-subject is

---

65. Ibid., 208–9.
66. Ibid., 381.

a search for direction in the movement of life.[67] Moreover, this search is a search for being, which is the "core of meaning."[68]

However, if the psyche is truly and fully sublimated to the spiritual intentionality driven by the pure desire to know, then the psyche must have an operator that corresponds to and is commensurate with the unlimited range of the pure desire to know. As Lonergan states:

> The principle of dynamic correspondence calls for a harmonious orientation on the psychic level, and from the nature of the case such an orientation would have to consist in some cosmic dimension, in some intimation of unplumbed depths, that, accrued to man's feelings, emotions, sentiments.[69]

In other words, the psyche must participate in the journey towards the known unknown, i.e., the notion of being, through some sensible presentation that spurs the affective dimensions of the human person. This is the role of the symbol, which "is the image as standing in correspondence with activities or elements on the intellectual level."[70]

Lonergan distinguishes the image as symbol from the same image as sign. The image as a symbol is pure potency that relates the subject to the known unknown, but the same image as sign is that image brought into an interpretation via conceptualization, other symbols, or a mythic narrative.[71] Hence, the symbol is related to the same notion of being to which understanding and judgment are related. Consequently, the interpretations of the symbol that transform it into a sign are not impoverishments of the symbol, per se, but actualizations towards the known unknown. This actualization does not mean that the sign exhausts the potency of the symbol. In fact, the sign must continue to operate as dynamically open to further questions in a manner

---

67. Doran, *Theology and the Dialectics of History*, 274.

68. Lonergan, *Insight*, 381.

69. Ibid.

70. Ibid., 557.

71. Myth here is used in a positive sense as denoting a narrative that situates the human person within the cosmos and can spur the human person into the mystery of being.

that nourishes the subject's intellectual activity. If the sign ceases to perform this nourishment, then it has severed itself from the symbol's original potency and ceases to function as a source for exploration by mistakenly judging the interpretation to have arrived at a totalizing framework for understanding the world. In the negative sense, this is the meaning of ideology.[72]

C. Compare and Contrast

With Doran and Ricoeur's underlying cognitional theories articulated, the first goal of this essay can be attained. Unlike Ricoeur's utilization and combination of Husserlian phenomenology and Kantian epistemology, Doran uses the intentionality analysis of Lonergan. This difference entails that Doran does not start from an understanding that consciousness is primordially 'consciousness of' but self-presence.[73] It is this difference that allows Doran to put the data of consciousness on an equal plane as the data of sense. By investigating the data of consciousness, self-appropriation reveals that it is not necessary to posit some third unconscious operation called the pure imagination. This is because the act of insight *into* psychic presentations and the autonomy of elemental experience giving rise to wonder provides a positive, conscious link between sensibility and intelligence. Moreover, this link paves the way for understanding how the work of thinking, conceiving, and judging are permeated by a pure desire to know that matches and is nourished by the surplus of meaning in the symbol. This consistency in the operative function of cognition that has the objective of Being allows Doran to understand the symbol as maintaining its integrity within and through the conceptual tools utilized by philosophy, theology, and personal discernment.

Hence, Ricoeur's understanding of intentionality and the processes of objectification inclines him towards Freud because Jung appears to attempt an integration of incompatible conceptual systems. Consequently, with Jung, both the insights gained through

---

72. Ibid., 566.
73. Ibid., 344–345.

psychoanalysis and the insights gained through phenomenology of religion are tarnished. Therefore, the best an inquirer can do is show how they are both potential aspects of the symbol and necessarily implied in action. However, by relying on Lonergan's intentionality analysis, Doran can have a different understanding of objectification that does not necessitate losing the integrity of the symbol. Insight bridges sensibility and intelligence, thereby making cognitive activity subsist within and maintain sensibility while the sensible participates in the finality of the pure desire to know. Therefore, although irreducible, intentional operations always have a sensible, psyche component giving rise to the feeling of clarity in insight, assurance in judgment, peace in a good conscience, and joy in love.[74]

Moreover, and crucially, intentional operations are able to stay in touch with the full surplus of meaning within the symbol as a psychic operator that continuously nourishes thought towards the known unknown. Consequently, Jung's teleological understanding of the symbol does not conflict with psychoanalytic methodology, and instead, it points to a way of integrating the archeological-teleological unity-in-tension within the symbol to the person's pursuit of Being.

III. Conclusion: Towards Finding Ricoeur's Place in Psychic Conversion

> I [Doran] do not believe Ricoeur highlights strongly enough the fact that the tension within symbolism points to a tension within the mythopoetic core of imagination itself. There seems to be in the psyche itself a teleological orientation toward being, truth, and value, as well as an archeological regressive tendency toward the inertness of non-living matter.[75]

This paragraph simultaneously encapsulates Ricoeur's unique contribution to psychic conversion and Doran's advancement. Ricoeur's contribution to psychic conversion is his insight into the tension that is the archeological-teleological unity-in-tension of the symbol, and

---

74. Doran, *Theology and the Dialectics of History,* 47.
75. Doran, *Subject and Psyche,* 154.

Doran's advancement is in applying this insight to the psyche's spontaneous, symbolic production. Hence, by utilizing Ricoeur's insight into the nature of the symbol, Doran was able to concretize the link between incommensurable and seemingly opposing schemes of recurrence, the organic and intentional spirit, by showing how the psyche's spontaneous, symbolic production is concretely participating in both schemes. Consequently, understanding the psychic censor as an emergent biological function negotiating between various, multilocular drives and perceptual reality does not exclude understanding the psychic censor as constructively aiding the pure desire to know and ultimately being-in-love.

That Ricoeur did not make this advancement himself should not be surprising if the arguments advanced thus far are correct. This is because although for Ricoeur the symbol concretely retains an archeological-teleological unity-in-tension, the universe of discourse through which one investigates the symbol determines what can be consciously thematized by inquirer by determining the inquirer's point of view. Hence, if an inquirer seeks to understand the psychic contribution to symbols, then they will stay within the limits of a Freudian, causal account.[76] Consequently, the symbols spontaneously produced with the psyche will not be "creations of meaning that take up the traditional symbols with their multiple significations and serve as the vehicle of new meaning."[77] Instead, these symbols will be fragments of the past, the organic, the archaeological. Nowhere, for Ricoeur, is this more the case than in respect to the symbols spontaneously produced in dreams:

> At the lowest level we come upon sedimented symbolism: here we find various stereotyped and fragmented remains of symbols, symbols so commonplace and worn with the use that they have nothing but a past. . . . Dreams provide a key only for the symbolism of the first level; the 'typical' dreams Freud appeals to in developing his theory of symbolism do not reveal the canonical

---

76. Ricoeur, "Art and Freudian Systematics," 208.
77. Ricoeur, *Freud and Philosophy*, 505.

form of symbols but merely their vestiges on the plane of sedimented expressions."[78]

The difference between Doran and Ricoeur, on this point, could not
be more stark. Dreams, for Doran, not only have the potential to be
vehicles of new meaning but are, in fact, the privileged site for this
new meaning to arise. This is because during sleep the psychic censor
is relaxed, which entails that images repressed during waking hours are
able indirectly to manifest. Moreover, since the psyche has a vertical
finality through its participation within the pure desire to know, these
symbolic expressions become the royal road to finding direction in the
movement of life, especially when one has lost their way.

This concluding section has shown both how close yet far Ricouer
is to Doran's development of psychic conversion. On the one hand,
Ricoeur's insight into archeological-teleological unity-in-tension concretely persisting within the symbol provides Doran with a concrete
link between the incommensurable and seemingly opposing schemes
of recurrence within the organic and intentional dimensions of the
person. However, on the other hand, Ricoeur's philosophical presuppositions place a serious roadblock to taking the seemingly small
step from the tension in the symbol to the tension in the mythopoetic
imagination or psyche.

---

78. Ibid., 504–5.

Part 3

APPROPRIATION
OF PSYCHIC CONVERSION

9

Psychic Conversion Manifested in Spiritual Direction: Tilling the Ground of "Universal Willingness"

Danielle Nussberger

Marquette University

The purpose of this chapter is to demonstrate the role of psychic conversion in relation to that of religious conversion in the ministry of spiritual direction. Each in their own way, both the directee and the director fundamentally seek an experience of religious conversion, one which Rose Mary Dougherty describes "as an act of prayer." She continues, "When I say 'an act of prayer,' I am referring to those times when we consciously choose to put ourselves in the way of grace, or to enter the sacred space of our True Self, or open ourselves to the Indwelling Mystery of our souls."[1] As the directee reflects upon the intimate moments of their life experience, multiple aspects of their being are laid bare, along with the Spirit's movements throughout these aspects. Through the director's careful listening, mirroring of the directee's words and feelings, and compassionate questioning, the gift of sanctifying grace is explicitly recognized, a gift that Robert M. Doran, SJ, explains ". . . is not conditioned by our knowledge or

---

1. Rose Mary Dougherty, "Experiencing the Mystery of God's Presence: The Theory and Practice of Spiritual Direction," in *Sacred is the Call: Formation and Transformation in Spiritual Direction Programs*, ed. Suzanne M. Buckley (New York: Crossroad Publishing Company, 2005), 28.

apprehension," "what Lonergan elsewhere calls 'the transition from the natural to the supernatural.'"[2] Being able to appreciate these glimmerings of religious conversion implies their relationship with ongoing stages of psychic conversion, as all forms of conversion (intellectual, moral, religious, and psychic) are bound up with one another.

The spiritual director's work is distinct from that of the psychologist, because the director is trained as an active listener who plumbs the depths of the psychic stratum to hear how the directee is experiencing ". . . God's gift of love flooding our hearts"[3] all the way down to ". . . the first, empirical level of consciousness (the psyche) that consists in the sensitive flow of sensations, memories, images, conations, emotions, associations, spontaneous intersubjective responses, bodily movements, and received meanings and values."[4] God is there in the directee's descriptions of their sensations, memories, images, emotions, associations, bodily movements, etc., bringing about their unique religious conversion through ". . . the self-appropriation of those dimensions of consciousness that are properly psychic."[5] Appropriating Doran's model for how religious conversion entails psychic conversion, the following pages will illustrate how the spiritual director can companion the directee in their psycho-spiritual transformation by using Tara Brach's development of the RAIN technique as an effective means of tilling the ground of "'universal willingness' or total being-in-love or charity."[6] The directee's cultivation of self-compassion that reorients their responses to emotions and the experiences from which they arise, fosters an expansive awareness of and empathy for their neighbors that opens the self to communion with others and with the Divine, nurturing their orientation toward Divine Love that

---

2. Robert M. Doran, *What is Systematic Theology?* (Toronto: University of Toronto Press, 2005), 108. The second part of the quotation from Doran is found in Bernard Lonergan, 'Mission and Spirit,' in *A Third Collection* 23.

3. Bernard Lonergan, *Method in Theology* (New York: Herder and Herder, 1972), 122.

4. Doran, *What is Systematic Theology?*, 111.

5. Doran, *What is Systematic Theology?*, 111.

6. Doran, *What is Systematic Theology?*, 112.

is supernaturally fulfilled through the sanctifying grace always at work in the directee's psycho-spiritual maturation.

Doran's Psychic Conversion and the Spiritual Director's Task

Explaining how the Holy Spirit's actions effecting religious conversion in the subject influence the entirety of human consciousness, and thereby involve psychic conversion, Doran writes:

> "The 'more' that God is doing consists fundamentally of created habits or (in *Insight*'s metaphysical terms) conjugate forms that are supernatural operators in human consciousness (thus the term 'operative grace'). If that is the case, then we may presume that the supernatural operators introduced into human consciousness by grace will affect both dimensions of consciousness (spiritual and psychic) . . . Within the context of the graced existential that is the topic of *Insight*'s chapter 20, psychic conversion will bring about a correspondence of the operators and processes occurring on the respective conscious levels of the spirit (the levels of insight, judgment, decision) and psyche, when all those operators have acquiesced as obediential potency to the reception of a set of habits created as free gift and have allowed those habits to become operative throughout living. *Within a strictly theological context, where religious conversion is primary, psychic conversion enables the acquiescence of the sensitive operator of psychic development to be obediential potency for the penetration of grace to the sensitive and primordially intersubjective levels of consciousness. With that acquiescence there are released requisite and appropriate images that are laden with affect oriented to God* [emphasis added].[7]

In keeping with Doran's insights, a spiritual director understands that when they listen to their directee's life experiences and their thoughts

---

7. Doran, *What is Systematic Theology*, 118–119.

and feelings about those experiences, they are witnessing the "requisite and appropriate images that are laden with affect oriented to God." Given that these images and feelings related to them are at the psychic level, the directee may not be entirely conscious of them until they hint at them with their words and their director highlights these words and explicitly questions their meaning, asking the directee to probe them further. In the give-and-take of spiritual direction, the psychic underpinnings of religious conversion are made known through the gradual process of a directee's reflections on their inner relationship with themselves, others, and God for which they use a unique idiom of affect and imagery that is the product of their personal history and their shared cultural and religious histories with the communities in which they have grown and to which they currently belong.

How Psychic Conversion Can Be Experienced Using the RAIN Method

There are several means a spiritual director can use to accompany a directee in exploring their emotions and desires and the images to which they appeal when accessing their emotions most effectively. This chapter will focus on the method that is known by the acronym of RAIN that stands for recognize (what is happening), allow (life to be just as it is), investigate (with a gentle, curious attention) and nurture (with loving presence), as it is articulated by Tara Brach in her book, *Radical Compassion: Learning to Love Yourself and Your World with the Practice of RAIN*.[8] Though Tara Brach does not use the language of psychic or religious conversion (nor is she a Christian theologian or spiritual director), she is a psychologist who relies upon the spiritual insights of the world's wisdom traditions to encourage an awakening

---

8. Tara Brach, *Radical Compassion: Learning to Love Yourself and Your World with the Practice of RAIN* (New York: Penguin Life, 2019), xix. Brach explains that she learned the RAIN technique "as a meditation guide by the senior Buddhist teacher Michele McDonald in the 1980s, and since then it has been adopted and adapted in various ways by mindfulness teachers. Over the past fifteen years, I've evolved my own approach to RAIN, adding a step (N-Nurture) that directly awakens self-compassion" (xx).

of one's psychic dimension that is intimately interconnected with one's spiritual and physical well-being. For Brach, as well as for many mindfulness, self-compassion-based mental health practitioners, loving attentiveness to personal psychic transformation is the groundwork for transcending the ego's biases and prejudices to establish the condition of freedom necessary for communal and social transformation.[9]

For example, addressing how important it is to recognize, allow, investigate, and nurture what is underneath our feelings of anger so that they can be transformed toward greater personal and social good, Brach writes:

> We've all been wounded by others—neglected, not seen, rejected, disrespected. Many of us—and those we love—have been abused or devalued and systemically oppressed because of our sexual orientation, gender identity, race, or religion. Anger has an intelligence: it is an essential survival emotion. We need to pay attention when it mobilizes our bodies and fills our minds with stories of wrongdoing. It alerts us to marshal our energies against obstacles to our well-being, to create better boundaries, to defend ourselves from physical threats, to make our needs or views heard when we've been silenced. And on a societal level, anger in response to oppression can energize the call for justice. Yet, as Buddhist teacher and author Ruth King writes, "anger is not transformative, it is initiatory." It's an energy we need to use wisely.[10]

Brach's apprehension of 1) what lies beneath our anger—a woundedness from being "abused or devalued and systematically oppressed because of our sexual orientation, gender identity, race, or religion," 2) how the anger itself ". . . mobilizes our bodies and fills our minds with stories of wrongdoing," and 3) how that anger properly understood can be the catalyst for individual and social purposefulness

---

9. Examples of other such practitioners and their research include Christopher K. Germer, *The Mindful Path to Self-Compassion: Freeing Yourself from Destructive Thoughts and Emotions* (New York: Guilford Press, 2009) and Kristin Neff, *Self-Compassion* (New York: William Morrow, 2015).

10. Brach, *Radical Compassion*, 141–142.

toward greater justice through compassion and love—is a concrete example of the process involved in Doran's notion of the self-appropriation of the psychic dimensions of consciousness. This is an instance of the appropriation of an emotion such as anger, of how that anger feels in our bodies, of memories of systematic oppression, and of the received meanings and values from these experiences. This example illuminates for us what Doran identifies as the "the key to this dimension of self-appropriation," ". . . the transformation of what in the sixth chapter of *Insight* Lonergan calls the repressive censorship into a constructive censorship that wants insight, rational judgement, and responsible decision, and so that admits into consciousness the sensitive and imaginal materials and the received meanings and values that will provide the data for insight."[11]

For Brach, the RAIN technique creates the circumstances for promoting a "constructive censorship that wants insight, rational judgement, and responsible decision." It does this by bringing into the light of consciousness, emotions such as anger and all that swirls underneath, around, and above them—including their believed meanings on the basis of prior individual and shared experience—in order to allow the emotions and their attending experiences to teach us a deeper wisdom that promotes more skillful judgements regarding how to respond to emotions and all that goes with them and how to make sound choices that respect one's own dignity and the dignity of others. The upshot of Brach's endorsement for RAIN is that it will help us to combat the undiscerning emotional reactivity that returns harm for harm, injustice for injustice, and violence for violence. In this way, it can contribute to informing the psychic conversion that Doran describes as occurring ". . . through the extension to the level of the sensitive psyche and of the preconscious neural functioning of the organism of the conversion process that promotes the condition of 'universal willingness' or total being-in-love or charity."[12] Brach terms the result of such psychic conversion, "presence." She writes:

---

11. Doran, *What is Systematic Theology?*, 112.

12. Doran, *What is Systematic Theology?*, 112.

When we've reconnected fully to presence, we can open to what is going on inside us—the changing flow of sensations, feelings, and thoughts—without any resistance. This allows us to live our life moments with clarity and compassion. The shift from being lost in unconscious mental and emotional reactivity to inhabiting our full presence is an awakening from trance.[13]

Brach's sense of "full presence" is an opening up of the self to allow the sensations and feelings of the psychic dimension and the thoughts that result from them to be there without resisting them so that we are not held in the grip of reacting to them. Instead, the emotions and desires therein teach us a wisdom that comes to us from the God who works through this deep, inner level of our being, and we are increasingly "awakened from trance" and from ". . . the bias of unconscious motivation . . ."[14] to live with the compassion and charity arising from our "created participation in the passive spiration that *is* the Holy Spirit."[15] Brach would agree with Doran that when one is immersed in such ongoing psycho-spiritual conversion:

There is released precisely the *mystery* that is at once symbol of an ever inexhaustible and uncomprehended absolute intelligence and love, sign of the fragments of complete intelligibility that have been grasped, and psychic force empowering living human bodies to a collaborative, joyful, courageous, wholehearted, intelligent adoption of the dialectical attitude that meets evil with a greater good.[16]

For those who employ the RAIN technique as Brach presents it, there is an invitation to be aware of and present to one's sensitive psyche (in emotions, sensations, bodily movements, images, etc.) to allow it

---

13. Brach, *Radical Compassion*, 3.

14. Lonergan defines bias as ". . . a block or distortion of intellectual development, and such blocks or distortions occur in four principal manners." The first of the four principal manners is the ". . . bias of unconscious motivation brought to light by depth psychology." See Lonergan, *Method in Theology*, 231.

15. Doran, *What is Systematic Theology?*, 108.

16. Doran, *What is Systematic Theology?*, 119.

to speak and be heard and received with compassionate openness and intelligent receptivity. The flourishing of such compassionate openness and intelligent receptivity toward the self produces a like compassionate openness and intelligent receptivity toward others and the world. The loving wisdom gained from the RAIN process instills an appreciation for the expansive self who is made for love, and it ignites in the self a transcending movement that seeks and finds greater interconnectedness with others in choosing the common good.[17]

With this background on Brach's assessment of RAIN's potential, a closer examination of its movement from recognizing, allowing, investigating, and nurturing, is in order. Brach familiarizes her audience with the technique by giving a personal example of her own implementation of it. She recollects an instance when she was apprehensively composing her remarks for an evening lecture, and her eighty-three-year-old mother came to her desiring to share an article from the *New Yorker* with her. Seeing her daughter's distress as she sat agitated in front of her computer screen, her mother set the magazine down on Brach's desk and quickly exited the room. Brach could sense an inner, psychic conflict manifesting itself in her body's tension and her nervous affect that was so apparent to her mother. She decided to apply the RAIN method at that moment to listen attentively to what was going on within her and to allow for a psycho-spiritual transformation to take root as insight emerged.[18]

She explains, "The first step was simply to Recognize (R) what was going on inside me—the circling of anxious thoughts and guilty feelings. The second step was to Allow (A) what was happening by breathing and letting be. Even though I didn't like what I was feeling, my intention was *not* to fix or change anything and, just as important, *not* to judge myself for feeling anxious or guilty."[19] By recognizing what was going on inside her, she accepted what we might call a graced invitation to bring the psychic dimension to awareness and to

---

17. Brach, *Radical Compassion*, 197–226.
18. Brach, *Radical Compassion*, 4.
19. Brach, *Radical Compassion*, 6.

allow it to communicate itself without stifling its disclosure through premature categorizing and censuring that would diminish and/or misunderstand its authentic content. Succumbing to self-condemnation would forestall the intent to go deeper into the organic, internal fluctuations that bespoke the body/mind/spirit's joint sensing of past and present circumstances contributing to her current state of being. Allowing by "breathing and letting be," she focused on the act of perceiving her inner processes, and she set the stage for the emergence of insight through the unconscious becoming conscious.

Next, she turned to Investigate (I) the feelings and their accompanying thoughts or beliefs:

> Now, with interest, I directed my attention to the feelings of anxiety in my body—a physical tightness, pulling and pressure around my heart. I asked the anxious part of me what it was believing, and the answer was deeply familiar: It believed I was going to fail. If I didn't have every teaching and story fleshed out in advance, I'd do a bad job and let people down. But that same anxiety made me unavailable to my mother, so I was also failing someone I loved dearly.[20]

Brach entered the Investigation stage by examining how her body manifested the conflict within her, and then she questioned what beliefs were being held tightly in the body's discomfort. She trusted that her body was communicating something important to her, giving her cues to how she was reacting to the conflict between preparing for her presentation and being present to her mother who wanted to discuss the *New Yorker* article with her. Her deep dive into her body's emotional state revealed: 1) that she was holding on to the negative belief that she was going to disappoint people if she was not sufficiently prepared for her talk, and 2) that her sense of herself as a failure was confirmed when her grasping at preparedness caused her to disappoint her mother by not being attentive to her. As her negative belief rose to the surface, she continued to examine her fear of inadequacy,

---

20. Brach, *Radical Compassion*, 6.

and she asked herself what the fearful part of her needed most in that moment: "I could immediately sense that it needed care and reassurance that I was not going to fail in any real way. It needed to trust that the teachings would flow through me, and to trust the love that flows between my mother and me."[21]

This need for solicitude and encouragement provided the transition to the fourth and last step of Nurturing (N). She spoke tenderly to the uneasiness within her and immediately felt a change within her body: "'It's okay, sweetheart. You'll be alright; we've been through this so many times before . . . trying to come through on all fronts.' I could feel a warm, comforting energy spreading through my body. Then there was a distinct shift: My heart softened a bit, my shoulders relaxed, and my mind felt more clear and open."[22] As we picture Brach sitting still in this graced state of calm presence, we have a vivid example of what it looks like when someone undergoes an instance of psychic conversion "that promotes the condition of 'universal willingness' or total being-in-love or charity."[23] Her language of her heart softening and her mind feeling more clear and open, indicates that she has cultivated a generous and welcoming posture toward reality as a whole, a compassionate awareness of herself and others that facilitates charitable action in participation with the Holy Spirit. As Brach deploys the RAIN technique to bring the unconscious dynamics of body and emotion to the conscious surface for the sake of insight that will spur rational judgment and responsible decision making with the goal of loving without reserve, she illustrates how such psychic conversion demands the practice of what Jesus identified as the second greatest commandment, "Love your neighbor as yourself" (Mark 12:31). To love her mother and to love those to whom she would offer her vocational talents, she had to nurture and love herself by partnering with the Holy Spirit in God's bringing love to life within her.

---

21. Brach, *Radical Compassion*, 7.
22. Brach, *Radical Compassion*, 7.
23. Doran, *What is Systematic Theology?*, 112.

The RAIN Method in the Context of Spiritual Direction

Tara Brach's *Radical Compassion* instructs her readers how to use the RAIN method themselves, much like she did when she brought the layers of unconscious desire and affect manifesting in her body and emotions, to consciousness. Like Brach, the RAIN practitioner can undergo an experience of psychic conversion that leads to psycho-spiritual growth in the gaining of insight and its application of right judgment and responsible decision making with a posture of "universal willingness" in charitable hospitality to others and to the world. This conversion process initiated by RAIN is not without its challenges and difficulties as one must "love one's neighbor as oneself," perhaps without having done so in the past. Nurturing self-compassion can be a supreme struggle when one has limited or no experience loving oneself because of having been marginalized by others and subsequently having internalized that marginalization in ways that caused further damage—from self-doubt to the extreme of self-loathing. For this reason, it can be extremely helpful for someone to have a spiritual director as a companion on this journey of psycho-spiritual conversion, someone who can mirror God's abiding love with the person by compassionately listening to them and supporting them in the graced process of self-discovery and healing toward a transformed way of being charitably present to themselves and others.

In their *Inviting the Mystic, Supporting the Prophet*, Katherine Marie Dyckman, S.N.J.M and L. Patrick Carroll, S.J. explain how spiritual directors are concerned ". . . not simply with the spiritual but with the whole person: body, mind, and spirit . . . Our concern encompasses the whole human being, embracing every deed and attitude, every thought and feeling, every job and relationship constituting the unique person before us . . . All of life is or can be a theophany, and our concern is with all the instruments and melodies, all the notes and movements of the song."[24] Note the repeated use of the

---

24. Katherine Marie Dyckman, S.N.J.M. and L. Patrick Carroll, S.J., *Inviting the Mystic, Supporting the Prophet: An Introduction to Spiritual Direction* (New York: Paulist Press, 1981), 20.

language of concern on the part of the spiritual director and on the wholeness of the directee that encompasses mind, body, and spirit and every thought and feeling. The director's concern is a participation in the Spirit's care for the directee. The Spirit's solicitude extends to every aspect of the directee's life by intimately working within the person's spirit, mind, and body, as the Spirit surrounds and impacts every thought and feeling to which the person is responding.

Given the Spirit's all-pervasive presence in the directee's life, it makes sense that Dyckman and Carroll would articulate a vision of all of life as a theophany played out as a song with various instruments, melodies, notes, and movements—all being directed by the Spirit. They make this explicit when they argue that spiritual direction is not ". . . 'direction' in the sense that the director is the one who tells the other what to do or how to do it. To the extent that there is a director in one's life of faith, that director is always and everywhere the Holy Spirit . . . Our relationship is not that . . . of a parent to a child, or of a teacher to a student, but a relationship that does whatever it can to facilitate God's own direction of us in our lives."[25] The Holy Spirit's direction is precisely what Doran recognizes as ". . . God's gift of love flooding our hearts"[26] all the way down to ". . . the first, empirical level of consciousness (the psyche) that consists in the sensitive flow of sensations, memories, images, conations, emotions, associations, spontaneous intersubjective responses, bodily movements, and received meanings and values."[27] The steps of the RAIN method are one way of identifying the spiritual director's task in witnessing to 'God's gift of love flooding the directee's heart.' The director accompanies the directee in the process of 1) Recognizing (R) the sensations, emotions, bodily movements, received meanings and values, etc. that are most prominent at a given time; 2) Allowing (A) them to be what they are by transitioning from "repressive censorship to constructive censorship,"[28]

25. Dyckman and Carroll, *Inviting the Mystic, Supporting the Prophet*, 20–21.

26. Bernard Lonergan, *Method in Theology* (New York: Herder and Herder, 1972), 122.

27. Doran, *What is Systematic Theology?*, 111.

28. Doran, *What is Systematic Theology?*, 112.

3) Investigating (I) them in a manner that leads to psychic conversion and its attendant insight, and Nurturing (N) the self with the compassion and love that are the Spirit's gifts to the directee.

Due to the director and directee's mutual understanding of the workings of the Spirit within, around, and between them, their attentiveness to the RAIN process will highlight the Spirit's role in the joint actualization of psychic and religious conversion through the Spirit's illumination of the psyche to till the ground of "universal willingness" for the full flowering of charity in will and deed. As an example of how this might look in practice, we will imagine how a spiritual director could use RAIN in partnership with someone who experienced something like what happened to Tara Brach after her tense preparation for her talk precluded a conversation with her mother.

Imaginative Exercise: A Practical Example of RAIN Used in Spiritual Direction

After the director welcomes the directee into their familiar sacred space where the Holy Spirit is intimately present, the directee shares how she is unsettled after a tense preparation for a presentation that made her unavailable to her mother, even though her mother expressed a desire to spend time with her daughter that day. In keeping with Dyckman and Carroll's integrated approach to spiritual direction as concern for all aspects of the human person—body, mind, and spirit—the director asks the directee how this feeling of unsettledness is showing up in her body, suggesting that the body signals to us what our emotions are and how they are affecting us, and that our attentiveness to our bodies is essential for our spiritual and mental well-being. The directee describes a tightness in her shoulders and chest, the same physical restriction of tenseness that had been there when she was designing her presentation. The director invites the directee to uncritically Recognize (R) the feelings that are embedded in the tightness of her chest and shoulders and to Allow (A) them to be there so that they can be authentically seen and heard by both her and her director. She recognizes her emotions as the all-too-familiar ones of fear and guilt. She allows herself to feel them, saying that the more she does so, the more she feels closed in on herself.

Now, the director encourages her to further Investigate (I) these feelings of fear and guilt (and their companion beliefs) that are closing her off from other parts of herself and from others. The director asks, "What do the fearful and guilty parts of you believe to be true?" The directee responds, "The fearful part of me believes that if I weren't solely focused on my work that day, I would never have been prepared enough or good enough to communicate the important message that I was responsible for getting across to my audience. I see my teaching as a vocation, and I want to be worthy of the calling God has given to me. At the same time, the guilty part of me believes that I wasn't a good daughter, because I didn't take a break from my work to spend time with my mother. God wants me to be a good teacher and a good daughter, and I believe I'm failing at both." The director pauses to give time for both the director and directee to acknowledge and reckon with these beliefs. Then, the director inquires, "Are there any other parts of you that would like to respond to what the fearful and guilty parts of you are voicing? Any other beliefs that would like to challenge those that say you are failing and that you are not good enough?" The directee indicates that she has had other experiences, both as a teacher and as a daughter, that she thought demonstrated she was at least doing fairly well in both roles. At those times, she remembers having felt proud of herself and having believed that she could succeed and do well. However, she longs to consistently perform better in these and all other aspects of her life, and her sense of being okay is not strong enough to outweigh her sense that she is failing much of the time.

Transitioning to the final stage of Nurturing (N), the director asks what the fearful and guilty parts of the directee need right now, that they might hear what other parts of her are voicing when they have felt proud and satisfied with who she is and what she has done. The directee is silent and then expresses a wish to be able to assure them that everything will be all right, that she has been and will be a skillful teacher and that her and her mother have a strong and loving relationship. She laments, "I wish I could encourage myself in this way, but I

don't know how. There are times when I just don't love myself enough
to be able to treat myself with mercy and tenderness." The director
replies, "What if you were to call upon the Holy Spirit to aid you in
doing what you feel you cannot do on your own right now? How
would the Holy Spirit treat you in this moment? What gifts would
the Spirit offer you?" The directee's despondency lightens when she
imagines herself being held in God's compassionate embrace and she
makes the psalmist's words her own, "You formed my inmost being;
you knit me in my mother's womb. I praise you, because I am wonderfully made; wonderful are your works! (Psalm 139: 13–14)"

A smile spreads across the directee's face as she desires to remember those words more often, especially when she is plagued by negative beliefs producing spiritual desolation that creates a false distance
between her and the God who loves her. As their meeting draws to
a close, the directee calls on her director to conclude with a prayer.
Following the directee's lead, the director appeals to the psalms' wisdom, exhorting God to defeat the enemies of our negative beliefs that
impede us from fully embracing our graced existence as charitable
creatures who are capable of self-compassion and compassion for all
others as a participation in the Spirit of love: "I call upon you; answer
me, O God. Turn your ear to me; hear my speech. Show your wonderful mercy, you who deliver with your right arm those who seek refuge from their foes. Keep me as the apple of your eye; hide me in the
shadow of your wings . . . Amen."

Tilling the Ground of "Universal Willingness" in Spiritual Direction

The foregoing imaginative exercise illustrates how spiritual direction's appropriation of the RAIN technique fosters a psychic conversion that tills the ground of "universal willingness." It does so by
presuming the action of the Spirit in every dimension of the directee's life, including the psychic dimension as it is unearthed through
awareness of the body, its feelings, and the beliefs that develop around
them when personally responding to one's emotions in ways that are

impacted by the dominant social and cultural messages one receives. The director and directee also assume the Spirit's activity in the act of proceeding through the steps of RAIN. The Spirit enables the Recognizing, Allowing, Investigating, and Nurturing necessary for the psyche to make itself known in ways that are usually hidden due to the human tendency to escape the body and its feelings, to dull the pain that accompanies negative emotion. As James and Evelyn Whitehead explain, "we learn to link these [negative] emotions to inadequacy and weakness. Soon we feel bad about feeling bad. Whenever guilt arises or loneliness stirs, the inner judgment automatically sounds: 'I should not be feeling like this!' Embarrassed by our negative emotions, we make haste to banish them."[29] The spiritual direction session is the sacred, safe space to dwell with these emotions in the company of the Spirit to allow them to speak to us and to allow us to speak to them a word that will honor them and direct them toward a larger vision that integrates body, mind, and spirit. The Spirit initiates: a) the religious conversion through which we welcome our "created participation in the passive spiration that *is* the Holy Spirit"[30] and b) the related psychic conversion that attends to our inner life's contribution to the enactment of charity by supporting a life-giving relationship with our bodies, feelings, and the beliefs around our emotions that opens our whole selves to receive and give love more freely.

To facilitate greater freedom in the directee's awareness of and responses toward her emotions, the director asks the directee what the fearful and guilty parts of her believe to be true. The director calls these 'parts' of the directee because people are not identical to their emotions; nor are they identical with the beliefs they have about their feelings. Consequently, the directee arrives at the insight that her beliefs around her feelings can change when they are better understood, especially when they are in dialogue with different beliefs grounded in the directee's direct experience of God as the one who lovingly calls her

---

29. Evelyn Eaton and James D. Whitehead, *Transforming our Painful Emotions: Spiritual Resources in Anger, Shame, Grief, Fear, and Loneliness* (New York: Orbis, 2010, Kindle Edition), 4.

30. Doran, *What is Systematic Theology?*, 108.

to be teacher and daughter because God trusts she can and will fulfill these roles to the best of her ability; this insight yields greater receptivity to the Spirit's communication and a related growth in the freedom to love herself and others.

This widening of the directee's openness to the Spirit and this broadening of her freedom to love, occur in the stage of Nurturing, during which the directee voices how difficult it can be for her to love herself; therefore, her director invites her to entertain how the Spirit might nurture her in ways she can thereafter imitate. She turns directly to scripture, to the Spirit's affirmation in Psalm 139 that she is indeed wonderfully made, divinely cherished from the moment the Spirit knit her in her mother's womb. She cannot deny what the Spirit declares to be true. To honor this truth, she must learn to treat herself with the same love and compassion shown to her by God. Coming to insight about one's worthiness in God's eyes generates right judgment regarding the like worthiness of others and responsible decision making for how to affirm others' inherent value through acts of compassion and justice that support the common good. The RAIN method's Nurturing stage helps sow the seeds of insight (along with the Investigation stage) as that insight is applied through practical instances of loving one's neighbor as oneself.

The spiritual direction relationship is abundantly grace-filled. It is an opportunity for the director and the directee to witness the Spirit at work in the director's empathetic listening and in the directee's sharing of intimate, personal experiences that are replete with divine summons for daily renewal and self-metamorphosis. The director and directee's joint practice of the RAIN technique and/or similar methods can contribute immensely to the ongoing process of psychic conversion that accompanies religious conversion.[31] What happens to one individual in the graced exchange of spiritual direction can have a domino effect

---

31. For a comparable approach to that of RAIN, see Lucy Abbott Tucker, "Embracing the Wisdom of the Body: Feelings and Spiritual Direction," in *Sacred is the Call: Formation and Transformation in Spiritual Direction Programs*, ed. Suzanne M. Buckley (New York: Crossroad Publishing Company, 2005), 101–109.

as each person unites with other people who have also been transformed by the Spirit all the way down to their psychic depths, engen-
dering a "psychic force [capable of] empowering living human bodies
to a collaborative, joyful, courageous, wholehearted, intelligent adoption of the dialectical attitude that meets evil with a greater good."[32]
May spiritual directors and directees reverence the gifts they give to
one another and receive from each other as they go forth to contribute
to communal flourishing and social regeneration.

---

32. Doran, *What is Systematic Theology?*, 119.

10

Christian Scripture and Psychic Conversion

Joseph K. Gordon

n chapter four of *Divine Scripture in Human Understanding*, I articulated a Lonerganian theological and philosophical anthropology as an account of the human location of Christian Scripture.[1] That chapter provided a basic heuristic resource for understanding the humanity of the authors of Scripture and the human dimensions of Scriptural interpretation, including relating Scripture to Bernard Lonergan's articulations of intellectual, moral, and religious conversions.[2] I was not able to do everything in that chapter that I originally intended.[3]

---

1. Joseph K. Gordon, *Divine Scripture in Human Understanding: A Systematic Theology of the Christian Bible* (Notre Dame, IN: University of Notre Dame Press, 2019), 113–163.

2. On those three types of conversion, see Bernard Lonergan, *Method in Theology*, in vol. 14 of Collected Works of Bernard Lonergan, ed. Robert M. Doran and John Dadosky (Toronto: University of Toronto Press, 2017), 223–229, 392–393. In subsequent citations I will utilize the abbreviation CWL for Collected Works of Bernard Lonergan.

3. For instance, I had initially hoped to locate Scripture in the dialectics of history as Doran explains them in *Theology and the Dialectics of History* (Toronto: University of Toronto, 1990). I was able to do some of that work in Joseph K. Gordon, "'Redrawing the Map': Insights from the Work of Robert M. Doran on the Place of Christian Scripture in the Dialectic of Culture," in *Intellect, Affect, and God: The Trinity, History, and the Life of Grace*, ed. Joseph Ogbonnaya and Gerard Whelan (Milwaukee, WI: Marquette University Press, 2021), 111–130. I argued there that Scripture is divinely given culture that mediates revelation and religious values through God's inspirational work in the composition and expression of its authors, redactors, &

Among other things, it did not address the important question of the relationship between Scripture and Robert M. Doran's notion of psychic conversion.[4] This chapter begins to address that deficiency.[5]

---

tradents. So composed and transmitted, God utilizes Scripture usefully in the transformation of persons through religious, moral, and intellectual conversion. Those persons so transformed subsequently create scriptural culture via the diverse carriers of meaning, and so transform social arrangements with a resulting transformation in the distribution of vital goods. Cultural products of engagement with Christian Scripture, of course, are enormously varied. They include homilies, works of scholarship, theological reflection, and the visual and plastic arts. I argued there that authentic scripture scholarship is a secularization to be affirmed and promoted. Authentic preaching, art, and incarnate meaning (saintliness) are authentic sacralizations to be promoted. Inauthentic scripture scholarship is a secularism to be resisted, and blasphemous homilies and other forms of spiritual abuse utilizing scripture are sacralizations to be resisted and denounced and repented of when committed. That chapter draws heavily on the ideas of Lonergan's "Sacralization and Secularization," in *Philosophical and Theological Papers 1965–1980*, in CWL 17, ed. Robert C. Crokon and Robert M. Doran (Toronto: University of Toronto Press, 2004), 259–281 and Doran's further reflections on Lonergan's work in that chapter in Doran's *The Trinity in History, Volume 1: Missions and Processions* (Toronto: University of Toronto, 2012), 227–258.

4. See Gordon, *Divine Scripture*, 332n183, 333n203. Neil Ormerod, one of the blind-peer reviewers of my manuscript, noted that the chapter called for an examination of the relationship between scripture and psychic conversion, but space and time limitations prevented me from adding one to that manuscript. This chapter remedies that deficiency. Lonergan recognized and affirmed the legitimacy of psychic conversion and the complement it added to his reflection on the personal transformations wrought by the other three conversions. See Bernard Lonergan, "Reality, Myth, Symbol," in *Philosophical and Theological Papers 1965*–1980, in CWL 17, eds. Robert C. Croken and Robert M. Doran (Toronto: University of Toronto, 2004), 390.

For other works on Scripture and psychic conversion, see Brian O. Sigmon's "Psychic Conversion in the Story of Joseph and His Brothers," in *Critical Realism and Christian Scripture*, ed. Joseph K. Gordon (Milwaukee, WI: Marquette University Press, forthcoming). See also Doran's own reflections on the general relevance of psychic conversion for hermeneutics in Robert M. Doran, "Psychic Conversion and Lonergan's Hermeneutics," in *Lonergan's Hermeneutics: Its Development and Application*, eds. Séan E. McEvenue and Ben F. Meyer (Washington, D.C.: Catholic University of America Press, 1989), 161–208.

5. I am grateful to Joseph Ogbonnaya for his invitation to write this piece in March of 2020. It has allowed me to revisit Bob's work on psychic conversion. And now, of course, Bob has gone on to his reward, so I offer this work in progress in his honor and memory. I am grateful for Bob's patience with me and encouragement to me in my own work. I now realize, much more than I did before, how gracious he was with me,

What are Psychic Conversion and Christian Scripture?

There are two compound nouns in the title of this chapter: Christian Scripture and psychic conversion. How are they related? One must have an attentive, intelligent, reasonable, and responsible understandings of both in order to do the work of relating them. I start with an all too brief account of the latter, psychic conversion. Doran concludes his article "Reception and Elemental Meaning" with this useful description:

> Whether [Psychic conversion] is defined from "below," as it were, as the transformation of the censorship over neural demands from a repressive to a constructive functioning, or explained from "above" in language that appeals to a healing of what Heidegger calls the forgetfulness of Being, *it is a transformation that effects a renewed link between the creative, inquiring human spirit and the materials, the elemental meaning, the mediated immediacy that at any given time constitute the starting point of the creative process*"[6]

Human consciousness is characterized by a tension between psyche and spirit in a dialectic of limitation and transcendence. The "materials, the elemental meaning, the mediated immediacy" that Doran refers to above, he elsewhere describes as the whole "complex flow of empirical consciousness," or "the sensitively experienced movement of

---

always, and I am only beginning to understand how significant, how liberating and empowering, his friendship and mentoring has been for me in my own formation as I pursue my vocation. *Ora pro me*, Bob.

    6. Robert M. Doran, "Reception and Elemental Meaning: An Expansion of the Notion of Psychic Conversion," *Toronto Journal of Theology* 20, no. 2 (2004): 155, italics mine for emphasis. Elsewhere he writes that "[psychic Conversion] is a reorientation of the specifically psychic dimension of the censorship exercised over images and affects by our habitual orientations, a conversion of that dimension of the censorship from exercising a repressive function to acting constructively in one's shaping of one's development." Robert M. Doran, *Theology and the Dialectics of History* (Toronto: University of Toronto Press, 1990), 9.

life, the pulsing flow of life" at the level of the psyche, the lowest of Lonergan's traditional four, or five, levels of consciousness.[7] Such psychic data constitute the dramatic pattern of our experience, received before adverted to, understood, and judged. We are born and develop and emerge into already existing worlds mediated by meaning, socialized and enculturated in a sea of symbols and words charged with feeling. Such givens constitute our horizon before we are aware of it as such. It is, according to Doran,

> a horizon constituted by meaning . . . prior to critical reflection on the part of the subject, largely the function of what Heidegger calls temporal and historical facticity, of 'being thrown' into existence in the world at this particular time and with these particular people, with their own horizons similarly determined for them by historical dialectics over which at the outset they have no control.[8]

The meanings and feelings and sensibilities of such thrownness are the givens of that lowest level of waking consciousness, the psychic level or psyche, which "occupies a middle ground between organism and spirit."[9] The psyche can be sublated by the higher levels of intelligence, reasonableness, responsibility, and love, of course, and it has its finality in such intellectual, moral, and ultimately religious self-transcendence. But it sets a limiting context upon, and provides the resources for, those higher levels. Even once one has objectified one's experience in intellectual conversion and self-appropriation, the pulsing flow of life, including imperceptible psychic undercurrents, continues. Even intellectual self-transcendence does not allow us some escape from the antecedent givens of our psyche in the dramatic patterning of our antecedent formation and experience.

Our dramatically patterned psychic experience is patterned with received relationships between feelings, meanings—in all carriers

---

7. Doran, *Theology and the Dialectics of History*, 46.

8. Robert M. Doran, *What is Systematic Theology?* (Toronto: University of Toronto Press, 2005), 137.

9. Doran, *Theology and the Dialectics of History*, 55.

whether intersubjective, elemental, symbolic, linguistic, or incarnate—and values. Such dramatic patterning is subject to distortion, or dramatic bias. The notion of "censorship," invoked in the first block quotation above, is of fundamental importance.[10] According to Doran, who builds on Lonergan and Sigmund Freud, our psyche exercises a pre-conscious censorship over images, possibly preventing our full consideration and use of the array of symbols that characterize our dramatically patterned experience. In psychic conversion, we are freed to objectify, consider, and make fruitful use of those images in the pulsing flow of life, in the work of participating in and promoting the increasing self-transcendence that comes from intellectual, moral, and religious conversion.

While intellectual, moral, and religious conversion involve conscious and conscientious decision from their inception, psychic conversion is at first spontaneous and passive, the "transformation of a preconscious psychic function."[11] As such, the work of identifying and understanding psychic conversion is even more difficult than the already difficult work of identifying and understanding intellectual, moral, and religious conversion. That difficultly presents us with unique challenges relative to Christian Scripture. I will discuss those difficulties in a moment.

The second compound noun in the title of this essay, Christian Scripture, is not simply definable either. It took me 458 pages to provide one provisional explanation of its referent in *Divine Scripture in Human Understanding*. I cannot reproduce that work here, of course, though it is immediately relevant to the work of this chapter. Instead of summarizing it, I will utilize a fairly common heuristic of the "three worlds of Scripture" to organize my reflection on the relationship between psychic conversion and the Bible.[12] In brief, the "world

---

10. See Doran, *Theology and the Dialectics of History*, 59–60.

11. See Elizabeth A. Murray, "Unmasking the Censor," in *Meaning and History in Systematic Theology: Essays in Honor of Robert M. Doran S.J.*, ed. John Dadosky (Milwaukee: Marquette University Press, 2009), 425.

12. See, for instance, chapters four, five, and six of Sandra M. Schneiders, *The Revelatory Text: Interpreting the New Testament as Sacred Scripture*, 2nd ed. (Collegeville, MN: Liturgical Press, 1999).

behind the text" represents or points to the historical context of the composition of a particular biblical text and includes a consideration of its author(s), audience(s), the social and cultural circumstances of its composition and delivery, and key extra-textual events relevant to its interpretation. The "world of the text" refers to the way that the words of the text are ordered literarily, generically, rhetorically, narratively, and (possibly) figurally. Finally, the "world in front of the text" refers to the presuppositions and contexts, whether adverted to or not, that readers and hearers bring to the text through their particular experiences of socialization, enculturation, and personal development.

I will treat psychic conversion in relationship to the world behind the text first and most briefly, then the world in front of the text, and finally the world of the text.

Psychic Conversion in/and the World Behind the Text

While Ben F. Meyer's judgment concerning the importance of the pursuit of authorial intention in biblical interpretation is salutary, what that judgment requires of scriptural readers complicates the question of how to relate psychic conversion to the world behind the text.[13] It is no small task to understand the intentions of the human authors of Sacred Scripture. The work of biblical scholarship demands the herculean effort of developing what Lonergan calls a "scholarly differentiation of consciousness."[14] Think of all that is required to learn ancient history through studying the literature and other material culture of the ancient contexts of scripture, not to mention the painstaking process of finding one's way into the alphabets, vocabularies, developments, and relations of multiple dead languages. Even with such formation, Lonergan helpfully reminds us

---

13. See Ben F. Meyer, "The Primacy of the Intended Sense of Texts," in *Lonergan's Hermeneutics: Its Development and Application*, eds. Sean E. McEvenue and Ben F. Meyer (Washington, D.C.: The Catholic University of America Press, 1989), 81–119.

14. Lonergan, *Method in Theology*, 257, 263,

that many scripture scholars have incomplete philosophical formation and so fail to raise and answer all of the relevant questions in the mediated phase of theology, especially those of the functional specialty of dialectic.[15]

Even those who are successful in developing the requisite scholarly differentiation of consciousness and who simultaneously possess the philosophical sophistication needed for the work of dialectic may be blind to the psychical nuances of ancient scriptural authors and audiences. Even if one was possessed of psychic self-awareness, though, there is a significant risk in "psychologizing" the biblical authors or biblical characters. Modern psychologists, dependent upon the theoretical frameworks of Freud, Jung, and countless others, have diagnosed the biblical characters and authors of both Testaments in a heavy-handed, careless way.[16] Psychological readings of the characters and authors of Scripture will always be limited by any deficiencies in their theoretical approaches, of course. Freudian or Jungian analyses will miss the mark to the extent that the theories of Freud and Jung are inadequate to the realities of the human psyche.[17] Such psychologizing readings are often ranked anachronism, as well, inadequate to the lower-blade of the biblical data. They frequently come from western and male-centric perspectives with all the benign and malign baggage such perspectives entail—especially individualism. The fact that much of the biblical literature bears witness to its

---

15. See Bernard Lonergan, "Exegesis and Dogma," in *Philosophical and Theological Papers 1958–1964*, vol 6 in CWL, ed. Robert C. Croken, Frederick E. Crowe, and Robert M. Doran (Toronto: University of Toronto Press, 1996), 153. For discussion, see Joseph K. Gordon, "The Truthfulness of Scripture: Bernard Lonergan's Contribution and Challenges for Protestants," *Method: Journal of Lonergan Studies* 6, no. 2 (2015), 47–53.

16. On the dangers of "psychologizing" the biblical authors and characters, see Wayne G. Rollins, *Soul and Psyche: The Bible in Psychological Perspective* (Minneapolis: Fortress Press, 1999), 62–65; Walter Wink, "Foreword," in *Psychological Insight into the Bible*, ed. Wayne G. Rollins and D. Andrew Kille (Grand Rapids: Eerdmans, 2007), xiii–xiv.

17. This is not to say that one cannot learn a tremendous amount from both. Doran's work bears witness to the relative truthfulness and usefulness of their work, especially to Jung's.

communal authorship, transmission, and redaction rules out individualistic approaches to the psychology of the biblical authors from the outset.[18]

Even though objectifications of human nature are historically conditioned, Lonergan shows how human nature is the same structured dynamism in all times and places. Humans have always been, are, and always will be experiencers, understanders, judgers, and deciders. Therefore, we might expect to find evidence in the text of something like intellectual, moral, and religious conversion, and psychic conversion for that matter, in the ancient persons "behind the texts" who produced those texts. It is difficult for me to surmise what kind of evidence would be required to affirm that a biblical author had or had not experienced any of the conversions, though. The judgment requires more reflection than I can give it at this point.[19] Certainly we can say that the biblical authors wrote from their own experience of relative psychological integrity and self-transcendence. In their experience of relative psychic health, the human authors of Scripture have deployed symbols and language to great effect in the commonsense conventions of their times and places. I will have much more to say on that soon.

Alongside the question of human intentions, and the psychic antecedents of those intentions preceding the composition of the texts of Scripture, Christian readers engage Scripture with the question of divine intentions in mind. But if the Triune God is truly transcendent—as I have argued in *Divine Scripture in Human Understanding* and contra

---

18. See Gordon, *Divine Scripture in Human Understanding*, 220.

19. In *Divine Scripture in Human Understanding* I express this judgment and suggest its relevance for the desiderata of a reappropriation, with significant corrections and transformations, of the ancient fourfold sense of Scripture. My thesis is that Scripture is eminently useful for facilitating the conversions in readers and hearers and that such conversions result in converted reading that reflects the exigencies of historical, philosophical, doctrinal, figural, typological, moral, spiritual, and eschatological readings. Secondarily, though, its usefulness as such must be in part because of the evidence of such transformations in its authors mediated in the words of the text as they stand written. See Gordon, *Divine Scripture in Human Understanding*, 369n179.

the proposals of process and open theologians—God's providence and inspiration do not admit of any sort of psychologizing at all.[20] Divine consciousness is not the passionateness of being, a tidal movement from the organic through the existential. God is not as one of us, that God should change God's mind (Num 23.19). God's biography cannot be written, despite the title and ostensive content of Jack Miles' *God: A Biography*.[21] Ergo God does not undergo psychic conversion but is its primary cause in human creatures, wherever and whenever and in whomever it occurs.

Since even such suggestions about the relevance of psychic conversion to understanding the authors, whether divine or human, and audiences of Scripture are questionable, or at the least that they demand more qualifications and reflection than I can offer at the moment, it will be more fruitful to move on to a consideration of psychic conversion relative to the world in front of the text.

Psychic Conversion in the World in Front of the Text

If we cannot responsibly or easily psychologize the biblical authors and characters to inquire whether they have experienced psychic conversion or not, perhaps we can ask the question about ourselves— have we, or have I, undergone this experience identified by the compound noun, "psychic conversion." And furthermore, if so, am I in the state or habit of being "psychically converted." Surely such an experience and state or habit would have profound implications for our reading, hearing, meditation upon, and teaching of Christian Scripture given the richness of its manifold elemental, symbolic, and linguistic meanings.

Yet asking the question requires the privilege of exposure to the language of "psychic conversion" in the first place. And exposure to that compound noun does not mean that I understand the reality to

---

20. See Gordon, *Divine Scripture in Human Understanding*, 85–94.
21. Jack Miles, *God: A Biography* (New York: Vintage Books, 1996).

which it refers. Finally, understanding the reality of psychic conversion does not mean that I have experienced that reality.[22]

As I noted above, psychic conversion is initially passive. It happens to one outside of that one's intentionality or decision. One does not at first choose for one's censor, for one's "organic mendacity," to be transformed.[23] Such transformation happens, though. I have often told my students that I am confident that I am wrong about things. If I should discover indeed that I am at fault, my hope is that I will consent and assent to the truth I have hitherto rejected. But experience shows us that we do not part with our cherished untruths easily. How much more difficult is it to move from unconscious censorship of symbols and other meanings that we reject "nonintentionally," (*nota bene*, I did not say "unintentionally"), because of our social and cultural malformation and stunted personal development that have shaped the dramatic patterning of our experience? The world in front of the text of Scripture, that is, the horizon of meanings and feelings each of us

---

22. I admit that part of the reason I have held off on commenting on psychic conversion and Scripture until now is a matter of personal deficiency. To this point in my career I have not felt confident that I understand completely what Doran was talking about and writing about when he talked and wrote about "psychic conversion." The work of this chapter provided me the exigence to return to what I had previously read about psychic conversion in *Theology and the Dialectics of History*, *What is Systematic Theology?*, and the first two volumes of *The Trinity in History*. It has also provided me the opportunity to read some of Doran's earlier work in *Subject and Psyche* and many of the essays in the volume *Theological Foundations: Psychic Conversion*. Lonergan once said that Doran was "remarkably creative" (see Pierrot Lambert, Charlotte Tansey, and Cathleen Going, eds. *Caring About Meaning: Patterns in the Life of Bernard Lonergan* (Montreal, Quebec: Thomas More Institute, 1982), 115). But Lonergan said that in the early 1980s, and Doran's remarkable creativity has unfolded for four more decades. My reconsideration of Doran's work has impressed upon me the truthfulness and significance of Lonergan's judgment forty years ago. Just as Lonergan did not stay still intellectually but constantly developed throughout his life, Doran's own work on psychic conversion kept developing as he explored the implications of his early discovery, first explained in print in *The Thomist* in 1977, through the publication of the second volume of *The Trinity in History* in 2019. I admit despite giving significant attention to that work and those developments in recent months, I can say with confidence that I have yet more to learn.

23. The phrase "organic mendacity" comes from Max Scheler and is quoted in Doran, *What is Systematic Theology?*, 140.

brings to the text, may in fact be profoundly transformed through the experience of psychic conversion. But how can one know whether one has actually undergone psychic conversion?

This uncertainty seems to lead us to an impasse in our consideration of psychic conversion and Christian Scripture. It is likely impossible, or at the least irresponsible, to comb the texts of scripture searching for evidence of a psychic conversion, a passive personal transformation that has only been identified and objectified in the past forty years. In "the world in front of the text," what we readers bring to Scripture, the experience of habitual psychic conversion would surely prove an invaluable resource for handling the symbolic and linguistic meanings of Scripture. That usefulness, though, depends upon one having experienced psychic conversion. And how can one know that one's censorship has truly been opened constructively to the flow of life, including those rich scriptural symbols? I can only pose those questions to readers of this chapter as an invitation, I cannot answer them for you. If we can go no further in our considerations of psychic conversion and the worlds behind and in front of the text, though, there is nevertheless one remaining world to consider, the "world of the text."

Psychic Conversion and the World of the Text

The "world of the text," once again, refers to the way that the particular words of scripture run rhetorically, generically, literarily, figurally, and symbolically. Given the importance of the discernment and use of symbols in psychic conversion, consideration of the symbols of scripture themselves likely provides the most fruitful point of entry for considering the relationship between that type of conversion and Christian Scripture. Scripture is not merely useful (see 2 Tim 3.16–17) intellectually, morally, and religiously.[24] One dimension of its usefulness is that its symbols are eminently suitable for provoking readers into the experience of psychic conversion.

---

24. For discussion of Scripture's usefulness for intellectual, moral, and religious conversion see Gordon, *Divine Scripture in Human Understanding*, 248–260.

"Divine revelation," as Lonergan explains it, is "God's entry and His taking part in [humanity's making of itself]."[25] Such revelation, for the Christian, is mediated through Sacred Scripture.[26] As I mentioned above, the words of Scripture are not theoretical but commonsense, and the elemental, symbolic, and dramatic meanings of the ancient words of Christian Scripture are notoriously slippery. Though Lonergan admits that symbols and other instantiations of dramatic and artistic meaning "are fairly unreliable in communicating truth," they nevertheless "have a particularly effective, and quite necessary, role in penetrating our sensibility and moving our affectivity."[27]

Given the importance of elemental, symbolic, dramatic, incarnate meaning in religious praxis, Doran has suggested that a Lonerganian understanding of divine revelation must begin from a focus on these types of meaning. Following Avery Dulles, he argues that it is best to think of revelation as "symbolic communication."[28] Such a suggestion will not please logicentric or rationalistic theologians, but it will help readers to measure up to the rich, emotionally charged particularity of the biblical texts. One only needs to think of how much of Scripture is narrative, or the evocative, emotionally dense psalms, the image saturated prophetic and apocalyptic literature, Jesus' use of parables, and the irony and symbolic fertility of the fourth gospel.[29] Even the wisdom literature and letters of Paul, though arguably more logicentric or rational, are suffused with potent imagery.[30] Christian readers must

---

25. Bernard Lonergan, "Theology in its New Context," in vol. 13 of CWL, ed. Robert M. Doran and John D. Dadosky (Toronto: University of Toronto, 2016), 54.

26. For much more on this, see Gordon, *Divine Scripture in Human Understanding*, 228–247.

27. Bernard Lonergan, *The Triune God: Doctrines*, vol. 11 of CWL, ed. Robert M. Doran and H. Daniel Monsour, trans. Michael G. Shields (Toronto: University of Toronto Press, 2009), 209.

28. Doran, *What is Systematic Theology?*, 137.

29. On the poetics of the Gospels in particular, see Olivier-Thomas Venard, *A Poetic Christ: Thomist Reflections on Scripture, Language, and Reality*, trans. Kenneth Oakes and Francesca Aran Murphy (New York: Bloomsbury T & T Clark, 2019).

30. For an examination of Paul's compelling use of imagery, see Gary S. Selby, *Not with Wisdom of Words: Nonrational Persuasion in the New Testament* (Grand Rapids: Eerdmans, 2016).

learn to deal with biblical symbolism well to understand and communicate what God has revealed about God's redemptive work. In *What is Systematic Theology?* Doran makes the striking assertion that

> The affirmed truth of the redemption, the doctrine of redemption, lies . . . in the domain of permanently elemental meaning. That is to say, it is possible that its meaning will always be better expressed in the symbolic, aesthetic, and/or dramatic terms of scripture, literature, and drama, and be lived forward from the narrative, than it will be formulated in the quasi-technical type of formulation that most dogmas provide.[31]

The symbolic, aesthetic, and dramatic forms of Scripture are divinely intended. Such forms have profound power that precedes important theoretical and doctrinal work and remains in force after such work is complete.

As I noted above, overly intellectualist approaches to divine revelation, Scripture itself, and the work of theological reflection may balk at the judgment that we should prioritize the symbolic and elemental in our considerations of revelation and Scripture. Such hesitation and resistance seems eminently reasonable to me, given the ease with which it is possible to utilize Scripture abusively and demonically. As I note in *Divine Scripture in Human Understanding*, Scripture has proven useful for countless programs other than God's redemptive work in history.[32] Its psychically charged symbolic language can be employed to sanction evil purposes. For those whose dramatic patterning is severely malformed through major and minor inauthenticity, the symbolic language and divine authority of scripture can be combined seamlessly for horrific effect. Such language can be, and has been, employed to increase scotomata and to practically drown hearers and devotees in the forgetfulness of being. Marx is at least partially right. Some forms of "biblical" religion are effective opiates for the masses.

---

31. Doran, *What is Systematic Theology?*, 22.

32. See Gordon, *Divine Scripture in Human Understanding*, 6, 258, and the literature cited therein.

The Bible as itself, as a symbol, possesses significant psychic power. Throughout Christian history, at least since the legalization and political ascendancy of Christianity in late antiquity, believers have found themselves thrown into horizons in which the text itself, the book itself, possesses or reflects absolute, divine, talismanic authority. Within such formation, or malformation, merely quoting the text can stop conversation, and thinking, completely.[33] The understandable response of many to such uses of Scripture has been to seek to dismantle the authority of Scripture completely by discrediting it.[34] For professing Christians that is not an option. It is possible, though, to relocate the authority of Scripture in the authority of the Triune God, which I have argued is expressed through God's love in creating, sustaining, and redeeming God's creation.[35]

When I am teaching I attempt to break the spell of "mythic [Bible] consciousness" by inviting listeners to pay attention to things in their own Bibles, text-critical issues in particular, that they have never noticed despite the fact that my audiences and classes have read Scripture their whole lives.[36] While it makes sense and is beautiful and faithful to carry the Evangeliary to the center of the cathedral for the reading of the Gospel, that fact does not efface the truth of the messiness of the transmission of those texts from the first century to the present. In fact, knowledge of Scripture's messy incarnate history should enhance such reverence.

---

33. Such power can be wielded effectively, even by those with little to no connection to institutional or traditional forms of Christianity. Think of the charade of our 45th president, if not actually commanding, at least taking advantage of the deployment of riot police and pepper spray on protestors, so that he could walk across Lafayette Square to be photographed, holding a Bible, in front of St. John's Church in Washington D.C. on June 1st 2020.

34. See, for instance, Hector Avalos, *The End of Biblical Studies* (Amherst, NY: Prometheus Books, 2007).

35. See Gordon, *Divine Scripture in Human Understanding*.

36. On "mythic consciousness" see Bernard Lonergan, *Insight*, vol. 3 of CWL, ed. Frederick E. Crowe and Robert M. Doran (Toronto: University of Toronto Press, 1992), 566–569.

The uses and abuses of the psychically charged imagery of Scripture call for a Christian response. That response will not be responsible if it ignores, downplays, or abandons those elemental, symbolic, and dramatic meanings. God has given Christian Scripture to us as it is with and not in spite of such psychically charged language. In the hands of responsible and faithful readers, the symbols of Scripture can and ought to be utilized to provoke people out of any forgetfulness of being which we might harbor. Authentic engagement with, and use of, scriptural meaning can facilitate the conversions, intellectual, moral, religious, and even psychic, which allow readers and hearers to find their way in the passionateness of being oriented towards God, that passionateness that is fulfilled in loving God and all that God loves.

I want to conclude with an experimental use of a symbol recurrent in Scripture as a means of illustrating the difference psychic conversion can have for Scriptural interpretation. I intend this exercise to be a metaphorical stick in the spokes, perhaps jarring at least some readers out of the flow, maybe even midwifing the experience of psychic conversion.

An Illustration from A Key Biblical Symbol: The Serpent

Serpents are mentioned frequently in both the Old and New Testaments. Very rare is the person who comes to serpent symbolism apart from intense feelings and value judgments. When somebody asks me to identify a snake, they will often ask me if it is a "good snake or a bad snake." Often, someone within earshot will interject "the only good snake is a dead snake" before I can respond. The language of good and bad, of course, reflects judgments of value. Most Americans, including American Christians, have been socialized and enculturated into the conviction that snakes are not just bad, but evil. And they ostensibly find ample support, divine authority in fact, for that judgment in the Christian Bible. Chapter nine of Ted Levin's *America's Snake: The Rise and Fall of the Timber Rattlesnake* begins with a list of nine biblical texts which imply or state that serpents are bad or evil (Gen 3.14; Ps

140.3; Matt 23.33; Rev 20.2; Gen 3.1; Ps 58.4–5; Dt 32.33; Isa 65.25; and Luke 10.19).[37]

For the transgression of the serpent in the garden, snakes are "cursed above animals" (Gen 3.14). The Bible says it, I believe it, that settles it. God has spoken. There is a necessary enmity between people and snakes, at least since the expulsion of our progenitors from the garden. To fulfill our vocation of dominion in God's creation entails, for many, that we stomp them out (Gen 3.15–16). In the eschaton, God will destroy "that ancient serpent, the devil" once and for all in eternal fire (Rev 20.2). The biblical evidence appears damning; snakes are evil and completely beyond redemption. What could be clearer? Such biblical imagery is invoked frequently when politicians are called "snakes in the grass." My parents, despite my love for serpents, would chastise me for losing things in plain sight. "If it was a snake, it would have bit you," they'd say. On more than one occasion, fellow Christians have questioned my sanity and spiritual well-being when they have discovered my appreciation of and admiration for serpents. When I attended church camp in rural Missouri in the summer of 1997, my ophidiophobic youth minister threatened to lock me indoors unless I promised not to search for snakes.

As James Charlesworth has shown in *The Good and Evil Serpent*, though, ancient peoples did not employ serpent imagery in exclusively negative ways. Many contemporary cultures and religious traditions appreciate and even revere snakes. While Charlesworth does identify 16 negative meanings of serpent imagery in Ancient Near Eastern and Greco-Roman cultures, he also discerns 29 different types of positive serpent symbolism.[38] It may surprise readers, American Christians in

---

37. Ted Levin, *America's Snake: The Rise and Fall of the Timber Rattlesnake* (Chicago: University of Chicago Press, 2016), 255–256.

38. James H. Charlesworth, *The Good and Evil Serpent: How a Universal Symbol Became Christianized* (New Haven, CT: Yale University Press, 2010). Charlesworth's archaeological and historical work is quite incredible as a work of scholarship. He exhaustively combs the ancient evidence, leaving no stone (seemingly literally), unturned, and then orders and categorizes it tidily. It is much less satisfying from a religious or theological perspective.

particular, that such positive serpent imagery is present within Christian Scripture alongside the negative. It is possible to take the positive snake imagery, and negative snake imagery, as both being divinely intended. The tension between such images could serve as a stumbling block to push readers and hearers towards self-transformation.

In general, my experience suggests to me that the dramatic patterning of American Christian piety includes an almost visceral abhorrence of serpents, justified and reinforced by the "snake-negative" texts of Sacred Scripture mentioned above. But American Christians also have a scotosis concerning "snake-positive" texts in the Bible. The positive serpent imagery in Scripture demands a response from someone with Christian commitment who is committed to the authority of Scripture. It also illustrates the potential that scriptural imagery has for instigating psychic conversion.

Prior to the serpent's deception in the second creation account of Genesis 2–3, the first creation account (Gen 1.1–2.4) affirms the created goodness of snakes. We read in Genesis 1.21 that God created and declared good "every living reptile" (LXX) on the sixth day. According to the narrative theological description of creation in Genesis 1, there are no bad snakes; all snakes are in fact created, judged, and recognized by God as good! Even the serpent that tempts Adam and Eve is given a superlative; it is called the "wisest" or "shrewdest" of all the animals in Genesis 3.1.

After Eden, the foreign sage Agur, son of Jakeh, declares that "the way of the snake on a rock" is "too wonderful" for him in Proverbs 30.18.[39] The first evangelist records Jesus telling his disciples to be as "wise as serpents," alluding to Genesis 3.1. That command suggests first that serpents are wise, and second, that disciples can and should learn from them (Matt 10.16). In Job, God commands that Job "ask the beasts and they will teach you," (Job 12.7–10) and creeping things are called upon to praise God in Psalm 148.10. Presumably they do so

---

39. All quotations from Scripture are from the *New Revised Standard Version, Anglicized Edition* (National Council of the Churches of Christ in the United States of America, 1989, 1995) unless otherwise noted.

in their own particular wisdom and goodness, simply by going about their wondrous serpentine ways. The picture of snakes emerging from these other texts is quite different from the one with which I began this section. But there is even more striking serpentine symbolism yet in Scripture.

Jesus explains his mission via anguine analogy in John 3.14, just two verses before the most famous text in the New Testament: "And just as Moses lifted up the serpent in the wilderness, so must the Son of Man be lifted up, that whoever believes in him may have eternal life. For God so loved the world that he gave his only Son, so that everyone who believes in him may not perish but may have eternal life. Indeed, God did not send the Son into the world to condemn the world, but in order that the world might be saved through him" (John 3.14; cf. Numbers 21.4–9). While the curse of the serpent creates, or reflects, the common enmity between humans and snakes, is it possible to believe that Christ's completed work ends not just the enmity between peoples (see Eph 2.14–16), but all enmity entirely?[40] If the serpent is cursed as Genesis indicates, surely that curse is reversed by the work of Christ lifted up on the cross. For Paul testifies that "he redeemed us . . . by becoming a curse for us—for it is written, 'Cursed is everyone who hangs on a tree'—" in Galatians 3.13.

That curse must be reversed eschatologically, for in Romans 8 Paul testifies that all of creation is groaning awaiting the consummation of God's work. If *ta panta*, that is "all things" will be reconciled in Christ, as the Pauline author testifies in Ephesians 1.8–10, surely snakes are among those things. For whatever the testimony of Revelation 20 about the destruction of "that ancient serpent, the devil," means (Rev 20.2). The prophet Isaiah, in his oracular description of God's holy mountain, says that

---

40. For intriguingly complementary interpretations of the enmity between humans and snakes, see Lynne A. Isbell, *The Fruit, the Tree, and the Serpent: Why We See So Well* (Cambridge, MA: Harvard University Press, 2009) and Joseph Fitzpatrick, *The Fall and the Ascent of Man: How Genesis Supports Darwin* (Lanham, NY: University Press of America, 2011).

The wolf shall live with the lamb,
   the leopard shall lie down with the kid,
the calf and the lion and the fatling together,
   and a little child shall lead them.
The cow and the bear shall graze,
   their young shall lie down together;
   and the lion shall eat straw like the ox.
The nursing child shall play over the hole of the asp,
   and the weaned child shall put its hand on the adder's den.
They will not hurt or destroy
   on all my holy mountain;
for the earth will be full of the knowledge of the Lord
as the waters cover the sea (Isaiah 11.6–9).

If asps and adders, no doubt representative of the dangerous, even deadly cobras and vipers native to the middle east, are present on God's holy mountain, I am confident that any created snake can get in. If God is reconciling all created things in Christ, then all snakes go to heaven.

Scripture abounds with archetypal symbols, those which are, according to Doran, "freighted with an emotional depth and a cross-cultural intelligibility that give one the sense of participating not only in one's own story, but also in a story that is everyone's or some universally accessible variant of the general patterns of human development."[41] Some of the positive serpent imagery in Scripture is arguably archetypal; their particular goodness, wisdom, and wonderful ways are suggestive of the goodness, beauty, and mystery of all created life. The negative serpent imagery is archetypal as well. Their danger and mystery also remind us of the universal experiences of fear, evil, and death. But serpents also function as an anagogic symbol, especially in John 3.14 and Isaiah 11.8, pointing to "nature's recreation and total transformation."[42]

---

41. Doran, *Theology and the Dialectics of History*, 270.

42. Doran, *Theology and the Dialectics of History*, 272–273. Doran cites Isaiah 11.6–9 as an example of anagogic symbolism in Scripture.

The ability to recognize, assess, and evaluate such symbols in Scripture can be a means of personal transformation, helping one to better understand and participate in the dynamics of creating and healing, progress and redemption, in history, and enabling one to diagnose, resist, and denounce evil and decline. The presence of such symbols in Scripture serves to provoke readers and hearers, moving us towards the God to whom they bear witness. The snake-positive, and even snake-redemptive, imagery in Scripture can serve as an impetus for readers and hearers of the text to undergo the experience of psychic conversion. It can jar them out of their received dramatic patterns, lifting their eyes beyond earthly archetypes to God.

Concluding Remarks

The quotation that I used from Doran's article "Reception and Elemental Meaning" ends with Doran mentioning the "starting point of the creative process."[43] Following the experience of psychic conversion, one is able to start the creative process anew, now forging "the first and only edition of oneself" with the resources of powerfully charged symbols.[44] Those who are able to operate on such symbols, whether through the experience of psychic conversion, or simply through healthy formation with respect to a certain symbol or symbol-set, can utilize such charged symbols to challenge and provoke others to psychic conversion. The language of Scripture is shot-through with such charged imagery, and, in faithful and responsible hands, can be deployed as the eminently divine useful instrument that it is. Teachers and counselors can thus utilize the text to help hearers and readers of the word to discern the contours of God's creative and redemptive work, and, in the limit, can help such readers and hearers find themselves in that work with its profound archetypal and anagogic resources.

---

43. Doran, "Reception and Elemental Meaning," 155.
44. Doran, *Theology and the Dialectics of History,* 55

11

Psychic Conversion and the Spiritual Exercises of St. Ignatius

Gerard Whelan SJ
Gregorian University, Rome

The death of Robert Doran in 2021 was a sad moment for all those who knew him and had been engaging with his work. At the same time, memorial testimonies to him seem to have provoked a curiosity about his thought among new audiences and one can hope that the reception of his thought will continue to deepen in academic circles. In this context, the initiative of Fr. Joseph Ogbonnaya in producing this book is timely, dedicated as it is to explaining the notion of psychic conversion and demonstrating its applicability to a variety of fields. In what follows, I explain how closely the notion of psychic conversion relates to themes found in *The Spiritual Exercises of St. Ignatius*.[1] The contribution unfolds in three parts. First, I outline how Doran explains psychic conversion, especially in his book *Theology and the Dialectics of History*.[2] Next, I identify some key themes

---

1. Ignatius of Loyola, *The Spiritual Exercises of St. Ignatius: A New Translation Based on Studies in the Language of the Autograph*, translated by Louis J. Puhl SJ (Chicago: University of Chicago Press, 1951).

2. Robert M. Doran, *Theology and the Dialectics of History* (Toronto: University of Toronto Press, 1990). When I studied with Bob Doran in the 1990's he used to say that this work adequately summarized all that he had written about psychic conversion in previous publications. For this reason, I refer mostly to this work. I acknowledge that Doran's notion of psychic conversion evolves after that time, as documented by Jeremy Blackwood elsewhere in this publication. However, Doran's development mostly involves the theological dimension of psychic conversion, something I identify as emerging already by 1990.

in the *Spiritual Exercises* that illuminate and are illuminated by this notion of psychic conversion. Finally, I offer a series of concluding reflections on the significance of making this link.

Part 1: Psychic Conversion and Grace

Already during his doctoral studies, Doran had been convinced that "the integral heuristic structure of the normative interiority of the subject has not been fully disengaged in Lonergan's writings," and that his own work would seek "to advance transcendental method through the discussion of psychic conversion."[3] This commitment on the part of Doran culminates in 1990 with the publication of *Theology and the Dialectics of History.* Subsequently, his work on this foundational notion undergoes some deepening, but he primarily turns to work in the functional specialty of systematics.[4]

The Vertical Finality of the Psyche

Doran's expansion of Lonergan's thought begins with a study of the role of the psyche in subjectivity, building on what Lonergan has to say about the "psychic censor" in *Insight,*[5] that "penetrates below the surface of consciousness to exercise its own domination and control and to effect, prior to conscious discrimination, its own selection and arrangements."[6] Doran builds on Lonergan's statement that, "primarily the censorship is constructive, it selects and arranges materials that

---

3. Doran, *Psychic Conversion and Theological Foundations* (Milwaukee, Marquette University Press, 1994), 28.

4. See, John D. Dadosky, "Introduction," in *Meaning and History in Systematic Theology: Essays in Honor of Robert Doran, SJ*, ed. John D. Dadosky, (Milwaukee: Marquette University Press, 2009.)

5. Bernard J. F. Lonergan, *Insight: A Study of Human Understanding,* ed. Frederick E. Crowe and Robert M. Doran, Collected Works of Lonergan 3 (Toronto: University of Toronto Press, 1992.) See especially, Chapter 6, "Common Sense and Its Subject," 196–331.

6. Lonergan, Insight, 213–14.

emerge in consciousness in a perspective that gives rise to an insight."[7] He adds to Lonergan's primarily Freudian writings a profound, and dialectical, engagement with the thought of Carl Jung.[8] He explains that the censor is related to the phenomenon of "complexes" at the level of the unconscious:

> All psychic energy is distributed into complexes . . . they provide us with the images that we need for insight, or offer us memories that help us to discover ways of responding to new situations, or spontaneously to acquiesce in the progress of reflection that anticipates judgment, or to apprehend genuine values in an affectively charged way that will lead to action consistent with our affective response.[9]

Doran next explores a second role of the psyche, a role that concerns images that have already been admitted to consciousness. He explains that the psyche represents "the sensitive flow of consciousness itself" and concludes that there are "two distinct sets of data of consciousness, the data of intentionality and the data of the psyche."[10] He also refers to this duality as existing between a pole constituted by "spirit" and one constituted by "psyche." He explains the former term (which has roots in Plato) is all that which Lonergan has differentiated concerning intentional consciousness. Explaining the latter term, he

---

7. Lonergan, *Insight*, 21.

8. Doran discusses Jung at some length in *Dialectics of History*. However, I also make use of yet more extensive discussion in Robert M. Doran, "Insight and Archetype," and, "Dramatic Artistry and the Third Stage of Meaning," in *Theological Foundations Volume 1: Intentionality and Psyche*, Marquette Studies in Theology, No. 8 (Milwaukee, WI: Marquette University Press, 1995), 231–278, and 279–310. The dialectical nature of Doran's engagement with Jung is evident in the following: "Jung is quite seriously deficient on a notion of human intentionality. My position heuristically integrates Jung's incredible familiarity with the human psyche with Lonergan's masterful treatment of intentionality" (Doran, "Insight and Archetype," 292).

9. Doran, *Dialectics of History*, 229.

10. Doran, *Dialectics of History*, 46. The theme of the duality of consciousness is so key to Doran's thought that it dictates the title of the book-length interview he gave toward the end of his life: *Consciousness in Two Ways: Robert Doran Remembers* (Milwaukee, WI: Marquette University Press, 2021).

states that psyche exhibits "a vertical finality toward participation in the life of the spirit."[11] He then explores the nature of this participation.

Doran describes how the psyche represents a principle of limitation in consciousness, whereas spirit represents a principle of transcendence. He thus speaks of a "finalistic tension of consciousness"[12] which is a "conscious dialectic of the subject"[13] and explains this tension with reference to Lonergan's notion of genetic method.[14] Lonergan outlines how the process of emergence in the universe is characterized by a tension between an integrator and an operator at every level of being and explains that, at the human level, this dialectic is expressed with the psyche functioning as integrator and spirit functioning as operator.[15]

Doran pays special attention to how this dialectic plays out in the "dramatic pattern of experience" that characterizes daily living, involving decisions that are intensely personal and which no moral authority can make for us. He explains that such decisions are guided by a "dramatically artistic affectivity,"[16] that wells up from the unconscious. He states that an authentic attending to feelings, so as to allow emerge a response to value, involves maintaining "a taut equilibrium or, perhaps better, creative tension, between the organic and the spiritual."[17] He stresses that, "affective integrity is a habitual abiding in a tension of opposites, an aesthetic detachment that allows there to emerge the inevitability of forms, an equilibrium."[18] He explains that

---

11. Doran, *Dialectics of History*, 51.

12. See Doran, *Dialectics of History*, 280–281 (referring to Lonergan, *Insight*, 484–507).

13. "To acknowledge the dialectic of psyche and intentionality within consciousness is to differentiate the dialectic of the subject into a twofold dialectic: between consciousness and the unconscious, and within consciousness itself" (Doran, *Dialectics of History*, 70, see also, 9).

14. Lonergan, *Insight*, 484–507.

15. "The dialectic [of spirit and psyche] itself is the humanly conscious form of the tension of limitation and transcendence that qualifies all development in the universe" (Doran, "Insight and Archetype," 280).

16. Doran, *Dialectics of History*, 57.

17. Doran, *Dialectics of History*, 57.

18. Doran, *Dialectics of History*, 57.

when decisions are made that emerge from such attentiveness to value, what results in consciousness is "the calm assurance and serenity" of a person who recognizes that "there can authentically be constituted the first and only edition of oneself."[19] It is based on such an account of the interaction of psyche and spirit that Doran begins to introduce a notion of psychic conversion:

> Psychic conversion is conversion to attentiveness in that streak of sensitive consciousness, to internal communication, to responsible activity in regard to neural demands, to an openness to negotiate them persuasively and patiently.[20]

Next, Doran explains that symbols play a key role in the life of the psyche and sets out to explain this. He recalls a definition provided by Lonergan: "A symbol is an image of a real or imaginary object that evokes a feeling or is evoked by a feeling."[21] Regarding how symbols can be evoked by a feeling, he points to the dreams we experience while sleeping constitute such symbols and express "our existential orientations as world constitutive and self-constitutive subjects."[22] Turning to the way in which feelings can be evoked by symbol, he draws particularly on what Lonergan says about the role "symbols of mystery"[23] can play in human living. Lonergan notes that, "even adequate self-knowledge and explicit metaphysics may contract, but cannot eliminate, a 'known unknown.'"[24] Lonergan adds that we need encouragement in allowing our pure desire pursuit to support us in this orientation toward a known unknown and that, for this to happen, we need recourse to symbols of mystery to help "control human living." He describes these symbols as, "dynamic

19. Doran, *Dialectics of History*, 57.

20. Doran, *Dialectics of History*, [85].

21. Doran, *Dialectics of History*, 58 (quoting Bernard J. F. Lonergan, *Method in Theology,* ed. Robert M. Doran, and John D. Dadosky, Collected Works of Lonergan 14 (Toronto: University of Toronto Press, 2017), 64).

22. Doran, *Dialectics of History*, 95.

23. Lonergan, *Insight*, 571.

24. Lonergan, *Insight*, 571.

images which make sensible to human sensitivity what human intelligence reaches for or grasps."[25]

Moving beyond a reference to Lonergan, Doran turns to the thought of Sigmund Freud and, especially, Karl Jung.[26] He acknowledges that Freud is the founder of the discipline of psychoanalysis but he identifies a reductionism in this Viennese thinker, who wanted to attribute unconscious operations, and their expression in the psyche, entirely to a "biological quantum,"[27] above all to a process whereby we seek to repress our sex drive. By contrast, he traces how Jung insists that, in addition to the kind of impulses described by Freud, there exists an impulse that wells up from the unconscious that prompts a "process of development toward wholeness," which, "Jung calls individuation."[28] He explains that the kind of symbols to which Jung refers must be engaged with intelligently by intentional consciousness in order to bear fruit in the decision-making of a self-transcending person. He recalls Freud's statement, "the dream is the royal road to the unconscious,"[29] and adds, "the close connection of images and affects renders the dream a royal road to psychic conversion."[30]

Next, Doran recognizes in Jung a distinction between at least two kinds of symbol. The first are "personal symbols" that employ images from one's own memory and are formed by, "one's affective habits and one's spontaneous apprehension of possible values."[31] The second are "archetypal symbols," which employ images from nature, which seem to have an "archaic" quality and to be shared with all other human

---

25. Lonergan, *Insight*, 571.

26. Doran states, "Freud and Jung entertained what eventually were to become dialectically opposed understandings of psychic energy and of its functioning in personal development," Doran, "Dramatic Artistry and the Third Stage of Meaning," 260. See also, *Dialectics of History*, Chapter 10, "A Clarification by Contrast," 295–352, where Doran conducts a dialectical analysis of the thought of Jung.

27. Doran, "Dramatic Artistry and the Third Stage of Meaning," 260.

28. Doran, "Dramatic Artistry and the Third Stage of Meaning," 266.

29. Doran, *Dialectics of History*, 85.

30. Doran, *Dialectics of History*, 85.

31. Doran, *Dialectics of History*, 60.

beings in some form of a "universal unconscious." Of these symbols he states:

> Certain symbolic combinations can be understood only by appealing to deeper and more 'impersonal' sources than any theory of personal repression would allow. The strange and numinous effect of these images can be explained only by a dimension of psychic energy that is at least relatively autonomous in relation to the personal ego . . . They can be made conscious only in their own time, which is not dependent on the ego's determination. And when they are made conscious, the ego's attitude then must be one of respectful negotiation, for they obviously are invested with the greatest potential for development.[32]

Doran stresses the importance of a kind of reverend attentiveness to symbol in dream analysis—both for archetypal symbols and personal symbols. He relates psychic conversion to the attitude of "reverence" and "contemplation" that Jung recommends for those involved in dream analysis, speaking of, "the role of contemplation in the aesthetic production of the dramatic form of conscious living,"[33] Recalling that psyche and spirit operate in a tension of "dialectic of contraries" with each other, Doran speaks of how the individual will recognize both "possibility," and "project" as she explores her interior life. He explains that the former is related to our psyche, and the latter to our spirit. Of the former, he states, "possibility is past and matter, origin and limitation." Of the latter, he states: "project is future and spirit, finality and transcendence." He then adds, "Psychic energy is their meeting ground. The dream proposes both to make of the possible a project, and to ensure that the project remains possible."[34] In a subtle shifting of Jung's notion of contemplation, Doran states that we should attend with reverence to the dimensions of both psyche and spirit in our subjectivity:

---

32. Doran, *Dialectics of History*, 316–317.
33. Doran, "Insight and Archetype," 295.
34. Doran, "Insight and Archetype," 293.

The contemplative spirit retrieves and heals memory, and in so doing projects a possible future into which a body can move . . . The first of the transcendental precepts calls for attentiveness. It is the imperative least elucidated by Lonergan. Its other name is contemplation, its activity receptivity, its prime data dreams, and its function the provision of the possibility without which the projects of intelligence, reason, and decision are folly and degradation.[35]

Victimization, Bias, and the Need for Healing

Doran next follows Lonergan in analyzing the problems that arise in the authentic functioning of the psychic censor, problems that culminate in a problem of "moral impotence" that can only be solved by supernatural intervention of God in human consciousness to solve the problem of evil.[36]

Lonergan describes the phenomenon of dramatic bias as a "scotosis," or blind-spot.[37] He explains the phenomenon by drawing on two concepts of Freud: repression, and inhibition. Regarding the former, he describes the way the psychic censor blocks the emergence to consciousness of certain images, "to prevent the emergence into consciousness of perspectives that would give rise to unwanted insights."[38] Regarding the latter, he describes how the repressing of images lead to distorted affectivity. He recalls that, in the logic of psychic functioning, images are always linked to affects. He explains that, while dramatic bias can be successful in repressing images, it is less successful in blocking associated affects. The result is that in the inhibited person, where, "these demands will emerge into consciousness with the affect detached from its initial object and attached to some associated and more or less incongruous object."[39] He notes

35. Doran, "Insight and Archetype," 297.

36. The issues of moral impotence and the supernatural solution are addressed in the final three chapters of *Insight* (Lonergan, *Insight*, 618–752.)

37. Lonergan, *Insight*, 214–215.

38. Lonergan, *Insight*, 216.

39. Lonergan, *Insight*, 216.

that the inhibited person is unlikely to respond authentically to value or to make good decisions.

Doran extends this analysis of Lonergan by reference to the finalistic tension of the subject. He explains that dramatic bias occurs when complexes have become "pathological":

> Our psychic energy can be blocked, fixed in inflexible patterns, driven by compulsions, plagued by obsessions, weighed down by general anxiety or specific fears, resistant to insight, true judgment, and responsible action.[40]

He explains that such blocked psychic energy is the result of a victimized psyche. He acknowledges that, in cases such as drug addiction, this victimization may be the result of "one's own self-destructiveness."[41] However, he insists that a far more common source of victimization are those hurts received in childhood, for which we are not personally responsible, insisting: "psychic spontaneity as such is not morally responsible for its own disorder."[42]

Next, Doran draws on the notion of a tension, or duality, in consciousness to describe how inauthenticity occurs by over-emphasizing either of the poles of this duality:

> The tendency of our sinful nature is a tendency to the displacement toward either the captivity of the spirit in the rhythms of mere sensitivity or the hubris that rejects our groundedness in the schemes of recurrence of the body on which we depend for the very images that are required if we are to understand anything whatever.[43]

To some extent, Doran attributes both hubris and "captivity of the spirit in the rhythms of mere sensitivity" to dramatic bias, for which the individual is not morally responsible. However, he also draws on

---

40. Doran, *Dialectics of History*, 229.

41. Doran, *Dialectics of History*, 232.

42. Doran, *Dialectics of History*, 232. Elsewhere Doran asserts: "Dramatic bias is the consequence of autonomous complexes beyond the reach of immediate self-determination" (*Dialectics of History*, 233).

43. Doran, *Dialectics of History*, 55.

Lonergan's account of other biases, especially individual bias and group bias,[44] to acknowledge that much inauthentic behavior is the product of "our sinful nature." It is to be noted that the way Doran explores a notion of hubris is one of the ways in which his ethics differs most clearly from that of Lonergan.[45] Indeed, in an interview given late in life, he expresses his agreement with John Dadosky who speaks of the danger of "intellectualist bias" in the community of Lonergan scholars, which may occur when individuals pursue intellectual conversion without developing a counter-balancing psychic conversion.[46]

Next, Doran expands his notion of psychic conversion to address the challenge of healing the woundedness of victimized consciousness:

> Psychic conversion is a transformation of the psychic component of what Freud calls 'the censor' from a repressive to a constructive agency in a person's development.[47]

Doran notes that, in spite of the unfreedom involved in dramatic bias, it is possible for individuals to employ their intentional self-transcendence, such as it is, to recognize that "something is wrong" with the way they function and to seek help. He explains how valuable it is to then take a series of steps: "first, one can recognize that the complex is a victim;" next, he states, "one can adopt an attitude of compassion in its regard": finally, he speaks of resorting to psychoanalysis as demonstrating a "willingness to cooperate with whatever redemptive forces are available to heal the disorder of darkness and to transform the contorted energies."[48]

---

44. Lonergan, *Insight*, 244–250.

45. Doran explores the relationship between his and Lonergan's approach to ethics in: "Discernment and Lonergan's Fourth Level of Consciousness," *Gregorianum* 89, no. 4 (2008), 790–902.

46. Doran, *Consciousness in Two Ways*: 18. See, John K Dadosky, "Desire, Bias, and Love: Revisiting Lonergan's Philosophical Anthropology," *Irish Theological Quarterly*, 77, no. 3 (2012), 244–264.

47. Doran, *Dialectics of History*, 59.

48. Doran, *Dialectics of History*, 239.

Doran recognizes that attending to victimization is common to most psychotherapeutic techniques and involves helping a person to an act of insight into hurts from the past that have caused pathological complexes. This, in turn, can result in a cathartic experience whereby one recognizes that this memory has been functioning destructively at an unconscious level and, by virtue of this insight, one gains some freedom from these negative effects. Nevertheless, Doran qualifies this appeal to psychoanalysis as the answer to dramatic bias. He explains how dramatic bias is associated with defence mechanisms that resist the insights of such analysis.[49] He suggests that a vicious circle easily emerges that regards, "the willingness to negotiate emotional darkness," and concludes that, easily, "the power of the [pathological] complex" can undermine the effectiveness of psychoanalysis to the point that, ultimately, it "negates the possibility of self-transcendent behavior."[50]

The Divine Solution for the Problem of Evil

Having explained how easily questions of moral impotence afflict efforts at healing by psychotherapeutic means, Doran asserts, "the freedom to deal compassionately with our own darkness must be given to us," and, invoking Lonergan's notion of the two ways of development states: "we cannot find that freedom in the creative vector of our own consciousness."[51] At this point, he follows the reasoning of Lonergan, as outlined in Chapter 20 of *Insight*.[52]

---

49. At this point, it is worth noting that Doran conducts an extensive critique of modern psychoanalysis claiming that, like Jung, they have an inadequate understanding of intentionality (Doran, *Dialectics of History*, 46. See also *Dialectics of History*, Chapter 9, "Reorienting Depth Psychology.")

50. Doran, *Dialectics of History*, 241. Parenthesis added by the present author.

51. Doran, Dialectics of History, 241–2. We might note that Doran is not stating that no psychotherapy works unless explicit reference is made to Christian principles of God's grace. Rather, he holds that God's grace is at work implicitly—or "anonymously—in all successful exercises of healing in psychotherapy. So it is that we note the reference to "willingness to cooperate with whatever redemptive forces" in the above quotation on psychotherapy.

52. Lonergan, *Insight*, Chapter 20, "Special Transcendent Knowledge," 709–752.

In that work, Lonergan sates, "because God is omniscient, he knows man's plight. Because he is omnipotent, he can remedy it, because he is good he wills to do so."[53] He adds, that the divine solution for the problem of evil "will be in some sense transcendent or supernatural. For what arises from nature is the problem."[54] Earlier in the work, Lonergan had introduced a metaphysical vocabulary to speak of habits of human behavior in terms of "conjugate forms." Now he states the supernatural intervention of God will involve the introduction of new "conjugate forms of faith and hope and charity."[55] Clearly, such reference to intellect and will implies that the individual is conscious of receiving God's grace. However, having explained how dramatic bias penetrates the unconscious, he begins to explore how grace "must also penetrate to the sensitive level and envelop it."[56] At this point, Lonergan states that the communication of the divine solution to human beings will need to include the use of symbols of the supernatural "mystery" into which the individual is being incorporated. He explains that, "man's sensitivity needs symbols that unlock its transforming dynamism."[57] He concludes:

> The full realization of the solution must include the sensible data that are demanded by man's sensitive nature and that will command his attention, nourish his imagination, stimulate his intelligence and will, release his affectivity, control his aggressivity, and, as central features of the world of sense, intimate its finality, its yearning for God.[58]

This statement is one of the places in Lonergan's work where he comes closest to Doran's thought on psychic conversion. And, certainly, Doran builds on these statements. The younger Jesuit states, "there is a transformation of the psyche under the influence of the supernatural or transcendent conjugate forms of faith, hope and charity."[59]

---

53. Lonergan, *Insight*, 716.
54. Lonergan, *Insight*, 716.
55. Lonergan, *Insight*, 744.
56. Lonergan, *Insight*, 744.
57. Lonergan, *Insight*, 744.
58. Lonergan, *Insight*, 745.
59. Doran, "Insight and Archetype," 304.

The Anagogic Symbol

Doran develops this theme by conducting a study of the thought of Karl Jung. He makes it clear that he plans to disagree with aspects of Jung's thought when he states, "because Jung lacked an adequate understanding of intentionality he fared poorly in treating the problem of evil."[60] He asserts that Jung's notions of archetypal symbol and personal symbol need to be complemented by an understanding of "anagogic symbol."[61] Introducing this kind of symbol, he explains that, "while they are taken from nature, they do not imitate nature as do archetypal symbols, but point to, intimate, the transformation of nature itself into a new creation."[62] He explains that they are "radically determined by one's participation in the divine solution to the problem of evil."[63] As with all symbols, he states that this kind of symbol is first experienced in our dream life.

> Anagogic dream symbols are preeminently characterized by these five elements. The feelings associated with them stretch our affective capacities to their inexpressible fulness; the known unknown that they intend is the incomprehensible mystery of God; their internal communication integrates the person precisely as a relation to this incomprehensible mystery; their archeology reaches to the creative source, and their teleology to the ultimate destiny, of everything; and their effectiveness is that of grace, and not simply of the transformative powers of nature.[64]

Following on dreams, Doran speaks of how figures such as poets and religious mystics will express anagogic symbols in artistic form. He describes how anagogic symbols will often reverse the natural symbolism of archetypes and offers the following example from the Hebrew scriptures:

---

60. Doran, "Insight and Archetype," 303.

61. Doran, explains that he draws on the thought of the literary critic, Northrop Frye, "for the distinction of archetypal and anagogic (while transposing his distinction from literary criticism to psychology and theology)" (*Dialectics of History*, 280.

62. Doran, "Insight and Archetype, 303.

63. Doran, "Insight and Archetype, 303.

64. Doran, *Dialectics of History*, 288.

The wolf shall dwell with the lamb,

. . . The sucking child shall play over the hole of the asp,

and the weaned child shall put his hand on the adder's den

(Isaiah 11.6–9).[65]

The Cross

Doran next explores the particular effectiveness of the cross of Jesus as an anagogic symbol. In order to do this, he first identifies a particular form of religious conversion that he calls soteriological conversion. He describes how this goes beyond a general confidence in the unconditional love of God to include a conviction that the divine solution to the problem of evil has already arrived in history. He states that, "the soteriological differentiation [of consciousness] is itself a conversion" and adds, "soteriological conversion implies a commitment to a certain insight about history."[66] Next, he analyzes why the cross of Jesus is such a potent symbol of healing.

Doran describes how the love of a fellow human can produce healing by helping victimized individuals to address their emotional darkness with compassion. He describes how individuals with victimized psyches put up any number of resistances to believing that the love of another is sincere, up to the point, sometimes, of inflicting harm on the one trying to love them. He adds that, often, what finally convinces such people is when the one who loves them is prepared to accept such harm and to enter into the "private hell"[67] of their suffering so as

---

65. This Biblical text is cited in Doran, *Dialectics of History*, 273. See also section, "The Anagogic Context of Psychological Experience," *Dialectics of History*, 284–286.

66. Doran, *Dialectics of History*, 173. Parenthesis added. Doran identifies how his insights into soteriological conversion and symbol also find a solid foundation in his mentor's thought (Doran, "Insight and Archetype," 304). In Chapter 20 of *Insight*, Lonergan speaks of how the supernatural solution impacts the level of "sensitivity and intersubjectivity" in the subject (*Insight*, 762–763) and even explores the links of psyche to bodiliness under the influence of God's solution: "It is to be noted that this transformation of sensitivity and intersubjectivity penetrates to the physiological level though the clear instances appear only in the intensity of mystical experience" (*Insight*, 763).

67. Doran states: "John Dunne has distinguished two types of human suffering. There is the hell of the night of private suffering, the suffering of isolation and

to suffer with them: "Healing will frequently be mediated precisely in and through the suffering of the lover due to the darkness of the beloved."[68] After first describing such love in terms of human interaction, Doran insists that, ultimately, love like this is "beyond human capacity."[69] He then explains that the symbol *par excellence* of a readiness to suffer for others is the cross of Jesus Christ and that, consequently, "Christianity has some genuine universal significance."[70] He describes how a Christian will mostly find the ability to love selflessly if he or she relates personally and explicitly to the symbol of the cross and so begin to exercise a "participation in the specifically paschal dimension of 'what Jesus did.'"[71] Doran concludes that it is only because of the divine intervention in history, completed in the self-sacrificing act of Jesus Christ (and the resurrection that followed it), that our damaged psyches find healing:

> Love alone releases one to be creatively self-transcendent . . . then life begins anew, everything changes, a new principle takes over . . . we are lifted above ourselves and carried along as parts within an ever more intimate and ever more liberating dynamic whole.[72]

Doran next brings to bear on Lonergan's reflection on the law of the cross[73] the fruits of his exploration of psychoanalysis. He suggests that individuals undergoing healing begin to feel an attraction to begin to live in "fidelity to the just and mysterious law of the cross."[74] This

victimization; and there is the night of the suffering of compassion and forgiveness . . . The hell of the night of private suffering is not redemptive. The night of the suffering of compassion and forgiveness is redemptive (*Dialectics of History*, 114).

68. Doran, *Dialectics of History*, 243–4.

69. Doran, *Dialectics of History*, 243–4.

70. Doran, *Dialectics of History*, 108. The significance of this claim to the universal significance of Christianity is immensely significant for a theology of religion.

71. Doran, *Dialectics of History*, 121.

72. Doran, *Dialectics of History*, 41.

73. Bernard J. F. Lonergan, *The Redemption,* trans. Michael G. Shields, ed. Robert M. Doran, H. Daniel Monsour, and Jeremy D. Wilkins, Collected Works of Lonergan 9 (Toronto: University of Toronto Press, 2018), 197.

74. Doran, *Dialectics of History*, 113.

includes an ability to recognize how bad behavior on the part of other individuals is often the product, at least in part, of a prior victimization. Spontaneously, individuals who have begun a process of healing desire to pass this on to others by returning good for evil. Thus, a process begins whereby the effort to assist in the healing of others, through an exercise in self-sacrificing love, becomes related to one's own journey of being healed. Doran notes that one needs to take care to be realistic about just who can be helped and who cannot, but concludes:

> Perhaps one knows oneself to be healed only when precisely the same material dynamics of victimization that once drove one into the hell of private suffering now can be responded to with compassion and forgiveness.[75]

Part 2: The Psyche and the *Spiritual Exercises of St. Ignatius*

The book called *The Spiritual Exercises of St. Ignatius*, was approved for publication by Pope Paul III in 1548. It was formulated by Ignatius as a means of inviting others to enjoy the spiritual experiences that he himself had enjoyed, and, above all, choose a state of life in which to express Christian discipleship. In its first paragraph, Ignatius describes the aim of this retreat experience:

> Just as taking a walk, journeying on foot, and running are bodily exercises, so we call Spiritual Exercises every way of preparing and disposing the soul to rid itself of all inordinate attachments, and, after their removal, of seeking and finding the will of God in the disposition of our life for the salvation of our soul.[76]

---

75. Doran, *Dialectics of History*, 245. In another contribution to this book, Jeremy Blackwood traces how Doran, in publications after *Dialectics of History*, deepens his analysis of psychic conversion and the law of the cross by reference to the thought of René Girard.

76. Ignatius, *The Spiritual Exercises of St. Ignatius*, no. 1. A numbered paragraph structure has long been used for citations from the *Spiritual Exercises*, and I limit my references to this.

The book produced by Ignatius is intended as a set of instructions for the one who will accompany the one undergoing these exercises.[77] The second paragraph cautions the one accompanying the retreatant to recognize the limits of the role she has to play.[78] He recommends that she present the instructions for daily prayer proposed by Ignatius "and add only a short or summary explanation." He stresses that the one accompanying is not a teacher but rather one who accompanies a process where the main drama is occurring directly between God and the soul of the retreatant. He explains:

> Now this produces greater spiritual relish and fruit than if one in giving the Exercises had explained and developed the meaning at great length. For it is not much knowledge that fills and satisfies the soul, but the intimate understanding and relish of the truth.[79]

The experience of the *Spiritual Exercises* is divided into four thematic "weeks," of variable length, usually amounting to thirty days. Broadly speaking, the First Week involves a reflection on one's sin and the receiving of the grace of forgiveness for this. The Second Week involves a reflection on the public life of Jesus, mostly as portrayed in the Gospels, and the invitation to make a life choice, or "election," concerning how best to follow Jesus. The Third Week involves a meditation on the passion of Our Lord and the Fourth Week meditates on the resurrection.

While the book of the *Spiritual Exercises* is not primarily intended as an object of academic study, since their first publication, considerable study of the text has been conducted, especially by Jesuits

---

77. Howard Grey SJ points out that Ignatius tended to avoid the term "spiritual director" in the *Spiritual Exercises* so as to encourage an approach of listening accompaniment on the part of one guiding the retreat. In what follows, I also avoid the term. See, Fr. Howard Grey SJ, a series of ten lectures delivered in Georgetown University, USA, "The Dynamics of the *Spiritual Exercises*" (https://president.georgetown.edu/initiatives/spiritual-exercises/), Lecture 1. These lectures represent the best of current approaches to the training of those who will accompany others in undergoing the *Spiritual Exercises*.

78. I adopt a terminological tactic of referring to the retreatant as "him" and the one accompanying him as "her."

79. Ignatius, *The Spiritual Exercises*, no. 2.

seeking to provide commentaries that expand on the sometimes lapidary instructions of Ignatius himself.[80] Over the centuries, these commentaries tended to have a dialectical relationship with the prevailing ideas in philosophy and theology. On the one hand, they tended to reflect current ideas on anthropology, theology, grace etc. On the other hand, an appeal to the *Spiritual Exercises* sometimes became a motive to intervene in current theological debates.[81] Around the time of Vatican II, a consensus emerged that the understanding of the *Spiritual Exercises*, and how to direct them, had been adversely affected by the mentality of Neo-Scholasticism. Figures such as Karl Rahner, and his brother and fellow Jesuit, Hugo, became prominent in providing new interpretations of the *Spiritual Exercises*.[82] Conversely, Karl Rahner would claim that the *Spiritual Exercises* were a major influence on his theological anthropology.[83] Lonergan did not provide any such reflection, but a small sub-genre of Lonergan studies emerged where individuals attempted to employ Lonergan's thought in this way. The most notable exercise of this kind is a book, *The Dynamics of Desire: Bernard J. F. Lonergan, S.J., on the Spiritual Exercises of St Ignatius of Loyola*, produced in 2006 by James Connor et. al.[84] This work is structured as a detailed commentary on the

---

80. A major survey of such commentaries was conducted by Joseph Maréchal in the early twentieth century. See Joseph Maréchal, S.J., Études sur la psychologie des mystiques, 2 vols (*Brussels, Édition Universelle*, 1937).

81. Philip Endean identifies how an article published in 1920 by Joseph Maréchal had a significant impact both on the study of the *Spiritual Exercises* at the time and on some current theological debates (Philip Endean S.J., "The Ignatian Prayer of the Senses," *The Heythrop Journal*, 31:4 (1990) 391–418, at 394, citing Joseph Maréchal, S.J., "Un essai de méditation orentée vers la contemplation," in Édudes sur la psychologie des mystiques, volume 2, 362–382.)

82. See, Karl Rahner SJ, *Spiritual Exercises* (London, Sheed, 1967): Hugo Rahner SJ, *Ignatius the Theologian* (London, Chapman, 1968.)

83. See, Harvey Egan, "The Mystical Theology of Karl Rahner," *The Way*, 52/2 (April 2013), 43–62.

84. James L. O'Connor SJ et. al., *The Dynamics of Desire: Bernard J. F. Lonergan, S.J., on the Spiritual Exercises of St Ignatius of Loyola* (Washington, D.C.: Woodstock Centre for Theological Reflection, 2006.) See also, Tad Dunne, *Spiritual Exercises for Today: Contemporary Presentation of the Classical Spiritual Exercises of Loyola* (New York: Harper Collins, 1991). A distinct line subgenre in Lonergan studies involves identifying the influence of Ignatius on Lonergan. See for e.g. Gordon Rixon, SJ., "Bernard Lonergan and Mysticism," *Theological Studies*, 62, no. 3 (2001), 479–497.

exercises presented in each of the four Weeks. To date, little study of the *Spiritual Exercises* has been attempted employing Doran's expansion on Lonergan's thought.[85] The following reflection seeks to begin such a line of reflection, which, ultimately, deserves to be treated at a similar length to the book of Connors.

The Cross and Repentance for Sin

There is one major way in which the First Week of the *Spiritual Exercises* converges with the thought of Doran: both stress the power of the symbol of the Cross of Christ to prompt genuine conversion. In the course of the First Week, Ignatius offers a series of exercises to guide a process of prayer that can take up to ten days. He invites retreatants to reflect on how God is a loving creator; on the first sin of the Angels; the sin of Adam and Eve: how sin spreads to the whole world; on hell; and, last but not least, one's own history of sin.[86] However, at regular intervals, Ignatius invites the retreatant to imagine that he is standing before the Cross of Christ:

Imagine Christ Our Lord present before you upon the cross, and begin to speak with him, asking how it is that though He is the Creator, He has stooped to become man, and to pass from eternal life to death here in time, that thus He might die for our sins. I shall also reflect upon myself and ask:

What have I done for Christ?

What am I doing for Christ?

What ought I to do for Christ?

As I behold Christ in this plight, nailed to the cross, I shall ponder upon what presents itself to my mind.[87]

---

85. I have made one attempt at relating Doran's thought to themes from the *Spiritual Exercises*: Gerard Whelan SJ, "Robert Doran and the Spiritual Exercises of St. Ignatius: A Dialogue with Joseph Maréchal on the Meaning of the Application of the Senses," in the e-journal, *Ignaziana, Revista di Ricerca Teologica*, 26(2018), 268–281. https://www.unigre.it/unigre/sito/PUG_HG_03O820150936/uv_papers/2017/Revista%20Ignaziana26-2018.pdf [2020-04-04].

86. Ignatius, *Spiritual Exercises*, nos. 40–90.

87. Ignatius, *Spiritual Exercises*, no. 52.

By such a repeated reflection on the cross, Ignatius hopes that the retreatant will undergo the affective experience that is the purpose of the First Week. This experience involves a series of steps: an appreciation of the unconditional love of God; an intense awareness of the sinful ways in which one has neither recognized this love nor responded authentically to it: an act of repentance; and an experience of being forgiven. Ignatius instructs the one accompanying the retreatant to look out for a moment of sincere repentance in the retreatant that is matched by a deep experience of God's forgiveness. He instructs her to delay or accelerate the conclusion of the First Week according to whether this event has occurred.[88]

Ignatius does not have the language of psychoanalysis at his disposal, but the compatibility with Doran is clear, who speaks of the unique effectiveness of the symbol of the cross in overcoming the defence mechanisms that oppose therapeutic insight and anagogic healing. Doran stresses the role of this symbol in healing victimization, but he also understands it as mediating an experience of forgiveness for these sins which we have committed consciously and freely.

Ignatian Contemplation

If the most obvious overlap between Ignatius and Doran lies in the First Week and their shared confidence in the symbolic power of the cross, the next most-clear overlap in their thought pertains to what has come to be called Ignatian Contemplation. As Ignatius moves the retreatant to the Second Week, he invites him to increasingly employ the powers of imagination in prayer. The link to Doran's thought is this: such a use of imagination can be interpreted as a form of "induced dreaming." Here one can recall all that Doran has said about three kinds of symbols that appear in our dream: personal, archetypal, and anagogic. Ignatian contemplation can be understood as a process of allowing the anagogic symbols of Christianity penetrate and transform both the conscious and the unconscious mind of the retreatant, thus helping to elicit a life-decision of discipleship on his part.

---

88. Ignatius, *Spiritual Exercises*, no. 71.

As with the First Week, the Second Week can take up to ten days, with each "Ignatian Day," involving four or five hours of silent prayer.[89] In the course of the Second Week, the retreatant is invited to engage imaginatively with the events of the life of Jesus, from his nativity to the days before his passion. At the beginning of his instructions for the Second Week, Ignatius recommends that each hour of prayer be structured in the same way.[90] At the beginning of the hour, one is invited to spend some minutes engaged with "three preludes." The first involves, "Calling to mind the history of the subject." This, usually, involves reading the text of the Gospel recommended for that hour. The second involves making a "Mental presentation of the place." This involves, as already described, attempting to apply one's imagination to the scene, usually placing oneself within it. Ignatius then outlines the third prelude. He states that the retreatant should not fear to state boldly the grace that is desired, and should "ask for an intimate knowledge of our Lord, who has become man for me, that I may love him more and follow him more closely."[91]

After these preludes, there follows the main body of the prayer period where the retreatant prays through the text, paying attention to what his imagination permits him to represent and what it does not. Toward the end of the hour of prayer, the retreatant is invited to devote some minutes to a final "Colloquy" where, "according to the light that I have received, I will beg for the grace to follow and imitate more closely our Lord."[92]

Three immediate observations on this structure of prayer are appropriate. First, the third prelude involves a prayer for an "intimate knowledge." and is clearly an affair of the psyche, where such feelings of intimacy will be registered. Second, such knowledge of our Lord is now expected to prompt a desire to "follow him more closely." Here we recognize a progression from the grace prayed for in the First Week, which primarily involved a passive experience of accepting God's

89. Ignatius, *Spiritual Exercises*, no. 72.
90. Ignatius, *Spiritual Exercises*, nos. 101–109.
91. Ignatius, *Spiritual Exercises*, no. 108.
92. Ignatius, *Spiritual Exercises*, no. 109.

forgiveness, to one that engages human free will as one decides how to respond to this love. Here one notes the relevance of Lonergan's distinction between "operative grace," which is the primary focus of the First Week, and "cooperative grace," which is key to the Second Week.[93] A third reflection is that the Colloquy indicates how different retreatants experience "light" received during prayer in diverse ways and at different times. This implies that the Second Week involves a process where graces may or may not be received and where different retreatants are likely to proceed at different paces.

Repetition and the Application of the Senses

The fact that during the Second Week no two retreatants will contemplate Gospel scenes in exactly the same way becomes evident when Ignatius speaks about "repetition" in the Ignatian Day. In his instructions, he proposes that, normally, the first two hours of prayer, employ two different Gospel texts. Strictly speaking, he preserves the term contemplation (*contemplación*) for these two hours, whereas he calls the next two hours "repetitions" (*repetición*.) During repetition, selected material from the first and second hours are repeated. Ignatius instructs: "In doing this, attention should always be given to some more important parts in which one has experienced understanding, consolation, or desolation."[94] Here Ignatius understands that the one who accompanies the retreatant has a key role to play. It should be she who decides just what passage should be repeated. Ignatius elaborates on the nature of consolation and desolation at length in an appendix to the *Spiritual Exercises*, where he provides twenty-two "Rules for the Discernment of Spirits"[95] and recommends that the one accompanying the retreatant invite him to read those rules as she judges appropriate

---

93. Lonergan's theology of grace is outlined in: J. Michael Stebbins, *The Divine Initiative: Grace, World-Order, and Human Freedom in the Early Writings of Bernard Lonergan* (Toronto: University of Toronto Press, 1995).

94. Ignatius, *Spiritual Exercises*, no. 118.

95. Ignatius, *Spiritual Exercises*, nos. 313–336.

for the moment through which he is passing. However, for one familiar with Doran's thought, a key insight into what Ignatius means by
consolation and desolation is already evident in the presentation Ignatius makes of the notion of repetition.

Interpreted in the light of Doran's thought, consolation can be
understood as the result of allowing one's consciousness and unconscious mind to accept an anagogic symbol as constitutive of its operating. In this context, returning in repetition to a passage where
consolation has occurred can have the obvious effect of deepening this
positive experience. By contrast, desolation can be understood occurring when one resists the influence of an anagogic symbol, usually
because one is trapped in pathological defence mechanisms. Revisiting such moments of desolation involves becoming increasingly aware
of one's resistance, and, if possible, its causes. Hopefully, this leads to
becoming more open to the advent of consolation. Here the role of one
accompanying the *Spiritual Exercises* is key. Left to his own devices, a
retreatant may be reluctant to revisit a part of a text that has provoked
a desolation—which can often be highly uncomfortable. The one
accompanying this retreatant may need to quietly insist that he return
to the occasion of his desolation and contemplate this scene further.
Here a principle applies that is well known in psychoanalysis: individuals are unlikely to identify and address their own defence mechanisms
without the aid of a therapist.

On the question of repetition in times of desolation, it might
help to offer some examples. It may occur that a retreatant who has
remained in desolation all day experiences an anagogic dream during
the night that changes everything for him, releasing a joyful affect and
allowing him to easily imagine himself in a Gospel scene that caused
him such problems the day before. Another example can be that when
the retreatant repeats a Gospel text that provoked desolation, he may
experience a flash of a hurtful memory from his own past. With the
help of good accompaniment, he can be helped to recognize that it
may be this real event, recalled in memory, that is a source of resistance
to the anagogic symbol. At this point, he can be encouraged to go "off
script" and begin a spontaneous dialogue with Jesus, as imagined in

the Gospel scene with which he has been praying. What can then follow is a breakthrough moment where the anagogic symbol overcomes resistance and the individual feels both loved and healed, and willing to consider questions of how to follow Jesus in his life-decisions.

The fifth hour of the Ignatian Day involves a particular kind of repetition which Ignatius calls an "Application of the Senses."[96] Here he instructs: "it will be profitable with the aid of the imagination to apply the five senses to the subject matter of the First and Second Contemplation (*contemplación*.)"[97] He then recommends:

> In seeing in imagination the persons, and in contemplating and meditating in detail the circumstances in which they are, and then in drawing some fruit from what has been seen . . . to hear what they are saying, or what they might say, and then by reflecting on oneself to draw some profit from what has been heard . . . to smell and to taste with the senses of smell and taste the infinite gentleness and sweetness of the divinity of the soul and of its virtues and of everything according to the person who is being contemplated reflecting on oneself and drawing profit from it.[98]

From a Doran perspective, it is striking how Ignatius employs terms that relate to the first level of consciousness and are registered in the psyche: sight, hearing, smell, taste. One can conclude that Ignatius is hoping that by the time of the fifth hour of the Ignatian Day resistance to the anagogic symbols proposed in the contemplation of that day has already been overcome and the appropriate steps—for that day—have been taken toward reflecting about how to respond to this love. At this stage—often held at midnight or in the early hours of the morning—the application of the senses involves a deepening, yet further, of the way that the anagogic symbol penetrates the psyche. This can be understood as allowing the dimension of operative grace in the symbol to come to the fore and to open oneself to a deeply

---

96. Ignatius, *Spiritual Exercises*, nos. 121–126.

97. Ignatius, *Spiritual Exercises*, nos. 121.

98. Ignatius, *Spiritual Exercises*, nos. 121–126.

mystical experience as one continues to contemplate it.[99] It seems clear that what Ignatius states in terms of the Application of the Senses is related to the spirit of contemplation that Jung advocates for attending to all dream symbols. Here one can also recall a statement by Lonergan describing how God's supernatural gifts can penetrate the different levels of the subject:

> It is to be noted that this transformation of sensitivity and inter-subjectivity penetrates to the physiological level though the clear instances appear only in the intensity of mystical experience.[100]

Discernment and Election

As already mentioned, overcoming resistance to anagogic symbols can release in the subject a desire for a life decision that employs the gifts of cooperative grace. Ignatius explains that a central aim of the Second Week is to help the retreatant make an "election" regarding the way he wants to follow the Lord in the future. With this in mind, he provides the one who accompanies the retreatant with a series of non-scriptural exercises for prayer that should be employed when she judges the time is right. A first set of exercises are introductory to the decision-making moment and have the aim of freeing the retreatant from "inordinate attachments" which might limit his freedom in being open to hearing God's will.[101] Then, exercises are proposed that are intended to directly accompany the making of a decision.[102]

---

99. Joseph Maréchal agrees with this point. He employs his interest in neurology and his emerging philosophy of transcendental Thomism to stress the importance of the "Application of the Senses," stating: "All our senses are susceptible to being transposed symbolically onto the level of ideas. A transposition grounded in affectivity" (Maréchal, "Application de sens," cols. 826–827. Cited in Endean, 397, note 13.)

100. Lonergan, *Insight*, 763.

101. See Ignatius, *Spiritual Exercises*, no. 1, mentioned above, which states the general purpose of the *Spiritual Exercises*. See also, "Introduction to the Consideration of Different States of Life," (no. 135); "A Meditation on Two Standards" (nos. 136–148); "Three Classes of Men" (nos. 149–157); and "Three Kinds of Humility" (nos. 165–168).

102. See, "Introduction to Making a Choice of a way of life"; "Matters About Which a Choice Should Be Made"; "Three Times When a Correct and Good Choice of a Way of Life May Be Made"; "Two Ways of Making A Choice Of a Way Of Life" (Ignatius, *Spiritual Exercises*, nos 169–184.)

Ignatius clarifies that the kind of decision to which he is referring is not one between good and evil, but rather: "that all matters of which we wish to make a choice be either indifferent or good in themselves."[103] Next, he is especially interested in the possibility of a retreatant making a decision regarding a state of life: "things that fall under an unchangeable choice, such as the priesthood, marriage, etc."[104] He then reminds the retreatant of the importance of remaining free from inordinate attachments. Next, he invites him to make a decision. He speaks of three ways in which people tend to make decisions. The first is "when God our Lord so moves and attracts the will that a devout soul without hesitation, or the possibility of hesitation, follows what has been manifested to it."[105] The second is, "when much light and understanding are derived through experience of desolations and consolations and discernment of diverse spirits."[106] The third is when one finds oneself "in a time of tranquillity . . . when the soul is not agitated by different spirits, and has free and peaceful use of its natural powers."[107] He explains that first and second ways of decision-making can occur relatively quickly and unambiguously. By contrast, the third way of decision-making can require more time.

Ignatius provides an extra set of exercises for the individual who finds himself in the third situation. A key moment in these exercises is where Ignatius stresses the importance of being "indifferent, without any inordinate attachment." He elaborates:

> I should be like a balance at equilibrium, without leaning to either side, that I might be ready to follow whatever I perceive is more for the glory and praise of God our Lord and for the salvation of my soul.[108]

---

103. Ignatius, *Spiritual Exercises*, no. 170.

104. Ignatius, *Spiritual Exercises*, no. 171. It should be noted that Ignatius also welcomes to undergo the *Spiritual Exercises* individuals who have already made their major life decisions, accepting that such individuals will make elections that have less major import for their life-direction.

105. Ignatius, *Spiritual Exercises*, no. 175.

106. Ignatius, *Spiritual Exercises*, no. 176.

107. Ignatius, *Spiritual Exercises*, no. 177.

108. Ignatius, *Spiritual Exercises*, no. 177.

He then instructs:

> I should beg God our Lord to deign to move my will, and to
> bring to my mind what I ought to do in this matter that would
> be more for His praise and glory.[109]

Overlaps with the thought of Doran are immediately evident here.
The image of "a balance at equilibrium," reminds one of Doran's reference to "taut equilibrium" and how, for Doran, the balance concerns
the "creative tension, between the organic and the spiritual."[110] Similarly, when Ignatius encourages the retreatant to pray that God will
"deign to move my will, and to bring to my mind what I ought to do"
one thinks of the way Doran describes a process of the psyche releasing into consciousness images that indicate decisions one should take.
Doran speaks of "an aesthetic detachment that allows there to emerge
the inevitability of forms," which results in their being constituted "the
first and only edition of oneself."[111]

In fact, from the point of view of Doran's analysis of symbol, what
is going on in the prayer of election is complex. It is not simply a question of opening oneself to the influence of an anagogic symbol. What is
at issue, now, is grace cooperating with human freedom as one decides
how to respond to the anagogic experience. Here, one recalls the quotation offered above, when the notion of anagogic dream symbols was
introduced. Of such dream symbols, Doran states, "their archeology
reaches to the creative source, and their teleology to the ultimate destiny,
of everything."[112] The point to note in the context of election, is that
the individual needs to draw on the creative source of his human nature
as well as the pull towards vertical finality provided by grace. We can
deduce that the way an individual responds to the call to discipleship of
Christ will have a lot to do with one's relationship with both archetypal
and personal symbols.[113] Furthermore, it is worth noting that Doran

---

109. Ignatius, *Spiritual Exercises*, no. 180.

110. Doran, *Dialectics of History*, 57 (quoting Lonergan, *Method in Theology*, 57).

111. Doran, *Dialectics of History*, 57.

112. Doran, *Dialectics of History*, 288.

113. Doran, *Dialectics of History*, 60.

acknowledges that his reflections on soteriological conversion and ana-gogic symbols remain relatively underdeveloped in *Theology and the Dialectics of History*.[114] In this respect, I hazard to suggest that reflection on the *Spiritual Exercises*, and not least the moment of election in the Second Week, can be a *locus theologicus* for deepening such a reflection.

In effect, Doran explains that all our natural capacities to symbol-ize exist in a relationship of obediential potency to anagogic symbols. When Doran explores the supernatural pole of this dialectic, he states "there is a transformation of psychic energy under the influence of the supernatural or transcendent conjugate forms or habits of faith and hope and charity"[115] and appeals to the interpreter "to understand the anagogic as the final hermeneutic determinant of the meaning and value of all other symbolic deliverances, including archetypal sym-bols."[116] By contrast, when speaking of the natural side of this dialectic, Doran recognizes that grace does not overwhelm nature, but rather, represents an elevation of the finality already present in it. On this theme, he continues to draw on Jung's insights into individuation and how there is a finalistic tension in consciousness between that aspect of the psyche that represents limitation, which he calls "possibility," and that which represents finality, "project." I find it helpful to reread the following statement, made in terms of the natural process of individu-ation, in terms of the process whereby the human notion of "project" becomes transformed by an encounter with anagogic symbols:

> Project is future and spirit, finality and transcendence, while pos-sibility is past and matter, origin and limitation. Project is con-sciousness, possibility the unconscious. Project is anticipation, possibility is memory. Psychic energy is their meeting ground. The dream proposes both to make of the possible a project, and to ensure that the project remains possible.[117]

---

114. Doran used to say this in the 1990s when I was studying with him. I leave it to others to judge to what degree he compensates for this deficiency in his later writings.

115. Doran, "Insight and Archetype," 304.

116. Doran, "Insight and Archetype," 305.

117. Doran, "Insight and Archetype," 293.

Conclusion

A purpose of this contribution has been to explain what Doran means by psychic conversion in the context of applying this notion to an understanding of the *Spiritual Exercises of St. Ignatius*. A number of final conclusions come to mind. One is that there remains much more to be said on the matter that has been discussed. One could hope for a book-length study of the *Spiritual Exercises* employing Doran's insights to parallel the one produced by James Connor et. al., which employs only Lonergan's thought for this purpose. Secondly, employing Doran's thought in the sub-discipline of the academic study of the *Spiritual Exercises* could, in my opinion, improve the way those who accompany retreatants are trained. A conclusion that emerges from these reflections is that it will help if the one accompanying the retreatant is both intellectually and psychically converted. Thirdly, the academic study of the *Spiritual Exercises* based on Doran's thought will need to include a dialectical engagement with other current interpreters of the *Spiritual Exercises*. Here one notes that, currently, many commentators apply some form of Rahnerian anthropology to the task of interpreting the *Spiritual Exercises*. One recalls that within the community of Lonergan studies there is a growing consensus that there exist in Rahner's thought counterpositions that need reversing.[118] One can conclude, therefore, that there is room to improve on some current interpretations of the *Spiritual Exercises*.[119] Finally, I recall that

---

118. E.g., Louis Roy, O.P., "Rahner's Epistemology and its Implications for Theology," in *Lonergan and Loyola: "I will Be Propitious to You in Rome,"* Lonergan Workshop, Volume 22 (Boston, Boston College, 2011), 422–439.

119. I have extended such a dialectical critique to Philip Endean where I suggest that he insufficiently distinguishes operative from cooperative grace when he criticizes the interpretation that Maréchal makes of the "Application of the Senses" (Whelan, "Robert Doran and the Spiritual Exercises of St. Ignatius," 281, note 56). Also of note, is the critique made by Franco Imoda SJ. of Harvey Egan (who helped Lonergan recognize Ignatian themes at play in Lonergan's thought.) Imoda who is a student of both Lonergan and Doran, suggests that Egan pays insufficient attention to the role that unconscious motivations play in the retreatant and how, during Ignatian contemplation retreatants can suffer from "a flight from the struggles from oneself that are so much part of growing" (Imoda, *The Spiritual Exercises and Psychology: The Breadth and Length and Height and Depth [Eph, 3,18]* [Rome: G&B Press, 1996], 72).

the *Spiritual Exercises* are not primarily intended to be studied but to be prayed through. For some time, I have had the dream that Jesuit retreat houses might organize Ignatian retreats for Lonergan scholars. If this book is devoted to explaining Doran's notion of psychic conversion at an academic level, one does well to note that psychic conversion is a deeply existential and, necessarily, grace-prompted event. Might more practical steps also be considered to help Lonergan scholars become more "grounded" by combining intellectual conversion with psychic conversion?

12

The Spiritual Texture of Trauma: Psychic Conversion, Mimetic Desire, and the Healing of the Damaged Self

RANDY ROSENBERG

Introduction

This essay is part of a larger project that attempts to develop a sapiential praxis vision of philosophy and theology in light of Pierre Hadot's interpretation of ancient philosophy through the lens of "spiritual exercises."[1] Hadot's insistence that philosophy requires a radical conversion invites the development of a robust schema of conversion—a schema that integrates contemporary insights into the relationship between brain, mind, and body. Attention to the body in the scholarship on spiritual practices has understandably focused on questions of sex, food, drink, and the other pleasures of life. Situating spiritual practices within the realm of the moderation of bodily appetites rightly speaks to the never-ending challenge of fashioning responsible and flourishing lives. And yet, the place of the body in the spiritual life ought not be limited to this angle. Advances in neuroscience and trauma theory have offered us glimpses of the depth of what lies beneath our conscious experience. It also gives us glimpses of the kinds of distorted situations that scar us and reveals the need for thicker accounts of conversion and healing. Such a situation beckons theologians to develop

---

1. Pierre Hadot, *Philosophy as a Way of Life: Spiritual Exercises from Socrates to Foucault*, ed. Arnold I. Davidson, trans. Michael Chase (Malded, MA: Blackwell, 1995).

a more layered and explanatory basis on which to conduct theological reflection on the performance of spiritual practices of healing.

An often-overlooked resource for this conversation is the work of Robert Doran, S.J. and his insistence that philosophers and theologians attend more closely to the neural and psychic dimensions of life, as they relate to the ongoing human quest for meaning, truth, goodness, and love. This essay connects Doran's work to the emerging body of research on trauma. My modest claim is that Doran provides a holistic framework for taking seriously on the one hand, the impact of trauma on the organismic and psychic realms of human interiority, and, on the other hand, the capacity for spiritual growth. His approach bears the resources for exploring both our own limitations and our capacity for self-transcendence. What is needed is a more adequate anthropological grounding for spiritual flourishing in the wake of trauma. Psychic scarring is real and attention to psychic conversion ought to be part of addressing the spiritual texture of trauma. As explained more at length below, I am treating the word "spirit" as the distinctively human dimension of the mind, determined by self-awareness and experienced in spontaneous questions, wonder, and dynamism to know and love. I refrain from treating the supernatural reality of grace in this essay. A fuller treatment of Doran's contribution would surely require the taking up of this task.

This essay proceeds in a threefold manner. (1) I present selected elements of psychiatrist Bessel van der Kolk's pioneering research on understanding and healing trauma. Mindful that the body of research on trauma is vast, van der Kolk serves as one thoughtful way into the neural and psychic dimensions of trauma. His work lends itself to a holistic framework. As he notes, traumatized persons organize their lives as if the trauma were still happening. Every encounter, relationship, and event is tainted by the past, with detrimental physiological and psychic effects. This is why it is critical, van der Kolk argues, that the treatment of trauma engages "the entire organism, body, mind, and brain" (53). (2) In light of this trauma research, I turn to Robert Doran's account of psychic conversion within a holistic framework that values both self-acceptance and self-transcendence. I write not as an expert in trauma, but as a philosophically oriented theologian sympathetic to Doran's overall vision. Thus, my aim is to begin, at least in an initial way, to integrate some of van der Kolk's insights into Doran's account of organismic-psychic-spiritual life. (3) Finally, I note Doran's later integration of the role of imitation and mimetic desire in human life. This dimension of his work invites connections to van der Kolk's own integration of research on mirror neurons. Mirror neurons enable the brain to vicariously mirror the actions and emotions of others. They reveal our deeply social nature, as well as the interpersonal dimension of trauma. I end this section by noting one example of scholarship on mimetic desire and trauma—a contribution that can enrich Doran's own work in this regard.

1. Van der Kolk on Understanding and Healing Trauma

The spiritual texture of the damaged self involves multilayered disintegration. Trauma induces damage to the fundamental structures of being human—a loss of trust in oneself, in others, and in God. Humiliation, guilt, and helplessness arise, and the human capacity for intimacy is disrupted by "intense and contradictory feelings of need and fear."[2] In this section, I turn to the work of psychiatrist Bessel van der Kolk, who has been studying posttraumatic stress since the 1970s.[3] As I mentioned above, trauma induces damage to the fundamental structures of being human. As the research on trauma continues to emerge, it is clear that trauma is not simply an event of the past. It leaves an imprint on the body, brain, and mind. Van der Kolk suggests that a healing program often requires a combination of (1) therapeutic conversations that allow us to understand what is going on in us as we process traumatic memories, (2) the facilitation of bodily experiences

2. Judith Herman, *Trauma and Recovery: The Aftermath of Violence--From Domestic Abuse to Political Terror* (New York: Basic Books, 1992), 56.

3. Bessel van der Kolk, *The Body Keeps the Score: Brain, Mind, and Body in the Healing of Trauma* (New York: Penguin Books, 2014).

that viscerally contradict the experiences of helplessness, rage, and brokenness from trauma, and (3) medications that mitigate excessive alarm reactions.[4] Van der Kolk's treatment of healing bodily experiences rightly calls into question the adequacy of talking about and narrating one's trauma. As he shows, trauma often causes victims to lose a sense of their bodies. Patients adapt by shutting down areas of the brain associated with the visceral feelings that accompany their terror.[5] Therapy in this context involves not primarily talking, but befriending the body. This physical self-awareness is "the first step in releasing the tyranny of the past."[6] The imprint on the body tends to shape "how the human organism manages to survive in the present."[7] For those who are not traumatized, the memory of a painful event eventually fades or is understood as something less severe. Traumatized people have difficulty making their story something that happened a long time ago.[8] Rather, as van der Kolk explains, "Trauma results in a fundamental reorganization of the way the mind and brain manage perceptions. It changes not only how we think and what we think about, but also our very capacity to think."[9] Although finding the right words in therapy can be profoundly meaningful, simply telling the story does not always mitigate the hormonal and physical response of bodies continuously on guard against assault. Long-lasting change requires the body to learn that the danger has passed. The implication is that healing requires not just out-narrating the damaging story, but in integrating other, bodily based processes for healing.[10] As van der Kolk explains, for over a century psychology and psychotherapy textbooks privileged the method of resolving distressing feelings through talking about them. The experience of trauma on the body, however, often limits the efficacy of conversation therapy. Even if one has insight into one's

---

4. Van der Kolk, *The Body Keeps the Score*, 3.
5. Van der Kolk, *The Body Keeps the Score*, 94.
6. Van der Kolk, *The Body Keeps the Score*, 103.
7. Van der Kolk, *The Body Keeps the Score*, 21.
8. Van der Kolk, *The Body Keeps the Score*, 19.
9. Van der Kolk, *The Body Keeps the Score*, 21.
10. Van der Kolk, *The Body Keeps the Score*, 21.

trauma, the rational dimension of the brain is often powerless against the emotional dimension of the brain's account of its own reality. Van der Kolk notes how difficult it is for people "to convey the essence of their experience." "It is so much easier," he writes, "for them to talk about what has been done to them—to tell a story of victimization and revenge—than to notice, feel, and put into words the reality of their internal experience."[11]

Van der Kolk's attention to the physical, neuronal, and hormonal responses to trauma is shaped by his own appropriation of the recent discovery of mirror neurons in the field of modern neuroscience. In 1994, Italian scientists fortuitously identified specialized cells in the cortex that enable the brain to vicariously mirror the actions of others. One scientist happened to notice that the monkey's brain cells were firing at the exact location where the motor command neurons were located, even though the monkey wasn't eating or moving. As van der Kolk notes, the monkey was watching the researcher, and his brain was mirroring the actions of the same.[12]

For van der Kolk, the discovery of mirror neurons offered ground-breaking insight into empathy, imitation, and synchrony. These neurons attune us to the intentions, actions, and emotional states of others. When we are emotionally in sync, our actions tend to follow suit, and this can be a very nurturing experience. We take on the same rhythms in voice and physical posture. But mirror neurons also make us vulnerable to the dark side of others. We can almost imitate their impulsivity, anger, anxiety, and depression.[13] In light of the literature on mirror neurons, trauma involves "not being seen, not being mirrored, and not being taken into account. Treatment needs to reactivate the capacity to safely mirror, and be mirrored, by others, but also to resist being hijacked by others' negative emotions."[14]

In addition to mirror neurons, Stephen Porges' polyvagal theory challenged scientists not to reduce the framing of trauma in terms of

11. Van der Kolk, *The Body Keeps the Score*, 47.
12. Van der Kolk, *The Body Keeps the Score*, 58.
13. Van der Kolk, *The Body Keeps the Score*, 58–9.
14. Van der Kolk, *The Body Keeps the Score*, 59.

fight or flight, but to give more weight to social relationships. As van der Kolk writes, Porges

> provided us with a more sophisticated understanding of the biology of safety and danger, one based on the subtle interplay between the visceral experiences of our own bodies and the voices and faces of the people around us. It explained why a kind of face or a soothing tone of voice can dramatically alter the way we feel. It clarified why knowing that we are seen and heard by the important people in our lives can make us feel calm and safe, and why being ignored or dismissed can precipitate rage reactions or mental collapse. It helped us understand why focused attunement with another person can shift us out of disorganized and fearful states.[15]

This emotional attunement and deep biological relatedness calls into question our culture's privileging of individuality and human autonomy. As van der Kolk suggests, our brains evolved to function as members of tribes. In reality we hardly exist as individual organisms: "We are part of that tribe even if we are by ourselves, whether listening to music (that other people created), watching a basketball game on television (our own muscles tensing as the players run and jump), or preparing a spreadsheet for a sales meeting (anticipating the boss's reactions)."[16] The majority of our life's energy is expelled in connecting with other people. Likewise, a great deal of our mental suffering involves disrupted relationships. For van der Kolk, feeling safe—having our lives infused with safe connections—is foundational to mental health and a flourishing life. Studies of disaster responses have shown that "social support is the most powerful protection against becoming overwhelmed by stress and trauma."[17] And reciprocity is critical to safe connections. It involves "being truly heard and seen by the people around us, feeling that we are held in someone else's mind and heart."

---

15. Van der Kolk, *The Body Keeps the Score*, 80.
16. Van der Kolk, *The Body Keeps the Score*, 80.
17. Van der Kolk, *The Body Keeps the Score*, 81.

Physiologically, we can only calm and heal when we have a visceral feeling of safety. "You don't need a history of trauma," writes van der Kolk, "to feel self-conscious and even panicked at a party with strangers--but trauma can turn the whole world into a gathering of aliens." Traumatized people often find themselves "chronically out of sync with the people around them."[18]

The tragic implications of early trauma are exhibited in a study conducted on a group from the Children's Clinic at the Massachusetts Mental Health Center. Researchers created test cards based on pictures cut out from magazines from the clinic waiting room. They compared the respective responses from children who were abused and children from the same violent neighborhoods who were not abused, but nevertheless witnessed their fair share of violence. One test card depicted a family scene with two kids smiling while watching their father repair a car. Children from both groups commented on the possible danger for the dad lying underneath the vehicle. Still, the children from the control group told stories with benign endings. Perhaps the car is repaired and they go out to lunch to celebrate. The traumatized kids, as van der Kolk tells us, came up with "gruesome tales:" "One girl said that the little girl in the picture was about to smash in her father's skull with a hammer. A nine-year-old boy who has been severely physically abused told an elaborate story about how the boy in the picture kicked away the jack, so that the car mangled his father's body and his blood spurted all over the garage."[19]

A similar pattern occurred when the children were shown an innocent picture of a pregnant woman near a window. When a seven-year-old girl who'd been sexually abused at age four observed the picture, "she talked about penises and vaginas" and repeatedly asked questions like "How many people have you humped?"[20] On the other hand, a seven-year-old girl from the control group picked up on the dreamy feel of the picture. In her imagination this was a widow who was looking out the

18. Van der Kolk, *The Body Keeps the Score*, 81.
19. Van der Kolk, *The Body Keeps the Score*, 109.
20. Van der Kolk, *The Body Keeps the Score*, 109.

window, grieving that her husband was gone. But ultimately the lady met a loving man who became a good father to the baby.[21]

In sum, the children who had not been abused still trusted in the essential goodness of the universe. Certainly there were sad and dangerous situations, but they could imagine ways out. They felt loved and maintained a sense of safety and security within their own families. The responses of the clinic children, however, were alarming. As van der Kolk explains, "The most innocent images stirred up intense feelings of danger, aggression, sexual arousal, and terror." For abused children, the world is dominated by danger and is full of triggers indicating that any stranger may at any moment be a "harbinger of catastrophe."[22]

As I pointed out above, for van der Kolk, healing often requires a combination of bodily experiences that viscerally contradict the experiences of helplessness, rage, and brokenness from trauma, and therapeutic conversations that allow us to understand what is going on in us as we process traumatic memories. We also possess an inbuilt system of control. We have the ability "to train our arousal system by the way we breath, chant, and move"—a principle that has permeated religious practices for centuries.[23] Studies have shown, for example, that ten weeks of yoga can significantly reduce PTSD. In contrast to Western psychiatric care and its emphasis on verbal therapies and drugs, other traditions have relied on movement, mindfulness, and rhythm.[24]

An effective way of facilitating body awareness is the practice of mindfulness. The core of trauma recovery is self-awareness. A life affected by trauma carries with it almost unbearable sensations. And avoidance of such emotions is rarely productive. As van der Kolk notes, "Body awareness puts us in touch with our inner world, the landscape of our organism. Simply noticing our annoyance, nervousness, or anxiety immediately helps us shift our perspective and opens up new options other than our automatic, habitual reactions. Mindfulness puts us in touch with the transitory nature of our feelings and perceptions. When

---

21. Van der Kolk, *The Body Keeps the Score*, 109–10.
22. Van der Kolk, *The Body Keeps the Score*, 110.
23. Van der Kolk, *The Body Keeps the Score*, 209.
24. Van der Kolk, *The Body Keeps the Score*, 210.

we pay focused attention to our bodily sensations, we can recognize the ebb and flow of our emotions and, with that, increase our control over them."[25] Traumatized are afraid of the feelings and sensations. Mindfulness enables one to calm down the sympathetic nervous system and avoid an acquiescence to continual fight or flight responses.[26]

Another healing practice is the nurturing of intentional relationships. Our bonds of attachment are the most important protection against threat. Whether we are children or adults, the presence and embrace of someone that we trust is the surest way to calm. Victims of trauma recover in "the context of relationships: with families, loved ones, AA meetings, veterans' organizations, religious communities, or professional therapists."[27] Such relationships provide "physical and emotional safety, including safety from feeling shamed, admonished, or judged, and bolster the courage to tolerate, face, and process the reality of what has happened."[28] Recovering requires a guide "who is not afraid of your terror and who can contain your darkest rage, someone who can safeguard the wholeness of you while you explore the fragmented experiences that you had to keep secret from yourself for so long."[29]

Related to this kind of relational therapy are forms of communal rhythms and synchrony. One of the effects of trauma is a "breakdown of attuned physical synchrony."[30] Healing often comes, not from analyzing words, but from the power of community expressed in music and rhythm. Van der Kolk describes this kind of experience that occurred at a support group for rape victims:

> The women sat slumped over—sad and frozen . . . I felt a familiar sense of helplessness, and, surrounded by collapsed people. I felt myself mentally collapse as well. Then one of the women started to hum, while gently swaying back and forth. Slowly a rhythm emerged; bit by bit other women joined in.

---

25. Van der Kolk, *The Body Keeps the Score*, 210.
26. Van der Kolk, *The Body Keeps the Score*, 211.
27. Van der Kolk, *The Body Keeps the Score*, 212.
28. Van der Kolk, *The Body Keeps the Score*, 212.
29. Van der Kolk, *The Body Keeps the Score*, 213.
30. Van der Kolk, *The Body Keeps the Score*, 215.

Soon the whole group was singing, moving, and getting up to dance. It was an astounding transformation: people coming back to life, faces becoming attuned, vitality returning to bodies.[31]

Communal activities like singing and playing bring about physical attunement, connection, humor, and joy.[32]

If feeling at home in one's body is the first step, treatment of trauma also involves therapeutic conversations. To take just one example, van der Kolk facilitates the psychotherapeutic practice of "creating structures" and "restructuring inner maps."[33] Unlike traditional psychotherapy, the aim is not to interpret and explain the past. The aim is to guide the imagination in physically re-experiencing the past in the present, and then reworking the past within safe and supportive structures. While this practice involves dialogue, it is a psychomotor therapy that "allows you to feel what you felt back then, to visualize what you saw, and to say what you could not say when it actually happened."[34] "It's as if," van der Kolk writes, "you could go back into the movie of your life and rewrite the crucial scenes. You can direct the role-players to do things they failed to do in the past, such as keeping your father from beating up your mother."[35] This form of therapy enables trauma victims to create new supplemental memories of, for example, growing up in affectionate settings safe from harm.[36] This involves re-scripting and re-narrating one's life.

2. The Holistic Framework of Robert Doran: Psychic Conversion and Self-Transcendence

The work of Robert Doran, S.J. offers a significant opening for attending to trauma in human experience, and does so within a holistic vision

---

31. Van der Kolk, *The Body Keeps the Score*, 216.
32. Van der Kolk, *The Body Keeps the Score*, 217.
33. Van der Kolk, *The Body Keeps the Score*, 298–310.
34. Van der Kolk, *The Body Keeps the Score*, 301.
35. Van der Kolk, *The Body Keeps the Score*, 301.
36. Van der Kolk, *The Body Keeps the Score*, 302.

of the human person—a point especially relevant to philosophers and theologians.[37] His framework is attentive to the biological, neurological, and psychic dimensions of human experience, while at the same time recognizing the human spiritual orientation to meaning, truth, goodness, and beauty—what, in the Catholic intellectual tradition, is considered a transcendent orientation—a natural desire for God.[38] This approach creates space for exploring our own vulnerability, on the one hand, and our call to transcendence, on the other hand. In other words, it accounts for both self-acceptance and self-transcendence.

For Doran, the human person is a totality of organism, psyche, and spirit and marked by an ongoing search for direction in the movement of life.[39] "The deepest desire of the human person is "to succeed in the drama of human existence by finding and holding to the direction that can be discovered in the movement of life."[40] In this frame, the world is more like a stage than it is a constellation of objects to be encountered or analyzed or manipulated. It envisions the person as a searcher, a pilgrim, on a quest for meaning, truth, goodness, and love. It is a tragedy in this view when social structures—families, communities, education—are so distorted or oppressive that they deprive people of the basic vital goods of safety, shelter, nutrition, as well as the psychic goods associated with our own interior peace and peace within our environment. And the absence of these goods makes it difficult to engage this quest for meaning—with this call to cooperate in making one's life a work of art. In other words, when you're hungry or fear that violence or abuse may come at any time, it is difficult to focus on the dramatic artistry of living, as exhibited above in the work of van der Kolk.

---

37. In this section, I draw mainly from Robert M. Doran, *Theology and the Dialectics of History* (Toronto: University of Toronto Press, 1990).

38. For my own treatment of this theme, see Randall S. Rosenberg, *The Givenness of Desire: Concrete Subjectivity and the Natural Desire to See Good* (Toronto: University of Toronto Press, 2017).

39. Doran, *Theology and the Dialectics of History*, 267.

40. Doran, *Theology and the Dialectics of History*, 358.

I offer here a brief overview of the tripartite structure that informs Doran's work.[41] It is important to note this is a heuristic structure, a tool, a way into the complex reality of the human person. Each dimension must be informed by ongoing scientific research and discovery. First, the level of an organism refers to the physical life form, bounded by space and time. It involves the physiological systems studied in physics, chemistry, biology, and medicine. The organismic dimension of being human requires satisfying life-sustaining biological needs. This is the realm of eating, resting, eliminating wastes, exercising, finding clothing and shelter, and releasing sexual tension. It aims for biological survival and health.

Second, the level of the psyche refers to the dimension of the human mind shared with other higher animals. This dimension includes emotions, imagery, and memory. It heavily informs our habitual responses that make up our personality. The psyche forms the organism's dispositional status. This realm aims to be at peace and to find comfort within one's environment.

Finally, the level of spirit is the distinctively human dimension of the mind, determined by reflexive awareness and experienced in wonder. The human spirit is oriented toward knowledge and love. The spirit expresses itself in experiencing, understanding, judgment, and decision. These cognitional-volitional operations transcend space and time—they are not intrinsically conditioned by space and time— and aim toward human authenticity. They are impelled by a call to be attentive, intelligent, reasonable, responsible, and loving. This is the self-transcendence of persons living lives of authenticity.

In light of this tripartite structure, Doran understands his vision as a psychology of orientation, which he contrasts with a psychology of passional motivation.[42] A psychology of passional motivation tends

---

41. In my description of the tripartite structure of organism, psyche, and spirit, I am especially drawing on Daniel A. Helminiak, *Religion and the Human Sciences: An Approach via Spirituality* (Albany: SUNY, 1998), 11. See also Carla Mae Streeter, *Foundations of Spirituality: The Human and the Holy: A Systematic Approach* (Collegeville: Liturgical Press, 2012), esp. Chapter 4.

42. Doran, *Theology and the Dialectics of History*, 218.

to understand the meaning and purpose of the human person solely in biological or even psychological terms. A psychology of orientation, on the other hand, integrates the organic and psychic levels, but envisions these dimensions as springboards to the distinctly spiritual dimensions of the person associated with this quest for meaning, truth, goodness, and love. It's one thing to honor the necessary role of biological survival or the role of the repressed sexual libido in the human quest, and it's another thing to reduce all of human reality to such biological or psychological dimensions. This framework attempts, in other words, to honor, and at the same time, reorient the depth-psychological tradition. It makes space for practices that foster both self-acceptance and self-transcendence.

The complexity of being human, then, involves navigating the relationship between organism, psyche, and spirit. The interlocking connections between organism and psyche, and between psyche and spirit reveal a vision of the person that takes seriously the reality of embodiment, so often underplayed in western philosophical traditions. This emphasis on embodiment opens up space for van der Kolk's insistence on the detrimental imprint trauma leaves on the body. For Doran, the notion of embodiment in psychic conversion can contribute to the "process of liberation from oppressive patterns of experience."[43]

> For the psyche is the locus of the embodiment of inquiry, insight, reflection, judgment, deliberation, and decision, just as it is the place of the embodiment of the oppressive forces from which we can be released by intentional operations. As the psyche is oriented to participation in the life of the intentional spirit, so intentionality is oriented to embodiment through the mass and momentum of feeling. Patterns of experience are either the distorted and alienated, or the integral and creative, embodiment of the human spirit. To the extent that our psychic sensitivity is victimized by oppression, the embodiment of the spirit is confined to an animal habitat, fastened on survival, intent on the satisfaction of its own deprivation of the humanum. To the extent that

---

43. Doran, *Theology and the Dialectics of History*, 61.

the psyche is released from oppressive patterns, the embodiment of the spirit is released into a human world, and indeed ultimately into the universe of being.[44]

As embodied subjects, we experience distortions, alienation, deprivation, as well as the mass and momentum of feeling of psychic life. But Doran also offers an account of healing:

> A true healing of the psyche would dissolve the affective wounds that block sustained self-transcendence; it would give the freedom required to engage in the constitution of a human world; but it would also render the psyche the medium of the embodiment of intentionality in the constitution of the person. As psychic conversion allows access to one's own symbolic system, and through that system to one's affective habits, one's spontaneous apprehension of possible values, so it makes of the psyche a medium of the embodiment of intentionality in the constitution of the human person. As the movement of consciousness 'from below' allows us to affirm the vertical finality of the psyche to participate in the life of the spirit, so the movement 'from above' enables us to affirm an orientation of the human spirit to embodiment in the constitution of the person.[45]

Returning to the interlocking relationship between organism, psyche, and spirit, Doran argues that the sensitive psyche occupies "a middle ground between the organism and spirit," since it participates in both.[46] On the one hand, the psyche is a "higher integration of neural manifolds" at the level of the organism. On the other hand, it "houses" the sensory apparatus operative in self-transcendence as we "feel our participation in the intelligibility, truth, and goodness of being . . ." Affective integrity, in Doran's vision, involves "abiding in the creative tension of matter and spirit."[47] Thus, this middle ground presents the

44. Doran, *Theology and the Dialectics of History*, 62.
45. Doran, *Theology and the Dialectics of History*, 62.
46. Doran, *Theology and the Dialectics of History*, 55.
47. Doran, *Theology and the Dialectics of History*, 55.

challenge of negotiating two relationships: the relation of the organism to the psyche and the relation of the psyche to the spirit.

This first relationship—that between the neural manifolds of the organism and the sensitive-imaginal realm of the psyche—beckons us to attend to the interaction between our unconscious and conscious minds. This dynamic is especially relevant to the impact of trauma. Following Lonergan, Doran speaks of a psychic censor that helps navigate this interaction.[48] Our neural activity attempts to find expression in our conscious psyche by producing images. But, if every neural demand found expression in our consciousness, this would create an overwhelming flow of images to process. This flooding of images requires, then, a psychic censor to select and arrange materials that emerge in consciousness. While this psychic censorship is necessary and so often operates in helpful, constructive modes, it can also be repressive. It can reject painful memories and feelings, and hence redirect them to the region of the unconscious. For Doran, psychic conversion (which is distinct from other forms of conversion—intellectual, moral, and religious) involves transforming this psychic censor away from a repressive mode of operating to constructive agency—an ongoing task that is integral to the difficult work of personal development.[49] Van der Kolk's treatment of healing bodily experiences rightly calls into question the adequacy of talking about and narrating one's trauma. It attends to this relationship between the neural and the psychic. Van der Kolk's work puts flesh on this relationship. As he shows, trauma often causes victims to lose a sense of their bodies. Patients adapt by shutting down areas of the brain associated with the visceral feelings that accompany their terror.[50] Therapy in this context involves, as explained above, not primarily talking, but finding security in our bodies, which is the genesis of overcoming the tyranny of our past. The relationship between the neural and the psychic can find

---

48. Doran, *Theology and the Dialectics of History*, 80, 180.
49. Doran, *Theology and the Dialectics of History*, 59–60.
50. Van der Kolk, *The Body Keeps the Score*, 94.

healing, as van der Kolk shows, in practices of mindfulness, intentional social relationships, yoga, and other forms of communal rhythms.

The second relationship—that between psyche and spirit—involves the connection between the images that emerge in consciousness and the insights needed to find direction in the movement of life. The flourishing psyche can create the conditions for and accompany the flourishing of the self-transcending human spirit. As a key dimension of self-appropriation, psychic conversion taps into one's own symbolic system "and through that system to one's affective habits and one's spontaneous apprehension of possible values."[51] Recall that for van der Kolk, feeling at home in one's body was foundationally crucial. But this should in no way minimize the importance of therapeutic conversations in the treatment of trauma. This feature of conversation therapy especially corresponds to the relationship between the psychic and the spirit. In Doran's account, psychic conversion involves navigating one's own symbolic narrative system, and the way these narratives impact our affective dispositions and spontaneous responses. It involves the transformation of the imagination from repressive, damaging symbols to healing, redemptive symbols. Van der Kolk's work also puts flesh on this dimension of psychic conversion. He has facilitated, as described above, psychotherapeutic practices of physically re-experiencing the past in the present, and then reworking the past in safe and supportive structures. This enables trauma victims to re-script and re-narrate their lives.

In sum, the interplay of organism, psyche, and spirit reveals the tensions that animate our own inner lives. And if we add our own psychic distortions to distortions in our families, communities, culture, we have a complicated situation on our hands. The blockages and resistances in our psyches, the wounding of our imaginations, tend to slow down or resist the full operations of the human spirit in its quest in the drama of human living. When organism, psyche, and spirit are in harmony, the human subject experiences affective self-transcendence that accompanies the higher level of spiritual self-transcendence. When integrated, affective self-transcendence can become

---

51. Doran, *Theology and the Dialectics of History*, 61.

"regular, easy, spontaneous, sustained, a way of life."[52] But psychic experience also reveals the fragility of our imaginations. The experience of trauma, painful memories, and wounded imaginations require psychic conversion.

3. Mimetic Desire and the Social Reality of Trauma

During the latter part of his career, Doran broadened his insights into the psyche by engaging the role of imitation, and especially imitative desire, in human experience.[53] In this way, Doran's framework makes space for engaging the impact of mirror neurons, along with the social dimension of trauma emphasized by van der Kolk. Doran's sage guide to the dynamics of imitation was the French intellectual, René Girard. Girard's account of mimetic desire, along with its anthropological emphasis on intersubjectivity, relationality, and the phenomenon of knowing and willing according to a model, enabled Doran to expand his own understanding of psychic life and complement his emphasis on the natural desire for meaning, truth, and goodness.[54]

Girard's fundamental insight is that our desires are imitative or mimetic, which is to say that they are rooted neither in ourselves or the objects we desire. Rather, our desires are elicited by models, whose desire we imitate in the hope of resembling them. Girard has written widely about the problematic nature of mimetic desire, especially its tendency toward conflict and violence. But the mimetic quality of childhood is indisputable. From our earliest days, our lives are shaped by wanting what others want. As Girard notes, all one has to do is "to watch two children or two adults who quarrel over some trifle."[55] In

52. Doran, *Theology and the Dialectics of History*, 51.

53. See especially Doran, *The Trinity in History: A Theology of the Divine Missions, vol. 1: Missions and Processions* (Toronto: University of Toronto Press, 2012), chapter 9.

54. Kevin Lenehan, "Girard and the Tasks of Theology," *Violence, Desire, and the Sacred, vol. 1: Girard's Mimetic Theory across the Disciplines*, ed. Scott Cowdell, Chris Fleming, and Joel Hodge (New York: Bloomsbury, 2012).

55. René Girard, *I See Satan Fall Like Lightning*, trans. James G. Williams (Maryknoll: Orbis, 2001), 8.

other words, "we tend to desire what our neighbor has or what our neighbor desires."[56] If this is true, then "rivalry exists at the very heart of human social relations. The rivalry, if not thwarted, would permanently endanger the harmony and even the survival of all human communities."[57] In sum, we are not, for Girard, "autonomous individuals," but rather "interdividuals" whose desires are socially mediated through a complex web of mediations.

In *The Trinity in History*, Doran established a framework for integrating natural desire (which corresponds to the dimension of "spirit" discussed above) and mimetic desire. According to Doran, Girard's mimetic desire corresponds to the desire elicited in the psychic dimension of consciousness to the polyphony or cacophony of our "sensations, memories, images, emotions, conations, associations, bodily movements, and spontaneous intersubjective responses."[58] But mimetic desire also "penetrates our spiritual orientation to the intelligible, the true and the real, and the good, for better and for worse."[59] In other words, distorted mimetic desire can infect the unfolding of the quest for authenticity, while positive mimesis may strengthen, enhance, and deepen our commitment to the exigencies of the mind and will. Positive models have the power to elicit the desire to be faithful to the natural desire for meaning, truth, and goodness. Doran's appropriation of Girard's work emphasizes that the psychic dimension of life is "precisely interdividual in many of its manifestations."[60] For Doran, psychic development entails the negotiation of this interdividual field, which often distorts the human spirit, on the one hand, and yet, if authentically negotiated, can allow the spiritual quest to flourish, on the other hand. Ideally, the intersubjective presence of the other would evoke our innate drive for self-transcendence.

Doran's heuristic structure of psychic conversion and van der Kolk's emphasis on the bodily dimensions of trauma invite insights

---

56. Girard, *I See Satan*, 8.

57. Girard, *I See Satan*, 8–9.

58. Doran, *Theology and the Dialectics of History*, 46.

59. Doran, *The Trinity in History*, 204.

60. Doran, *The Trinity in History*, 206.

from mimetic theory. Scott Garrels has urged a collaborative effort between mimetic scholars and the empirical sciences, which includes the research on mirror neurons noted by van der Kolk.[61] There is a remarkable convergence between researchers of human imitation in animal and human life and mimetic theory. Garrels argues that imitation research, when viewed through the prism of mimetic theory, illuminates "not only the building blocks of relatedness, mindfulness, and meaningfulness but also the mechanisms of distortion, disillusionment, and violence."[62] Mimetic theory challenges scientists working on imitation research "to better appreciate and understand the incredible nature of human life, culture, and religion, an appreciation that is essential in transforming human culture and relationships through infinitely more imaginative and nonviolent ways of relating."[63] Now that we understand scientifically how ubiquitous imitation is in human affairs it is time to look more deeply into the contributions of mimetic theory to illuminate the constructive and destructive potential of human imitation. This requires attention to the dual nature of human relationships, marked as they are by both modeling and rivalry. The dual nature of drama among toddlers, after all, only foreshadows the envy, rivalry, and conflict that permeate adult life. A key contribution of mimetic theory to the other sciences is its focus on human desire. Since we do not know what to desire, we tend to observe others and imitate their desires. Thus, modeling occurs for good and for ill. At worst, models and imitators end up desiring the same object, and hence their relationship becomes infected with rivalrous desire—a desire that can spread (unlike animal rivalries) throughout entire communities.

This van der Kolk-Doran conversation can be especially bolstered by Martha Reineke's research on mimetic theory and trauma. Reineke's *Intimate Domain: Desire, Trauma, and Mimetic Theory* connects the explanatory power of Girard's mimetic theory with an "examination

---

61. Scott Garrels, "Imitation, Mirror Neurons, and Mimetic Desire: Convergence Between the Mimetic Theory of René Girard and Empirical Research on Imitation," *Contagion: Journal of Violence, Mimesis, and Culture* Vol. 12–13 (2006): 47–86.

62. Garrels, "Imitation, Mirror Neurons, and Mimetic Desire," 80.

63. Garrels, "Imitation, Mirror Neurons, and Mimetic Desire," 80.

of family life: sensory experience, trauma, and intimacy."[64] Reineke argues that sensory experience can be a "vehicle for positive mimesis" and can open up avenues for transformation. Reineke develops a "corporeal hermeneutics"—indicating that the "evocation of bodily expressiveness" through movement is constitutive to narrative meaning, a stance that resonates deeply with van der Kolk and Doran.[65] She animates notions of affective memory and sensory experience. Such a turn helps one account for both the trauma that results from violence and the healing transformation made possible by positive mimesis.[66]

Reineke makes the case that Girard's treatment of families requires more nuance. Girard was committed to protecting childhood desire from Freudian imposition. In doing so, Girard tended to offer an overly idyllic picture of early childhood. But perhaps, Reineke contends, psychoanalytic theory can offer the nuance of family dynamics that Girard needs. Family life is the earliest site of mimetic relationships—a domain which shapes our negotiation of mimetic desire later in life. Reineke argues that Girard does not do justice to mimetic desire in children, along with the conflicts between children and parents. Parent, child, and sibling conflicts can be just as traumatic as other interpersonal conflicts.[67]

Building on the psychoanalysis of Juliet Mitchell, Reineke distinguishes vertical relations (children and parents) and lateral relations (siblings). Drawing on Sophocles' *Antigone*, she identifies an "Antigone complex," which has to do with the fraught relationships between siblings, dominated as they are by anxiety about getting replaced in parental affection, along with corresponding fears about violent jealousies.[68] Think not only of twins, but of Cain and Abel, Jacob and Esau, and Romulus and Remus—stories that have dominated the religious and cultural imagination.

---

64. Martha J. Reineke, *Intimate Domain: Desire, Trauma, and Mimetic Theory* (East Lansing: Michigan State University Press, 2014), xii.

65. Reineke, *Intimate Domain*, xxxiii.

66. Reineke, *Intimate Domain*, xxxiv.

67. Reineke, *Intimate Domain*, xvi.

68. Reineke, *Intimate Domain*, xLiii.

Reineke offers an interpretation of Sophocles Theban Cycle—
Oedipus the King, Oedipus at Colonus, and *Antigone.* Oedipus himself
in *Oedipus the King* and *Oedipus at Colonus* reveal a wounded man—
but a man never released from his trauma. Instead, the trauma is transferred to his daughter, Antigone. And the play *Antigone* "demonstrates
that only intimacy heals, opening us to time—a time for others lived
in accord with an ethics of intimacy."[69] The mourning of Antigone
herself "permits the reliving and reworking of loss associated with
traumatic violence in order to repair a wounded existence." Reineke
argues that the "affective and bodily features of Antigone's mourning"
occupy a central role.[70] "Just as trauma is contagious, so also is healing
when sensory experiences reverse the effects of trauma and open up a
future to intimacy." As figures of Greek tragedy work through trauma,
they "begin their journey to healing with embodied, nonvocal forms
of communication."[71] Their stories reveal lives imbued with "traumatic
repetition." Resonant with van der Kolk's emphasis on the healing of
the body through ritual synchrony, Reineke writes: "Living in utter
isolation from others by virtues of silences that attest to the severing
of ties with human community, their bodily communication, in movement and gesture, eventually creates a bridge that opens up the future
for a life inclusive of others."[72]

Conclusion

In conclusion, I highlight three key insights of this essay. *First, the
connection between trauma and the flourishing of the human spirit
requires a holistic framework.* Spiritual healing should not be treated
as an extrinsic religious structure grafted on the human being. Rather,
treatment of trauma must be attentive to the interrelated realms of
organism, psyche, and the spirit. Doran's heuristic framework provides

---

69. Reineke, *Intimate Domain,* 138.
70. Reineke, *Intimate Domain,* 139.
71. Reineke, *Intimate Domain,* 153.
72. Reineke, *Intimate Domain,* 153.

a more adequate anthropological grounding to spiritual formation and practice. Spiritual flourishing entails healing from damages that have occurred at the level of organism and psyche. *Second, Doran's account of the twofold relationship involved in psychic conversion—the neural to the psychic, and the psychic to the spiritual—helped us map out van der Kolk's claim that the "body keeps the score" and integrate his insights into a larger philosophical and theological vision.* Van der Kolk's suggestion that a healing program often requires a combination of bodily experiences and therapeutic conversation put flesh on the bones of Doran's vision of holistic self-transcendence. *Third, healing from trauma requires interpersonal attunement to the deeply social, mimetic structure of human living.* Doran's connection between psychic life and the role of mimetic desire opens up connections to both scientific research on mirror neurons and the role of mimetic desire in the life of subjects, communities, and cultures. Doran's expanded framework creates space for the relational healing and communally rhythmic synchrony described by van der Kolk. Such a vision of healing was bolstered by Reineke's corporal hermeneutics, and her expansion of the explanatory power of Girard's mimetic theory into the realm of sensory experience, trauma, and intimacy.

Part 4

PSYCHIC CONVERSION AND CONTEMPORARY THEOLOGICAL ISSUES

13

A Perspective on Psychic Conversion: Healing the Wound of Replacement Theory

Cyril Orji
University of Dayton

ernard Lonergan speaks of religious, moral, and intellectual conversion, suggesting that they can occur in one's life in any order, depending on one's existential situation.[1] But what he says about interiority and development of feelings in *Method in Theology* as they relate to self-transcendence leaves open the possibility of a fourth basic form of conversion that complements the existing three. Some think the fourth conversion is affective conversion because of what Lonergan says about affective self-transcendence. Robert Doran recognizes the need for affective self-transcendence. But he chooses to call the fourth of Lonergan's conversion a psychic conversion, not just because of its psychological resonances, but fundamentally because of the many references Lonergan makes to the psyche and symbols.[2] Very much like religious, moral, and intellectual conversion that can occur in any order at any stage in a person's life, Doran also says

---

1. See Bernard Lonergan, Collected Works of Bernard Lonergan, vol.14, *Method in Theology*, edited by Robert M. Doran and John D. Dadosky (Toronto: University of Toronto Press, 2017).

2. See Robert M. Doran, *Theology and the Dialectics of History* (Toronto: University of Toronto Press, 1990).

psychic conversion can occur at any point in one's life, depending on one's existential situation.

Many, including those within the Lonergan circle, are befuddled by what Doran means by psychic conversion. They want to know what psychic conversion entails and whether it is not a misrepresentation of Lonergan's idea. It is precisely questions such as these that this essay addresses. However, I do not intend to offer an elaborate discussion of psychic conversion here, since I have done that elsewhere.[3] What I intend to do rather is show the place and value of psychic conversion in a person's life, especially in the light of the psychic wounds that biases and prejudices generate in the minds of persons in society. My context is the United States. The issue I use to elucidate my point is the Great Replacement theory—a theory that proponents and enthusiasts use to scuttle the movement towards equity and fairness. Although the symbolism of psychic wound stemming from racism affects both per-petrators and victims alike, the limitation of space permits me to focus only on the psychic wound of the perpetrator. The nuts and bolts of my argument is that the Replacement theory is a manifestation of a psychic wound that afflicts a person in their fixed or chosen horizon. It is a clever and convenient way of denying racism and still not be held responsible for being racist. Replacement theory is a gaslighting and a psychologically astute way of making the perpetrator believe the victim is the problem. The psychic wound it generates on the perpetrators leads to the aberration of sensibilities. My conclusion is that psychic conversion can aid the re-establishment of the loss of sensibilities stem-ming from the psychic wounds.

I do not intend to rehash how and when Doran made a break-through in psychic conversion. That account has been given by Doran who detailed how the idea of psychic conversion crystalized for him in graduate school at Marquette.[4] But it is pertinent that I mention that Doran's breakthrough work on psychic conversion came as a result of

---

3. See my forthcoming book on *Lonergan and Racism*, University of Toronto Press.

4. See Robert M. Doran, "Two Ways of Being Conscious: The Notion of Psychic Conversion," *Method: Journal of Lonergan Studies* 3 (2012), 1–17.

the connections he was making between the philosophy of Martin Heidegger, the depth psychology of Carl C. Jung, and the mimetic theory of Rene Girard in the light of what Lonergan says in *Insight*[5] and *Method in Theology* about the psyche and the affective development of a person. For Doran, understanding what characterizes affective self-transcendence is key to grasping what he means by psychic conversion. In the light of racism and the willful denial of racism that harm the victim and destroy the psyche of the perpetrators, psychic conversion should not be seen as a theory, but a cure and a remedy. Racism comes in different shades and forms. Its psychic damage fundamentally remains the same. The Replacement theory is a form of denial of racism. Its psychic damage also fundamentally remains the same as racism.

I begin by explaining the Great Replacement theory and how it is feeding the loss of affective dimension in our intersubjective encounter. I explain it in the backdrop of what Lonergan says about the two ways we are conscious as human beings. In one way, we are conscious through our sensibilities—we sense and imagine, have our desires and fears, delights and sorrows, joys and sadness. In another way, we are conscious through our intellectuality—by raising relevant questions and finding correct answers. Lonergan furthermore states that "we are more active when we consciously inquire in order to understand, understand in order to utter a word, weigh evidence in order to judge, deliberate in order to choose, and exercise our will in order to act."[6] Great Replacement is a repression of these human ways of being conscious. Doran accepts Lonergan's basic premise that we are conscious in two ways—through our sensibility (sensing, imagining, desiring, fearing, delighting, etc.) and through our intellectuality (understanding, judging, and deciding). Doran also furthers Lonergan's argument

---

5. See Bernard Lonergan, Collected Works of Bernard Lonergan, vol. 3, *Insight: A Study of Human Understanding*, edited by Frederick E. Crowe and Robert M. Doran (Toronto: University of Toronto Press, 1997).

6. Bernard Lonergan, *Triune God: Systematics*, translated by Michael G. Shields and edited by Robert M. Doran and H. Daniel Monsour (Toronto: University of Toronto Press), 139.

that our sensitive and intellectual consciousness can be impaired and distorted. There can be no better example of what distorts and impairs a person's sensitive and intellectual consciousness as the biases that are evoked to feed the Replacement theory. What goes by Replacement theory not only distorts a person's sensitive consciousness, but also their levels of understanding, judgment, and decision. Thus, I explain Replacement theory as a psychic resistance to raising further critical questions. Since the theory is deliberately invoked by its enthusiasts to promote fear and foster an ideology of exclusion, I show that Replacement theory is an instance of the psychic contagion that Lonergan suggests is deliberately provoked and exploited by activists, political leaders, and pseudo-religious leaders.[7] The antidote of the contagion is psychic conversion. Just as religious conversion has something to do with loving correctly and moral conversion has something to do with deciding correctly and intellectual conversion has something to do with understanding and judging correctly, psychic conversion has something to do with attending correctly to one's empirical consciousness. For empirical consciousness penetrates all of these dimensions (experiencing, understanding, judging, deciding, and loving) in a person as that person is changed and moves from one level to another.[8]

Replacement Theory—A Cumulatively Misinterpreted Experience

Lonergan painstakingly worked out the matter of bias in chapters six and seven of *Insight*. His conclusion on the matter was informed by three theoretical analysis of human history that aid his theological investigations. His first approximation is that human beings always do what is intelligent and reasonable and that when they do the intelligent and reasonable it results in human progress and promote the good of

---

7. Lonergan, *Method in Theology*, 56–7.

8. Robert Doran, "What Does Bernard Lonergan Mean by Conversion," Unpublished Paper (2011); online: https://lonerganresource.com/pdf/lectures/What%20Does%20Bernard%20Lonergan%20Mean%20by%20Conversion.pdf; accessed July 4, 2022.

order. His second approximation is the radical inverse insight—that people can be biased and when they are biased they are unintelligent and unreasonable in their choices and decisions. Its implication is decline in the human person and denouement of the good of order. I will get to the third approximation that deals with redemption and reversal later in the section on Psychic Conversion. Let me elaborate on the second approximation, since it speaks to the obtuseness and unintelligence of the dramatic bias that goes in the name of the Great Replacement theory. When Lonergan speaks of decline in a person and society, he speaks of it as at times stemming from false or erroneous beliefs. For, "Besides the false beliefs there is the false believer."[9] The Replacement theory instantiates a human person's mimetic dimension of consciousness. The mimetic dimension results from the human lack of intelligence that wreaks havoc on society. For a long time the Replacement theory was ignored by the academic community and policy makers in the United States. It was viewed and dismissed as a white supremacist rhetoric. But the events of the last several years in which mass shooters have claimed to have drawn their inspiration from the theory have shown why the rhetoric can no longer be ignored. The Replacement theory is fast making its way into mainstream consciousness and this rings danger.

The origin of the Replacement theory goes back to the early twentieth century when some French nationalist writers, like the novelist-politician and anti-Semite, Maurice Barres (1862–1923) and Edouard Drumont (1844–1917), began denouncing as evil, Jews, aliens, Marxists, Kantian intellectuals, grands bourgeois, and liberals of all kinds. Barres for one thought that -these people were eating away at the body-politic of the French nation and that they were bringing France to ruin.[10] In truth, Barres' revolutionary idea was a reflection of the ideas that were already gaining ground in European intellectual circles. At the time, the same revolutionary ideas in Europe had produced Arthur Moeller van den Bruck, Julius Langbeh, and Adolf

---

9. Lonergan, *Method in Theology*, 44.

10. See Zeev Sternhell, "Nationalism Socialism and Anti-Semitism: The Case of Maurice Barres," *Journal of Contemporary History* 8 (1973), 47–66, 47.

Sticker in Germany, Karl Lueger and George Schonerer in Austria, and Carducci, Corraduni, and d'Annunzio in Italy.[11] While these revolutionaries all espoused, in one form or another, a range of theories that would later be called "the Great Replacement," the person who popularized the idea the most was the French dystopian fiction novelist, Jean Raspail (1925–2020).

Raspail thought that European whites were being replaced in their countries by non-white immigrants. He captured his xenophobic ideas in a fictional work, *Le Camp des Saints* [The Camp of the Saints] (1973).[12] In this controversial novel, Raspail details what, according to his imagination, was the impending loss of white culture. He details a flotilla of "bestial feces-eating" Indian migrants finding its way to the southern coast of France. He describes them as waves of "refugees, whose race, religion, language, and culture are different from our own." They are, according to him, fleeing famine, misery, and despair. Instead of turning away the "grotesque little beggars from the streets of Calcutta," he writes, the ruling elites choose to "empty out all our hospital beds" for the "cholera-ridden and leprous wretches." "Armed only with their weakness and their numbers, overwhelmed by misery, encumbered with starving brown and black children, ready to disembark on our soil." In Raspail's imagination, "To let them in would destroy us. To reject them would destroy them." The result of the hospitality was, white women being forced into "whorehouse" for Hindus. He blames the ruling elites for failing to respond and allowing France to be overrun by migrants from the Third world.

Raspail depicts the pope as a social activist and the church as an organ of social activism. He blames the media for promoting white (racial) guilt that are chipping away Western values. He also blames society for buying into the white guilt syndrome—that in trying to make amends for white guilt, society has looked the other way while the Third World immigrants flood European borders. Police officers that should enforce laws are more concerned with racial guilt than

---

11. Ibid.

12. See Jean Raspail, *The Camp of the Saints*, translated by Norman Shaipro [No facts of publication; no page numbers].

enforcing the laws. The military that should be defending the sovereignty of the nation is more concerned with racial guilt than their defense duties. All the channels that are supposed to protect European interests have become negligent because of white guilt. They have all joined forces with the Third world immigrants. European culture is changed forever and white race is lost.

Raspail's xenophobic vitriol comes down to, white race was lost because there was no will or belief on the part of the whites to defend their race. People with similar caste of mind have made *Le Camp des Saints* a must-read. In fact, *Le Camp des Saints* is "a must-read within the white supremacist circle" who take the book as their own canonical text.[13] Stephen Miller (a senior advisor for policy and director of Speech writing to former President Trump), Marine Le Pen (French lawyer and politician who ran for France's presidential election in 2012, 2017, and 2022), and Iowa Representative Steve King who suggested that the book should be imprinted in everyone's brain, have all touted the book in recent years.[14] Many others have also used Raspail's book and ideas to stoke fears of immigrants. Some of these anti-immigration enthusiasts consider Raspail to be the model prophet-intellectual. They take as dogma what Raspail details in his novel, not minding that the book is a fiction. Raspail's book inspired the French novelist and ideologue Renaud Camus (1946—) who in turn wrote *The Great Replacement* (2012) and *You Will Not Replace Us* (2018). Camus used these books to promote the false idea that white people are being reverse colonized by Third World immigrants who are flooding the door steps of European nations in record numbers.[15]

The ideas promoted by Camus in his two fictions have promoted all kinds of prejudices. In the United States where the prejudice or

13. Elian Peitier and Nicholas Kullish, "A Racist Book's Malign and Lingering Influence," *The New York Times* (Nov. 22, 2019); online: https://www.nytimes.com/2019/11/22/books/stephen-miller-camp-saints.html; accessed June 27, 2022.

14. Ibid.

15. See Renaud Camus, *You Will Not Replace Us* (Chez L'auteur, 2018); James Biser Whisker and John R. Coe, *The Great Replacement Theory* (Independently Published, 2022); Sarah Burley, *Great Replacement Theory and the USA: We Must Secure the Existence of Our People and the Future of White Children* (Kindle Edition, 2022).

bias is triggered automatically and unintentionally, some have taken to describing it as implicit bias. Like all prejudices, implicit bias comes in different shades and forms. But one constant in all its manifestations is that implicit bias affects a person's judgments and decisions. A law enforcement personnel with a high level of implicit bias against black people is more likely to categorize a black person's phone or toy as a gun. The induced and automatically triggered bias makes a non-weapon seem lethal. There are far too many examples in the United States of an unarmed black person who died in the custody of law enforcement personnel. Conversely, a black person with a high degree of implicit bias against the police is going to expect to be treated unfairly by the police because of the few rotten apples who have given a bad name to the police when in actual fact a vast majority of police officers and law enforcement personnel are judicious and very professional. A teacher or college professor with a high level of implicit bias is more likely to think of a high-energy black kid as "disruptive" and "less cooperative." Many black kids have been expelled from school in the United States for their high energy that biased teachers pass off as "disruptive." A physician with a high level of implicit bias against ethnic minorities is hardly going to give the best treatment to that ethnic minority. Numerous studies have shown that health care professionals display implicit bias towards patients of color—that they display the same level of implicit bias as the general population.[16] Implicit bias is broad in scope and cuts across ethnicity, race, and gender. A better term for this bias that manifests preconsciously is dramatic bias. There are some who question whether implicit bias is not just a convenient cover for racist behavior. They argue that to say a prejudicial behavior is implicit is to so deny culpability. This objection cannot easily be dismissed. This is why Lonergan offers a better category for conceptualizing this insidious bias. I have detailed the merit of the argument for dramatic bias in a different work.[17]

---

16. See Chloe FitzGerald and Samia Hurst, "Implicit Bias in Healthcare Professionals: A Systematic Review," *Medical Ethics* 18 (2017), 1–18.

17. See my forthcoming book on *Lonergan and Racism*, University of Toronto Press.

Replacement Theory as a Form of Dramatic Bias

Lonergan's elaborate discourse on bias is in *Insight* where he calls it scotoma and a distortion of intellectual development. The scotoma occurs in four principal ways—dramatic bias, individual bias, group bias, and general bias of common sense. I will refer the reader to *Insight* for detailed analyses of these discussions.[18] What I would like to allude to here is that Replacement theory, in so far as it is preconscious and unconscious, is a form of dramatic bias. The distortion feeds on false Philosophies and false historical narratives. It uses these narratives and philosophies to make negative evaluations of one group and its members relative to another and does it preconsciously.[19] The faulty non-existent ontologies of Replacement theory are induced by repression and inhibition that fundamentally undermine the psyche. The inhibition and repression generate a subtle, and in some cases, a manifestly clear intellectual bias. There are far too many instances of the latent and overt expressions of the theory in the United states. As hinted earlier, in the last two decades, replacement theory has become a catch-word in white supremacists circle, including fringe groups who now wish to express their biases in subtle ways. They have at times used other phrases that essentially suggest the same idea, such as "You Will Not Replace Us." The idea "that Western elites, sometimes manipulated by Jews, want to 'replace' and disempower white Americans— has become an engine of racist terror, helping inspire a wave of mass shootings."[20] There are also far too many examples of how this dramatic bias aligns with group bias, another incomplete development of intelligence at the group level, in the United States and around the world to undermine the psyche:

- In 2017, a group that gathered for a two-day rally in Charlottesville, Virginia, most of whom were white supremacists and Ku

---

18. See Lonergan, *Insight*, 244–67.

19. For more on dramatic bias, see Lonergan, *Insight*, 214–31.

20. Nicholas Confessore and Karen Yourish, "A Fringe Conspiracy Theory, Fostered Online, Is Refashioned by the G.O.P.," *The New York Times* (May 15, 2022), online: https://www.nytimes.com/2022/05/15/us/replacement-theory-shooting-tucker-carlson.html; accessed June 27, 2022.

Klux Klan, referenced the "Great Replacement" and chanted "You
will not replace us"

- In 2018, the shooter at the Tree of Life Synagogue in Pittsburgh
blamed Jews for allowing immigrant "invaders" into the US. In his
blog post he said he was motivated by "the Great Replacement"
- In 2019, the man who attacked and killed 51 people at two
mosques in Christchurch, New Zealand described his manifesto
as "The Great Replacement"
- In 2019, the Walmart shooter in El Paso TX who targeted Latino
immigrants blamed the "Hispanic invasion" and cited the Great
Replacement
- In 2019, a white supremacist killed one and injured three at a
Synagogue in Poway, California. In a letter he posted online, he
claimed that the Jews were responsible for the genocide of "white
Europeans"
- In 2022, the white gunman in Buffalo who targeted black people
and killed 10 posted online that the shoppers came from a culture
that sought to "ethnically replace my own people."

It would be easy to ignore Replacement theory if it was espoused
only by a few fringe elements. But sadly, Replacement theory is no
longer fringe. The contagion has taken center stage and is in main
stream channels. If psychic contagion is a matter of sharing another's emotion without adverting to it,[21] then the repeated references
to the replacement theory by some in main stream channels, especially when speaking about Latino and Haitian immigrants, show
how fast the contagion has spread. "We can't restore our civilization
with somebody else's babies," tweeted one prominent politician. The
tweet validates what Lonergan says in *Method in Theology*, "Such
contagion seems to be the mechanism of mass excitement in panics,
revolutions, revolts, demonstrations, strikes, where in general there
is a disappearance of personal responsibility, a domination of drives
over thinking, a decrease of the intelligence level, and a readiness for

---

21. Lonergan, *Method in Theology*, 56.

submission to a leader."[22] The polls also bear out this line of reasoning. An April 2022 poll by the Southern Poverty Law Center (SPLC) that examines the extent to which extremist beliefs and narratives that mobilize the hard right have been absorbed by the American public life not only found the Great Replacement theory to be trending mainstream, but also that nearly 7 in 10 of the 1500 Republicans surveyed "agree to at least some extent that demographic changes in the United States are deliberately driven by liberal and progressive politicians attempting to gain political power by "replacing more conservative white voters."[23] The SPLC survey is consistent with an earlier 2021 study in which nearly half of the Republicans polled by the Associated Press and the National Opinion Research Center (NORC) agree, at least to some extent, that there is a deliberate intent to replace native born Americans with immigrants.[24] While the SPLC survey was not designed to measure prejudice or bigotry, but to examine the extent to which certain groups feel threatened or persecuted by another, it is still easy to see how one group feels the existence of another group is an existential threat to their own. The very notion that one group can be perceived as inherently harmful to another group's existence is foundational to extremism and to bias. It is as ludicrous as the idea that societal changes or movement to build an equitable society pose a threat to white people.[25] The former Prime Minister of Great Britain, Boris Johnson, could not have stated any better his "one insight into human beings," which is, "that genius and talent and enthusiasm and imagination are evenly

22. Ibid., 57.

23. See Cassie Miller, "SPLC Poll Finds Substantial Support for 'Great Replacement' Theory and Other Hard-Right Ideas," online: https://www.splcenter.org/news/2022/06/01/poll-finds-support-great-replacement-hard-right-ideas; accessed June 27, 2022.

24. See Phillip Bump, "Nearly Half of Republicans Agree with 'Great Replacement Theory,'" *Washington Post* (May 9, 2022), online: https://www.washingtonpost.com/politics/2022/05/09/nearly-half-republicans-agree-with-great-replacement-theory/; accessed June 27, 2022.

25. Miller, "SPLC Poll Finds Support for 'Great Replacement Theory' and Other Hard-Right Ideas."

distributed" among peoples, "But opportunity is not."[26] This is an essential insight the replacement theorists miss or fail to grasp. To think that another group's existence is a threat to one's own existence because they seek equal opportunities, or to think that the movement toward an equitable society is a threat to the privileged, is naïve, to say the least. It is analogous to the philosophical thinking that only intuitions are sensitive.

In sum, the Great Replacement theory touches on the bias of the unconscious, which Lonergan painstakingly worked out in *Insight*, and which Doran elaborated on in many of his writings. As a form of naïve realism, the Great Replacement thinks of knowing as taking a good look. I noted earlier Lonergan's quip—that besides the false beliefs there is the false believer. The nuptial union of false beliefs and false believer has helped turn what was a trickle into a flood of masses who now hold on to the Replacement theory. To undo any false belief, Lonergan suggests that we begin by looking into the manner in which the false belief came to be accepted in the first place, so that one can "try to discover and correct the carelessness, the credulity, the bias that led one to mistake the false for the true."[27] This is precisely what I have done with the history and origins of the Replacement theory. But it is one thing to uncover the error, it is another thing to find a good remedy. Again to invoke Lonergan, "Mere hunting for errors can leave one a personal and cultural wreck without convictions and commitments."[28] Hence I turn next to a "commitment" that can help bring a solution—psychic conversion.

Psychic Conversion—A Form of Therapy

Earlier I alluded to Lonergan's three approximation of history, explaining the first two and deferring on the third. The third of Lonergan's

26. See full transcript of Boris Johnson's resignation speech as British Prime Minister on July 7, 2022, online: https://www.telegraph.co.uk/politics/2022/07/07/boris-johnson-resignation-speech-downing-street-prime-minister/; accessed July 7, 2022.

27. Lonergan, *Method in Theology*, 44.

28. Ibid.

approximation of history is the redemptive process resulting from God's gift of grace and the manifestation of this love in Christ Jesus. It is to this realm that psychic conversion belongs. Lonergan writes regarding conversion in general:

> Religious conversion goes beyond moral. Questions for intelligence, for reflection, for deliberation reveal the eros of the human spirit, its capacity and its desire for self-transcendence. But that capacity meets fulfilment, that desire turns to joy, when religious conversion transforms the existential subject into a subject in love, a subject held, grasped, possessed, owned through a total and so an other-worldly love. Then there is a new basis for all valuing and all doing good. In no way are the fruits of intellectual or moral conversion negated or diminished. On the contrary, all human pursuit of the true and the good is included within and furthered by a cosmic context and purpose and, as well, there now accrues to man the power of love to enable him to accept the suffering involved in undoing the effects of decline.[29]

The dramatic bias we have identified as Replacement theory shows human inability to transcend the limitations of their understanding and a person's inability to move beyond their lust to maintain their own personal advantages and comfort. Lonergan explains that this kind of egoism and aberration is easy to maintain and difficult to correct. "Egoists do not turn altruists overnight. Hostile groups do not easily forget their grievances, drop their resentments, overcome their fears and suspicions."[30] In psychological terms, it will take a significant amount of cognitive restructuring to give up years of resentments and suspicions. In theological terms, psychic conversion can act as a form of cognitive restructuring. One of the books Lonergan depended on while working out the four scotosis of the dramatic subject is Hebert Fingarette's *The Self in Transformation*[31] in which Fingarette conceived

---

29. Ibid., 242.

30. Ibid, 52.

31. See Herbeert Fingarette, *The Self in Transformation: Psychoanalysis, Philosophy and the Life of the Spirit* (New York: Basic Books, 1963).

neurosis as cumulatively misinterpreted experience.[32] Lonergan appropriates Fingarette, showing us that in any cumulatively misinterpreted experience, "both the experience and the misinterpretation are conscious though not adverted to, identified, named, distinguished from other experience and interpretations."[33]

Psychic conversion does not work in isolation. It presupposes the existence of religious, moral, and intellectual conversion. In practical terms, psychic conversion can help a person expand their circle of friends to include those who may seem foreign to them.[34] In his essay on friendship in which he appropriates Pope Francis' *Fratelli Tutti*, John Dadosky interprets the Pope as emphasizing our need to transcend ourselves through an encounter with others.[35] Like all scotoma and aberrations of understanding, the dramatic bias of Replacement theory is a limited horizon that undermines a person's ability to transcend themselves and make friends beyond their limited circle. Replacement theory is a repressive censor. The repressor puts a limit to what a person knows and is interested in. It limits their horizon only to what is convenient to them. What Doran calls psychic conversion functions as the transformation of the censor from a repressive to a constructive role in a person's development.[36]

Let me say a few words about the psyche before I return to psychic conversion. In explaining some key Christian doctrines, Lonergan locates "a sensitive psychic component of both the dialectic of the subject and the dialectic of community."[37] In the same vein, in explaining the mediation of Christ, Lonergan gives a general overview

32. Bernard Lonergan, "Insight Revisited," in Collected Works of Bernard Lonergan, vol., 13: *A Second Collection*, edited by Robert M. Doran and John D. Dadosky (Toronto: University of Toronto Press, 2016), 221–33, 228.

33. Ibid.

34. John Dadosky has captured this notion of expanding our circle of friends and neighbors. See John Dadosky, "Family and Friendship: The Implicit Ecclesiologies *ad extra* in Pope Francis' *Fratelli Tutti* and the Legacy of Vatican II's Dual Theologies of the Church," *Gregorianum* 103 (2022), 519–37.

35. Ibid., 525.

36. Doran, "Two Ways of Being Conscious" 8.

37. Ibid., 9.

of mediation, a term he traces back to Aristotle who distinguished between first principles (which are immediate and admit of no middle term because they cannot be proven) and conclusions (which are mediated by a middle term that is inserted between subject and predicate), Lonergan employs a wide range of examples—mechanical, organic, and psychic—to elucidate what is entailed in mediation. It is informative that when citing a psychic example Lonergan points to anger (or the irascible, in scholastic language), the very form of emotion that fuels Replacement theory. He shows how anger is immediate in aggression. While anger is immediate in aggressivity, it is at the same time mediated to consciousness through the senses—eyes, voice, jutting jaw, raised arm, forward step, violent images, one-track thinking, and vigor of the will[38]—the exact same way the sentiments behind Replacement theory are mediated. As anger grows and one tends towards explosion, "there is a mutual mediation or a feedback from the results of the anger to its causes."[39] We can see the mutual mediation in Replacement theory in politics and social movements from the examples we cited in the previous sections. Following Lonergan and shedding light on what Lonergan says about mutual mediation of emotions, such as anger, Doran shows that the psyche is the flow of sensations, memories, images, affects, conations, spontaneous intersubjective responses that accompany a person's intellectual and moral activities.[40] Doran correctly understands Lonergan as identifying the psyche with the empirical consciousness, i.e., the level of experience (as distinct from the levels of understanding, judgment, and decision.[41]

To return to conversion, Lonergan was clear about how a person's horizon can be bounded like "the line at which earth and sky appear to meet."[42] Since the range of our vision, like the scope of our knowledge

---

38. Bernard Lonergan, "The Mediation of Christ in Prayer," *Method: Journal of Lonergan Studies* 2 (1984), 1–20, 3–4; online: https://lonerganresource.com/pdf/journals/Method_Vol_2_No_1.pdf; accessed July 4, 2022.

39. Ibid., 5.

40. Robert Doran, "What Does Lonergan Mean by Conversion," Unpublished Paper (2011).

41. Doran, "Two Ways of Being Conscious," 12–13.

42. Lonergan, *Method in Theology*, 221.

PERSPECTIVES ON PSYCHIC CONVERSION

and interests are bounded, a shift in horizon is needed in the quest for self-transcendence. It is the movement into a new horizon, which involves an about-face and a new beginning, that Lonergan calls conversion.[43] He speaks of conversion as intellectual when it clarifies or eliminates myths about objectivity and knowing, such as the myth that black and brown people are coming to replace white people. He speaks of conversion as moral when it changes the criterion of one's decisions and choices from satisfactions to values.[44] With respect to Replacement theory, it will mean changing the parameters by which we judge the ethnic other and make decisions with respect to them. He speaks of conversion as religious when one is grasped by ultimate concerns and begins to love in an unrestricted manner. To be in love with a transcendent God means to be in love with someone. That "someone" includes the alien other and the ethnic other, i.e., people outside of our geographical frontiers. And to love them means loving them without qualifications or conditions or reservations or limits. In Dadosky's terms, this will entail making friends with them and regarding them as part of our family. This is Lonergan's essential point about self-transcendent love. This is what he means by "When someone transcendent is my beloved, he is in my heart, real to me from within me. When that love is the fulfillment of my unrestricted thrust to self-transcendence through intelligence and truth and responsibility, the one that fulfills that thrust must be supreme in intelligence, truth, and goodness."[45] Psychic conversion is a transformation of a person's conscious knowing and willing. It is a movement away from the psychic resistance to know truly and to love truly. Doran describes it as "the movement away from this resistance toward a new way of life in which one's sensitive desires begin to reach out toward a condition in which they will match and support the self-transcendence of the pure desire that is the spirit of inquiring consciousness itself."[46]

43. Ibid., 223.
44. Ibid., 225.
45. Ibid., 105.
46. Doran, *Theology and the Dialectics of History*, 52.

Psychic conversion re-establishes the two sensible and intellectual ways of knowing that may have been distorted. It "establishes or reestablishes a link that should never have been broken, the link between the intentional operations of understanding, judgment, and decision, and the tidal movement that begins before consciousness, emerges into consciousness in the form of dream images and affects, continues to permeate intentional operations in the form of feelings, and reaches beyond these operations and states in the interpersonal relations and commitments that constitute families, communities, and religions."[47] Conversion, however, is hardly ever instantaneous. It is mediated and happens incrementally and over time. Psychic conversion, in like manner, happens over time. Psychic conversion "does not mean affective self-fulfillment. It is a matter of establishing the connections in consciousness between one's waking orientation as a cognitive, moral, and religious being and the underlying movement of life with its affective and imaginal components."[48] As a flow of sensations, memories and images that undergird a person's intersubjective responses, "If you are asking a question, there is an affective dimension to that experience, not just an intellectual component. If you arrive at a satisfactory answer to your question, there is a change in you that is not only intellectual but also affective; you feel differently from the way you felt while you were confused and asking questions."[49]

Conclusion

Since many want to know what psychic conversion is and how it is relevant in society, our demonstration has been motivated by the desire to show the many relevancies of psychic conversion. The fact of racism, particularly its subliminal undertones, as evidenced in the Great Replacement theory, validates the need for psychic conversion. Lonergan speaks of conversion as something that affects all of

---

47. Doran, "Two Ways of Being Conscious," 7.
48. Doran, "What Does Lonergan Mean by Conversion."
49. Ibid.

a person's conscious and intentional operations. He speaks of conversion as directing a person's gaze, pervading the person's imagination, and releasing the symbols that penetrate the depths of the person's psyche. It is worth noting that Lonergan makes allusion to the psyche and more vividly speaks of conversion as penetrating the "depths of the psyche."[50] It is when a person's about-face has penetrated the depths of the psyche that conversion "enriches his understanding, guides his judgments, reinforces his decisions."[51] This is why I have argued for psychic conversion as a solution to the Great Replacement theory. If conversion is a change of direction and a change for the better that Lonergan says it is,[52] it will require a psychic re-orientation for proponents and believers in Replacement theory to drop their misleading fears, errors, and ideologies with respect to immigrants and ethnic minorities. It will take psychic conversion to seek friendship with God as it bears on friendship with the ethnic other. "The friendship with God is connected to the presence of charity where presumably the just are able to return God's favor through loving acts of benevolence."[53] At a recent American Theological Society (ATS) Conference (2022), someone reminded us that there are two energies in the world: love and fear and that fear is delusional and has the need to control because it is ego-driven. This person reminded us that "fear is actually a call to love." It is psychic conversion that can turn the negative energy, fear, into a positive energy, love.

---

50. Lonergan, Method in Theology, 126.
51. Ibid.
52. Ibid., 51.
53. Dadosky, "Family and Friendship," 530.

14

"Give the Quietus to the Daemon": Psychic Conversion, Redemption, and Antiblackness[1]

Jeremy W. Blackwood, PhD

ernard Lonergan (1904–1984) predicted that, as civilization unravels, "human activity settles down to a decadent routine, and initiative becomes the privilege of violence"[2]—a violence to be opposed by, not a new set of ideas or human achievements in human terms, but a "higher viewpoint" within which to make those achievements.[3] For Lonergan, that higher viewpoint consisted in an imitation of and participation in the cross of Christ that he called the "law of the cross."[4] Yet, as one of my graduate students recently exclaimed in simple but accurate language, *performing the law of the cross is hard!* The difficulty is not simply born of the meanings and values to which we hold; it is felt, emotional, visceral.

Robert M. Doran (1939–2021) engaged in an extensive analysis of this affective component throughout his career. Beginning with a

---

1. This work benefitted from feedback at the 2021 Lonergan Workshop. I thank the participants for their comments.

2. Bernard J. F. Lonergan, *Insight: A Study of Human Understanding,* ed. Frederick E. Crowe and Robert M. Doran, Collected Works of Lonergan 3 (Toronto: University of Toronto Press, 1992), 8.

3. Lonergan, *Insight,* 233.

4. Bernard J. F. Lonergan, *The Redemption,* trans. Michael G. Shields, ed. Robert M. Doran, H. Daniel Monsour, and Jeremy D. Wilkins, Collected Works of Lonergan 9 (Toronto: University of Toronto Press, 2018), 197.

hypothesis about what he called "psychic conversion," he argued for recognition of the sensitive-psychic component that accompanied the conscious-intentional elements in Lonergan's work, and he later extended that account to incorporate the mimetic analyses of René Girard (1923–2015).

This essay will describe key components of Doran's work on psychic conversion and then illustrate the contribution it could make to dealing with one major issue in contemporary American discourse, namely, the racial injustice known as antiblackness. A first section will narrate Doran's insights into psychic conversion and its connection to Girardian analysis, including its relevance to Lonergan's understanding of redemption and the law of the cross. A second section will then describe the plague of antiblackness that infects the social order and cultural meanings and values of the United States. A concluding comment will suggest ways to understand some components of the solution to antiblackness via Doran's work.

I. Doran's Development on Psychic Conversion

Doran understood his engagement with the affective dimension of subjectivity to have always had a theological *telos*.[5] Its later development in terms of the law of the cross and Girard develops further this original conception. Those later moves brought to fruition Doran's earliest efforts at working out the distinction and link between the intentional and the affective dimensions of consciousness. At no point did Doran consider his work in this area to be a replacement for or significant correction of Lonergan's positions, however. Doran envisaged himself to be complementing Lonergan's work by raising and answering further questions.[6]

Doran first shared his hypothesis with Lonergan on a short set of notes in November 1973, where he proposed the following:

---

5. Robert M. Doran, *What is Systematic Theology?* (Toronto: University of Toronto Press, 2005), ix.

6. See, for example, Robert M. Doran, "Psychic Conversion," *The Thomist* 41, no. 2 (1977), 232.

. . . there is a sublation of the imaginal, and principally of the symbolic revelations of dreams (through which feelings are released from
their muteness) on the part of the whole of attentive, intelligent, reasonable, responsible, cooperative-intersubjective waking consciousness. Thus, in addition to the attentive, intelligent, reasonable, and
responsible appropriation of one's rational self-consciousness,
there is the attentive, intelligent, reasonable, and responsible
appropriation and negotiation of one's irrationality. . . .
    This sublation effects a conversion of the existential subject.
This conversion is called psychic conversion.
    Psychic conversion is the issuing of the existential subject
into the capacity to distinguish symbolic positions from symbolic counterpositions, mystery from myth. This capacity is
therapeutic, involving a healing of affect.[7]

Lonergan's reply explicitly affirmed the basic hypothesis: "As far as
I can see your account of my position is accurate. In the same sense, I
think your work is a needed complement to my own."[8]

    A few years later (1977), Doran would publish and refine his
approach:

the exigence for self-appropriation recognized and heeded by
Lonergan, when it extends to the existential subject, to what
Lonergan would regard as the fourth level of intentional consciousness, becomes an exigence for psychic self-appropriation,
calling for the release of what C. G. Jung calls the transcendent
function, the mediation of psyche with intentionality in an
intrasubjective collaboration heading toward individuation.
The release of the transcendent function is a fourth conversion,

7. Robert M. Doran, "Twenty-Five Methodological Theses," unpublished notes,
November 18, 1973; now published as Robert M. Doran, *Conscious in Two Ways:
Robert M. Doran Remembers,* ed. Joseph Ogbonnaya, Jeremy W. Blackwood, and
Gregory Lauzon (Milwaukee: Marquette University Press, 2021), 105–09. The cited
statements are found on pages 105–06.
    8. Doran, *Conscious in Two Ways,* 111. See also John D. Dadosky, "Introduction,"
in *Meaning and History in Systematic Theology: Essays in Honor of Robert Doran, SJ,*
ed. John D. Dadosky, (Milwaukee: Marquette University Press, 2009), 10 n3.

beyond the religious, moral, and intellectual conversions specified by Lonergan. I call it psychic conversion.[9]

Doran saw the opening for the psychological component in Lonergan's recognition of "a twofold mediation of immediacy by meaning":
that is, one when we objectify cognitional process and another when
we discover and accept feelings in psychotherapy.[10] Essentially, Doran
argued, the second form of immediacy is always imaginal and is not
accessible by direct encounter, as are, for example, the operations of
experiencing, understanding, judging, or deciding that we encounter in the first form. Thus, psychotherapy is needed to work on those
images and affects, and Doran named the point at which we achieved
access to them 'psychic conversion.'[11]

In these early conceptions, the prompt for the development toward
this conversion was the realization that one's deciding, judging, and
understanding were inadequate.[12] Lonergan had stated that the typical sequence of conversion was religious to moral to intellectual[13] but,
Doran argued, if that were the case, then there would be something
pre-critical about one's religious and moral conversions, as they would
have occurred prior to intellectual conversion.[14] Then, once intellectual conversion occurs, one would run the risk of rejecting moral and
religious conversion because their content was pre-critical, unless one
could negotiate the content of moral and religious conversion in ways
that are not reducible to and eliminable in this critical shift in the criterion of the real. Doran had the insight that, because our converted
pursuit of the good relies on a grasp of value in intentional feelings, the
appropriation of one's imaginal-affective field that psychic conversion

---

9. Doran, "Psychic Conversion," 201.

10. Doran, "Psychic Conversion," 204.

11. Doran, "Psychic Conversion," 205.

12. Doran, "Psychic Conversion," 210.

13. Bernard J. F. Lonergan, *Method in Theology*, ed. Robert M. Doran, and John
D. Dadosky, Collected Works of Lonergan 14 (Toronto: University of Toronto Press,
2017), 228–29.

14. Doran, "Psychic Conversion," 207 and 208.

enables, allows us to critically *understand*, rather than just pre-critically *perform*, the authentic operation made possible by moral and religious conversion, and only in that fuller sense can we be said to have truly appropriated our own conscious-intentional subjectivity.[15]

This argument depends upon Doran's suspicion that "basic terms and relations, as psychological, are also explanatory."[16] In other words, the field of imagery and affect on which our intelligence draws for its understandings and which conditions our grasps of value at the existential level is intelligible as such a field, even if its content is not that of intelligent operation. Engagement with it therefore need not be regression to pre-criticality.[17] Instead, the imaginal-affective dimension can be grasped as the field out of which arise the images needed for insight. By grasping it that way, we can address the authenticity of that imaginal-affective field to achieve therapeutic gains, where 'therapeutic' is defined, at least in part, as a movement toward authenticity in all the dimensions of consciousness.

The second period[18] of Doran's career came to a more precise definition of psychic conversion: "a transformation of the subject [that is] a reorientation of the specifically psychic dimension of the censorship exercised over images and affects by our habitual orientations, a conversion of that dimension of the censorship from exercising a repressive function to acting constructively in one's shaping of one's own development."[19] The issue at hand, as we just saw, is authenticity: the two dimensions of consciousness allow for a distinction between a "pneumopathology" (unauthenticity in one's conscious operations) and a "psychopathology" (unauthenticity in one's negotiation of image and affect) in the unconverted.[20]

---

15. Doran, "Psychic Conversion," 202, 205 n15, and 208–209.

16. Doran, "Psychic Conversion," 231.

17. Doran, "Psychic Conversion," 212.

18. See Dadosky, "Introduction," 9–10.

19. Robert M. Doran, *Theology and the Dialectics of History* (Toronto: University of Toronto Press, 1990), 9.

20. Doran, *Theology and the Dialectics of History*, 48. See also Doran, "Psychic Conversion," 216.

Finally, in Doran's third period, we see the issue pressed farther into the theological dimension:

> Psychic conversion is to be understood as the transformation especially of the psychic dimension of the censorship, the dimension affected by what Lonergan calls 'dramatic bias.' The transformation occurs through the extension to the level of the sensitive psyche and of the preconscious neural functioning of the organism of the conversion process that promotes the condition of 'universal willingness' or total being-in-love or charity.[21]

These definitions, however, call for further explanation: What is it that psychic conversion *does*?

Conversion As Psychic

For Doran, these psychological data both cannot be ignored and must be understood in relation to the data on our own acts of insight and judgment, moral evaluation and decision-making, and love.[22] Operationally defined, then, psychic conversion is a "self-appropriation which begins when one attentively, intelligently, reasonably, and responsibly learns to negotiate the symbolic configurations of dispositional immediacy."[23] The term 'conversion' applied because it consisted in a shift in the subject's use of her own indeliberate psychological field of imagery and affect *from* holding back uncomfortable imagery and affect, which risked neglecting the materials needed for accurate insight, *to* offering forth the materials needed for insight even when and if they are uncomfortable or painful.[24]

This self-transcending shift then provided the criterion by which psychic performance was to be normed,[25] a norming that gains its

---

21. Doran, *What is Systematic Theology?*, 112.

22. Doran, *Theology and the Dialectics of History*, 44. See also Doran, *What is Systematic Theology?*, 110.

23. Doran, "Psychic Conversion," 230.

24. Doran, *Theology and the Dialectics of History*, 53 and 75. See also Doran, *What is Systematic Theology?*, 111.

25. Doran, *Theology and the Dialectics of History*, 54.

significance from the fact that insights, judgments, moral deliberations and decisions, and love are conditioned by the imaginal-affective field.[26] That is, self-transcending authenticity in conscious-intentional operations is accompanied by a corresponding form of self-transcendence by and in which one's field of images and affects supports and sustains the authentic performance of knowing and choosing.[27] All of this, Doran argued, means that rather than supporting any intellectualist effort to *eliminate* these depths, psychic conversion allows for and makes authentic the *appropriation* of the depths for use in an explanatory way by which we can differentiate between symbolic expressions of authentic positions and symbolic expressions of unauthentic counterpositions.[28]

Later, Doran drew out another implication: psychic conversion opened the subject up to receive properly the aesthetic component of the revelation of God in Christ.[29] As Lonergan had noted, conscious intentionality is "preceded, accompanied, and transcended by an aesthetic-dramatic operator" to which psychic conversion gave access.[30] Insofar as it provides the imagery into which insights are had and conditions the affectivity in which values are grasped, the imaginal-affective component could then offer to theology a further source for its reflections on the symbols of the religious tradition.[31]

Psyche and Social Reality

Doran conceived of the aberrations that psychic conversion heals as originating in social interactions between human beings. A psyche that has been the subject of a harmful social order (whether between two people

26. Doran, *Theology and the Dialectics of History*, 47.

27. Doran, *Theology and the Dialectics of History*, 55.

28. Doran, *Theology and the Dialectics of History*, 61. On Lonergan's use of the terms 'position' and 'counterposition,' see Lonergan, *Insight*, 413–414.

29. Doran, *What is Systematic Theology?*, 92.

30. Doran, *What is Systematic Theology?*, 114, citing Bernard J. F. Lonergan, "Philosophy and the Religious Phenomenon," in *Philosophical and Theological Papers 1965–1980*, ed. Robert C. Croken and Robert M. Doran, Collected Works of Lonergan 17 (Toronto: University of Toronto Press, 2004), 401–402.

31. Doran, *What is Systematic Theology?*, 119; see 117–119 for the larger point.

or between sweeping, civilization-level components) connects images and affects in ways that make the calling forth of appropriate images painful, decreasing the chance that appropriate images will be made available for the operations of understanding, judgment, and moral deliberation and action.[32] In such cases, a subject can develop an "organic mendacity" in which their imaginal-affective field conditions their conscious-intentional operations in such a way that the subject is led to selfish results without having had to deliberately choose them as egoistically beneficial.[33]

In such cases, there has been a corruption in the way that meaning and value are received from the human beings around us. In *What Is Systematic Theology?* (2005) Doran argued strenuously for a renewed notion of empirical consciousness, one that would include not simply the reception of data of sense and consciousness in the movement from experience up to decision, but also the reception of meaning and value from our fellow human beings in the top-down movement from valuing to attending.[34] While the first movement generates original meaning within an individual subject who then may communicate it outwardly, the second movement is one's reception of ordinary meaning that other subjects have generated.[35] This reception of meaning and value penetrates to the sensitive-psychic or imaginal-affective level, so the reception of distorted meaning and value has a concomitant distorting effect on the imaginal-affective field. Simply put, as a result of disordered meaning and value, images, meanings, and values that should be pleasing feel unpleasant, while images, meanings, and values that should be unpleasant feel pleasing. This distortion impinges upon the calling forth of needed images and affects, leading

---

32. Doran, *Theology and the Dialectics of History*, 62. For an earlier form of this argument, see Doran, "Psychic Conversion," 218–219, citing there Erich Neumann, *Depth Psychology and a New Ethic*, trans. Eugene Rolfe (New York: G. P. Putnam, 1969).

33. See, for example, Robert M. Doran, "The Nonviolent Cross: Lonergan and Girard on Redemption," *Theological Studies* 71 (2010), 49, where he is quoting Max Scheler, *Ressentiment*, trans. William H. Holdheim (New York: Free Press of Glencoe, 1961), 77–78.

34. Doran, *What is Systematic Theology?*, 125.

35. See Lonergan, *Insight*, 302, and Doran, *What is Systematic Theology?*, 124–33.

to misunderstandings as well as poor judgments of fact and value. Subjects then produce further corrupted meaning and value, which is then received by others who are, in turn, damaged by it, and who then produce additional corrupted meaning and value, and so on.[36]

For Doran, this analysis draws on and specifies what Lonergan called "the passionateness of being."[37] Understood as a "tidal movement" stretching from the pre-conscious elements on which intentionality acts, passing up through the levels of such intentionality, and finding a terminus when one falls in love, this "passionateness" is in a sense the subject's experience of participation in what we might call the flow of the unfolding of the emerging universe.[38] Negotiation of the imaginal-affective field, then, is a significant—though not the only—part of our authentic participation in the entire universe created by God. Without such negotiation, our participation in that universe is stunted, biased toward a disincarnate conception of subjectivity, and disconnected from concerns about the authenticity and health of the very field out of which our conscious-intentional operations of meaning and valuing gather their material.

Psychic Conversion as Theological Tool

By the publication of 2019's *The Trinity in History* volume, occurrences of the explicit term 'psychic conversion' were significantly reduced,[39] and Doran was developing and expanding his account.[40] As mentioned above, Doran had hit upon the significance of the imaginal-affective

---

36. See Doran, *What is Systematic Theology?*, 126. Here, Doran is citing Lonergan, *Insight*, 243.

37. Bernard J. F. Lonergan, "Mission and the Spirit," in *A Third Collection*, ed. Robert M. Doran, and John D. Dadosky, Collected Works of Lonergan 16 (Toronto: University of Toronto Press, 2017), 29. Cited at Doran, *What is Systematic Theology?*, 27; see also 112–113.

38. See, for example, Jeremy W. Blackwood, *"And Hope Does Not Disappoint": Love, Grace, and Subjectivity in the Work of Bernard J. F. Lonergan, S. J.* (Milwaukee: Marquette University Press, 2017), 116.

39. Doran, *The Trinity in History, Vol. 2*, 256.

40. Doran, *What is Systematic Theology?*, 109.

field and its proper negotiation for our reception of revelation. Revelation is carried primarily by a symbolic medium, the proper understanding of which requires a converted psyche to enable engagement with one's own symbolic reservoir in order to connect it with that of the revealed truth of God found in Tradition and Scripture.[41]

The central (though certainly not only) theological locus on which this symbolic-imaginal-affective issue turns is the question of redemption. Doran affirmed that "any articulation of redemption must remain irretrievably elemental, esthetic, dramatic, ultimately narrative in form"[42] precisely because there is a sense in which the meanings we receive from others (such as the content of revelation) oftentimes (though not always) have a "permanently elemental" character.[43] Doran argued that redemption is found in a set of events, some of its meaning is only expressible symbolically, and therefore, subsequent expression of that meaning in an explanatory-technical mode does not reproduce, but only "set[s] within a conceptual field," the meaning itself.[44] In other words, for Doran, a systematic-explanatory articulation of the meaning of the redemption leaves behind the symbolic-imaginal-affective precisely *as* symbolic-imaginal-affective and, effectively, *replaces it with an explanatory account of* the symbolic-imaginal-affective aspects of the redemption. But since the symbolic-imaginal-affective *as such* is intrinsic to the very meaning of the redemption, leaving it behind loses part of the full meaning of the redemption.[45]

Understood within the larger social and even cosmic context, we are reminded that redemption is not easily accomplished. The early Doran understood Jungian psychology as a process by which "the whole of subjectivity will be afforded an optimum degree of life and development, as the subject continues on the journey to individuation."[46] Yet that social and cosmic context, and specifically any efforts

41. Doran, *What is Systematic Theology?*, 122–124.
42. Doran, "The Nonviolent Cross," 50.
43. Doran, *What is Systematic Theology?*, 129.
44. Doran, *What is Systematic Theology?*, 22.
45. Doran, *What is Systematic Theology?*, 22–23.
46. Doran, "Psychic Conversion," 214.

at individuation, run up against a significant, recurrent problem: violence.[47] Doran's insight into psychic conversion addresses the need for "softening the human heart or refashioning the human self [that] requires that social and psychological reflexes relied upon and reinforced 'since the foundation of the world' be overridden," as Gil Bailie put it.[48] Not until his engagement with René Girard, however, did this dimension become fully clear.

Psychic Conversion and Girard

What Is Systematic Theology? contains little explicit mention of Girard.[49] Five years after its publication, however, Doran affirmed the value of Girard's work in relation to Lonergan in precisely the context of violence just noted:

> Lonergan has articulated the structure of what he calls the transcendental intentions or notions of intelligibility, truth and being, and the good. Girard has elucidated the mimetic, indeed acquisitively mimetic and potentially violent, character of a great deal of human desire. Each thinker is a contributor to what perhaps we may call a hermeneutics of desire.[50]

In the later portion of his life and career, Doran drew attention to Girard more and more. He argued that Girard described the "principal instance" of dramatic bias[51] in such a way as to specify[52] and offer the best account of or approach to psychic conversion.[53]

---

47. Robert J. Daly, "Phenomenology of Redemption? Or Theory of Sanctification?," *Theological Studies* 74 (2013), 361.

48. Gil Bailie, *Violence Unveiled: Humanity At the Crossroads* (New York: Crossroad, 1995), 216, quoting Mt 13:35. Cited in Daly, "Phenomenology of Redemption?" 358.

49. Doran, *What is Systematic Theology?*, 24 contains the only mention of Girard in the body of the book. In footnotes, he connects Girard to redemption (212 n10) and *ressentiment* (224 n69).

50. Doran, "The Nonviolent Cross," 47.

51. Doran, *The Trinity in History, Vol. 1*, 211.

52. Doran, *The Trinity in History, Vol. 1*, 224.

53. Doran, *The Trinity in History, Vol. 2*, 22, 25. See also Doran, *The Trinity in History, Vol. 1*, 354 n12 and Doran, *The Trinity in History, Vol. 1*, 354 n14.

In theological terms, Doran came to believe that Girard offers a way to understand a dimension of redemption that Lonergan had not (or at least, had not fully) taken into account: namely, the affective. Where Lonergan offered a systematic-theological way of understanding how, through the cross, God transformed violence and death into a meaningful means of salvation, Girard allowed Doran to extend this analysis to more readily incorporate the second way of being conscious.

> For my present purposes, it is the relation of the two ways of being conscious that is significant. They interact, and the relative autonomy of the second may be compromised by the gradual and unnoticed infiltration of acquisitive mimetic desire into the very performance of operations of understanding, judging, and deciding.[54]

Lonergan's theology of redemption finds its focus in what he termed 'the law of the cross,' in which he sought to transpose soteriology into the terms of the third stage of meaning, rooting it in conscious operations.[55] In Lonergan's account, the simplicity, goodness, and intelligibility of God mean that the universe God created is good and just to the extent that it is intelligible.[56] Yet there are evils in the universe, and evils are absences of good and intelligibility, so a question arises concerning how a universe with these lacunae remains both just and intelligible. The necessary distinction arises when we realize that God does not will the evils in the same way that God wills the goods: God wills the goods directly, permits but does not will the evil of sin, and in willing a just, intelligible universe, indirectly wills intelligibly connected consequences, including the evils that are the consequences of sin. Created minds thus confront the fact that the universe is a complex, rather than a simple, intelligibility. The universe's whole order must include some way for intelligibility and justice to be drawn out of those lacunae.

---

54. Doran, "The Nonviolent Cross," 49.

55. William P. Loewe, "Sebastian Moore, Redemptive Transformation, and the Law of the Cross," *The Downside Review* 136, no. 3 (2018), 179.

56. This summary owes a significant debt to Charles Hefling, "A Perhaps Permanently Valid Achievement: Lonergan on Christ's Satisfaction," *Method: Journal of Lonergan Studies* 10, no. 1 (1992), 56.

The law of the cross is precisely that mechanism. It includes three steps: (1) sin in the universe gives rise to the evil of death; (2) this evil of death should be responded to not in kind, but out of love; and (3) God will then bless this transformation with renewed life.[57] Doran is clear that the law of the cross does not mean mere submission to the old law, mere passive acceptance of the evil.[58] At the same time, the law does not eliminate the evils, but rather transforms them into something new.[59] That something new is the "supreme good" that is "the whole Christ, head and members," and for Doran this consists in a new community of interpersonal relations grounded on the personal subsistent relations that the Trinitarian persons are.[60]

Ligita Ryliškytė has helpfully reminded us of the cosmic range of this supreme good, but in so doing she suggests that Doran denies the cosmic reach of the end into which the evils are transformed.[61] It's more likely that Doran focused his attention on the new interpersonal community, not because he took a position contrary to Lonergan and neglected the cosmic dimension, but because both men held that it is in and through the new interpersonal community that that cosmic dimension is reached. In one of his last published articles, Doran argued that

the covenant purposes of God 'always envisioned the redemption of the whole world' and now are explicitly 'call[ing] into being a trans-national and transcultural community' to *catalyze the new law on earth* that comes from the establishment of God's reign. The ultimate end, beyond even the community of the new

---

57. For this concise way of putting it, see Loewe, "Sebastian Moore, Redemptive Transformation, and the Law of the Cross," 179.

58. Doran, *The Trinity in History, Vol. 1*, 239. For another approach, see Ligita Ryliškytė, "Conversion: Falling Into Friendship Like No Other," *Theological Studies* 81, no. 2 [2020], 392.

59. Mark T. Miller, "Imitating Christ's Cross: Lonergan and Girard on How and Why," *The Heythrop Journal* LIV (2013), 866.

60. Doran, *The Trinity in History, Vol. 1*, 232–34, citing Lonergan, *The Redemption*, 197.

61. Ryliškytė, "Conversion."

covenant, is the redeemed world itself, where redemption as end is coterminous with the reign of God.[62]

In this article, he explicitly connected the new community to the integral scale of values before adding that the point of the community is the "continued mediation of the ultimate end, which is the redemption of human history itself in the reign of God in accord with the social grace that is manifest whenever, and to the extent that, the scale of values is realized in history."[63] As the quote above suggests, however, the reign of God is not restricted simply to human community. Doran's entire discussion here takes place in light of a distinction he drew between redemption as end *in history* and redemption as end *beyond history*—the latter of which is eschatological.[64] In the historical unfolding of redemption, the new community entered upon by participating in the law of the cross is the means by which the scale of values is enacted, and the enactment of the scale of values is, in turn, the means by which the whole universe is redeemed.

Doran's approach accords with Lonergan's perspective in *Insight*, the *Redemption* text, and the *Supplement*. In *Insight* Lonergan argued that the expansion of the influence of human intelligence through human history includes generating both the social *and the material* conditions for further insight and decision.[65] Thus, the expansion of the higher viewpoint occasioned by the law of the cross includes the alteration of the wider cosmos in an intelligent, reasonable, and responsible manner.

Similarly, in the *Redemption* text, the extrinsic end (the divine essence) is brought to the intrinsic end (the universal order)[66] through the rational material to which certain components of the gift of the

---

62. Robert M. Doran, "Redemption as End and Redemption as Mediation," *Gregorianum* 101, no. 4 (2020), 936–37, citing N. T. Wright, *Jesus and the Victory of God* (Minneapolis: Fortress Press, 1996), 219. Doran's emphasis.

63. Doran, "Redemption as End and Redemption as Mediation," 938.

64. Doran, "Redemption as End and Redemption as Mediation," 927.

65. Lonergan, *Insight*, 252–53.

66. Lonergan, *The Redemption*, 221.

extrinsic end are ordered.[67] Lonergan states explicitly, for example, that the intrinsic end achieved by communicating the extrinsic end is

> the order of the universe [but] in a way such that (1) it is an order of persons in the communication of the divine good, (2) this order is brought about through the wisdom of apprehension . . . and through the charity of the will, and, finally, (3) the wisdom of this apprehension is attained in this life through faith, and in the life to come through the vision of God.[68]

As for the *Supplement*, there we find that the body of Christ is a universal order participating in and for the sake of the divine goodness.[69] Here seems to be the crux of Ryliškytė's needed emphasis on the cosmic. However, Lonergan's argument in the *Supplement* makes human beings central to the overall plan, as "what divine wisdom has ordered and divine goodness has chosen comes into existence through human beings who understand, judge, and consent."[70] There is a hierarchy in the body of Christ,[71] and the incarnation is for the sake of communication to the "intellectual creatures"[72] in that hierarchy who could be the recipients of grace and the gifts of the Spirit.[73] This encompasses all human beings,[74] because it has to do with "the human good of order"[75] and its changes "for better or worse."[76] God uses the fact that human causality extends out into the universe through our

---

67. Lonergan, *The Redemption*, 205.

68. Lonergan, *The Redemption*, 221.

69. Lonergan, *The Redemption*, 625–29.

70. Lonergan, *The Redemption*, 583. See also Jeremy W. Blackwood, "Law of the Cross and the Mystical Body of Christ," in *Intellect, Affect, and God: The Trinity, History, and the Life of Grace*, ed. Joseph Ogbonnaya, and Gerard Whelan S.J., (Milwaukee: Marquette University Press, 2021), 278–279.

71. Lonergan, *The Redemption*, 629 and 631.

72. Lonergan, *The Redemption*, 633.

73. Lonergan, *The Redemption*, 635.

74. Lonergan, *The Redemption*, 633. See also 635.

75. Lonergan, *The Redemption*, 639.

76. Lonergan, *The Redemption*, 579.

understanding and willing,[77] especially as that causality is more effective when performed communally.[78]

Lonergan thus argues that the focus of the incarnation was God's relationship with human beings and human beings' relationships with one another, and then through that the redemption is connected to the rest of the cosmos. This accords with Ryliškytė's observation that "[t]he proximate referent of God's salvific intent, however, is the transformation of the human being."[79] The transformed individual is never plucked free from the communal or cosmic context, however, so it seems clear that Doran's focus on the transformation of human community was not disagreeing with Lonergan or neglecting the cosmic dimension, but rather focusing on interpersonal community as the means by which God achieves that cosmic, eschatological consummation.

When it comes to the role of René Girard's work in understanding redemption, Doran interprets Girard as addressing the imaginal-affective or psychic dimension alongside Lonergan's systematic-theological law of the cross. Girard analyzed the issue in terms of desire. For him, all human desiring arises from our imitation of one another and is therefore mimetic (imitative).[80] This is a positive attribute insofar as it allows us to learn new things, but it can become a source of problems. Because we learn to desire from others, and they are desiring certain objects, then our imitative desiring seeks those same object(s). Two individuals, then—the model and the imitator—can become rivals for the same object of desire. Other people are drawn in, as they imitate the rivals. The situation intensifies, communal bonds weaken and, eventually, collapse. The violent feelings seek release, and people tend to direct them onto someone—a scapegoat—who, after being chosen, is (originally, for Girard) killed or (later) cast out or (even later) replaced symbolically by an animal or other ritual.

---

77. Lonergan, *The Redemption*, 575.

78. Lonergan, *The Redemption*, 579.

79. Ryliškytė, "Conversion."

80. For a helpful overview of Girard's position, see Charles Hefling, "About What Might a 'Girard-Lonergan "Conversation"' be?," *Lonergan Workshop* 17 (2002), 97–100.

This expulsion really does lessen the violence; it serves as a safety valve providing the community with an outlet, as they blame this killed or expelled person for the breakdown of community. Their belief is reinforced when, precisely because they've cast out this object of their vitriol, peace returns to the community. The troubling aspect, however, is that this scapegoat mechanism only works if people believe it works. If people were to realize that, in fact, the scapegoat did not actually do anything to cause the violence and breakdown of community or to heal it upon expulsion, then killing or expelling them would do no good.

Girard interprets the Israelite Scriptures as moving in the direction of revealing this mechanism and the Gospel narrative as disclosing, in the person of Jesus of Nazareth, how the scapegoat mechanism worked to kill a truly innocent person. In other words, he maintains that Christianity's core is, in fact, the revelation that the scapegoating mechanism is based on a falsehood.

Development as a human being, then, is for Girard the emergence from being enmeshed in the relatively undifferentiated "interdividual" field in which mimetic desire arises, feeds off of, and results in conflict with other human beings, and the reaching of a point of personal differentiation and refusal to participate in the mimetic rivalry and scapegoating. He then interprets Christianity as fostering precisely this kind of growth in authenticity.

Psyche, Mimesis, and Redemption

As was mentioned above, Doran draws the law of the cross and Girard together by elaborating on the significance of desire for both Lonergan and Girard. Whereas the latter considers desire to be something that arises from imitation of other persons, the former distinguishes a form of desire intrinsic to the human spirit, one that manifests in questions seeking understanding, reflective grasp of the truth, and discernment of value and proper courses of action.[81]

---

81. See, for example, Doran, *The Trinity in History, Vol. 1*, 197–99.

Doran argued that Lonergan provided the heuristic structure of conscious intentionality in relation to which Girard offered data to be understood.[82] I think a question can be raised here, however, about whether and to what degree a Girardian framework should be thought to reside at the level of the "upper blade" heuristic or the "lower blade" of the data to be understood. To the extent that the Girardian analysis describes and even explains intrinsic dynamics of human affectivity, then one could argue that mimesis, its manifestation in terms of rivalry, and the tendency toward violence in individual incarnate subjects all express aspects of the imaginal-affective component *of the heuristic*. In such a case, the data to be understood would be, not the Girardian contribution in general, but specific instances of grasps of meaning, truth, value, and decisions as conditioned by affectivity taking the form, at least in part, of mimetic structures of rivalry and violence.

No matter what we say about the heuristic, the two forms of desire pertain to the law of the cross differently, as Doran understands it:

> [L]iberation from psychic bias is given only through the grace that enables one to live by what Lonergan calls the Law of the Cross. . . . That grace also liberates the intersubjective psyche from mimetic violence and rivalry and that liberation is itself, among other things, freedom for development in attentiveness, intelligence, reasonableness, and responsibility, that is, for development precisely in the habits and operations that Lonergan regards as crucial to the determination of the genuineness of cultural and religious traditions and convictions.[83]

In other words, the law of the cross involves decisions one makes in accord with one's grasp of value and truth, and the Girardian insights offer a way to understand the imaginal-affective dimension that conditions those grasps.[84] Grace, in enabling our participation in the law of the cross, penetrates to this imaginal-affective dimension in such a

---

82. Doran, "The Nonviolent Cross," 51.
83. Doran, *The Trinity in History, Vol. 1*, 248.
84. Doran, *The Trinity in History, Vol. 1*, 318. See also 248.

way that the mimetic component of that field is drawn to a healthy orientation that fosters, rather than detracts from, the operations of attending, understanding, judging, and deciding.

The challenge resides in the fact that, rather than turning our desires in a healthy direction that would enhance our grasps of truth and value, human history has been a story of our letting mimetic rivalry run its course and then purging our desires by using the scapegoat mechanism. As Robert Daly has noted, this mimetic tendency is deeply rooted and has been discerned across neurobiology, psychology, physiology, and more.[85] Our need for some way of dealing with desire is thus also deeply rooted, and the question becomes whether or not we can find a way of doing so if the scapegoat mechanism is unveiled and removed.[86] Doran understands this deep rooting theologically in terms of original sin by suggesting that our failure to reject this mimetic cycle results in the evil consequences with which we now must contend, and he raises a question about the extent to which those consequences prompt further failures to reject the cycle and its accompanying basic sins.[87] The problem isn't just further mimetic rivalry, scapegoating, and violence as a passive unfolding of consequences, either; the beneficiaries of systematized injustice actively utilize the elevation of bias in order to deteriorate human relations by cultivating mimetic rivalry and violent scapegoating. Even those resisting such systems often end up engaging in the very elevation of bias and scapegoating from which they have been made to suffer, as they make into scapegoats those who are maintaining the unjust systems.

We therefore need some alternative, and Daly expresses well the core of Doran's contention: "if it is a Christian story that we are trying to tell and by which we are trying to live, the only way to do that is by imitating the desire of Jesus," and in doing so, we will be following the

---

85. See Daly, "Phenomenology of Redemption?" 361–62. Daly cites Scott R. Garrels, "Imitation, Mirror Neurons, and Mimetic Desires: Convergence Between the Mimetic Theory of René Girard and Empirical Research on Imitation," *Contagion: Journal of Violence, Mimesis, and Culture* 12–13 (2006), 68.

86. Daly, "Phenomenology of Redemption?" 361–62.

87. Doran, "The Nonviolent Cross," 58.

path of "a nonacquisitive, nonrivalrous mimesis that does not scape-goat victims but identifies with them. . . ."[88] The supreme good into which the evils are transformed via the law of the cross therefore must have some dimension that corresponds to this imaginal-affective field Doran identified in terms of psychic conversion and, later, with reference to Girardian analysis. There must be an imitation of Christ, a Christoformity arising from mimetic imitation of Jesus in pursuit of the same object Jesus desired—namely union with God, holiness. Moreover, the interpersonal relational structures arising within that supreme good must be structures fostering such holiness in and through, but not reducible to, a refusal and reversal of the scapegoating mechanism.[89]

II. Antiblackness: Psyche, Society, and Redemption in the United States

Redemption is never an abstraction.[90] If, as I've suggested, the inclusion of Girard offers us a further heuristic element, rather than data on which the Lonerganian heuristic should go to work, then what might be a set of data on which the Lonergan-Girard heuristic could prove helpful? As an example of such an issue, we will conclude this article by looking at antiblackness as a specific evil with dimensions ranging from interpersonal-relational structures to individual conscious-intentional operations. In this section, we will briefly examine Katie Grimes' succinct account of antiblackness to draw out ways in which Doran's approach could prove helpful in understanding and negotiating some of the relevant theological issues.

---

88. Daly, "Phenomenology of Redemption?" 364. See also Daly, "Phenomenology of Redemption?" 365.

89. Doran, "The Nonviolent Cross," 56, 58–59. Doran is not arguing for a reductionist account of redemption in Girardian terms, but for understanding the penetration of redemption into one's psychic field. See Doran, "The Nonviolent Cross," 60 and Doran, *The Trinity in History, Vol. 2*, 133–35.

90. See Mary Gerhart, "Bernard Lonergan's 'Law of the Cross': Transforming the Sources and Effects of Violence," *Theological Studies* 77, no. 1 (2016), 95.

The Sin of Antiblackness

Antiblackness is an example of deviated interpersonal relations that corrupt meaning and value, impinging upon the imaginal-affective field as it conditions our understanding, judging, deciding, and loving. To elaborate on that example, we will draw on Katie Grimes' recent overview of antiblackness, where she notes the distinction between white supremacy and an "antiblackness supremacy" that "alone seeks to preserve the association between both blackness and black people and slave status."[91]

This link matters because Africanized slavery differs qualitatively, not just quantitatively, from other injustices and forms of slavery.[92] First, Africanized slavery images and conceives of the slave master in terms of pardon: slavery is considered to be better than what the slave deserves—namely, death. Slavery, then, is therefore a *reprieve* that should be accepted as such—and thus seen as justified—in the mind of the slave. Moreover, since the master's gratuitous mercy preserves the slave's life, the slave is placed in a position of all-encompassing ontological debt, and therefore subservience, toward the master.[93]

Second, Africanized slavery is linked to a specific body type in a unique way. As Grimes puts it, "Africanized slavery did not enslave people who happened to be black; it instead enslaved people solely because they were black."[94] This is contrasted with other forms of slavery and indentured servitude, because in those cases the physical body was not the reason for treating the person as enslaved or enslavable. One's debt, one's need to pay for immigration, one's criminal status, and more served to justify the servitude—it was not the ontological status of one's very own body.

---

91. Katie Grimes, "Antiblackness," *Theological Studies* 81, no. 1 (2020), 171–172.

92. Grimes, "Antiblackness," 173. While being quite clear that in no way does the recognition of this difference minimize or neglect other forms of injustice and even other forms of racism, at the same time, Grimes notes that recognizing the variations in forms of oppression makes more authentic our understanding of each of those forms (see 176).

93. Grimes, "Antiblackness," 173.

94. Grimes, "Antiblackness," 175.

Third, interpersonal relations among and with Africanized slaves were denied legitimacy. The sole legitimate relationship was that between slave and master, and no connection to heritage or tradition, no commitment to one another in marriage or family, no parental bond was given validity. While indentured servants, even those placed in such a condition involuntarily, retained their family connections and identity via heritage and social connection, this was denied to Africanized slaves.[95]

Africanized slavery, then, relies on the idea that all black people are considered to belong to a category ontologically deserving of death and therefore enslavable in themselves as a form of gratuitous mercy, rather than as a response to a certain contingent condition. In turn, all other people are considered to be of a category that, while their contingent condition *may* result in a situation like indentured servitude, is in itself ontologically deserving of life and so their servitude could not be understood as a beneficent preservation from a death ontologically deserved. For Grimes, this is why we still see seemingly lingering effects of past racial injustice in America: since slavery was founded on an ontological value claim about black bodies, even when the specific institution of slavery was eliminated, the same imaging and conception of black bodies in those value terms continued by merely changing form.[96] What we encounter are not just lingering effects, but continued manifestations of the same root issue, and so a continuation of Africanized slavery in different forms. Antiblackness is not simply a residual effect of the racist history of the United States but is instead a present reality continuing the basic sin and evil consequences of racism.

In relation to Doran's understanding of the imaginal-affective dimension, Girardian analysis, and redemption as described above, antiblackness depends, in part, on particular construals of the affect-imagery link, the affectivity-value judgment link, and mimetic antagonism and scapegoating arising from and causing a corrupted imaginal-affective field in subjects who perpetuate it. Antiblackness corrupts the connection

---

95. Grimes, "Antiblackness," 173–174.
96. Grimes, "Antiblackness," 177.

between the image of black bodies and affectivity in the minds of those whose social orders are structured around Africanized slavery. Because values are grasped in intentional feelings, antiblackness generates negative judgments of value about human beings with black bodies in subjects' conscious operations of evaluation and decision. Moreover, the categorization of blacks through this association in the imaginal-affective field makes them an object of both mimetic rivalry and scapegoating. Within the social framework of antiblackness, gains by those with black bodies are considered to be at the expense of persons who are considered to be of a distinct and higher ontological value. Thus, rivalry can ensue when, for example, people with black skin receive preferential treatment designed to counteract the negative value status assigned to them in virtue of their blackness. In addition, black people are positioned in such a way that they are vulnerable to *scapegoating*, as they become the object on which the vitriol and violence of others' mimetic rivalries is directed as an outlet. As Bill Moyers relates, Lyndon Johnson understood this principle well: "'If you can convince the lowest white man he's better than the best colored man, he won't notice you're picking his pocket. Hell, give him somebody to look down on, and he'll empty his pockets for you.'"[97] There arises a vicious circle: black bodies are linked to negative affectivity, the negative affectivity results in negative value judgments, the negative value judgments feed into scapegoating, and because black bodies are scapegoats, they are linked to negative affectivity, perpetuating the cycle.

Conclusion: A Call for Change

Doran's work in bringing the imaginal-affective dimension to the fore deepens and extends our understanding of what must be done to combat antiblackness. Rooted in Lonergan's own approach, Ryliškytė emphasizes the analogy of reconciliation to understand what is operative in Christ's performance of the law of the cross.[98] The satisfaction wrought

---

97. Bill Moyers, "What a Real President Was Like," *The Washington Post*, 1988.

98. Because this is grounded in Lonergan, Ryliškytė is not alone. See Lonergan, *The Redemption*, 497, 547.

by the passion, death, and resurrection of Christ is powered by Christ's charity, and that charity restores relationship. In the case of sin, however—like that of the antiblackness that denies the ontological value of black bodies and so denies their being made in the image of God—the form charity must take is that of repentance.[99] Such repentance must incorporate both an acceptance of one's own responsibility and a deliberate decision to repair the situation, and only if there occur such graced inner operations can just social organization—including the eradication of antiblackness—be achieved and interpersonal relationship restored.[100]

This cruciform path, though, involves "purgation," as Ryliškytė emphasizes in drawing our attention to the cruciform criterion of religious conversion.[101] Scripturally, we can identify the roots of this position in the cruciform context of the Pauline quote Lonergan linked to religious conversion: Romans 5:5.[102] While that verse does refer to the gift of God's own love for God poured into our hearts, the subsequent verses make clear its cost:

> For Christ, while we were still helpless, yet died at the appointed time for the ungodly. Indeed, only with difficulty does one die for a just person, though perhaps for a good person one might even find courage to die. But God proves his love for us in that while we were still sinners Christ died for us. How much more then, since we are now justified by his blood, will we be saved through him from the wrath. Indeed, if, while we were enemies, we were reconciled to God through the death of his Son, how much more, once reconciled, will we be saved by his life. Not only that, but we also boast of God through our Lord Jesus Christ, through whom we have now received reconciliation.[103]

---

99. Ryliškytė, "Conversion," 387.

100. Ryliškytė, "Conversion," 391.

101. Ryliškytė, "Conversion," 376.

102. See Lonergan, *Method*, 101, 261, 291.

103. Romans 5:6–11, NABRE.

Such a purgation must, in part, address the imaginal-affective field, and this would include the ways in which we associate affect with the images into which we have our insights and the ways in which image and affect influence our value judgments. What's called for is a change in the link between imagery and affect in order to break the cycle by which scapegoating comes into play in antiblackness. We can no longer associate the image of black bodies with the negative affectivity that leads to false value judgments about black human beings and the justification of their being made the scapegoat. Doran expressed this component well in his early explanations of psychic conversion:

> No outward tinkerings with the world and no social ameliora-
> tion can give the quietus to the daemon, to the gods or devils
> of the human soul, or prevent them from tearing down again
> and again what consciousness has built. Unless they are assigned
> their place in consciousness and culture, they will never leave
> mankind in peace.[104]

With respect to this issue of antiblackness, human beings who benefit from it must be willing to acknowledge its reality, accept responsibility for our part—however complex, multifaceted, and indeliberate—and resolve to make amends. Such amends must include deliberate attention to the associations made between black bodies and the affectivity that conditions value judgments. It must also include a firm resolve to refuse to participate in the scapegoat mechanism, including especially its manifestations that turn attention to black persons as objects of violence—no matter how refined, organized, rationalized, or sanctioned.

In order to do this, we must be willing to become ourselves the object of rivalry and scapegoating violence, as we are confronted with whataboutisms, pushed to the defensive, and reputationally, verbally, and perhaps even physically assaulted, and we must refuse to respond to such accruing contagion with further violence. While we must

---

104. Doran, "Psychic Conversion," 218, citing Neumann, *Depth Psychology and a New Ethic*, 394.

never make the mistake of thinking that our position equates to that of those against whom antiblackness has been directed, we must accept the fact that, in Mark Miller's words, "Our vocation is to love; but in this fallen world, love cannot avoid suffering."[105] Ultimately, the goal is to participate in the communication of the cruciform divine good in such a way that all will be called to repentance.

In this example, we can see the value of Doran's notion of psychic conversion and its development in Girardian terms. Without that notion, we may understand many dynamics of redemption and of its manifestation in the world, but our understanding will include an oversight of an intrinsic component of the decline and evil of sin and, thus, of its undoing and of the unfolding of the Kingdom of God.

---

105. Miller, "Imitating Christ's Cross," 875.

15

Decolonization and Psychic Conversion: A Theological Appraisal of the Challenges of Africa's Developmental Strides from the Prism of Robert Doran's Psychic Conversion

MARK OBETEN

MARQUETTE UNIVERSITY

Introduction

The quest for decolonization in Africa concerns all aspects of her life, including theological contributions towards development. For a continent with a checkered history of slave trade and colonization and currently bedeviled with varied challenges of underdevelopment and leadership loopholes, Africa has consistently been positioned in the last rung of the ladder of development.[1] Decades after the end of colonial regimes and the institution of indigenous governments, this paper engages the reality and extent of freedom from the western powers. It

---

1. According to the UNDP 2020 Human Development Index (HDI), of Africa's 53 countries assessed, only Mauritius made the list of countries with Very High HDI ranking: first in Africa and 66th in the world; 8 other countries are in the high HDI and 14 in the medium HDI categories. More than half of Africa (30 countries) are in the bottom class of low HDI. Note that the population of Mauritius is a paltry 98, 000 people, compared to Africa's population. (https://en.wikipedia.org/wiki/List_of_countries_by_Human_Development_Index#cite_note-2020_components-2). Retrieved on September 4, 2021.

argues among other things that, political independence without economic and psychical freedom is a half measure. It maintains that this situation of neocolonialism,[2] in which most governments still depend directly or indirectly on the western influence and approval to act, is a major clog in the wheel of progress and development of Africa.

The goal of this paper is not just to lament and call out the injustice and brutality of colonization as this might simply amount to crying over spilled milk. Of course, it is my intention to state the woes of colonialism but more than that, to essentially stir the African conscience and stimulate it to further action against the western grasp of her destiny. In other words, this paper argues that the developmental challenge of the African continent is not dissociated from her experience of slave trade and colonialism. It appreciates the political, intellectual, moral, and even religious decolonization drives so far but then argues that the psychic element in the struggle for freedom, which has not been significantly attended to, must now be explored with the intensity and intentionality with which political independence was pursued in the mid-twentieth century. It turns to Robert Doran, influenced as he was by the thoughts of Bernard Lonergan on conversion, to argue that the cycle of change on the march to wholesome authenticity never reaches completion without the sublation[3] of the religious, moral and intellectual conversion of the existential subject (the African). The beauty of this lies in the fact that psychic conversion does

---

2. Professor of Political Theology in the Department of World Religion, World Church, Notre Dame University Indiana, Emmanuel Katongole's exposition of and commentary on the radical revolution of Thomas Sankara in Upper Volta is an excellent account of the plight of Africa and the need for a reorientation of self-image and nation building. Emmanuel Katongole, *The Sacrifice of Africa: A Political Theology* (Grand Rapids: Wm. B. Eerdmans Publishing Co., 2011), chapter four, "daring to Reinvent the Future."

3. Sublation is term that Lonergan used to represent a kind of growth or transformation in which the new improved level of a thing comes about without destroying the 'lesser' level. It is replacement without annihilation. A new tradition for example does not necessarily have to abolish the old one since it is able to demonstrate an advancement of the older tradition rather than annihilation. More light is shed on this in my treatment of Psychic conversion later in this piece.

not destroy moral, religious or intellectual conversion but improves the subject in its own way, as an internal force.

Tracing The Roots of Underdevelopment in Africa to Colonization

The Janus-faced situation of the continent of Africa is one that is fed by the tributaries of several levels of binarism. There is an admixture of hope and despair demonstrated by the stories of the stinkingly rich in a constant effort to overshadow the fragrantly poor of the society. Interestingly, one is right about the stench of riches and the aroma of poverty that oozes out of the same continent, the same country and in some cases the opposite sides of the same street. The situation immediately begs the question as to the sincerity of the stories being told. This doubt is worsened by the fact that evidence abound as to people and governments that have cried for and received help for the fight against poverty and illiteracy but have embezzled the proceeds from such campaigns. Yet there are also stories of genuine activities of individuals and organizations that have positively impacted so many and given them a push in the upward movement from poverty to stability in life.

The discovery, manufacture, and advancement of modes of transportation has led to a huge realization of the interdependence of human beings from different parts of the world. The interaction between the West and sub-Saharan Africa since the fifteenth century gradually inaugurated an era of transatlantic slave trade, a system that has come to be referred to as a Western imperialism in which more than ninety percent of Africa lost sovereignty and control of their natural resources.[4] Attempts to check this sad reality led to the abolition of slave trade in 1886.

Sadly, while efforts to abolish slave trade in Africa were reaching their zenith, the scramble and partitioning of the African continent in an all-European Berlin conference on Africa in 1884 inaugurated the

---

4. Michael Hunt, *The World Transformed 1945 to the Present* (New York: Oxford University Press, 2017), 264.

era of colonialism to perpetuate Europe's hold on African peoples and resources.[5] A traditional African sense of simplicity and hospitality was taken advantage of and battered by the European invaders. According to Robert Boyce, "Indeed, there was no form of trickery that was not practiced upon these poor black children of Africa. . . . the African commercial exploiter was face to face with a more simple-minded race and he took a mean advantage of his position with the native black."[6] This is derogatory but true—trickery feasted on simplicity! In the following sections, I will point to a few concrete examples of the relationship between colonialism and underdevelopment in Africa.

Ethnicity and the Western Conspiracy

A close look at the present-day map of Africa will show how colonization brought about a forced amalgamation of peoples who had very little or nothing in common and bundled them under the same country. This is how one might explain the cascade of civil wars and heightened communal clashes that have continued to plague and ripple through the continent, without prejudice to the existence of inter-tribal attritions prior to colonialism. To this day, Africans identify themselves more by ethnicity, Yoruba, Igbo, Tutsi, Maasai, rather than by nationality.[7]

The colonizers did not leave Africa without offering their colonies a seat on a keg of gunpowder, a crocodile smile, as strategy to perpetuate their strangle on the African continent. For example, in the case of Nigeria, renowned literary giant, Chinua Achebe maintained that the Igbos who were the most qualified in many sectors in the Nigerian government at the eve of the independence were never appointed to leadership roles. For him, this might only be explained as continuity with

---

5. Ibid.

6. Robert Boyce, "The Colonization of Africa" in *Journal of the Royal African Society*, 10.40, (1911): 395.

7. Cyril Orji, *Ethnic and Religious Conflict in Africa: an analysis of Bias, decline and conversion based on the Works of Bernard Lonergan*, (Milwaukee: Marquette University Press, 2008), 132.

the grand plan of the colonizers who had strategized to carefully ensure that the nation's *independence* was enshrined in *dependence*. According to Achebe, "the ploy in the Nigerian context was simple and crude: Get the achievers out and replace them with less qualified individuals from the desired ethnic background so as to gain access to the resources of the state."[8] No doubt, this subtle seed of discord did not take too long to bear fruits. By 1966, Nigeria had her first military coup and soon after, a civil war that would claim no less than three million lives was underway. Ethnicity was a telling factor in this civil war. Rather than pursuing nation-building and development, Nigeria got engaged in civil war, ethnic clashes, and flagrant nepotism. Thus, the British kept the doors open for continued dominance and exploitation in the country's affairs. The same is true for a great many other African countries.

It is instructive to note that whether it was colonization by indirect rule in British West Africa or by the French Assimilation Policy; be it the Portuguese *Assimmilado* or even the Belgian imperialist Congo, there was a clear sense of deception, oppression and intimidation in the administration of the African peoples and resources under colonial rule. Thanks also to the philosophical and psychological branding of Africans as subhuman with infantile mentality in the works of such scholars as Lucien Levy-Bruhl, David Hume and Immanuel Kant, there was no limit to the dehumanization of the African in the colonial era.[9] The end of slavery therefore did not benefit the African perceived as subhuman. There is a strong connection between the twin evils of slavery and colonialism and the situation of underdevelopment in Africa.

Education System and the Denigration of African Languages

Perhaps the most devastating blow against the Africans was the hijack and disintegration of the African system of education, a direct attack

---

8. Chinua Achebe, *There was a Country: A Memoir,* (New York: Penguin, 2013), 76.
9. George Omaku Ehusani, *An Afro-Christian Vision "OZOVEHE!": Toward A More Humanized World* (Lanham: University Press of America, 1991), 77–79.

on the African psyche and mindset. The African system of education was soon to be judged worthless and defunct and quickly replaced by an educational system convoluted with school curriculum that was not just foreign to the African but also designed to perpetuate African servitude and dependence on the West. The content of these curricula was not suitable for the African experience and need. Not just the language but also the very concepts they identified were strange to the African child in his native environment. Hence, education became a medium of oppression with the result that decades after colonization, the African is stuck with a reconstructed mental framework patterned to serve the western constructs of modernity and epistemology.[10] African systems of education, like her religions and other elements of her culture, were contemptuously written off and this content sunk into the African through this western education mold.

Consequently, Colonization meant that the African who sought formal education could no longer think in his native and comfortable tongue but was forced to think in a foreign language and to communicate this thought in that same foreign language. Apart from the difficulty involved in this process, the African child was also cut off his root with the proscription of vernacular in schools. Language was no longer a vehicle, but an obstacle, an end it itself. This system of education also meant that the African child grew up considering his own mother tongue as worthless or at most, second best in relation to the language of the colonizers. Of course, it is common knowledge that human beings are not equally talented with the gift of learning and communicating with foreign languages. Hence, the language factor became a very big setback in the progress of Africa as intelligent kids were labelled dullards and prevented from contributing their wisdom and skills to nation building, no thanks to the challenge of foreign language. [11]

---

10. Gwinyai H. Muzorewa, *The Origins and Development of African Theology* (Eugene, Oregon: Wipf and Stock Publishers, 1987), 84. Muzorewa argued that in terms of religious decolonization, African theology that strives to build on a western epistemological framework (philosophy) cannot serve to construct a relevant African theology since there is a marked difference in western and African thought patterns.

11. Cyril Orji, *A Semiotic Approach to the Theology of Inculturation* (Eugene: Pickwick Publications, 2015) 91.

What is Psychic Conversion?

Psychic conversion is Robert Doran's contribution to Bernard Lonergan's theology in respect to conversion. Bernard Lonergan's works demonstrate that the combating of bias is critical to the subject matter of conversion. The idea of self-transcendence is the key driver of conversion and herein lies the capacity for transforming oneself and world.[12] Bernard Lonergan identified a three-fold dimension to conversion: intellectual, moral and religious and Doran introduced a fourth, psychic conversion. In Lonergan, authenticity and self-transcendence play a pivotal role in the understanding of human development at the individual and communal levels. Little wonder then the operations of experience, understanding and judgment combine to authenticate knowledge. Arriving at this authentic knowledge is always the implication of an intellectual conversion where one must have moved from a shallow or totally wrong notion to a fuller or truer knowledge, through experience, insight, judgement and decision. Since the three-fold categories of conversion must work towards authenticating the human experience of the subject, knowledge after intellectual conversion must inform the choices of the individual and mean a movement from what satisfies to what is of a higher value. This way, transformation (or transvaluation) positions the subject to being in love with God and being truly committed to his labor of love in a religious sense.[13]

The interaction of intellectual, moral and religious conversion authenticates human transformation. "Conversion is not merely a change or even development; rather, it is a radical transformation on which follows, on all levels of living, an interlocked series of changes and developments. What hitherto was unnoticed becomes vivid and present. What has been of no concern becomes a matter of high import."[14] For Lonergan, conversion is not a one-off experience but

---

12. Orji, *Ethnic and Religious Conflicts in Africa,* 200.

13. Bernard Lonergan, *Method in Theology. Collected Works of Bernard Lonergan. Vol. 14.* eds. Robert M. Doran and John D. Dadosky (Toronto: University of Toronto Press, 2017), 224–226.

14. Lonergan, *Method in Theology,* cited in Doran, *Subject and Psyche,* 218.

a repeated cycle of movements leading to authenticity: "It involves an about-face; it comes out of the old by repudiating characteristic features; it begins a new sequence that can keep revealing even greater depth and breadth and width. Such an about-face and new beginning is what is meant by conversion."[15] Thus, conversion is transformation that begins from the individual level and then becomes interpersonal, communal and societal. It might well be understood as overgrowing individual, communal and even general biases[16] by a radical transformation occasioned by this about-face movements in the horizontal and vertical directions in the exercise of freedom.

Robert Doran on Psychic Conversion

But how can conversion be authentic if it is not holistic or if it leaves out the psyche, the mental, and inner force of human activities and decision-making? Such a question motivated Doran to seeking a way of better understanding and maximizing the benefits of Lonergan's contribution to the theme of conversion. The end result of Doran's study in this regard was the introduction of a fourth level of conversion - psychic conversion. Doran maintains openly that psychic conversion makes sense and finds its relevance within the framework of Lonergan's three-fold conversion. For Doran, "Psychic conversion is integrally related to the religious, moral and intellectual conversion specified by Lonergan as qualifying authentic human subjectivity."[17]

Psychic conversion is inspired by Doran's appropriation of feelings and symbols as significant additions to engaging the Lonergan understanding of conversion: "I am maintaining that the emergence of the capacity to disengage the symbolic constitution of the feelings in which the primordial apprehension of values occurs satisfies Lonergan's notion

---

15. Lonergan, *Method in Theology*, 223.

16. Bernard Lonergan, *Insight: A Study of Human Understanding* (Toronto: University of Toronto Press, 1992), 232–269. This reference is to the seventh chapter of *Insight* where Lonergan has a broad treatment of common sense and the various levels of bias.

17. Doran, *Subject and Psyche*, 217.

of conversion but also that it is something other than the three conversions of which he speaks."[18] Doran's conversion also goes through the series of development, setback and renewal. It is indeed a beginning.

According to Doran, "the conscious capacity for the sublation of the imaginal is effected by a conversion on the part of the existential subject."[19] The notion of sublation, which he takes from Lonergan, is very momentous to the comprehension of psychic conversion and how it can be a tool for decolonization and development. Doran emphasizes that psychic conversion does not claim to displace Lonergan's three levels of conversion nor present itself as the perfect form of, or the completion of the conversion cycle. Instead, he asserts that,

> . . . like any other conversion, psychic conversion is not the goal but the beginning. As religious conversion is not the mystic's cloud of unknowing, as moral conversion is not moral perfection, as intellectual conversion is not methodological craftsmanship, so psychic conversion is not unified affectivity or total integration with intentionality or immediate release from psychic imprisonment.[20]

Thus, Doran stresses that psychic conversion is a beginning; a moment when a person begins to take seriously the need to make decisions from a more authentic consciousness of fuller knowledge and higher value rather than from the throne of ego. This conversion helps to make for a more holistic view of the situation and takes the long-term best approach to life and decisions. Doran explains further, noting that,

> [Psychic conversion] is, at the beginning, no more than the obscure understanding of the nourishing potential of the psyche to maintain the vitality of conscious living by a continuous influx of energy; the hint that one's psychic being can be transformed so as to aid one in the quest for individual authenticity; the suspicion that coming to terms with one's dreams will profoundly

---

18. Doran, *Subject and Psyche*, 219.
19. Doran, *Subject and Psyche*, 217.
20. Doran, *Subject and Psyche*, 220.

change one's ego by ousting it from its central and dominating position in one's conscious living, by shifting the birthplace of meaning gradually but progressively to a deeper center which is simultaneously a totality, the self.[21]

Meanwhile, the capacity of the psyche for a deeper level of consciousness[22] properly positions the individual to desire and to appreciate the changes that come from harnessing the psychic component by breaking forth from an egoistic dominance. But what exactly does to break from the ego mean, does it mean constantly suppressing the ego to the point of extinction? Doran makes clear that the ego does not become absent in one who has undergone (or is undergoing) psychic conversion as it remains a constitutive part of the authentic subject. Rather, the transformation is such that the ego is dominated by the psyche, a higher faculty, in making choices that are all-encompassing, that thus keeps the ego's excesses under check:

It seems therefore that psychic conversion is a process of development in which the subject trains itself through a pattern of choices in which it chooses activities that lead to wholeness and authenticity. In this way it suppresses the ego and weakens or replaces its control over the choices made by the subject. Hence is the movement from a lower level of psychic engagement to a more holistic and integral vision of life. The relationship between psyche and intentionality is also unearthed in the dialectic of psyche and intentionality whereby the ego, while not annihilated, is sublated without negation to make way for a superior and more authentic faculty to dominate that existential subject that has thus become self-transcending.[23]

---

21. Doran, *Subject and Psyche*, 220.

22. In a 2012 article, Doran maintained that "the human psyche has a constitutive role to play in the establishment of integrity" and that to stress the spiritual over the psychic or vice versa would lead to distortion in the dialectics of the community and eventually a breakdown of the scale of values. Robert Doran, "Two Ways of Being Conscious: The Notion of Psychic Conversion" in *Method: Journal of Lonergan Studies, n.s.,* vol. 3 No 110 (Spring 2013) 1–17, 10.

23. Doran, *Subject and Psyche*, 241–242.

It is from this position of the psyche's dominance over the ego that the transition from individual to communal relevance of psychic conversion is made and thus leads to the transformation of society. One can notice and transpose the capacity of psychic conversion to confront distortions that frustrate the subject's orientation towards authenticity. Therein, psychic conversion also has capacity to make a meaningful contribution in the transformation of the African society, held back as it is from actualizing its potentials in the unfortunate drawback of neocolonialism.

Two rather deep questions give bearing to Doran's engagement with the quest for a psychic conversion, positioning his theory as naturally relevant to the interest of this paper. First, he enquires: "how do we recover the story in which is verified the authenticity or inauthenticity both of our judgment of value and of our consequent cognitional value?"[24] This question is equally critical to the African situation as regards decolonization. It is asking in essence, how sure are the Africans that they are addressing the real issues militating against progress and development in the continent? Given the intentionally designed mental distortion by a foreign, colonial educational system and a rather twisted history, how sure is the African that he is addressing his own story rather than a different story imposed by western powers and the negative ripple effects therefrom?

Doran poses a second question thus: "How do we move from this recovery to assume our distinct historical responsibility for the concrete process of the human good?"[25] This second enquiry targets the indigenous responsibility for retelling the African story and steering of the wheels of progress in the continent. So, Doran's take off questions challenge the African to raise the right questions as well as take responsibility for addressing the issues properly.

Similarly, in *Lonergan, Social Transformation and Sustainable Human development,* Professor of Theology and Director of the Marquette Lonergan Project, Dr. Joseph Ogbonnaya, has argued that psychic conversion has a definite benefit to any discussion on the

---

24. Doran, *Psychic Conversion and Theological Foundations,* 2nd Edition (Milwaukee: Marquette University Press, 2006), 170.

25. Doran, Ibid.

316 PERSPECTIVES ON PSYCHIC CONVERSION

development of the human (African) society by aiding human authenticity. According to Ogbonnaya, "a depressed or Schizophrenic individual finds it difficult to fully contribute to societal development or transformation. Leaders with dramatic biases can wreak havoc to the development of a country or continent as the case may be."[26] He cites the ease with which African leaders obtain loans from developmental proposals but divert and embezzle these funds to selfish and albeit, personal projects. Psychic conversion thus becomes an important prescription to the leadership ineptitude of the African elite on the one hand. On the other hand, it can empower the people to demand accountability from the administrators of their commonwealth. Indeed, it demands a transvaluation of the African elitist psyche, a procedure that must begin from that individual level and then ripple into society.

Given Doran's qualification of psychic conversion as the "transformation of what Lonergan (following Freud but with a somewhat different meaning) calls the censor, from a repressive to a constructive intra-subjective agency in personal development,"[27] Ogbonnaya further holds that "psychic conversion, by transforming the repressed censor to a constructive censor, promotes insights that make for societal development. Authentic individuals faithful to the transcendental precepts are needed for the progress and development of peoples, psychic conversion, social progress and development in this regard."[28] Thus, an appreciation of psychic conversion can lead Africans to emancipate themselves from mental slavery, decades after slave trade and colonialism are said to have ended.

The enduring benefit of reflecting on decolonization in terms of conversion in the Lonerganian intellectual milieu is that this three (now four)-fold conversion can help African leaders and people to break forth from their intellectual traditions, see and accept the fuller

---

26. Joseph Ogbonnaya, *Lonergan, Social Transformation and Sustainable Human Development* (Eugene, OR: Pickwick Publications, 2013) 126.

27. Doran, *Theological Foundations*, cited in Ogbonnaya, *Lonergan, Social transformation and Sustainable human Development*, 125.

28. Ogbonnaya, *Lonergan, Social Transformation and Sustainable Human Development*, 126.

knowledge from the bigger picture and make the radical change required. This intellectual conversion soon crystalizes into a moral transvaluation, and the religious transformation engenders the commitment that speaks of the urgency with which a psychic conversion can engender decolonization and development.

Psychic Conversion and the Task of Decolonization

If the human person is naturally a political animal and the African person notoriously religious, whence shall we make an entry into psychic conversion? According to Orobator, ". . . centuries of colonial domination of Africa have resulted in a historical psychological conditioning of Africans that manifests itself as a defeatist mentality, a self-perception incapable of envisioning progress, and perpetual confinement in a straitjacket of misery."[29] I find this elocution very concise in projecting the cause and stating the current and persistent degree of Africa's developmental challenges in the quest for self-identification and self-reliance.

Franz Fanon once held that "colonialism is not simply content to impose its rule upon the present and future of a dominated country. Colonialism is not satisfied merely with holding a people in its grip and emptying the native's brain of all forms and content. By a form of perverse logic, it turns to the past of the oppressed people and distorts it, disfigures, and destroys it."[30] It is in this light that the question regarding the nature of freedom gained at independence from colonial rule takes its relevance even today. If colonialism is structured to place a grip on both the present and the future and is used to distort the African's mindset to servitude, how authentically realistic then is the independence? Thus, the need to continue the struggle for independence albeit through decolonization and precisely through a psychic

---

29. Agbonkhianmeghe E. Orobator, "*Caritas in Veritate* and Africa's Burden of (Under)Development" *Theological Studies, 71 (2010)*, 322.

30. Walter D. Mignolo, "Delinking: The Rhetoric of Modernity, The Logic of Coloniality and The Grammar of De-coloniality" in *Cultural Studies*, 21:2, 449–514.

conversion that repositions the African in a more confident and forward-looking posture.

Another significant contribution to the subject of decolonization is recorded in the resounding chord struck by Mignolo when he asserts that "Decolonial thinking and doing aims to delink from the epistemic assumptions common to all the areas of knowledge established in the western world since the European Renaissance and through the European Enlightenment. . . . the sustained effort to re-orient our human communal praxis of living."[31] Indeed there is an obvious need for the African to rethink her way of living and progressing in relating with the western powers. This is so because Africa's encounter with colonialism reflects to a great extent, the economic interests of imperial powers and has been linked to other social dynamics, including the cultural change.[32]

Psychic Conversion and Deferred Gratification

The problems of Africa have built up through decades and centuries and hence need sustained efforts over a period. Unfortunately, the idea of planting trees for unborn generations to eat of their fruits seems to be very far from the African Elites. The psyche of the African political elites is only open to instant gratification. Everyone wants to reap the harvest of their 'labor' not just within their lifetime but, and this is unfortunate, they want the harvest during their time in office. It is to this thinking pattern that Doran's psychic conversion throws the challenge of a deferred gratification.

Worse still, religion, and more precisely, prosperity gospel in Africa is a principal culprit of the instant gratification philosophy and a critical factor in the continent's developmental setback. The steady growth and spread of religious adherence have not meant a concomitant

---

31. Walter D. Mignolo and Catherine E. Walsh, *On Decoloniality: Concepts, Analytics and Praxis* (Durham: Duke University Press, 2018), 106.

32. Chima J. Korieh, ed., *Africa's Encounter with Christianity and Social Change: The Essays of Felix K. Ekechi* (Glassboro, NJ: Goldline and Jacob Publishing Company, 2020), 3.

growth in the struggle for freedom. On the contrary, Muzorewa indicts religion as promoting rather than combating the slavery of Africans. Hence, he calls for spiritual and psychological freedom as an important cause to be pursued by religion: "the spiritual and psychological dimensions of freedom need to be explored in order to give spiritual depth to the nationalist dimension of freedom."[33] Religion seems to be promoting a false notion that liberation from hardship and economic backwardness depends solely on how much prayer, fasting and tithing people can boast of. It is crucial to ensure that religion does not end up being a new form of slavery. The need to demand the freedom of Christians from the regimes of oppressive psychological bondage in their search for economic freedom cannot be overemphasized. It is in this light that psychic conversion emphasizes that religion experiences conversion from prosperity gospel and its preachers. It must refrain from preaching a cross-less Christianity and make sure to promote diligence and the reward of hard work.

In his treatment of Transcendence and Limitation in *Psychic Conversion and Theological Foundation,* Doran argues that a lasting solution to the problems of society must go beyond short term to long range solutions. According to him, "the long-range point of view is honored only when integrity is pursued for its own sake, and to pursue integrity is to act from the tense unity of transcendence and limitation."[34] Here Doran makes sure to explain that transcendence is not just about a higher force or spirit but precisely about the subject transcending itself in its authentic maturation.

Furthermore, in a characteristically interesting nuance in his entire treatment of psychic conversion and its capacity for sublation without nihilation, Doran insists that the short-term solutions are not bad or useless. Just as we may not run away from limitation and hope to solve all our problems from a transcendental perspective, the short-term solutions must go on without overlooking the perhaps more important need for solutions that are transcendental and long reaching. Says

---

33. Muzorewa, *Origins and Development of African Theology,* 61.
34. Doran, *Psychic Conversion and Theological Foundations,* 172.

Doran, "to neglect the need of our sensitivity for an ordered response to values is to deny transcendence and to cripple limitation . . . when the order of values is compacted into the social and particular goods, transcendence is distorted into a megalomanic drive to power and domination."[35] Hence, an attempt to build a strong and self-reliant Africa needs such a balance that does not fall to any extremes, "only by maintaining integrity with our bodily and psychic limitations can we be genuinely transcendent"![36]

The balance between transcendence and limitation finds a practical resonance in Emmanuel Katongole's call for sustained commitment to Africa's overall development: "there is a type of social reorientation that is needed for a new future to take shape in Africa. Three stand out: intellectual clarity, revolutionary madness, and commitment and sacrifice."[37] And it is this type of social transformation that this paper likens to psychic conversion. Kantongole demonstrates this reorientation by calling forth Sankara's reforms in Upper Volta, present-day Burkina Faso. Thomas Sankara's revolution, properly speaking, dared to reinvent the future and this focused more on boosting the self-image and esteem of the Upper Voltans. Sankara called for and implemented a change of heart and orientation in terms of a *social reconversion*. According to Katongole, Sankara spoke of his revolutionary madness as the "total reconversion" of the entire state machinery, with its laws, administration, courts, police, and army as a "qualitative transformation of our minds."[38] Sankara's Campaigns bore great fruits but found no continuity in the successive administrations. Yet, it stands out as a great example of how effective the psyche can be in Africa's advancement endeavors.

The application of Psychic conversion to the process of decolonization is therefore a summons to a more visionary leadership in Africa. A leadership that is future oriented without neglecting the present.

---

35. Doran, Ibid.
36. Doran, Ibid.
37. Katongole, *The Sacrifice of Africa,* 89.
38. Katongole, *The Sacrifice of Africa,* 97.

There is a socio-political dimension to this viewpoint. It is able to question the notion among African leaders that the salvation of Africa must come from the West and must be in the here and now. Hence, African leaders tend to seek and secure foreign loans to address certain infrastructure problems without any workable plans for paying back these loans and in this way, they end up leaving behind hardship and an ever-increasing debt burden on the future generations.

Doran argues that there is a need to pay attention to both the infrastructure and the superstructure: "psychic conversion is an instrument for the differentiation and appropriation of cross-cultural modes of psychic symbolization. . . . A cultural infrastructure consists of the transactions that constitute the fabric of everyday life. The superstructure emerges from disciplined reflection on the infrastructure."[39] Thus, in proposing the superstructure as a more important engagement, Doran admits that superstructure and infrastructure are not mutually exclusive and must be proportionally attended to.

Conclusion

By and large, decolonization is a commitment to liberate masses of Africans from their subservience to a collective oppressive colonial mentality and memory.[40] There is a need to expand the understanding and pursuit of conversion in the religious environment or atmosphere in the continent of Africa. In this paper, I have attempted to establish that there is a grave need for development in Africa by building a background to the current challenges of Africa and linking this to slave trade and colonialism and pointing out that the immediate culprit for this situation is the ineptitude of the African elites. This background was then weaved into Doran's Psychic Conversion as influenced by Bernard Lonergan. Hence the argument of this writeup has been that psychic conversion is an essential part of decolonization and ipso

---

39. Doran, *Psychic Conversion and Theological Foundations*, 9.

40. Orobator, *"Caritas in Veritate* and Africa's Burden of (Under)Development,"
323.

facto, a radical catalyst for development in Africa. This fourth level in the conversion of a person leads to and shapes the conversion of society. Psychic consciousness and thus conversion would see to the empowerment of the African mindset to a transcendence that neither denies nor neglect its limitation. Thus, attending to the psyche will help Africa to discover not only the story of her decline but also the elements that are still available for reversing the course of that story[41]

41. Doran, *Psychic Conversion and Theological Foundations*, 173.

16

Psychic Conversion and Catholic Higher Education

ANDREA STAPLETON

iberal arts education has for millennia aimed to serve as more than a trade school, but to develop students to conceive of the world more broadly. The definition of "value" of education has evolved, depending on broader cultural values and societal structures. Currently in the United States, for example, there is some debate about the value of higher education and liberal arts education. This debate is driven out of economic pragmatism and seen through a capitalistic lens. This leaves many colleges and universities—especially more financially constrained ones—with the question of how best to prioritize academic programming without compromising the value of their service to students.

Of course, students who pursue higher education acquire more than career skills and content knowledge but develop as whole persons. This chapter will consider some models of development in terms of the aims of higher education, specifically, Catholic Higher Education (CHE). How do Bernard Lonergan's and Robert Doran's ideas of conversion add to these approaches to student development, and, more broadly, help strengthen the mission of CHE and its relationships to the students, Church, and society?

The learning environment in education transcends the classroom. Developmental psychology has informed approaches to serving students' overall human development through the college years with advances in the field of student affairs, which has seen dramatic evolution over the last century. Research in student affairs has furthered understanding about the student as learner through the whole experience of college, not just in the classroom, and introduced manners of nurturing the student beyond academic development. The theories that contribute to the field have evolved not only with educational models and new approaches in developmental and therapeutic psychology, but also with cultural changes, with new awareness of human development and in response to changing times and contexts which have elucidated the needs of students and driven better responses to their needs as whole persons, i.e., physical, psychological, social, contextual, etc. Additionally, more recent attention to mental health care has added mental health services and normalized mental health education.

This concern for the development of the whole student has also called upon student support professionals to offer holistic care to the students that reflect the uniqueness of an institution. The whole higher educational experience does not just focus on serving the student but orienting the student to the broader world.

Secular and faith-based institutions alike attend to whole student development and to orienting students to the broader social context, through academic content, social awareness, and contextual learning opportunities. One may ask what makes a faith-based institution unique? Is not the pursuit of social justice, for example, the same from one institution to the next? What prepares students to better respond to the needs of society, to be "good" citizens, how are these criteria determined, and does a faith-based institution have anything unique to offer? Specifically, what does CHE have to offer?

With regard to the value of liberal arts schools, particularly Catholic colleges and universities, we ask what is—or could be—the qualitative difference in the ways that the institutions 1) orient the student to the broader world, 2) identify and respond to the needs of the day in which the student is 3) prepared to serve in a manner that advances 4) "the good." Here we will find a great use for the method of Bernard Lonergan and the addition of Robert Doran's work particularly *Theology and the Dialectics of History*.

Catholic Higher Education

There is no shortage of discussion over what it means to be a Catholic college or university, or "how Catholic" an institution is. Some of CHE's contemporary conundrum concerns questions about the identity of the school, how it expresses its religiosity, its relationship to the church, and the depth of its lived mission.[1]

A Catholic college or university's Catholic identity may be challenged by the philosophical question of what it means to be a Catholic university or college in changing contexts, the concern over the authority of the magisterium and local church, the integration of the Catholic Intellectual Tradition amidst concerns about protecting academic freedom, the methods for integrating Catholic social teaching and morality, and the increase of religious and philosophical plurality (and ambivalence) among its students, staff, and faculty. All these challenges to the culture of an institution may impact participation in the communal events and shared symbolism, all of which express and deepen communal commitment to shared meaning and purpose.

These questions suggest some of the differences in faith-based higher education compared to its secular counterpart. For instance, what does responsible participation in society mean in secular compared to religious contexts? The Catholic lens provides this distinction, and therefore because the school's mission and identity are theologically based, modes by which CHE develops its outcomes, develops institutional culture, and informs student development and pedagogy, are all shaped by theology.

Intellectual Tradition and Faith Tradition

To say that the Catholic college or university is a theological institution is to acknowledge that it is 1) rooted in a particular tradition with a particular narrative and mission, 2) it mediates meaning in a particular way of helping to orient all in its community to the broader society, 3) it lives in

---

1. For an excellent discussion of this, see John Haughey, SJ, *Where is Knowing Going? The Horizons of the Knowing Subject*, (Georgetown University Press, 2009).

fidelity to the teachings of the church *while* engaging in meaning derived through different disciplines. Insofar as theology is traditionally defined as faith seeking understanding, CHE exemplifies theology as a process.

Lonergan's method invites the theological process to be free of bias, engage in dialectical processes, set new foundations, and to communicate authentically and invite communion with authentic participation. Where better to intersect the ever-advancing knowledge of society and culture as it unfolds with the commitments of a living faith that is directed to enact its mission in the world than through education? While local churches are predominantly comprised of Catholics, the university ministers to diverse backgrounds, including people with no faith affiliation. More than that, all are invited to engage the world through its values-based approach, which is informed by the Christian faith and theological premises, in a balance of upholding its Catholic identity while demonstrating its universal and inclusive principles. The Catholic institution invites critical inquiry and discourse to responsibly advance knowledge in every field, while yet situated in an environment that recognizes the capacity for transcendence in our world, with an aim towards promoting the good.

In this sense, CHE exemplifies Lonergan's method in theology. How, then, may Lonergan's method, complemented by Doran's psychic conversion, help CHE define its missional responsibilities and to better understand the way in which it serves students and the world they will shape?

The goals, the mission of the university, and its operations are constituted by the institution's relationships among student, its ecclesial relationship, and the external community which it serves. Its authenticity in mission depends on its fidelity to and responsiveness to these relationships.

Saint John Paul II, in *Ex corde ecclesia*, identifies the Catholic university as "born from the heart of the church . . . a promising sign of the fecundity of the Christian mind in the heart of every culture." Through its unique role in cultivating the intellect while informed in the light of faith, it is enabled "to include the moral, spiritual and religious dimension in its research, and to evaluate the attainments of science and technology in the perspective of the totality of the human person." For the Catholic university, more is at stake than training professionals, or advancing the various disciplines, but to discover the "very meaning of the human person."[2]

Communications and the Catholic University . . .

When the institution cultivates a culture that discusses individuals and society this way, in which the subject, society, and world are situated in a transcendent history, in a graced world, CHE's mission is set apart from a secular mission. The individual's aims and orientation to society may be seen differently, and social justice work may be grounded in different values informing its aims.

The university is a mediator of meaning, and as such, it has such transformative impact for this critical period of life. For, as Lonergan points out, meaning is not only about cognitive learning, but the stages of coming to know. Regardless of the age of the student, the experience of being educated shapes the subject into a knowing, conscious subject.

Meaning is mediated by history, through symbol, by community. CHE offers meaning through a culture that is steeped in the story of the human as a being that is transformed by love, and that transforms others by being in love. Those in Christian contexts are offered the opportunity to discover and experience transcendent love. When we consider the problems of the world and the solutions that we aim to teach our students, this answer has already been given in the original divine solution and can be apprehended through the scale of values. This is worked out through the subject's conversion, which may be religious, intellectual, or moral. This is where Doran's work on psychic conversion fleshes out this process of development. Lonergan says,

> Besides the immediate world of the infant and the adult's world mediated by meaning, there is the mediation of immediacy by meaning when one objectifies cognitional process

---

2. John Paul II. *Apostolic Constitution Ex Corde Ecclesia* [On Catholic Universities]. Aug. 15, 1990. Holy See. http://w2.vatican.va/content/john-paulii/en/apost_constitutions/documents/hf_jpii_apc_15081990_ex-corde-ecclesiae.html, 5-9.

in transcendental method and when one discovers, identifies, accepts one's submerged feelings in psychotherapy.[3]

This chapter will examine how the formation of students may be enhanced when treating the whole person as capable of transcendence and self-differentiation, and how such a contribution might inform models of student development.

All of this raises key questions much outside the scope of this chapter, but which may serve as important implications for further study:

- How do we understand our role as Catholic higher education in our ecclesial mission serving in a secular context, regarding the development of students and the transformation of society?

- How can a theological perspective on human authenticity inform current models and practices in student development?

- What does this mean for Catholic colleges and universities in terms of service to students as participants and agents in transforming society?

- How can this perspective help missions of Catholic higher education live their missions more authentically, communicate their mission in a way that sets them apart as unique approaches to education, which will add value to society, not just for the sake of democracy, but for enriching cultural values?

Principles of Student Development

Secular approaches to student development in the student affairs profession

In the latter half of the 20th century, student affairs professionals developed some key principles, in the light of advancing discussion about their role in the outcomes of higher education. There is a general consensus around these themes regarding values, virtues, and outcomes.

---

3. Bernard Lonergan, *Method in Theology*, Toronto: University of Toronto Press, 1971, Location 1297.

While we see that these are valuable aims, which are oriented toward more than career skills, I propose that they could be strengthened for Catholic higher education with the complement of Lonergan's notion of conversion and Doran's model of psychic conversion.

Key outcomes for higher education students generally fall into the categories of psychosocial development (Self-awareness and inter-personal sensitivity), intellectual development, and life-skills development.[4] Student Affairs professionals generally agree that these values are essential to the profession: altruism, equality, aesthetics, freedom, human dignity, justice, truth, and community.[5]

Emerging from these values, we see that social justice is one of the outcomes in higher education, and it is based on the principles of human dignity, equality, and community. The "higher" purpose of social justice advocacy, in these models, however, is concern towards responsible citizenship and the preservation of democratic principles.[6] The goal to educate democratic citizens, may not, thus, be a universal value nor may it hold its value over time and in changing contexts. Still, this aim does provide some framework for cultivating an institutional culture in which ethics are expected.

In the mid-1980s, student affairs professionals adopted the following principles to construct an ethical framework for student development: respecting autonomy, doing good, doing no harm, being faithful (in the sense of fidelity to relationships), being just.[7]

Virtues are also believed to inform student decision making. According to Tom Beauchamp and James Childress, virtue is defined

---

4. F.A. Hamrick, N.J. Evans, and J.H. Schuh, *Foundations of student affairs practice: How philosophy, theory and research strengthen educational outcomes*, San Francisco: Jossey-Bass, 2002, 88.

5. Ibid, 82.

6. F.A. Hamrick, "Democratic citizenship and student activism," *Journal of College Student Development*, 1998, 449–459.

7. T. Beauchamp and J. Childress, *Principles of biomedical ethics* (4th ed.)., New York: Oxford University Press, 1994. See also K. Kitchener, "Ethical principles and ethical decisions in student affairs." In H. Canon and R. Brown (Eds.), *Applied ethics in student services* (New Directions for Student Services No. 30, pp. 17–30), San Francisco: Jossey-Bass, 1985.

as "a trait of character that is socially valued, and moral virtue is a trait that is morally valued."[8] According to Naomi Meara, Lyle Schmidt, and Jeanne Day in 1996, there are four virtues in service professions: prudence, integrity, respectfulness, benevolence.[9]

The American Catholic Colleges and Universities, the American College Personnel Association, and the National Association for Student Personnel Administrators examined the implications of *Ex corde* for Student Affairs Practices and produced a framework for student development professionals for Catholic higher education, *Principles of Good Practice for Student Affairs at Catholic Colleges and Universities*. The eight principles are summarized here:

1. Welcomes students into a vibrant campus community that celebrates God's love;

2. Grounds policies, practices, and decisions in the teachings and tradition of the Church;

3. Integrates faith and reason;

4. Offers opportunities for students to experience, reflect upon, and act from a commitment to justice, mercy, and compassion, and in light of Catholic social teaching;

5. Sets high standards of personal behavior and responsibility through the formation of character and virtues;

6. Invites and accompanies students into the life of the Catholic Church through prayer, liturgy, sacraments and spiritual direction;

7. Offers dialogue among religious traditions and with contemporary culture;

8. Assists students in discerning their vocations.[10]

---

8. Ibid.

9. Meara, N. M., Schmidt, L. D., & Day, J. D. (1996). Principles and virtues: A foundation for ethical decisions, policies, and character. *The Counseling Psychologist,* 24(1), 4–77.

10. Association of Catholic Colleges and Universities, Association for Student Affairs at Catholic Colleges and Universities, and the Jesuit Association of Student Personnel Administrators, *Principles of Good Practice for Student Affairs at Catholic Colleges and Universities*, 2nd ed., 2009.

Clearly, secular and faith-based models are both concerned with values-based development which orient students to interpersonal good and the good of society, but CHE seeks these aims in terms of its ecclesial commitment.

Development and Conversion

Here we will look at different models of human development: some perspectives from psychological theories used by student affairs professionals, and the methods of Lonergan and Doran.

Two approaches to human development

1. Humanistic-existential theory of development

In the humanistic-existential theories, the foci are responsibility and freedom that will facilitate personal growth. They are based on the idea that people possess the capacity for self-awareness and choice. They combine the humanistic idea of a basically good human nature and order of society where one looks out for others, and choices are made in the interest of well-being for self and others. The existentialist contribution regards the ability to make authentic and responsible choices.[11]

This model accounts for the desires of the person, which lead to an authentic and free life, and considers that this way of life is contingent on others' abilities to live a free and authentic life as well. Thus, a just social order derives from authentic interpersonal relationships and individuals' orientation to society.

This model emphasizes that identity development is bound to psychosocial and intellectual development. According to Bill Hettler's Model of Wellness, wellness is a state of "complete physical, mental, and social well-being," which consist of six components of wellness that must be balanced and require commitment to maintain this

---

11. Center for Substance Abuse Treatment. "Brief Interventions and Brief Therapies for Substance Abuse." *Treatment Improvement Protocol (TIP) Series, No. 3.* Rockville (MD), 1999. https://www.ncbi.nlm.nih.gov/books/NBK64947/

equilibrium: physical, intellectual, social/emotional, spiritual, environmental, and occupational.[12]

A "good" society in this model builds on Maslow's idea wherein society fosters the "fullest development of human potentials" adding that a good society is one that maximizes the extent to which people can actualize their wants," meaning their highest order desires, such as those that constitute self-determination. Actualization, in this context, is a fulfillment and an orientation of desires, and some progression in life or relationships as a response to those desires.[13]

2. Cognitive-Structural Theories of Development

Cognitive-Structural theories explain how people make meaning from experiences and how they make decisions based on levels of knowing and reflecting. These are commonly sequential operations, during which individuals progress through stages of knowing or certainty about their knowledge, followed by reflection and evaluation of this knowledge, which leads them to reflection on their convictions and form commitments to their values.

Lawrence Kohlberg is well known for explaining sequential stages in moral development, whereby the individual gains autonomy through six stages of moral reasoning. Bill Perry also follows a sequential pattern of nine stages of development, grouped into four stages, during which the individual gains more certainty in their knowledge of the world through their experiences, through others' perspectives, and their reasoning and reflection upon the various perspectives informing their judgments. Similar to Kohlberg's thought, the individual begins by relying on authority to determine what is "right" and progresses through stages of increased autonomy, based on the assimilation of

---

12. Dallas Long, "Theories and Models of Student Development," In L. J. Hinchliffe & M. A. Wong (Eds.), *Environments for student growth and development: Librarians and student affairs in collaboration*, Chicago: Association of College & Research Libraries, 2012, 41–55.

13. Mick Cooper, "The Fully Functioning Society: A Humanistic–Existential Vision of an Actualizing, Socially Just Future," *Journal of Humanistic Psychology*, Volume: 56 Issue: 6, Nov 1, 2016, 581–594.

knowledge and evaluation of it. Finally, knowledge and reflection, while weighing multiple perspectives and solutions, lead the person to recognize that knowledge and commitment to values evolve.

P.M. King and K.S. Kitchener later developed the reflective judgment model, which consists of three basic stages: Pre-reflective, during which knowledge begins with observation, quasi-reflective, in which knowledge is uncertain and subjective, and reflective, whereby knowledge is actively constructive and conclusions should be drawn from multiple sources and continuously evaluated.[14]

Conversion, Psychic Conversion

The work of Bernard Lonergan, who described the transcendental method and three types of conversion: religious, moral, and intellectual, and Robert Doran's work on psychic conversion and the dialectics of history, may contribute to these models and serve to unite secular approaches to development with the faith-based aims of CHE. In *Theology and the Dialectics of History*, Doran demonstrates how a person not only influences community, society, and culture, but they are also products of it. More specifically, these structures are mutually reinforcing. That is to say that just as the authentic individual may contribute to the authenticity of their community and culture, so too the authenticity of the community will inform the authentic development of the individual. So, it goes also for group bias and individual bias.

The Individual and Psychic Conversion

The person is a being capable of transcending, oriented to others in community, and to God, and comes to understand themselves through their conscious participation in these relationships. While a person may simply exist inattentively, their full participation in life

---

14. P.M. King, and K.S. Kitchener, "Reflective judgment: Theory and research on the development of epistemic assumptions through adulthood," *Educational Psychologist*, 39(1), 2004, 5–18. https://doi.org/10.1207/s15326985ep3901_2

and in society rest on how intentionally they respond to their calling to become fully aware of the meaning of their life and their purpose. Transcendent love, that is, the love that draws us out of our individual solitude and calls forth what we are to be and what we are to do as a being-in-relationship, gives us the answer and direction to our existential questions. This is realized, according to Lonergan, "when the isolation of the individual was broken and he (*sic*) spontaneously functioned not just for himself (*sic*) but for others as well."[15]

As one who is capable of exercising one's consciousness, an individual, according to Carl Jung and Doran, lives in a tension of opposites. The person who "succeeds in giving validity to his widened consciousness . . . creates a tension of opposites that provides the stimulation which culture needs for its further progress."[16] Doran expounds upon Jung's work, recognizing that the person's aim is to be integrated, not to give in to the polarization that is natural to the human experience. The exercise of consciousness that leads one to become fully integrated leads one's desires to become known and the direction forward to become available. As a knower, there is peace in recognizing that the spirit of inquiry is sustained "by the gift of divine and human love working from above," and so, affective integrity is recognized through falling in love, and this results in one's authentically becoming "constituted the first and only edition of oneself."[17] This exercise of consciousness not only reveals oneself but also reveals the desires that lay open the path forward. This is the basis of the individual's decision making and is essential for authentic human development.

Thus, consciousness is not an act of knowing, but an act of presence. Consciousness unveils a person's character, their values and judgements as it builds upon the questions and experience that constitute one's reality and brings clarity to the person through the

---

15. *Method in Theology*, 289.

16. Robert M. Doran, *Theology and the Dialectics of History* (Toronto: University of Toronto Press, 1990), 88. Cf. Carl Jung, "On the nature of the psyche," Collected Works of C. G. Jung, Vol. 8: Structure and Dynamics of the Psyche, 2nd ed., Princeton, NJ: Princeton University Press, 1972, p. 167–173.

17. *Theology and Dialectics of History*, 89.

transcendental precepts. Consciousness is the basis of the person's transcendence, where the subject begins with the question and becomes a person responsibly able to judge and to morally act. As Lonergan has shown us, this begins by simply paying attention to one's questions.

Consciousness is also being present to one's feelings, one's experiences and responses to life's movement. Feelings may lead one either toward one's development or to aberration. For feelings are linked to apprehension of values. Feelings reveal values and thus reveal one's existential orientation. Feelings indicate what we love and what we don't love. What we love, we value. And it is why consciousness matters a great deal, for the presence to one's feelings, what one loves, what one desires, and what one moves towards, will determine how one manages the tension, whether it will move the individual towards transcendence or to keep them limited.[18]

Psychic conversion leads the knowing subject to the question of the intelligible, to the virtually unconditioned, and reveals existential desires and purpose. Doran illustrates this process of discernment through the practice of the Ignatian Spiritual Exercises, whereby one begins by apprehending the value in feelings after asking all the questions there are to ask. The reflection continues through a process of being drawn in different directions, of having to make a choice that upsets the tension in one direction or another. Finally, the third reflection makes judgments while holding the equilibrium, values-based judgments because the person is integral, and attentive to feelings but not disrupted by them.

Like religious, moral, and intellectual conversion, psychic conversion clears the way to achieve authenticity. The human person, as an individual and in the context of community, society, and in relationship with God, has the capacity to be a genuine human, the one true self anyone has or can become "true to" throughout one's lifetime. Within the deep dimensions of the conscious lies a person's experiences

---

18. Doran's principle of transcendence and limitation builds upon Jung and Lonergan and suggests that our integrity depends on holding the tension of opposites in equilibrium, which is a dialectic of contraries, not contradictories.

of "the very movement of life, the passionateness of being, in which it is our task to find direction."[19]

Psychic conversion occurs through the process of censorship over neural demands, which is either constructive or repressive. Neural demands constitute part of the unconscious and the demands are for "conscious integration and psychic representation." The neural demands provide images to the person which reveal the person's true needs and desires. Freud and Jung suggested that this process of censorship is informed by the habits of our intellect and affect that determine what we will allow to be revealed. We may repress what is held in our unconscious, or we may be open to them. Transcendence is possible when the censorship is constructive, which is to say that the censorship does not repress the needed insights for the person to accept their desires, to become the person they need to be. When constructive, the conscious reveals the desires of the person. When constructive, the person wants and is open to insights, which are revealed and then may move the person forward. The transformation of the psyche occurs through the ongoing habits of openness and readiness for the emergence of the images required for insights which continue to reveal the person's deepest needs and desires.[20]

Like intellectual, moral, and religious conversion, psychic conversion is guided by the transcendental precepts. "One has to acquire the skills and learning of a competent human being in some walk of life."[21] The differentiation of consciousness will allow one to develop the habits that will cumulatively shape the process of censorship so that the "underlying neural manifold becomes an ever more pliable support and instrument of artistic world constitution and concomitant self-constitution, and the censorship becomes character, habit, virtue."[22] This, according to Doran, is how one develops into an integrated subject.

Conversely, however, one may reject the opportunities to be attentive, intelligent, reasonable, and responsible, and flee from one's own

---

19. Doran, *Theology and Dialectics of History*, 1019.
20. *Theology and Dialectics of History*, 103.
21. Ibid., 115.
22. Ibid., 113.

responsibility to understand their own subjectivity or their orientation in the world. This rejection of one's own task in life—the task to become oneself authentically—will lead to the repression of one's desires, and the psyche will censor those images that need to emerge to develop. Doran explains, "one's development becomes aberrant, and heads in the limit to the breakdown, disintegration, collapse of the failed artist, of the person who has not found, or has found and then lost, the direction that can be discovered or missed in the movement of life."[23] The rejection of one's responsibility to the transcendental precepts will lead to the scotosis that perpetuates individual bias. It upsets the balance in the tension within the psyche and leads to a failure of genuineness.

Love, according to both Doran and Lonergan, is the remedy to the distortion of bias. Experiencing love in intimacy, in community, and love of God leads to the reflective understanding of values and judgements. Feelings reveal values, and the scale of values are constituted by love, and these values, vital, social, cultural, personal, and religious are normative for measuring affective integrity. The more one experiences love and responds to love and the values that it illuminates, the more integrated the person will be. Loving is not a function of the psychic process but an integration of it, which transforms the process and yields a transformation in the subject.[24] Responses to feelings of love, and authentic encounters with others, all mediate meaning. Symbols also communicate these encounters, and symbols both mediate meaning and are integrated into the process of psychic conversion.

Society, Culture, the Dialectic of Society and Culture:

Doran situates the individual within the social and cultural framework. The development of an individual and their integrity are situated within a context that is religious, social and cultural. These values can inform a global social order, which, in a process of emergence, are dependent on the future of humanity and its progress.[25]

---

23. Ibid.
24. Ibid., 130–133.
25. Ibid., 715.

The scale consists of vital, social, cultural, personal, and religious values. Vital values are the values conducive to health and strength, grace and vigor. Social values consist of a social order whose schemes of recurrence guarantee vital values to the whole community. Cultural values are the meanings, values, and orientations informing the living and operating of the community. Personal value is the authentic subject as originating value in the community. And religious value is the grace that enables the subject, the culture, the community, to be authentic. At each successive level we are carried to a greater degree of self-transcendence in our affective and effective response.[26]

Like the dialectic of the individual, dialectical tension also constitutes society and culture. Authenticity is a function of the principle of limitation and transcendence on the social and cultural levels, just as it is for individuals. Just as the individual may be converted (or not), so may the society and culture. Yet again, the meaning that informs the values of a society and culture will determine its integrity.

Cultural integrity, Doran says, is impossible without persons of integrity. The integrity of culture and institutions is a "function of the meanings and values that inform them." The scale of values is the heart of society's structure. Above all of this, however, just as conversion "is the work of grace in personal life, so too the originating values of authentic culture are God's instruments for the renewal of the face of the earth."[27]

The integrated person who contributes to society's values is a person who has responded to the gift of grace. And so, religious values give the possibility of personal integrity. Cultural integrity depends on moral and intellectual conversion to give the conditions for genuine cultural values to promote the integral dialectic of community, and all the numerous social structures that constitute it.[28] Problems at the level of social values, then, rest on the integrity of the individuals in it and can only be resolved by "proportionate changes at the level of culture."[29]

---

26. Ibid., 144.
27. Ibid., 145.
28. Ibid., 151.
29. Ibid., 136.

The possibility of personal integrity is conditioned by religious values, and cultural values are conditioned by personal integrity. Collaboratively, the integrity of society will give authentic and integral science and scholarship and a just social order. A just social order is the only path to address global injustice, with all the myriad structures that, altogether, determine a world of equity or inequity.[30]

> In the present situation this responsibility involves contributing to the constitution of an emerging set of meanings and values to inform a way of life that can order the political, economic, and technological relations of a globally interdependent human community. The transformation of culture on a global scale is the condition of the possibility of a human infrastructural order of society. That transformation will take the form of a pattern of meanings and values, publicly expressed in symbolic forms that emerge from the retrieval . . . of our currently available, historically transmitted knowledge about and attitudes toward the word, God, ourselves, and the sense of our lives.[31]

As with the individual with a differentiated conscious, meaning and value in culture will inform the direction and outcomes of society's advances, in science, technology, humanities, and the human sciences. If unity is grounded in integration, conversion, and intentional consciousness, it will shift the meanings and values that will set the course for society's institutions. This may have a cumulative effect and is evident in cultural change and the change in social and economic priorities.

The distortion of sin leads individuals, society, and culture to limitation, and the more entrenched and reinforcing these distortions become, the farther from the path of transcendence. In Lonergan's understanding, bias is the state of sin into which we are born. Sin is the rejection of the person—or collectively, the culture—to embark on their existential task to be authentic. Grace disrupts this refusal grounds intentionality. But the effects of sin are cumulative: it begins with disorder in individual psyche and leads to the distortion of dialectics in communities and cultures. These are mutually reinforcing.

---

30. Ibid., 148.
31. Ibid., 717.

This mutual reinforcement establishes ever more rigid schemes of recurrence in history limiting the potential of the human spirit to raise and answer the right questions, and binding its powers of effecting the changes that are required to set things right at the three levels of personal, cultural, and social value. [32]

The Church, theology, and university as mediators of meaning and change

The distortions present in culture may be described as the problem of evil. Whereas bias is the distortion, the answer is in religious values, the response to grace, where intellectual conversion and psychic conversion free individuals and societies toward genuineness. Not only the Christian religion, but the world religions and their dialogue will provide a community square for the exchange of differentiated consciousness, a sharing of horizons. Thus, religion is not only concerned with its own tradition, but is interested in mediating meaning intended to transform human beings and cultures.

For Christians, these symbols and meanings may originate only in the original divine answer: the law of the cross. When the community of the Christian church recognizes itself as the suffering servant of God to the world, it welcomes into the community the grace that is essential for the transformation that will orient people to themselves, God, and their world.

The divinely originated solution has already been given as a remedy to the problem of evil. Yet to be efficacious, it depends on its allowance into the dimensions of the human psyche. This is an act of freedom of individuals to accept the free offer of God's grace. This relationship between the individual and God leads to the authentic community of disciples, the community of suffering servants.

An intellectual collaboration is needed that would assume the integrity of culture as its principal responsibility, and that would

---

32. Ibid., 748.

meet this responsibility by reorienting both the human sciences and commonsense practicality in such a way as to promote in society and history an integral dialectic between spontaneous intersubjectivity and the practical creation of technological, economic, and political institutions.[33]

The work of the church requires the community of faithful to act as the servant of God in the world. Ecclesial ministry along with CHE should reflect the suffering servant on a redemptive mission. It is the responsibility of both institutions to reverse the cycle of decline in society.[34] Theology helps to engage the historical situation with the church's ecclesial mission.

> Theology mediates first and foremost the self-understanding of the church. A contemporary theology must call the church to understand its discipleship in the present situation, a discipleship that would catalyze a global network of communities as an alternative to the competing and escalating distortions of the dialectic of community that constitute this situation.[35]

This, then, is not only the role of the church, but extends to the Catholic college or university, especially as it intersects the broader reaches of knowledge and of society.

Psychic Conversion's Contribution to Catholic Higher Education

"A real healing of the psyche heads toward affective self-transcendence, precisely for the sake of the intentional self-transcendence through which we can become collaborators in the constitution of a human world that is truly worthwhile."[36]

---

33. Ibid., 526.
34. Ibid., 554.
35. Ibid., 600.
36. Ibid., 85.

While the church has a mission for the whole world, it uses symbols and narrative shared exclusively by those within the community. But when ministry neglects to connect the symbols, tradition, and narrative with the human experience, the symbols and rituals may fail to invite them to attend to their own existential questions. The transcendental method begins with the subject and their question. It is for all humans.

The university has as its primary task to lead students from one point to another in their knowledge. It is inherently a space for the process of inquiry and transcendence. In Lonergan and Doran's terms, this is the opportunity to lead people to a new horizon. Insofar as the Catholic college or university facilitates intellectual, moral, and religious conversion through pedagogy and through community, its goal is to orient students in society as conscious and intentional subjects.

Doran's psychic conversion utilizes depth psychology to release the person's real self and desires even more fully. Beyond Lonergan's three types of conversions, psychic conversion engages the subject as feeling and can elevate the person's presence to themselves, as it then leads them into a transcendent process where they engage meaning from other sources. Doran's approach to psychic conversion makes a person present—conscious—to self. This calls forth the genuineness that then can be true in its response to the other realms of meaning.

This process may give added dimension to the humanist-existential method and cognitive-structural theories of development. Like those methods, the transcendental method leads students into a process of knowing, deciding, and making values judgements. Doran's psychic conversion helps students towards authentic development, by making judgments of value based on the genuine attention and response to one's true desires. If the two aforementioned models prove helpful for colleges and universities to create a sense of autonomous decision-making and a sense of concern for the common good, Doran's approach can ground it in a real sense and experience of transcendent meaning.

Psychic conversion thus provides new foundations for social justice activities and orients the subject in a more profound way to the world that they seek to change. Again, this is compatible with the two models of development as it adds religious context to social justice, not in the sense of moral "duty," but in the sense of existential purpose. It may add to the experience students have of evaluating different viewpoints and establishing their commitments. The information gained about social-historical contexts, scientific contexts, etc., gained through their intellectual pursuits, can be discerned in terms of a framework that grounds these pursuits for social change with a different lens and purpose, even if the question of God remains unthematic. For the transcendental method needs only to invite the subject to ask the question.

The transcendental method, and specifically psychic conversion, will also assist the Catholic principles of student development, for it provides the community with the method to ground the Catholic context of all the services it provides for the students, it allows the symbols and narrative that mediate meaning entry into work with students, and into the community, and situates the pursuit of social transformation, the values that unite the community to shared purpose, in the law of the cross. It could enliven campus ministries immensely, giving opportunity to pursue spiritual paths by those who may not have embraced the Christian story, but still yearn to understand themselves as part of a universal story. Additionally, there are wide openings in this method to talk about vocation in a way that is appealing and authentic and inclusive.

Doran's method of psychic conversion invites people to become authentic, to find their paths, simply by honestly allowing their true selves to come forth, and to respond to that message from within with further questions. The "leading out" of higher education begins always with a question and an honest look at the answers and inviting for further questions. Not only will this lead students to their own genuineness, but they will call for the same authenticity in their community, society, and culture, as they are better equipped to respond authentically to meaning and to identify distortion.

The focus on conversion as Lonergan and Doran understand it, strengthens Catholic identity by presenting more than just the Christian narrative, but a pursuit of truth born from inquiry. The Catholic college or university is at once a place to pursue questions of faith as well as academic inquiry. While some people imagine the religious context may stifle their freedom of inquiry, the methods of Lonergan and Doran instead encourage freedom to inquire, and freedom to reflect as full humans who do not need to be threatened in any way by religious narrative, but simply to inquire and be attentive to themselves as full, genuine human beings.

Because the university, unlike a church community, is multi-religious, the method unites people into common meaning, beginning with the question of what it means to exist, and to meet one another through the process of becoming genuine. Like the transcendental method, academia strives to cultivate authentic, knowing subjects who have grown through the cyclical nature of inquiry and knowledge.

Further, the culture will better understand and embrace authenticity. When the religious community becomes better able to handle authentic individuals, the biases that divide communities, especially those that result in exclusionary practices, will be clearly exposed as distortions in the dialectics of the community. Religious communities that set an expectation to accept symbols and meanings that are imposed, not genuinely mediated, cannot lead to authentic foundations, and will lead to inauthentic practices. Unfortunately, we have seen this too often in religious contexts, and reinforced by tradition codified by history: religious symbols used to divide and justify distortion, bias, and exclusion.

The transcendental method can strengthen the mission of the school and provide community insofar as it mediates meaning and orients the individuals, the community, in shared values as it understands its service to the world. Thus, the value of the faith-based higher education is that it provides a strong foundation for encouraging authentic development, and authentic community that need not separate meaning found in the intellect from meaning found in feeling or in faith. Rather, it provides an opportunity and method to integrate meaning and a language to ground healing and hope for individuals, communities, society, and cultures.

17

Cura Personalis and the Psychological Analogy of the Trinity in Contemporary Psychotherapeutic Practices

CECILLE MEDINA-MALDONADO

MARQUETTE UNIVERSITY

O ver the last half century, Trinitarian theology has received a revival of sorts.[1] Long gone are the days of separating the Trinity in two into the so-called "economic" or "immanent" Trinities. While Karl Rahner proposed his axiom on the two Trinities,[2] Bernard Lonergan (and later, Robert Doran) expounded the four-point hypothesis of the Trinity.[3] In the cases of all these theologians, it was apparent that the Trinity is more than a concept; the Trinity is a personal God who we are called to imitate and ultimately be grafted into divine life through participation. To be a whole person—that is, to be a person in the fullest sense—is to imitate and participate in the life of the Trinitarian God most closely.

---

1. Dadosky, John D. "God's Eternal Yes!: An Exposition and Development of Lonergan's Psychological Analogy of the Trinity," *Irish Theological Quarterly* 2016 Vol. 81 (4): 397–419, see especially notes 1–2.

2. "*The 'economic' Trinity is the 'immanent' Trinity and the 'immanent' Trinity is the 'economic' Trinity.*" Rahner, Karl, *The Trinity*, trans. Joseph Donceel. London: Burns & Oates, 1970, pp. 22.

3. Lonergan, Bernard. *The Triune God: Systematics*. Eds. Robert M. Doran and Daniel H. Monsour. Toronto: University of Toronto Press, 2007, pp. 470–73.

The whole person, not coincidentally, is a key concept in Jesuit higher education;[4] it is crucial to the development of the Jesuit-educated healthcare provider. Medicine in this context is meant to treat the whole person—*cura personalis*. The whole person, comprised of one's body, mind, and soul, is meant to be cared for in its fullness. In the cases of various physical illnesses, this is somewhat straightforward. Many physical ailments and illnesses require physiological treatment in addition to psychological care. It is effectively standard procedure to provide psychological support services for patients with long-term, chronic, or palliative care.

When approaching a patient in long-term care, or simply a patient requiring only psychological or mental healthcare, I argue that it is important to remember that the patient—a whole person—is called to be an imitation of Trinitarian life.[5] We are called to see Christ in others—and by extension, we are called to see the Trinity in others. What I attempt to do in this work is understand how the Trinity can be mirrored and imitated in contemporary psychotherapy. What I aim to do in my work is to connect Lonergan and Doran's Trinitarian theology with the practice of mindfulness. I believe that the psychological analogy of the Trinity, per Augustine, and later appropriated by Lonergan and Doran, has a rough counterpart in the modern psychotherapeutic tool called self-compassion. To explain this, I will first expound the psychological analogy of the Trinity and its relationship with Lonergan and Doran's work. Then, I will explain the connection between the modern theologians' work and modern psychology. Finally, I will connect self-compassion to the psychological analogy of the Trinity. I hope to show that the Trinity remains quite relevant in all contexts, particularly healthcare and treating the whole person.

---

4. Peters, Catherine. "Cura Personalis: the Incarnational Heart of Jesuit Education," *Jesuit Higher Education: A Journal*: Vol. 11: No. 1, Article 3.

5. Though outside the scope of this work, an identical statement can be made for the healthcare provider. Further study on supporting whole-person education and coping strategies for healthcare workers would prove beneficial for medical providers, particularly after the grueling years marking the COVID-19 pandemic.

Augustine's psychological analogy of the Trinity is based in his understanding of human love.[6] Augustine's work—is stated thusly: "the mind, and the knowledge by which it knows itself, and the love by which it loves itself." In his work, *De Trinitate*, Augustine attempted to find an appropriate metaphor or analogy for the Trinity. The divine substance—an analogue for the human mind—was one of his most innovative contributions. In Augustine's thought, the mind is the divine substance itself, finding its closest analogue in God the Creator; the knowledge by which it knows itself finds its closest analogue in God the Son (Jesus); the love by which it loves itself finds its closest analogue in God the Spirit (the Holy Spirit).[7] Thus the human being can see in themselves how the Trinitarian relations might operate by observing one's own inner workings. In very simple terms, it is the acknowledgement that I am a subject; I know myself as a subject; I love myself as a subject.

Augustine and later, both Lonergan and Doran, use specific terms to describe the way in which these concepts play out in the human psyche. These terms are memoria, understanding, and will. Memory is understood as the mind, filled with human memories that shape and color our world; it is "understood precisely as the condition under which the mind is present to itself, function[ing] as the analogue for the divine Father."[8] Memory or memories inform the way we live and provide biases, both helpful and unhelpful, when constructing our human experience. Divine memory, God Godself, is naturally free of such biases. Understanding is the knowledge of such memories; I can understand that I have memories and I can recall memories. Will is the love; I will to remember memories; I will to act upon memories; I will to understand memories; I will to act in accordance with the helpful or unhelpful biases within my memories. These three terms—memory,

---

6. Drilling, Peter D. "The Psychological Analogy of the Trinity: Augustine, Aquinas, and Lonergan." *Irish Theological Quarterly* 2006 Vol. 71, pp. 320–337.

7. Ibid., pp. 323–326.

8. Doran, Robert M. *The Trinity in History: Missions and Processions* vol. 1 (Toronto: University of Toronto Press), 2012: p. 37.

understanding, and will—cooperate and operate within themselves and independently, just as the relations of the Trinity do.

The psychological analogy of the Trinity is one of the pillars by which to construct Bernard Lonergan's contribution to Trinitarian theology, alongside his own work in what is arguably his *magnum opus*, *Insight*. This concept of acknowledgement of self-as-subject, knowing the self as subject, and loving oneself (and hopefully, others, as God loves others) as subject is at the heart of what it means to be an authentic human person; it surprises no one that this authentic human consciousness is reflected in Lonergan's understanding of the Trinity, particularly with the reliance on Augustine's analogy. In terms of human consciousness, the psychological analogy has analogues in the Trinity as the Father as originating love, the Son as judgment of value expressing that love, and the Spirit as originated loving.[9] This divine love is manifested in judgments of value, which carry out in decisions that are acts of loving.[10]

Lonergan and Doran join Augustine's notion of the psychological analogy of the Trinity with Aquinas' contributions in the four-point hypothesis:

> Thus there is established an analogy for understanding Trinitarian processions that obtains in the supernatural order itself. This analogy joins Augustine in positing *memoria* as the first step, where *memoria* is the retrospective appropriation of the condition in which one finds oneself gifted by unconditional love. *Memoria* and the judgment of value (faith) that follows from it as *verbum spirans amorem* participate in active spiration. The charity that flows from them participates in passive spiration.[11]

Practically speaking, it is often difficult to understand how to incorporate the inner workings of what is termed the "immanent" Trinity,

---

9. Lonergan, "Christology Today: Methodological Reflections," in *A Third Collection: Papers by Bernard J.F. Lonergan S.J.*, ed. Frederick E. Crowe (New York: Paulist, 1985) 93–94.

10. Ibid.

11. Doran, *Missions and Processions*, pp. 33–34.

that is, the Trinity as relations in and of themselves, in our own lives. Though we know we are made in the image and likeness of God—a Trinitarian God, no less—the concept of imitating the divine relations, per Doran's understanding, involves quite a bit of grace. More specifically, it requires what Doran terms as *sanctifying grace*. This is the type of grace that makes one holy; it makes one more like God.

The concept I'd like to explore most closely in relation to love of self within the psychological analogy of the Trinity is the concept of self-compassion, as developed by contemporary psychotherapist Kristen Neff. Self-compassion, put simply, is a concept that aims to bring kindness to oneself; it is "simply compassion directed inward."[12] It encourages sympathy and kindness for oneself, much like compassion for another encourages sympathy and kindness for another. Self-compassion grew out of the need to recognize one's own self-worth amid mental health crises. Where unhelpful, critical, or distorted thoughts abound, self-compassion aims to curtail the unhelpful stream of negativity towards oneself. It is not self-pity or self-indulgence; it is a concept that works to recognize and value one's own humanity. It is a somewhat "standalone" concept in psychotherapy, relying on various therapeutic techniques to work its full effectiveness.

Self-compassion, as defined by its main creator, Neff, has three main components. First, self-compassion prioritizes self-kindness over self-judgment. Self-kindness, for the purposes of our study, most closely mirrors the understanding that human beings are fallen creatures. Human persons are imperfect and are prone to sin. These sins carry us forward, despite our best efforts. If we were to engage in Lonerganian terms, we might consider this as the awareness that we have dramatic biases—we have wounds in our psyche that impact our ability to experience the world around us. As Neff defines self-kindness:

> Self-kindness means that we soothe and comfort ourselves when in pain. It is internally offering ourselves the same support and kindness that we would offer to a dear friend who was

---

12. Germer, Christopher K. and Kristin D. Neff, "Self-Compassion in Clinical Practice," *Journal of Clinical Psychology* Aug. 2013, Vol. 26, Issue 8, pp. 856–867.

suffering--offering a kind ear and a hug instead of a criticism and a smack. It also means taking care of ourselves for our long-term benefit, putting ourselves on the priority list.[13]

Again, it is the recognition that we have sin; we have dramatic biases. Rather than ignoring them or berating ourselves for our damaged psyche, we can have compassion on ourselves for being born into the human condition. This is not an endorsement of such trauma, but rather recognition that the trauma is valid and present, and that it impacts our day-to-day human experiencing. Not only is it recognition of the trauma, but it is *kindness and loving* in the face of such trauma. It is the reminder, a remembrance, a memory, that we are very much loved by God, who is the originator of love.

Second, self-compassion is defined by finding common humanity, rather than isolation. Per Neff's definition:

> Common humanity involves recognizing that suffering is part of the shared human condition. None of us is unique in suffering. To be human is to accept that pain, challenge, failure, and misfortune happen to everyone. Every lawyer feels fear and doubt sometimes, and every attorney encounters major obstacles. It's just part of being in the legal profession—and being human.[14]

This point aims to recognize that we are not alone in our suffering; for our study, again, this most closely most closely mirrors the understanding that human beings are fallen creatures. Human persons are imperfect and are prone to sin. While there is no sin for the persons of the Trinity, the very fact that Jesus became Incarnate and has shared in our common humanity means there is shared suffering between the Triune God and human persons. There is no solitude when there are shared experiences of humanity and suffering, or even of sharing in the divine essence. The Trinity is never truly alone; having relations both among the persons of the Trinity and the relations beyond the Trinity

---

13. Neff, Kristen D. "Self-Compassion: An Alternative Conceptualization of a Healthy Attitude Toward Oneself," Self and Identity, 2003 (2:2), at 85–102.

14. Ibid.

poured out on creation, the Trinity has community and unity in its very essence. This concept—common humanity—helps ground us to judgments of fact. Common humanity allows us to affirm—give the *yes!*—or perhaps *no!*—to the insight we have made.

Mindfulness is known as "the awareness that arises through intentionally attending in an open, caring, and discerning way."[15] Neff and her co-authors further this definition by saying that mindful awareness

> [I]nvolves a *knowing* and *experiencing* of life as it arises and passes away each moment. It is a way of relating to all experience- positive negative, and neutral—in an open, kind, and receptive manner. This awareness involves freedom from grasping and wanting anything to be different than it is. It simply *knows* what is truly occurring here and now, allowing us to see the nature of reality clearly and with compassion, without all of our conditioned patterns of perception clouding awareness.[16]

Unsurprisingly, mindfulness fits well into Lonergan's study of human consciousness; mindfulness is a tremendously useful skill in identifying one's thought patterns. Furthermore, mindfulness can assist the self in understanding oneself, hopefully to lead one to love oneself as a subject.

Mindfulness, in fact, is at the heart of self-compassion. Mindfulness permeates all three pillars of self-compassion. This is again unsurprising, given Lonergan's contributions to the study of human consciousness. Being aware of one's thought patterns and constantly reevaluating them in light of experience, data, and judgments allows one to see—fully see—where their biases lie, or where they fail to act as an authentic human being.

Mindfulness, per my understanding, mirrors the way in which the divine relations relate to one another. I connect this with Aquinas'

---

15. Shapiro, S.L. and Carlson, L.E. (2017). *The art and science of mindfulness:* Integrating mindfulness into psychology and the helping professions. Washington, D.C.: American Psychology Press, p. 8.

16. Shapiro, Shauna, Ronald Siegel, and Kristin D. Neff, "Paradoxes of Mindfulness," *Mindfulness* (2018): 9: 1693–1701.

concept of intelligible emanations, and later, Lonergan's development of intelligible emanations in his study of human consciousness. The three intelligible emanations in Aquinas' work[17] are given to human consciousness as follows: the first emanation is what we might know as insight, an *a-ha* moment caused by the data of human experience; the second emanation comes from the understanding that one's insight is true; finally, the third emanation is a judgment of truth; it is an affirmation that truth has been achieved. Upon affirmation of this truth, action may be taken—a decision is made. When applied as mindfulness in self-compassion, it is again, tremendously easy to illustrate the pattern of human consciousness that Lonergan laid out in *Insight* and then appropriated to the psychological analogy of the Trinity.

What I would like to offer now is an example of an imaginative exercise—I would like to walk you through an exercise in mindfulness with an eye on how the Trinity and self-compassion tie together. This is my attempt to illustrate in social terms what I have been attempting to illustrate in academic terms. I will be walking through an exercise in self-compassion and noting where I find glimpses of the Trinity—as understood through the psychological analogy—within the exercise itself.

Our exercise for mindfulness and self-compassion begins with remembering something that is causing us pain, stress, or anxiety. It may very well be anxiety over an upcoming deadline, assignment, or professional responsibility! Simply remembering something that causes stress, pain, anxiety, or any unpleasurable emotion will do. As the subject remembers a stressor, the subject ought to observe their thoughts surrounding the stressor, particularly thoughts about themselves as subject.

Let us employ the example of presenting one's research at an academic conference. What kinds of anxieties might a presenter have before sharing their work at a conference? Perhaps thinking that they are inadequate—what one might know as 'impostor syndrome' in academic circles. Such a subject might think or believe the following: "I am woefully inadequate." This is a judgment of the self; it is a

---

17. ST 1, 27, art. 1 and 2.

judgment that is unkind. Recognizing the unkindness of this judgment allows one to see how that judgment may be a detriment to authentic human experience. If I am, in fact, woefully inadequate, then perhaps the feedback I receive on my work will be colored with this unpleasant self-judgment; perhaps the feedback I receive on my work will be discarded as irrelevant because I am woefully beyond repair.[18]

To practice self-kindness in this situation, I can recognize that anxiety or feelings of inadequacy are perfectly normal for human beings in stressful situations. After all, when Adam and Eve ate from the tree of the knowledge of good and evil, they hid from the Lord. When Cain killed his brother, he too hid himself. While presenting work at a conference does not constitute such egregious sins, the innate human desire to hide or experience fear before others is built into our very makeup. I am human; therefore, I will experience fear. Recognizing that my feelings are part of the human condition and not an indictment of my own morality or goodness, I can move onto the next step in mindfulness.

I now turn to the notion of common humanity. To do this is to realize that all persons feel inadequate at some point. I recognize, as a person of faith, that all persons have a primordial wound to their psyche; all persons feel inadequate or doubt their self-worth. The thought that one is inadequate—while potentially unhelpful when it disrupts authentic human experiencing—is not a unique thought in human experience at all. It is an important thought and one shared by many persons, but it is not so unique that it is cause for isolation.[19]

---

18. Those familiar with Lonergan's work on biases will see the development of either dramatic biases or individual biases in the subject. These biases stem partly from the fallen human condition. Without practicing self-compassion or spiritual exercises in detachment, it's remarkably easy to see how individuals become bogged down by their psyches to the point of spiritual, professional, or personal decline.

19. Indeed, as a person of faith and as a scholar of the Trinity, I go further in seeing the commonalities among all human persons. With the Trinity as the model for human behavior (as well as humanity's *telos*, to be union with God and one another), I can envision the way in which God the Father expresses compassion for the Son as a perfect example of self-compassion. The compassion poured out on humanity is the self-same compassion we are called to give ourselves *and* one another.

I remind myself that it is not my personal human condition that causes me to fear or feel inadequate; all persons are wounded by the same ancient pain that continues to tug at us and guide our decisions. In short, by recognizing the state of the whole human condition, I decide to merely observe my thoughts as they come. I choose not to over-identify with the feelings of inadequacy. I neither deny nor suppress the thoughts; I simply recognize they are part of a shared, lived human experience. I choose to be governed by the task at hand—that of sharing my work—rather than succumbing to the breakdown that would prevent me from achieving my goals.

Where, then, is the Trinity in each of these steps towards self-compassion? As with all of creation, there are vestiges of the Trinity in each step. The whole person—the subject—is a Trinitarian person. The practice of self-compassion requires reflection and insight into one's own thoughts while recognizing the parallels with other persons. Finally, the practice of self-compassion spurs one to make a decision—to choose to observe one's thoughts and feelings, rather than act rashly as a result of them.

The entirety of this structure is an exercise in employing the mental cognitive processes outlined in Lonergan's *Insight* but framed in Trinitarian language. Dramatic biases fuel the thought distortions that require psychotherapeutic tools. This damage to our *memoria*, our psyche, is the starting point for many mental health breakdowns. In the context of a patient already experiencing chronic illness or palliative care, I suggest it further alienates them or isolates them, exacerbating the severity of their physical illness.[20]

The recognition of common humanity and its struggles mirrors the Trinity in its relations and relationships. To be a fully human person is to be in relationship; the isolation that stems from dramatic or individual biases, left unchecked without the reality that others

---

20. This is not unlike the way in which Jesus the Healer not only restored physical function to the sick and wounded but enabled them to re-enter the communities from which they were shunned. Treating the whole person and recalling the human's place in relationship and community is part of what constitutes this model of 'care for the whole person.'

struggle with similar burdens, feeds into greater loneliness. The compassion extended upon ourselves ought to be extended to others; the compassion that God pours out on his Son through the Holy Spirit is the same compassion that we are given and called to give others.

Choosing then, to observe one's thoughts and feelings, detaches oneself from the biases that threaten to cloud one's knowledge and will. One's *memoria* is observed at a healthy distance, so that the knowledge or understanding of one's experience is accurately grasped. When true knowledge and experience are grasped, action and decision follow. In this therapeutic tool, the Trinity cannot be divided into immanent or economic; it cannot be divided by Person or Relation. The inner workings of the mind are mirrored in the outer actions of the human person. When infused with self-reflection and recognition of others, the subject heals spiritually and psychologically.

Self-compassion is but one method of treating a patient made in the image and likeness of the Trinitarian God. What Augustine, Lonergan, and Doran contribute to Trinitarian theology and theological anthropology is the notion that understanding of the self is essential to self-appropriation and transcendence. In the case of patients with chronic illnesses—or rather, *any* person ambling through life with wounds seen and unseen—healthcare providers can incorporate psychotherapeutic techniques with the aim of healing the whole person. Ultimately, like Christ, the healthcare provider re-incorporates the patient into relationship with others, with the self, and promotes healing on both physical and spiritual planes.

Select Bibliography

Achebe, Chinua. *There was a Country: A Memoir.* New York: Penguin, 2013.

Begley, Sharon. *Train Your Mind Change Your Brain: How a New Science Reveals Our Extraordinary Potential to Transform Ourselves,* New York: Ballantine Books, 2007.

Boggs, James Lee. *Racism and the Class Struggle.* New York: Monthly Review Press, 1970.

Bohm, David. *Quantum Theory.* Englewood Cliffs, New Jersey: Prentice-Hall, 1958.

Bohr, Neils. *Atomic Theory and the Description of Nature.* New York: Macmillan, 1934.

Brach, Tara *Radical Compassion: Learning to Love Yourself and Your World with the Practice of RAIN* (New York: Penguin Life, 2019)

Brantley, Jeffrey, M.D. *Calming Your Anxious Mind: How Mindfulness and Compassion Can Free You from Anxiety, Fear, and Panic.* California: Raincoast Books, 2003.

Clayton, Philip. *Mind and Emergence: From Quantum to Consciousness.* New York: Oxford University Press, 2004.

Conn, Walter. *Conscience: Development and Self-Transcendence.* Birmingham, Alabama: Religious Education Press, 1981.

Dadosky, John D. *Meaning and History in Systematic Theology: Essays in Honor of Robert Doran, S.J.* Ed. John D. Dadosky. Milwaukee: Marquette University Press, 2009.

Doidge, Norman, M.D. *The Brain that Changes Itself.* New York: Penguin Group, 2007.

Doran, Robert M. *Conscious in Two Ways,* edited by Joseph Ogbonnaya, Jeremy W. Blackwood, and Gregory Lauzon (Milwaukee: Marquette University Press, 2021).

――――. *The Trinity in History: A Theology of the Divine Missions, vol. 1: Missions and Processions.* Toronto: University of Toronto Press, 2012.

――――. *What is Systematic Theology?* (Toronto: University of Toronto Press, 2005).

――――. *Theological Foundations I: Intentionality and Psyche.* Milwaukee: Marquette University Press, 1995

――――. *Subject and Psyche.* 2nd ed. Milwaukee: Marquette University Press, 1994.

――――. *Theology and The Dialectics of History.* Toronto: University of Toronto Press, 1990.

――――. *Psychic Conversion and Theological Foundations: Toward A Reorientation of the Human Sciences.* California: Scholars Press, 1981.

Douglas, Kelly Brown. *Stand Your Ground: Black Bodies and the Justice of God.* Maryknoll, N.Y.: Orbis Books, 2015.

Dyckman, Katherine Marie S.N.J.M. and Carroll, L. Patrick S.J., *Inviting the Mystic, Supporting the Prophet: An Introduction to Spiritual Direction* (New York: Paulist Press, 1981.

Fitzpatrick, Joseph. *The Fall and the Ascent of Man: How Genesis Supports Darwin* (Lanham, NY: University Press of America, 2011).

Freud Sigmund. *Civilization and Its Discontents. Translated and Edited by James Strachey. New York: W.W. Norton & Company,* 2010.

――――. *The Ego and the Id.* Translated by Joan Riviere. Edited by James Strachey. New York: W.W. Norton & Company, 1989.

Gendlin, Eugene. *Experiencing and the Creation of Meaning.* Illinois: Northwestern University Press, 1997.

――――. *Focusing,* 2nd ed. New York: Bantam Books, 1981.

――――. *Let Your Body Interpret Your Dreams.* Illinois: Chiron Publications, 1986.

Gordon, Joseph K. *Divine Scripture in Human Understanding: A Systematic Theology of the Christian Bible.* Notre Dame, IN: University of Notre Dame Press, 2019.

Gregson, Vernon. Ed. *The Desires of the Human Heart: An Introduction to the Theology of Bernard Lonergan.* New York: Paulist Press, 1988.

Herman, Judith *Trauma and Recovery: The Aftermath of Violence— From Domestic Abuse to Political Terror* (New York: Basic Books, 1992).

Hunt, Michael. *The World Transformed 1945 to the Present.* New York: Oxford University Press, 2017.

Ignatius of Loyola, *The Spiritual Exercises of St. Ignatius: A New Translation Based on Studies in the Language of the Autograph,* translated by Louis J. Puhl SJ (Chicago: University of Chicago Press, 1951).

Jacobs, Jane. *The Nature of Economies.* New York: The Modern Library, 2000.

Jung, C. G. *Memories, Dreams, Reflections.* Edited by Aniela Jaffe. Trans. Richard and Clara Winston. New York: Vintage Books, 1989.

Jung, Carl. *Psychology and Religion.* New Haven: Yale University Press, 1960.

Kabat-Zinn, Jon, Ph.D. *Full Catastrophe Living: Using the Wisdom of Your Body and Mind to Face Stress, Pain, and Illness.* New York: Dell Publishing, 1990.

Kolk, Bessel van der *The Body Keeps the Score: Brain, Mind, and Body in the Healing of Trauma.* New York: Penguin Books, 2014.

Lamb, Matthew. Ed. *Creativity and Method: Essays in Honor of Bernard Lonergan, S.J.* Milwaukee, WI: Marquette University Press, 1981.

Lawrence, Frederick G. *The Fragility of Consciousness: Faith, Reason, and The Human Good.* Toronto: University of Toronto Press, 2017.

Levin, Ted. *America's Snake: The Rise and Fall of the Timber Rattlesnake.* Chicago: University of Chicago Press, 2016.

Lonergan, Bernard J. F. *The Redemption.* Trans. Michael G. Shields, ed. Robert M. Doran, H. Daniel Monsour, and Jeremy D. Wilkins,

Collected Works of Lonergan 9 Toronto: University of Toronto Press, 2018.

―――. *Method in Theology*, CWL 14 edited by Robert M. Doran and John D. Dadosky. Toronto: University of Toronto Press, 2017.

―――. *The Triune God: Doctrines*. Vol. 11 of CWL, ed. Robert M. Doran and H. Daniel Monsour, trans. Michael G. Shields. Toronto: University of Toronto Press, 2009.

―――. Bernard Lonergan, *Verbum: Word and Idea in Aquinas*. Eds. Frederick E. Crowe and Robert M. Doran, CWL 2 Toronto: University of Toronto Press, 1997.

―――. *Insight: A Study of Human Understanding Collected Works of Bernard Lonergan. Vol. 3.* Edited by Frederick E. Crowe and Robert M. Doran. Toronto: University of Toronto Press, 1992.

McNamara, Patrick. *The Neuroscience of Religious Experience*. Cambridge: Cambridge University Press, 2009.

Mignolo Walter D. and Walsh, Catherine E. *On Decoloniality: Concepts, Analytics and Praxis* Durham: Duke University Press, 2018.

Muzorewa, Gwinyai H. *The Origins and Development of African Theology* (Eugene, Oregon: Wipf and Stock Publishers, 1987.

Neumann, Erich. *The Origins and History of Consciousness. Vol 1*, Trans. R. F. C. Hull (New York: Harper and Brothers, 1954).

Nietzsche, Friedrich. *The Genealogy of Morals*. Trans. Maudemarie Clark and Alan J. Swensen Indianapolis: Hackett Publishing Company, Inc., 1998.

Ogbonnaya, Joseph. *Lonergan, Social Transformation and Sustainable Human Development* (Eugene, OR: Pickwick Publications, 2013).

Ogbonnaya Joseph and Gerard Whelan S.J. Ed. Intellect, Affect, and God: The Trinity, History, and the Life of Grace. Milwaukee, WI: Marquette University Press, 2021.

Orji, Cyril. *Ethnic and Religious Conflict in Africa: An Analysis of Bias, Decline and Conversion Based on the Works of Bernard Lonergan.* Milwaukee: Marquette University Press, 2008.

Powers, W. T. *Behavior: The Control of Perception.* Chicago: Aldine, 1973.

Ricoeur, Paul. *Freedom and Nature: The Voluntary and the Involuntary* (1950). Translated by Erazim V. Kohák, Evanston, IL: Northwestern University Press, 2007.

———.*The Conflict of Interpretation: Essays in Hermeneutics* (1969). Edited by Don Ihde. Evanston, IL: Northwestern University Press, 2007.

———. *Oneself as another*. Translated by Kathleen Blamey. Chicago: University of Chicago Press, 1992.

———. *Time and Narrative, vol. 3* (1985). Translated by Kathleen Blamey and David Pellauer. Chicago: University of Chicago Press, 1988.

———. *Fallible Man* (1960). Translation by Charles A. Kelbley. New York: Fordham University Press, 1986.

———. *Interpretation Theory: Discourse and the Surplus of Meaning*. Fort Worth, TX: TCU Press, 1976.

———. *Freud and Philosophy: An Essay on Interpretation*. Translated by Denis Savage. New Haven: Yale University Press, 1970.

———. *The Symbolism of Evil* (1967). Translated by Emerson Buchanan. Boston: Beacon Press, 1969.

Scheler, Max. *Ressentiment.* Trans. William W. Holdeim. New York: Schocken Books, 1972.

Shaw, Christopher. *Toward a Theory of Neuroplasticity.* Edited by Jill McEachern. Philadelphia: Psychology Press, 2001.

Strasser, Stephan *Phenomenology of Feeling,* trans. Robert E. Wood. Pittsburgh: Duquesne University Press, 1977.

Wittgenstein, Ludwig *Philosophical Investigations.* Ed. P. M. S. Hacker and Joachim Schulte. Trans. G. E. M. Anscombe, P. M. S. Hacker, and Joachim Schulte, Fourth Edition Malden, MA: Blackwell Publishing, 2009.

Author Bios

Blackwood, Jeremy W. a graduate of Marquette University, Milwaukee, WI, is associate professor of theology at the Sacred Heart Seminary, Milwaukee. He is the author of *And Hope Does Not Disappoint":* *Love, Grace, and Subjectivity in the Work of Bernard J. F. Lonergan, S. J.* (2017), and co-edited with Joseph Ogbonnaya and Gregory Lauzon, *Robert M. Doran, Conscious in Two Ways: Robert M. Doran Remembers* (2021). In addition to book chapters, his articles have appeared in *Method: Journal of Lonergan Studies, Theological Studies, Irish Theological Studies, Lonergan Review*, etc.

Copeland, M. Shawn is Professor *emerita* of Systematic Theology in the Department of Theology at Boston College, and Theologian-in-Residence at Saint Katharine Drexel Roman Catholic Parish, Boston, Massachusetts. She is an internationally recognized scholar and award-winning writer—the author and/or editor of eight books including *Enfleshing Freedom: Body, Race, and Being* 2nd ed (2023) and 135 articles and book chapters on spirituality, theological anthropology, political theology, social suffering, gender, and race. Most recently she and Laurie Cassidy co-edited *Desire, Darkness, and Hope: Theology in a Time of Impasse: Engaging the Thought of Constance Fitz-Gerald, OCD* (2021).

Dadosky, John Ph.D., S.T.D. is professor of theology and philosophy at Regis—St. Michael's School of Theology/University of Toronto. He is author of *The Structure of Religious Knowing* (SUNY Press, 2004), *The Eclipse and Recovery of Beauty* (University of Toronto Press, 2014), co-editor of four volumes of the Collected Works of Bernard Lonergan, including *Method in Theology* (2017) and the final archival volume. His book *Image to Insight: The Art of William Hart*

McNichols (2018), won a 2019 New Mexico-Arizona book award. He has numerous articles in Lonergan studies and a range of topics on philosophical theology, systematic theology, interreligious dialogue with Buddhism, and intercultural theology.

Gordon, Joseph K. is Professor of Theology at Johnson University and directs the Critical-Realist Hermeneutics team in the International Institute for Method in Theology. The author of *Divine Scripture in Human Understanding* (Notre Dame, 2019/2022) and editor of *Critical Realism and the Christian Scriptures* (Forthcoming Marquette University), his articles, scientific notes, and poetry appear in Theological Studies, *Nova et Vetera, The Lonergan Review, Method: Journal of Lonergan Studies, Macrina Magazine, Herpetological Review*, and elsewhere. A certified master herpetologist and southern Appalachian naturalist, he is working on a book on snakes and theology and an introduction to Lonergan's life and work (Cascade).

Heaps, Jonathan specializes in the work of Bernard Lonergan with a special focus on questions of embodiment. He has published articles in *Heythrop Journal, American Catholic Philosophical Quarterly*, and *Theological Studies*, as well as numerous chapters in edited volumes. His forthcoming book, *The Ambiguity of Being: Bernard Lonergan and the Problems of the Supernatural*, will appear with the Catholic University of America Press. He lives in Austin, TX.

Hemmer, Ryan (Ph.D., Marquette University) is editor-in-chief at Fortress Press in Minneapolis, Minnesota. He is the author of *The Death and Life of Speculative Theology: A Lonergan Idea* (2023) and is a member of the editorial council of Streets.mn, a land use and transportation news publication covering the Twin Cities and Greater Minnesota.

McDonald, Mary Jo is a theologian, spiritual director, and retired hospital chaplain. Holding a Master of Divinity and Doctorate of Theology from Regis College at the Toronto School of Theology, her doctoral thesis aimed to develop an understanding of the body's participation in the thrust of, what Bernard Lonergan, S.J., articulated as, one's intentional spirit toward healing and wholeness. Following this doctoral work, her further research interests have been in developing the spiritual practice and understanding of how focusing on one's felt sense in the body aids in the process of releasing previously repressed images into consciousness. Mary Jo is a founding member of the Contemplative Women of St. Anne, a contemplative lay association formed and inspired by way of a desire to both retrieve and honor feminine spirituality and mysticism.

Medina-Maldonado, Cecille is a doctoral student in systematic theology at Marquette University. Her research interests include Trinitarian theology, especially the contributions of Bernard Lonergan and Robert Doran, and the connection between the Trinity, deification, and grace. She contributed "Bias, Conversion, and Grace in the Time of a Pandemic," in *Intellect, Affect, and God: The Trinity, History and the Life of Grace, Essays in Honor of Robert M. Doran, S.J.,* eds. Joseph Ogbonnaya and Gerard Whelan, S.J. (Marquette University Press, 2021, pp. 213–228). She is also interested in Catholic bioethics, particularly reproductive ethics. She has received degrees from the University of Illinois at Urbana-Champaign and Loyola University Chicago.

Murray, Elizabeth Professor Emerita, retired recently from LMU, where she taught for 35 years, and served as Department Chair and Director of the Philosophy Graduate Program. She is the author of *Anxiety: A Study of the Affectivity of Moral Consciousness* (1986). She co-edited *Understanding and Being* (1980, re-edited 1990); and she co-edited *The Lonergan Reader* (1997). She has written extensively on Lonergan and on other thinkers including Plato, Aristotle, Kierkegaard, Nietzsche, Freud, and Sartre. She was a founding member of the West Coast Methods Institute, founded by Timothy Fallon, S.J. in 1984. In 1994, she founded the Lonergan Philosophical Society.

Nussberger, Danielle Ph.D. is an associate professor of systematic theology at Marquette University in Milwaukee, WI. She specializes in systematic theology and spirituality. She has specific interests in the intersection between spirituality and theology, action and contemplation, and prayer and spiritual direction. She has written on such topics as: contemplation and the vocation of the theological educator, the spirituality of Lúcás Chan's biblical ethics, Hans Urs von Balthasar and Constance Fitzgerald on Holy Saturday and the dark night of *impasse*, sainthood in John Henry Newman and Hans Urs von Balthasar, and feminism and Catholic thought.

Obeten, Mark is a PhD student in the department of theology at Marquette University, Wisconsin. Mark has Bachelor of Sacred Theology degree from the Saints Peter and Paul Seminary, Ibadan in affiliation to the Pontifical Urbaniana University in Rome and a Master of Theological Studies degree from the St John's School of Theology, Collegeville, Minnesota. He has theological interests in inculturation theology, Lonergan studies, and interfaith dialogue in Africa.

Ogbonnaya, Joseph is associate professor of Theology at Marquette University, Milwaukee, WI. He is the director of the Marquette Lonergan Project and the International Institute for Method in Theology. He is the author of *African Perspectives on Culture and World Christianity* (2017), *African Catholicism and Hermeneutics of Culture* (2014), *Lonergan, Social Transformation and Sustainable Human Development* (2013), *Moral Integrity & Igbo Cultural Value (2011)*, *Deepening the Christian Faith (2011)* as well as co-editor of *Conscious in Two Ways: Robert M. Doran Remembers (2021)*, *Intellect, Affect, and God: The Trinity, History, and the Life of Grace* (2021), *Everything is Connected: Towards a Globalization with a Human Face and Integral Ecology* (2019), *Christianity and Culture Collision* (2016) and *The Church as Salt and Light* (2011).

Orji, Cyril is Professor of Systematic Theology and Core Integrated Study at the University of Dayton, Ohio, USA. He specializes in fundamental and constructive theology, with particular emphasis on the theology and philosophy of Bernard Lonergan, which he brings into conversation with the works of the American pragmatist and semiotician, Charles Sanders Peirce, and the German Lutheran theologian, Wolfhart Pannenberg. He has published numerous journal articles. He has also published several books, including, *Exploring Theological Paradoxes* (2023), *Unmasking the African Ghost: Theology, Politics, and* *the Nightmare of Failed States (2022), A Semiotic Christology* (2021), *An Introduction to Religious and Theological Studies,* 2nd edition (Cascade, 2021). *A Semiotic Approach to the Theology of Incultura- tion* (2015), *The Catholic University and the Search for Truth* (2013), *Ethnic and Religious Conflicts in Africa: An Analysis of Bias and Con- version Based on the Work of Bernard Lonergan* (Marquette Univer- sity Press, 2008).

Rosenberg, Randall S. is associate professor of theology at St Louis University, Missouri. He is the author of *The Givenness of Desire: Con- crete Subjectivity and the Natural Desire to See God* (Toronto: Uni- versity of Toronto Press, 2017), *The Vision of Saint John XXIII* (New York: Paulist Press, April 15, 2014), and co-editor of *The Fragility of Consciousness: Faith, Reason, and the Human Good* (Selected Essays of Frederick G. Lawrence) (Toronto: University of Toronto Press, 2017). His articles have appeared in *Theological Studies, Irish Theolog- ical Studies, Nova et Vetera*, Gregorianum, *Logos: A Journal of Catholic Thought and Culture,* etc.

Sandschafer, Cody is a doctoral student in Religious Studies at Mar- quette University. His work examines the social and interpersonal dimensions of subjectivity in light of the doctrine of creation and soteriological accounts derived from Transcendental Thomism and Liberation Theology. He is also an editorial assistant at Syndicate Network and has curated or is in the process of curating numerous symposiums ranging from topics covering *creatio ex nihilo* to ethics in artificial intelligence. His work has been presented at Lonergan on the Edge, the Society of Ancient Greek Philosophy, and Psychology and the Other.

Stapleton, Andrea J. serves as the Vice President for Mission and Justice at Mount Mary University in Milwaukee, Wisconsin. She has taught theology and served in administration in several universities and seminaries. She has written and spoken nationally on Catholic higher education, theology, and diversity and equity in higher edu- cation. Her work includes spiritual and pastoral ministry and non- profit leadership. Stapleton's research focuses on Lonergan Studies, ecclesiology, sacramental theology, feminist theology, and religious pluralism. She is the first recipient of the M. Shawn Copeland Award for Lonergan Studies in Contextual Theology from the Lonergan Center at Marquette University.

Whelan, S.J., Gerard is an Irish Jesuit and Chairman of the Department of Fundamental Theology at the Pontifical Gregorian University, Rome. He directs the "Lonergan Project" at the university and is author of *Redeeming History: Social Concern in Bernard Lonergan and Robert Doran* (Rome, G&B Press, 2013) and *A Discerning Church: Pope Francis, Lonergan, and a Theological Method for the Future* (Paulist Press, 2019.) Before coming to Rome, he lived in Africa for fourteen years. He has published articles and book chapters relating Doran's thought to parish work, integral ecology, and the Spiritual Exercises of St. Ignatius.

Index Names

Index